Wilbur Smith

The World's Greatest and Most Popular Writer of Epic Adventure

'Wilbur Smith rarely misses a trick'
Sunday Times

'The world's leading adventure writer'
Daily Express

'Action is the name of Wilbur Smith's game and he is a master'
Washington Post

'The pace would do credit to a Porsche, and the invention is as bright and explosive as a firework display'
Sunday Telegraph

'A violent saga set in Boer War South Africa, told with vigour and enthusiasm . . . Wilbur Smith spins a fine tale'
Evening Standard

'An epic novel . . . it would be hard to think of a theme that was more appropriate today . . . Smith writes with a great passion for the soul of Africa'
   Today

'I read on to the last page, hooked by its frenzied inventiveness piling up incident upon incident . . . mighty entertainment'
   Yorkshire Post

'There is a streak of genuine poetry, all the more attractive for being unfeigned'
   Sunday Telegraph

' . . . action follows action . . . mystery is piled on mystery . . . tales to delight the millions of addicts of the gutsy adventure story'
   Sunday Express

'Action-crammed'
   Sunday Times

'Rattling good adventure'
   Evening Standard

The novels of Wilbur Smith

The Courtneys:
   When the Lion Feeds
   The Sound of Thunder
   A Sparrow Falls

The Courtneys of Africa:
   The Burning Shore
   Power of the Sword
   Rage

The Ballantyne novels:
   A Falcon Flies
   Men of Men
   The Angels Weep
   The Leopard Hunts in Darkness

Also:
   The Dark of the Sun
   Shout at the Devil
   Gold Mine
   The Diamond Hunters
   The Sunbird
   Eagle in the Sky
   The Eye of the Tiger
   Cry Wolf
   Hungry as the Sea
   Wild Justice
   Golden Fox
   Elephant Song

When the Lion Feeds
The Sound of Thunder

Wilbur Smith was born in Central Africa in 1933. He was educated at Michaelhouse and Rhodes University.

He became a full-time writer in 1964 after the successful publication of *When the Lion Feeds*, and has since written twenty novels, meticulously researched on his numerous expeditions worldwide.

He normally travels from November to February, often spending a month skiing in Switzerland, and visiting Australia and New Zealand for sea fishing. During his summer break, he visits environments as diverse as Alaska and the dwindling wilderness of the African interior. He has an abiding concern for the peoples and wildlife of his native continent, an interest strongly reflected in his novels.

He is married to Danielle, to whom his last nineteen books have been dedicated.

WILBUR SMITH

When the Lion Feeds

The Sound of Thunder

Mandarin

A Mandarin Paperback
WHEN THE LION FEEDS
THE SOUND OF THUNDER

When the Lion Feeds first published in Great Britain 1964
by William Heinemann Ltd
Mandarin paperback edition published 1991
The Sound of Thunder first published in Great Britain 1966
Mandarin paperback edition published 1992
First published together in this omnibus edition 1993
by Mandarin Paperbacks
an imprint of Reed Consumer Books Ltd
Michelin House, 81 Fulham Road, London sw3 6rb
and Auckland, Melbourne, Singapore and Toronto

When the Lion Feeds copyright © Wilbur Smith 1964
The Sound of Thunder copyright © Wilbur Smith 1966
This omnibus edition copyright © Wilbur Smith 1993

A CIP catalogue record for this title
is available from the British Library
ISBN 0 7493 1474 5

Printed and bound in Great Britain
by Cox & Wyman Ltd, Reading

When the Lion Feeds

This book is for
Elfreda and Herbert James Smith
with love

Part I
Natal

I

A single wild pheasant flew up the side of the hill almost brushing the tips of the grass in its flight. It drooped its wings and hung its legs as it reached the crest and then dropped into cover. Two boys and a dog followed it up from the valley: the dog led, with his tongue flopping pink from the corner of his mouth, and the twins ran shoulder to shoulder behind him. Both of them were sweating in dark patches through their khaki shirts, for the African sun still had heat although it stood half-mast down the sky.

The dog hit the scent of the bird and it stopped him quivering: for a second he stood sucking it up through his nostrils, and then he started to quarter. He worked fast, back and forth, swinging at the end of each tack, his head down and only his back and his busy tail showing above the dry brown grass. The twins came up behind him. They were gasping for breath for it had been a hard pull up the curve of the hill.

'Keep out to the side, you'll get in my way,' Sean panted at his brother and Garrick moved to obey. Sean was his senior by four inches in height and twenty pounds in weight: this gave him the right to command. Sean transferred his attention back to the dog.

'Put him up, Tinker. Seek him up, boy.'

Tinker's tail acknowledged Sean's instructions, but he held his nose to the ground. The twins followed him, tensed for the bird to rise. They carried their throwing sticks ready and moved forward a stealthy pace at a time, fighting to control their breathing. Tinker found the bird crouched flat in the grass; he jumped forward giving tongue for the first time, and the bird rose. It came up fast on noisy wings, whirling out of the grass.

Sean threw; his kerrie whipped past it. The pheasant swung away from the stick, clawing at the air with frantic wings and Garrick threw. His kerrie cartwheeled up, hissing, until it smacked into the pheasant's fat brown body. The bird toppled, feathers flurried from it and it fell. They went after it. The pheasant scurried broken-winged through the grass ahead of them, and they shouted with excitement as they chased it. Sean got a hand to it. He broke its neck and stood laughing, holding the warm brown body in his hands, and waited for Garrick to reach him.

'Ring-a-ding-a-doody, Garry, you sure gave that one a beauty!'

Tinker jumped up to smell the bird and Sean stooped and held it so he could get his nose against it. Tinker snuffled it, then tried to take it in his mouth, but Sean pushed his head away and tossed the bird to Garrick. Garrick hung it with the others on his belt.

'How far do you reckon that was – fifty feet?' Garrick asked.

'Not as much as that,' Sean gave his opinion. 'More like thirty.'

'I reckon it was at least fifty. I reckon it was farther than any you've hit today.' Success had made Garrick bold. The smile faded from Sean's face.

'Yeah?' he asked.

'Yeah!' said Garrick. Sean pushed the hair off his forehead with the back of his hand, his hair was black and soft and it kept falling into his eyes.

'What about that one down by the river? That was twice as far.'

'Yeah?' asked Garrick.

'Yeah!' said Sean truculently.

'Well, if you're so good, how did you miss this one – hey? You threw first. How come you missed, hey?'

Sean's already flushed face darkened and Garrick realized suddenly that he had gone too far. He took a step backwards.

'You'd like to bet?' demanded Sean. It was not quite clear to Garrick on what Sean wished to bet, but from past experience he knew that whatever it was the issue would be settled by single combat. Garrick seldom won bets from Sean.

'It's too late. We'd better be getting home. Pa will clobber us if we're late for dinner.' Sean hesitated and Garrick turned, ran back to pick up his kerrie then set off in the direction of home. Sean trotted after him, caught up with him and passed him. Sean always led. Having proved conclusively his superior prowess with the throwing sticks Sean was prepared to be forgiving.

Over his shoulder he asked, 'What colour do you reckon Gypsy's foal will be?'

Garrick accepted the peace-offering with relief and they fell into a friendly discussion of this and a dozen other equally important subjects. They kept running: except for an hour, when they had stopped in a shady place by the river to roast and eat a couple of their pheasants, they had run all day.

Up here on the plateau it was grassland that rose and fell beneath them as they climbed the low round hills and dropped into the valleys. The grass around them moved with the wind: waist-high grass, soft dry grass the colour of ripe wheat. Behind them and on each side the grassland rolled away to the full range of the eye, but suddenly in front of them was the escarpment. The land cascaded down into it, steeply at first then gradually levelling out to become the Tugela flats. The Tugela river was twenty miles away across the flats, but today there was a haze in the air so they could not see that far. Beyond the river, stretched far to the north and a hundred miles east to the sea, was Zululand. The river was the border. The steep side of the escarpment was cut by vertical gulleys and in the gulleys grew dense, olive-green bush.

Below them, two miles out on the flats, was the homestead of Theunis Kraal. The house was a big one, Dutch-gabled and smoothly thatched with combed grass. There were horses in the small paddock: many horses, for the twins' father was a wealthy man. Smoke from the cooking fires blued the air over the servants' quarters and the sound of someone chopping wood carried faintly up to them.

Sean stopped on the rim of the escarpment and sat down in the grass. He took hold of one of his grimy bare feet and twisted it up into his lap. There was a hole in the ball of his heel from which he had pulled a thorn earlier in the day and now it was plugged with dirt. Garrick sat down next to him.

'Man, is that going to hurt when Ma puts iodine on it!' gloated Garrick. 'She'll have to use a needle to get the dirt out. I bet you yell – I bet you yell your head off !'

Sean ignored him. He picked a stalk of grass and started probing it into the wound. Garrick watched with interest. Twins could scarcely have been less alike. Sean was already taking on the shape of a man: his shoulders were thickening, and there was hard muscle forming in his puppy fat. His colouring was vivid: black hair, skin brown from the sun, lips and cheeks that glowed with the fresh young blood beneath their surface, and blue eyes, the dark indigo-blue of cloud shadow on mountain lake.

Garrick was slim, with the wrists and ankles of a girl. His hair was an undecided brown that grew wispy down the back of his neck, his skin was freckled, his nose and the rims of his pale blue eyes were pink with persistent hay fever. He was fast losing interest in Sean's surgery. He reached across and fiddled with one of Tinker's pendulous ears, and this broke the rhythm of the dog's panting; he gulped twice and the saliva dripped from the end of his tongue. Garrick lifted his head and looked down the slope. A little below where they were sitting was the head of one of the bushy gullies. Garrick caught his breath.

'Sean, look there – next to the bush!' His whisper trembled with excitement.

'What's it?' Sean looked up startled. Then he saw it.

'Hold Tinker.' Garrick grabbed the dog's collar and pulled his head around to prevent him seeing and giving chase. 'He's the biggest old inkonka in the world,' breathed Garrick. Sean was too absorbed to answer.

The bushbuck was picking its way warily out of the thick cover. A big ram, black with age; the spots on his haunches were faded like old chalk marks. His ears pricked up and his spiral horns held high, big as a pony, but stepping daintily, he came out into the open. He stopped and swung his head from side to side, searching for danger, then he trotted diagonally down the hill and disappeared into another of the gullies. For a moment after he had gone the twins were still, then they burst out together.

'Did you see him, hey – did you see them horns?'

'So close to the house and we never knew he was there –'

They scrambled to their feet jabbering at each other, and Tinker was infected with their excitement. He barked around them in a circle. After the first few moments of confusion Sean took control simply by raising his voice above the opposition.

'I bet he hides up in the gulley every day. I bet he stays there all day and comes out only at night. Let's go and have a look.'

Sean led the way down the slope.

On the fringe of the bush, in a small cave of vegetation that was dark and cool and carpeted with dead leaves, they found the

6

ram's hiding-place. The ground was trampled by his hooves and scattered with his droppings and there was the mark of his body where he had lain. A few loose hairs, tipped with grey, were left on the bed of leaves. Sean knelt down and picked one up.

'How are we going to get him?'

'We could dig a hole and put sharpened sticks in it,' suggested Garrick eagerly.

'Who's going to dig it – you?' Sean asked.

'You could help.'

'It would have to be a pretty big hole,' said Sean doubtfully. There was silence while both of them considered the amount of labour involved in digging a trap. Neither of them mentioned the idea again.

'We could get the other kids from town and have a drive with kerries,' said Sean.

'How many hunts have we been on with them? Must be hundreds by now, and we haven't even bagged one lousy duiker – let alone a bushbuck.' Garrick hesitated and then went on. 'Besides, remember what that inkonka did to Frank Van Essen, hey? When it finished sticking him they had to push all his guts back into the hole in his stomach!'

'Are you scared?' asked Sean.

'I am not, so!' said Garrick indignantly, then quickly, 'Gee, it's almost dark. We'd better run.'

They went down the valley.

2

Sean lay in the darkness and stared across the room at the grey oblong of the window. There was a slice of moon in the sky outside. Sean could not sleep: he was thinking about the bush-buck. He heard his parents pass the door of the bedroom; his stepmother said something and his father laughed: Waite Court-ney had a laugh as deep as distant thunder.

Sean heard the door of their room close and he sat up in bed. 'Garry.' No answer.

'Garry.' He picked up a boot and threw it; there was a grunt. 'Garry.'

'What you want?' Garrick's voice was sleepy and irritable.

'I was just thinking – tomorrow's Friday.'

'So?'

'Ma and Pa will be going into town. They'll be away all day. We could take the shotgun and go lay for that old inkonka.'

Garrick's bed creaked with alarm.

'You're mad!' Garrick could not keep the shock out of his voice. 'Pa would kill us if he caught us with the shotgun.' Even as he said it he knew he would have to find a stronger argument than that to dissuade his brother. Sean avoided punishment if possible, but a chance at a bushbuck ram was worth all his father's right arm could give. Garrick lay rigid in his bed, search-ing for words.

'Besides, Pa keeps the cartridges locked up.'

It was a good try, but Sean countered it.

'I know where there are two buckshots that he has forgotten about: they're in the big vase in the dining-room. They've been there over a month.'

Garrick was sweating. He could almost feel the sjambok curl-ing round his buttocks, and hear his father counting the strokes: eight, nine, ten.

'Please, Sean, let's think of something else. . . .'

8

Across the room Sean settled back comfortably on his pillows. The decision had been made.

3

Waite Courtney handed his wife up into the front seat of the buggy. He patted her arm affectionately then walked around to the driver's side, pausing to fondle the horses and settle his hat down over his bald head. He was a big man, the buggy dipped under his weight as he climbed up into the seat. He gathered up the reins, then he turned and his eyes laughed over his great hooked nose at the twins standing together on the veranda.

'I would esteem it a favour if you two gentlemen could arrange to stay out of trouble for the few hours that your mother and I will be away.'

'Yes, Pa,' in dutiful chorus.

'Sean, if you get the urge to climb the big blue gum tree again then fight it, man, fight it.'

'All right, Pa.'

'Garrick, let us have no more experiments in the manufacture of gunpowder – agreed?'

'Yes, Pa.'

'And don't look so innocent. That really frightens the hell out of me!'

Waite touched the whip to the shiny round rumps in front of him and the buggy started forward, out along the road to Ladyburg.

'He didn't say anything about not taking the shotgun,' whispered Sean virtuously. 'Now you go and see if all the servants are out of the way – if they see us, they'll kick up a fuss. Then come round to the bedroom window and I'll pass it out to you.'

Sean and Garrick argued all the way to the foot of the escarpment. Sean was carrying the shotgun across one shoulder, hanging onto the butt with both hands.

'It was my idea, wasn't it?' he demanded.

'But I saw the inkonka first,' protested Garrick. Garrick was bold again: with every yard put between him and the house his fear of reprisal faded.

'That doesn't count,' Sean informed him. 'I thought of the shotgun, so I do the shooting.'

'How come you always have the fun?' asked Garrick, and Sean was outraged at the question.

'When you found the hawk's nest by the river, I let you climb for it. Didn't I? When you found the baby duiker, I let you feed it. Didn't I?' he demanded.

'All right. So I saw the inkonka first, why don't you let me take the shot?'

Sean was silent in the face of such stubbornness, but his grip on the butt of the shotgun tightened. In order to win the argument Garrick would have to get it away from him – this Garrick knew and he started to sulk. Sean stopped among the trees at the foot of the escarpment and looked over his shoulder at his brother.

'Are you going to help – or must I do it alone?'

Garrick looked down at the ground and kicked at a twig. He sniffed wetly; his hayfever was always bad in the mornings.

'Well?' asked Sean.

'What do you want me to do?'

'Stay here and count to a thousand slowly. I'm going to circle up the slope and wait where the inkonka crossed yesterday. When you finish counting come up the gulley. Start shouting when you are about halfway up. The inkonka will break the same way as yesterday – all right?'

Garrick nodded reluctantly.

'Did you bring Tinker's chain?'

Garrick pulled it from his pocket, and at the sight of it the dog backed away. Sean grabbed his collar, and Garrick slipped it on. Tinker laid his ears flat and looked at them reproachfully.

'Don't let him go. That old inkonka will rip him up. Now start counting,' said Sean and began climbing. He kept well out to the left of the gulley. The grass on the slope was slippery under his feet, the gun was heavy and there were sharp lumps of rock in the grass. He stubbed his toe and it started to bleed, but he kept on upwards. There was a dead tree on the edge of the bush that Sean had used to mark the bushbuck's hide. Sean climbed above it and stopped just below the crest of the slope where the moving grass would break up the silhouette of his head on the skyline. He was panting. He found a rock the size of a beer barrel to use as a rest for the gun, and he crouched behind it. He laid the stock of the gun on the rock, aimed back down the hill and traversed the barrels left and right to make sure his field of fire was clear. He imagined the bushbuck running in his sights and he felt excitement shiver along his forearms, across his shoulders and up the back of his neck.

'I won't lead on him – he'll be moving fairly slowly, trotting most probably. I'll go straight at his shoulders,' he whispered.

He opened the gun, took the two cartridges out of his shirt pocket, slid them into the breeches and snapped the gun closed. It took all the strength of both his hands to pull back the big fancy hammers, but he managed it and the gun was double-loaded and cocked. He laid it on the rock in front of him again and stared down the slope. On his left the gulley was a dark-green smear on the hillside, directly below him was open grass where the bushbuck would cross. He pushed impatiently at the hair on his forehead: it was damp with sweat and stayed up out of his eyes.

The minutes drifted by.

'What the hell is Garry doing? He's so stupid sometimes!' Sean muttered and almost in answer he heard Garrick shout below him. It was a small sound, far down the slope and muffled by the bush. Tinker barked once without enthusiasm; he was also sulking, he didn't like the chain. Sean waited with his forefinger on one trigger, staring down at the edge of the bush. Garrick shouted again – and the bushbuck broke from cover.

It came fast into the open with its nose up and its long horns held flat against its back. Sean moved his body sideways swinging the gun with its run, riding the pip of the foresight on its black shoulder. He fired the left barrel and the recoil threw him off balance; his ears hummed with the shot and the burnt powder smoke blew back into his face. He struggled to his feet still holding the gun. The bushbuck was down in the grass, bleating like a lamb and kicking as it died.

'I got him,' screamed Sean. 'I got him first shot! Garry, Garry! I got him, I got him!'

Tinker came pelting out of the bush dragging Garry behind him by the chain and, still screaming, Sean ran down to join them. A stone rolled under his foot and he fell. The shotgun flew out of his hand and the second barrel fired. The sound of the explosion was very loud.

When Sean scrambled onto his feet again Garrick was sitting in the grass whimpering – whimpering and staring at his leg. The blast of the shotgun had smashed into it and churned the flesh below the knee into tatters – bursting it open so the bone chips showed white in the wound and the blood pumped dark and strong and thick as custard.

'I didn't mean it. . . . Oh God, Garry, I didn't mean it. I slipped. Honest, I slipped.' Sean was staring at the leg also. There was no colour in his face, his eyes were big and dark with horror. The blood pumped out onto the grass.

'Stop it bleeding! Sean, please stop it. Oh, it's sore! Oh! Sean, please stop it!'

Sean stumbled across to him. He wanted to vomit. He unbuckled his belt and strapped it round the leg, and the blood was warm and sticky on his hands. He used his sheathed knife to twist the belt tight. The pumping slowed and he twisted harder.

'Oh, Sean, it's sore! It's sore. . . .' Garrick's face was waxy-white and he was starting to shiver as the cold hand of shock closed on him.

'I'll get Joseph,' Sean stammered. 'We'll come back quickly as we can. Oh, God, I'm sorry!' Sean jumped up and ran. He fell, rolled to his feet and kept running.

They came within an hour. Sean was leading three of the Zulu servants. Joseph, the cook, had brought a blanket. He wrapped Garrick and lifted him and Garrick fainted as his leg swung loosely. As they started back down the hill Sean looked out across the flats: there was a little puff of dust on the Ladyburg road. One of the grooms was riding to fetch Waite Courtney.

They were waiting on the veranda of the homestead when Waite Courtney, came back to Theunis Kraal. Garrick was conscious again. He lay on the couch: his face was white and the blood had soaked through the blanket. There was blood on Joseph's uniform and blood had dried black on Sean's hands. Waite Courtney ran up onto the veranda; he stooped over Garrick and drew back the blanket. For a second he stood staring at the leg and then very gently he covered it again.

Waite lifted Garrick and carried him down to the buggy. Joseph went with him and they settled Garrick on the back seat. Joseph held his body and Garrick's stepmother took the leg on her lap to stop it twisting. Waite Courtney climbed quickly into the driver's seat: he picked up the reins, then he turned his head and looked at Sean still standing on the veranda. He didn't speak, but his eyes were terrible – Sean could not meet them. Waite Courtney used the whip on the horses and drove them back along the road to Ladyburg: he drove furiously with the wind streaming his beard back from his face.

Sean watched them go. After they had disappeared among the trees he remained standing alone on the veranda; then suddenly he turned and ran back through the house. He ran out of the kitchen door and across the yard to the saddle-room, snatched a bridle down from the rack and ran to the paddock. He picked a bay mare and worked her into a corner of the fence until he could slip his arm around her neck. He forced the bit into her mouth, buckled the chin strap and swung up onto her bare back.

He kicked her into a run and put her to the gate, swaying back as her body heaved up under him and falling forward on her neck as she landed. He gathered himself and turned her head towards the Ladyburg road.

It was eight miles to town and the buggy reached it before Sean. He found it outside Doctor Van Rooyen's surgery: the horses were blowing hard, and their bodies were dark with sweat. Sean slid down off the mare's back; he went up the steps to the surgery door and quietly pushed it open. There was the sweet reek of chloroform in the room. Garrick lay on the table, Waite and his wife stood on each side of him, and the doctor was washing his hands in an enamel basin against the far wall. Ada Courtney was crying silently, her face blurred with tears. They all looked at Sean standing in the doorway.

'Come here,' said Waite Courtney, his voice flat and expressionless. 'Come and stand here beside me. They're going to cut off your brother's leg and, by Christ, I'm going to make you watch every second of it!'

4

They brought Garrick back to Theunis Kraal in the night. Waite
Courtney drove the buggy very slowly and carefully and Sean
trailed a long way behind it. He was cold in his thin khaki shirt,
and sick in the stomach with what he had seen. There were
bruises on his upper arm where his father had held him and
forced him to watch.

The servants had lanterns burning on the veranda. They were
standing in the shadows, silent and anxious. As Waite carried
the blanket-wrapped body up the front steps one of them called
softly in the Zulu tongue. 'The leg?'

'It is gone,' Waite answered gruffly.

They sighed softly all together and the voice called again. 'He
is well?'

'He is alive,' said Waite.

He carried Garrick through to the room that was set aside for
guests and sickness. He stood in the centre of the floor holding
the boy while his wife put fresh sheets on the bed; then he laid
him down and covered him.

'Is there anything else we can do?' asked Ada.

'We can wait.'

Ada groped for her husband's hand. 'Please, God, let him live,'
she whispered. 'He's so young.'

'It's Sean's fault!' Waite's anger flared up suddenly. 'Garry
would never have done it on his own.' He tried to disengage
Ada's hand.

'What are you going to do?' she asked.

'I'm going to beat him! I'm going to thrash the skin off him!'

'Don't, please don't.'

'What do you mean?'

'He's had enough. Didn't you see his face?'

Waite's shoulders sagged wearily and he sat down on the
armchair beside the bed. Ada touched his cheek.

15

'I'll stay here with Garry. You go and try to get some sleep, my dear.'

'No,' Waite said. She sat down on the side of the chair and Waite put his arm around her waist. After a long while they slept, huddled together on the chair beside the bed.

5

The days that followed were bad. Garrick's mind escaped from the harness of sanity and ran wild into the hot land of delirium. He panted and twisted his fever-flushed face from side to side; he cried and whimpered in the big bed; the stump of his leg puffed up angrily and the stitches were drawn so tight it seemed they must tear out of the swollen flesh. The infection oozed yellow and foul-smelling onto the sheets.

Ada stayed by him all that time. She swabbed the sweat from his face and changed the dressings on his stump, she held the glass for him to drink and gentled him when he raved. Her eyes sunk darkly into their sockets with fatigue and worry, but she would not leave him. Waite could not bear it. He had the masculine dread of suffering that threatened to suffocate him if he stayed in the room: every half hour or so he came in and stood next to the bed and then he turned away and went back to his restless wandering around the house. Ada could hear his heavy tramp along the corridors.

Sean stayed in the house also: he sat in the kitchen or at the far end of the veranda. No one would speak to him, not even the servants; they chased him when he tried to sneak into the bedroom to see Garrick. He was lonely with the desolate loneliness of the guilty – for Garry was going to die, he knew it by the evil silence that hung over Theunis Kraal. There was no chatter nor pot-clatter from the kitchens, no rich deep laughter from his father: even the dogs were subdued. Death was at Theunis Kraal. He could smell it on the soiled sheets that were brought through to the kitchen from Garrick's room; it was a musky smell, the smell of an animal. Sometimes he could almost see it: even in bright daylight sitting on the veranda he sensed it crouched near him like a shadow on the edge of his vision. It had no form as yet. It was a darkness, a coldness

17

that was gradually building up around the house, gathering its strength until it could take his brother.

On the third day Waite Courtney came roaring out of Garrick's room. He ran through the house and out into the stable yard. 'Karlie. Where are you? Get a saddle onto Rooiberg. Hurry, man, hurry – damn you. He's dying, do you hear me, he's dying.'

Sean did not move from where he sat against the wall next to the back door. His arm tightened around Tinker's neck and the dog touched his cheek with a cold nose; he watched his father jump up onto the stallion's back and ride. The hooves beat away towards Ladyburg and when they were gone he stood up and slipped into the house: he listened outside Garrick's door and then he opened it quietly and went in. Ada turned towards him, her face was tired. She looked much older than her thirty-five years, but her black hair was drawn back behind her head into a neat bun and her dress was fresh and clean. She was still a beautiful woman despite her exhaustion. There was a gentleness about her, a goodness that suffering and worry could not destroy. She held out her hand to Sean and he crossed and stood beside her chair and looked down at Garrick. Then he knew why his father had gone to fetch the doctor. Death was in the room – strong and icy cold hovered over the bed. Garrick lay very still: his face was yellow, his eyes were closed and his lips were cracked and dry.

All the loneliness and the guilt came swelling up into Sean's throat and choked him into sobs, sobs that forced him to his knees and he put his face into Ada's lap and cried. He cried for the last time in his life, he cried as a man cries – painfully, each sob tearing something inside him.

Waite Courtney came back from Ladyburg with the doctor. Once more Sean was driven out and the door closed. All night he heard them working in Garrick's room, the murmuring of their voices and the scuff of feet on the yellow wood floor. In the morning it was over. The fever was broken and Garrick was alive. Only just alive – his eyes were sunk into dark holes like those of a skull. His body and his mind were never to recover completely from that brutal pruning.

It was slow – a week before he was strong enough to feed himself. His first need was for his brother, before he was able to talk above a whisper it was, 'Where's Sean?'

And Sean, still chastened, sat with him for hours at a time.

Then when Garrick slept Sean escaped from the room, and with a fishing-rod or his hunting sticks and Tinker barking behind him went into the veld. It was a measure of Sean's repentance that he allowed himself to be contained within the sick-room for such long periods. It chafed him like ropes on a young colt: no one would ever know what it cost him to sit quietly next to Garrick's bed while his body itched and burned with unexpended energy and his mind raced restlessly.

Then Sean had to go back to school. He left on a Monday morning while it was still dark. Garrick listened to the sounds of departure, the whicker of the horses outside on the driveway and Ada's voice reciting last minute instructions: 'I've put a bottle of cough mixture under your shirts, give it to Fräulein as soon as you unpack. Then she'll see that you take it at the first sign of a cold.'

'Yes, Ma.'

'There are six vests in the small case – use a new one every day.'

'Vests are sissy things.'

'You will do as you're told, young man.' Waite's voice, 'Hurry up with your porridge – we've got to get going if I'm to have you in town by seven o'clock.'

'Can I say goodbye to Garry?'

'You said goodbye last night – he'll still be asleep now.'

Garrick opened his mouth to call out, but he knew his voice would not carry. He lay quietly and listened to the chairs scraping back from the dining-room table, the procession of footsteps out onto the veranda, voices raised in farewells and at last the wheels of the buggy crunching gravel as they moved away down the drive. It was very quiet after Sean had left with his father.

After that the weekends were, for Garrick, the only bright spots in the colourless passage of time. He longed for them to come and each one was an eternity after the last – time passes slowly for the young and the sick. Ada and Waite knew a little of how he felt. They moved the centre of the household to his room: they brought two of the fat leather armchairs from the lounge and put them on each side of his bed and they spent the evenings there. Waite with his pipe in his mouth and a glass of brandy at his elbow, whittling at the wooden leg he was making and laughing his deep laugh, Ada with her knitting and the two of them trying to reach him. Perhaps it was this conscious effort that was the cause of their failure, or perhaps it is impossible to reach back down the years to a small boy. There is always that reserve, that barrier between the adult and the secret world of youth. Garrick laughed with them and they talked together, but it was not the same as having Sean there. During the day Ada had the running of a large household and there were fifteen thousand acres of land and two thousand head of cattle that needed Waite's attention. That was the loneliest time for Garrick. If it had not been for the books, he might not have been able to bear it. He read everything that Ada brought to him: Stevenson, Swift, Defoe, Dickens and even Shakespeare. Much of it he didn't understand, but he read hungrily and the opium of the printed word helped him through the long days until Sean came home each Friday.

When Sean came home it was like a big wind blowing through the house. Doors slammed, dogs barked, servants scolded and feet clattered up and down the passages. Most of the noise was Sean's, but not all of it. There were Sean's followers: youngsters from his class at the village school. They accepted Sean's authority as willingly as did Garrick, and it was not only Sean's fists that won this acceptance but also the laughter and the sense of excitement that went with him. They came out to Theunis Kraal in droves that summer, sometimes as many as three on one bare-backed pony: sitting like a row of sparrows on a fence rail. They came for the added attraction of Garry's stump. Sean was very proud of it.

'That's where the doc sewed it up,' pointing to the row of stitch marks along the pink fold of scar tissue.

'Can I touch it, man?'

'Not too hard or it'll burst open.' Garrick had never received attention like this in his life before. He beamed round the circle of solemn, wide-eyed faces.

'It feels funny – sort of hot.'

'Was it sore?'

'How did he chop the bone – with an axe?'

'No.' Sean was the only one in a position to answer technical questions of this nature. 'With a saw. Just like a piece of wood.' He made the motions with his open hand.

But even this fascinating subject couldn't hold them for long and presently there would be a restlessness amongst them.

'Hey, Sean, Karl and I know where there's a nest of squawkers

– you wanta have a look?' or 'Let's go and catch frogs,' and Garrick would cut in desperately.

'You can have a look at my stamp collection if you like. It's in the cupboard there.'

'Naw, we saw it last week. Let's go.'

This was when Ada, who had been listening to the conversation through the open kitchen door, brought in the food. Koeksusters fried in honey, chocolate cakes with peppermint icing, watermelon konfyt and half a dozen other delicacies. She knew they wouldn't leave until it was finished and she knew also that there'd be upset stomachs when it was, but that was preferable to Garrick lying alone and listening to the others riding off into the hills.

The weekends were short, gone in a breathless blur. Another long week began for Garrick. There were eight of them, eight dreary weeks before Doctor Van Rooyen agreed to let him sit out on the veranda during the day. Then suddenly the prospect of being well again became a reality for Garrick. The leg that Waite was making was nearly finished: he shaped a leather bucket to take the stump and fitted it to the wood with flatheaded copper nails; he worked carefully, moulding the leather and adjusting the straps that would hold it in place. Meanwhile, Garrick exercised along the veranda, hopping beside Ada with an arm around her shoulder, his jaws clenched with concentration and the freckles very prominent on his face that had been without the sun for so long. Twice a day Ada sat on a cushion in front of Garrick's chair and massaged the stump with methylated spirits to toughen it for its first contact with the stiff leather bucket.

'I bet old Sean'll be surprised, hey? When he sees me walking around.'

'Everyone will,' Ada agreed. She looked up from his leg and smiled.

'Can't I try it now? Then I can go out fishing with him when he comes on Saturday.'

'You mustn't expect too much, Garry, it's not going to be easy at first. You will have to learn to use it. Like riding a horse – you remember how often you fell off before you learned to ride.'

'But can I start now?'

Ada reached for the spirits bottle, poured a little into her cupped hand and spread it on the stump. 'We'll have to wait

21

until Doctor Van Rooyen tells us you're ready. It won't be long now.'

It wasn't. After his next visit Doctor Van Rooyen spoke to Waite as they walked together to the doctor's trap.

'You can try him with the peg-leg – it'll give him something to work for. Don't let him overtire himself and watch the stump doesn't get rubbed raw. We don't want another infection.'

'Peg-leg.' Waite's mind echoed the ugly word as he watched the trap out of sight. 'Peg-leg': he clenched his fists at his sides, not wanting to turn and see the pathetically eager face behind him on the veranda.

6

'Are you sure that's comfortable?' Waite squatted in front of Garrick's chair adjusting the leg and Ada stood next to him.

'Yes, yes, let me try it now. Gee, old Sean will be surprised, hey? I'll be able to go back with him on Monday, won't I?' Garrick was trembling with eagerness.

'We'll see,' Waite grunted non-committally. He stood up and moved round beside the chair.

'Ada, my dear, take his other arm. Now listen, Garry, I want you to get the feel of it first. We'll help you up and you can just stand on it and get your balance. Do you understand?'

Garrick nodded vigorously.

'All right, then up you come.'

Garrick drew the leg towards him and the tip scraped across the wooden floor. They lifted him and he put his weight on it.

'Look at me – I'm standing on it. Hey, look I'm standing on it.' His face glowed. 'Let me walk, come on! Let me walk.'

Ada glanced at her husband and he nodded. Together they led Garrick forward. He stumbled twice but they held him. Klunk and klunk again the peg rang on the floor boards. Before they reached the end of the veranda Garrick had learned to lift the leg high as he swung it forward. They turned and he stumbled only once on the way back to the chair.

'That's fine, Garry, you're doing fine,' laughed Ada.

'You'll be on your own in no time,' Waite grinned with relief. He had hardly dared to hope it would be so easy, and Garrick fastened on his words. 'Let me stand on my own now.'

'Not this time, boy, you've done well enough for one day.'

'Oh, gee, Pa. Please. I won't try and walk, I'll just stand. You and Ma can be ready to catch me. Please, Pa, please.'

Waite hesitated and Ada added her entreaty. 'Let him, dear, he's done so well. It'll help build up his confidence.'

'Very well. But don't try to move,' Waite agreed. 'Are you

23

ready, Garry? Let him go!' They took their hands off him cautiously. He teetered slightly and their hands darted back.

'I'm all right – leave me.' He grinned at them confidently and once more they released him. He stood straight and steady for a moment and then he looked down at the ground. The grin froze on his face. He was alone on a high mountain, his stomach turned giddily within him and he was afraid, desperately unreasonably afraid. He lurched violently and the first shriek tore from him before they could hold him. 'I'm falling. Take it off! Take it off!'

They sat him in the chair with one swift movement.

'Take it off! I'm going to fall!' The terrified screams racked Waite as he tore at the straps that held the leg.

'It's off, Garry, you're safe. I'm holding you.' Waite took him to his chest and held him, trying to quieten him with the strength of his arms and the security of his own big body, but Garrick's terrified struggling and his shrieks continued.

'Take him to the bedroom, get him inside.' Ada spoke urgently and Waite ran with him, still holding him against his chest.

Then for the first time Garrick found his hiding-place. At the moment when his terror became too great to bear he felt something move inside his head, fluttering behind his eyes like the wings of a moth. His vision greyed as though he was in a mist bank. The mist thickened and blotted out all sight and sound. It was warm in the mist – warm and safe. No one could touch him here for it wrapped and protected him. He was safe.

'I think he's asleep,' Waite whispered to his wife, but there was a puzzled expression in his voice. He looked carefully at the boy's face and listened to his breathing.

'It happened so quickly though – it isn't natural. And yet – and yet he looks all right.'

'Do you think, we should call the doctor?' Ada asked.

'No.' Waite shook his head. 'I'll just cover him up and stay with him until he wakes.'

He woke in the early evening, sat up and smiled at them as though nothing had happened. Relaxed and shyly cheerful, he ate a big supper and no one mentioned the leg. It was almost as though Garrick had forgotten about it.

7

Sean came home on the following Friday afternoon. He had a black eye – not a fresh one; it was already turning green round the edges of the bruise. Sean was very reticent on the subject of how he had obtained it. He brought with him also a clutch of flycatchers' eggs which he gave to Garrick, a live red-lipped snake in a cardboard box which Ada immediately condemned to death despite Sean's impassioned speech in its defence, and a bow carved from M'senga wood which was, in Sean's opinion, the best wood for a bow.

His arrival wrought the usual change in the household of Theunis Kraal – more noise, more movement and more laughter.

There was a huge roast for dinner that evening, with potatoes baked in their jackets. These were Sean's favourite foods and he ate like a hungry python.

'Don't put so much in your mouth,' Waite remonstrated from the head of the table, but there was a fondness in his voice. It was hard not to show favouritism with his sons. Sean accepted the rebuke in the spirit it was given. 'Pa, Frikkie Oberholster's bitch had pups this week, six of them.'

'No,' said Ada firmly.

'Gee, Ma, just one.'

'You heard your mother, Sean.' Sean poured gravy over his meat, cut a potato in half and lifted one piece to his mouth. It had been worth a try. He hadn't really expected them to agree.

'What did you learn this week?' Ada asked. This was a nasty question. Sean had learned as much as was necessary to avoid trouble – no more.

'Oh, lots of things,' he replied airily and then to change the subject. 'Have you finished Garry's new leg yet, Pa?'

There was a silence. Garrick's face went expressionless and he dropped his eyes to his plate. Sean put the other half of the potato in his mouth and spoke around it.

25

'If you have, me and Garry can go fishing up at the falls tomorrow.'

'Don't talk with your mouth full,' snapped Waite with unnecessary violence. 'You've got the manners of a pig.'

'Sorry, Pa,' Sean muttered. The rest of the meal passed in uneasy silence and as soon as it finished Sean escaped to the bedroom. Garry went with him hopping along the passage with one hand on the wall to balance himself.

'What's Pa so mad about?' Sean demanded resentfully as soon as they were alone.

'I don't know.' Garrick sat on the bed. 'Sometimes he just gets mad for nothing – you know that.'

Sean pulled his shirt off over his head, screwed it into a ball and threw it against the far wall.

'You'd better pick it up, else there'll be trouble,' Garrick warned mildly. Sean dropped his pants and kicked them after the shirt. This show of defiance put him in a better mood. He walked across and stood naked in front of Garrick.

'Look,' he said with pride. 'Hairs!'

Garrick inspected them. Indisputably they were hairs.

'There aren't very many.' Garrick couldn't disguise the envy in his voice.

'Well, I bet I've got more than you have,' Sean challenged. 'Let's count them.'

But Garrick knew himself to be an outright loser; he slipped off the bed and hopped across the room. Steadying himself against the wall he stooped and picked up Sean's discarded clothing, he brought it back and dropped it in the soiled linen basket beside the door. Sean watched him and it reminded him of his unanswered question.

'Has Pa finished your leg yet, Garry?'

Garry turned slowly, he swallowed and nodded once, a quick jerky movement.

'What's it like? Have you tried it yet?'

The fear was on Garrick again. He twisted his face from side to side as though seeking an escape. There were footsteps in the passage outside the door. Sean dived at his bed and snatching up his nightgown pulled it over his head as he slid between the sheets. Garrick was still standing beside the clothes basket when Waite Courtney came into the room. 'Come on, Garry, what's holding you up?'

Garrick hurried across to his bed and Waite looked at Sean. Sean grinned at him with all the charm of his good looks and Waite's face softened into a grin also. 'Nice to have you home again, boy.' It was impossible to be angry with Sean for long.

He reached out and took a handful of Sean's thick black hair. 'Now I don't want to hear any talking in here after the lamp's out – do you understand?'

He tugged Sean's head from side to side gently, embarrassed by the strength of his feeling for his son.

8

The next morning Waite Courtney rode back to the homestead for his breakfast when the sun was high. One of the grooms took his horse and led it away to the paddock and Waite stood in front of the saddle room and looked around him. He looked at the neat white posts of the paddock, at the well-swept yard, at his house filled with fine furniture. It was a good feeling to be rich – especially when you knew what it was like to be poor. Fifteen thousand acres of good grassland, as many cattle as the land would carry, gold in the bank. Waite smiled and started across the yard.

He heard Ada singing in the dairy.

> 'How rides the farmer
> Sit, sit, so
> Sit, sit, so – tra la
> The Capetown girls say
> Kiss me quick
> Kiss me quick – tra la.'

She had a clear sweet voice and Waite's smile broadened – it was a good feeling to be rich and to be in love. He stopped at the door of the dairy; because of the thick stone walls and heavy thatch it was cool and dark in the room. Ada stood with her back to the door, her body moving in time to the song and the turning of the butter churn. Waite watched her a moment, then he walked up behind her and put his arms around her waist.

Startled, she turned within his arms and he kissed her on the mouth. 'Good morning, my pretty maid.'

She relaxed against him. 'Good morning, sir,' she said.

'What's for breakfast?'

'Ah, what a romantic fool I married!' She sighed, 'Come along, let's go and see.'

She took off her apron, hung it behind the door, patted her

hair into place and held her hand out to him. They walked hand-in-hand across the yard and into the kitchen. Waite sniffed loudly.

'Smells all right. Where are the boys?'

Joseph understood English though he could not speak it. He looked up from the stove.

'Nkosi, they are on the front veranda.'

Joseph had the typical moon-round face of the Zulu, when he smiled his teeth were big and white against the black of his skin.

'They are playing with Nkosizana Garry's wooden leg.'

Waite's face flushed. 'How did they find it?'

'Nkosizana Sean asked me where it was and I told him you had put it in the linen cupboard.'

'You bloody fool!' roared Waite. He dropped Ada's hand and ran. As he reached the lounge he heard Sean shout and immediately there was the sound of someone falling heavily on the veranda. He stopped in the middle of the lounge floor; he couldn't bear to go out and face Garrick's terror. He felt sick with dread and with his anger at Sean.

Then he heard Sean laugh. 'Get off me, man, don't just lie there.'

And then, incredibly, Garrick's voice. 'Sorry, it caught in the floor boards.'

Waite walked across to the window and looked out onto the veranda. Sean and Garrick lay in a heap together near the far end. Sean was still laughing and on Garrick's face was a set nervous smile. Sean scrambled up. 'Come on. Get up.'

He gave Garrick his hand and dragged him to his feet. They stood clinging to each other, Garrick balancing precariously on his peg. 'I bet if it was me I could just walk easy as anything,' said Sean.

'I bet you couldn't, it's jolly difficult.'

Sean let go of him and stood back with his arms spread ready to catch him. 'Come on.'

Sean walked backwards in front of him and Garrick followed unsteadily, his arms flapping out sideways as he struggled to keep his balance, his face rigid with concentration. He reached the end of the veranda and caught onto the rail with both hands. This time he joined in Sean's laughter.

Waite became aware that Ada was standing beside him; he

glanced sideways at her and her lips formed the words 'come away.' She took his arm.

9

At the end of June 1876 Garrick went back to school with Sean. It was almost four months since the shooting. Waite drove them. The road to Ladyburg was through open forest, two parallel tracks with the grass growing in between – it brushed the bottom of the buggy. The horses trotted in the tracks, their hooves silent on the thick powder dust. At the top of the first rise Waite slowed the horses and turned in his seat to look back at the homestead. The early sun gave the whitewashed walls of Theunis Kraal an orange glow and the lawns around the house were brilliant green. Everywhere else the grass was dry in the early winter and the leaves of the trees were dry also. The sun was not yet high enough to rob the veld of its colour and light it only with the flat white glare of midday. The leaves were golden and russet and red-brown, the same red-brown as the bunches of Afrikander cattle that grazed among the trees. Behind it all was the back-drop of the escarpment, striped like a zebra with the green black bush that grew in its gullies.

'Look, there's a hoopoe, Sean.'

'Yeah, I saw it long ago. That's a male.'

The bird flew up from in front of the horses: chocolate and black and white wings, its head crested like an Etruscan helmet.

'How do you know?' challenged Garrick.

''Cause of the white in its wings.'

'They've all got white in their wings.'

'They haven't – only the males.'

'Well, all the ones I've seen got white in their wings,' said Garrick dubiously.

'Perhaps you've never seen a female. They're jolly rare. They don't come out of their nests much.'

Waite Courtney smiled and turned back in his seat. 'Garry's right, Sean, you can't tell the difference by their feathers. The male's a little bigger, that's all.'

'I told you,' said Garrick, brave under his father's protection.

'You know everything,' muttered Sean sarcastically. 'I suppose you read it in all those books, hey?'

Garrick smiled complacently. 'Look, there's the train.'

It was coming down the escarpment, dragging a long grey plume of smoke behind it. Waite started the horses into a trot. They went down to the concrete bridge over the Baboon Stroom.

'I saw a yellow fish.'

'It was a stick, I saw it too.'

The river was the boundary of Waite's land. They crossed the bridge and went up the other side. In front of them was Ladyburg. The train was running into the town past the cattle sale pens; it whistled and shot a puff of steam high into the air.

The town was spread out, each house padded around by its orchard and garden. A thirty-six ox team could turn in any of the wide streets. The houses were burnt brick or whitewashed, thatched or with corrugated-iron roofs painted green or dull red. The square was in the centre and the spire of the church was the hub of Ladyburg. The school was on the far side of town.

Waite trotted the horses along Main Street. There were a few people on the side walks; they moved with early morning stiffness beneath the flamboyant trees that lined the street and every one of them called a greeting to Waite. He waved his whip at the men and lifted his hat to the women, but not high enough to expose the bald dome of his head. In the centre of town the shops were open, and standing on long thin legs in front of his bank was David Pye. He was dressed in black like an undertaker.

'Morning, Waite.'

'Morning, David,' called Waite a little too heartily. It was not six months since he had paid off the last mortgage on Theunis Kraal and the memory of debt was too fresh in his mind; he felt as embarrassed as a newly released prisoner meeting the prison governor on the street.

'Can you come in and see me after you've dropped off your boys?'

'Have the coffee ready,' agreed Waite. It was well known that no one was ever offered coffee when they called on David Pye. They went on down the street, turned left at the far end of Church Square, passed the courthouse and down the dip to the school hostel.

There were half a dozen Scotch carts and four-wheelers standing in the yard. Small boys and girls swarmed over them unloading their luggage. Their fathers stood in a group at one end of the yard – brown-faced men, with carefully brushed beards, uncomfortable in their suits which still showed the creases of long hanging. These men lived too far out for their children to make the daily journey into school. Their land sprawled down to the banks of the Tugela or across the plateau halfway to Pietermaritzburg.

Waite stopped the buggy, climbed down and loosened the harness on his horses and Sean jumped from the outside seat to the ground and ran to the nearest bunch of boys. Waite walked across to the men; their ranks opened for him, they smiled their welcomes and in turn reached for his right hand. Garrick sat alone on the front seat of the buggy, his leg stuck out stiffly in front of him and his shoulders hunched as though he were trying to hide.

After a while Waite glanced back over his shoulder. He saw Garrick sitting alone and he made as if to go to him, but stopped immediately. His eyes quested among the swirl of small bodies until they found Sean. 'Sean.'

Sean paused in the middle of an animated discussion. 'Yes, Pa.'

'Give Garry a hand with his case.'

'Aw, gee, Pa – I'm talking.'

'Sean!'Waite scowled with both face and voice.

'All right, I'm going.' Sean hesitated a moment longer and then went back to the buggy.

'Come on, Garry. Pass the cases down.'

Garrick roused himself and climbed awkwardly over the back of the seat. He handed the luggage down to Sean who stacked it beside the wheel, then turned to the group that had followed him across.

'Karl, you carry that. Dennis, take the brown bag. Don't drop it, man, it's got four bottles of jam in it.' Sean issued his instructions.

'Come on, Garry.'

They started off towards the hostel and Garrick climbed down from the buggy and limped quickly after them.

'You know what, Sean?' said Karl loudly. 'Pa let me start using his rifle.'

33

Sean stopped dead, and then more with hope than conviction, 'He did not!'

'He did,' Karl said happily. Garrick caught up with them and they all stared at Karl.

'How many shots did you have?' asked someone in an awed voice.

Karl nearly said, 'Six' but changed it quickly.

'Oh, lots – as many as I wanted.'

'You'll get gun-shy – my Pa says if you start too soon you'll never be a good shot.'

'I never missed once,' flashed Karl.

'Come on,' said Sean and started off once more – he had never been so jealous in his life. Karl hurried after him.

'I bet you've never shot with a rifle, Sean, I bet you haven't, hey?' Sean smiled mysteriously while he searched for some new topic; he could see that Karl was going to kick the subject to death.

From the veranda of the hostel a girl ran to meet him.

'It's Anna,' said Garrick.

She had long brown legs, skinny; her skirts fussed about them as she ran. Her hair was black, her face was small with a pointed chin. 'Hello, Sean.'

Sean grunted. She fell in beside him, skipping to keep pace with him.

'Did you have a nice holiday?'

Sean ignored her, always coming and trying to talk to him, even when his friends were watching.

'I've got a whole tin of shortbread, Sean. Would you like some?' There was a flash of interest in Sean's eyes; he half turned his head towards her, for Mrs Van Essen's shortbread was rightly famous throughout the district, but he caught himself and kept grimly on towards the hostel.

'Can I sit next to you in class this term, Sean?'

Sean turned furiously on her. 'No, you can't. Now go away – I'm busy.'

He went up the steps. Anna stood at the bottom; she looked as though she was going to cry and Garrick stopped shyly beside her.

'You can sit next to me if you like,' he said softly.

She glanced at him, looking down at his leg. The tears cleared and she giggled. She was pretty. She leaned towards him.

'Peg-leg,' she said and giggled again. Garrick blushed so vividly, and suddenly his eyes watered. Anna put both hands to her mouth and giggled through them, then she turned and ran to join her friends in front of the girls' section of the hostel. Still blushing, Garrick went up the steps after Sean; he steadied himself on the banisters.

Fräulein stood at the door of the boys' dormitory. Her steel-rimmed spectacles and the iron grey of her hair gave her face an exaggerated severity, but this was relieved by the smile with which she recognized Sean.

'Ah, my Sean, you have come.' What she actually said was, 'Ach, mein Sean, you haf gom.'

'Hello, Fräulein.' Sean gave her his number one very best smile.

'Again you have grown,' Fräulein measured him with her eyes. 'All the time you grow, already you are the biggest boy in the school.'

Sean watched her warily, ready to take evasive action if she attempted to embrace him as she did sometimes when she could no longer contain her feelings. Sean's blend of charm, good looks and arrogance had completely captured her Teutonic heart.

'Quickly, you must unpack. School is just now starting.' She turned her attention to her other charges and Sean, with relief, led his men through into the dormitory.

'Pa says that next weekend I can use his rifle for hunting, not just targets,' Karl steered the conversation back.

'Dennis, put Garry's case on his bed.' Sean pretended not to hear.

There were thirty beds arranged along the walls, each with a locker beside it. The room was as neat and cheerless as a prison or a school. At the far end a group of five or six boys sat talking. They looked up as Sean came in but no greetings were exchanged – they were the opposition.

Sean sat down on his bed and bounced experimentally, it was hard as a plank, Garrick's peg thumped as he walked down the dormitory and Ronny Pye, the leader of the opposition, whispered something to his friends and they all laughed, watching Garrick. Garrick blushed again and sat down quickly on his bed to hide his leg.

'I guess I'll shoot duiker first before Pa lets me shoot kudu or bushbuck,' Karl stated and Sean frowned.

35

'What's the new teacher like?' he asked.

'He looks all right,' one of the others answered. 'Jimmy and I saw him at the station yesterday.'

'He's thin and got a moustache.'

'He doesn't smile much.'

'I suppose next holiday Pa will take me shooting across the Tugela,' Karl said aggressively.

'I hope he's not too keen on spelling and things,' Sean declared. 'I hope he doesn't start all that decimal business again, like old Lizard did.'

There was a round of agreement and then Garrick made his first contribution. 'Decimals are easy.'

There was a silence while they all looked at him.

'I might even shoot a lion,' said Karl.

IO

There was a single schoolroom to accommodate the youngest upwards of both sexes. Double desks; on the walls a few maps, a large set of multiplication tables and a picture of Queen Victoria. From the dais Mr Anthony Clark surveyed his new pupils. There was a hushed anticipation; one of the girls giggled nervously and Mr Clark's eyes sought the sound, but it stopped before he found it.

'It is my unfortunate duty to attempt your education,' he announced. He wasn't joking. Long ago his sense of vocation had been swamped by an intense dislike for the young: now he taught only for the salary.

'It is your no more pleasant duty to submit to this with all the fortitude you can muster,' he went on, looking with distaste at their shining faces.

'What's he saying?' whispered Sean without moving his lips.

'Shh,' said Garrick.

Mr Clark's eyes swivelled quickly and rested on Garrick. He walked slowly down the aisle between the desks and stopped beside him; he took a little of the hair that grew at Garrick's temple between his thumb and his forefinger and jerked it upwards. Garrick squeaked and Mr Clark returned slowly to his dais.

'We will now proceed. Standard Ones kindly open your spelling books at page one. Standard Twos turn to page fifteen. . . .' He went on allocating their work.

'Did he hurt you?' breathed Sean. Garrick nodded almost imperceptibly and Sean conceived an immediate and intense hatred for the man. He stared at him.

Mr Clark was a little over thirty years old – thin, and his tight three-piece suit emphasized this fact. He had a pale face made sad by his drooping moustache, and his nose was upturned to such a degree that his nostrils were exposed; they pointed out of his face like the muzzle of a double-barrelled shotgun. He lifted his head from the list he held in his hand and aimed his nostrils straight at Sean. For a second they stared at each other.

'Trouble,' thought Mr Clark; he could pick them unerringly. 'Break him before he gets out of control.'

'You, boy, what's your name?'

Sean turned elaborately and looked over his shoulder. When he turned back there was a little colour in Mr Clark's cheeks. 'Stand up.'

'Who, me?'

'Yes, you.'

Sean stood.

'What's your name?'

'Courtney.'

'Sir!'

'Courtney, sir.'

They looked at each other. Mr Clark waited for Sean to drop his eyes but he didn't.

'Big trouble, much bigger than I thought,' he decided and said aloud, 'All right, sit down.'

There was an almost audible relaxation of tension in the room. Sean could sense the respect of the others around him; they were proud of the way he had carried it off. He felt a touch on his shoulder. It was Anna, the seat behind him was as close as she could sit to him. Ordinarily her presumption would have annoyed him, but now that small touch on his shoulder added to his glow of self-satisfaction.

An hour passed slowly for Sean. He drew a picture of a rifle in the margin of his spelling book then rubbed it out carefully, he watched Garrick for a while until his brother's absorption with his work irritated him.

'Swot,' he whispered, but Garrick ignored him.

Sean was bored. He shifted restlessly in his seat and looked at the back of Karl's neck – there was a ripe pimple on it. He picked up his ruler to prod it. Before he could do so Karl lifted his hand as if to scratch his shoulder but there was a scrap of paper between his fingers. Sean put down the ruler and surreptitiously reached for the note. He held it in his lap, on it was written one word.

'Mosquitoes.'

Sean grinned. Sean's imitation of a mosquito was one of the

many reasons why the previous schoolmaster had resigned. For six months old Lizard had believed that there were mosquitoes in the room – then for the next six months he had known there were not. He had tried every ruse he could think of to catch the culprit, and in the end it had got him. Every time the monotonous hum began the tic in the corner of his mouth became more noticeable.

Now Sean cleared his throat and started to hum. Instantly the room was tense with suppressed laughter. Every head, including Sean's, was bent studiously over a book. Mr Clark's hand hesitated in writing on the blackboard but then went on again evenly.

It was a clever imitation; by lowering and raising the volume Sean gave the effect of an insect moving about the room. A slight trembling at his throat was the only sign that he was responsible.

Mr Clark finished writing and turned to face the room. Sean did not make the mistake of stopping, he allowed the mosquito to fly a little longer before settling.

Mr Clark left his dais and walked down the row of desks furthest from Sean. Once or twice he paused to check the work of one of his pupils. He reached the back of the room and moved across to Sean's row. He stopped at Anna's desk.

'It is unnecessary to loop your L's like that,' he told her. 'Let me show you.' He took her pencil and wrote, 'You see what I mean. To show off when writing is as bad as showing off in your everyday behaviour.'

He handed her back her pencil and then pivoting on one foot he hit Sean a mighty crack across the side of the head with his open hand. Sean's head was knocked sideways and the sound of the blow was very loud in the quiet room.

'There was a mosquito sitting on your ear,' said Mr Clark.

II

In the following two years Sean and Garrick made the change from child to young manhood. It was like riding a strong current, being swept with speed along the river of life.

There were parts of the river that flowed steadily:

Ada was one of these. Always understanding, with the ability to give her understanding expression, unchanging in her love for her husband and the family she had taken as her own.

Waite was another. A little more grey in his hair but big as ever in body, laugh and fortune.

There were parts of the river that ran faster:

Garrick's reliance on Sean. He needed him more strongly each month that passed, for Sean was his shield. If Sean was not there to protect him when he was threatened, then he used his final refuge: he crawled back into himself, into the warm dark mists of his mind.

They went to steal peaches: the twins, Karl, Dennis and two others. There was a thick hedge around Mr Pye's orchard and the peaches that grew on the other side of it were as big as a man's fist. They were sweet as honey but tasted even sweeter when taken on the plunder account. You reached the orchard through a plantation of wattle trees.

'Don't take too many off one tree!' Sean ordered. 'Old Pye will notice it as sure as anything.'

They came to the hedge and Sean found the hole.

'Garry, you stay here and keep cats for us. If anyone comes

give a whistle.' Garrick tried not to show his relief, he had no stomach for the expedition.

Sean went on. 'We'll pass the peaches out to you – and don't eat any until we're finished.'

'Why doesn't he come with us?' asked Karl.

"Cause he can't run, that's why. If he gets caught they'll know who the rest of us are for sure and we'll all get it.'

Karl was satisfied. Sean went down on his hands and knees and crawled into the hole in the hedge and one at a time the others followed him until Garrick was left alone.

He stood close to the hedge, drawing comfort from its protecting bulk. The minutes dragged by and Garrick fidgeted nervously – they were taking an awfully long time.

Suddenly there were voices, someone was coming through the plantation towards him. Panic beat up inside him and he shrank back into the hedge, trying to hide; the idea of giving a warning never even entered his head.

The voices were closer and then through the trees he recognized Ronny Pye: with him were two of his friends. Each of them was armed with a slingshot and they walked with their heads thrown back, searching the trees for birds.

For a time it seemed they would not notice Garrick in the hedge; but then, when they had almost passed, Ronny turned his head and saw him. They stared at each other, ten paces apart, Garrick crouched against the hedge and Ronny's expression of surprise slowly changing to one of cunning. He looked around quickly, to make sure that Sean was not there.

'It's old Hobble-dee-hoy,' he announced and his friends came back and stood on each side of him.

'What're you doing, Peg-leg?'

'Rats got your tongue, Peg-leg?'

'No, termites got his leg!' – laughter aimed to hurt.

'Talk to us, Peg-leg.' Ronny Pye had ears that stood out on each side of his head like a pair of fans. He was small for his age which made him vicious and his hair was ginger.

'Come on. Talk to us, Peg-leg.'

Garrick moistened his lips with his tongue, already there were tears in his eyes.

'Hey, Ronny, make him walk for us, like this.' One of the others gave a graphic imitation of Garrick's limp. Again laughter, louder now, more confident and they closed in on him. 'Show us how you walk.'

Garrick swung his head from side to side searching for an escape.

'Your brother's not here,' crowed Ronny. 'No good looking for him, Peg-leg.'

He caught a hold of Garrick's shirt and pulled him out of the hedge.

'Show us how you walk.'

Garrick plucked ineffectually at Ronny's hand.

'Leave me, I'll tell Sean. I'll tell Sean unless you leave me.'

'All right, I'll leave you,' agreed Ronny and with both hands shoved him in the chest. 'Don't come my way – go that way!' Garrick stumbled backwards.

One of the others was ready for him. 'Don't come my way – go that way!' and pushed him in the back. They formed a ring around him and kept him staggering between them.

'Go that way!'

'Go that way!'

The tears were streaked down his cheeks now. 'Please, please stop.'

'Please, please,' they mimicked him.

Then, with a rush of relief, Garrick felt the fluttering start behind his eyes – their faces dimmed, he hardly felt their hands upon him. He fell and his face hit the ground, but there was no pain. Two of them stooped over him to lift him, and there was dirt mixed with the tears on his cheeks.

Sean came through the hedge behind them; the front of his shirt bulged with peaches. For a second he crouched on his hands and knees while he took in what was happening, then he came out of his crouch at a run. Ronny heard him, dropped Garrick and turned.

'You've been pinching Pa's peaches,' he shouted. 'I'll tell –'

Sean's fist hit him on the nose and he sat down. Sean swung towards the other two but they were already running, he chased them a few paces and then came back for Ronny, but he was too late. Ronny was dodging away between the trees holding his face and his nose was bleeding onto his shirt.

'Are you all right, Garry?' Sean knelt beside him, trying to wipe the dirt off his face with a grubby handkerchief. Sean helped him to his feet, and Garrick stood swaying slightly with his eyes open but a remote and vacant smile on his lips.

There were landmarks along the course of the river. Some of them small as a pile of rocks in shallow water:

Waite Courtney looked at Sean across the breakfast table at Theunis Kraal. The fork-load of egg and grilled gammon stopped on the way to his mouth.

'Turn your face towards the window,' he commanded suspiciously. Sean obeyed. 'What the hell is that on your face?'

'What?' Sean ran his hand over his cheek.

'When did you last bath?'

'Don't be silly, my dear.' Ada touched his leg under the table. 'It isn't dirt – it's whiskers.'

'Whiskers, are they?' Waite peered closely at Sean and started to grin, he opened his mouth to speak and Ada knew instantly that he was going to make a joke – one of those ponderous jokes of his, as subtle as an enraged dinosaur, that would wound Sean deep in his half-formed manhood. Quickly she cut in, 'I think you should buy him a razor, don't you, Waite?'

Waite lost the thread of his joke, he grunted and put the egg into his mouth.

'I don't want to cut them,' said Sean and flushed scarlet.

'They'll grow quicker if you shave them a bit at first,' Ada told him.

Across the table from her Garrick fingered his jowls wistfully.

Some of the landmarks were big as headlands:

Waite fetched them from school at the beginning of the December holidays. In the confusion of loading their cases onto the buggy and shouting farewells to Fräulein and to their friends, some of whom they would not see for another six weeks, the twins did not notice that Waite was acting strangely.

It was only later when the horses were heading for home at twice their normal speed that Sean asked, 'What's the hurry, Pa?'

'You'll see,' said Waite, and both Garrick and Sean looked at

43

him with sudden interest. It had been an idle question of Sean's but Waite's answer had them immediately intrigued. Waite grinned at the bombardment of questions but he kept his answers vague. He was enjoying himself. By the time they reached Theunis Kraal the twins were in a frenzy of curiosity.

Waite pulled the horses up in front of the house and one of the grooms ran to take the reins. Ada was waiting on the veranda and Sean jumped down and ran up the steps to her. He kissed her quickly. 'What's happening?' he pleaded. 'Pa won't tell us but we know it's something.'

Garrick hurried up the steps also. 'Go on, tell us.' He caught hold of her arm and tugged it.

'I don't know what you're talking about,' Ada laughed. 'You'd better ask your father again.'

Waite climbed up after them, put one arm around Ada's waist and squeezed her.

'I don't know where they got this idea from,' said Waite, 'but why not tell them to go and have a look in their bedroom? They might as well have their Christmas presents a bit earlier this year.'

Sean beat Garrick to the lounge and was far in the lead by the time he reached the door of their bedroom.

'Wait for me,' called Garrick desperately. 'Please wait for me.'

Sean stopped in the doorway.

'Jesus Christ,' he whispered – they were the strongest words he knew. Garrick came up behind him and together they stared at the pair of leather cases that lay on the table in the middle of the room – long flat cases, heavy polished leather with the corners bound in brass.

'Rifles!' said Sean. He walked slowly to the table as though he were stalking the cases, expecting them at any moment to vanish.

'Look!' Sean reached out to touch with one finger the gold lettering stamped into the lid of the nearest case. 'Our names on them even.'

He sprung the locks and lifted the lid. In a nest of green baize, perfumed with gun oil, glistened a poem in steel and wood.

'Jesus Christ,' said Sean again. Then he looked over his shoulder at Garrick. 'Aren't you going to open yours?'

Garrick limped up to the table trying to hide his disappointment: he had wanted a set of Dickens so badly.

In the river there were whirlpools:

The last week of the Christmas holidays and Garrick was in bed with one of his colds. Waite Courtney had gone to Pietermaritzburg for a meeting of the Beef Growers' Association and there was very little work to do on the farm that day. After Sean had dosed the sick cattle in the sanatorium paddock and ridden an inspection around the south section he returned to the homestead and spent an hour talking to the stableboys, then he drifted up to the house. Garry was asleep and Ada was in the dairy making butter. He asked for and got an early lunch from Joseph and ate it standing in the kitchen. While he ate he thought over the problem of how to fill the afternoon. He weighed the alternatives carefully. Take the rifle and try for duiker along the edge of the escarpment or ride to the pools above the White Falls and fish for eels. He was still undecided after he had finished eating so he crossed the yard and looked into the cool dimness of the dairy.

Ada smiled at him across the churn. 'Hello, Sean, I suppose you want your lunch.'

'Joseph gave it to me already, thanks, Ma.'

'Joseph has already given it to me,' Ada corrected mildly. Sean repeated it after her and sniffed the dairy smell – he liked the cheesy warmth of new butter and the tang of the cow dung smeared on the earth floor.

'What are you going to do this afternoon?'

'I came to ask you if you wanted venison or eels – I don't know if I want to go fishing or shooting.'

'Eels would be nice – we could jelly them and have them for dinner tomorrow when your father comes home.'

'I'll get you a bucket full.'

He saddled the pony, hung his tin of worms on the saddle and with his pole over his shoulder rode towards Ladyburg. He crossed the Baboon Stroom bridge and turned off the road to follow the stream up to the falls. As he skirted the wattle plantation below the Van Essens' place he realized he had made a mistake in picking this route. Anna, with her skirts held up to her knees, came pelting out from among the trees. Sean kicked the pony into a trot and looked straight ahead.

'Sean – hey, Sean.'

She was ahead of him, running to intercept him; there was no chance of evading her so he stopped the pony.

'Hello, Sean.' She was panting and her face was flushed.

'Hello,' he gruffed.

'Where are you going?'

'There and back to see how far it is.'

'You're going fishing – may I come with you?' She smiled appealingly. Her teeth were small and white.

'No, you talk too much; you'll frighten the fish.'

He started the pony.

'Please, I'll be quiet; honest I will.' She was running next to him.

'No.' He flicked the reins and pulled away from her. He rode for a hundred yards then looked round and she was still following with her black hair streaming out behind her. He stopped the pony and she caught up with him.

'I knew you'd stop,' she told him through her gasps.

'Will you go home? I don't want you following me.'

'I'll be quiet as anything – honest I will.'

He knew she'd follow him right up to the top of the escarpment and he gave in. 'All right, but if you say a word, just one single word, I'll send you home.'

'I promise – help me up, please.'

He dragged her onto the pony's rump and she sat sideways with her arms round his waist. They climbed the escarpment. The path ran close beside the White Falls and they could feel the spray blowing off them fine as mist. Anna kept her promise until she was sure they'd gone too far for Sean to send her back alone. She started talking again. When she wanted an answer from him, which wasn't very often, she squeezed his waist and Sean grunted. Sean knee-haltered the pony, and left him among the trees above the pools. He hid his saddle and bridle in an ant-bear hole and they walked down through the reeds to the water. Anna ran ahead of him and when he came out on to the sandbank she was throwing pebbles into the pool.

'Hey, stop that! You'll frighten the fish,' Sean shouted.

'Oh. I'm sorry. I forgot.'

She sat down and wriggled her bare toes into the sand. Sean baited his hook and lobbed it out into the green water – the current drifted his float in a wide circle under the far bank and they both watched it solemnly.

'It doesn't seem as though there are any fish here,' Anna said.

46

'You've got to be patient – you can't expect to catch one right away.'

Anna drew patterns in the sand with her toes and five minutes passed slowly. 'Sean –'

'Ssh!'

Another five minutes.

'Fishing's a silly old thing.'

'Nobody asked you to come,' Sean told her.

'It's hot here!' Sean didn't answer

The high reed beds shut out any breeze and the white sand threw the sun's heat back at them. Anna stood up and wandered restlessly across the sand to the edge of the reeds. She picked a handful of the long spear-shaped leaves and plaited them together.

'I'm bored,' she announced.

'Well, go home then.'

'And I'm hot.'

Sean pulled his line in, inspected the worms and cast them out again. Anna stuck her tongue out at his back.

'Let's have a swim,' she suggested.

Sean ignored her. He stuck the butt of his rod into the sand, pulled his hat down to shield his eyes from the glare and leaned back on his elbows with his legs stretched out in front of him. He could hear the sand crunching as she moved and then there was another silence. He started to worry what she was doing, but if he looked around it would be a show of weakness.

'Girls!' he thought bitterly.

There was the sound of running feet just behind him. He sat up quickly and started to turn. Her white body flashed past him and hit the water, with a smack like a rising trout. Sean jumped up. 'Hey, what're you doing?'

'I'm swimming,' laughed Anna, waist-deep in green water, with her hair slicked wetly down her shoulders and over her breasts. Sean looked at those breasts, white as the flesh of an apple and nippled in dark pink, almost red. Anna dropped onto her back and kicked the water white.

'*Voet sak*, little fishes! Scat, little fishes,' she gurgled.

'Hey, you mustn't do that,' Sean said half-heartedly. He wanted her to stand up again, those breasts gave him a strange tight feeling in his stomach, but Anna knelt with the water up

47

to her chin. He could see them through the water. He wanted her to stand up.

'It's lovely! Why don't you come in?' She rolled on her stomach and ducked her head under the water; the twin ovals of her bottom broke the surface and Sean's stomach tightened again.

'Are you coming in?' she demanded, rubbing the water out of her eyes with both hands. Sean stood bewildered – within a few seconds his feelings towards her had undergone a major revolution. He wanted very much to be in the water with all those mysterious white bulges – but he was shy.

'You're scared! Come on, I give you guts to come in.' She teased him. The challenge pricked him.

'I'm not scared.'

'Well, come on then.'

He hesitated a few seconds longer, then he threw off his hat and unbuttoned his shirt. He turned his back on her while he dropped his pants then spun round and dived into the pool, thankful for the cover it gave him. His head came out and Anna pushed it under again. He groped and caught her legs, straightened up and threw her on her back. He dragged her towards the shallows, where the water wouldn't cover her. She was thrashing her arms to keep her head out and screaming delightedly. Sean's heels snagged a rock and he fell, letting go of her; before he could recover she had leapt on him and strad- dled his back. He could have thrown her off, but he liked the feel of her flesh on his – warm through the cool water, slippery with wetness. She picked up a handful of sand and rubbed it into his hair. Sean struggled gently. She threw her arms round his neck and he could feel the whole length of her body along his back. The tightness in his stomach moved up into his chest and he wanted to hold her. He rolled over and reached for her but she twisted out of his hands and dived back into the deep again. Sean splashed after her but she kept out of his reach, laughing at him.

At last they faced each other, still chin deep, and Sean was getting angry. He wanted to hold her. She saw the change of his mood and she waded to the bank, walked to his clothes and picked up his shirt. She dried her face on it, standing naked and unashamed – she had too many brothers for modesty. Sean watched the way her breasts changed shape as she lifted her arms, he looked at the lines of her body and saw that her once skinny legs had filled out; her thighs touched each other all the way up to the base of her belly and there she wore the dark triangular badge of womanhood. She spread the shirt out on the sand and sat down upon it, then she looked at him.

'Are you coming out?'

He came out awkwardly, covering himself with his hands. Anna moved over on the shirt. 'You can sit down, if you like.'

He sat hurriedly and drew his knees up under his chin. He watched her from the corner of his eye. There were little goose-pimples round her nipples from the cold water. She was aware that he was watching her and she pulled back her shoulders, enjoying it. Sean felt bewildered again – she was so clearly in control now. Before she had been someone to growl at but now she was giving the orders and he was obeying.

'You've got hairs on your chest,' Anna said, turning to look at him. Sparse and silky though they were, Sean was glad that he had them. He straightened out his legs.

'And you're much bigger there than Frikkie.' Sean tried to pull up his knees again but she put her hand on his leg and stopped him.

'Can I touch you?'

Sean tried to speak but his throat had closed and no sound came through it. Anna did not wait for an answer.

'Oh, look! It's getting all cheeky – just like Caribou's.'

Caribou was Mr Van Essen's stallion.

'I always know when Pa is going to let Caribou service a mare, he tells me to go and visit Aunt Lettie. I just hide in the plantation. You can see the paddock jolly well from the plantation.'

Anna's hand was soft and restless, Sean could think of nothing else.

'Do you know that people service, just like horses do?' she asked.

Sean nodded, he had attended the biology classes conducted by Messrs Daffel and Company in the school latrines. They were quiet for a while, then Anna whispered.

'Sean, would you service me?'

'I don't know how,' croaked Sean.

'I bet horses don't either the first time, nor people for that matter,' Anna said. 'We could find out.'

They rode home in the early evening, Anna sitting up behind Sean, her arms tight round his waist and the side of her face pressed between his shoulders. He dropped her at the back of the plantation.

'I'll see you at school on Monday,' she said and turned to go.

'Anna –'

'Yes?'

'Is it still sore?'

'No,' and then, after a moment's thought, 'it feels nice.'

She turned and ran into the wattle trees.

Sean rode slowly home. He was empty inside; it was a sad feeling and it puzzled him.

'Where are the fish?' asked Ada.

'They weren't biting.'

'Not even one?'

Sean shook his head and crossed the kitchen.

'Sean.'

'Yes, Ma.'

'Is something wrong?'

'No' – quick denial – 'No, I'm fine.' He slipped into the passage.

Garrick was sitting up in bed. The skin around his nostrils was inflamed and chapped; he lowered the book he was reading and smiled at Sean as he came into the room. Sean went to his own bed and sat on it.

'Where have you been?' Garrick's voice was thick with cold.

'Up at the pools above the falls.'

'Fishing?'

Sean didn't answer, he leaned forward on the bed with his elbows on his knees. 'I met Anna, she came with me.'

Garrick's interest quickened at the mention of her name and he watched Sean's face. Sean still had that slightly puzzled expression.

'Garry,' he hesitated; he had to talk about it. 'Garry, I screwed Anna.'

Garrick drew in his breath with a small hiss. He went very pale, only his nose was still red and sore-looking.

'I mean,' Sean spoke slowly as though he were trying to explain it to himself, 'I mean really screwed her, just like we've talked about. Just like. . . .' He made a helpless gesture with his hands, unable to find the words. Then he lay back on the bed.

'Did she let you?' Garrick's voice was almost a whisper.

'She asked me to,' Sean said. 'It was slippery – sort of warm and slippery.'

And then later, long after the lamp was out and they were both in bed, Sean heard Garrick's soft movements in the darkness. He listened for a while until he was certain.

'Garry!' He accused him loudly.

'I wasn't, I wasn't.'

'You know what Pa told us. Your teeth will fall out and you'll go mad.'

'I wasn't, I wasn't.' Garrick's voice was choked with his cold and his tears.

'I heard you,' said Sean.

'I was just scratching my leg. Honestly, honestly, I was.'

And at the end the river plunged over the last waterfall and swept them into the sea of manhood.

Mr Clark had not been able to break Sean. He had provoked instead a bitter contest in which he knew himself to be slowly losing ground, and now he was afraid of Sean. He no longer made Sean stand, for Sean was as tall as he was. The contest had been on for two years; they had explored each other's weaknesses and knew how to exploit them.

Mr Clark could not bear the sound of anyone sniffing; perhaps subconsciously he took it as mockery of his own deformed nose. Sean had a repertoire that varied from a barely audible connoisseur testing-the-bouquet-of-brandy sniff to a loud hawking in the back of his throat.

'Sorry, sir, I can't help it. I've got a bit of a cold.'

But then, to even the score, Mr Clark had realized that Sean was vulnerable through Garrick. Hurt Garrick even a little and you were inflicting almost unbearable agony on Sean.

It had been a bad week for Mr Clark. His liver, weakened by persistent bouts of malaria, had been troubling him. He had suffered with a bilious headache for three days now; there had been unpleasantness with the Town Council about the terms on which his contract was to be renewed; Sean had been in good sniffing form the day before and Mr Clark had had about as much as he was prepared to take.

He came into the schoolroom and took his place on the dais; he let his eyes move slowly over his pupils until they came to Sean.

'Just let him start,' thought Mr Clark. 'Just let him start today and I'll kill him.'

The seating had been rearranged in the last two years. Sean and Garrick had been separated and Garrick was now at the front of the room where Mr Clark could reach him easily. Sean was near the back.

'English Readers,' said Mr Clark. 'Standard Ones turn to page five. Standard Twos turn to –'

Garrick sniffed wetly, hayfever again.

Mr Clark shut his book with a snap.

'Damn you!' he said softly, and then, his voice rising, 'Damn you!' Now he was shaking with rage, the edges of his nostrils were white and flared open.

He came down from the dais to Garrick's desk. 'Damn you! Damn you – you bloody little cripple,' he screamed and hit Garrick across the face with his open hand. Garrick cupped both hands over his cheek and stared at him.

'You dirty little swine,' Mr. Clark mouthed at him. 'Now you're starting it too.'

He caught a handful of Garrick's hair and pulled his head down so that his forehead hit the top of the desk. 'I'll teach you. By God, I'll teach you.'

'I'll show you.' Bump.

'I'll teach you.' Bump.

It took Sean that long to reach them. He grabbed Mr Clark's arm and pulled him backwards. 'Leave him alone! He didn't do anything!'

Mr Clark saw Sean's face in front of him – he was passed all reason – the face that had tormented him for two long years. He bunched his fist and lashed out at it.

Sean staggered back from the blow, the sting of it made his eyes water. For a second he lay sprawled across one of the desks, watching Clark and then he growled.

The sound sobered Clark, he backed away but only two paces before Sean was on him. Hitting with both hands, grunting with each punch, Sean drove him against the blackboard. Clark tried to break away but Sean caught the collar of his shirt and dragged him back – the collar tore half loose in his hand and Sean hit him again. Clark slid down the wall until he was sitting against it and Sean stood panting over him.

'Get out,' said Clark. His teeth were stained pink by the blood in his mouth and a little of it spilled out onto his lips. His collar stood up at a jaunty angle under one ear.

There was no sound in the room except Sean's breathing.

'Get out,' said Clark again and the anger drained out of Sean leaving him trembling with reaction. He walked to the door.

'You too,' Clark pointed at Garrick. 'Get out and don't come back!'

'Come on, Garry,' said Sean.

Garrick stood up from his desk and limped across to Sean and together they went out into the school yard.

'What are we going to do now?' There was a big red lump on Garrick's forehead.

'I suppose we'd better go home.'

'What about our things?' asked Garrick.

'We can't carry all that – we'll have to send for them later. Come on.'

They walked out through the town and along the road to the farm. They had almost reached the bridge on the Baboon Stroom before either of them spoke again.

'What do you reckon Pa will do?' asked Garrick. He was only putting into words the problem that had occupied them both since they left the school.

'Well, whatever he does, it was worth it.' Sean grinned. 'Did you see me clobber him, hey? Smackeroo – right in the chops.'

'You shouldn't have done it, Sean. Pa's going to kill us. Me too and I didn't do anything.'

'You sniffed,' Sean reminded him.

They reached the bridge and leaned over the parapet side by side to watch the water.

'How's your leg?' asked Sean.

'It's sore – I think we should rest a bit.'

'All right, if you say so,' Sean agreed.

There was a long silence, then, 'I wish you hadn't done it, Sean.'

'Well, wishing isn't going to help. Old Nose-Holes is as punched up as he'll ever be and all we can do is think of something to tell Pa.'

'He hit me,' said Garrick. 'He might have killed me.'

'Yes,' agreed Sean righteously, 'and he hit me too.'

They thought about it for a while.

'Perhaps we should just go away,' suggested Garrick.

'You mean without telling Pa?' The idea had attraction.

'Yeah, we could go to sea or something,' Garrick brightened.

'You'd get seasick, you even get sick in a train.'

Once more they applied their minds to the problem. Then Sean looked at Garrick, Garrick looked at Sean and as though by agreement they straightened up and started off once more for Theunis Kraal.

Ada was in front of the house. She had on a wide-brimmed straw hat that kept her face in shadow and over one arm she carried a basket of flowers. Busy with her garden, she didn't notice them until they were halfway across the lawn and when she did she stood motionless. She was steeling herself, trying to get her emotions under control; from experience she had learned to expect the worst from her stepsons and be thankful when it wasn't as bad as that.

As they came towards her they lost momentum and finally halted like a pair of clockwork toys running down.

'Hello,' said Ada.

'Hello,' they answered her together.

Garrick fumbled in his pocket, drew out a handkerchief and blew his nose. Sean stared up at the steep Dutch-gabled roof of Theunis Kraal as though he had never seen it before.

'Yes?' Ada kept her voice calm.

'Mr Clark said we were to go home,' announced Garrick.

'Why?' Ada's calm was starting to crack.

'Well –' Garrick glanced at Sean for support. Sean's attention was still riveted on the roof.

'Well . . . You see Sean sort of punched him in the head until he fell down. I didn't do anything.'

Ada moaned softly, 'Oh, no!' She took a deep breath. 'All right. Start at the beginning and give me the whole story.'

They told it in relays, a garbled rush of words, interrupting each other and arguing over the details. When they had finished Ada said, 'You better go to your room. Your father is working in the home section today and he'll be back for his lunch soon. I'll try and prepare him a little.'

The room had the cheery atmosphere of a condemned cell.

'How much do you reckon he'll give us?' asked Garrick.

'I reckon until he gets tired, then he'll rest and give us some more,' Sean answered.

They heard Waite's horse come into the yard. He said something to the stable boy and they heard him laugh; the kitchen door slammed and there was half a minute of suspense before they heard Waite roar. Garrick jumped nervously.

For another ten minutes they could hear Waite and Ada talking in the kitchen, the alternate rumble and soothing murmur. Then the tap of Ada's feet along the passage and she came into the room.

'Your father wants to see you – he's in the study.'

Waite stood in front of the fireplace. His beard was powdered with dust and his forehead as corrugated as a ploughed land with the force of his scowl.

'Come in,' he bellowed when Sean knocked and they filed in and stood in front of him. Waite slapped his riding-whip against his leg and the dust puffed out of his breeches.

'Come here,' he said to Garrick and took a handful of his hair. He twisted Garrick's face up and looked at the bruise on his forehead.

'Hmm,' he said. He let go of Garrick's hair and it stood up in a tuft. He threw the riding-whip on the stinkwood desk.

'Come here,' he said to Sean. 'Hold out your hands – no, palms down.'

The skin on both hands was broken and one knuckle was swollen and puffy looking.

'Hmm,' he said again. He turned to the shelf beside the fireplace, took a pipe out of the rack and filled it from the stone jar of tobacco.

'You're a pair of bloody fools,' he said, 'but I'll take a chance and start you on five shillings a week all found. Go and get your lunch . . . we've got work to do this afternoon.'

They stared at him a moment in disbelief and then back towards the door.

'Sean.' Sean stopped, he knew it was too good to be true. 'Where did you hit him?'

'All over, Pa, anywhere I could reach.'

'That's no good,' Waite said. 'You must go for the side of his head – here,' he tapped the point of his jaw with his pipe, 'and keep your fists closed tight or you'll break every finger in your hands before you're much older.'

'Yes, Pa.'

The door closed softly behind him and Waite allowed himself to grin.

'They've had enough book learning anyway,' he said aloud and struck a match to his pipe; when it was drawing evenly he blew out smoke.

'Christ, I wish I could have watched it. That little pen-pusher will know better than to tangle with my boy again.'

12

Now Sean had a course along which to race. He was born to run and Waite Courtney led him out of the stall in which he had fretted and gave him his lead. Sean ran, unsure of the prize, unsure of the distance; yet he ran with joy, he ran with all his strength.

Before dawn, standing with his father and Garrick in the kitchen, drinking coffee with hands cupped around the mug, Sean felt excitement for each coming day.

'Sean, take Zama and N'duti with you and make sure there are no strays in the thick stuff along the river.'

'I'll only take one herdboy, Pa, you'll need N'duti at the dipping tank.'

'All right, then. Try and meet us back at the tank before midday, we've got to push through a thousand head today.'

Sean gulped the remains of his coffee and buttoned his jacket. 'I'll get going then.'

A groom held his horse at the kitchen door. Sean slid his rifle into the scabbard and went up into the saddle without putting his foot into the steel; he lifted a hand and grinned at Waite, then he swung the horse and rode across the yard. The morning was still dark and cold. Waite watched him from the doorway.

'So goddamned sure of himself,' thought Waite. Yet he had the son he had hoped for and he was proud.

'What you want me to do, Pa?' Garrick asked beside him.

'Well, there are those heifers in the sick paddock –'

Waite stopped. 'No. You'd better come with me, Garry.'

Sean worked in the early morning when the sunlight was tinted as a stage effect, all golden and gay, and the shadows were long and black. He worked in the midday sun and sweated in the heat; in the rain; in the mist that swirled down grey and damp from the plateau; in the short African twilight, and came home in the dark. He loved every minute of it.

He learned to know cattle. Not by name, for only the trek oxen were named, but by their size and colour and markings, so that by running his eye over one of the herds he knew which animals were missing.

'Zama, the old cow with the crooked horn. Where is she?'

'Nkosi,' no longer the diminutive Nkosizana – little lord.

'Nkosi, yesterday I took her to the sick paddock, she has the worm in her eye.'

He learned to recognize disease almost before it started. The way a beast moved and held its head. He learned the treatment for them. Screw worm – kerosene poured into the wound until the maggots fell out like a shower of rice. Ophthalmia – rinse the eye with permanganate. Anthrax and quarter-evil – a bullet and a bonfire for the carcass.

He delivered his first calf among the acacia trees on the bank of the Tugela; he did it alone with his sleeves rolled up above the elbows and the soapy feel of the slime on his hands. Afterwards, while the mother licked it and it staggered at each stroke of the tongue, Sean felt a choking sensation in his throat.

All this was not enough to burn up his energy. He played while he worked.

Practising his horsemanship: swinging from the saddle and running beside his horse, up again and over the other side, standing on the saddle at full gallop and then opening his legs and smacking down on his backside – his feet finding the stirrups without groping.

Practising with his rifle until he could hit a running jackal at a hundred and fifty paces, cutting the fox-terrier-sized body in half with the heavy bullet.

Then there was much of Garrick's work to do also.

'I don't feel very well, Sean.'

'What's, wrong?'

'My leg's sore, you know how it chafes if I ride too much.'

'Why don't you go home, then?'

'Pa says I've got to fix the fence round the Number Three dip tank.' Garrick leaned forward on his horse to rub his leg, giving a brave little smile.

'You fixed it last week,' Sean protested.

'Yes – but the wires sort of came loose again.' There was always a strange impermanency about any repairs that Garrick effected.

'Have you got the wire cutters?' and Garrick produced them with alacrity from his saddle bag.

'I'll do it,' said Sean.

'Hell, man, thanks a lot,' and then a second's hesitation. 'You won't tell Pa, will you?'

'No – you can't help it if your leg's sore,' and Garrick rode home, sneaked through to his bedroom and escaped with Jim Hawkins into the pages of *Treasure Island*.

From this work came a new emotion for Sean. When the rain brought the grass out in green and filled the shallow pans on the plateau with water it was no longer simply a sign that the birdnesting season had begun and that the fishing in the Baboon Stroom would improve – now it meant that they could take cattle up from the valley, it meant that there would be fat on the herds they drove into the sale pens at Ladyburg, it meant that another winter had ended and again the land was rich with life and the promise of life. This new emotion extended to the cattle also. It was a strong, almost savage feeling of possession,

It was in the late afternoon. Sean was sitting on his horse among trees, looking out across open vleiland at the small herd that was strung out before him. They were feeding, heads down, tails flicking lazily. Between Sean and the main body of cattle was a calf – it was three days old, still pale-beige in colour and unsure of its legs. It was trying them out, running clumsy circles in the short grass. From the herd a cow lowed and the calf stopped dead and stood with its legs splayed awkwardly under it and its ears up. Sean grinned and picked up the reins from his horse's neck; it was time to start back for the homestead.

At that moment he saw the lammergeyer: it had already begun its stoop at the calf, dropping big and dark brown from the sky, wings cocked back and its talons reaching for the strike. The wind rustled against it with the speed of its dive.

Sean sat paralysed and watched. The eagle hit the calf and Sean heard bone break, sharp as the snap of a dry stick, and then the calf was down in the grass struggling feebly with the eagle crouched on top of it.

For a second longer Sean sat, dazed with the speed at which it had happened. Then hatred came on him. It came with a violence that twisted his stomach. He hit his horse with his heels and it jumped forward. He drove it at the eagle and as he rode he screamed at it, a high-pitched formless sound, an animal expression of hate.

The eagle turned its head, looking at him sideways with one eye. It opened its great yellow beak and answered his scream, then it loosed its claws from the calf and launched itself into the air. Its wings flogged heavily and it moved low along the ground, gaining speed, lifting, drawing away from Sean.

Sean pulled his rifle from the scabbard and hauled his horse back onto its haunches. He threw himself out of the saddle and levered open the breech of the rifle.

The eagle was fifty yards ahead of him rising fast now. Sean slipped a cartridge into the breech, closed it and brought the rifle up in one continuous movement.

It was a difficult shot. Moving away from him and rising, the beat of its wings jerking its body. Sean fired. The rifle jumped back into and the gunsmoke whipped away on the wind, so he could watch the bullet connect.

The eagle collapsed in the air. It burst like a pillow in a puff of feathers and fell with its six-feet-long wings fluttering limply. Before it hit the ground Sean was running.

It was dead when he reached it, but he reversed his rifle: holding it by the muzzle, he swung the butt down from above his head onto its body. At the third blow the butt of his rifle broke off, but he kept on hitting. He was sobbing with fury.

When he stopped and stood panting the sweat was running down his face and his body was trembling. The eagle was a squashy mess of broken flesh and feathers.

The calf was still alive. The rifle was jammed. Sean knelt beside it with tears of anger burning his eyes and killed it with his hunting-knife.

13

So strong was this new feeling that Sean could hate even Garrick. He did not hate for long, though. Sean's anger and his hatred were quick things, with flames like those of a fire in dry grass: hot and high but soon burnt out and afterwards the ashes dead with no smouldering.

Waite was away when it happened. For three consecutive years Waite Courtney had been nominated for the chairmanship of the Beef Growers' Association and each time he had stood down. He was human enough to want the prestige the office carried with it, but he was also sensible to the fact that his farm would suffer from his frequent absences. Sean and Garrick had been working for two years when the annual election of office bearers came around again.

The night before Waite left for the meeting in Pietermaritzburg he spoke to Ada. 'I had a letter from Bernard last week, my dear,' he was standing before the mirror in their bedroom trimming his beard. 'They insist that I stand for the chair this year.'

'Very wise of them,' said Ada. 'They'd have the best man if you did.'

Waite frowned with concentration as he snipped at his whiskers. She believed so unquestioningly in him that he seldom doubted himself. Now looking at his face in the mirror he wondered how much of his success was owed to Ada's backing.

'You can do it, Waite.' Not a challenge, not a question, but a calm statement of fact. When she said it he believed it.

He laid the scissors down on the chest of drawers and turned to her. She sat cross-legged on the bed in a white nightgown, her hair was down in a dark mass around her shoulders. 'I think Sean can look after things here,' she said, and then quickly, 'and of course Garry.'

'Sean's learning fast,' Waite agreed.

'Are you going to take the job?'

Waite hesitated. 'Yes,' he nodded and Ada smiled.

'Come here,' she held out her hands to him.

Sean drove Waite and Ada to the station at Ladyburg: at the last minute Waite had insisted that she go with him, for he wanted her to be there to share it with him.

Sean put their luggage into the coach and waited while they talked with the small group of cattlemen who were going up to the meeting. The whistle blew and the travellers scattered to their compartments. Ada kissed Sean and climbed up. Waite stayed a second longer on the platform.

'Sean, if you need any help go across to Mr Erasmus at Lion Kop. I'll be back on Thursday.'

'I won't need any help, Pa.'

Waite's mouth hardened. 'Then you must be God, he's the only one who never needs help,' Waite said harshly. 'Don't be a bloody fool – if you run into trouble ask Erasmus.'

He climbed up after Ada. The train jerked, gathered speed and ran out towards the escarpment. Sean watched it dwindle, then he walked back to the buggy. He was master of Theunis Kraal and he liked the feeling. The small crowd on the platform was dispersing and out of it came Anna.

'Hello, Sean.' She had on a green cotton dress that was faded with washing, her feet were bare. She smiled with her small white teeth and watched his face.

'Hello, Anna.'

'Aren't you going up to Pietermaritzburg?'

'No, I've got to look after the farm.'

'Oh!'

They waited in silence, uncomfortable before so many people. Sean coughed and scratched the side of his nose.

'Anna, come on. We've got to get home.' One of her brothers called from in front of the ticket office and Anna leaned towards Sean.

'Will I see you on Sunday?' she whispered.

'I'll come if I can. But I don't know – I've got to look after the farm.'

'Please try, Sean.' Her face was earnest. 'I'll be waiting for you,

I'll take some lunch and wait all day. Please come, even if it's only for a little while.'

'All right, I'll come.'

'Promise?'

'Promise.'

She smiled with relief. 'I'll wait for you on the path above the waterfall.'

She turned and ran to join her family and Sean drove back to Theunis Kraal. Garrick was lying on his bed reading.

'I thought Pa told you to get on with the branding of those new cattle we bought on Wednesday.'

Garrick laid down his book and sat up. 'I told Zama to keep them in the kraal until you got back.'

'Pa told you to get on with it. You can't keep them there all day without feed or water.'

'I hate branding,' muttered Garrick. 'I hate it when they moo like that as you burn them, and I hate the stink of burning hair and skin – it gives me a headache.'

'Well someone's got to do it. I can't, I've got to go down and mix new dip into the tanks for tomorrow.' Sean was losing his temper. 'Hell, Garry, why are you always so damn helpless?'

'I can't help it, I can't help it if I've only got one leg.' Garrick was close to tears again. The reference to his leg had the desired effect – Sean's temper steadied instantly.

'I'm sorry,' Sean smiled his irresistible smile. 'I tell you what. I'll do the branding – you fix the tanks. Get the drums of dip loaded onto the Scotch cart, take a couple of the stable boys with you to help. Here are the keys of the storeroom.' He tossed the bunch onto the bed beside Garrick. 'You should be finished before dark.'

At the door he turned.

'Garry, don't forget to do all six tanks – not just the ones near the house.'

So Garrick loaded six drums of dip onto the Scotch cart and went off down the hill. He was home well before dark. The front of his breeches was stained with the dark, tarry chemical and some of it had soaked into the leather of his single riding-boot. As he came out of the kitchen into the passage Sean shouted from the study. 'Hey, Garry, did you finish them?'

Garrick was startled. Waite's study was a sacred place, the inner sanctum of Theunis Kraal. Even Ada knocked before going into it and the twins went there only to receive punishment. Garrick limped along the passage and pushed open the door.

Sean sat with his boots on top of the desk and his ankles neatly crossed. He leaned back in the swivel chair.

'Pa will kill you,' Garrick's voice was shaky.

'Pa's in Pietermaritzburg,' said Sean.

Garrick stood in the doorway and looked around the room. It was the first time he had really seen it. On every previous visit he had been too preoccupied with the violence to come and the only item in the room he had studied closely was the seat of the big leather easy chair as he bent over the arm of it and exposed his backside to the sjambok.

Now he looked at the room. The walls were panelled to the ceiling, the wood was dark yellow and polished. The ceiling was fancy plaster, in a pattern of oak leaves. A single lamp hung from the centre of it on a brass chain. You could walk into the fireplace of brown chipped stone and there were logs laid ready for the match.

Pipes and tobacco jar on the ledge beside the fireplace, guns in a rack along one wall, a bookcase of green and maroon leather bound volumes: encyclopaedias, dictionaries, books on travel and farming, but no fiction. There was an oil painting of Ada on the wall opposite the desk, the artist had captured a little of her serenity: she wore a white dress and carried her hat in her hand. A magnificent set of Cape buffalo horns above the fireplace dominated the room with their great crenellated bosses and wide sweep to the tips.

It was a man's room, with loose dog-hairs on the leopard-skin rugs, and the presence of the man strongly there – it even smelled of Waite. It was as distinctively his as the tweed coat and Terai hat that hung behind the door.

Next to where Sean sat the cabinet was open and a bottle of brandy stood on top of it. Sean had a goblet in his hand.

'You're drinking Pa's brandy,' Garrick accused.

'It's not bad.' Sean lifted the glass and inspected the liquid; he took a careful sip and held it in his mouth, preparing himself to swallow. Garrick watched him with awe and Sean tried not to blink as it went down his throat.

'Would you like some?'

Garrick shook his head and the fumes came up Sean's nose and his eyes ran.

'Pa will kill you!' said Garrick again.

'Sit down,' ordered Sean, his voice husky from the brandy. 'I want to work out a plan for the time Pa's away.'

Garrick advanced on the armchair, but before he reached it he changed his mind – the associations were too painful. He went to the sofa instead and sat on the edge.

'Tomorrow,' Sean held up one finger, 'we'll dip all the cattle in the home section. I've told Zama to start bringing them early – you did do the tanks, didn't you?'

Garrick nodded and Sean went on.

'On Saturday,' Sean held up his second finger, 'we'll burn fire breaks along the top of the escarpment. The grass is dry as hell up there. You take one gang and start near the falls, I'll ride down to the other end, near Fredericks Kloof. On Sunday. . .' Sean said and then paused. On Sunday Anna.

'I want to go to church on Sunday,' said Garrick quickly.

'That's fine,' agreed Sean. 'You go to church.'

'Are you going to come?'

'No,' said Sean.

Garrick looked down at the leopard-skin rugs that covered the floor – he didn't try to persuade Sean for Anna would be at the service. Perhaps afterwards, if Sean wasn't there to distract her, he could drive her home in the buggy. He started a day dream and wasn't listening as Sean went on talking.

In the morning it was full daylight by the time Sean reached the dip tank. He pushed a small herd of stragglers before him and they came out through the trees and stirrup high grass into the wide area of trampled earth around the tank. Garrick had started running cattle through the dip and there were about ten head already in the draining kraal at the far end, standing wet and miserable, their bodies dark with dip.

Sean drove his herd through the gates of the entrance kraal into the solid pack of brown bodies that were already there. N'duti slid the bars of the gate back into place to hold them.

'I see you, Nkosi.'

'I see you, N'duti. Plenty of work today!'

'Plenty,' agreed N'duti, 'always plenty of work.'

Sean rode around the kraal and tied his horse beneath one of the trees, then walked across to the tank. Garrick was standing by the parapet and leaning against one of the columns that supported the roof.

'Hello, Garry, how's it going?'

'Fine.'

Sean leaned over the parapet next to Garry. The tank was twenty feet long and eight wide, the surface of the liquid was below ground level. Around the tank was a low wall and over it a roof of thatch to prevent rain diluting the contents.

The herdboys drove the cattle up to the edge and each beast hesitated on the brink.

'E'yapi, E'yapi,' screamed the herdboys and the push of bodies behind it forced it to jump. If one was stubborn, Zama leaned over the railing of the kraal, grabbed its tail and bit it.

Each beast jumped with its nose held high and its forefeet gathered up under its chest; it disappeared completely under the oil black surface and came up again swimming frantically along the tank until its hooves touched the sloping bottom at the far end and it could lumber up into the draining kraal.

'Keep them moving, Zama,' shouted Sean.

Zama grinned at him and bit with big white teeth into a reluctant tail.

The ox was a heavy animal and it splashed a drop up onto Sean's cheek as he leaned over the wall. Sean did not bother to wipe it off, he went on watching.

'Well, if we don't get top prices for this lot at the next sale then the buyers don't know good cattle,' he said to Garry.

'They're all right,' agreed Garry.

'All right? They're the fattest oxen in the district.' Sean was about to enlarge on the theme, but suddenly he was aware of discomfort – the drop of dip was burning his cheek. He wiped it off with his finger and held it to his nose; the smell of it stung his nostrils. For a second he stared at it stupidly and the spot on his cheek burned like fire.

He looked up quickly. The cattle in the draining kraal were milling restlessly and as he looked one of them staggered sideways and bumped against the railing.

'Zama!' shouted Sean, and the Zulu looked up. 'Stop them. For God's sake don't let any more through.'

There was another ox poised on the edge. Sean snatched off his hat and jumped up onto the wall, he beat the ox in the face with his hat trying to drive it back, but it sprang out into the tank. Sean caught hold of the railing and stepped into the space it had left on the edge of the tank.

66

'Stop them,' he shouted. 'Get the bars in, don't let any more through.'

He spread his arms across the entrance, holding onto the railing on each side, kicking at the faces of the cattle in front of him.

'Hurry, damn you, get the bars in,' he shouted. The oxen pressed towards him, a wall of horned heads. Pushed forward by those behind and held back by Sean they started to panic; one of them tried to jump over the railing. As it swung its head its horn raked Sean's chest, up across the ribs, ripping his shirt.

Behind him Sean felt the wooden bars being dropped into place, blocking the entrance to the tank, and then Zama's hands on his arm pulling him up out of the confusion of horns and hooves. Two of the herdboys helped him over the railing and Sean shrugged their hands off as soon as he was on the ground.

'Come on,' he ordered and ran to his horse.

'Nkosi, you are bleeding.'

Blood had splotched the front of Sean's shirt but he felt no pain. The cattle that had been through the dip were now in terrible distress. They charged about the kraal, bellowing pitifully; one of them fell and when it got to its feet again its legs were shaking so that it could barely stand.

'The river,' shouted Sean, 'get them down to the river. Try and wash it off. Zama, open the gate.'

The Baboon Stroom was a mile away. One of the oxen died before they could get them out of the kraal, another ten before they reached the river. They died in convulsions, with their bodies shuddering and their eyes turned back into their heads.

Sean drove those that remained down the bank into the river. The water was clear and as each beast went into it, the dip washed off in a dark brown cloud.

'Stand here, Zama. Don't let them come out.'

Sean swam his horse to the far bank and turned back the oxen that were trying to climb it.

'Nkosi – one is drowning,' called N'duti and Sean looked across the river. A young ox was in convulsions in the shallows: its head was under water and its feet thrashed the surface.

Sean slid off his horse and waded out to it. The water was up to his armpits. He tried to hold its head out and drag it to the bank.

'Help me, N'duti,' he shouted, and the Zulu came into the

river. It was a hopeless task: each time the ox lunged it pulled them both under with it. By the time they got the ox to the bank it was dead.

Sean sat in the mud beside the body of the ox: he was exhausted and his lungs ached with the water he had breathed.

'Bring them out, Zama,' he gasped. The survivors were standing in the shallows or swimming in aimless circles. 'How many?' asked Sean. 'How many are dead?'

'Two more while you were in the water. Altogether thirteen, Nkosi.'

'Where's my horse?'

'It ran, and I let it go. It will be back at the house.'

Sean nodded.

'Bring them up to the sick paddock. We must watch them for a few days.'

Sean stood up and started walking back towards the dip tank. Garrick was gone, and the main herd was still in the kraal. Sean opened the gate and turned them loose. He felt better by then, and as his strength returned with it came his anger and his hatred. He started along the track towards the homestead. His boots squelched as he walked and he hated Garrick more strongly with each step. Garrick had mixed the dip. Garrick had killed his cattle and Sean hated him,

As Sean came up the slope below the house he saw Garrick standing in the yard. Garrick saw him also; he disappeared into the kitchen and Sean started to run. He went in through the kitchen door and nearly knocked down one of the servants,

'Garrick,' shouted Sean. 'Damn it – where are you?'

He searched the house; once quickly and then again thoroughly. Garrick was gone, but the window of their bedroom was open and there was a dusty boot print on the sill. Garrick had gone over it.

'You bloody coward,' howled Sean and scrambled out after him. He stood a second, with his head swinging from side to side and his fists opening and closing.

'I'll find out,' he howled again. 'I'll find you wherever you're hiding.'

He started across the yard towards the stables and halfway there he saw the door of the dairy was closed. When he tried it he found it was locked from inside. Sean backed away from it and then charged it with his shoulder – the lock burst and the door flew open. Sean skidded across the room and came up against the far wall. Garrick was trying to climb out of the window, but it was small and high up. Sean caught him by the seat of his pants and pulled him down.

'Whatcha do to the dip, hey? Whatcha do to it?' He shouted in Garrick's face.

'I didn't mean to. I didn't know it'd kill them.'

'Tell me what you did.' Sean had hold of the front of his shirt and was dragging him towards the door.

'I didn't do anything. Honest I didn't know.'

'I'm going to hammer you anyway, so you might as well tell me.'

'Please, Sean, I didn't know.'

Sean jammed Garrick against the doorway and held him there with his left hand – his right hand he drew back with the fist bunched.

'No, Sean. Please, no.'

And suddenly the anger was gone from Sean, his hands sank back to his sides.

'All right – just tell me what you did,' he said coldly. His anger was gone but not his hatred.

'I was tired and it was getting late and my leg was hurting,' whispered Garrick, 'and there were still four more tanks to do, and I knew you'd check that all the drums were empty, and it was so late . . . and . . .'

'And?'

'And so I emptied all the dip into the one tank . . . but I didn't know it would kill them, truly I didn't.'

Sean turned away from him and started walking slowly back towards the house. Garrick stumbled after him.

'I'm sorry, Sean, honest I'm sorry. I didn't know that. . .'

Sean walked ahead of him into the kitchen and slammed the door in his face. He went through into Waite's study. From the bookshelf he lifted down the heavy leather-covered stock register and carried it to the desk. He opened the book, picked up a pen and dipped it. For a moment he stared at the page and then in the 'deaths' column he wrote the number *13* and after it the words 'dip poisoning'. He pressed down so hard with the pen that the nib cut the paper.

It took Sean and the herdboys all the rest of that day and the next to bale out the tank, refill it with clean water and mix in fresh dip. He saw Garrick only at meals and they didn't speak.

The next day was Sunday. Garrick went into town early, for the church service started at eight o'clock. When he had gone Sean began his preparations. He shaved – leaning close to the mirror and handling the cut-throat gingerly, shaping his side burns and clearing the hair from the rest of his face until his skin was smooth and fresh-looking. Then he went through to the master-bedroom and helped himself to a generous portion of his father's brilliantine, taking care to screw the lid back on the bottle and replace it exactly as he had found it. He rubbed the brilliantine into his hair and sniffed its perfume appreciatively. He combed his hair over his forehead, parted it down the centre and polished it into a gloss with Waite's silver-backed brushes. Then a clean white shirt, breeches worn only once before, boots as shiny as his hair – and Sean was ready.

The clock on the mantelpiece in the lounge assured him that he was well ahead of time. To be exact, he was two hours early. Eight o'clock now: church didn't end until nine and it would be another hour before Anna could escape from under the eyes of her family and reach the rendezvous above the falls. He settled down to wait. He read the latest copy of the *Natal Farmer*. He had read it three times before for it was a month old, and now even the excellent article on 'Stomach parasites in Cattle and Sheep' had lost much of its punch. Sean's attention wandered – he thought about the day ahead and felt the familiar movement within his breeches. This necessitated a rearrangement for the breeches were tight fitting. Then fantasy palled; Sean was a doer not a thinker, and he went through to the kitchen to solicit a cup of coffee from Joseph. When he had finished it, there was still half an hour to go.

'The hell with it,' said Sean and shouted for his horse. He climbed the escarpment, letting his horse move diagonally up the slope and at the top he dismounted and let it blow. Today he could see the course of the Tugela river out across the plain – it was a belt of dark green. He could count the roofs of the houses in Ladyburg and the church spire, copper clad, shone in the sunlight like a beacon fire.

He mounted again and rode along the edge of the plateau until he reached the Baboon Stroom above the falls. He followed it back and forded it at a shallow place, lifting his feet up on the saddle in front of him to keep his boots dry. He off-saddled next to the pools and knee-haltered his horse, then he followed the path until it dropped over the edge of the plateau into the thick forest that surrounded the falls. It was cool and damp in the forest with moss growing on the trees, for the roof of leaves and creepers shut out the sun. There was a bottle-bird in the undergrowth.

'Glug, glug, glug,' it said, like water poured from a bottle, and its call was almost drowned in the ceaseless thunder of the falls.

Sean spread his handkerchief on a rock beside the path, sat down on it and waited. Within five minutes he was fidgeting impatiently – within half an hour he was grumbling aloud.

'I'll count to five hundred. . . . If she hasn't come by then I'm not going to wait.'

He counted and when he reached the promised figure he stopped and peered anxiously down the path. There was no sign of Anna.

'I'm not going to sit here all day,' he announced and made no effort to stand up. A fat yellow caterpillar caught his eye; it was on the trunk of a tree farther down the slope. He picked up a pebble and threw it. It bounced off the tree an inch above the caterpillar.

'Close,' Sean encouraged himself and stooped for another stone. After a while he had exhausted the supply of pebbles around his feet and the caterpillar was still moving leisurely up the trunk. Sean was forced to go out on a foraging expedition for more pebbles. He came back with both hands full and once more took up his position on the rock. He piled the pebbles between his feet and reopened the bombardment. He aimed each throw with the utmost concentration and with his third pebble he hit squarely and the caterpillar popped in a spurt of green juice. Sean felt cheated. He looked around for a new target and instead found Anna standing beside him.

'Hello, Sean.' She had on a pink dress. She carried her shoes in one hand and a small basket in the other. 'I brought some lunch for us.'

'What took you so long?' Sean stood up and wiped his hands on his breeches. 'I thought you weren't coming.'

'I'm sorry – everything went wrong.'

There was an awkward pause and Anna, flushed slightly as

Sean looked at her. Then she turned and started up the path. 'Come on – I'll race you to the top.'

She ran fast on bare feet, holding her skirts up to her knees and she was out in the sunshine before Sean caught her. He put his arms around her from behind and they fell together into the grass beside the path. They lay holding each other, laughing and panting at the same time.

'The service went on and on – I thought it would never finish,' said Anna, 'and afterwards –'

Before she could finish Sean covered her mouth with his and immediately her arms came up around his neck. They kissed with the tension building up steadily between them until Anna was moaning softly and moving her body against his. Sean released her mouth and moved his lips down across her cheek to her neck.

'Oh, Sean, it's been so long. It's been a whole week.'

'I know.'

'I've missed you so – I thought about you every day.'

Sean had his face pressed into her neck, he didn't answer.

'Did you miss me, Sean?'

'Hmm,' Sean murmured and lifted his mouth to take the lobe of her ear between his teeth.

'Did you think about me while you were working?'

'Hmm.'

'Tell me properly, Sean, say it properly.'

'I missed you, Anna, I thought about you all the time,' lied Sean and kissed her on the mouth. She clung to him and Sean's hand went down, right down to her knee and then up again under her clothes. Anna caught his wrist and held his hand away. 'No, Sean, just kiss me.'

Sean waited until her grip relaxed and then tried again, but this time she twisted away from him and sat up. 'Sometimes I think that's all you want to do.'

Sean felt his temper coming up, but he had the good sense to check it.

'That's not true, Anna. It's just that I haven't seen you for so long and I've missed you so much.'

She softened immediately and reached out to touch his cheek. 'Oh, Sean, I'm sorry. I don't mind really, it's just that – oh, I don't know.' She scrambled to her feet and picked up the basket. 'Come on, let's go on to the pools.'

They had a special place. It was walled in by the reeds and shaded by a big tree that grew on the bank above; the sand was washed clean and white. Sean spread his saddle blanket for them to sit on. They could hear the river, close by but hidden, and the reeds rustled and nodded their fluffy heads with each breath of the wind.

'– and I couldn't get rid of him,' Anna chattered as she knelt on the blanket and unpacked the basket. 'He just sat there and every time I said something he blushed and wriggled on his seat. In the end I just told him, "I'm sorry, Garry, I have to go!" '

Sean scowled. The mention of Garrick had reminded him of the dip; he hadn't forgiven him yet.

'And then when I got into the house I found that Pa and Frikkie were fighting. Ma was in tears and the other kids were locked in the bedroom.'

'Who won?' asked Sean with interest.

'They weren't really fighting – they were just shouting at each other. They were both drunk.'

Sean was always slightly shocked at Anna's casual reference to her family's drinking habits. Everybody knew about Mr Van Essen and his two eldest boys but Anna didn't have to talk about it. Once Sean had tried to correct her. 'You shouldn't say things like that about your Pa. You should respect him.'

And Anna had looked at him calmly and asked, 'Why?' which was a difficult question. But now she changed the subject.

'Do you want to eat yet?'

'No,' said Sean and reached for her. She fought back, shrieking demurely until Sean held her down and kissed her. Then she lay quietly, answering his kisses.

'If you stop me now I'm going to get mad,' whispered Sean and deliberately unfastened the top button of her dress. She watched his face with solemn eyes and her hands stayed on his shoulders until he had undone her blouse down to the waist and then with her fingers she traced the bold black curves of his eyebrows.

'No, Sean, I won't stop you. I want to as well, I want to as much as you do.'

There was so much to discover and each thing was strange and wonderful and they were the first to find it. The way the muscles stood out down the side of his chest beneath his arms and yet left a place where she could see the outline of his ribs.

73

The texture of her skin, smooth and white with the faint blue suggestion of veins beneath. The deep hollow down the centre of his back – pressing her fingers into it she could feel his spine. The down on her cheeks, so pale and fine he could see it only in the sunlight. The way their lips felt against each other and the tiny flutter of tongues between. The smell of their bodies, one milky warm and the other musky and vigorous. The hair that covered his chest and grew thicker under his arms, and hers: startlingly dark against white skin, a small silky nest of it. Each time there was something new to find and greet with soft sounds of delight.

Now, kneeling before her as she lay with her head thrown back and her arms half-raised to receive him, Sean suddenly bowed his head and touched her with his mouth. The taste of her was clean as the taste of the sea.

Her eyes flew open. 'Sean, no, you mustn't – oh no, you mustn't.' There were lips within lips and a bud as softly resilient as a tiny green grape. Sean found it with the tip of his tongue.

'Oh, Sean, you can't do that. Please, please, please.' And her hands were in the thick hair at the back of his head holding him there.

'I can't stand it any more, come over me . . . quickly, quickly, Sean.'

Filling like a sail in a hurricane, swollen and hard and tight, stretched beyond its limit until it burst and was blown to shreds in the wind and was gone. Everything gone. The wind and the sail, the tension and the wanting, all gone. There was left only the great nothingness which is peace. Perhaps a kind of death; perhaps death is like that. But, like death, not an ending – for even death contains the seeds of resurrection. So they came back from peace to a new beginning, slowly at first and then faster until they were two people again. Two people on a blanket among reeds with the sunlight white on the sand about them.

'Each time it's better and better – isn't it, Sean?'

'Ah!' Sean stretched, arching his back and spreading his arms.

'Sean, you do love me, don't you?'

'Sure. Sure I love you.'

'I think you must love me to have done' – she hesitated – 'to do what you did.'

'I just said so, didn't I?' Sean's attention wandered to the basket. He selected an apple and polished it on the blanket.

'Tell me properly. Hold me tight and tell me.'

'Hell, Anna, how many times have I got to say it?' Sean bit into the apple. 'Did you bring any of your Ma's shortbread?'

It was coming on night when Sean got back to Theunis Kraal. He turned his horse over to one of the grooms and went into the house. His body tingled from the sun, and he felt the emptiness and sadness of after-love, but it was a good sadness, like the sadness of old memories.

Garrick was in the dining-room, eating alone. Sean walked into the room and Garrick looked up nervously.

'Hello, Garry.' Sean smiled at him and Garrick was momentarily dazzled by it. Sean sat down in the chair beside him and punched him lightly on the arm.

'Have you left any for me?' His hatred was gone.

'There's plenty,' Garrick nodded eagerly. 'Try some of the potatoes, they're jolly good.'

14

'They say the Governor sent for your Pa while he was in Pietermaritzburg. Had him alone for nearly two hours.' Stephen Erasmus took the pipe out of his mouth and spat down onto the railway lines. In his brown homespun and *veldschoen* he did not look like a rich cattleman. 'Well, we don't need a prophet to tell us what it was about, do we?'

'No, sir,' Sean agreed vaguely. The train was late and Sean wasn't listening. He had an entry in the stock register to explain to his father and he was mentally rehearsing his speech.

'*Ja*, we know what it's about all right.' Old Erasmus put the pipe back between his teeth and spoke around it. 'It's been two weeks now since the British Agent was recalled from Cetewayo's kraal at Gingindhlovu. *Liewe Here!* in the old days we'd have called out the Commando long ago.' He packed his pipe, pushing down onto the glowing tobacco with a calloused forefinger. Sean noticed that the finger was twisted and scarred by the trigger-guards of a hundred heavy rifles.

'You've never been on commando have you, *Jong*?'

'No, sir.'

'About time you did then,' said Erasmus, 'about bledy time.'

Up on the escarpment the train whistled and Sean started guiltily.

'There she is.' Erasmus stood up from the bench on which they were sitting and the station master came out from his office with a rolled red flag in his hand. Sean felt his stomach sink slowly until it stopped somewhere just above his knees.

The train ran in past them, whooshing steam and brake-whining. The single passenger coach stopped precisely opposite the wooden platform. Erasmus came forward and took Waite's hand.

'*Goeie More*, Steff.'

'*More*, Waite. They tell me you're the new chairman now. Well done, man.'

'Thanks. Did you get my telegram?' Waite spoke in Afrikaans.

'Ja. I got it. I told the others, we'll all be out at Theunis Kraal tomorrow.'

'Good,' Waite nodded. 'You'll stay for lunch, of course. We've got a lot to talk about.'

'Is it what I think it is?' Erasmus grinned wickedly. The tobacco had stained his beard yellow around his mouth and his face was brown and wrinkled.

'I tell you all about it tomorrow, Steff.' Waite winked at him, 'but in the meantime you'd better get that old muzzle-loader of yours out of moth-balls.'

They laughed, one deep down and the other a rusty old laugh.

'Grab the bags, Sean. Let's get home.' Waite took Ada's arm and they walked with Erasmus to the buggy. Ada had on a new dress, blue with leg o'mutton sleeves and a picture hat; she looked lovely but a little worried as she listened to them talking. It's strange how women can never face the prospect of war with the same boyish enthusiasm as their men.

'Sean!' Waite Courtney's roar carried clearly from his study along the corridor and through the closed door of the sitting-room. Ada dropped her knitting into her lap and her features set into an expression of unnatural calm. Sean stood up from his chair.

'You should have told him earlier,' Garrick said in a small voice. 'You should have told him during lunch.'

'I didn't get a chance.'

'Sean!' Another blast from the study.

'What's happened now?' asked Ada quietly.

'It's nothing, Ma. Don't worry about it.'

Sean crossed to the door.

'Sean,' Garrick's stricken voice, 'Sean, you won't – I mean you don't have to tell –' He stopped and sat hunched in his chair, his eyes full of desperate appeal.

'It's all right, Garry, I'll fix it.'

Waite Courtney stood over the desk. Between his clenched fists the stock register lay open. He looked up as Sean came in and closed the door.

'What's this?' He prodded the page with a huge square-tipped finger. Sean opened his mouth and then closed it again.

'Come on. I'm listening.'

'Well, Pa –'

'Well, Pa – be buggered. Just tell me how you've managed to massacre half the cattle on this farm in a little over a week?'

'It's not half the cattle – it's only thirteen.' Sean was stung by the exaggeration.

'Only thirteen,' bellowed Waite, '*only* thirteen. God Almighty, shall I tell you how much that is in cash? Shall I tell you how much that is in hard work and time and worry?'

'I know, Pa.'

'You know,' Waite was panting. 'Yes, you know everything. There's nothing anyone can tell you, is there? Not even how to kill thirteen head of prime oxen.'

'Pa –'

'Don't Pa me, by Jesus.' Waite slammed the heavy book closed. 'Just explain to me how you managed it. What's "dip poisoning"? What the bloody hell is "dip poisoning"? Did you give it to them to drink? Did you stick it up their arses?'

'The dip was too strong,' said Sean.

'And why was the dip too strong? How much did you put in?'

Sean took a deep breath, 'I put in four drums.'

There was silence and then Waite asked softly, '*How much?*'

'Four drums.'

'Are you mad? Are you raving bloody mad?'

'I didn't think it would harm them.' His carefully rehearsed speech forgotten, Sean unconsciously repeated the words he had heard from Garrick. 'It was getting late and my leg was –' Sean bit the sentence off and Waite stared at him, then the confusion cleared from his face.

'Garry!' he said.

'No,' shouted Sean. 'It wasn't him, I did it.'

'You're lying to me.' Waite came round from behind the desk. There was a note of disbelief in his voice. To his knowledge it was the first time it had ever happened. He stared at Sean and then his anger was back more violently than before. He had forgotten the oxen – it was the lie that concerned him now. 'By Christ, I'll teach you to tell the truth.' He snatched up his sjambok from the desk.

'Don't hit me, Pa,' Sean warned him, backing away. Waite threw up the sjambok and swung it down overarm. It hissed softly and Sean twisted away from it, but the tip of the lash

78

caught his shoulder. Sean gasped at the pain and lifted his hand to it.

'You lying little bastard!' shouted Waite and swung the whip sideways as though he were scything wheat, and this time it curled around Sean's chest under his uplifted arm. It split his shirt like a razor cut and the cloth fell away to expose the red ridged welt across his ribs and around his back.

'Here's some more!' Waite lifted the sjambok again and as he stood with his arm thrown back and his body turned off balance he knew he had made a mistake. Sean was no longer clutching the whip marks; his hands were held low and his fists were bunched. At the corners his eyebrows were lifted, giving an expression of satanical fury to his face. He was pale and his lips were drawn back tight, showing his teeth. His eyes, no longer blue but burning black, were on a level with Waite's.

'He's coming for me.' Waite's surprise slowed his reflexes, he couldn't bring his whip-arm down before Sean was on him. Sean hit him, standing solidly on both feet, bringing the full weight of his body into the punch, hurling it into the middle of Waite's exposed chest.

Heart punched, strength oozing out of him, Waite staggered back against the desk. The sjambok fell out of his hand and Sean went after him. Waite had the sensation of being a beetle in a saucer of treacle: he could see and think but he could barely move. He saw Sean take three quick paces forward, saw his right hand cocked like a loaded rifle, saw it aimed at his defenceless face.

In that instant, while his body moved in slow motion but his mind raced, the scales of paternal blindness dropped from Waite Courtney's eyes and he realized that he was fighting a man who matched him in strength and height, and who was his superior in speed. His only advantage lay in the experience he had gathered in forty years of brawling.

Sean threw his punch: it had all the power of the first one and Waite knew that he could not survive that in his face – and yet he could not move to avoid it. He dropped his chin onto his chest and took Sean's fist on the top of his head. The force of it flung him backwards over the desk, but as it hit he heard the brittle crackle of Sean's fingers breaking.

Waite dragged himself to his knees, using the corner of the desk as a support, and looked at his son. Sean was doubled up with pain, holding his broken hand against his stomach. Waite pulled himself to his feet and sucked in big breaths of air, he felt his strength coming back.

'All right,' he said, 'if you want to fight – then we fight.' He came round the desk, moving slowly, his hands ready, no longer underestimating his man.

'I am going to knock the daylights out of you,' announced Waite. Sean straightened up and looked at him. There was agony in his face now, but the anger was there also. Something surged up inside Waite when he saw it.

He can fight and he's game. Now we'll see if he can take a beating. Rejoicing silently Waite moved in on him, watching Sean's left hand, disregarding the broken right for he knew what pain was in it. He knew that no man could use a hand in that condition.

He shot out his own left hand, measuring with it, trying to draw Sean. Sean side-stepped, moving in past it. Waite was wide open for Sean's right, his broken right, the hand he could not possibly use – and Sean used it with all his strength into Waite's face.

Waite's brain burst into bright colours and darkness, he spun sideways, falling, hitting the leopard-skin rug with his shoulder and sliding with it across the floor into the fireplace. Then in the darkness he felt Sean's hands on him and heard Sean's voice.

'Pa, oh, my God, Pa. Are you all right?'

The darkness cleared a little and he saw Sean's face, the anger gone from it and in its place worry that was almost panic.

'Pa, oh, my God! Please, Pa.'

Waite tried to sit up, but he could not make it. Sean had to help him. He knelt next to Waite holding him, fumbling helplessly with his face, trying to brush the hair back off his forehead, stroking the rumpled beard into place. 'I'm sorry, Pa, truly I'm sorry. Let me help you to the chair.'

Waite sat in the chair and massaged the side of his jaw. Sean hovered over him, his own hand forgotten.

'What you want to do – kill me?' asked Waite ruefully.

'I didn't mean it. I just lost my temper.'

'I noticed,' said Waite, 'I just happened to notice that.'

'Pa – about Garry. You don't have to say anything to him, do you?'

Waite dropped his hand from his face and looked at Sean steadily.

'I'll make a bargain with you,' he said, 'I'll leave Garry out of it if you'll promise me two things. One: You never lie to me again.'

Sean nodded quickly.

'Two: If anybody ever takes a whip to you again you swear to me you'll give him the same as you just gave me.'

Sean started to smile and Waite went on gruffly. 'Now let's have a look at your hand.'

Sean held it out and Waite examined it, moving each finger in turn. Sean winced.

'Sore?' asked Waite. *He hit me with that. Sweet Jesus, I've bred me a wild one.*

'A little.' Sean was white-faced again.

'It's a mess,' said Waite. 'You'd better get into town right away and let Doctor Van have a go at it.'

Sean moved towards the door.

'Hold on.' Sean stopped and Waite pulled himself out of his chair. 'I'll come with you.'

'I'll be all right, Pa, you stay and rest.'

Waite ignored this and walked towards him.

'Really, Pa, I'll be all right on my own.'

'I'm coming with you,' Waite said harshly; and then softly, almost inaudibly, 'I want to, dammit.'

He lifted his arm as though to put it around Sean's shoulders, but before it touched him he let it drop back to his side and together they went out into the corridor.

15

With two fingers in splints Sean handled his knife awkwardly at lunch the next day, but his appetite was unimpaired. As was only right and fitting he took no part in the conversation except on the rare occasions that a remark was addressed directly to him. But he listened, his jaws chewing steadily and his eyes moving from speaker to speaker. He and Garry sat side by side in a backwater of the luncheon board while the guests were grouped in order of seniority around Waite.

Stephen Erasmus by age and wealth was in the right-hand seat; opposite him Tim Hope-Brown, just as wealthy but ten years younger; below him Gunther Niewenhuizen, Sam Tingle and Simon Rousseau. If you added it all together you could say that Waite Courtney had about a hundred thousand acres of land and half a million sterling sitting around his table. They were brown men – brown clothing, brown boots and big brown, calloused, hands. Their faces were brown and battered-looking and now that the meal was in its closing stages their usual reserve was gone and there was a tendency among them to talk all at the same time and to perspire profusely. This was not entirely a consequence of the dozen bottles of good Cape Mossel that Waite had provided nor of the piles of food they had eaten – it was more than that. There was a sense of expectancy among them, an eagerness they were finding it difficult to suppress.

'Can I tell the servants to clear away, Waite?' Ada asked from the end of the table.

'Yes, thank you, my dear. We'll have coffee in here, please.'

He stood up and fetched a box of cigars from the sideboard and carried it to each of his guests in turn. When the ends were cut and the tips were glowing, every man leaning back in his chair with a recharged glass and a cup of coffee in front of him, Ada slipped out of the room and Waite cleared his throat for silence.

'Gentlemen.' They were all watching him. 'Last Tuesday I spent two hours with the Governor. We discussed the recent developments across the Tugela.'

Waite lifted his glass and sipped at it, then held it by the stem and rolled it between his fingers as he went on.

'Two weeks ago the British Agent at the Zulu king's kraal was recalled. Recalled is perhaps the wrong word – the king offered to smear him with honey, and tie him over an ant-hill, an offer that Her Britannic Majesty's Agent declined with thanks. Shortly thereafter he packed his bags and made for the border.'

There was a small ruffle of laughter.

'Since then Cetewayo has collected all his herds which were grazing near the Tugela and driven them into the north; he has commanded a buffalo hunt for which he has decided he will need *all* his impis – twenty thousand spears. This hunt is to be held along the banks of the Tugela, where the last buffalo was seen ten years ago.' Waite sipped at his glass, watching their faces. 'And he has ordered that all wounded game is to be followed across the border.'

There was a sigh then, a murmur from them. They all knew that this was the traditional Zulu declaration of war.

'So, man, what are we going to do about it. Must we sit here and wait for them to come and burn us out?'

Erasmus leaned forward watching Waite.

'Sir Bartle Frere met Cetewayo's Indunas a week ago. He has given them an ultimatum. They have until January the eleventh to disband the impis and take the Queen's Agent back into Zululand. In the event that Cetewayo disregards the ultimatum, Lord Chelmsford is to command a punitive column of regulars and militia. The force is being assembled now and will leave Pietermaritzburg within the next ten days. He is to cross the Tugela at Rorke's Drift and engage the impis before they break out. It is intended to end this constant threat to our border and break the Zulu nation for ever as a military power.'

'It's about bledy time,' said Erasmus.

'His Excellency has gazetted me full colonel and ordered me to raise a commando from the Ladyburg district. I have promised him at least forty men fully armed, mounted and provisioned who will be ready to join Chelmsford at the Tugela. Unless any of you object I am appointing you gentlemen as my captains and

83

I know I can rely upon you to help me make good my promise to His Excellency.'

Suddenly Waite dropped his stilted manner and grinned at them. 'You will collect your own pay. It will be in cattle, as usual.'

'How far north has Cetewayo driven his herds?' asked Tim Hope-Brown.

'Not far enough, I'll warrant,' cackled Stephen Erasmus.

'A toast,' said Simon Rousseau jumping to his feet and holding up his glass. 'I give you a toast: the Queen, Lord Chelmsford and the Royal Herds of Zululand.'

They all stood and drank it, and then suddenly embarrassed by their display they sat down again, coughing awkwardly and shuffling their feet.

'All right,' said Waite, 'let's get down to details. Steff, you'll be coming and your two eldest boys?'

'Ja, three of us and my brother and his son. Put down five, Erasmus.'

'Good. What about you Gunther?'

They began the planning. Men, horses and wagons were marshalled on paper; each of the captains was allotted a series of tasks. There was question, answer and argument that filled the hours before the guests left Theunis Kraal. They rode in a bunch, trippling their horses, sitting slack and long-legged in the saddles, moving up the far slope along the road to Ladyburg. Waite and his sons stood on the front step and watched them go.

'Pa –' Garry tried tentatively for Waite's attention.

'Yes, boy?' Waite kept his eyes on the group. Steff Erasmus turned in the saddle and waved his hat above his head, Waite waved back.

'Why do we have to fight them, Pa? If the Governor just sent somebody to talk to them, then we wouldn't have to fight.'

Waite glanced at him, frowning slightly.

'Anything worth having is worth fighting for, Garry. Cetewayo has raised twenty thousand spears to take this from us –' Waite swept his arm in a circle that took in the whole of Theunis Kraal. 'I think it's worth fighting for – don't you, Sean?'

'You bet,' Sean nodded eagerly.

'But couldn't we just make a treaty with them?' Garry persisted.

'Another cross on a piece of paper.' Waite spoke with fierce disdain. 'They found one like that on Piet Retrief's body – hell of a lot of good it did him.'

Waite walked back into the house with his sons following him.

He lowered himself into his armchair, stretched his legs out in front of him and smiled at Ada. 'Damn good lunch, my dear.' He clasped his hands over his stomach, belched involuntarily and was immediately contrite. 'I beg your pardon – it just slipped out.'

Ada bent her head over her sewing to hide her smile.

'We've got a lot to do in the next few days.' He turned his attention back to his sons. 'We'll take one mule wagon and a pair of horses each. Now about ammunition. . . .'

'But, Pa, couldn't we just –?' Garry started again.

'Shut up,' said Waite, and Garry subsided miserably into one of the other chairs.

'I've been thinking,' announced Sean.

'Not you as well,' growled Waite. 'Damn it to hell, here's your chance to win your own cattle and. . . .'

'That's just what I've been thinking,' Sean cut in. 'Everybody will have more cattle than they know what to do with. The prices will drop way down.'

'They will at first,' admitted Waite, 'but in a year or two they'll climb back again.'

'Shouldn't we sell now? Sell everything except the bulls and breeding cows, then after the war we'll be able to buy back at half the price.'

For a moment Waite sat stunned and then slowly his expression changed.

'My God, I never thought of that.'

'And Pa,' Sean was twisting his hands together in his enthusiasm, 'we'll need more land. When we bring the herds back across the Tugela there won't be enough grazing to go round. Mr Pye has called the mortgages on Mount Sinai and Mahoba's Kloof. He's not using the land. Couldn't we lease them from him now before everybody starts looking for grazing?'

'We had a lot to do before you started thinking,' said Waite softly, 'but now we've really got to work.'

He searched his pockets, found his pipe and while he filled it with tobacco he looked at Sean. He tried to keep his face neutral but the pride kept showing.

'You keep thinking like that and you'll be a rich man one day.' Waite could not know how true his prophecy would prove – the time was still remote when Sean could drop the purchase price of Theunis Kraal across a gaming table, and laugh at the loss.

16

The Commando was moving out on New Year's Day. New Year's Eve was set down for a double celebration: 'Welcome 1879', and 'God speed the Ladyburg Mounted Rifles'. The whole district was coming into town for the *braaivleis* and dancing that was being held in the square. Feast the warriors – laugh, dance and sing, then form them up and march them out to war.

Sean and Garry rode in early. Ada and Waite were to follow later in the afternoon. It was one of those bright days of a Natal summer: no wind and no clouds, the kind of day when the dust from a wagon hangs heavy in the air. They crossed the Baboon Stroom and from the farther ridge looked down across the town and saw the wagon dust on every road leading into Ladyburg.

'Look at them come,' said Sean; he screwed up his eyes against the glare and stared at the north road. 'That will be the Erasmus wagon. Karl will be with them.'

The wagons looked like beads on a string.

'That's the Petersens',' said Garry, 'or the Niewehuisens'.'

'Come on,' shouted Sean, and slapped the free end of his reins across his horse's neck. They galloped down the road. The horses they rode were big glossy animals, with their manes cropped like English hunters.

They passed a wagon. There were two girls sitting beside mama on the box seat, the Petersen sisters. Dennis Petersen and his father were riding ahead of the wagon.

Sean whooped as he raced past the wagon and the girls laughed and shouted something that was lost in the wind.

'Come on, Dennis,' howled Sean as he swept past the two sedately trotting outriders. Dennis's horse reared and then settled in to run, chasing Sean. Garry trailed them both.

They reached the cross roads, lying flat along their horses' necks, pumping the reins like jockeys. The Erasmus wagon was trundling down to meet them.

'Karl,' Sean called as he held his horse a little to stand in the stirrups. 'Karl. Come on, man, catch a wayo, Cetewayo!'

They rode into Ladyburg in a bunch. They were all flush-faced and laughing, excited and happy at the prospect of dancing and killing.

The town was crowded, its streets congested with wagons and horses and men and women and girls and dogs and servants.

'I've got to stop at Pye's store,' said Karl, 'come with me – it won't take long.'

They hitched their horses and went into the store; Sean, Dennis and Karl walked noisily and talked aloud. They were men, big sun-burned raw-boned men, muscled from hard work, but uncertain of the fact that they were men. Therefore, walk with a swagger and laugh too loud, swear when Pa isn't listening and no one will know you have your doubts.

'What are you going to buy, Karl?'

'Boots.'

'That'll take all day – you'll have to try them on. We'll miss half the fun.'

'There'll be nothing doing for another couple hours,' protested Karl. 'Wait for me, you chaps.'

Karl sitting on the counter, trying boots on his large feet, was not a spectacle that could hold Sean's interest for long. He drifted away amongst the piles of merchandise that cluttered Pye's store. There were stacks of pick handles, piles of blankets, bins of sugar and salt and flour, shelves of groceries and clothing, overcoats and women's dresses and hurricane-lamps and saddles hanging from the roof, and all of it was permeated by the peculiar smell of a general dealer's store: a mixture of paraffin, soap and new cloth.

Pigeon to its coop, iron to magnet. . . . Sean's feet led him to the rack of rifles against the far wall of the room. He lifted down one of the Lee Metford carbines and worked the action; he stroked the wood with his fingertips, then he weighed it in his hands to feel the balance and finally brought it up to his shoulder.

'Hello, Sean.' His ritual interrupted, Sean looked up at the shy voice.

'It's Strawberry Pie,' he said smiling. 'How's school?'

'I've left school now. I left last term.'

Audrey Pye had the family colouring but with a subtle difference – instead of carrot her hair was smoked copper with glints in it. She was not a pretty girl, her face was too broad and flat, but she had that rare skin that too seldom goes with red hair: creamy unfreckled purity.

'Do you want to buy anything, Sean?'

Sean placed the carbine back in the rack.

'Just looking,' he said. 'Are you working in the store now?'

'Yes.' She dropped her eyes from Sean's scrutiny. It was a year since he'd last seen her. A lot can change in a year; she now had that within her blouse which proved she was no longer a child. Sean eyed it appreciatively and she glanced up and saw the direction of his eyes; the cream of her skin clouded red. She turned quickly towards the trays of fruit.

'Would you like a peach?'

'Thanks,' said Sean and took one.

'How's Anna?' asked Audrey.

'Why ask me?' Sean frowned.

'You're her beau, aren't you?'

'Who told you that?' Sean's frown became a scowl.

'Everybody knows that.'

'Well, everybody's wrong.' Sean was irritated by the suggestion that he was one of Anna's possessions. 'I'm nobody's beau.'

'Oh!' Audrey was silent a moment, then, 'I suppose Anna will be at the dance tonight?'

'Most probably.' Sean bit into the furry golden peach and studied Audrey. 'Are you going, Strawberry Pie?'

'No,' Audrey answered wistfully. 'Pa won't let me.'

How old was she? Sean made a quick calculation ... three years younger than he was. That made her sixteen. Suddenly Sean was sorry she wouldn't be at the dance.

'That's a pity,' he said. 'We could have had some fun.' Linking them together, with the plural 'we', Sean threw her into confusion again. She said the first words she could think of, 'Do you like the peach?'

'Hmm.'

'It's from our orchard.'

'I thought I recognized the flavour.' Sean grinned and Audrey laughed. Her mouth was wide and friendly when she laughed. 'I knew you used to pinch them. Pa knew it was you. He used to say he'd set a mantrap in that hole in the hedge.'

'I didn't know he'd found that hole – we used to cover it up each time.'

'Oh, yes,' Audrey assured him, 'we knew about it all the time. It's still there. Some nights when I can't sleep I climb out of my bedroom window and go down through the orchard, through the hedge into the wattle plantation. It's so dark and quiet in the plantation at night – scary, but I like it.'

'You know something,' Sean spoke thoughtfully. 'If you couldn't sleep tonight and came down to the hedge at ten o'clock, you might catch me pinching peaches again.'

It took a few seconds for Audrey to realize what he had said. Then the colour flew up her face again and she tried to speak but no words came. She turned with a swirl of skirt and darted away among the shelves. Sean bit the last of the flesh off the peach pip and dropped it on the floor. He was smiling as he walked across to join the others.

'Hell's teeth, Karl, how much longer are you going to be?'

17

There were fifty or more wagons outspanned around the perimeter of the square but the centre was left open, and here the
braaivleis pits were burning, the flames already sinking to form
glowing beds. Trestle-tables stood in two lines near the fires and
the women worked at them cutting meat and boerwors, butter-
ing bread, arranging platoons of pickle bottles, piling the food on
trays and sweetening the evening with their voices and laughter.

In a level place a huge buck-sail was spread for the dancing
and at each corner a lantern hung on a pole. The band was
tuning with squeaks from the fiddles and preliminary asthma
from the single concertina.

The men gathered in knots amongst the wagons or squatted
beside the braaivleis pits, and here and there a jug pointed its
base briefly at the sky.

'I don't like to be difficult, Waite,' Petersen came across to
where Waite was standing with his captains, 'but I see you've
put Dennis in Gunther's troop.'

'That's right.' Waite offered him the jug and Petersen took it
and wiped the neck with his sleeve.

'It's not you, Gunther,' Petersen smiled at Gunther
Niewehuisen, 'but I would be much happier if I could have
Dennis in the same troop as myself. Keep an eye on him, you
know.'

They all looked at Waite to hear what he would say. 'None
of the boys are riding with their fathers. We've purposely
arranged it that way. Sorry, Dave.'

'Why?'

Waite Courtney looked away, over the wagons at the furious
red sunset that hung above the escarpment. 'This isn't going to
be a bushbuck shoot, Dave. You may find that you'll be called
upon to make decisions that will be easier for you if you're not
making them about your own son.'

There was a murmur of agreement and Steff Erasmus took his pipe out of his mouth and spat into the fire. 'There are some things it is not pretty for a man to see. They are too hard for him to forget. He should not see his son kill his first man, also he should not see his son die.'

They were silent then, knowing this truth. They had not spoken of it before because too much talk softens a man's stomach, but they knew death and understood what Steff had said. One by one their heads turned until they were all staring across the square at the gathering of youngsters beyond the fires. Dennis Petersen said something but they could not catch the words and his companions laughed.

'In order to live a man must occasionally kill,' said Waite, 'but when he kills too young, he loses something . . . a respect for life: he makes it cheap. It is the same with a woman, a man should never have his first woman until he understands about it. Otherwise that too becomes cheap.'

'I had my first when I was fifteen,' said Tim Hope-Brown. 'I can't say it made them any cheaper; in fact I've known them to be bloody expensive.'

Waite's big boom led the laughter.

'I know your old man pays you a pound a week but what about us, Sean?' protested Dennis, 'we aren't all millionaires.'

'All right, then,' Sean agreed, 'five shillings in the pool. Winner takes the lot.'

'Five bob is reasonable,' Karl opined, 'but let's get the rules clear so there's no argument afterwards.'

'Kills only, woundings don't count,' said Sean.

'And they have to be witnessed,' insisted Frikkie Van Essen. He was older than the others; his eyes were already a little bloodshot for he had made a start on the evening's drinking.

'All right, dead Zulus only and a witness to each kill. The highest score takes the pool.' Sean looked around the circle of faces for their assent. Garry was hanging back on the fringe. 'Garry will be banker. Come on, Garry, hold out your hat.'

They paid the money into Garrick's hat and he counted it.

'Two pounds – from eight of us. That's correct.'

'Hell, the winner will be able to buy his own farm.'

They laughed.

'I've got a couple of bottles of smoke hidden in my saddle bags,' Frikkie said. 'Let's go and try them.'

The hands of the clock on the church tower showed quarter before ten. There were silver-edged clouds around the moon, and the night had cooled. Rich meaty smelling steam from the cooking pits drifted across the dancers, fiddles sawed and the concertina bawled the beat, dancers danced and the watchers clapped in time and called encouragement to them. Someone whooped like a Highlander in the feverish pattern of movement, in the fever of fun. Dam the dribble of minutes with laughter, hold the hour, lay siege against the dawn!

'Where are you going, Sean?'

'I'll be back just now.'

'But where are you going?'

'Do you want me to tell you, Anna, do you really want to know?'

'Oh, I see. Don't be long. I'll wait for you by the band.'

'Dance with Karl.'

'No, I'll wait for you, Sean. Please don't be long. We've got such a little time left.'

Sean slipped through the circle of wagons, he kept in the tree shadow along the sidewalk, round the side of Pye's store and down the lane, running now, jumped the ditch and through the barbed wire fence. It was dark in the plantation and quiet as she had said; dead leaves rustled and a twig popped under his feet. Something ran in the darkness, scurry of small feet. Sean's stomach flopped over: nerves, only a rabbit. He came to the hedge and searched for the hole, missed it and turned back, found it and through into the orchard. He stood with his back against the wall of vegetation and waited. The trees were moon grey and black below. He could see the roof of the house beyond them. He knew she'd come, of course. He had told her to.

The church clock chimed the hour and then later the single stroke of the quarter hour. Angry now, damn her! He went up through the orchard, cautiously staying in shadow. There was a light in one of the side windows, he could see it spilling out into a yellow square on the lawn. He circled the house softly.

She was at the window with the lamp behind her. Her face was dark but lamplight lit the edges of her hair into a coppery halo. There was something of yearning in her attitude, leaning

93

forward over the sill. He could see the outline of her shoulders through the white cloth of her gown.

Sean whistled, pitching it low to reach her only, and she started at the sound. A second longer she stared out from light into the dark and then she shook her head, slowly and regretfully from side to side. She closed the curtains and through them Sean saw her shadow move away. The lamp went out.

Sean went back through the orchard and the plantation. He was trembling with anger. From the lane he heard the music in the square and he quickened his pace. He turned the corner and saw the lights and movement.

'Silly little fool,' he said out loud, anger still there but something else as well. Affection? Respect?

'Where have you been? I've waited nearly an hour.' Possessive Anna.

'There and back to see how far it is.'

'Funny! Sean Courtney, where have you been?'

'Do you want to dance?'

'No.'

'All right, don't then.'

Karl and some of the others were standing by the cooking pits. Sean started for them.

'Sean, Sean, I'm sorry.' Penitent Anna. 'I'd love to dance, please.'

They danced, jostled by other dancers, but neither of them spoke until the band stopped to wipe their brows and wet dry throats.

'I've got something for you, Sean.'

'What is it?'

'Come, I'll show you.'

She led him from the light among the wagons and stopped by a pile of saddles and blankets. She knelt and opened one of the blankets and stood up again with the coat in her hands.

'I made it for you. I hope you like it.'

Sean took it from her. It was sheepskin, tanned and polished, stitched with love, the inside wool bleached snowy white.

'It's beautiful,' Sean said. He recognized the labour that had gone into it. It made him feel guilty: gifts always made him feel guilty.

'Thank you very much.'

'Try it on, Sean.'

Warm, snug at the waist, room to move in the shoulders; it enhanced his considerable bulk. Anna stood close to him, arranging the collar.

'You look nice in it,' she said. Smug pleasure of the giver.

He kissed her and the mood changed. She held him tight around the neck. 'Oh, Sean, I wish you weren't going.'

'Let's say goodbye properly.'

'Where?'

'My wagon.'

'What about your parents?'

'They've gone back to the farm. Pa's coming in tomorrow morning. Garry and I are sleeping here.'

'No, Sean, there are too many people. We can't.'

'You don't want to,' Sean whispered. 'It's a pity because it might be the last time ever.'

'What do you mean?' She was suddenly still and small in his arms.

'I'm going away tomorrow. You know what might happen?'

'No. Don't talk like that. Don't even think it.'

'It's true.'

'No, Sean, don't. Please don't.'

Sean smiled in the darkness. So easy, so very easy.

'Let's go to my wagon.' He took her hand.

18

Breakfast in the dark, cooking fires around the square, voices quiet, men standing with their wives, holding the small children in farewell. The horses saddled, rifles in the scabbards and blanket rolls behind, four wagons drawn up in the centre of the square with the mules in the traces.

'Pa should be here any minute. It's nearly five o'clock,' said Garry.

'They're all waiting for him,' agreed Sean. He shrugged at the weight of the bandolier strapped over his shoulder.

'Mr Niewehuizen has made me one of the wagon drivers.'

'I know,' said Sean. 'Can you handle it?'

'I think so.'

Jane Petersen came towards them.

'Hello, Jane. Is your brother ready yet?'

'Nearly. He's just saddling up.'

She stopped in front of Sean and shyly held out a scrap of green-and-yellow silk.

'I've made you a cockade for your hat, Sean.'

'Thanks, Jane. Won't you put it on for me?' She pinned up the brim of Sean's hat; he took it back from her and set it at a jaunty angle on his head.

'I look like a general now,' he said and she laughed at him. 'How about a goodbye kiss, Jane?'

'You're terrible,' said little Jane and went away quickly, blushing. Not so little, Sean noticed. There were so many of them you hardly knew where to start.

'Here's Pa,' announced Garry, as Waite Courtney rode into the square.

'Come on,' said Sean and untied his horse. From all around the square, men were leading out their horses.

'See you later,' said Garry and limped off towards one of the waiting mule wagons.

Waite rode at the head of the column. Four troops of fifteen men in double file, four wagons behind them, and then the loose horses driven by black servants.

They moved out across the square, through the litter of the night's festivities, and into the main street. The women watched them in silence, standing motionless with the children gathered around them. These women had seen men ride out before against the tribes; they did not cheer for they too were wise in the ways of death, they had learned that there is no room for glory in the grave.

Anna waved to Sean. He did not see her for his horse was skittish and he was past her before he had it under control. She let her hand drop back to her side and watched him go. He wore the skeepskin coat.

Sean did see the coppery flash and the swiftly-blown kiss from the upstairs window of Pye's store. He saw it because he was looking for it. He forgot his injured pride sufficiently to grin and wave his hat.

Then they were out of the town, and at last even the small boys and dogs that ran beside them fell back and the column trotted out along the road to Zululand.

The sun came up and dried the dew. The dust rose from under the hooves and drifted out at an angle from the road. The column lost its rigidity as men spurred ahead or dropped back to ride with their friends. They rode in groups and straggles, relaxed and cheerfully chatting, as informal as a party out for a day's shooting. Each man had taken to the field in the clothing he considered most suitable. Steff Erasmus wore his church suit, but he was the most formally attired of the group. They had only one standard item of uniform among them: this was the green-and-yellow cockade. However, even here there was scope for individual taste: some wore them on their hats, some on their sleeves and others on their chests. They were farmers, not fighting men, but their rifle scabbards were battered with use, their bandoliers worn with easy familiarity and the wood of their gun butts was polished from the caress of their hands.

It was middle afternoon before they reached the Tugela.

'My God, look at that!' whistled Sean. 'I've never seen so many people in one place in my life before.'

'They say there are four thousand,' said Karl.

'I know there are four thousand.' Sean ran his eyes over the camp. 'But I didn't know four thousand was that many.'

The column was riding down the last slope to Rorke's Drift. The river was muddy brown and wide, rippling over the shallows of the crossing place. The banks were open and grassy with a cluster of stone-walled buildings on the near side. In a quarter-mile radius around the buildings Lord Chelmsford's army was encamped. The tents were laid out in meticulous lines, row upon row with the horses picketed between them. The wagons were marshalled by the drift, five hundred at least, and the whole area swarmed with men.

The Ladyburg Mounted Rifles, in a solid bunch that over-flowed the road behind their Colonel, came down to the perimeter of the camp and found their passage blocked by a sergeant in a dress coat and with a fixed bayonet.

'And who be you, may I ask?'

'Colonel Courtney — and a detachment of the Ladyburg Mounted Rifles.'

'What's that? Didn't catch it.'

Waite Courtney stood in his stirrups and turned to face his men.

'Hold on there, gentlemen. We can't all talk at once.'

The hubbub of conversation and comment behind him faded and this time the sergeant heard him.

'Ho! Beg your pardon, sir. I'll call the orderly officer.'

The orderly officer was an aristocrat and a gentleman. He came and looked at them. 'Colonel Courtney?' There was a note of disbelief in his voice.

'Hello,' said Waite with a friendly smile. 'I hope we are not too late for the fun.'

'No, I don't believe you are.' The officer's eyes fastened on Steff Erasmus. Steff lifted his top hat politely. *'More, Meneer.'* The bandoliers of ammunition looked a little out of place slung across his black frockcoat.

The officer tore his eyes away from him. 'You have your own tents, Colonel?'

'Yes, we've got everything we need.'

'I'll get the sergeant here to show you where to make camp.'

'Thank you,' said Waite.

The officer turned to the sergeant. So carried away was he that he took the man by the arm. 'Put them far away. Put them on the other side of the Engineers –' he whispered frantically. 'If the General sees this lot. . . .' He shuddered, but in a genteel fashion.

19

Garrick first became conscious of the smell. Thinking about it served as a rallying point for his attention and he could start to creep out of the hiding-place in his mind. For Garrick, these returns to reality were always accompanied by a feeling of light-headedness and a heightening of the senses. Colours were vivid, skin sensitive to the touch, tastes and smells sharp and clear.

He lay on a straw mattress. The sun was bright, but he was in shade. He lay on the veranda of the stone-walled hospital above Rorke's Drift. He thought about the smell that had brought him back. It was a blending of corruption and sweat and dung, the smell of ripped bowels and congealing blood.

He recognized it as the smell of death. Then his vision came into focus and be saw the dead. They were piled along the wall of the yard where the cross-fire from the store and the hospital had caught them; they were scattered between the buildings, and the burial squads were busy loading them onto the wagons. They were lying down the slope to the drift, they were in the water and on the far bank. Dead Zulus, with their weapons and shields strewn about them. Hundreds of them, Garrick thought with astonishment: no, thousands of them.

Then he was aware that there were two smells; but both of them were the smells of death. There was the stink of the black, balloon-bellied corpses swelling in the sun and there was the smell from his own body and the bodies of the men about him, the same smell of pain and putrefaction but mixed with the heaviness of disinfectant. Death wearing antiseptic – the way an unclean girl tries to cover her menstrual odour.

Garrick looked at the men around him, They lay in a long row down the veranda, each on his own mattress. Some were dying and many were not but on all of them the bandages were stained with blood and iodine. Garrick looked at his own body. His left arm was strapped across his bare chest and he felt the ache start beating within him, slow and steady as a funeral drum. There were bandages around his head. I'm wounded – again he was astonished. How? But how?

'You've come back to us, Cocky,' cheerful Cockney from beside him. 'We thought you'd gone clean bonkers.'

Garrick turned his head and looked at the speaker; he was a small monkey-faced man in a pair of flannel underpants and a mummy suit of bandages.

'Doc said it was shock. He said you'd come out of it soon enough.' The little man raised his voice, 'Hey, Doc, the hero is completely mentos again.' The doctor came quickly, tired-looking, dark under the eyes, old with overwork.

'You'll do,' he said, having groped and prodded. 'Get some rest. They're sending you back home tomorrow.' He moved away for there were many wounded, but then he stopped and looked back. He smiled briefly at Garrick, 'I doubt it will ease the pain at all but you've been recommended for the Victoria Cross. The General endorsed your citation yesterday. I think you'll get it.'

Garrick stared at the doctor as memory come back patchily,

'There was fighting,' Garrick said.

'You're bloody well tooting there was!' the little man beside him guffawed.

'Sean !' said Garrick. 'My, brother! What happened to my brother?' There was silence then and Garrick saw the quick shadow of regret in the doctor's eyes. Garrick struggled into a sitting position.

'And my Pa. What happened to my father?'

'I'm sorry,' said the doctor with simplicity, 'I'm afraid they were both killed.'

Garrick lay on his mattress and looked down at the Drift. They were clearing the corpses out of the shallows now, splashing as they dragged them to the bank. He remembered the splashing as Chelmsford's army had crossed. Sean and his father had been among the scouts who had led the column, three troops of the Ladyburg Mounted Rifles and sixty men of the Natal Police. Chelmsford had used these men who knew the country over which the initial advance was to be made.

Garrick had watched them go with relief. He could hardly believe the good fortune that had granted him a squirting dysentery the day before the ultimatum expired and the army crossed the Tugela.

'The lucky bastards,' protested one of the other sick as they watched them go. Garrick was without envy: he did not want to go to war, he was content to wait here with thirty other sick men and a garrison of sixty more to hold the Drift while Chelmsford took his army into Zululand.

Garrick had watched the scouts fan out from the Drift and disappear into the rolling grassland, and the main body of men and wagons follow them until they too had crawled like a python into the distance and left a well-worn road behind them through the grass.

He remembered the slow slide of days while they waited at the Drift. He remembered grumbling with the others when they were made to fortify the store and the hospital with bags and biscuit tins filled with sand. He remembered the boredom.

Then, his stomach tightening, he remembered the messenger.

'Horseman coming.' Garrick had seen him first. Recovered from his dysentery he was doing sentry duty above the Drift.

'The General's left his toothbrush behind, sent someone back for it,' said his companion. Neither of them stood up. They watched the speck coming across the plain towards the river.

'Coming fast,' said Garrick. 'You'd better go and call the Captain.'

'I suppose so,' agreed the other sentry. He trotted up the slope to the store and Garrick stood up and walked down to the edge of the river. His peg sank deep into the mud.

'Captain says to send him up to the store when he gets here.' Garrick's companion came back and stood beside him.

'Something funny about the way he's riding,' said Garrick, 'he looks tired.'

'He must be drunk. He's falling about in the saddle like it's Saturday night.'

Garrick gasped suddenly, 'He's bleeding, he's wounded.'

The horse plunged into the Drift and the rider fell forward onto its neck; the side of his shirt was shiny black with blood, his face was pale with pain and dust. They caught his horse as it came out of the water and the rider tried to shout but his voice was a croak. 'In the name of God prepare yourselves. The Column's been surrounded and wiped out. They're coming – the whole black howling pack of them. They'll be here before nightfall.'

'My brother,' said Garrick. 'What happened to my brother?'

'Dead,' said the man. 'Dead, they're all dead.' He slid sideways off his horse.

They came, the impis of Zulu in the formation of the bull, the great black bull whose head and loins filled the plain and whose horns circled left and right across the river to surround them. The bull stamped with twenty thousand feet and sang with ten thousand throats until its voice was the sound of the sea on a stormy day. The sunlight reflected brightly from the spear blades as it came singing to the Tugela.

'Look! Those in front are wearing the helmets of the Hussars,' one of the watchers in the hospital exclaimed. 'They've been looting Chelmsford's dead. There's one wearing a dress coat and some are carrying carbines.'

It was hot in the hospital for the roof was corrugated-iron and the windows were blocked with sandbags. The rifle slits let in little air. The men stood at the slits, some in pyjamas, some stripped to the waist and sweating in the heat.

'It's true then, the Column has been massacred.'

'That's enough talking. Stand to your posts and keep your mouths shut.'

The impis of Zulu crossed the Tugela on a front five hundred yards wide. They churned the surface to white with their crossing.

'My God! Oh, my God!' whispered Garrick as he watched them come. 'We haven't got a chance, there are so many of them.'

'Shut up. Damn you,' snapped the sergeant at the Gatling machine-gun beside him and Garry covered his mouth with his hand.

' – Grabbed O'Riley by the neck
Shoved his head in a pail of water
Rammed that pistol up his –'

sang one of the malaria cases in delirium and somebody else laughed, shrill hysteria in the sound.

'Here they come!'

'Load!'

The metallic clashing of rifle mechanism. 'Hold your fire, men. Fire on command only.'

The voice of the bull changed from a deep sonorous chant to

the shrill ululation of the charge – high-pitched frenzy of the blood squeal.

'Steady, men. Steady. Hold it. Hold your fire.'

'Oh, my God!' whispered Garrick softly, watching them come black up the slope. 'Oh, my God! – please don't let me die.'

'Ready!'

The van had reached the wall of the hospital yard. Their plumed head-dresses were the frothy crest of a black wave as they came over the wall.

'Aim!'

Sixty rifles lifted and held, aimed into the press of bodies.

'Fire!'

Thunder, then the strike of bullets into flesh, a sound as though a handful of gravel had been flung into a puddle of mud. The ranks reeled from the blow. The clustered barrels of the Gatling machine-gun jump – jump – jumped as they swung, cutting them down so they fell upon each other, thick along the wall. The stench of burnt black powder was painful to breathe.

'Load!'

The bullet-ravaged ranks were re-forming as those from behind came forward into the gaps.

'Aim!'

They were coming again, solid black and screaming halfway across the yard.

'Fire!'

Garrick sobbed in the shade of the veranda and pressed the fingers of his right hand into his eye sockets to squeeze out the memory.

'What's the trouble, Cocky?' The Cockney rolled painfully onto his side and looked at Garrick.

'Nothing!' said Garrick quickly. 'Nothing!'

'Coming back to you, is it?'

'What happened? I can only remember pieces of it.'

'What happened!' The man echoed his question, 'What didn't happen!'

'The doctor said –' Garrick looked up quickly, 'He said the General had endorsed my citation. That means Chelmsford's alive. My brother and my father – they must be alive as well!'

'No such luck, Cocky. The Doc's taken a fancy to you – you with one leg doing what you did – so he made inquiries about your folk. It's no use.'

'Why?' asked Garrick desperately. 'Surely if Chelmsford's alive they must be too?'

The little man shook his head. 'Chelmsford's made a base camp at a place called Isandhlwana. He left a garrison there with all the wagons and supplies. He took a flying column out to raid, but the Zulus circled around him and attacked the base camp, then they came on here to the Drift. As you know, we held them for two days until Chelmsford's flying column came to help us.'

'My folk – what happened to them?'

'Your father was at the Isandhlwana camp. He didn't escape. Your brother was with Chelmsford's column but he was cut off and killed in one of the skirmishes before the main battle.'

'Sean dead?' Garrick shook his head. 'No, it's not possible. They couldn't have killed him.'

'You'd be surprised how easily they did it,' said the Cockney. 'A few inches of blade in the right place is enough for the best of them.'

'But not Sean – you didn't know him. You couldn't understand.'

'He's dead, Cocky. Him and your Pa and seven hundred others. The wonder is we aren't too.' The man wriggled into a more comfortable position on his mattress. 'The General made a speech about our defence here. Finest feat of arms in the annals of British courage – or something like that.'

He winked at Garrick. 'Fifteen citations for the old V.C. – you's one of them. I ask you, Cocky, isn't that something? What's your girl friend going to do when you come home with a mucking great gong clanking around on your chest, hey?'

He stared at Garrick and saw the tears oozing in oily lines down his cheeks.

'Come on, Cock. You're a bloody hero.' He looked away from Garrick's grief. 'Do you remember that part – do you remember what you did?'

'No,' Garrick's voice was husky. *Sean. You can't leave me alone. What am I going to do, now that you're gone?*

'I was next to you. I saw it all. I'll tell you about it,' said the Cockney.

As he talked so the events came back and fitted into sequence in Garrick's mind.

'It was on the second day, we'd held off twenty-three charges.'

Twenty-three, was it as many, as that? Garrick had lost count; it might have been but a single surging horror. Even now he could taste the fear in the back of his throat and smell it rancid in his own sweat.

'Then they piled wood against the hospital wall and set fire to it.' Zulus coming across the yard carrying bundles of faggots, falling to the rifles, others picking up the bundles and bringing them closer until they too died and yet others came to take their place. Then flames pale yellow in the sunlight, a dead Zulu lying on the bonfire his face charring, and the smell of him mingled with the smoke.

'We knocked a hole in the back wall and started to move the sick and wounded out through it and across to the store.'

The boy with the assegai through his spine had shrieked like a girl as they lifted him.

'Them bloody savages came again as soon as they saw we were pulling out. They came from that side.' He pointed with his bandaged arm, 'where the chaps in the store couldn't reach them, and there was only you and I and a couple of others at the loopholes – everyone else was carrying the wounded.'

There had been a Zulu with the blue heron feathers of an Induna in his head-dress. He had led the charge. His shield was dried oxhide dappled black and white, and at his wrists and ankles were bunches of war rattles. Garrick had fired at the instant the Zulu half-turned to beckon to his warriors – the bullet sliced across the tensed muscles of his belly and unzipped it like a purse. The Zulu went down on his hands and knees with his entrails bulging out in a pink and purple mass.

'They reached the door of the hospital and we couldn't fire on them from the angle of the windows.'

The wounded Zulu started to crawl towards Garrick, his mouth moving and his eyes fastened on Garrick's face. He still had his assegai in his hand. The other Zulus were beating at the door and one of them ran his spear blade through a crack in the woodwork and lifted the bar. The door was open.

Garrick watched the Zulu crawling towards him through the dust with his pink wet bowels swinging like a pendulum under him. The sweat was running down Garrick's cheeks and dripping off the end of his chin, his lips were trembling. He lifted his rifle and aimed into the Zulu's face. He could not fire.

'That's when you moved, Cocky. I saw the bar lifted out of

its brackets and I knew that in the next second there'd be a mob of them in through the door and we'd stand no chance against their spears at close range.'

Garrick let go his rifle and it rattled on the concrete floor. He turned away from the window. He could not watch that crippled, crawling thing. He wanted to run, to hide. That was it – to hide. He felt the fluttering start behind his eyes, and his sight began to grey.

'You were nearest to the door. You did the only thing that could have saved us. Though I know I wouldn't have had the guts to do it.'

The floor was covered with cartridge cases – brass cylinders shiny and treacherous under foot. Garrick stumbled; as he fell he put out his arm.

'Christ,' the little Cockney shuddered, 'to put your arm into the brackets like that – I wouldn't have done it.'

Garrick felt his arm snap as the mob of Zulus threw themselves against the door. He hung there staring at his twisted arm, watching the door tremble and shake as they beat against it. There was no pain and after a while everything was grey and warm and safe.

'We fired through the door until we had cleared them away from the other side. Then we were able to get your arm free, but you were out cold. Been that way ever since.'

Garrick stared out across the river. He wondered if they had buried Sean or left him in the grass for the birds.

Lying on his side Garrick drew his legs up against his chest, his body was curled. Once as a brutal small boy he had cracked the shell of a hermit crab. Its soft fat abdomen was so vulnerable that its vitals showed through the transparent skin. It curled its body into the same defensive attitude.

'I'll reckon you'll get your gong,' said the Cockney.

'Yes,' said Garrick. He didn't want it. He wanted Sean back.

20

Doctor Van Rooyen gave Ada Courtney his arm as she stepped down from the buggy. In fifty years he had not obtained immunity from other people's sorrow. He had learned only to conceal it: no trace of it in his eyes, or his mouth, or his lined and whiskered face.

'He's well, Ada. They did a good job on his arm: that is, for military surgeons. It will set straight.'

'When did they arrive?' asked Ada.

'About four hours ago. They sent all the Ladyburg wounded back in two wagons.'

Ada nodded, and he looked at her with the professional shield of indifference, hiding the shock he felt at the change in her appearance. Her skin was as dry and lifeless as the petals of a pressed flower, her mouth had set determinedly against her grief and her widow's weeds had doubled her age.

'He's waiting for you inside.' They walked up the steps of the church and the small crowd opened to let them pass. There were subdued greetings for Ada and the usual funereal platitudes. There were other women there wearing black, with swollen eyes.

Ada and the doctor went into the cool gloom of the church. The pews had been pushed against the wall to make room for the mattresses. Women were moving about between them and men lay on them.

'I'm keeping the bad ones here, where I can watch them,' the doctor told her. 'There's Garry.'

Garrick stood up from the bench on which he was sitting. His arm was slung awkwardly across his chest. He limped forward to meet them, his peg tapped loudly on the stone floor.

'Ma, I'm –' he stopped. 'Sean and Pa – '

'I've come to take you home, Garry.' Ada spoke quickly, flinching at the sound of those two names.

'They can't just let them lie out there, they should –'

'Please, Garry. Let's go home,' said Ada. 'We can talk about it later.'

'We are all very proud of Garry,' said the doctor.

'Yes,' said Ada. 'Please, let's go home, Garry.' She could feel it there just below the surface and she held it in: so much sorrow confined in so small a place. She turned back towards the door, she mustn't let them see it. She mustn't cry here in front of them, she must get back to Theunis Kraal.

Willing hands carried Garrick's bags out to the buggy and Ada took the reins. Neither of them spoke again until they crossed the ridge and looked down at the homestead.

'You're the master of Theunis Kraal now, Garry,' said Ada softly and Garrick stirred uneasily on the seat beside her. He didn't want it, he didn't want the medal. He wanted Sean.

21

'I hope you don't mind me coming,' said Anna, 'but I had to talk to you.'

'No. I'm glad you did. Truly I'm glad,' Garrick assured her earnestly. 'It's so good to see you again, Anna. It feels like forever since we left.'

'I know, and so much – so much has happened. My Pa and yours. And – and Sean.' She stopped. 'Oh, Garry, I just can't believe it yet. They've told me and told me but I can't believe it. He was so – so alive.'

'Yes,' said Garrick, 'he was so alive.'

'He talked about dying the night before he left. I hadn't even thought about it until then.' Anna shook her head in disbelief, 'and I never dreamed it could happen to him. Oh, Garry, what am I going to do?'

Garrick turned and looked at Anna. The Anna he loved, Sean's Anna. But Sean was dead. He felt an idea move within him, not yet formed in words, but real enough to cause a sick spasm of conscience. He shied away from it.

'Oh, Garry. What can I do?'

She was asking for help, the appeal was apparent in her voice. Her father killed at Isandhlwana, her elder brothers still with Chelmsford at Tugela, her mother and the three small children to feed. How blind of him not to see it!

'Anna, can I help you? Just tell me.'

'No, Garry. I don't think anyone can.'

'If it's money –' He hesitated discreetly. 'I'm a rich man now. Pa left the whole of Theunis Kraal to Sean and I, and Sean isn't – ' She looked at him without answering.

'I can lend you some to tide you over –' blushed Garrick, 'as much as you need.'

She went on staring at him while her mind adjusted itself.

Garrick master of Theunis Kraal, he was rich, twice as rich as Sean would have been. And Sean was dead.

'Please, Anna. Let me help you. I want to, really I do.'

He loved her, it was pathetically obvious – and Sean was dead.

'You will let me, Anna?'

She thought of hunger and bare feet, dresses washed until you could see through them when you held them to the light, petticoats patched and cobbled. And always the fear, the uncertainty you must live with when you are poor. Garry was rich and alive, Sean was dead.

'Please tell me you will.' Garrick leaned forward and took her arm, he gripped it fiercely in his agitation and she looked into his face. You could see the resemblance, she thought, but Sean had strength where here there was softness and uncertainty. The colour was wrong also, pale sand and paler blue instead of brutal black and indigo. It was as though an artist had taken a portrait and with a few subtle strokes had altered its meaning completely so as to make it into an entirely different picture. She did not want to think about his leg.

'It's sweet of you, Garry,' she said, 'but we've got a little in the bank and the plot is free of debt. We've got the horses; we can sell them if we have to.'

'What is it then? Please tell me.'

She knew then what she was going to do. She could not lie to him – it was too late for that. She would have to tell him, but she knew that the truth would not make any difference to him. Well, perhaps a little – but not enough to prevent her getting what she wanted. She wanted to be rich, and she wanted a father for the child she carried within her.

'Garry, I'm going to have a baby.'

Garrick's chin jerked up and his breathing jammed and then started again.

'A baby?'

'Yes, Garrick. I'm pregnant.'

'Whose? Sean's?'

'Yes, Garry. I'm going to have Sean's baby.'

'How do you know, are you sure?'

'I'm sure.'

Garrick pulled himself out of his chair and limped across the veranda. He stopped against the railing and gripped it with his good hand; the other was still in the sling. His back was turned to Anna and he stared out across the lawns of Theunis Kraal to the lightly-forested slope beyond.

Sean's baby. The idea bewildered him. He knew that Sean and Anna did that together. Sean had told him and Garrick had not resented it. He was jealous, but only a little, for Sean had let him share in it by telling him and so some of it had belonged to him also. But a baby. Sean's baby.

Slowly the full implication came to him. Sean's baby would be a living part of his brother, the part that had not been cut down by the Zulu blades. He had not completely lost Sean. Anna – she must have a father for her child, it was unthinkable that she could go another month without marrying. He could have both of them, everything he loved in one package. Sean and Anna. She must marry him, she had no other choice. Triumph surged up within him and he turned to her.

'What will you do, Anna?' He felt sure of her now. 'Sean's dead. What will you do?'

'I don't know.'

'You can't have the baby. It would be a bastard.' He saw her wince at the word. He felt very certain of her.

'I'll have to go away – to Port Natal.' She spoke without expression in her voice. Looking calmly at him, knowing what he would say, 'I'll leave soon,' she said, 'I'll be all right. I'll find some way out.'

Garrick watched her face as she spoke. Her head was small on shoulders wide for a girl, her chin was pointed, her teeth were slightly crooked but white – she was very pretty despite the catlike set of her eyes.

'I love you, Anna,' he said. 'You know that, don't you?'

She nodded slowly and her hair moved darkly on her shoulders. The cat eyes softened contentedly. 'Yes, I know, Garry.'

'Will you marry me?' He said it breathlessly.

'You don't mind? You don't mind about Sean's baby?' she said, knowing he did not.

'I love you, Anna.' He came towards her clumsily and she looked up at his face. She did not want to think about the leg.

'I love you, nothing else matters.' He reached for her and she let him hold her.

'Will you marry me, Anna?' He was trembling.

'Yes.' Her hands were quiescent on his shoulders. He sobbed

softly and her expression changed to one of distaste, she made the beginnings of a movement to push him away but stopped herself.

'My darling, you won't regret it. I swear you won't,' he whispered.

'We must do it quickly, Garry.'

'Yes. I'll go into town this afternoon and speak to Padre – '

'No! Not here in Ladyburg,' Anna cut in sharply. 'People will have too much to say. I couldn't stand it.'

'We'll go up to Pietermaritzburg,' Garrick acquiesced.

'When, Garry?'

'As soon as you like.'

'Tomorrow,' she said. 'We'll go tomorrow.'

22

The Cathedral in Pietermaritzburg stands on Church Street. Grey stone with a bell-tower and iron railings between the street and the lawns. Pigeons strut puff-chested on the grass.

Anna and Garrick went up the paved path and into the semi-dark of the Cathedral. The stained glass window had the sun behind it, making the interior glow weirdly with colour. Because they were both nervous they held hands as they stood in the aisle.

'There's no one here,' whispered Garrick.

'There must be,' Anna whispered back. 'Try through that door there.'

'What shall I say?'

'Just tell him we want to get married.'

Garrick hesitated.

'Go on.' Anna still whispered, pushing him gently towards the door of the vestry.

'You come with me,' said Garrick. 'I don't know what to say.'

The priest was a thin man with steel-rimmed spectacles. He looked over the top of them at the nervous pair in the doorway and shut the book on the desk in front of him.

'We want to get married,' Garrick said and blushed crimson.

'Well,' said the priest drily, 'you have the right address. Come in.'

He was surprised at their haste and they argued a little, then he sent Garrick down to the Magistrates' Court for a special licence. He married them, but the ceremony was hollow and unreal. The drone of the priest's voice was almost lost in the immense cavern of the Cathedral as they stood small and awed before him. Two old ladies who came in to pray stayed on gleefully to witness for them, and afterwards they both kissed Anna and the priest shook Garrick's hand. Then they went out again into the sunlight. The pigeons still strutted on the lawn and a mule wagon rattled down Church Street with the coloured driver singing and cracking his whip. It was as though nothing had happened.

'We're married,' said Garrick doubtfully.

'Yes,' agreed Anna, but she sounded as though she didn't believe it either.

They walked back to the hotel side by side. They didn't talk or touch each other. Their luggage had been taken up to their room and the horses had been stabled. Garrick signed the register and the clerk grinned at him.

'I've put you in Number Twelve, sir, it's our honeymoon suite.' One of his eyelids drooped slightly and Garrick stammered in confusion.

After dinner, an excellent dinner, Anna went up to the room and Garrick sat on in the lounge drinking coffee. It was almost an hour later that he mustered the courage to follow her. He crossed the drawing-room of their suite, hesitated at the bedroom door then went in. Anna was in bed. She had pulled the bedclothes up to her chin and she looked at him with her inscrutable cat's eyes.

'I've put your nightshirt in the bathroom, on the table,' she said.

'Thank you,' said Garrick. He stumbled against a chair as he crossed the room. He closed the door behind him, undressed quickly and leaning naked over the basin splashed water onto his face; then he dried and pulled the nightshirt over his head. He went back into the bedroom: Anna lay with her face turned away from him. Her hair was loose on the pillow, shining in the lamplight.

Garrick sat on the edge of the chair. He lifted the hem of his nightshirt above his knee and unfastened the straps of his leg, laid the peg carefully beside the chair and massaged the stump with both hands. It felt stiff. He heard the bed creak softly and he looked up. Anna was watching him, staring at his leg. Hurriedly Garrick pulled down his nightshirt to cover the protruding slightly enlarged end with its folded line of scar-tissue. He stood up, balancing, and then hopped one-legged across to the bed. He was blushing again.

He lifted the edge of the blankets and slipped into the bed and Anna jerked violently away from him.

'Don't touch me,' she said hoarsely.

'Anna. Please don't be scared.'

'I'm pregnant, you mustn't touch me.'

'I won't. I swear I won't.'

She was breathing hard, making no attempt to hide her revulsion.

'Do you want me to sleep in the drawing-room, Anna? I will if you say so.'

'Yes,' she said, 'I want you to.'

He gathered his dressing-gown from the chair and stooping picked up his leg. He hopped to the door and turned back to face her. She was watching him still.

'I'm sorry, Anna, I didn't mean to frighten you.' She did not answer him and he went on.

'I love you. I swear I love you more than anything in the world. I wouldn't hurt you, you know that, don't you? You know I wouldn't hurt you?'

Still she did not answer and he made a small gesture of appeal, the wooden leg clutched in his hand and the tears starting to fill his eyes. 'Anna. I'd kill myself rather than frighten you!'

He went quickly through the door and closed it behind him. Anna scrambled out of the bed and with her nightdress flurrying around her legs she ran across the room to the door and turned the key in the lock.

23

In the morning Garrick was bewildered to find Anna in a mood of girlish gaiety. She had a green ribbon in her hair and her green frock was faded but pretty. She chattered happily through breakfast and while they were having their coffee she leaned across the table and touched Garrick's hand. 'What shall we do today, Garry?'

Garrick looked surprised, he hadn't thought that far ahead. 'I suppose we'd better catch the afternoon train back to Ladyburg,' he said.

'Oh, Garry,' Anna pouted effectively. 'Don't you love me enough to give me a honeymoon?'

'I suppose –' Garrick hesitated and then 'of course, I didn't think of it.' He grinned excitedly. 'Where can we go?'

'We could take the mail boat down the coast to Capetown,' Anna suggested.

'Yes!' Garrick adopted the idea immediately. 'It'll be fun.'

'But, Garry –' Anna's eagerness faded. 'I only have two old dresses with me.' She touched her clothes. Garrick sobered also while he grappled with this new problem. Then he found the solution.

'We'll buy you some more!'

'Oh, Garry, could we? Could we really?'

'We'll buy you all you can use, more than you can use. Come on, finish your coffee and we'll go into town and see what they have.'

'I'm finished.' Anna stood up from the table ready to go.

24

They had a stateroom on the *Dunottar Castle* from Port Natal to Capetown. There were other young people aboard. Anna, in her elegant new clothing and sparkling with excitement, formed the centrepiece of a gay little group that played deck games, dined, danced and flirted as the mailboat drove south through the sunny, golden days of early autumn.

At first Garrick was content to stay unobtrusively close to Anna. He was there to hold her coat, fetch a book or carry a rug. He watched her fondly, revelling in her success, hardly jealous when she almost disappeared behind a palisade of attentive young men, not resenting the sofa which formed his uncomfortable bed in the drawing-room of their suite.

Then gradually there came a realization among their travelling companions that Garrick was paying for most of the refreshments and other little expenses that came up each day. They became aware of him and of the fact that he appeared to be the richest of the group. From there it needed only a small adjustment to their thinking to admit Garrick to the circle. The men addressed remarks directly at him and some of the other girls flirted with him openly and sent him on small errands. Garrick was at once overjoyed and appalled by these attentions, for he could not cope with the lightning exchange of banter that flickered around him and left him stammering and blushing. Then Garrick found how easy it really was.

'Have a dram, old chap?'

'No, really. I don't, you know.'

'Nonsense, everybody does. Steward, bring my friend here a whisky.'

'Really, no really I won't.'

And of course Garrick did. It tasted foul and he spilt a little on Anna's evening dress; while he wiped it up with his handkerchief she whispered a barbed reprimand and then laughed gaily at a joke from the moustached gentleman on her right. Garrick shrank miserably back in his chair and forced down the rest of the whisky. Then slowly and exquisitely the glow came upon him, starting deep own inside him and spreading out warmly to the very tips of his fingers.

'Have another one, Mr Courtney?'

'Yes, thanks. I'll have the same again, but I think it's my round.' He had the next drink. They were sitting in deck-chairs on the upper deck in the shelter of the superstructure, there was a moon and the night was warm. Someone was talking about Chelmsford's Zulu campaign.

'You're wrong on that point,' Garrick said clearly. There was a small silence.

'I beg your pardon!' the speaker glanced at him with surprise. Garrick leaned forward easily in his chair and began talking. There was a stiffness at first but he made a witticism and two of the women laughed. Garrick's voice strengthened. He gave a quick and deep-sighted résumé of the causes and effects of the war. One of the men asked a question. It was a sharp one but Garrick saw the essence of it and answered neatly. It was all very clear and he found the words without effort.

'You must have been there,' one of the girls hazarded.

'My husband was at Rorke's Drift,' said Anna quietly, looking at him as though he were a stranger. 'Lord Chelmsford has cited him for the award of the Victoria Cross. We are waiting to hear from London.'

The party was silent again, but with new respect.

'I think it's my round, Mr Courtney. Yours is whisky, isn't it?'

'Thank you.'

The dry musty taste of the whisky was less offensive this time; he sipped it thoughtfully and found that there was a faint sweetness in the dry.

As they went down to their staterooms later that night Garrick put his arm around Anna's waist.

'What fun you were tonight!' she said.

'Only a reflection of your charm, my darling, I am your mirror.' He kissed her cheek and she pulled away, but not violently.

'You're a tease, Garry Courtney.'

Garrick slept on his back on the sofa with a smile on his face and no dreams, but in the morning his skin felt tight and dry and there was a small ache behind his eyes. He went through to the bathroom and cleaned his teeth; it helped a little but the ache behind his eyes was still there. He went back to the drawing-room and rang for the cabin steward.

'Good morning, sir.'

'Can you bring me a whisky and soda?' Garry asked hesitantly.

'Certainly, sir.'

Garry did not put the soda into it but drank it neat, like medicine. Then afterwards miraculously the glow was there again, warming him. He had hardly dared to hope for it.

He went through to Anna's cabin. She was rosy with sleep, her hair a joyous tangle on the pillow.

'Good morning, my darling.' Garrick stooped over her and kissed her, and his hand moved to cover one of her breasts through the silk of her gown.

'Garry, you naughty boy.' She slapped his wrist, but jokingly.

There was another honeymoon couple aboard returning to their farm near Capetown – seventy-five acres of the finest vines on the whole of the Cape Peninsula, the man's own words. Anna and Garrick were forced by sheer persistence to accept their invitation to stay with them.

Peter and Jane Hugo were a delightful pair. Very much in love, rich enough, popular and in demand with Capetown society. With them Anna and Garrick spent an enchanted six weeks.

They went racing at Milnerton.

They swam at Muizenberg in the warm Indian Ocean. They picnicked at Clifton and ate crayfish, fresh caught and grilled over open coals. They rode to hounds with the Cape Hunt and caught two jackals after a wild day's riding over the Hottentots' Holland. They dined at the Fort and Anna danced with the Governor.

They went shopping in the bazaars that were filled with treasures and curiosities from India and the Orient, Whatever Anna wanted she was given. Garry bought himself something as well – a silver flask, beautifully worked and set with cornelians. It fitted into the inside pocket of his coat without showing a bulge. With its help Garrick was able to keep pace with the rest of the company.

Then the time came for them to leave. The last night there were only the four of them for dinner and it was sad with the regret of present parting, but happy with the memory of shared laughter.

Jane Hugo cried a little when she kissed Anna goodnight. Garry and Peter lingered on downstairs until the bottle was finished and then they walked upstairs together and shook hands outside Garry's bedroom. Peter spoke gruffly. 'Sorry to see you two go. We've got used to having you round. I'll wake you early and we can go out for a last early morning ride before the boat leaves.'

Garry changed quietly in the bathroom and went through to the bedroom. His peg made no sound on the heavily carpeted floor. He crossed to his own bed and sat down to unstrap his peg.

'Garry,' Anna whispered.

'Hullo, I thought you were asleep.'

There was a stirring and Anna's hand came out from under the bedclothes, held towards him in invitation.

'I was waiting to say goodnight to you.'

Garry crossed to her bed, suddenly awkward again.

'Sit down for a minute,' said Anna and he perched on the edge of her bed. 'Garry, you don't know how much I've enjoyed these last weeks. They've been the happiest days of my whole life. Thank you so much, my husband.'

She reached up and touched his cheek. She looked small and warm curled up in the bed.

'Kiss me goodnight, Garry.'

He leaned forward to touch her forehead with his lips but she moved quickly and took it full on her mouth.

'You can come in, if you like,' she whispered, her mouth still against his. She opened the bedclothes with one hand.

So Garry came to her when the bed was warm, and the wine still sang a little in her head and she was ready in the peculiar passion of early pregnancy. It should have been so wonderfully good.

Impatient now, ready to lead him, she reached down to touch and then stilled into surprised disbelief. Where there should have been hardness, male and arrogant, there was slackness and uncertainty.

Anna started to laugh. Not even the shotgun blast had hurt as deeply as that laugh.

'Get out,' she said through the cruel laughter. 'Go to your own bed.'

25

Anna and Garrick had been married two full months when they came back to Theunis Kraal. Garrick's arm was out of plaster, Peter Hugo's doctor had fixed that for him.

They took the road that by-passed the village and crossed the Baboon Stroom bridge. At the top of the rise Garry pulled the horses to a halt and they looked out across the farm.

'I can't understand why Ma moved into town,' said Garrick. 'She didn't have to do that. There's plenty of room for everybody at Theunis Kraal.'

Anna sat silently and contentedly beside him. She had been relieved when Ada had written to them at Port Natal after they had telegraphed her the news of their marriage. Young as she was Anna was woman enough to recognize the fact that Ada had never liked her. Oh, she was sweet enough when they met, but Anna found those big dark eyes of hers disconcerting. They looked too deep and she knew they found the things she was trying to hide.

'We'll have to go and see her as soon as we can. She must come back to the farm – after all Theunis Kraal is her home too,' Garrick went on. Anna moved slightly in her seat, *let her stay in the house in Ladyburg, let her rot there*, but her voice was mild as she answered, 'Theunis Kraal belongs to you now, Garry, and I'm your wife. Perhaps your stepmother knows what's best.' Anna touched his arm and smiled at him, 'Anyway we'll talk about it some other time. Let's get home now, it's been a long drive and I'm very tired.'

Immediately concerned, Garrick turned to her. 'I'm terribly sorry, my dear. How thoughtless of me.' He touched the horses with the whip and they went down the slope towards the homestead.

The lawns of Theunis Kraal were green and there were cannas in bloom, red and pink and yellow.

It's beautiful, thought Anna, *and it's mine. I'm not poor any more*. She looked at the gabled roof and the heavy yellow wood shutters on the windows as the carriage rolled up the drive.

There was a man standing in the shade of the veranda. Anna and Garrick saw him at the same time. He was tall with shoulders as wide and square as the crosstree of a gallows, he stepped out of the shadow and came down the front steps into the sunlight. He was smiling with white teeth in a brown burnt face; it was the old irresistible smile.

'Sean,' whispered Anna.

26

Sean really noticed him for the first time when they stopped to water the horses. They had left Chelmsford's Column the previous noon to scout towards the north-east. It was a tiny patrol – four mounted white men and a half-a-dozen Nongaai, the loyal Native troops from Natal.

He took the reins from Sean's hands. 'I will hold your horse while you drink.' His voice had a resonance to it and Sean's interest quickened. He looked at the man's face and liked it immediately. The whites of the eyes had no yellow in them and the nose was more Arabic than negroid. His colour was dark amber and his skin shone with oil.

Sean nodded. There is no word in the Zulu language for 'thank you', just as there are no words for 'I am sorry'.

Sean knelt beside the stream and drank. The water tasted sweet for he was thirsty; when he stood again there were damp patches on his knees and water dripping from his chin.

He looked at the man who was holding his horse. He wore only a small kilt of civet-cat tails: no rattles nor cloak, no headdress. His shield was black rawhide and he carried two short stabbing spears.

'How are you called?' Sean asked, noticing the breadth of the man's chest and the way his belly muscles stood out like the static ripples on a windswept beach.

'Mbejane.' Rhinoceros.

'For your horn?' The man chuckled with delight, his masculine vanity tickled.

'How are you called, Nkosi?'

'Sean Courtney.'

Mbejane's lips formed the name silently and then he shook his head.

'It is a difficult name.' He never said Sean's name – not once in all the years that were to follow.

'Mount up,' called Steff Erasmus. 'Let's get moving.'

They swung up onto the horses, gathered the reins and loosened the rifles in the scabbards. The Nongaai who had been stretched out resting on the bank stood up.

'Come on,' said Steff. He splashed through the stream. His horse gathered itself and bounded up the far bank and they followed him. They moved in line abreast across the grassland, sitting loose and relaxed in their saddles, the horses trippling smoothly.

At Sean's right stirrup ran the big Zulu, his long extended stride easily pacing Sean's horse. Once in a while Sean dropped his eyes from the horizon and looked down at Mbejane; it was a strangely comforting feeling to have him there.

They camped that night in a shallow valley of grass. There were no cooking fires; they ate biltong for supper, the black strips of dried salt meat, and washed it down with cold water.

'We're wasting our time. There hasn't been a sign of Zulu in two days' riding,' grumbled Bester Klein, one of the troopers.

'I say we should turn back and rejoin the Column, We're getting farther and farther away from the centre of things – we're going to miss the fun when it starts.'

Steff Erasmus wrapped his blanket more closely about his shoulders: the night's first chill was on them.

'Fun, is it?' He spat expertly into the darkness. 'Let them have the fun, if we find the cattle.'

'Don't you mind missing the fighting?'

'Look, you, I've hunted bushmen in the Karroo and the Kalahari, I've fought Xhosas and Fingoes along the Fish river, I went into the mountains after Moshesh and his Basutos. Matabele, Zulu, Bechuana – I've had fun with all of them. Now four or five hundred head of prime cattle will be payment enough for any fun we miss.' Steff lay back and adjusted his saddle behind his head. 'Anyway what makes you think there won't be guards on the herds when we find them. You'll get your fun – I promise you.'

'How do you know they've got the cattle up here?' insisted Sean.

'They're here,' said Steff, 'and we'll find them.' He turned his head towards Sean. 'You've got the first watch, keep your eyes open.' He tilted his top hat forward over his face, groped with his right hand to make sure his rifle lay beside him and then spoke from under the hat, 'Goodnight.' The others settled down into their blankets: fully-dressed, boots on, guns at hand. Sean moved out into the darkness to check the Nongaai pickets.

There was no moon, but the stars were fat and close to earth; they lit the land so that the four grazing horses were dark blobs against the pale grass. Sean circled the camp and found two of his sentries awake and attentive. He had posted Mbejane on the north side and now he went there. Fifty yards in front of him he picked up the shape of the small bush beside which he had left Mbejane. Suddenly Sean smiled and sank down onto his hands and knees, he cradled his rifle across the crooks of his elbows and began his stalk. Moving flat along the ground silently, slowly he closed in on the bush. Ten paces from it he stopped and lifted his head, careful to keep the movement inchingly slow. He stared, trying to find the shape of the Zulu among the scraggy branches and bunches of leaves. The point of a stabbing spear pricked him below the ear in the soft of his neck behind the jaw bone. Sean froze but his eyes rolled sideways and in the starlight he saw Mbejane kneeling over him holding the spear.

'Does the Nkosi seek me?' asked Mbejane solemnly, but there was laughter deep down in his voice. Sean sat up and rubbed the place where the spear had stung him.

'Only a night ape sees in the dark,' Sean protested.

'And only a fresh caught catfish flops on its belly,' chuckled Mbejane,

'You are Zulu,' Sean stated, recognizing the arrogance, although he had known immediately from the man's face and body that he was not one of the bastard Natal tribes who spoke the Zulu language but were no more Zulu than a tabby-cat is a leopard.

'Of Chaka's blood,' agreed Mbejane, reverence in his voice as he said the old king's name.

'And now you carry the spear against Cetewayo, your king?'

'My king?' The laughter was gone from Mbejane's voice. 'My king?' he repeated scornfully.

There was silence and Sean waited. Out in the darkness a jackal barked twice and one of the horses whickered softly.

'There was another who should have been king, but he died with a sharpened stick thrust up into the secret opening of his body, until it pierced his gut and touched his heart. That man was my father,' said Mbejane. He stood up and went back into the shelter of the bush and Sean followed him. They squatted side by side, silent but watchful. The jackal cried again up above the camp and Mbejane's head turned towards the sound.

'Some jackals have two legs,' he whispered thoughtfully. Sean felt the tingle along his forearms.

'Zulus?' he asked. Mbejane shrugged, a small movement in the darkness.

'Even if it is, they will not come for us in the night. In the dawn, yes, but never in the night.' Mbejane shifted the spear in his lap. 'The old one with the tall hat and grey beard understands this. Years have made him wise, that's why he sleeps so sweetly now but mounts up and moves in the darkness before each dawn.'

Sean relaxed slightly. He glanced sideways at Mbejane.

'The old one thinks that some of the herds are hidden near here.'

'Years have made him wise,' repeated Mbejane. 'Tomorrow we will find the land more broken, there are hills and thick thorn bush. The cattle will be hidden among them.'

'Do you think we'll find them?'

'Cattle are difficult to hide from a man who knows where to look.'

'Will there be many guards with the herds?'

'I hope so,' answered Mbejane, his voice a purr. His hand crept to the shaft of his assegai and caressed it. 'I hope there will be very many.'

'You would kill your own people, your brothers, your cousins?' asked Sean.

'I would kill them as they killed my father.' Mbejane's voice was savage now. 'They are not my people. I have no people. I have no brothers – I have nothing.'

Silence settled between them again, but slowly the ugliness of Mbejane's mood evaporated and in its place came a sense of companionship. Each of them felt comforted by the other's presence. They sat on into the night.

27

Mbejane reminded Sean of Tinker working a bird, he had the same half-crouched gait and the same air of complete absorption. The white men sat their horses in silence watching him. The sun was well up already and Sean unbuttoned his sheepskin coat and pulled it off. He strapped it onto the blanket roll behind him.

Mbejane had moved out about fifty yards from them and now he was working slowly back towards them. He stopped and minutely inspected a wet pat of cow dung.

'Hierdie Kaffir verstaan wat hy doen,' opined Steff Erasmus approvingly, but no one else spoke. Bester Klein fidgeted with the hammer of his carbine; his red face was already sweaty in the rising heat.

Mbejane had proved right, they were in hilly country. Not the smoothly rounded hills of Natal but hills with rocky crests, deeply gullied and ravined between. There was thorn forest and euphorbia covering the sides of the hills with a lattice work of reptile grey trunks, and the grass was coarse and tall.

'I could use a drink,' said Frikkie Van Essen and wiped his knuckles across his lips.

'Chee peep, chee peep,' a barbet called stridently in the branches of the kaffir boom tree under which they waited. Sean looked up; the bird was brown and red among the scarlet flowers which covered the tree.

'How many?' asked Steff and Mbejane came to stand at his horse's head.

'Fifty – no more,' he answered.

'When?'

'Yesterday, after the heat of the day they moved slowly down the valley. They were grazing. They cannot be more than half an hour's ride ahead of us.'

Steff nodded. Fifty head only, but there would be more.

'How many men with them?'

Mbejane clucked his tongue disgustedly. 'Two *umfaans*.' He pointed with his spear at a dusty place where the print of a half grown boy's bare foot showed clearly. 'There are no men.'

'Good,' said Steff. 'Follow them.'

'They told us that if we found anything we must go back and report,' protested Bester Klein quickly. 'They said we shouldn't start anything on our own.'

Steff turned in his saddle, 'Are you frightened of two *umfaans*?' he asked coldly.

'I'm not frightened of anything, it's just what they told us.' Klein flushed redder in his already red face.

'I know what they told us, thank you,' said Steff. 'I'm not going to start anything, we're just going to have a look.'

'I know you,' burst out Klein. 'If you see cattle you'll go mad for them. All of you, you're greedy for cattle like some men are for drink. Once you see them you won't stop.' Klein was a railway ganger.

Steff turned away from him. 'Come on, let's go.'

They rode out of the shade of the kaffir boom tree into the sunlight, Klein muttering softly to himself and Mbejane leading them down the valley.

The floor of the valley sloped gradually and on each side of them the ground rose steep and rocky. They travelled quickly with Mbejane and the other Nongaai thrown out as a screen and the horsemen cantering in a line with their stirrups almost touching.

Sean levered open the breech of his rifle and drew out the cartridge. He changed it for another from the bandolier across his chest.

'Fifty head is only ten apiece,' complained Frikkie.

'That's a hundred quid – as much as you earn in six months.' Sean laughed with excitement and Frikkie laughed with him.

'You two keep your mouths shut and your eyes open.' Steff's voice was phlegmatic, but he couldn't stop the excitement from sparkling in his eyes.

'I knew you were going to raid,' sulked Klein. 'I knew it, sure as fate.'

'You shut up also,' said Steff and grinned at Sean.

They rode for ten minutes; then Steff called softly to the

Nongaai and the patrol halted. No one spoke and every man stood with his head alert and his ears straining.

'Nothing,' said Steff at last. 'How close are we?'

'Very close,' Mbejane answered. 'We should have heard them from here.'

Mbejane's exquisitely muscled body was shiny with sweat and the pride of his stance set him apart from the other Nongaai. There was a restrained eagerness about him, for the excitement was infectious.

'All right, follow them,' said Steff. Mbejane settled the rawhide shield securely on his shoulder and started forward again.

Twice more they stopped to listen and each time Sean and Frikkie were more restless and impatient.

'Sit still,' snapped Steff. 'How can we hear anything with you moving about?'

Sean opened his mouth, but before he could answer they all heard an ox low mournfully ahead of them among the trees.

'That's it!'

'We've got them!'

'Come on!'

'No, wait!' Steff ordered. 'Sean, take my farlookers and climb up that tree. Tell me what you can see.'

'We're wasting time,' argued Sean. 'We should – '

'We should learn to do as we're damn well told,' said Steff. 'Get up that tree.'

With the binoculars slung around his neck, Sean clambered upwards until he sat high in a crotch of two branches. He reached out and broke off a twig which obscured his vision, then exclaimed immediately, 'There they are, right ahead of us!'

'How many?' Steff called up to him.

'A small herd – two herdboys with them.'

'Are they among the trees?'

'No,' said Sean, 'they're in the open. Looks like a patch of swamp.'

'Make sure there aren't any other Zulus with them.'

'No –' Sean started to answer but Steff cut him short.

'Use the glasses, dammit. They'll be hiding if they're there.'

Sean brought up the glasses and focused them. The cattle were fat and sleek skinned, big horned and bodies dappled black on white. A cloud of white tick-birds hovered over them. The two herdboys were completely naked, youngsters with the thin legs

131

and the disproportionately large genitals of the Africans. Sean turned the glasses slowly back and forth searching the patch of swamp and the surrounding bush. At last he lowered them.

'Only the two herdboys,' he said.

'Come down then,' Steff told him.

The herdboys fled as soon as the patrol rode out into the open. They disappeared among the fever trees on the far side of the swamp.

'Let them go,' laughed Steff. 'The poor little buggers are going to be in enough trouble as it is.'

He spurred his horse forward into the vivid green patch of swamp grass. It was lush: thick and tall enough to reach his saddle.

The others followed him in with the mud squelching and sucking at the hooves of the horses. They could see the backs of the cattle showing above the grass a hundred yards ahead of them. The tick-birds circled squawking.

'Sean, you and Frikkie cut around to the left –' Steff spoke over his shoulder and before he could finish the grass around them was full of Zulus, at least a hundred of them in full war dress.

'Ambush!' yelled Steff. 'Don't try and fight, too many of them. Get out!' and they dragged him off his horse.

Horses panicked in the mud, whinnying as they reared. The bang of Klein's rifle was almost drowned in the triumphant roar of the warriors. Mbejane jumped to catch the bridle of Sean's horse; he dragged its head around.

'Ride, Nkosi, quickly. Do not wait.'

Klein was dead, an assegai in his throat and the blood bursting brightly from the corners of his mouth as he fell backwards.

'Hold on to my stirrup leather.' Sean felt surprisingly calm. A Zulu came at him from the side; Sean held his rifle across his lap and fired with the muzzle almost in the man's face. It cut the top off his head. Sean ejected the cartridge case and reloaded.

'Ride, Nkosi!' Mbejane shouted again. He had made no effort to obey Sean: his shield held high he barged into two of the attackers and knocked them down into the mud. His assegai rose and fell, rose and fell.

'*Ngi Dhla*,' howled Mbejane. 'I have eaten.' Fighting madness on him, he jumped over the bodies and charged. A man stood to meet him and Mbejane hooked the edge of his shield under his and jerked it aside, exposing the man's left flank to his blade.

'*Ngi Dhla*,' Mbejane howled again.

He had torn an opening in the ring of attackers and Sean rode for it, his horse churning heavily through the mud. A Zulu caught at his reins and Sean fired with his muzzle touching the man's chest. The Zulu screamed.

'Mbejane,' shouted Sean. 'Take my stirrup!'

Frikkie Van Essen was finished; his horse was down and Zulus swarmed over him with red spears.

Leaning out of the saddle Sean circled Mbejane's waist with his arm and plucked him out of the mud. He struggled wildly but Sean held him. The ground firmed under his horse's hooves, they were moving faster. Another Zulu stood in their way with his assegai ready. With Mbejane kicking indignantly under one arm and his empty rifle in his other hand Sean was helpless to defend himself. He shouted an obscenity at the Zulu as he rode down on him. The Zulu dodged to one side and darted in again. Sean felt the sting of the blade across his shin and then the shock as it went on into his horse's chest. They were through, out of the swamp and into the trees.

Sean's horse carried him another mile before it fell. The assegai had gone in deep. It fell heavily but Sean was able to kick his feet out of the irons and jump clear. He and Mbejane stood looking down at the carcass – both of them were panting.

'Can you run in those boots?' asked Mbejane urgently.

'Yes.' They were light *veldschoen*.

'Those breeches will hold your legs.' Mbejane knelt swiftly and with his assegai cut away the cloth until Sean's legs were bare from the thighs down. He stood up again and listened for the first sounds of pursuit. Nothing.

'Leave your rifle, it is too heavy. Leave your hat and your bandolier.'

'I must take my rifle,' protested Sean.

'Take it then,' Mbejane flashed impatiently. 'Take it and die. If you carry that they'll catch you before noon.'

Sean hesitated a second longer and then he changed his grip, holding the rifle by the barrel like an axe. He swung it against the trunk of the nearest tree. The butt shattered and he threw it from him.

'Now we must go,' said Mbejane.

Sean glanced quickly across at his dead horse, the leather thongs held his sheepskin coat onto the saddle. All Anna's hard work wasted, he thought wryly. Then following Mbejane he started to run.

The first hour was bad; Sean had difficulty matching his step to that of Mbejane. He ran with his body tensed and soon had a stabbing stitch in his side. Mbejane saw his pain and they stopped for a few minutes while Mbejane showed him how to relax it away. Then they went on with Sean running smoothly. Another hour went by and Sean had found his second wind.

'How long will it take us to get back to the main army?' grunted Sean.

'Two days perhaps . . . don't talk,' answered Mbejane.

The land changed slowly about them as they ran. The hills not so steep and jagged, the forest thinned and again they were into the rolling grassland.

'It seems we are not being followed.' It was half an hour since Sean had last spoken.

'Perhaps,' Mbejane was non-committal. 'It is too soon yet to tell.'

They ran on side by side, in step so their feet slapped in unison on the hard-baked earth.

'Christ, I'm thirsty,' said Sean.

'No water,' said Mbejane, 'but we'll stop to rest a while at the top of the next rise.'

They looked back from the crest. Sean's shirt was soaked with sweat and he was breathing deeply but easily.

'No one following us,' Sean's voice was relieved. 'We can slow down a bit now.'

Mbejane did not answer. He also was sweating heavily but the way he moved and held his head showed he was not yet beginning to tire. He carried his shield on his shoulder and the blade of the assegai in his other hand was caked with black, dry blood. He stared out along the way they had come for fully five minutes before he growled angrily and pointed with his assegai.

'There! Close to that clump of trees. Can you see them?'

'Oh, hell!' Sean saw them: about four miles behind, on the edge of the forest where it thinned out, a black pencil line drawn on the brown parchment of grassland. But the line was moving.

'How many of them?' asked Sean.

'Fifty,' hazarded Mbejane. 'Too many.'

'I wish I had brought my rifle,' muttered Sean.

'If you had they would be much closer now – and one gun against fifty –' Mbejane left it unfinished.

'All right, let's get going again,' said Sean.

'We must rest a little longer. This is the last time we can stop before nightfall.'

Their breathing had slowed. Sean took stock of himself: he was aching a little in the legs, but it would be hours yet before he was really tired. He hawked a glob of the thick gummy saliva out of his throat and spat it into the grass. He wanted a drink but knew that would be fatal folly.

'Ah!' exclaimed Mbejane. 'They have seen us.'

'How do you know?' asked Sean.

'Look, they are sending out their chasers.' From the head of the line a trio of specks had detached themselves and were drawing ahead.

'What do you mean?' Sean scratched the side of his nose uneasily. For the first time he was feeling the fear of the hunted – vulnerable, unarmed, with the pack closing in.

'They are sending their best runners ahead to force us beyond our strength. They know that if they push us hard enough – even though they break their own wind while they do it – we will fall easily to the others that follow.'

'Good God,' Sean was now truly alarmed. 'What are we going to do about it?'

'For every trick, there is a trick,' said Mbejane. 'But now we have rested enough, let us go.'

Sean took off down the hill like a startled duiker, but Mbejane pulled him up sharply.

'That is what they want. Run as before.' And once again they fell into the steady lope, swinging long-legged and relaxed.

'They're closer,' said Sean when they reached the top of the next hill. Three specks were now well ahead of the others.

'Yes.' Mbejane's voice was expressionless. They went over the crest and down the other side, the slap-slap-slap of their feet together and their breathing an unaltering rhythm: suck blow, suck blow.

There was a tiny stream in the bottom of the valley, clean water rippling over white sand. Sean jumped it with only a single longing glance and they started up the far slope. They were just short of the crest when behind them they heard a thin distant shout. He and Mbejane looked round. On the top of the hill they had just left, only a half a mile away, were the three Zulu runners, and as Sean watched they plunged down the slope towards him with their tall feather head-dresses bobbing and their leopard-tail kilts swirling about their legs. They had thrown aside their shields, but each man carried an assegai.

'Look at their legs,' exulted Mbejane. Sean saw that they ran with the slack, blundering steps of exhaustion.

'They are finished, they have run too hard.' Mbejane laughed. 'Now we must show them how afraid we are: we must run like the wind, run as though a hundred Tokoloshe* breathe on our necks.'

It was only twenty paces to the crest of the slope and they pelted panic-stricken up and over the top. But the instant they were out of sight Mbejane caught Sean's arm and held him.

'Get down,' he whispered. They sank into the grass and then crawled back on their stomachs until they lay just below the crest.

Mbejane held his assegai pointed forward, his legs were gathered up under him and his lips were drawn back in a half grin.

Sean searched in the grass and found a rock the size of an orange. It fitted neatly into his right hand.

They heard the Zulus coming, their horny bare feet pounding up the hill and then their breathing, hoarse hissing gasps, closer and closer until suddenly they came up over the crest. Their momentum carried them down to where Sean and Mbejane stood up out of the grass to meet them. Their fatigue-grey faces crumbled into expressions of complete disbelief; they had expected to find their quarry half a mile ahead of them. Mbejane killed one with his assegai, the man did not even lift his arms to parry the thrust; the point came out between his shoulders.

Sean hurled the rock into the face of another. It made a sound like a ripe pumpkin dropped on a stone floor; he fell backwards with his assegai spinning from his hand.

The third man turned to run and Mbejane landed heavily on his back, bore him down and then sat astride his chest, pushed his chin back and cut his throat.

Sean looked down at the man he had hit; he had lost his head-

---

* A chimera of Zulu mythology.

dress and his face had changed shape. His jaw hung lopsided, he was still moving feebly.

I have killed three men today, thought Sean, *and it was so easy.*

Without emotion he watched Mbejane come across to his victim. Mbejane stooped over him and the man made a small gasping sound then lay still. Mbejane straightened up and looked at Sean.

'Now they cannot catch us before dark.'

'And only a night ape can see in the dark,' said Sean. Remembering the joke, Mbejane smiled; the smile made his face younger. He picked up a bunch of dry grass and wiped his hands on it.

The night came only just in time to save them. Sean had run all day and at last his body was stiffening in protest; his breathing wheezed painfully and he had no moisture left to sweat with.

'A little longer, just a little longer.' Mbejane whispered encouragement beside him.

The pack was spread out, the stronger runners pressing a scant mile behind them and the others dwindling back into the distance.

'The sun is going; soon you can rest.' Mbejane reached out and touched his shoulder; strangely, Sean drew strength from that brief physical contact. His legs steadied slightly and he stumbled less frequently as they went down the next slope. Swollen and red, the sun lowered itself below the land and the valleys were full of shadow.

'Soon now, very soon.' Mbejane's voice was almost crooning. He looked back: the figures of the nearest Zulu were indistinct. Sean's ankle twisted under him and he fell heavily; he felt the earth graze the skin from his cheek and he lay on his chest with his head down.

'Get up,' Mbejane's voice was desperate. Sean vomited painfully, a cupful of bitter bile.

'Get up,' Mbejane's hands were on him, dragging him to his knees.

'Stand up or die here,' threatened Mbejane. He took a handful of Sean's hair and twisted it mercilessly. Tears of pain ran into Sean's eyes and he swore and lashed out at Mbejane.

'Get up,' goaded Mbejane and Sean heaved to his feet.

'Run,' said Mbejane, half-pushing him and Sean's legs began to move mechanically under him. Mbejane looked back once more. The nearest Zulu was very close but almost merged into the fading twilight. They ran on, Mbejane steadying Sean when he staggered, Sean grunting in his throat with each step, his mouth hanging open, sucking air across a swollen tongue.

Then quickly, in the sudden African transition from day to night, all colour was gone from the land and the darkness shut down in a close circle about them. Mbejane's eyes flicked restlessly back and forth, picking up shapes in the gloom, judging the intensity of the light. Sean reeled unseeing beside him.

'We will try now,' decided Mbejane aloud. He checked Sean's run and turned him right at an acute angle on their original track, now they were heading back towards the hunters at a tangent that would take them close past them but out of sight in the darkness.

They slowed to a walk, Mbejane holding Sean's arm across his shoulders to steady him, carrying his assegai ready in his other hand. Sean walked dully, his head hanging.

They heard the leading pursuers passing fifty paces away in the darkness and a voice called in Zulu, 'Can you see them?'

'*Aibo!*' Negative answered another.

'Spread out, they, may try to turn in the dark.'

'*Yeh-bo!*' Affirmative.

Then the voices were passed and silence and night closed about them once more. Mbejane made Sean keep walking. A little bit of moon came up and gave them light and they kept going with Mbejane gradually working back onto a course towards the southeast. They came to a stream at last with trees along its bank. Sean drank with difficulty, for his throat was swollen and sore. Afterwards they curled together for warmth on the carpet of leaves beneath the trees and they slept.

28

They found Chelmsford's last camp on the following afternoon: the neat lines of black camp fires and the flattened areas where the tents had stood, the stakes which had held the horse pickets and the piles of empty bully-beef tins and five-pound biscuit tins.

'They left two days ago,' said Mbejane.

Sean nodded, not doubting the correctness of this. 'Which way did they go?'

'Back towards the main camp at Isandhlwana.'

Sean looked puzzled.

'I wonder why they did that.'

Mbejane shrugged. 'They went in haste – the horsemen galloped ahead of the infantry.'

'We'll follow them,' said Sean.

The spoor was a wide road for a thousand men had passed along it and the wagons and gun carriages had left deep ruts.

They slept hungry and cold beside the spoor and the next morning there was frost in the low places when they started out.

A little before noon they saw the granite dome of Isandhlwana standing out against the sky and unconsciously they quickened their pace. Isandhlwana, the Hill of the Little Hand. Sean was limping for his boot had rubbed the skin from one heel. His hair was thick and matted with sweat and his face was plastered with dust.

'Even army bully beef is going to taste good,' said Sean in English, and Mbejane did not answer for he did not understand, but he was looking ahead with a vaguely worried frown on his face.

'Nkosi, we have seen no one for two days' march. It comes to me that we should have met patrols from the camp before now.'

'We might have missed them,' said Sean without much

interest, but Mbejane shook his head. In silence they went on. The hill was closer now so they could make out the detail of ledge and fissure that covered the dome in a lace-work pattern.

'No smoke from the camp,' said Mbejane. He lifted his eyes and started visibly.

'What is it?' Sean felt the first tingle of alarm.

'N'yoni,' said Mbejane softly and Sean saw them. A dark pall, turning like a wheel slowly, high above the hill of Isandhlwana, still so far off that they could not distinguish the individual birds: only a shadow, a thin dark shadow in the sky. Watching it Sean was suddenly cold in the hot noonday sun. He started to run.

There was movement below them on the plain. The torn canvas of an overturned wagon flapped like a wounded bird, the scurry and scuffle of the jackals and higher up the slope of the kopje the hunch-shouldered trot of a hyena.

'Oh, my God!' whispered Sean. Mbejane leaned on his spear; his face was calm and withdrawn but his eyes moved slowly over the field.

'Are they dead? Are they all dead?' The question required no answer. He could see the dead men in the grass, thick about the wagons and then scattered more thinly back up the slope. They looked very small and inconsequential. Mbejane stood quietly waiting. A big black kolbes vulture planed across their front, the feathers in its wing-tips flated like the fingers of a spread hand. Its legs dropped, touched and it hopped heavily to rest among the dead, a swift transformation from beautiful flight to obscene crouching repose. It bobbed its head, ruffled its feathers and waddled to dip its beak over a corpse that wore the green Hunting Tartan of the Gordons.

'Where is Chelmsford? Was he caught here also?'

Mbejane shook his head. 'He came too late.'

Mbejane pointed with his spear at the wide spoor that skirted the battlefield and crossed the shoulder of Isandhlwana towards the Tugela. 'He has gone back to the river. He has not stopped even to bury his dead.'

Sean and Mbejane walked down towards the field. On the outskirts they picked their way through the debris of Zulu weapons and shields; there was rust forming on the blades of the assegais. The grass was flattened and stained where the dead had lain, but the Zulu dead were gone – sure sign of victory.

They came to the English lines. Sean gagged when he saw what had been done to them. They lay piled upon each other, faces already black, and each one of them had been disembowelled. The flies crawled in their empty stomach cavities.

'Why do they do that?' he asked. 'Why do they have to hack them up like that?'

He walked on heavily past the wagons. Cases of food and drink had been smashed open and scattered in the grass, clothing and paper and cartridge cases lay strewn around the dead, but the rifles were gone. The smell of putrefaction was so thick that it coated his throat and tongue like castor oil.

'I must find Pa,' Sean spoke quietly in almost a conversational tone. Mbejane walked a dozen paces behind him. They came to the lines where the Volunteers had camped. The tents had been slashed to tatters and trampled into the dust. The horses had been stabbed while still tethered to their picket lines; they were massively bloated. Sean recognized Gypsy, his father's mare. He crossed to her.

'Hello, girl,' he said. The birds had taken her eyes out; she lay on her side, her stomach so swollen that it was as high as Sean's waist. He walked around her. The first of the Ladyburg men lay just beyond. He recognized all fifteen of them although the birds had been at them also. They lay in a rough circle, facing outwards. Then he found a sparse trail of corpses leading up towards the shoulder of the mountain. He followed the attempt that the Volunteers had made to fight their way back towards the Tugela and it was like following a paper chase. Along the trail, thick on each side of it, were the marks where the Zulus had fallen.

'At least twenty of them for every one of us,' whispered Sean, with a tiny flicker of pride. He climbed on up and at the top of the shoulder, close under the sheer rock cliff of Isandhlwana, he found his father.

There were four of them, the last four: Waite Courtney, Tim Hope-Brown, Hans and Nile Erasmus. They lay close together. Waite was on his back with his arms spread open, the birds had taken his face away down to the bone, but they had left his beard and it stirred gently on his chest as the wind touched it. The flies, big metallic green flies, crawled thick as swarming bees in the open pit of his belly.

Sean sat down beside his father. He picked up a discarded felt hat that lay beside him and covered his terribly mutilated face. There was a green-and-yellow silk cockade on the hat, strangely gay in the presence of so much death. The flies buzzed sullenly and some came to settle on Sean's face and lips. He brushed them away.

'You know this man?' asked Mbejane.

'My father,' said Sean, without looking up.

'You too.' Compassion and understanding in his voice, Mbejane turned away and left them alone.

'I have nothing', Mbejane had said. Now Sean also had nothing. There was hollowness: no anger, no sorrow, no ache, no reality even. Staring down at this broken thing, Sean could not make himself believe that this was a man. Meat only; the man had gone.

Later Mbejane came back. He had cut a sheet of canvas from one of the unburned wagons and they wrapped Waite in it. They dug his grave. It was hard work for the soil was thick with rock and shale. They laid Waite in the grave, with his arms still widespread in *rigor mortis* beneath the canvas for Sean could not bring himself to break them. They covered him gently and piled rocks upon the place. They stood together at the head of the grave.

'Well, Pa –' Sean's voice sounded unnatural. He could not make himself believe he was talking to his father.

'Well, Pa –' he started again, mumbling self-consciously. 'I'd like to say thanks for everything you've done for me.' He stopped and cleared his throat. 'I reckon you know I'll look after Ma and the farm as best I can – and Garry also.' His voice trailed away once more and he turned to Mbejane.

'There is nothing to say.' Sean's voice was surprised, hurt almost.

'No,' agreed Mbejane. 'There is nothing to say.'

For a few minutes longer Sean stood struggling to grapple with the enormity of death, trying to grasp the utter finality of it, then he turned away and started walking towards the Tugela. Mbejane walked a little to one side and a pace behind him. *It will be dark before we reach the river*, thought Sean. He was very tired and he limped from his blistered heel.

29

'Not much farther,' said Dennis Petersen.

'No,' Sean grunted. He was irritated at statement of the obvious; when you come out of Mahoba's Kloof and have the Baboon Stroom next to the road on your left hand, then it is five miles to Ladyburg. As Dennis had said: not much farther.

Dennis coughed in the dust. 'That first beer is going to turn to steam in my throat.'

'I think we can ride ahead now.' Sean wiped at his face, smearing the dust. 'Mbejane and the other servants can bring them in the rest of the way.'

'I was going to suggest it.' Dennis was obviously relieved. They had almost a thousand head of cattle crowding the road ahead of them and raising dust for them to breathe. It had been two days' drive from Rorkes Drift where the Commando had disbanded.

'We'll hold them in the sale pens tonight and send them out tomorrow morning – I'll tell Mbejane.'

Sean clapped his heels into his horse and swung across to where the big Zulu trotted at the heels of the herd. A few minutes' talk and then Sean signalled to Dennis. They circled out on each side of the herd and met again on the road ahead of it.

'They've lost a bit of condition,' grumbled Dennis looking back.

'Bound to,' said Sean. 'We've pushed them hard for two days.'

A thousand head of cattle, five men's share of Cetewayo's herds – Dennis and his father, Waite, Sean and Garrick – for even dead men drew a full share.

'How far ahead of the others do you reckon we are?' asked Dennis.

'Dunno,' said Sean. It wasn't important and any answer would be only a guess: pointless question is just as irritating as obvious statement. It suddenly occurred to Sean that but a few months previously a question like that would have started a discussion and argument that might have lasted half an hour. What did that mean? It meant that he had changed. Having answered his own question, Sean grinned sardonically.

'What're you laughing at?' asked Dennis.

'I was just thinking that a lot has changed in the last few months.'

'Ja,' said Dennis and then silence except for the broken beat of their hooves. 'It's going to seem funny without Pa,' Dennis said wistfully. Mr Petersen had been at Isandhlwana. 'It's going to seem funny being just Ma, the girls and me on the farm.'

They didn't speak again for a while. They were thinking back across the brief months and the events that had changed their lives.

Neither of them yet twenty years of age, but already head of his family, a holder of land and cattle, initiated into grief and a killer of men. Sean was older now with new lines in his face, and the beard he wore was square and spade-shaped. They had ridden with the Commandos who had burned and plundered to avenge Isandhlwana. At Ulundi they had sat their horses behind the ranks of Chelmsford's infantry in the hot sun, quietly waiting as Cetewayo massed his impis and sent them across open ground to overwhelm the frail square of men. They had waited through the din of the regular, unhurried volleys and watched the great black bull of Zulu tearing itself to shreds against the square. Then at the end the ranks of infantry had opened and they had ridden out, two thousand horsemen strong, to smash for ever the power of the Zulu empire. They had chased and hunted until the darkness had stopped them and they had not kept score of the kill.

'There's the church steeple,' said Dennis.

Sean came back slowly out of the past. They were at Ladyburg.

'Is your stepmother out at Theunis Kraal?' asked Dennis.

'No, she's moved into town – the cottage on Protea Street.'

'I suppose she doesn't want to be in the way now that Anna and Garry are married,' said Dennis.

Sean frowned quickly,

'How do you like old Garry getting Anna?' Dennis chuckled and shook his head. 'I reckon you could have got twenty-to-one odds he didn't have a chance.'

Sean's frown became a scowl. Garry had made him look such a damn fool – Sean hadn't finished with Anna.

'Have you heard from them yet? When are they coming home?'

'The last time we heard was from Pietermaritzburg; they sent a wire to Ma just to say they were married. She got it a couple of days before I arrived home from Isandhlwana. That was two months ago; as far as I know we haven't heard since.'

'I suppose Garry's so firmly settled on the nest they'll have to prise him off with a crowbar.' Dennis chuckled again, lewdly. Sean had a sudden and shockingly vivid mental picture of Garry on top of Anna; her knees were up high, her head was thrown back and her eyes were closed; she was making that little mewing sound.

'Shut up, you dirty bastard,' snarled Sean.

Dennis blinked. 'Sorry, I was only joking.'

'Don't joke about my family, he's my brother.'

'And she was your girl, hey?' murmured Dennis.

'Do you want a punch?'

'Cool down, man, I was joking.'

'I don't like that kind of joke, see?'

'All right. All right. Cool down.'

'It's dirty, that's dirty talk.' Sean was trying desperately to shut out the picture of Anna; she was in wild orgasm, her hands pleading at the small of Garrick's back.

'Jesus, since when have you become a saint?' asked Dennis and, urging his horse into a gallop, drew ahead of Sean; he kept going along the main street towards the hotel. Sean considered calling him back, but finally let him go.

Sean turned right into a shady side street. The cottage was the third house down, Waite had purchased it three years before as an investment. It was a charming little place, set among trees in a small green garden with flowers: thatched, whitewashed and surrounded by a wooden picket fence. Sean hitched his horse at the gate and went up the path.

There were two women in the sitting-room when he pushed the door open. They both stood up, surprise instantly becoming delight as they recognized him. It warmed him inside to see it – it's good to be welcome.

'Oh Sean, we weren't expecting you.' Ada came quickly to him. He kissed her and saw that sorrow had left its marks on

145

her. He felt vaguely guilty that Waite's death had not wrought so obvious a change in him. He held her away at arm's length.

'You're beautiful,' he said. She was thin. Her eyes were too big for her face and the grief was in them like shadows in the forest, but she smiled and laughed at him.

'We thought you'd be back on Friday. I'm so glad you've come earlier.'

Sean looked past Ada.

'Hello, Strawberry Pie.' She was hovering impatiently for his attention.

'Hello, Sean.' She flushed a little with his eyes on her, but she did not drop hers.

'You look older,' she said, hardly noticing the dust that caked his skin, powdered his hair and eyelashes, and reddened his eyes.

'You've just forgotten what I look like,' he said, turning back to Ada.

'No, I'd never do that,' whispered Audrey so softly that neither of them heard her. She felt swollen up inside her chest.

'Sit down, Sean.' Ada led him to the big armchair across from the fireplace. There was a daguerreotype of Waite on the mantel.

'I'll get you a cup of tea.'

'How about a beer, Ma?' Sean sank into the chair.

'Of course – I'll get it.'

'No.' Audrey flew across the room towards the kitchen. 'I'll get it.'

'They're in the pantry, Audrey,' Ada called after her, and then to Sean, 'She's such a sweet child.'

'Look again,' Sean smiled. 'She's no child.'

'I wish Garry –' Ada cut herself short.

'What do you wish?' Sean prompted her. She was quiet for a moment, wishing that Garrick could have found a girl like Audrey instead of –

'Nothing,' she said to Sean and came to sit near him.

'Have you heard from Garry again?' asked Sean.

'No. Not yet, but Mr Pye says he had a cheque come through the bank – cashed in Capetown.'

'Capetown?' Sean raised a dusty eyebrow. 'Our boy's living life to the hilt.'

'Yes,' said Ada, remembering the size of that cheque. 'He is.'

Audrey came back into the room: she had a large bottle and

146

a glass on a tray. She crossed to Sean's chair. Sean touched the bottle; it was cold.

'Quickly, wench,' Sean encouraged her. 'I'm dying of thirst.'

The first glass emptied in three swallows, Audrey poured again and, with the replenished glass in his fist, Sean settled back comfortably in the chair.

'Now,' said Ada, 'tell us all about it.'

In the warmth of their welcome – his muscles aching pleasantly, the glass in his hand – it was good to talk. He had not realized that there was so much to tell. At the first hint of slackening in his flow of speech either Ada or Audrey was ready with a question to keep him going.

'Oh, my goodness,' gasped Audrey at last. 'It's nearly dark outside, I must go.'

'Sean,' Ada stood up. 'Will you see that she gets home safely?'

They walked side by side in the half darkness, under the flamboyants. They walked in silence until Audrey spoke.

'Sean, were you in love with Anna?' She blurted out the question and Sean experienced his standard reaction: quick anger. He opened his mouth to blast her, then checked. It was a nice question. Had he been in love with Anna? He thought about it now for the first time, phrasing the question with care that he might answer it with truth. He felt a sudden rush of relief and he was smiling when he told her.

'No, Strawberry Pie, no, I was never in love with Anna.' The tone of his voice was right, he wasn't lying. She walked on happily beside him.

'Don't bother to come up to the house.' She noticed for the first time his stained and dirty clothing that might embarrass him in front of her parents. She wanted it to be right from the start.

'I'll watch you till you get to the door,' said Sean.

'I suppose you'll be going out to Theunis Kraal tomorrow?' she asked.

'First thing in the morning,' Sean assured her. 'There's a hell of a lot of work to do.'

'But you'll be coming to the store?'

'Yes,' said Sean and the way he looked at her made her blush and hate her redhead's skin which betrayed her so easily.

She went quickly up the path and then stopped and looked back.

'Sean, please don't call me Strawberry Pie any more.'

Sean chuckled. 'All right, Audrey, I'll try to remember.'

30

Six weeks had gone since his return from the Zulu Campaign, Sean reflected, six weeks that had passed in a blur of speed. He sipped coffee from a mug the size of a German beer *stein*, sitting in the centre of his bed with his nightshirt hitched up to his waist and his legs crossed in comfortable Buddha fashion. The coffee was hot; he sipped noisily and then exhaled steam from his mouth.

The last six weeks had been full – too full for brooding grief or regret, although in the evenings, when he sat in the study with Waite's memory all about him, the ache was still there.

The days seemed to pass before they had fairly begun. There were three farms now: Theunis Kraal and the other two rented from old man Pye. He had stocked them with the looted cattle and the purchases he had made since his return. The price of prime beef had dropped to a new low, with nearly a hundred thousand cattle brought back from Zululand and Sean could afford to be selective in his buying. He could also afford to wait while the price climbed up again.

Sean swung his legs off the bed and walked across the room to the washstand. He poured water from the jug into the basin and tested it tentatively with one finger. It was so cold it stung. He stood hesitating in his ridiculously feminine nightshirt, with dark chest hairs curling out above the elaborately embroidered front. Then he mustered his courage and plunged his face into the basin; he scooped water with both hands and poured it over the back of his neck, massaged it into his hair with hooked fingers and emerged at last blowing heavily with water dripping down onto his nightshirt. He towelled, stripped off the damp garment and stood naked peering out of the window. It had lightened enough for him to make out the smoky swirl of drizzle and mist beyond the pane.

'A hell of a day,' he grumbled aloud, but his tone was

deceptive. He felt excitement for this day; he was fresh and sharp-edged, hungry for breakfast, ready to go for there was work to do.

He dressed, hopping on one leg as he got into his breeches, stuffing in the tails of his shirt and then sitting on the bed to pull on his boots. Now he was thinking about Audrey – he must try and get into town tomorrow to see her.

Sean had decided on matrimony. He had three good reasons. He had found that it was easier to get into the Bank of England's vaults than to get under Audrey's petticoats without marrying her. When Sean wanted something no price was too high to pay.

Living at Theunis Kraal with Garry and Anna, Sean had decided that it would be pleasant to have his own woman to cook for him, mend his clothes and listen to his stories, for Sean was feeling a little left out.

The third consideration, by no means the least significant, was Audrey's connections with the local bank. She was one of the very few weaknesses in old man Pye's armour. He might even weigh in with Mahoba's Kloof Farm as a wedding present, though even the optimist in Sean realized that this hope was extravagant. Pye and his money were not easily parted.

Yes, Sean decided, he would have to find time to get into town and tell Audrey – in Sean's mind it wasn't a question of asking her. Sean brushed his hair, combed his beard, winked at himself in the mirror and went out into the passage. He could smell breakfast cooking and his mouth started to water.

Anna was in the kitchen. Her face was flushed from the heat of the stove.

'What's for breakfast, little sister?'

She turned to him, quickly brushing the hair off her forehead with the back of her hand.

'I'm not your sister,' she said, 'I wish you wouldn't call me that.'

'Where's Garry?' Sean asked as though he had not heard her protest.

'He's not up yet.'

'The poor boy's exhausted, no doubt.' Sean grinned at her and she turned away in confusion. Sean looked at her bottom without desire. Strange that Anna being Garry's wife should kill his appetite for her. Even the memory of what they had done before was vaguely obscene, incestuous.

'You're getting fat,' he said noticing the new heaviness of her body. She ducked her head but did not answer and Sean went on, 'I'll have four eggs, please, and tell Joseph not to dry them out completely.'

Sean went through into the dining-room and Garry came in through the side door at the same moment. His face was still vacant from sleep. Sean got a whiff of his breath; it smelled of stale liquor.

'Good morning, Romeo,' said Sean and Garry grinned sheepishly. His eyes were bloodshot and he hadn't shaved.

'Hello, Sean. How did you sleep?'

'Beautifully, thank you. I take it that you did also.' Sean sat down and spooned porridge from the tureen.

'Have some?' he asked Garry.

'Thanks.' Sean passed him the plate. He noticed how Garry's hand shook. *I'll have to talk to him about letting up on the bottle a trifle.*

'Hell, I'm hungry.' They talked the jerky, disconnected conversation of the breakfast table. Anna came through and joined them. Joseph brought the coffee.

'Have you told Sean yet, Garry?' Anna spoke suddenly, clearly and with decision.

'No.' Garry was taken by surprise, he spluttered his coffee.

'Told me what?' Sean asked. They were silent and Garrick fluttered his hand nervously. This was the moment he had been dreading – what if Sean guessed, what if he knew it was his baby and took them away, Anna and the baby, took them away and left Garry with nothing. Haunted by wild unreasonable fears, Garrick stared fixedly across the table at his brother.

'Tell him, Garry,' commanded Anna.

'Anna's going to have a baby,' he said. He watched Sean's face, saw the surprise change slowly to delight, felt Sean's arm close round his shoulders in a painful hug, almost crushing him.

'That's great,' Sean exulted, 'that's wonderful. We'll have the house full of kids in no time if you keep that up, Garry. I'm proud of you.'

Grinning stupidly with relief Garrick watched Sean hug Anna more gently and kiss her forehead.

'Well done, Anna, make sure it's a boy. We need cheap labour around here.'

He hasn't guessed, thought Garrick, *he doesn't know and it will be mine, No one can take it away from me now.*

That day they worked in the south section. They stayed together, Garry laughing in happy confusion at Sean's banter. It was delightful to have Sean give him so much attention. They finished early; for once Sean was in no mood for work.

'My reproductive brother, every barrel loaded with buck-shot.' Sean leaned across and punched Garry's shoulder. 'Let's knock it off and go into town. We can have a few quick ones to celebrate at the hotel and then go and tell Ada.'

Sean stood up in the stirrup and yelled above the moo and mill of the herd.

'Mbejane, bring those ten sick ones up to the house and don't forget that tomorrow we are going to fetch cattle from the sale pens.'

Mbejane waved in acknowledgement and Sean turned back to Garrick.

'Come on, let's get the hell out of here.'

They rode side by side, globules of moisture covering their oilskins and shining on Sean's beard. It w: till cold and the escarpment was hidden in the wet mist.

'It's real brandy-drinking weather,' said Sean and Garrick did not answer. He was frightened again. He didn't want to tell Ada. She would guess. She guessed everything, she would know it was Sean's child. You couldn't lie to her.

The horses' hooves plopped wetly in the mud. They reached the spot where the road forked and climbed over the ridge to Ladyburg.

'Ada's going to love being a grandma,' chuckled Sean, and at that moment his horse stumbled slightly, broke its gait and started favouring its near fore. Sean dismounted, lifted the hoof and saw the splinter driven deep into the frog.

'Damn it to hell,' he swore. He bent his head, gripped the hilt of the splinter with his teeth and drew it out.

'Well, we can't go into Ladyburg now, that leg will be sore for days.' Garry was relieved; it put off the time when he must tell Ada.

'Your horse isn't lame. Off you go, man, give her my love.' Sean looked up at him.

'We can tell her some other time. Let's get back home,' Garry demurred.

'Go on, Garry, it's your baby. Go and tell her.'

Garrick argued until he saw Sean's temper rising, then with a sigh of resignation he went and Sean led his own horse back to Theunis Kraal. Now that he was walking the oilskin was uncomfortably hot and heavy, Sean took it off and slung it over the saddle.

Anna was standing on the *stoep* as he came up to the homestead.

'Where's Garry?' she called.

'Don't worry. He's gone into town to see Ada. He'll be back by supper-time.'

One of the stable boys came to take Sean's horse. They talked together and then Sean stooped to lift the injured hoof. His breeches tightened across his buttocks and enhanced the long moulded taper of his legs. Anna looked at him. He straightened up and his shoulders were wide beneath the damp white linen of his shirt. He smiled at her as he came up the steps of the *stoep*. The rain had made his beard curl and he looked like a mischievous pirate.

'You must take better care of yourself now.' He put his hand on her upper arm to lead her inside. 'You can't stand around in the cold any more.' They went in through the glass doors. Anna looked up at him, the top of her head on a level with his shoulder.

'You're a damn fine woman, Anna, and I'm sure you're going to make a fine baby.' It was a mistake, for as he said it his eyes softened and his face turned down towards her. He let his arm drop around her shoulders.

'Sean!' She said his name as though it were an exclamation of pain. She moved quickly, fiercely within the circle of his arm, her body flattened itself against his and her hands went up to catch in the thick hair at the back of his head. She pulled his face down and her mouth opened warm and wet across his lips, her back arched and thrust her thighs against his legs. She moaned softly as she kissed him. For startled seconds Sean stood imprisoned in her embrace, then he tore his face away.

'Are you mad?' He tried to push her from him, but she fought her way back through his fending hands. She locked her arms around him and pressed her face against his chest.

'I love you. Please, please. I love you. Just let me hold you, that's all. I just want to hold you.' Her voice was muffled by the damp cloth of his shirt. She was shivering.

'Get away from me.' Roughly Sean broke her hold and almost threw her backwards onto the couch beside the fireplace.

'You're Garry's wife now, and you'll soon be the mother of his child. Keep your hot little body for him.' Sean stood back from her with his anger starting to mount.

'But I love you, Sean. Oh, my God, if I could only make you understand how I've suffered, living here with you and not being able to touch you even.'

Sean strode across to where she sat. 'Listen to me.' His voice was harsh, 'I don't want you. I never loved you, but now I could no more touch you than I could go with my own mother.' She could see the revulsion in his face. 'You're Garry's wife; if ever again you look at another man I'll kill you.'

He lifted his hands holding them with the fingers crooked ready. 'I'll kill you with my bare hands.'

His face was close to hers. She could not bear the expression in his eyes: she lashed out at him. He pulled back in time to save his eyes, but her nails gouged bloody lines across his cheek and down the side of his nose. He caught her wrists and held her while a thin trickle of blood dribbled down into his beard. She twisted in his hands, jerking her body from side to side, and she screamed at him.

'You swine, you dirty, dirty swine. Garry's wife, you say. Garry's baby, you say.' She threw her head back and laughed wildly through her screaming. 'Now I'll tell you the truth. What I have within me you gave me. It's yours! Not Garry's!' Sean let go her wrists and backed away from her.

'It can't be,' he whispered, 'you must be lying.' She followed him.

'Don't you remember how you said goodbye to me before you went to war? Don't you remember that night in the wagon? Don't you remember – don't you? Don't you?' She was talking quietly now, using her words to wound him.

'That was months ago. It can't be true,' Sean stammered, still moving away from her.

'Three and a half months,' she told him. 'Your brother's baby will be a little early, don't you think? But lots of people have premature babies –' Her voice droned on steadily, she was shivering uncontrollably now and her face was ghostly pale. Sean could stand it no longer.

'Leave me, leave me alone. I've got to think. I didn't know.' He brushed past her and went out into the passage. She heard the door of Waite's study slam shut and she stood still in the centre of the floor. Gradually her panting came under control and the storm surf of her anger abated to expose the black reefs of hatred beneath. She crossed the floor, went down the passage and into her own bedroom. She stood in front of the mirror and looked at herself.

'I hate him,' her lips formed the words in the mirror. Her face was still pale. 'There's one thing I can take from him. Garry's mine now, not his.'

She pulled the pins from her hair and let them drop onto the floor; her hair fell down her back. She shook it onto her shoulders then lifted her hands and tangled it into confusion. Her teeth closed on her own lips, she bit until she tasted blood.

'Oh, God, I hate him, I hate him,' she whispered through the pain. Her hands came down onto the front of her dress. She tore it open, then in the mirror looked without interest at the round bosses of her nipples that were already darkening with the promise of fruition. She kicked off her shoes.

'I hate him.' She stooped and her hands went up under her skirts into the petticoats. She loosened her pantaloons and stepped out of them; she held them across her chest to tear them, then threw them next to the bed. She swept her arm across the top of her dressing-table: one of the bowls hit the floor and burst with a splash of face-powder and there was the sudden pungent reek of spilled perfume. She crossed to the bed and dropped onto it. She lifted her knees and her petticoats fell back like the petals of a flower: her white legs and lower body were the stamen.

Just before nightfall there was a shy knock on her door.

'What is it?' she asked.

'The Nkosikazi has not told me what I should cook for dinner,' Old Joseph's voice was raised respectfully.

'There will be no dinner tonight. You and all the servants may go.'

'Very well, Nkosikazi.'

Garrick came home in the dark. He had been drinking; she heard him stagger as he crossed the *stoep*, and his voice slur as he called.

'Hallo. Where's everybody? Anna! Anna! I'm back.' Silence for a while as he lit one of the lamps and then the hurried thump, thump of his peg along the passage and his voice again edged with alarm.

'Anna, Anna, where are you?'

He pushed the door open and stood with the lamp in his hand. Anna rolled away from the light, pressing her face into the pillow and hunching her shoulders. She heard him set the lamp down on the dressing-table, felt his hands pulling down her skirts to cover Her nakedness, then gently turn her to face him. She looked into his face and saw the uncomprehending horror in it.

'My darling, oh Anna, my darling, what's happened?' He stared at her broken lips and her breasts. Bewildered he turned his head and looked at the bottles on the floor, at her torn pantaloons. His face hardened and came back to her.

'Are you hurt?' She shook her head.

'Who? Tell me who did it.' She turned away from him again, hiding her face.

'My darling, my poor darling. Who was it – one of the servants?'

'No,' her voice stifled with shame.

'Please tell me, Anna. What happened?'

She sat up quickly and threw her arms about him, holding him hard so her lips were near his ear. 'You know, Garry, You know who did it.'

'No, I swear I don't, please tell me.'

Anna drew her breath in deep, held it a second then breathed it out. 'Sean!'

Garrick's body convulsed in her arms, she heard him grunt as though he had been hit. Then he spoke. 'This too. Now this too.'

He loosened her hands from his neck and pushed her gently down onto the pillows. He crossed to the cupboard, opened one of the drawers and took out Waite's service pistol.

He's going to kill Sean, she thought. Garrick went out of the room without looking at her again. She waited with her hands clenched at her sides and her whole body stretched tightly. When the shot came at last it was surprisingly muted and unwarlike. Her body relaxed, her hands opened and she began to cry softly.

31

Garry limped down the passage. The pistol was heavy and the checkered grip rough in his hand. There was light showing under the study door at the end of the passage. It was unlocked. Garrick went in.

Sean sat with his elbows on the desk and his face in his hands but he looked up as Garrick came in through the door. The scratches had already dried black across his cheek, but the flesh around them was red and inflamed. He looked at the pistol in Garrick's hand.

'She has told you.' There was no question or expression in his voice.

'Yes.'

'I hoped that she wouldn't,' said Sean. 'I wanted her to spare you that at least.'

'Spare me?' Garrick asked. 'What about her? Did you think of her?'

Sean did not answer, instead he shrugged and laid back tiredly in his chair.

'I never realized before what a merciless swine you are,' choked Garrick. 'I have come to kill you.'

'Yes.' Sean watched the pistol come up. Garrick was holding it with both hands, his sandy hair hung forward onto his forehead.

'My poor Garry,' Sean said softly and immediately the pistol started to shake. It sank until Garrick held it, still with both hands between his knees. He crouched over it, blubbering — chewing at his lips to stop himself. Sean started out of his chair to go to him, but Garrick recoiled against the door-jamb.

'Keep away from me,' he yelled, 'don't touch me.' He threw the pistol, the sharp edge of the hammer cut across Sean's forehead, jerking his head back. The pistol glanced off and hit the wall behind him. It fired and the bullet splintered the panelled woodwork.

'We're finished,' Garrick screamed. 'We're finished for ever.' He groped wildly for the door and stumbled out into the passage, through the kitchens into the rain. He fell many times as the grass caught his peg, but each time he scrambled up and kept running. He sobbed with each step in the utter darkness of the night.

At last the growl of the rain-engorged Baboon Stroom blocked his way. He stood on the bank with the drizzle blowing into his face.

'Why me, why always me?' He screamed his agony into the darkness. Then with a rush of relief as strong as the torrent in the river-bed below him he felt the moth flutter its wings behind his eyes. The warmth and the greyness closed about him and he sank down onto his knees in the mud.

32

Sean took very little with him: his bedroll, a rifle and a spare horse. Twice in the darkness he lost the path to Mbejane's kraal but each time his horse found it again. Mbejane had built his big grass beehive hut well away from the quarters of the other servants, for he was Zulu of royal blood. When at last Sean came to it there were a few minutes of sleepy stirring and muttering within before Mbejane, with a blanket draped around his shoulders and an old paraffin lamp in his hand, came out to Sean's shouts.

'What is it, Nkosi?'

'I am going, Mbejane.'

'Where to?'

'Wherever the roads lead. Will you follow?'

'I will get my spears,' said Mbejane.

Old man Pye was still in his office behind the bank when they reached Ladyburg. He was counting the sovereigns and stacking them in neat golden piles and his hands were as gentle on them as a man's hands on the body of the woman he loves, but he reached quickly for the open drawer at his side as Sean shouldered the door open.

'You don't need that,' said Sean and Pye lifted his hand guiltily off the pistol.

'Good gracious! I didn't recognize you, my boy.'

'How much have I got credited to my account?' Sean cut through the pleasantries.

'This isn't banking hours, you know.'

'Look here, Mr Pye, I'm in a hurry. How much have I got?'

Pye climbed out of his chair and crossed to the big iron safe. Shielding it with his body he tumbled the combination and swung open the door. He brought the ledger across to the desk.

'Carter – Cloete – Courtney,' he muttered as he turned the pages. 'Ah – Ada – Garrick – Sean. Here we are. Twelve hundred and ninety-six pounds eight and eight pence; of course, there are last month's accounts at the store still unpaid.'

'Call it twelve hundred then,' said Sean. 'I want it now and while you are counting it you can give me pen and paper.'

'Help yourself, there on the desk.'

Sean sat at the desk, pushed the piles of gold out of his way, dipped the pen and wrote. When he had finished he looked up at old Pye.

'Witness that, please.'

Pye took the paper and read it through. His face went limp with surprise.

'You're giving your half share of Theunis Kraal and all the cattle to your brother's first born!' he exploded.

'That's right, please witness it.'

'You must be mad,' protested Pye. 'That's a fortune you're giving away. Think what you're doing – think of your future. I had hoped that you and Audrey –' He stopped himself and went on. 'Don't be a fool, man.'

'Please witness it, Mr Pye,' said Sean and, muttering under his breath, Pye signed quickly.

'Thank you.' Sean folded the document, slipped it into an envelope and sealed it. He put it away inside his coat.

'Where's the money?' he asked.

Pye pushed a canvas bag across to him. His expression was one of disgust; he wanted no truck with fools.

'Count it,' he said.

'I'll take your word for it,' said Sean and signed the receipt.

Sean rode out past the sale-pens and up the escarpment along the road to Pietermaritzburg. Mbejane trotted at his stirrup leading the spare horse. They stopped at the top of the escarpment. The wind had blown the clouds open and the starlight came through. They could see the town below them with here and there a lighted window.

I should have said goodbye to Ada, Sean thought. He looked down the valley towards Theunis Kraal. He could see no light. He touched the letter in the inside pocket of his coat.

'I'll post it to Garry from Pietermaritzburg,' he spoke aloud.

'Nkosi?' asked Mbejane.

'I said, "It's a long road, let us begin." '

'Yes,' agreed Mbejane. 'Let us begin.'

Part II

Witwatersrand

I

They turned north from Pietermaritzburg and climbed steadily up across bleak grassland towards the mountains. On the third day they saw the Drakensberg, jagged and black as the teeth of an ancient shark along the skyline.

It was cold; wrapped in his kaross Mbejane trailed far behind Sean. They had exchanged perhaps two dozen words since they left Pietermaritzburg for Sean had his thoughts and they were evil company. Mbejane was keeping discreetly out of his way. Mbejane felt no resentment, for a man who had just left his home and his cattle was entitled to brood. Mbejane was with sadness himself – he had left a fat woman in his bed to follow Sean.

Mbejane unplugged his small gourd snuff-box, picked a pinch and sniffed it delicately. He looked up at the mountains. The snows upon them were turning pink in the sunset and in a little while now they would make camp, and then again perhaps they would not. It made no difference.

Sean rode on after dark. The road crossed another fold in the veld and they saw the lights in the valley below.

'Dundee', Sean thought without interest. He made no effort to hasten his horse but let it amble down towards the town. Now he could smell the smoke from the coal mine, tarry and thick in the back of his throat. They entered the main street. The town seemed deserted in the cold. Sean did not intend stopping – he would camp on the far side; but when he reached the hotel he hesitated. There was warmth in there and laughter and the sound of men's voices and he was suddenly aware that his fingers were stiff with cold.

'Mbejane, take my horse. Find a place to camp beyond the town and make a fire so I won't miss you in the dark.'

Sean climbed down and walked into the bar. The room was full, miners most of them – he could see the grey coal dust etched into their skins. They looked at him incuriously as he crossed to the counter and ordered a brandy. He drank it slowly, making no attempt to join the loud talk around him.

The drunk was a short man but built like Table Mountain, low, square and solid. He had to stand on tiptoe to put his arm around Sean's neck.

'Have a drink with me, *Boetie.*' His breath smelt sour and old.

'No thanks.' Sean was in no mood for drunks.

'Come on, come on,' the drunk insisted; he staggered and Sean's drink slopped onto the counter.

'Leave me alone.' Sean shrugged the arm away.

'You've got something against me?'

'No. I just feel like drinking alone.'

'You don't like my face, maybe?' The drunk held it close to Sean's. Sean didn't like it.

'Push off, there's a good fellow.'

The drunk slapped the counter.

'Charlie, give this big ape a drink. Make it a double. If he don't drink it, I ram it down his throat.'

Sean ignored the proffered glass. He swallowed what remained in his own and turned for the door. The drunk threw the brandy in his face. The spirit burned his eyes and he hit the man in the stomach. As his head came down Sean hit him again – in the face. The drunk spun sideways, fell and lay bleeding from his nose.

'What you hit him for?' Another miner was helping the drunk into a sitting position.

'It wouldn't cost you nothing to have a drink with him.' Sean felt the hostility in the room; he was the outsider.

'This boy is looking for trouble.'

'He's a tough monkey. We know how to handle tough monkeys.'

'Come on, let's sort this bastard out.'

Sean had hit the man as a reflex action. He was sorry now, but his guilt evaporated as he saw them gathering against him. Gone too was his mood of depression and in its place was a sense of relief. This was what he needed.

There were six of them moving in on him in a pack. Six was a fairly well-rounded number. One of them had a bottle in his hand and Sean started to smile. They were talking loudly, spreading courage and waiting for one of their fellows to start it.

Sean saw movement out of the side of his eye and jumped back to cover it with his hands ready.

'Steady on there,' a very English voice soothed him. 'I have come to offer my services. It seems to me you have adversaries and to spare.' The speaker had stood up from one of the tables behind Sean. He was tall, with a gauntly ravaged face and an immaculate grey suit.

'I want them all,' said Sean.

'Damned unsporting.' The newcomer shook his head. 'I'll buy the three gentlemen on the left if your price is reasonable.'

'Take two as a gift and consider yourself lucky.' Sean grinned at him and the man grinned back. They had almost forgotten the impending action in the pleasure of meeting.

'Very decent of you. May I introduce myself – Dufford Charley-wood.' He shifted the light cane into his left hand and extended his right to Sean.

'Sean Courtney.' Sean accepted the hand.

'Are you bastards going to fight or what?' protested one of the miners impatiently.

'We are, dear boy, we are,' said Duff and moved lightly as a dancer towards him, swinging the cane. Thin as it was it made a noise like a well-hit baseball along the man's head.

'Then there were five,' said Duff. He flicked the cane and, weighted with lead, it made a most satisfactory swish. Like a swordsman he lunged into the throat of the second miner. The man lay on the floor and made a strangling noise.

'The rest are yours, Mr Courtney,' said Duff regretfully.

Sean dived in low, spreading his arms to scoop up all four pairs of legs at once. He sat up in the pile of bodies and started punching and kicking.

'Messy, very messy,' murmured Duff disapprovingly. The yelps and thuds gradually petered into silence and Sean stood up. His lip was bleeding and the lapel was torn off his jacket.

'Drink?' asked Duff.

'Brandy, please.' Sean smiled at the elegant figure against the bar. 'I won't refuse another drink this evening.'

They took the glasses to Duff's table, stepping over the bodies as they went.

'Mud in your eye!'

'Down the old red lane!'

Then they studied each other with frank interest, ignoring the clearing up operations being conducted around them.

'You are travelling?' asked Duff.

'Yes, are you?'

'No such luck. I am in the permanent employ of Dundee Collieries Ltd.'

'You work here?' Sean looked incredulous for Duff was a peacock among pigeons.

'Assistant Engineer,' nodded Duff. 'But not for long; the taste of coal-dust sticks in my craw.'

'May I suggest something to wash it out?'

'A splendid idea,' agreed Duff.

Sean brought the drinks to the table.

'Where are you headed?' asked Duff.

'I was facing north when I started,' shrugged Sean, 'I just kept going that way.'

'Where did you start from?'

'South.' Sean answered abruptly.

'Sorry, I didn't mean to pry.' Duff smiled. 'Yours is brandy, isn't it?'

The barman came round from behind the counter and crossed to their table.

'Hello, Charlie,' Duff greeted him. 'I take it you require compensation for the damage to your fittings and furniture?'

'Don't worry about it, Mr Charleywood. Not often we have a good barney like that. We don't mind the odd table and chair as long as it's worth watching. Have it on the house.'

'That's extremely good of you.'

'That's not what I came across for, Mr Charleywood. I've got something I'd like you to take a look at, you being a mining chap and all. Could you spare a minute, sir?'

'Come on, Sean. Let's see what Charlie's got for us. My guess is it's a beautiful woman.'

'It's not actually, sir,' said Charlie seriously and led the way through into the back room. Charlie reached up and took a lump of rock down from one of the shelves. He held it out to Duff. 'What do you make of that?'

Duff took it and weighed it in his hand, then peered closely at it. It was glassy grey, blotched with white and dark-red and divided by a broad black stripe.

'Some sort of conglomerate.' Duff spoke without enthusiasm. 'What's the mystery?'

'Friend of mine brought it down from Kruger's Republic on the other side of the mountains. He says it's gold bearing. They've made a big strike at a place called Witwatersrand just outside Pretoria. Of course, I don't put much store by these rumours 'cos you hear them all the time: diamonds and gold, gold and diamonds.'

Charlie laughed and wiped his hands on his apron.

'Anyway my friend says the Boers are selling mining licences to them as want to dig for the stuff. Thought I'd just get you to have a look.'

'I'll take this with me, Charlie, and pan it in the morning. Right now my friend and I are drinking.'

2

Sean opened his eyes the next morning to find the sun burning in through the window above his bed. He closed them again hurriedly and tried to remember where he was. There was a pain in his head that distracted him and a noise. The noise was a regular croaking rattle; it sounded as though someone was dying. Sean opened his eyes and turned his head slowly. Someone was in the bed across the room. Sean groped for a boot and threw it; there was a snort and Duff's head came up. For a second he regarded Sean through eyes as red as a winter sunset and then he subsided gently back into the blankets.

'Keep it down to a bellow,' whispered Sean. 'You are in the presence of grave illness.'

A long time later a servant brought coffee.

'Send word to my office that I am sick,' commanded Duff.

'I have done so.' The servant clearly understood his master. He went on, 'There is one outside who seeks the other Nkosi.' He glanced at Sean. 'He is greatly worried.'

'Mbejane. Tell him to wait,' said Sean.

They drank coffee in silence, sitting on the edge of their beds.

'How did I get here?' asked Sean.

'Laddie, if you don't know, then nobody does.' Duff stood up and crossed the room to find fresh clothing. He was naked and Sean saw that although he was slim as a boy his body was finely muscled.

'My God, what does Charlie put in his liquor?' complained Duff as he picked up his jacket.

He found the lump of rock in the pocket, brought it out and tossed it onto the packing-case that served as a table. He regarded it sourly as he finished dressing, then he went to the great pile of bachelor debris that filled one corner of the room. He scratched around and came out with a steel pestle-and-mortar and a battered black gold pan.

'I feel very old this morning,' he said as he started to crush the rock to powder in the mortar. He poured the powder into the pan, carried it out to the corrugated iron water tank beside the front door and filled the pan from the tap.

Sean followed him and they sat together on the front step. Duff worked the pan, using a practised dip and swing that set the contents spinning like a whirlpool and slopped a little over the front lip with each turn. He filled it again with clean water.

Suddenly Sean felt Duff stiffen beside him. He glanced at his face and saw that his hangover had gone; his lips were shut in a thin line and his bloodshot eyes were fastened on the pan.

Sean looked down and saw the gleam through the water, like the flash of a trout's belly as it turns to take the fly. He felt the excitement prickle up his arms and lift the hair on his neck.

Quickly Duff splashed fresh water into the pan; three more turns and he flicked it out again. They sat still, not speaking, staring at the golden tail curved round the bottom of the pan.

'How much money have you got?' Duff asked without looking up.

'Little over a thousand.'

'As much as that. Excellent! I can raise about five hundred but I'll throw in my mining experience. Equal partners – do you agree?'

'Yes.'

'Then why are we sitting here? I'm going down to the bank. Meet me on the edge of town in half an hour.'

'What about your job?' Sean asked.

'I hate the smell of coal – the hell with my job.'

'What about Charlie?'

'Charlie is a poisoner – the hell with Charlie.'

3

They camped that night in the mouth of the pass with the mountains standing up before them. They had pushed the pace all that afternoon and the horses were tired – they turned their tails to the wind and cropped at the dry winter grass.

Mbejane built a fire in the shelter of a red stone outcrop and they huddled beside it brewing coffee, trying to keep out of the snow-cold wind, but it came down off the mountains and blew a plume of sparks from the fire. They ate; then Mbejane curled up beside the fire, pulled his kaross over his head and did not move again until morning.

'How far is it to this place?' Sean asked.

'I don't know,' Duff admitted. 'We'll go up through the pass tomorrow – fifty or sixty miles through the mountains – and then we'll be out into the high veld. Perhaps another week's riding after that.'

'Are we chasing rainbows?' Sean poured more coffee into the mugs.

'I'll tell you when we get there.' Duff picked up his mug and cupped his hands around it. 'One thing's certain – that sample was stinking with gold. If there's much of that stuff around somebody's going to get rich.'

'Us, perhaps?'

'I've been on gold stampedes before. The first ones in make the killings. We might find the ground for fifty miles around as thick with claim pegs as quills on a porcupine's back.' Duff sipped noisily at his coffee. 'But we've got money – that's our ace in the hole. If we peg a proposition we've got capital to work it. If we're too late we can buy claims from the brokers. If we can't, well, there're other ways of getting gold than grubbing for it – a store, a saloon, a transport business, take your pick.'

Duff flicked the coffee grounds out of his mug. 'With money in your pocket you're somebody; without it anyone can kick you in the teeth.' He took a long black cheroot out of his top pocket and offered it to Sean. Sean shook his head and Duff bit the tip from the cheroot and spat it into the fire. He picked up a burning twig and lit it, sucking with content.

'Where did you learn mining, Duff?'

'Canada.' The wind whipped the smoke away from his mouth as Duff exhaled.

'You've been around?'

'I have, laddie. It's too damn cold to sleep; we'll talk instead. For a guinea I'll tell you the story of my life.'

'Tell me first, I'll see if it's worth it!' Sean pulled the blanket up around his shoulders and waited.

'Your credit is good,' agreed Duff. He paused dramatically. 'I was born thirty-one years ago, fourth and youngest son to the sixteenth Baron Roxby – that is, not counting the others who never made it to puberty.'

'Blue blood,' said Sean.

'Of course, just look at my nose. But please don't interrupt. Very early in the game my father, the sixteenth Baron, dispelled with a horsewhip any natural affection we may have owed him. Like Henry the Eighth he preferred children in the abstract. We kept out of his way and that suited everybody admirably. A sort of armed truce.

'Dear father had two great passions in life: horses and women. During his sixty-two glorious years he acquired a fine collection of both. My fifteen-year-old cousin, a comely wench as I recall, was his last and unattained ambition. He took her riding every day and fingered her most outrageously as he helped her in and out of the saddle. She told me about it with giggles.

'However father's horse, a commendably moral creature, cut short the pursuit by kicking father on the head, presumably in the middle of one of these touching scenes. Poor father was never the same again. In fact so much was he altered by this experience that two days later, to the doleful clangour of bells and a collective sigh of relief from his sons and his neighbours who owned daughters, they buried him.'

Dufford leaned forward and prodded the fire.

'It was all very sad. I or any of my brothers could have told father that not only was my cousin comely but she had the family sporting instincts developed to a remarkable degree After all who should know better than we? We were her cousins and

171

you know how cousins will be cousins. Anyway father never found out and to this day I feel guilty – I should have told him. He would have died happier . . . Do I bore you?'

'No, go on. I've had half a guinea's worth already,' Sean laughed.

'Father's untimely decease made no miraculous changes in my life. The seventeenth Baron, brother Tom, once he had the title was every bit as tight-fisted and unpleasant as father had been. There I was at nineteen on an allowance too small to enable me to pursue the family hobbies, gathering mould in a grim old castle forty miles from London, with the development of my sensitive soul being inhibited by the undiluted company of my barbaric brothers.

'I left with three months' advance allowance clutched in my sweaty palm and the farewells of my brothers ringing in my ears. The most sentimental of these was "don't bother to write".

'Everybody was going to Canada: it seemed like a good idea so I went too. I made money and spent it. I made women and spent them also, but the cold got to me in the end.'

Duff's cheroot had died; he re-lit it and looked at Sean.

'It was so cold you couldn't urinate without getting frostbite on your equipment, so I began to think of lands tropical, of white beaches and sun, of exotic fruits and even more exotic maidens. The peculiar circumstances that finally decided me to leave are painful to recall and we will not dwell upon them. I left, to say the least, under a cloud. So here you see me freezing slowly to death, with a bearded ruffian for company and not an exotic maiden within a day's ride.'

'A stirring tale – well told,' applauded Sean.

'One story deserves another – let's hear your tale of woe.'

Sean's smile slid off his face. 'Born and bred here in Natal. Left home a week or so ago, also in painful circumstances.'

'A woman?' asked Duff with deep compassion.

'A woman,' agreed Sean.

'The sweet bitches,' sighed Duff. 'How I love them.'

4

The pass ran like a twisted gut through the Drakensberg. The mountains stood up sheer and black on each side of them, so they rode in shadow and saw the sun only for a few hours in the middle of the day. Then the mountains dropped away and they were out into the open.

Open was the word for the high veld. It stretched away flat and empty, grass and brown grass dwindling to a distant meeting with the pale empty sky. But the loneliness could not blunt the edge of their excitement: each mile covered, each successive camp along the ribbon road ground it sharper until at last they saw the name in writing for the first time. Forlorn as a scarecrow in a ploughed land the signpost pointed right and said, 'Pretoria', pointed left and said, 'Witwatersrand'.

'The Ridge of White Waters,' whispered Sean. It had a ring to it that name – a ring like a hundred millions in gold.

'We're not the first,' muttered Duff. The left-hand fork of the road was deeply scored by the passage of many wagons.

'No time to worry about that.' Sean had the gold sickness on him now. 'There's a little speed left in these mokes – let's use it.'

It came up on the horizon as a low line above the emptiness, a ridge of hills like a hundred others they had crossed. They went up it and from the top looked down. Two ridges ran side by side, north and south, four miles or so apart. In the shallow valley between they could see the flash of the sun off the swamp pools that gave the hills their name.

'Look at them,' groaned Sean.

The tents and wagons were scattered along the length of the valley and in between them the prospect trenches were raw wounds through the grass. The trenches were concentrated along a line down the centre of the valley.

'That's the strike of the reef,' said Duff, 'and we're too late –
it's all pegged!'

'How do you know?' protested Sean.

'Use your eyes, laddie. It's all gone.'

'There might be some they've overlooked.'

'These boys overlook nothing. Let's go down and I'll show
you.' Duff prodded his horse and they started down. He spoke
over his shoulder to Sean. 'Look up there near that stream –
they aren't wasting time. They've got a mill going already. It's
a four-stamp rig by the looks of it.'

They rode into one of the larger encampments of tents and
wagons; there were women at work around the fires and the
smell of food brought saliva jetting from under Sean's tongue.
There were men also, sitting among the wagons waiting for their
suppers.

'I'm going to ask some of these characters what's going on
here,' said Sean. He climbed down off his horse and tossed the
reins to Mbejane. Duff watched him with a wry grin as he tried
in succession to engage three different men in conversation.
Each time Sean's victim avoided his eyes, mumbled vaguely and
withdrew. Sean finally gave up and came back to the horses.

'What's wrong with me,' he asked plaintively. 'Have I got a
contagious clap?'

Duff chuckled. 'They've got gold sickness,' he said. 'You're a
potential rival. You could die of thirst and not one of them
would spit on you, lest it gave you strength to crawl out and
peg something they hadn't noticed.'

He sobered. 'We're wasting time. There's an hour left before
dark, let's go and have a look for ourselves.'

They trotted out towards the area of mauled earth. Men were
working pick and shovel in the trenches, some of them lean and
tough-looking with a dozen natives working beside them; others
fat from an office stool, sweating and gritting teeth against the
pain of blistered palms, their faces and arms burnt angry red by
the sun. All of them greeted Sean and Duff with the same
suspicious hostility.

They rode slowly towards the north and every hundred yards
with sickening regularity they came across a claim peg with a
cairn of stones around its foot and the scrap of canvas nailed to
it. Printed in crude capitals on the canvas was the owner's name
and his licence number.

Many of the claims were as yet untouched and on these Duff dismounted and searched in the grass, picking up pieces of rock and peering at them before discarding them again. Then once more they moved on with sinking spirits and increasing exhaustion. They camped after dark on the open windy ridge and while the coffee brewed they talked.

'We're too late.' Sean scowled into the fire.

'We've got money, laddie, just remember that. Most of these gentlemen are broke – they are living on hope, not beef and potatoes. Look at their faces and you'll see despair starting to show. It takes capital to work reef gold: you need machinery and money for wages, you have to pipe in water and pile rock, you need wagons and time.'

'Money's no good without a claim to work,' brooded Sean.

'Stay with me, laddie. Have you noticed how many of these claims haven't been touched yet? They belong to speculators and my guess is that they are for sale. In the next few weeks you'll see the men sorted out from the boys –'

'I feel like packing up. This isn't what I expected.'

'You're tired. Sleep well tonight and tomorrow we'll see how far this reef runs – then we'll start some scheming.'

Duff lit one of his cheroots and sucked on it: in the firelight his face was as gaunt as a Red Indian's. They sat on in silence for a while, then Sean spoke.

'What's that noise?' It was a dull tom-tom beat in the darkness.

'You'll get used to that if you stay around here much longer,' said Duff. 'It's the stamps on that mill we saw from the high ground. It's a mile or so farther up the valley; we'll pass it in the morning.'

They were on the move again before the sun was up and they came to the mill in the morning's uncertain light. The mill crouched black and ugly on the smooth curve of the ridge, defiant as a quixotic monster. Its jaws thumped sullenly as it chewed the rock; it snorted steam and screeched metallically.

'I didn't realize it was so big,' said Sean.

'It's big all right,' agreed Duff, 'and they cost money, they don't give them away. Not many men around here can afford a set-up like that.'

There were men moving around the mill, tending its needs, feeding it rock and fussing about the copper tables over which its gold-laden faeces poured. One of the men came forward to offer them the usual hospitality. 'This is private ground. We don't want sightseers around here – keep on going.'

He was a dapper little man with a round brown face and a derby hat pulled down to his ears. His moustache bristled like the whiskers of a fox terrier.

'Listen, Francois, you miserable bloody earthworm, if you talk to me like that I'll push your face around the back of your head,' Duff told him, and the dapper one blinked uncertainly and came closer, peering up at them.

'Who are you? Do I know you?'

Duff pushed his hat back so the man could see his face.

'Duff!' crowed the little man delightedly. 'It's old Duff.' He bounced forward to take Duff's hand as he dismounted. Sean watched the orgy of reunion with amusement. It lasted until Duff managed to bring it under control and lead the little Afrikander across to make the introduction.

'Sean, this is Francois du Toit. He's an old friend of mine from the Kimberley diamond fields.'

Francois greeted Sean and then relapsed once more into the excited chorus of 'Gott, it's good to see you old Duff.' He pounded Duff's back despite the nimble footwork that Duff was using to spoil his aim. Another few minutes of this passed before Francois composed himself to make his first coherent statement.

'Listen, old Duff, I'm just in the middle of cleaning the amalgam tables. You and your friend go down to my tent. I'll be with you in half an hour, tell my servant to make you some breakfast. I won't be long, man. Gott, man, it's good to see you.'

'An old lover of yours?' asked Sean when they were alone.

Duff laughed. 'We were on the diamond fields together. I did him a favour once – pulled him out of a caving drive when the rock fall had broken his legs. He's a good little guy and meeting him here is the proverbial answer to a prayer. What he can't tell us about this goldfield no one else can.'

Francois came bustling into the tent well under the promised half hour and during breakfast Sean was an outsider in a conversation where every exchange began, 'Do you remember –? or 'What happened to old so and so?'

Then, when the plates were empty and the coffee mugs filled, Duff asked, 'So, what are you doing here, Franz? Is this your own outfit?'

'No, I'm still with the Company.'

'Not that whoreson Hradsky?' Duff registered mock alarm. 'Tha – tha that's ta – ta – terrible,' he imitated a stutter.

'Cut it out, Duff.' Francois looked nervous. 'Don't do that, you want me to lose my job?'

Duff turned to Sean with an explanation. 'Norman Hradsky and God are equals, but in this part of the world God takes his orders from Hradsky.'

'Cut it out, Duff.' Francois was deeply shocked but Duff went on imperturbably.

'The organization through which Hradsky exercises his divine powers is referred to with reverently bated breath as "The Company". In actual fact its full and resounding title is The South African Mining and Lands Company. Do you get the picture?'

Sean nodded smiling and Duff added as an afterthought, 'Hradsky is a bastard and he stutters.'

It was too much for Francois. He leaned across and caught Duff's arm. 'Please, man. My servant understands English, cut it out, Duff.'

'So the Company has started on these fields, hey? Well, well, it must be pretty big,' mused Duff and Francois followed with relief onto safer ground.

'It is! You just wait and see, it's going to make the diamond fields look like a church bazaar!'

'Tell me about it,' said Duff.

'They call it the Rotten Reef or the Banket or the Heidelberg Reef – but in fact there are three reefs, not one. They run side by side like layers in a sandwich cake.'

'All three have pay gold?' Duff shot the question and Francois shook his head. There was a light in his eyes; he was happy talking gold and mining.

'No – you can forget about the outer reef, just traces there. Then there's the Main Reef. That's a bit better, it's as much as six feet thick in places and giving good values, but it's patchy.'

Francois leaned eagerly across the table; in his excitement his thick Afrikaans accent was very noticeable.

'The bottom reef is the winner, we call it the Leader Reef. It's only a few inches thick and some places it fades out altogether, but it's rich. There's gold in it like plums in a pudding. It's rich, Duff, I'm telling you that you won't believe it until you see it!'

'I'll believe you,' said Duff. 'Now tell me where I can get some of this Leader Reef for myself.'

Francois sobered instantly, a shutter dropped over his eyes and hid the light that had shone there a moment before.

'It's gone. It's all gone,' he said defensively. 'It's all been pegged, you've come too late.'

'Well, that's that,' said Duff and a big silence settled on the gathering. Francois fidgeted on his stool, chewing at the ends of his moustache and scowling into his mug. Duff and Sean waited quietly; it was obvious that Francois was wrestling with himself, two loyalties tearing him down the middle. Once he opened his mouth and then closed it again; he blew on his coffee to cool it and the heat came off it in steam.

'Have you got any money?' He fired the question with startling violence.

'Yes,' said Duff.

'Mr Hradsky has gone down to Capetown to raise money. He has a list of a hundred and forty claims that he will buy when he gets back.' Francois paused guiltily. 'I'm only telling you this because of what I owe you.'

'Yes, I know.' Duff spoke softly. Francois took an audible breath and went on.

'On the top of Mr Hradsky's list is a block of claims that belongs to a woman. She is willing to sell and they are the most likely-looking propositions on the whole field.'

'Yes?' Duff encouraged him.

'This woman has started an eating-house about two miles from here on the banks of the Natal Spruit. Her name is Mrs Rautenbach, she serves good food. You could go and have a meal there.'

'Thanks, Francois.'

'I owed it to you,' Francois said gruffly, then his mood changed quickly and he chuckled. 'You'll like her, Duff, she's a lot of woman.'

Sean and Duff went to eat lunch at Mrs Rautenbach's. It was an unpainted corrugated-iron building on a wooden frame and the sign above the veranda said in letters of red and gold 'Candy's Hotel. High-class cuisine. Free toilet facilities. No drunks or horses admitted. Proprietor Mrs Candella Rautenbach.'

They washed off the dust in the enamel basin which stood on

the veranda, dried themselves on the free towel and combed in the free mirror on the wall.

'How do I look?' asked Duff.

'Ravishing,' said Sean, 'but you don't smell so good. When did you last bath?'

They went into the dining-room and found it almost full, but there was an empty table against the far wall. The room was hot and thick with pipe smoke and the smell of cabbage. Dusty, bearded men laughed and shouted or ate silently and hungrily. They crossed the room to the table and a coloured waitress came to them.

'Yes?' she asked. Her dress was damp at the armpits.

'May we have the menu?'

The girl looked at Duff with faint amusement. 'Today we got steak and mashed potatoes with pudding afterwards.'

'We'll have it,' Duff agreed.

'You sure as hell won't get nothing else,' the girl assured him and trotted back to the kitchen.

'The service is good,' Duff enthused. 'We can only hope that the food and the proprietress are of the same high standard.'

The meat was tough but well flavoured and the coffee was strong and sweet. They ate with appreciation until Sean who was facing the kitchen stopped his fork on its way to his mouth. A hush was on the room.

'Here she is,' he said.

Candy Rautenbach was a tall and bright, shiny blonde and her skin was Nordic flawlessness as yet unspoiled by the sun. She filled the front of her blouse and the back of her skirt with a pleasant abundance. She was well aware of and yet not disconcerted by the fact that every eye in the room was on one of those areas. She carried a ladle which she twitched threateningly at the first hand that reached out to pinch her rump, the hand withdrew and Candy smiled sweetly and moved on among the tables. She stopped occasionally to chat with her customers and it was clear that many of these lonely men came here not only to eat. They watched her avidly, grinning with pleasure when she spoke to them. She reached their table and Sean and Duff stood up. Candy blinked with surprise.

'Sit down, please.' The small courtesy had touched her. 'You are new here?'

'We got in yesterday,' Duff smiled at her. 'And the way you cook a steak makes me feel as though I were home again.'

'Where are you from?' Candy looked at the two of them with perhaps just a shade more than professional interest.

'We've come up from Natal to have a look around. This is Mr Courtney – he is interested in new investments and he thought that these goldfields might provide an outlet for some of his capital.'

Sean just managed to stop his jaw dropping open and then quickly assumed the slightly superior air of a big financier as Duff went on.

'My name is Charleywood. I am Mr Courtney's mining adviser.'

'Pleased to meet you. I am Candy Rautenbach.' She was impressed.

'Won't you join us for a few minutes, Mrs Rautenbach?' Duff drew back a chair for her and Candy hesitated.

'I have to check up in the kitchen – perhaps later.'

'Do you always lie so smoothly?' Sean spoke with admiration when Candy had gone.

'I spoke no untruths,' Duff defended himself.

'No, but the way you tell the truth! How the hell am I going to play up to the role you have created for me?'

'You'll learn to live with it, don't worry. Just look wise and keep your mouth shut,' Duff advised. 'What do you think of her anyway?'

'Toothsome,' said Sean.

'Decidedly palatable,' agreed Duff.

When Candy came back Duff kept the conversation light and general for a while, but when Candy started asking some sharp questions it was immediately apparent that her knowledge of geology and mining was well above average and Duff remarked on it.

'Yes, my husband was in the game. I picked it up from him.' She reached into one of the pockets of her blue and white checked skirt and brought out a small handful of rock samples. She put them down in front of Duff. 'Can you name those?' she asked. It was the direct test, she was asking him to prove himself.

'Kimberlite. Serpentine. Feldspar.' Duff reeled them off and Candy relaxed visibly.

'As it happens I have a number of claims pegged along the Heidelberg Reef. Perhaps Mr Courtney would care to have a look at them. Actually, I am negotiating at the moment with The South African Mining and Lands Company who are very interested.'

Sean made his solitary but valuable contribution to the conversation. 'Ah yes,' he nodded sagely. 'Good old Norman.'

Candy was shaken – not many men used Hradsky's Christian name. 'Will tomorrow morning be convenient?' she asked.

5

That afternoon they bought a tent from a disillusioned hopeful who had thrown up his job on the Natal Railways to make the pilgrimage to Witwatersrand and now needed money to get home. They pitched it near the Hotel and went down to the Natal Spruit to take a long overdue bath. That night they held a mild celebration on the half bottle of brandy that Duff produced from his saddlebag and the next morning Candy took them out to the claims. She had twenty of them pegged right along the Banket. She led them to a spot where the reef outcropped.

'I'll leave you two to look around. If you're interested we can talk about it when you come to the Hotel. I've got to get back now, there'll be hungry mouths to feed.'

Duff escorted Candy to her horse, giving her his arm across the rough ground and helping her into the saddle in a manner he must have learned from his father. He watched her ride away then came back to Sean. He was elated.

'Tread lightly, Mr Courtney, walk with reverence for beneath your feet lies our fortune.'

They went over the ground, Sean like a friendly bloodhound and Duff cruising with the restless circling of a tiger shark. They inspected the claim notices, paced out the boundaries and filled their pockets with chips of rock, then they rode back to their tent and Duff brought out his pestle, mortar and pan. They took them down to the bank of the Natal Spruit and all afternoon crushed the rock and worked the pan. When they had tested the last sample Duff gave his judgement.

'Well, there's gold – and I'd say it's payable gold. It's not nearly as rich as the one we panned at Dundee but that must have been a selected piece of the Leader Reef!' He paused and looked seriously at Sean. 'I think it's worth a try. If the Leader Reef is there we'll find it and in the meantime we won't lose money by working the main reef.'

Sean picked up a pebble and tossed it into the stream in front of him. He was learning for the first time the alternate thrill and depression of gold sickness when one minute you rode the lightning and the next you dropped abruptly into the depths. The yellow tails in the pan had looked pathetically thin and undernourished to him.

'Supposing you're right and supposing we talk Candy into selling her claims, how do we go about it? That four-stamp mill looked a devilishly complicated and expensive bit of machinery to me, not the kind of thing you can buy over the counter in every general dealer's store.'

Duff punched his shoulder and smiled lopsidedly at him. 'You've got your Uncle Duff looking after you. Candy will sell her claims – she trembles when I touch her, a day or two more and she'll be eating out of my hand. As for the mill . . . When I came out to this country I fell in with a rich Cape farmer whose lifelong ambition had been to have his own gold mine. He selected a ridge which in his undisputed wisdom as a grower of grapes he considered to be an ideal place for his mine. He hired me to run it for him, purchased a mill of the latest and most expensive vintage and prepared himself to flood the market with gold. After six months when we had processed vast quantities of assorted quartz, schist and earth and recovered sufficient gold to fit into a mouse's ear without touching the sides, my patron's enthusiasm was somewhat dampened and he dispensed with my invaluable services and closed the circus down. I left for the diamond fields and as far as I know the machinery is still lying there waiting for the first buyer with a couple of hundred pounds to come and pick it up.' Duff stood up and they walked back towards the tent. 'However, first things first. Do you agree that I should continue the negotiations with Mrs Rautenbach?'

'I suppose so.' Sean was feeling more cheerful again. 'But are you sure your interest in Mrs Rautenbach is strictly line of duty?'

Duff was shocked. 'Don't think for a minute that my intentions are anything but to further the interests of our partnership. You can't believe that my animal appetite plays any part in what I intend doing?'

'No, of course not,' Sean assured him. 'I hope you can force yourself to go through with it.'

Duff laughed. 'While we are on the subject I think this is as good a time as any for you to develop a stomach ailment and retire to your lonely bed. From now on until we've got the agreement signed your boyish charm will be of no great value in the proceedings. I'll tell Candy that you've given me authority to act on your behalf.'

Duff combed his curls, put on the clothes that Mbejane had washed for him and disappeared in the direction of Candy's Hotel. Time passed slowly for Sean; he sat and chatted with Mbejane, drank a little coffee and when the sun went down retired to his tent. He read one of Duff's books by the light of the hurricane lamp but could not concentrate on it; his mind kept straying to thoughts of blonde hair. When someone scratched on the canvas door he leapt up with a confused hope that Candy had decided to come and deal with him direct. It was the coloured girl from the Hotel, her crinkly black hair at odds with what he had been thinking.

'Madame says she's sorry to hear about your sickness and to tell you to have two spoons of this,' she told him and offered Sean the bottle of castor oil.

'Tell your mistress, thank you very much.'

Sean accepted the medicine and started to close the tent flap again.

'Madame told me to stay and make sure that you took two full spoons − I have to take the bottle back and show her how much you've had.'

Sean's stomach cringed. He looked at the coloured girl standing resolute in the doorway, determined to carry out her instructions. He thought of poor Duff doing his duty like a man − he could do no less. He swallowed down the thick clinging oil with his eyes closed then went back to his book. He slept uneasily starting up occasionally to look at the empty bed across the tent. The medicine drove him out into the cold at half past two in the morning. Mbejane was curled up next to the fire and Sean scowled at him. His regular contented snoring seemed a calculated mockery. A jackal yelped miserably up on the ridge, expressing Sean's feelings exactly, and the night wind fanned his bare buttocks.

Duff came home in the dawning. Sean was wide awake.

'Well, what happened?' he demanded.

Duff yawned. 'At one stage I began to doubt whether I was man enough. However, it worked out to the satisfaction of all concerned. What a woman!' He pulled off his shirt and Sean saw the scratches across his back.

'Did she give you any castor oil?' Sean asked bitterly.

'I'm sorry about that.' Duff smiled at him sympathetically. 'I tried to dissuade her – truly I did. She's a very motherly person. Most concerned about your stomach.'

'You still haven't answered my question. Did you make any progress with the claims?'

'Oh that –' Duff pulled the blankets up under his chin. 'We disposed of that early on in the proceedings. She'll take a down payment of ten pounds each on them and give us an option to buy the lot at any time during the next two years for ten thousand. We arranged that over dinner. The rest of the time was devoted, in a manner of speaking, to shaking hands over the deal. Tomorrow afternoon – or rather this afternoon – you and I'll ride across to Pretoria and get a lawyer to write up an agreement for her to sign. But right now I need some sleep. Wake me at lunch time. Goodnight, laddie.'

Duff and Sean brought the agreement back from Pretoria the following evening. It was an impressive four-page document full of 'in so much as' and 'party of the first part.' Candy led them to her bedroom and they sat around anxiously while she read it through twice.

She looked up at last and said, 'That seems all right – but there is just one other thing.' Sean's heart sank and even Duff's smile was strained. It had all been too easy so far.

Candy hesitated and Sean saw with faint surprise that she was blushing. It was a pleasant thing to see the peach of her cheeks turning to ripe apple and they watched it with interest, their tension lessening perceptibly. 'I want the mine named after me.'

They nearly shouted with relief.

'An excellent idea! How about the Rautenbach Reef Mine?'

Candy shook her head. 'I'd rather not be reminded of him – we'll leave him out of it.'

'Very well – let's call it the Candy Deep. A little premature, I suppose, as we are still at ground level, but pessimism never pays,' suggested Duff.

'Yes, that's lovely,' Candy enthused, flushing again but this time with pleasure. She scrawled her name across the bottom of the document while Sean fired out the cork of the champagne which Duff had bought in Pretoria. They clinked glasses and Duff gave the toast 'To Candy and the Candy Deep – may one grow sweeter and the other deeper with each passing day.'

6

'We'll need labour, about ten natives to start with. That'll be your problem,' Duff told Sean. It was the following morning and they were eating breakfast in front of the tent. Sean nodded but didn't try to answer until he had swallowed his mouthful of bacon.

'I'll get Mbejane onto that right away. He'll be able to get us Zulus, even if he has to drive them here with a spear at their backs.'

'Good – in the meantime you and I'll ride back to Pretoria again to buy the basic equipment. Picks, shovels, dynamite and the like.' Duff wiped his mouth and filled his coffee cup. 'I'll show you how to start moving the overburden and stacking the ore in a dump. We'll pick a site for the mill and then I'll leave you to get on with it while I head south for the Cape to see my farmer friend. God and the weather permitting ours will be the second mill working on these fields.'

They brought their purchases back from Pretoria in a small ox wagon. Mbejane had done his work well. There were a dozen Zulus lined up for Sean's approval next to the tent with Mbejane standing guard over them like a cheerful sheepdog. Sean walked down the line stopping to ask each man his name and joke with him in his own language. He came to the last in the line. 'How are you called?'

'My name is Hlubi, Nkosi.'

Sean pointed at the man's well-rounded paunch bulging out above his loincloth.

'If you come to work for me, we'll soon have you delivered of your child.'

They burst out in delighted laughter and Sean smiled at them affectionately: proud simple people, tall and big-muscled, completely defenceless against a well-timed jest. Through his mind flashed the picture of a hill in Zululand, a battlefield below it and the flies crawling in the pit of an empty stomach. He shut the picture out quickly and shouted above their laughter.

'So be it then – sixpence a day and all the food you can eat. Will you sign on to work for me?'

They chorused their assent and climbed up onto the back of the wagon. Sean and Duff took them out to the Candy Deep and they laughed and chattered like children going on a picnic.

It took another week for Duff to instruct Sean in the use of dynamite, to explain how he wanted the first trenches dug and to mark out the site for the mill and the dump. They moved the tent up to the mine and worked twelve hours every day. At night they rode down to Candy's Hotel to eat a full meal and then Sean rode home alone. He was so tired by evening that he hardly envied Duff the comfort of Candy's bedroom; instead he found himself admiring Duff's stamina. Each morning he looked for signs of fatigue in his partner but, although his face was lean and gaunt as ever, his eyes were just as clear and his lopsided smile just as cheerful.

'How you do it beats me,' Sean told him the day they finished marking out the mill site.

Duff winked at him. 'Years of practice, laddie, but between you and me the ride down to the Cape will be a welcome rest.'

'When are you going?' Sean asked.

'Quite frankly I think that every day I stay on here increases the risk of someone else getting in before us. Mining machinery is going to be at a premium from now on. You have got things well in hand now . . . What do you say?'

'I was starting to think along the same lines,' Sean agreed. They walked back to the tent and sat down in the camp chairs, from where they could look down the length of the valley. The week before about two dozen wagons had been outspanned around Candy's Hotel, but now there were at least two hundred and from where they sat they could count another eight or nine encampments, some even larger than the one around Candy's place. Wood and iron buildings were beginning to replace the canvas tents and the whole veld was criss-crossed with rough roads along which mounted men and wagons moved without apparent purpose.

The restless movement, the dust clouds raised by the passage of men and beasts, and the occasional deep crump, crump of dynamite firing in the workings along the Banket – all heightened the air of excitement, of almost breathless expectancy that hung over the whole goldfield.

'I'll leave at first light tomorrow,' Duff decided. 'Ten days' riding to the railhead at Colesberg and another four days by train will get me there. With luck I'll be back in under two months.' He wriggled round in his chair and looked directly at Sean. 'After paying Candy her two hundred pounds and with what I spent in Pretoria I've only got about a hundred and fifty left. Once I get to Paarl I'll have to pay out three or four hundred for the mill, then I'll need to hire twenty or thirty wagons to bring it up here – say eight hundred pounds altogether to be on the safe side.'

Sean looked at him. He had known this man a few short weeks. Eight hundred was the average man's earnings for three years. Africa was a big land, a man could disappear easily. Sean loosened his belt and dropped it onto the table; he unbuttoned the money pouch.

'Give me a hand to count it out,' he told Duff.

'Thanks,' said Duff and he was not talking about the money. With trust asked for so simply and given so spontaneously the last reservations in their friendship shrivelled and died.

7

When Duff had gone Sean drove himself and his men without mercy. They stripped the overburden off the Reef and exposed it across the whole length of the Candy claims, then they broke it up and started stacking it next to the mill site. The dump grew bigger with every twelve-hour day worked. There was still no trace of the Leader Reef but Sean found little time to worry about that. At night he climbed into bed and slept away his fatigue until another morning called him back to the workings. On Sundays he rode across to Francois's tent and they talked mining and medicines. Francois had an enormous chest of patent medicines and a book titled *The Home Physician*. His health was his hobby and he was treating himself for three major ailments simultaneously. Although he was occasionally unfaithful, his true love was sugar diabetes. The page in *The Home Physician* which covered this subject was limp and grubby from the touch of his fingers. He could recite the symptoms from memory and he had all of them. His other favourite was tuberculosis of the bone; this moved around his body with alarming rapidity taking only a week to leave his hip and reach his wrist. Despite his failing health, however, he was an expert on mining and Sean picked his brain shamelessly. Francois's sugar diabetes did not prevent him from sharing a bottle of brandy with Sean on Sunday evenings. Sean kept away from Candy's Hotel – that shiny blonde hair and peach skin would have been too much temptation. He couldn't trust himself not to wreck his new friendship with Duff by another importunate affair, so instead he sweated away his energy in the trenches of the Candy Deep.

Every morning he set his Zulus a task for the day, always just a little more than the day before. They sang as they worked and it was very seldom that the task was not complete by nightfall. The days blurred into each other and turned to weeks which quadrupled like breeding amoebae and became months. Sean began to imagine Duff giving the Capetown girls a whirl with his eight hundred pounds. One evening he rode south for miles along the Cape road, stopping to question every traveller he met and when he finally gave up and returned to the goldfields he went straight to one of the canteens to look for a fight. He found a big, yellow-haired German miner to oblige him. They went outside and for an hour they battered each other beneath a crisp Transvaal night sky surrounded by a ring of delighted spectators. Then he and the German went back into the canteen, shook each other's bleeding hands, drank a vow of friendship together and Sean returned to the Candy Deep with his devil exorcized for the time being.

The next afternoon Sean was working near the north boundary of the claims; at this point they had burrowed down about fifteen feet to keep contact with the reef. Sean had just finished marking the shot holes for the next blast and the Zulus were standing around him taking snuff and spitting on their hands before attacking the rock once more.

'Mush, you shag-eared villains. What's going on here, a trade union meeting?' The familiar voice came from above their heads, Duff was looking down at them. Sean scrambled straight up the side of the trench and seized him in a bear hug. Duff was thinner, his jowls covered with a pale stubble and his curly hair white with dust. When the fury of greeting had subsided a little Sean demanded, 'Well, where's the present you went to fetch me?'

Duff laughed, 'Not far behind, all twenty-five wagons full of it.'

'You got it then?' Sean roared.

'You're damn right I did! Come with me and I'll show you.'

Duff's convoy was strung out four miles across the veld, most of the wagons double-teamed against the enormous weight of the machinery. Duff pointed to a rust-streaked cylinder that completely filled one of the leading wagons.

'That is my particular cross, seven tons of the most spiteful, stubborn and evil boiler in the world. If it's broken the wagon axle once it's broken it a dozen times since we left Colesberg, not to mention the two occasions on which it capsized itself – once right in the middle of a river.'

They rode along the line of wagons.

'Good God! I didn't realize there'd be so much.' Sean shook

his head dubiously. 'Are you sure you know how it all fits together?'

'Leave it to your Uncle Duff. Of course, it's going to need a bit of work done on it, after all it's been lying out in the open for a couple of years. Some of it was rusted up solid, but the judicious use of grease, new paint and the Charleywood brain will see the Candy Deep plant breaking rock and spitting out gold within a month.' Duff broke off and waved to a horseman coming towards them. 'This is the transport contractor. Frikkie Malan – Mr Courtney, my partner.'

The contractor pulled up next to them and acknowledged the introduction. He wiped the dust off his face with the sleeve of his shirt.

'*Gott*, man, Mr Charleywood, I don't mind telling you that this is the hardest money I've ever worked for. Nothing personal – but I'll be *vragtig* glad to see the last of this load.'

8

Duff was wrong; it took much longer than a month. The rust had eaten deep into parts of the machinery and each bolt they twisted open was red with the scaly cancer. They worked the usual twelve-hour day chipping and scraping, filing and greasing, knuckles knocked raw against steel and palms wet and red where the blisters had burst. Then one day suddenly and miraculously they were finished. Along the ridge of the Candy Deep, neat and sweet smelling in its new paint, thick with yellow grease and waiting only to be fitted together, lay the dismembered mill.

'How long has it taken us so far?' Duff asked.

'It seems like a hundred years.'

'Is that all?' Duff feigned surprise. 'Then I declare a holiday – two day's of meditation.'

'You meditate, brother – I'm going to do some carousing.'

'That's an excellent alternative – let's go!'

They started at Candy's place but she threw them out after the third fight so they moved on. There were a dozen places to drink at and they tried them all. Others were celebrating, because the day before old Kruger, the President of the Republic, had given official recognition to the goldfields. This had the sole effect of diverting the payments for mining licences from the pockets of the farmers who owned the land into the Government coffers. No one worried about that, except possibly the farmers. Rather it was an excuse for a party. The canteens were packed with swearing, sweating men. Duff and Sean drank with them.

The Crown and Anchor boards were doing a steady business in every bar and the men who crowded around them were the new population of the goldfields. Diggers bare to the waist and caked with dirt, salesmen with loud clothes and louder voices selling everything from dynamite to dysentery cure, an evangelist peddling salvation, gamblers mining pockets, gentlemen trying to keep the tobacco juice off their boots, boys new-flown from home and wishing themselves back, Boers bearded and drab-suited, drinking little but watching with inscrutable eyes the invaders of their land. Then there were the others, the clerks and farmers, the rogues and contractors listening greedily to the talk of gold.

The coloured girl, Martha, came to find Sean and Duff on the afternoon of the second day. They were in a mud-brick and thatch hut called The Tavern of the Bright Angels. Duff was doing a solo exhibition of the Dashing White Sergeant partnered by a chair; Sean and the fifty or so other customers were beating the rhythm on the bar counter with glasses and empty bottles.

Martha skittered across to Sean, slapping at the hands that tried to dive up her skirts and squealing sharply every time her bottom was pinched. She arrived at Sean's side flushed and breathless.

'Madame says you must come quickly – there's big trouble,' she gasped and started to run the gauntlet back to the door. Someone flipped up her dress behind and a concerted masculine roar approved the fact that she wore nothing under the petticoats.

Duff was so engrossed in his dancing that Sean had to carry him bodily out of the bar and dip his head in the horse trough outside before he could gain his attention.

'What the hell did you do that for?' spluttered Duff and swung a round-arm punch at Sean's head. Sean ducked under it and caught him about the body to save him falling on his back.

'Candy wants us – she says there's big trouble.'

Duff thought about that for a few seconds, frowning with concentration, then he threw back his head and sang to the tune of 'London's Burning',

> 'Candy wants us – Candy wants us
> We don't want Candy, we want brandy.'

He broke out of Sean's grip and headed back for the bar. Sean caught him again and pointed him in the direction of the Hotel. Candy was in her bedroom. She looked at the two of them as they swayed arm-in-arm in the doorway.

'Did you enjoy your debauch?' she asked sweetly. Duff mumbled and tried to straighten his coat. Sean tried to steady him as his feet danced an involuntary sideways jig.

'What happened to your eye?' she asked Sean and he fingered

it tenderly; it was puffed and blue. Candy didn't wait for an answer but went on, still sweetly:

'Well, if you two beauties want to own a mine by tomorrow you'd better sober up.'

They stared at her and Sean spoke deliberately but nevertheless indistinctly.

'Why, what's the matter?'

'They're going to jump the claims, that's the matter. This new proclamation of a State goldfield has given the drifters the excuse they've been waiting for. About a hundred of them have formed a syndicate. They claim that the old titles aren't legal any more; they are going to pull out the pegs and put in their own.'

Duff walked without a stagger across to the washbasin beside Candy's bed; he splashed his face, towelled it vigorously then stooped and kissed her. 'Thanks, my sweet.'

'Duff, please be careful,' Candy called after them.

'Let's see if we can't hire a few mercenaries,' Sean suggested.

'Good idea, we'll try and find a few sober characters – there should be some in Candy's dining-room.'

They made a short detour on their way back to the mine and stopped at Francois's tent; it was dark by then and Francois came out in a freshly ironed nightshirt. He raised an eyebrow when he saw the five heavily armed men with Sean and Duff.

'You going hunting?' he asked.

Duff told him quickly and Francois was hopping with agitation before he had finished.

'Steal my claims, the thunders, the stinking thunders!' He rushed into his tent and came out again with a double-barrelled shotgun.

'We'll see, man, we'll see how they look full of buckshot.'

'Francois, listen to me,' Sean shouted him down. 'We don't know which claims they'll go to first. Get your men ready and if you hear shooting our way come and give us a hand – we'll do the same for you.'

'Ja, ja, we'll come all right – the dirty thunders.' His nightshirt flapping around his legs Francois trotted off to call his men.

'Mbejane and the other Zulus were cooking dinner, squatting round the three-legged pot. Sean rode up to them.

'Get your spears,' he told them. They ran for their huts and almost immediately came crowding back.

'Nkosi, where's the fight?' they pleaded, food forgotten.

'Come on, I'll show you.'

They placed the hired gunmen amongst the mill machinery from where they could cover the track which led up to the mine. The Zulus they hid in one of the prospect trenches. If it developed into a hand-to-hand fight the syndicate was in for a surprise. Duff and Sean walked a little way down the slope to make sure their defenders were all concealed.

'How much dynamite have we got?' Sean asked thoughtfully. Duff stared at him a second, then he grinned.

'Sufficient, I'd say. You're full of bright ideas this evening.' He led the way back to the shed which they used as a storeroom.

In the middle of the track a few hundred yards down the slope they buried a full case of explosive and placed an old tin can on top of it to mark the spot. They went back to the shed and spent an hour making grenades out of bundles of dynamite sticks, each with a detonator and a very short fuse. Then they settled down huddled into their sheepskin coats, rifles in their laps and waited.

They could see the lights of the encampments straggled down the valley and hear an occasional faint burst of singing from the canteens, but the moonlit road up to the mine remained deserted. Sean and Duff sat side by side with their backs against the newly painted boiler.

'How did Candy find out about this, I wonder?' Sean asked.

'She knows everything. That hotel of hers is the centre of this goldfield and she keeps her ears open.'

They relapsed into silence again while Sean formed his next question.

'She's quite a girl – our Candy.'

'Yes,' agreed Duff.

'Are you going to marry her, Duff ?'

'Good God!' Duff straightened up as though someone had stuck a knife into him. 'You going mad, laddie, or else that was a joke in the worst possible taste.'

'She dotes on you and from what I've seen you're fairly well disposed towards her.' Sean was relieved at Duff's quick rejection of the idea. He was jealous, but not of the woman.

'Yes, we've got a common interest, that I won't deny – but marriage!' Duff shivered slightly, not altogether from the cold. 'Only a fool makes the same mistake twice.'

Sean turned to him with surprise. 'You've been married before?' he asked.

'With a vengeance. She was half Spanish and the rest Norwegian, a smoking bubbly mixture of cold fire and hot ice.' Duff's voice went dreamy. 'The memory has cooled sufficiently for me to think of it with a tinge of regret.'

'What happened?'

'I left her.'

'Why?'

'We only did two things well together and one of them was fight. If I close my eyes I can still see the way she used to pout with those lovely lips and bring them close to my ear before she hissed out a particularly foul word, then – hey ho! back to bed for the reconciliation.'

'Perhaps you made the wrong choice. You look around, you'll see millions of happily, married people.'

'Name me one,' challenged Duff and the silence lengthened as Sean thought.

Then Duff went on, 'There's only one good reason for marriage, and that's children.'

'And companionship – that's another good reason.'

'Companionship from a woman?' Duff cut in incredulously. 'Like perfume from garlic. They're incapable of it. I suppose it's the training they get from their mothers, who are after all women themselves, but how can you be friends with someone who suspicions every little move you make, who takes your every action and weighs it on the balance of he loves me, he loves me not?' Duff shook his head unhappily. 'How long can a friendship last when it needs an hourly declaration of love to nourish it? The catechism of matrimony, "Do you love me, darling?" "Yes, darling, of course I do, my sweet." It's got to sound convincing every time otherwise tears.'

Sean chuckled.

'All right, it's funny – it's hilarious until you have to live with it,' Duff mourned. Have you ever tried to talk to a woman about anything other than love? The same things that interest you leave them cold. It comes as a shock the first time you try talking sense to them and suddenly you realize that their attention is not with you – they get a slightly fixed look in their eyes and you know they are thinking about that new dress or whether to invite Mrs Van der Hum to the party, so you stop talking and that's another mistake. That's a sign; marriage is full of signs that only a wife can read.'

'I hold no brief for matrimony, Duff, but aren't you being a little unfair, judging everything by your own unfortunate experience?'

'Select any woman, slap a ring on her third finger and she becomes a wife. First she takes you into her warm, soft body, which is pleasant, and then she tries to take you into her warm, soft mind, which is not so pleasant. She does not share, she possesses – she clings and she smothers. The relation of man to woman is uninteresting in that it conforms to an inescapable pattern, nature has made it so for the very good reason that it requires us to reproduce; but in order to obtain that result every love, Romeo and Juliet, Bonaparte and Josephine not excepted, must lead up to the co-performance of a simple biological function. It's such a small thing – such a short-lived, trivial little experience. Apart from that man and woman think differently, feel differently and are interested in different things. Would you call that companionship?'

'No, but is that a true picture? Is that all there is between them?' Sean asked.

'You'll find out one day. Nature in her preoccupation with reproduction has planted in the mind of man a barricade; it has sealed him off from the advice and experience of his fellowmen, inoculated him against it. When your time comes you'll go to the gallows with a song on your lips.'

'You frighten me.'

'It's the sameness of it all that depresses me – the goddamn monotony of it.' Duff shifted his seat restlessly then settled back against the boiler. 'The interesting relationships are those in which sex the leveller takes no hand – brothers, enemies, master and servant, father and son, man and man.'

'Homosexuals?'

'No, that's merely sex out of step and you're back to the original trouble. When a man takes a friend he does it not from an uncontrollable compulsion but in his own free choice. Every friendship is different, ends differently or goes on for ever. No chains bind it, no ritual or written contract. There is no question of forsaking all others, no obligation to talk about it – mouth it up and gloat on it the whole time.' Duff stood up stiffly. 'It's one of the good things in life. How late is it?'

Sean pulled out his watch and tilted its face to catch the moonlight. 'After midnight – it doesn't look as if they're coming.'

'They'll come – there's gold here, another uncontrollable compulsion. They'll come. The question is when.'

The lights along the valley faded out one by one, the deep singsong voices of the Zulus in the prospect trench stilled and a small cold wind came up and moved the grass along the ridge of the Candy Deep. Sitting together, sometimes drowsing, sometimes talking quietly, they waited the night away. The sky paled, then pinked prettily. A dog barked over near Hospital Hill and another joined it. Sean stood up and stretched, he glanced down the valley towards Ferrieras Camp and saw them. A black moving blot of horsemen, overflowing the road, lifting no dust from the dew-damp earth, spreading out to cross the Natal Spruit then bunching together on the near bank before coming on.

'Mr Charleywood, we have company.'

Duff jumped up.

'They might miss us and go onto the Jack and Whistle first.'

'We'll see which road they take when they come to the fork. In the meantime let's get ready. Mbejane,' shouted Sean and the black head popped out of the trench.

'Nkosi?'

'Are you awake? They are coming.'

The blackness parted in a white smile. 'We are awake.'

'Then get down and stay down until I give the word.'

The five mercenaries were lying belly down in the grass, each with a newly-opened packet of cartridges at his elbow. Sean hurried back to Duff and they crouched behind the boiler.

'The tin can shows up clearly from here. Do you think you can hit it?'

'With my eyes closed,' said Sean.

The horsemen reached the fork and turned without hesitation towards the Candy Deep, quickening their paces as they came up the ridge. Sean rested his rifle across the top of the boiler and picked up the speck of silver in his sights.

'What's the legal position, Duff?' he asked out of the corner of his mouth.

'They've just crossed our boundary – they are now officially trespassers,' Duff pronounced solemnly.

One of the leading horses kicked over the tin can and Sean

fired at the spot on which it had stood. The shot was indecently loud in the quiet morning and every head in the syndicate lifted with alarm towards the ridge, then the ground beneath them jumped up in a brown cloud to meet the sky. When the dust cleared there was a struggling tangle of downed horses and men. The screams carried clearly up to the crest of the ridge.

'My God,' breathed Sean, appalled at the destruction.

'Shall we let them have it, boss?' called one of the hired men.

'No,' Duff answered him quickly. 'They've had enough.'

The flight started, riderless horses, mounted men and others on foot were scattering back down the valley. Sean was relieved to see that they left only half a dozen men and a few horses lying in the road.

'Well, that's the easiest fiver you've ever earned,' Duff told one of the mercenaries. 'I think you can go home now and have some breakfast.'

'Wait, Duff.' Sean pointed. The survivors of the explosion had reached the road junction again and there they were being stopped by two men on horseback.

'Those two are trying to rally them.'

'Let's change their minds, they're still within rifle range.'

'They are not on our property any more,' disagreed Sean. 'Do you want to wear a rope?'

They watched while those of the syndicate who had had enough fighting for one day disappeared down the road to the camps and the rest coagulated into a solid mass at the crossroad.

'We should have shot them up properly while we had the chance,' grumbled one of the mercenaries uneasily. 'Now they'll come back – look at that bastard talking to them like a Dutch uncle.'

They left their horses and spread out, then they started moving cautiously back up the slope. They hesitated just below the line of boundary pegs then ran forward, tearing up the pegs as they came.

'All together, gentlemen, if you please,' called Duff politely and the seven rifles fired. The range was long and the thirty or so attackers ran doubled up and dodging. The bullets had little effect at first, but as the distance shortened men started falling. There was a shallow donga running diagonally down the slope and as each of the attackers reached it he jumped down into it and from its safety started a heated reply to the fire of Sean's men. Bullets spanged off the machinery, leaving bright scars where they struck.

Mbejane's Zulus were adding their voices to the confusion.

'Let us go down to them now, Nkosi.'

'They are close – let us go.'

'Quiet down, you madmen, you'd not go a hundred paces against those rifles,' Sean snarled impatiently.

'Sean, cover me,' whispered Duff. 'I'm going to sneak round the back of the ridge, rush them from the side and lob a few sticks of dynamite into that donga.'

Sean caught his arm, his fingers dug into it so that Duff winced.

'You take one step and I'll break a rifle butt over your head – you're as bad as those Blacks. Now keep shooting and let me think.' Sean peered over the top of the boiler but ducked again as a bullet rang loudly against it, inches from his ear. He stared at the new paint in front of his nose, put his shoulder against it; the boiler rocked slightly. He looked up and Duff was watching him.

'We'll walk down together and lob that dynamite,' Sean told him. 'Mbejane and his bloodthirsty heathens will roll the boiler in front of us. These other gentlemen will cover us, we'll do this thing in style.'

Sean called the Zulus out of the trench and explained to them. They chorused their approval of the scheme and jostled each other to find a place to push against the boiler. Sean and Duff filled the front of their shirts with the dynamite grenades and lit a short length of tarred rope each.

Sean nodded to Mbejane.

'Where are the children of Zulu?' sang Mbejane, shrilling his voice in the ancient rhetorical question.

'Here,' answered his warriors braced ready against the boiler.

'Where are the spears of Zulu?'

'Here.'

'How bright are the spears of Zulu?'

'Brighter than the Sun.'

'How hungry are the spears of Zulu?'

'Hungrier than the locust.'

'Then let us take them to the feeding.'

'Yeh-bo.' Explosive assent and the boiler revolved slowly to the thrust of black shoulders.

'*Yeh-bo.*' Another reluctant revolution.

'*Yeh-bo.*' It moved more readily.

'*Yeh-bo.*' Gravity caught it. Ponderously it bumped down the slope and they ran behind it. The fire from the donga doubled its volume, rattling like hail against the huge metal cylinder. The singing of the Zulus changed its tone also; the deep-voiced chanting quickened, climbed excitedly, and became the blood trill. That insane, horrible squealing made Sean's skin crawl, tickled his spine with the ghost fingers of memory, but it inflamed him also. His mouth opened and he squealed with them. He touched the first grenade with the burning rope then flung it in a high spluttering sparking arc. It burst in the air above the donga. He threw again. Crump, crump. Duff was using his explosive as well. The boiler crashed over the lip of the donga and came to rest in a cloud of dust; the Zulus followed it in, spreading out, still shrieking, and now their assegais were busy. The white men broke, clawed frantically out of the ravine and fled, the Zulus hacking at them as they ran.

When Francois arrived with fifty armed diggers following him the fight was over.

'Take your boys down to the camps. Comb them out carefully. We want every one of those that got away,' Duff told him. 'It's about time we had a little law and order on this field.'

'How will we pick out the ones that were in on it?' asked Francois.

'By their white faces and the sweat on their shirts you will know them,' Duff answered.

Francois and his men went, leaving Sean and Duff to clean up the battlefield. It was a messy job – the stabbing spears had made it so. They destroyed those horses that the blast had left still half alive and they gleaned more than a dozen corpses from the donga and the slope below it. Two of them were Zulus. The wounded, and there were many, they packed into a wagon and took them down to Candy's Hotel.

It was early afternoon by the time they arrived. They threaded the wagon through the crowd and stopped it in front of the Hotel. It seemed the entire population of the goldfield was there, packed around the small open space in which Francois was holding his prisoners.

Francois was almost hysterical with excitement. He was sweeping the shotgun around in dangerous circles as he harangued the crowd. Then he darted back to prod one of the prisoners with the twin muzzles.

'You thunders,' he screamed. 'Steal our claims – hey – steal our claims.'

At that moment he caught sight of Duff and Sean bringing the wagon through the press.

'Duff, Duff. We got them. We got the whole lot of them.' The crowd backed respectfully away from the menace of that circling shotgun and Sean flinched as it pointed directly at him for a second.

'So I see, Francois,' Duff assured him. 'In fact, I have seldom seen anyone more completely had.'

Francois's prisoners were swathed in ropes; they could move only their heads and as additional security a digger with a loaded rifle stood over each of them. Duff climbed down off the wagon.

'Don't you think you should slacken those ropes a little?' Duff asked dubiously.

'And have them escape?' Francois was indignant.

'Do you think they'd get very far?'

'No, I don't suppose so.'

'Well, another half hour and they'll all have gangrene – look at that one's hand already, a beautiful shade of blue.'

Reluctantly Francois conceded and told his men to untie them.

Duff pushed his way through the crowd and climbed the steps of the Hotel. From there he held up his hands for silence.

'There have been a lot of men killed today – we don't want it to happen again. One way we can prevent it is to make sure that this lot get what they deserve.' Cheers were led by Francois.

'But we must do it properly. I suggest we elect a committee to deal with this affair and with any other problems that crop up on these fields. Say ten members and a chairman.'

More cheers.

'Call it the Diggers' Committee,' shouted someone and the crowd took up the name enthusiastically.

'All right, the Diggers' Committee it is. Now we want a chairman, any suggestions?'

'Mr Charleywood,' shouted Francois.

'Yes, Duff – he'll do.'

'Yes, Duff Charleywood.'

'Any other suggestions?'

'No,' roared the crowd.

'Thank you, gentlemen.' Duff smiled at them. 'I am sensible of the honour. Now, ten members.'

'Jock and Trevor Heyns.'

'Karl Lochtkamper.'

'Francois du Toit.'

'Sean Courtney.'

There were fifty nominations. Duff baulked at counting votes so the committee was elected by applause. He called the names one at a time and judged the strength of the response to each. Sean and Francois were among those elected. Chairs and a table were brought out onto the veranda and Duff took his seat. With a water-jug he hammered for silence, declared the first session of the Diggers' Committee open and then immediately fined three members of the crowd ten pounds each for discharging firearms during a meeting – gross contempt of Committee. The fines were paid and a proper air of solemnity achieved.

'I'll ask Mr Courtney to open the case for the prosecution.'

Sean stood up and gave a brief description of the morning's battle, ending, 'You were there, Your Honour, so you know all about it anyway.'

'So I was,' agreed Duff. 'Thank you, Mr Courtney. I think that was a very fair picture you presented. Now,' he looked at the prisoners, 'who speaks for you?'

There was a minute of shuffling and whispering, then one of them was pushed forward. He pulled off his hat and blushed purple.

'Your Worship,' he began, then stopped, wriggling with embarrassment.

'Your worship.'

'You've said that already.'

'I don't rightly know where to begin, Mr Charleywood – I mean Your Honour, sir.'

Duff looked at the prisoners again.

'Perhaps you'd like to reconsider your choice.'

Their first champion was withdrawn in disgrace and a fresh one sent forward to face the Committee. He had more fire.

'You bastards got no right to do this to us,' he started and Duff promptly fined him ten pounds. His next attempt was more polite.

'Your Honour, you can't do this to us. We had our rights, you know, that new proclamation and all, I mean, them old titles wasn't legal no more now, was they? We just came along as peaceful as you please, the old titles not being legal, we got a right to do what we done. Then you bastards, I mean Your Honour, dynamited us and like we had a right to protect ourselves, I mean after all, didn't we, sir?'

'A brilliant defence most ably conducted. Your fellows should be grateful to you,' Duff complimented him, then turned to his Committee. 'Well now, how say you merry gentlemen. Guilty or not guilty?'

'Guilty.' They spoke together and Francois added for emphasis, 'the dirty thunders.'

'We will now consider sentence.'

'String them up,' shouted someone and instantly the mood changed. The mob growled: an ugly sound.

'I'm a carpenter, I'll whip you up a handsome set of gallows in no time at all.'

'Don't waste good wood on them. Use a tree.'

'Get the ropes.'

'String them up.'

The crowd surged in, lynch mad. Sean snatched Francois's shotgun and jumped up onto the table.

'So help me God, I'll shoot the first one of you that touches them before this court says so.' They checked and Sean pressed his advantage. 'At this range I can't miss. Come on, try me – there's two loads of buckshot in here. Someone will get cut in half.' They fell back still muttering.

'Perhaps you've forgotten, but there's a police force in this country and there's a law against killing. Hang them today and it'll be your turn tomorrow.'

'You're right, Mr Courtney, it'll be cruel heartless murder. That it will,' wailed the spokesman.

'Shut up, you bloody fool,' Duff snarled at him and someone in the crowd laughed. The laughter caught on and Duff sighed silently with relief. That had been very close.

'Give them the old tar and feathers.'

Duff grinned. 'Now you're talking sense. Who's got a few barrels of tar for sale?' He looked round. 'What, no offers? Then we'll have to think of something else.'

'I've got ten drums of red paint – thirty shillings each, good imported brand.' Duff recognized the speaker as a trader who had opened a general dealer's store down at Ferrieras Camp.

'Mr Tarry suggests paint. What about it?'

'No, it comes off too easily – that's no good.'

'I'll let you have it cheap – twenty-five shillings a drum.'

'No – stick your ruddy paint,' the crowd booed him.

'Give them a twist on Satan's Roulette Wheel,' shouted another voice, and the crowd clamoured agreement.

'That's it – give them the wheel.'

'Round and round and round she goes – where she stops nobody knows,' roared a black-bearded digger from the roof of the shanty across the road. The crowd howled.

Sean watched Duff's expression – the smile had gone. He was weighing it up. If he stopped them again they might lose all patience and risk the shotgun. He couldn't chance it.

'All right. If that's what you want.' He faced the terrified cluster of prisoners. 'The sentence of this court is that you play roulette with the devil for one hour and that you then leave this goldfield – if we catch you back here again you'll get another hour of it. The wounded are excused the first half of the sentence. I think they've had enough. Mr du Toit will supervise the punishment.'

'We'd prefer the paint, Mr Charleywood,' pleaded the spokesman again.

'I bet you would,' said Duff softly, but the crowd was carrying them away already, out towards the open veld beyond the Hotel. Most of them had staked claims of their own and they didn't like claim jumpers. Sean climbed down off the table.

'Let's go and have a drink,' Duff said to him.

'Aren't you going to watch?' asked Sean.

'I've seen it done once before down in the Cape. That was enough.'

'What do they do?'

'Go and have a look, I'll be waiting for you at the Bright Angels. I'll be surprised if you stay the full hour.'

By the time Sean joined the crowd most of the wagons had been gathered from the camps and drawn up in a line. Men swarmed round them fitting jacks under the axles to lift the big back wheels clear of the ground. Then the prisoners were hustled forward – one to each wheel. Eager hands lifted them and held them while their wrists and ankles were lashed to the rim of the wheel with the hub in the middle of their backs and their arms and legs spread-eagled like stranded starfish. Francois hurried along the line checking the ropes and placing four diggers at each wheel, two to start it and another two to take over when those were tired. He reached the end, came back to the centre again, pulled his watch from his pocket, checked the time, then shouted.

'All right – turn them, *kerels*.'

The wheels started moving, slowly at first then faster as they built up momentum. The bodies strapped to them blurred with the speed.

'Round and round and round she goes – round and round and round she goes,' chanted the crowd gleefully.

Within minutes there was a burst of laughter from the end of the line of wagons. Someone had started vomiting, it sprayed from him like yellow sparks from a catherine wheel. Then another and another joined in, Sean could hear them retching and gasping as the centrifugal force flung the vomit up against the back of their throats and out of their noses. He waited a few more minutes but when their bowels started to empty he turned away gagging and headed for the Bright Angel.

'Did you enjoy it?' asked Duff.

'Give me a brandy,' answered Sean.

9

With the Diggers' Committee dispensing rough justice a semblance of order came to the camps. President Kruger wanted no
part in policing the nest of ruffians and cut-throats which was
growing up just outside his Capital and he contented himself
with placing his spies among them and leaving them to work
out their own salvation. After all, the field was far from proved
and the chances were that in another year the veld would again
be as deserted as it had been nine months before. He could afford
to wait; in the meantime the Diggers' Committee had his tacit
sanction.

While the ants worked, cutting down into the reef with pick
and with dynamite, the grasshoppers waited in the bars and
shanties. So far only the Jack and Whistle mill was turning out
gold, and only Hradsky and Francois du Toit knew how much
gold was coming out of it. Hradsky was still in Capetown crusad-
ing for capital and Francois spoke to no one, not even to Duff,
about the mill's productivity.

The rumours flew like sand in a whirlwind. One day it seemed
that the reef had pinched out fifty feet below the surface, and
the next the canteens buzzed with the news that the Heyns
brothers had gone down a hundred feet and were pulling out
nuggets the size of musket balls. Nobody knew but everybody
was prepared to guess.

Up at the Candy Deep, Duff and Sean worked on relentlessly.
The mill took shape on its concrete platform, its jaws open for
the first bite at the rock. The boiler was swung up onto its cradle
by twenty sweating, singing Zulus. The copper tables were fitted
up ready to be smeared with quicksilver. There was no time to
worry about the reef nor the dwindling store of money in Sean's
cash belt. They worked and they slept – there was nothing else.
Duff took to sharing Sean's tent up on the ridge and Candy had
her featherbed to herself again.

On the twentieth of November they fired the boiler for the first time. Tired and horny-handed, their bodies lean and tempered hard with toil, they stood together and watched the needle creek up round the pressure gauge until it touched the red line at the top.

Duff grunted. 'Well, at least we've got power now.' Then he punched Sean's shoulder 'What the hell are you standing here for – do you think this is a Sunday School picnic? There's work to do, laddie.'

On the second of December they fed the mill its first meal and watched the powdered rock flow across the amalgam tables. Sean threw his arm round Duff's neck in an affectionate half-Nelson, Duff hit him in the stomach and pulled his hat down over his eyes, they drank a glass of brandy each at supper and laughed a little but that was all. They were too tired to celebrate. From now on one of them must be in constant attendance on that iron monster. Duff took the first night shift and when Sean went up to the mill next morning he found him weaving on his feet, his eyes sunk deep in dark sockets.

'By my reckoning we've run ten tons of rock through her. Time to clean the tables and see just how much gold we've picked up.'

'You go and get some sleep,' said Sean and Duff ignored him.

'Mbejane, bring a couple of your savages here, we're going to change the tables.'

'Listen, Duff, it can wait an hour or two. Go and get your head down.'

'Please stop drivelling – you're as bad as a wife.'

Sean shrugged. 'Have it your own way, show me how you do it then.'

They switched the flow of powdered rock onto the second table that was standing ready; then with a broad bladed spatula Duff scraped the mercury off the copper top of the first table, collecting it in a ball the size of a coconut.

'The mercury picks up the tiny particles of gold,' he explained to Sean as he worked, 'and lets the grains of rock wash across the table and fall off into the dump. Of course it doesn't collect it all, some of it goes to waste.'

'How do you get the gold out again?'

'You put the whole lot in a retort and boil off the mercury – the gold stays behind.'

'Hell of a waste of mercury, isn't it?'

'No, you catch it as it condenses and use it again. Come on, I'll show you.'

Duff carried the ball of amalgam down to the shed, placed it in the retort and lit the blow-lamp. With the heat on it the ball dissolved and started to bubble. Silently they stared at it. The level in the retort fell.

'Where's the gold?' Sean asked at last.

'Oh, shut up,' Duff snapped impatiently, and then, repentant, 'Sorry, laddie, I feel a bit jaded this morning.'

The last of the mercury steamed off and there it was, glowing bright, molten yellow. A drop of gold the size of a pea. Duff shut off the blow-lamp and neither of them spoke for a while. Then Sean asked, 'Is that all?'

'That, my friend, is all,' agreed Duff wearily. 'What do you want to do with it – fill a tooth?'

He turned towards the door with a droop to his whole body.

'Keep the mill running, we might as well go down with our colours flying.'

10

It was a miserable Christmas dinner. They ate it at Candy's Hotel. They had credit there. She gave Duff a gold signet ring and Sean a box of cigars. Sean had never smoked before but now the sting of it in his lungs gave him a certain masochistic pleasure. The dining-room roared with men's voices and cutlery clatter, the air was thick with the smell of food and tobacco smoke while in one corner – marooned on a little island of gloom – sat Sean, Duff and Candy.

Once Sean lifted his glass at Duff and spoke like an undertaker's clerk. 'Happy Christmas.'

Duff's lips twitched back in a dead man's grin. 'And the same to you.'

They drank. Then Duff roused himself to speak. 'Tell me again – how much have we got left? I like to hear you say it; you have a beautiful voice, you should have played Shakespeare.'

'Three pounds and sixteen shillings.'

'Yes, yes, you got it just right that time – three pounds and sixteen shillings – now to really make me feel Christmassy, tell me how much we owe.'

'Have another drink,' Sean changed the subject.

'Yes, I think I will, thank you,'

'Oh please, you two, let's just forget about it for today,' pleaded Candy. 'I planned for it to be such a nice party – look, there's Francois! Hey, Francois – over here!'

The dapper du Toit bustled across to their table.

'Happy Christmas, kerels, let me buy you a drink.'

'It's nice to see you.' Candy gave him a kiss. 'How are you? You're looking fine.'

Francois sobered instantly. 'It's funny you should say that, Candy. As a matter of fact I'm a bit worried.' He tapped his chest and sank down into an empty chair. 'My heart, you know, I've been waiting for it to happen, and then yesterday I was up at the mill, just standing there, you understand, when suddenly it was as though a vice was squeezing my chest. I couldn't breathe – well, not very well anyway. Naturally I hurried back to my tent and looked it up. Page eighty-three. Under "Diseases of the Heart".' He shook his head sadly. 'It's very worrying. You know I wasn't a well man before, but now this.'

'Oh, no,' wailed Candy. 'I can't stand it – not you too.'

'I'm sorry, have I said something wrong?'

'Just in keeping with the festive spirit at this table.' She pointed at Duff and Sean. 'Look at their happy faces – if you'll excuse me I'm going to check up in the kitchen.' She went.

'What's wrong, old Duff ?'

Duff flashed his death's head grin across the table at Sean.

'The man wants to know what's wrong – tell him.'

'Three pounds sixteen shillings,' said Sean and Francois looked puzzled.

'I don't understand.'

'He means we're broke – flat broke.'

'*Gott*, I'm sorry to hear that, Duff, I thought you were going good. I've heard the mill running all this month, I thought you'd be rich by now.'

'The mill's been running all right and we've recovered enough gold to block a flea's backside.'

'But why, man? You are working the Leader Reef, aren't you?'

'I'm beginning to think this Leader Reef of yours is a bedtime story.'

Francois peered into his glass thoughtfully.

'How deep are you?'

'We've got one incline shaft down about fifty feet.'

'No sign of the Leader?' Duff shook his head and Francois went on.

'You know when I first spoke to you a lot of what I said was just guessing.'

Duff nodded.

'Well, I know a bit more about it now. What I am going to tell you is for you alone – I'll lose my job if it gets out, you understand?'

Duff nodded again.

'So far the Leader Reef has only been found at two places. We've got it on the Jack and Whistle and I know the Heyns brothers have struck it on the Cousin Jock Mine. Let me draw it for you.' He picked up a knife and drew in the gravy on the bottom of Sean's plate. 'This is the Main Reef running fairly straight. Here I am, here is the Cousin Jock and here you are in between us. Both of us have found the Leader and you haven't. My guess is it's there all right – you just don't know where to look.

'At the far end of the Jack and Whistle claims the Main Reef and the Leader are running side by side two feet apart but by the time they reach the boundary nearest to the Candy Deep they've opened up to seventy feet apart. Now on the boundary of the Cousin Jock they're back to fifty feet apart. To me it seems that the two reefs form the shape of a long bow, like this.' He drew it in. 'The Main Reef is the string and the Leader Reef is the wood. I'm telling you, Duff, if you cut a trench at right-angles to the Main Reef you'll find it – and when you do you can buy me a drink.'

They listened gravely and when Francois finished Duff leaned back in his chair. 'If we'd known this a month ago! Now how are we going to raise the money to cut this new trench and still keep the mill running?'

'We could sell some of our equipment,' suggested Sean.

'We need it, every scrap of it, and besides if we sold one spade the creditors would be on us like a pack of wolves, howling for their money.'

'I'd make you a loan if I had it – but with what Mr Hradsky pays me –' Francois shrugged. 'You'll need about two hundred pounds. I haven't got it.'

Candy came back to the table in time to hear Francois's last remark.

'What's this all about?'

'Can I tell her, Francois?'

'If you think it will do any good.'

Candy listened, then thought for a moment. 'Well, I've just bought ten plots of ground in Johannesburg, this new Government village down the valley, so I'm short myself. But I could let you have fifty pounds if that would help.'

'I've never borrowed money from a lady before – it'll be a new experience. Candy, I love you.'

'I wish you meant that,' said Candy, but luckily for Duff his hearing failed him completely just as Candy spoke. He went on hurriedly.

'We'll need another hundred and fifty or so – let's hear your suggestions, gentlemen.'

There was a long silence, then Duff started to smile and he was looking at Sean.

'Don't tell me, let me guess,' Sean forestalled him. 'You're going to put me out to stud?'

'Close – but not quite right. How are you feeling, laddie?'

'Thank you, I'm all right.'

'Strong?'

'Yes.'

'Brave?'

'Come on, Duff, let's have it. I don't like that look in your eye.'

Duff pulled a notebook out of his pocket and wrote in it with a stump of pencil. Then he tore out the page and handed it to Sean. 'We'll have posters like this put up in every canteen on the goldfields.'

Sean read it:

> ON NEW YEAR'S DAY MR SEAN COURTNEY HEAVYWEIGHT CHAMPION OF THE TRANSVAAL REPUBLIC WILL STAND TO MEET ALL COMERS IN FRONT OF CANDY'S HOTEL FOR
> A PURSE OF FIFTY POUNDS ASIDE.
> Spectators' Fee, 2s. All Welcome.

Candy was reading it over his shoulder. She squeaked.

'That's wonderful. I'll have to hire extra waiters to serve drinks and I'll run a buffet luncheon. I suppose I could charge two shillings a head?'

'I'll fix the posters,' Francois was not to be outdone, 'and I'll send a couple of my chaps down to put up a ring.'

'We'll close the mill down until New Year – Sean will have to get a lot of rest. We'll put him on light training only. No drinking, of course, and plenty of sleep,' said Duff.

'It's all arranged then, is it?' asked Sean. 'All I've got to do is go in there and get beaten to a pulp?'

'We're doing this for you, laddie, so that you can be rich and famous.'

'Thank you, thank you very much.'

'You like to fight, don't you?'

'When I'm in the mood.'

'Don't worry, I'll think up some dirty names to call you – get you worked up in no time.'

II

'How are you feeling?' Duff asked for the sixth time that morning.

'No change since five minutes ago,' Sean reassured him.

Duff pulled out his watch, stared at it, held it to his ear and looked surprised that it was still ticking.

'We've got the challengers lined up on the veranda. I've told Candy to serve them free drinks – as much as they want. Every minute we can wait here gives them a little longer to take on a load of alcohol. Francois is collecting the gate money in my valise; as you win each bout the stakes will go into it as well. I've got Mbejane stationed at the mouth of the alley beside the Hotel. If there's a riot one of us will throw the bag to him and he'll head for the long grass.'

Sean was stretched out on Candy's bed with his hands behind his head. He laughed. 'I can find no fault with your planning. Now for pity's sake calm down, man. You're making me nervous.'

The door burst open and Duff leapt out of his chair at the crash. It was Francois, he stood in the doorway holding his chest.

'My heart,' he panted. 'This is doing my heart no good.'

'What's happening outside?' Duff demanded.

'We've collected over fifty pounds gate money already. There's a mob up on the roof that haven't paid, but every time I go near them they throw bottles at me.'

Francois cocked his head on one side. 'Listen to them.' The noise of the crowd was barely softened by the flimsy walls of the Hotel. 'They won't wait much longer – you'd better come out before they start looking for you.'

Sean stood up. 'I'm ready.'

Francois hesitated.

'Duff, you remember Fernandes, that Portuguese from Kimberley?'

'Oh no!' Duff anticipated him. 'Don't tell me he's here.'

Francois nodded. 'I didn't want to alarm you but some of the local boys clubbed in and telegraphed south for him. He arrived on the express coach half an hour ago. I had hoped he wasn't going to make it in time, but –' He shrugged.

Duff looked at Sean sadly.

'Bad luck, laddie.'

Francois tried to soften the blow. 'I told him it was first come first served. He's sixth in the line so Sean will be able to make a couple of hundred quid anyway – then we can always say he's had enough and close the contest.'

Sean was listening with interest. 'This Fernandes is dangerous?'

'They were thinking of him when they invented that word,' Duff told him.

'Let's go and have a look at him.'

Sean led the way out of Candy's room and down the passage.

'Did you get hold of a scale to weigh them with?' Duff asked Francois as they hurried after Sean.

'No, there's not one on the fields that goes over a hundred and fifty pounds – but I have Gideon Barnard outside.'

'How does that help us?'

'He's a cattle dealer – all his life he's been judging animals on the hoof. He'll give us the weights to within a few pounds.'

Duff chuckled. 'That'll have to do then. Besides I doubt we'll be claiming any world titles.'

Then they were out on the veranda blinking in the brightness of the sun and the thunder of the crowd.

'Which is the Portuguese?' whispered Sean – he needn't have asked. The man stood out like a gorilla in a cage of monkeys. A shaggy coating of hair began on his shoulders and continued down his back and chest, completely hiding his nipples and exaggerating the bulge of his enormous belly.

The crowd opened a path for Sean and Duff and they walked along it to the ring. Hands slapped Sean's back but the well-wishes were drowned in the churning sea of sound. Jock Heyns was the referee – he helped Sean through the ropes and ran his hands over his pockets.

'Just checking,' he apologized. 'We don't want any scrap iron in the ring.' Then he beckoned to a tall, brown-faced fellow who was leaning on the ropes chewing tobacco.

'This is Mr Barnard our weighing steward. Well, what do you say, Gideon?'

The steward hosed a little juice from the side of his mouth. 'Two hundred and ten.'

'Thank you.' Jock held up his hands and after a few minutes was rewarded with a comparative silence.

'Ladies and Gentlemen.'

'Who you talking to, Guvnor?'

'We are privileged to have with us today – Mr Sean Courtney.'

'Wake up, *Boet*, he's been with us for months.'

'The heavyweight champion of the Republic.'

'Why not make it the world, cock, he's got just as much right to that title.'

'Who will fight six bouts –'

'If it lasts that long.'

'– for his title and a purse of fifty pounds each.'

Sustained cheering.

'The first challenger – at two hundred and ten pounds – Mr Anthony –'

'Hold on,' Sean shouted, 'who says he's first?'

Jock Heyns bad taken a deep breath to bellow the name, he let it escape with a hiss. 'It was arranged by Mr du Toit.'

'If I fight them, then I pick them – I want the Port . . .'

Duff's hand whipped over Sean's mouth and his whisper was desperate. 'Don't be a bloody fool – take the easy ones first. Use your head – we aren't doing this for fun, we're trying to finance a mine, remember?'

Sean clawed Duff's hand off his mouth. 'I want the Portuguese,' he shouted.

'He's joking,' Duff assured the crowd, then turned on Sean fiercely. 'Are you mad? That dago's a man-eater, we're fifty pounds poorer before you start.'

'I want the Portuguese,' repeated Sean with all the logic of a small boy picking the most expensive toy in the shop.

'Let him have the dago,' shouted the gentlemen on the hotel roof and Jock Heyns eyed them nervously; it was clear that they were about to add a few more bottles to the argument.

'All right,' he agreed hastily. 'The first challenger, at –' he glanced at Barnard and repeated after him, 'two hundred and fifty-five pounds – Mr Felezardo da Silva Fernandes.'

In a storm of hoots and applause the Portuguese waddled down off the veranda and into the ring. Sean had seen Candy at the dining-room window and he waved to her. She blew him a two-handed kiss and at that instant Trevor Heyns, the timekeeper, hit the bucket which served as a gong and Sean heard Duff's warning shout. Instinctively he started to duck. There was a flash of lightning inside his skull and he found himself sitting in amongst the legs of the first line of spectators.

'The bastard King hit me,' Sean complained loudly. He shook his head and was surprised to find it still attached to his body. Someone poured a glass of beer over him and it steadied him. He felt his anger flaming up through his body.

'Six,' counted Jock Heyns.

The Portuguese was standing at the ropes. 'Come back, Leetle Sheet, I haf some more for you, not half.'

Sean's anger jumped in his throat.

'Seven, eight.'

Sean gathered his legs under him.

'I kiss your mother.' Fernandes puckered his lips and smacked them. 'I love your sister, like this.' He demonstrated graphically.

Sean charged. With the full weight of his run behind it, his fist thudded into the Portuguese's mouth, then the ropes caught Sean and catapulted him back into the crowd once more.

'You weren't even in the ring, how could you hit him?' protested one of the spectators who had broken Sean's fall. He had money on Fernandes.

'Like this!' Sean demonstrated. The man sat down heavily and had nothing further to say. Sean hurdled the ropes. Jock Heyns was halfway through his second count when Sean interrupted him by lifting the reclining Portuguese to his feet, using the tangled bush of his hair as a handle. He balanced the man on his unsteady legs and hit him again.

'One, two, three . . .' resignedly Jock Heyns began his third count, this time he managed to reach ten.

There was a howl of protest from the crowd and Jock Heyns struggled to make himself heard above it.

'Does anyone want to lodge a formal objection?'

It seemed that there were those who did.

'Very well, please step into the ring. I can't accept shouted comments.' Jock's attitude was understandable – he stood to lose a considerable sum if his decision were reversed. But Sean was patrolling the ropes as hungrily as a lion at feeding time. Jock waited a decent interval, then held up Sean's right arm.

'The winner – ten minutes for refreshments before the next bout. Will the keepers please come and fetch their property.' He gestured towards the Portuguese.

'Nice going, laddie, unorthodox perhaps but beautiful to watch.' Duff took Sean's arm and led him to a chair on the veranda.

'Three more to go, then we can call it a day.' He handed Sean a glass.

'What's this?'

'Orange juice.'

'I'd prefer something a little stronger.'

'Later, laddie.'

Duff collected the Portuguese purse and dropped it into the valise while that gentleman was being carried from the ring by his straining sponsors and laid to rest at the far end of the veranda.

Mr Anthony Blair was next. His heart was not in the encounter. He moved prettily enough on his feet but always in the direction best calculated to keep him out of reach of Sean's fists.

'The boy's a natural long-distance champ.'

'Watch it, Courtney, he'll run you to death.'

'Last lap, Blair, once more round the ring and you've done five miles.'

The chase ended when Sean, now sweating gently, herded him in a corner and there dispatched him.

The third challenger had by this time developed a pain in his chest.

'It hurts like you wouldn't believe it,' he announced through gritted teeth.

'Does it sort of gurgle in your lungs as you breathe?' asked Francois.

'Yes, that's it – gurgles like you wouldn't believe it.'

'Pleurisy,' diagnosed du Toit with more than a trace of envy in his voice.

'Is that bad?' the man asked anxiously.

'Yes it is. Page one hundred and sixteen. The treatment is –'

'Then I won't be able to fight, Hell, that's bad luck,' the invalid complained cheerfully.

'It's exceptionally bad luck,' agreed Duff. 'It means you'll have to forfeit your purse money.'

'You wouldn't take advantage of a sick man?'

'Try me,' Duff suggested pleasantly.

The fourth contestant was a German. Big, blond and happy-faced. He stumbled three or four times on his way to the ring, tripped over the ropes and crawled to his corner on hands and knees; once there he was able to regain his feet with a little help from the ring post. Jock went close to him to smell his breath and before he could dodge, the German caught him in a bear hug and led him into the opening steps of a waltz. The crowd loved it ind there were no objections when at the end of the dance Jock declared Sean the winner on a technical knock-out. More correctly the decision should have gone to Candy who had provided the free drinks.

'We can close down the circus now if you want to, laddie,' Duff told Sean. 'You've made enough to keep the Candy Deep afloat for another couple of months.'

'I haven't had a single good fight out of the lot of them. But I like the looks of this last one. The others were for business; this one I'll have just for the hell of it.'

'You've been magnificent – now you deserve a little fun,' agreed Duff.

'Mr Timothy Curtis. Heavyweight champion of Georgia, U.S.A.' Jock introduced him.

Gideon Barnard put his weight at two hundred and ten pounds, the same as Sean's. Sean shook his hand and from the touch of it knew he was not going to be disappointed.

'Glad to know you.' The American's voice was as soft as his grip was hard.

'Your servant, sir,' said Sean and hit the air where the man's head had been an instant before. He grunted as a fist slogged into his chest under his raised right arm and backed away warily. A soft sigh blew through the crowd and they settled down contentedly. This was what they had come to see.

The red wine was served early; it flew in tiny drops every time a punch was thrown or received. The fight flowed smoothly around the square of trampled grass. The sound of bone on flesh was followed immediately by the growl of the crowd and the seconds between were filled with the hoarse breathing of the two men and the slither, slither of their feet.

'Yaaaa!' Through the tense half silence ripped a roar like that of a mortally wounded foghorn. Sean and the American jumped apart startled, and turned with everyone else to face Candy's Hotel. Fernandes was with them again; his mountain-wide hairiness seemed to fill the whole veranda. He picked up one of Candy's best tables and holding it across his chest tore off two of its legs as though they were the wings of a roasted chicken.

'Francois, the bag!' shouted Sean. Francois snatched it up and threw it high over the heads of the crowd. Sean held his breath as he followed its slow trajectory, then he blew out again with relief as he saw Mbejane field the pass and vanish around the corner of the Hotel.

'Yaaaa!' Fernandes gave tongue again. With a table leg in each hand he charged the crowd that stood between him and Sean; it scattered before him.

'Do you mind if we finish this some other time?' Sean asked the American.

'Of course not. Any time at all. I was just about to leave myself.'

Duff reached through the ropes and caught Sean's arm.

'There's someone looking for you – or had you noticed?'

'It might just be his way of showing friendliness.'

'I wouldn't bet on it – are you coming?'

Fernandes rumbled to a halt, braced himself and threw. The table leg whirred like a rising pheasant an inch over Sean's head, ruffling his hair with the wind of its passage.

'Lead on, Duff.' Sean was uncomfortably conscious of the fact that Fernandes was again in motion towards him, still armed with a long oak, and that three very thin ropes were all that stood between them. The speed that Sean and Duff turned on then made Mr Blair's earlier exhibition seem like that of a man with both legs in plaster, Fernandes, carrying top weight as he was, never looked like catching them.

Francois came up to the Candy Deep just after midday with the news that the Portuguese, after beating three of his sponsors into insensibility, had left on the noon coach back to Kimberley.

Duff uncocked his rifle. 'Thanks, Franz, we were waiting lunch for him. I thought he might call on us.'

'Have you counted the takings?'

'Yes, your commission is in that paper bag on the table.'

'Thanks, man, let's go down and celebrate.'

'You go and have one for us.'

'Hey, Duff, you promised –' Sean started.

'I said later – in three or four weeks' time. Now we've got a little work to do, like digging a trench fifty feet deep and three hundred yards long.'

'We could start first thing tomorrow.'

'You want to be rich, don't you?' asked Duff.

'Sure, but –'

'You want nice things, like English suits, French champagne and –'

'Yes, but –'

'Well, stop arguing, get off your fat arse and come with me.'

12

The Chinese use firecrackers to keep the demons away. Duff and Sean applied the same principle. They kept the mill running; as long as its clunking carried across the valley to the ears of their creditors all was well. Everyone accepted the fact that they were working a payable reef and left them alone, but the money they fed into the front of the mill had halved its value by the time it came out of the other side in those pathetic little yellow pellets.

In the meantime they cut their trench, tearing into the earth in a race against Settlement Day. They fired dynamite and as the last stones dropped back out of the sky they were in again, coughing with the fumes, to clear the loosened rock and start drilling the next set of holes. It was summer, the days were long, and while it was light they worked. Some evenings they lit the last fuses by lantern light.

Sand fell through the hour-glass faster than they had bargained for, the money dribbled away and on the fifteenth of February Duff shaved himself, changed his shirt and went to see Candy about another loan. Sean watched him walk away down the slope. They had sold the horses a week before, and he said a small prayer – the first for many years.

Duff came back in the late morning. He stood on the edge of the trench and watched Sean tamping in the charges for the next cut. Sean's back was shiny with sweat; each individual muscle standing out in relief, swelling and subsiding as he moved.

'That's the stuff, laddie, keep at it.'

Sean looked up with dust-reddened eyes. 'How much?' he asked.

'Another fifty, and this is the last – or so she threatens.'

Sean's eyes fastened on the package Duff held under his arm. 'What's that?'

He could see the stains seeping through the brown paper and the saliva flooded out from under his tongue.

'Prime beef chops – no mealie meal porridge for lunch today.' Duff grinned at him.

'Meat.' Sean caressed the word. 'Underdone – bleeding a little as you bite it, a trace of garlic, just enough salt.'

'And you beside me, singing in the wilderness,' agreed Duff. 'Cut out the poetry, light those fuses and let's go and eat.'

An hour later they walked side by side along the bottom of their trench, Mbejane and his Zulus crowding behind them. Sean belched. 'Ah, pleasant memory, I'll never be able to look another plate of mealie meal in the face again.'

They reached the end, where the freshly broken earth and rock lay piled. Sean felt the thrill start in his hands, tingle up his arms and squeeze his lungs. Then Duff's fingers were biting into his shoulder; he could feel them trembling.

It looked like a snake, a fat grey python crawling down one wall of the trench, disappearing under the heap of new rubble and out the other side.

Duff moved first, he knelt and picked up a piece of the reef, a big grey mottled lump of it and he kissed it.

'It must be it, hey, Duff? It must be the Leader?'

'It's the end of the rainbow.'

'No more mealie meal,' Sean said softly and Duff laughed. Then Sean laughed. Wildly, crazily, together they howled their triumph.

13

'Let me hold it again,' said Sean.

Duff passed it across to him.

'Hell, it's heavy.'

'There's nothing heavier,' agreed Duff.

'Must be all of fifty pounds.'

Sean held the bar in two hands, it was the size of a cigar box. 'More!'

'We've retrieved all our losses in two days' working.'

'And some to spare, I'd say.'

Sean placed the gold bar on the table between them. It shone with little yellow smiles in the lantern light and Duff leaned forward and stroked it; its surface felt knobbly from the rough casting.

'I can't keep my hands off it,' he confessed sheepishly.

'I can't either!' Sean reached out to touch it. 'We'll be able to pay Candy out for the claims in another week or two.'

Duff started. 'What did you say?'

'I said we'd be able to pay Candy out.'

'I thought I wasn't hearing things.' Duff patted his arm indulgently. 'Listen to me, laddie, I'll try and put it simply. How long have we got the option on these claims for?'

'Three years.'

'Correct – now the next question. How many people on these fields have any money?'

Sean looked mystified. 'Well, we have now and – and . . .'

'No one else, that is until Hradsky gets back,' Duff finished for him.

'What about the Heyns brothers? They've cut open the Leader Reef.'

'Certainly, but it won't do them any good, not until their machinery arrives from England.'

'Go on!' Sean wasn't quite sure where Duff was leading.

'Instead of paying Candy out now we are going to use this' –
he patted the gold bar – 'and all its little brothers to buy up
every likely claim we can lay, our hands on. For a start there
are Doc Sutherland's claims between us and the Jack and
Whistle. Then we are going to order a couple of big ten-stamp
mills and when those are spilling out gold we'll use it to buy
land, finance brick works, engineering shops, transport companies and the rest. I've told you before there are more ways of
making gold than digging for it.'

Sean was staring at him silently.

'Have you got a head for heights?' asked Duff.

Sean nodded.

'You're going to need it, because we are going up where the
eagles fly – you are about to be a party to the biggest financial
killing this country has ever seen.'

Sean lit one of Candy's cigars; his hand was a little unsteady.

'Don't you think it would be best to – well – not try and go
too quickly. Hell, Duff, we've only been working the Leader for
two days –'

'And we've made a thousand pounds,' Duff interrupted him.
'Listen to me, Sean, all my life I've been waiting for an opportunity like this. We're the first in on this field, it's as wide open
as the legs of a whore. We're going to go in and take it.'

The next morning Duff had the good fortune to find Doc
Sutherland early enough to talk business with him, before be
began the day's drinking. Another hour would have been too
late. As it was Doc knocked over his glass and fell out of his
chair before he finally signed away twenty-five claims to Sean
and Duff. The ink was hardly dry on the agreement before Duff
was riding down to Ferrieras Camp to look for Ted Reynecke
who held the claims on the other side of the Cousin Jock. Up
on the Candy Deep Sean nursed the mill and bit his nails.
Within seven days Duff had bought over one hundred claims and
committed them to forty thousand pounds in debts.

'Duff, you're going mad.' Sean pleaded with him. 'We'll lose
everything again.'

'How much have we pulled out of the Candy Deep so far?'

'Four thousand.'

'Ten per cent of what we owe in ten days – and with a
miserable little four-stamp mill at that. Hold on to your hat,
laddie, tomorrow I'm going to sign up for the forty claims on

the other side of the Jack and Whistle. I would have had them today but that damned Greek is holding out for a thousand pounds apiece. I'll have to give it to him, I suppose.'

Sean clutched his temples.

'Duff – please, man, we're in over our necks already.'

'Stand back, laddie, and watch the wizard work.'

'I'm going to bed – I suppose I'll have to take your shift again in the morning if you're determined to spend tomorrow ruining us.'

'That's not necessary, I've hired that Yankee – Curtis. You know, your sparring partner. It turns out he's a miner and he's willing to work for thirty a month. So you can come to town with me and watch me make you rich. I'm meeting the Greek at Candy's Hotel at nine o'clock.'

14

At nine o'clock Duff was talking and Sean sat silently on the edge of his chair; at ten the Greek had still not put in an appearance, Duff was moody and Sean was garrulous with relief. At eleven Sean wanted to go back to the mine.

'It's an omen, Duff, God looked down and he saw us sitting here all ready to make a terrible mistake. "No," he said, "I can't let them do it – I'll have the Greek break a leg – I can't let it happen to such nice boys." '

'Why don't you go and join a Trappist monastery?' Duff checked his watch. 'Come on, let's go!'

'Yes, sir!' Sean stood up with alacrity. 'We'll get back in plenty of time to clean the tables before lunch.'

'We're not going home, we're going to look for the Greek.'

'Now listen, Duff.'

'I'll listen later – come on.'

They rode across to the Bright Angels, left the horses outside and walked in together. It was dark in the canteen after the sunshine outside, but even in the gloom a group at one of the tables caught their attention immediately. The Greek sat with his back to them; the line of his parting seemed to be drawn with white chalk and a ruler through the oily black waves of his hair. Sean's eyes switched from him to the two men that sat across the table from him. Jews, there was no mistaking it, but there any similarity ended. The younger one was thin with smooth olive skin drawn tight across the bold bones of his cheeks; his lips were very red and his eyes, fringed with girl's lashes, were toffee-brown and melting. In the chair beside him was a man with a body that had been shaped in wax then held near a hot flame. Shoulders rounded to the verge of deformity drooped down over a pear-shaped body; with difficulty they supported the great Taj Mahal domed head. His hair was styled in the fashion of Friar Tuck, thick only around the ears. But the eyes – the flickering yellow eyes – there was nothing comical about them.

'Hradsky,' hissed Duff, then his expression changed. He smiled as he walked across to the table.

'Hello, Nikky, I thought we had an appointment.'

The Greek twisted quickly in his chair.

'Mr Charleywood, I'm sorry, I was held up.'

'So I see, the woods are full of highwaymen.'

Sean saw the flush start to come up out of Hradsky's collar then sink back again.

'Have you sold?' Duff asked.

The Greek nodded nervously.

'I'm sorry, Mr Charleywood, but Mr Hradsky paid my price and no haggling – cash money, too!'

Duff let his eyes wander across the table.

'Hello, Norman. How's your daughter?'

This time the flush escaped from Hradsky's shirt and flooded over his face. He opened his mouth, his tongue clucked twice, then he closed it again.

Duff smiled, he looked at the younger Jew. 'Say it for him, Max.'

The toffee eyes dropped to the table top. 'Mr Hradsky's daughter is very well.'

'I believe she married soon after my involuntary departure from Kimberley.'

'That is correct.'

'Wise move, Norman, much wiser than having your bully boys run me out of town. That wasn't very nice of you.'

No one spoke.

'We must get together some time and have a chat about old times. Until then, fa – fa – fare ye we – we – well.'

On the way back to the mine Sean asked, 'He's got a daughter? If she looks like him you were lucky to escape.'

'She didn't – she was like a bunch of ripe grapes with the bloom on them.'

'I can hardly credit it.'

'Neither could I. The only conclusion I could reach was that Max did that job for him as well.'

'What's the story about Max?'

'He's the Court Jester. Rumour has it that after Hradsky has finished hanging it out, Max shakes it for him.'

Sean laughed and Duff went on, 'But don't underestimate Hradsky. His stutter is his only weakness and with Max to talk for him he's overcome that. Beneath that monumental skull is a brain as quick and merciless as a guillotine. Now that he's arrived on this goldfield there's going to be some action; we'll have to gallop to keep up with him.'

Sean thought for a few seconds, then, 'Talking about action, Duff, now that we've lost the Greek's claims and won't have to use all our ready money satisfying him, let's give some thought to ordering new machinery to work the claims we have got.'

Duff grinned at him.

'I sent a telegram to London last week. There'll be a pair of brand new ten-stamp mills on the water to us before the end of the month.'

'Good God, why didn't you tell me?'

'You were worried enough as it was – I didn't want to break your heart.'

Sean opened his mouth to blast Duff out of the saddle, Duff winked at him before he could talk and Sean's lips trembled. He felt the laughter in his throat, he tried to stop it but it swamped him.

'How much is it going to cost us?' he howled through his mirth.

'If you ask that question once more, I'll strangle you,' Duff laughed back at him. 'Rest content in the knowledge that if we're going to have enough to honour the bills of lading when those mills arrive at Port Natal, we'll have to run a mountain of Leader Reef through our little rig during the next few weeks.'

'What about the payments on the new claims?'

'That's my department – I'll worry about that.'

And so their partnership crystallized; their relationship was established over the weeks that followed. Duff with his magic tongue and his charming, lopsided grin was the one who negotiated, who poured the oil on the storm waters churned up by impatient creditors. He was the storehouse of mining knowledge which Sean tapped daily, he was the conceiver of schemes, some wild, others brilliant. But his fleeting nervous energy was not designed to bring them to fruition. He lost interest quickly and it was Sean who finally rejected the least likely Charleywood brain children and adopted the others that were more deserving; once he had made himself stepfather to them he reared them as though they were his own. Duff was the theorist, Sean the practician. Sean could see why Duff had never found success before, but at the same time he recognized that without him he would be helpless. He watched with profound admiration the way that Duff used the barely sufficient flow of gold from the Candy Deep to keep the mill running, pay the tradesmen, meet the claim monies as they fell due and still save enough for the new machinery. He was a man juggling with live coals: hold one too long and it burns, let one fall and all fall. And Duff, deep-down-uncertain Duff, had a wall to put his back against. His speech never showed it but his eyes did when he looked at Sean. Sometimes he felt small next to Sean's big body and bigger determination, but it was a good feeling: like being on a friendly mountain.

They put up new buildings around the mill: storerooms, a smelting house and cabins for Sean and Curtis. Duff was sleeping at the Hotel again. The location for the Natives sprawled haphazard down the back slope of the ridge, retreating a little each week as the white mountain of the mine dump grew and pushed it back. The whole valley was changing. Hradsky's new mills arrived and stood up along the ridge, tall and proud until their own dumps dwarfed them. Johannesburg, at first a mere pattern of surveyors' pegs, sucked the scattered encampments onto her grassy chequerboard and arranged them in a semblance of order along her streets.

The Diggers' Committee, its members tired of having to scrape their boots every time they went indoors, decreed public latrines be erected. Then, flushed with their own audacity, they built a bridge across the Natal Spruit, purchased a water cart to lay the dust on the streets of Johannesburg and passed a law prohibiting burials within half a mile of the city centre. Sean and Duff as members of the Committee felt it their duty to demonstrate their faith in the goldfield, so they bought twenty-five plots of ground in Johannesburg, five pounds each to be paid within six months. Candy recruited all her customers and in one weekend of frantic effort they razed her Hotel to the ground, packed every plank and sheet of iron onto their wagons, carried it a mile down the valley and re-erected it on her own land in the centre of the township. During the party she gave them on that Sunday night they nearly succeeded in dismantling it for the second time. Each day the roads from Natal and the Cape fed more wagons, more men into the Witwatersrand goldfield. Duff's suggestion that the Diggers' Committee levy a guinea a head from all newcomers to help finance the public works was reluctantly rejected, the general feeling being that if it led to civil rebellion there were more newcomers than Committee members and no one fancied being on the losing side.

One morning, when he came out to the mine, Duff brought a telegram with him. He handed it to Sean without comment. Sean read it. The machinery had arrived.

'Good God, it's three weeks early.'

'They must have had a downhill sea, or a following wind or whatever it is that makes ships go faster,' muttered Duff.

'Have we got enough to pay the bill?' asked Sean.

'No.'

'What are we going to do?'

'I'll go and see the little man at the bank.'

'He'll throw you out in the street.'

'I'll get him to give us a loan on the claims.'

'How the hell are you going to do that – we haven't paid for them yet.'

'That's what you call financial genius. I'll simply point out to him that they're worth five times what we bought them for.' Duff grinned. 'Can you and Curtis carry on here without me for today while I go and arrange it?'

'You arrange it and I'll happily give you a month's holiday.'

When Duff came back that afternoon he carried a paper with him. It had a red wax seal in the bottom corner, across the top it said 'Letter of Credit' and in the middle, standing out boldly from the mass of small print, was a figure that ended in an impressive string of noughts.

'You're a bloody marvel,' said Sean.

'Yes, I am rather, aren't I?' agreed Duff.

15

The Heyns brothers' machinery was on the same ship. Jock and Duff rode down to Port Natal together, hired a hundred wagons and brought it all back in one load.

'I'll tell you what I'll do with you, Jock, I'll wager you that we get our mills producing before you do. Loser pays for the transport on the whole shipment,' Duff challenged him when they reached Johannesburg where, in Candy's new bar-room, they were washing the dust out of their throats.

'You're on!'

'I'll go further, I'll put up a side bet of five hundred.'

Sean prodded Duff in the ribs.

'Gently, Duffy – we can't afford it.' But Jock had already snapped up the bet.

'What do you mean we can't afford it?' whispered Duff. 'We've got nearly fifteen hundred pounds left on the letter of credit.'

Sean shook his head. 'No, we haven't.'

Duff pulled the paper from his inside pocket and tapped Sean's nose with it. 'There – read for yourself.'

Sean took it out of Duff's hand.

'Thanks, old chap, I'll go and pay the man now.'

'What man?'

'The man with the wagons.'

'What wagons?'

'The wagons that you and Jock hired in Port Natal. I've bought them.'

'The hell you say!'

'It was your idea to start a transport business. Just as soon as they've offloaded they'll be on their way again to pick up a shipment of coal from Dundee.'

Duff grinned at him. 'Don't you ever forget an idea? All right, laddie, off you go – we'll just have to win the bet, that's all.'

One of the mills they placed on the Candy Deep, the other

on the new claims beyond the Cousin Jock Mine. They hired two gangs from among the unemployed in Johannesburg. Curtis supervised one of them and Sean the other, while Duff darted back and forth keeping an eye on both. Each time he passed the Cousin Jock he spent a few minutes checking Trevor and Jock's progress.

'They've got the edge on us, Sean; their boilers are up and holding pressure already,' he reported fretfully, but the next day he was smiling again.

'They didn't mix enough cement in the platform – it started to crumble as soon as they put the crusher on it. They'll have to cast it again. That set them back three or four days.'

The betting down in the canteens fluctuated sharply with each change of fortune. Francois came up to the Candy Deep one Saturday afternoon. He watched them work, made a suggestion or two, then remarked, 'They're giving three-to-one against you at the Bright Angels; they, reckon the Heynses will be finished by next weekend.'

'Go down and put another five hundred pounds on for me,' Duff told him, and Sean shook his head despairingly.

'Don't worry, laddie, we can't lose – that amateur mining engineer, Jock Heyns, has assembled his crusher jaws all arse-about-face. I only noticed it this morning – he's in for a surprise when he tries to start up. He'll have to strip the whole damn rig.'

Duff was right – they brought both their mills into production a comfortable fifteen hours before the Heyns brothers. Jock rode over to see them with his jaw on his chest. 'Congratulations.'

'Thanks, Jock, did you bring your cheque book?'

'That's what I came to talk about. Can you give me a little time?'

'Your credit's good,' Sean assured him, 'come and have a drink and let me sell you some coal.'

'Ah, yes, I heard your wagons arrived back this morning. What price are you charging?'

'Fifteen pounds a hundredweight.'

'Good God. You bloody bandit, I bet it cost you less than five shillings a hundredweight.'

'A man's entitled to a reasonable profit,' protested Sean.

It had been a long hard pull up to the top of the hill but Sean and Duff had arrived at last and from there it was downhill all the way. The money poured in.

The geological freak that had bowed the Leader Reef away from the Main across the Candy Deep claims had, at the same time, enriched it – injected it full of the metal. Francois was there one evening when they put the ball of amalgam into the retort. His eyes bulged as the mercury boiled away; he stared at the gold the way a man watches a naked woman.

'*Gott!* I'm going to have to call you two thunders "Mister" from now on.'

'Have you ever seen richer reef, Francois?' Duff gloated.

Francois shook his head slowly. 'You know my theory about the reef being the bed of an old lake – well this bears it out. The kink in your reef must have been a deep trench along the bottom of the lake. It would have acted as a natural gold trap. Hell, man, what luck. With your eyes closed you have picked the plum out of the pudding. The Jack and Whistle is half as rich as this.'

Their overdraft at the bank dropped like a barometer in a hurricane; the tradesmen started greeting them with a smile; they gave Doc Sutherland a cheque which would have kept even him in whisky for a hundred years. Candy kissed them both when they paid her out in full, plus interest at seven per cent. Then she built herself a new Hotel, double storied, with a crystal chandelier in the dining-room and a magnificent bedroom suite on the second floor done out in maroon and gold. Duff and Sean rented it immediately but with the express understanding that if ever the Queen visited Johannesburg they would allow her to use it. In anticipation Candy called it the Victoria Rooms.

Francois, with a little persuasion, agreed to take over the running of the Candy Deep. He moved his possessions, one chest of clothes and four chests of patent medicines, across from the Jack and Whistle. Timothy Curtis was the manager of the mill on the new claims; they named it the Little Sister Mine. Although not nearly as rich as the Candy Deep it was producing a sweet fortune each month, for Curtis worked as well as he fought.

By the end of August Sean and Duff had no more creditors: the claims were theirs, the mills were theirs and they had money to invest.

'We need an office of our own here in town. We can't run this show from our bedrooms' complained Sean.

'You're right,' agreed Duff, 'we'll build on that corner plot nearest the market square.' The plan was for a modest little four-room building, but it finally expanded to two stories, stinkwood floors, oak panelling and twenty rooms. What they couldn't use they rented.

'The price of land has trebled in three months,' said Sean, 'and it's still moving.'

'You're right – now's the time to buy,' Duff agreed. 'You're starting to think along the right lines.'

'It was your idea.'

'Was it?' Duff looked surprised.

'Don't you remember your "up where the eagles fly" speech?'

'Don't you forget anything?' asked Duff.

They bought land: one thousand acres at Orange Grove and another thousand around Hospital Hill. Their transport wagons, now almost four hundred strong, plied in daily from Port Natal and Lourenço Marques. Their brickfields worked twenty-four hours a day, seven days a week, to try to meet the demand for building materials.

It took Sean almost a week to dissuade Duff from building an Opera House but he succeeded and instead they joined most of the other members of the Diggers' Committee in financing a different type of pleasure palace. At Duff's suggestion they called it the Opera House. They recruited the performers not from the great companies of Europe but from the dock areas of Capetown and Port Natal and chose as the conductor a Frenchwoman of vast experience named Blue Bessie after the colour of her hair. The Opera House provided entertainment on two levels. For the members of the Committee and the other emergent rich there was a discreet side entrance, a lavishly furnished lounge where one could buy the finest champagne and discuss the prices on the Kimberley Stock Exchange, and beyond the lounge were a series of tastefully decorated retiring-rooms. For the workers there was a bare corridor to queue in, no choice for your money and a five-minute time limit. In one month the Opera House produced more gold than the Jack and Whistle mine.

By December there were millionaires in Johannesburg: Hradsky, the Heyns brothers, Karl Lochtkamper, Duff Charleywood, Sean Courtney and a dozen others. They owned the mines, the land, the buildings and the city: the aristocracy of the Witwatersrand, knighted with money and crowned with gold.

A week before Christmas, Hradsky, their unacknowledged but undoubted king, called them all to a meeting in one of the private lounges of Candy's Hotel.

'Who the hell does he think he is,' complained Jock Heyns, 'ordering us round like a bunch of kaffirs.'

'*Verdammt Juden!*' agreed Lochtkamper.

But they went, every last man of them, for whatever Hradsky did had the smell of money about it and they could no more resist it than a dog can resist the smell of a bitch in season.

Duff and Sean were the last to arrive and the room was already hazed with cigar smoke and tense with expectation. Hradsky sagged in one of the polished leather armchairs with Max sitting quietly beside him; his eyes flickered when Duff walked in but his expression never changed. When Duff and Sean had found chairs Max stood up. 'Gentlemen, Mr Hradsky has invited you here to consider a proposition.'

They leaned forward slightly in their chairs and there was a glitter in their eyes like hounds close upon the fox.

'From time to time it is necessary for men in your position to find capital to finance further ventures and to consolidate past gains; on the other hand those of us who have money lying idle will be seeking avenues for investment.' Max cleared his throat and looked at them with his sad brown eyes.

'Up to the present there has been no meeting-place for these mutual needs such as exists in the other centres of the financial world. Our nearest approach to it is the Stock Exchange at Kimberley which, I'm sure you will agree, is too far removed to be of practical use to us here at Johannesburg. Mr Hradsky has invited you here to consider the possibility of forming our own Exchange and, if you accept the idea, to elect a chairman and governing body.'

Max sat down and in the silence that followed they took up the idea, each one fitting it into his scheme of thinking, testing it with the question 'How will I benefit?'.

'*Ja*, it's dom fine idea.' Lochtkamper spoke first.

'Yes, it's what we need.'

'Count me in.'

While they schemed and bargained, setting the fees, the place and the rules, Sean, watched their faces. The faces of bitter men, happy men, quiet ones and big bull-roarers but all with one common feature – that greedy glitter in the eyes. It was midnight before they finished.

Max stood up again.

'Gentlemen, Mr Hradsky would like you to join him in a glass of champagne to celebrate the formation of our new enterprise.'

'This I can't believe; the last time he paid for drinks was back in 'sixty,' declared Duff. 'Quickly somebody – find a waiter before he changes his mind.'

Hradsky hooded his eyes to hide the hatred in them.

16

With its own Stock Exchange and bordel Johannesburg became a city. Even Kruger recognized it; he deposed the Diggers' Committee and sent in his own police force, sold monopolies for essential mining supplies to members of his family and Government, and set about revising his tax laws with special attention to mining profits. Despite Kruger's efforts to behead the gold-laying goose, the city grew, overflowed the original Government plots and spread brawling and blustering out into the surrounding veld.

Sean and Duff grew with it. Their way of life changed swiftly; their visits to the mines fell to a weekly inspection and they left it to their hired men. A steady river of gold poured down from the ridge to their offices on Eloff Street, for the men they hired were the best that money could find.

Their horizons closed in to encompass only the two panelled offices, the Victoria Rooms and the Exchange. Yet within that world Sean found a thrill that he had never dreamed existed. He had been oblivious to it during the first feverish months; he had been so absorbed in laying the foundations that he could spare no energy for enjoying or even noticing it.

Then one day he felt the first voluptuous tickle of it. He had sent to the bank for a land title document he needed, expecting it to be delivered by a junior clerk – but instead the sub-manager and a senior clerk filed respectfully into his office. It was an exquisite physical shock and it gave him a new awareness. He noticed the way men looked at him as he passed them on the street. He realized suddenly that over fifteen hundred human beings depended on him for their livelihood.

There was satisfaction in the way a path cleared for him and Duff as they crossed the floor of the Exchange each morning to take their places in the reserved leather armchairs of the members' lounge. When Duff and he leaned together and talked quietly before the trading began, even the other big fish watched them. Hradsky with his fierce eyes hooded by sleepy lids, Jock and Trevor Heyns, Karl Lochtkamper – any of them would have given a day's production from their mines to overhear those conversations.

'Buy!' said Sean.

'Buy! Buy! Buy!' clamoured the pack and the prices jumped as they hit them, then slumped back as they sucked their money away and put it to work elsewhere.

Then one March morning in 1886 the thrill became so acute it was almost an orgasm. Max left the chair at Norman Hradsky's side and crossed the lounge towards them. He stopped in front of them, lifted his sad eyes off the patterned carpet and almost apologetically proffered a loose sheaf of papers.

'Good morning, Mr Courtney. Good morning, Mr Charleywood. Mr Hradsky has asked me to bring this new share issue to your attention. Perhaps you would be interested in these reports, which are, of course, confidential, but he feels they are worthy of your support.'

You have power when you can force a man who hates you to ask for your favours. After the first advance by Hradsky they worked together often. Hradsky never acknowledged their existence by word or look. Each morning Duff called a cheerful greeting across the full width of the lounge, 'Hello, chatterbox,' or 'Sing for us, Norman.'

Hradsky's eyes would flicker and he would sag a little lower into his chair, but before the bell started the day's trading Max would stand up and come across to them, leaving his master staring into the empty fireplace. A few soft sentences exchanged and Max would walk back to Hradsky's side.

Their combined fortunes were irresistible: in one wild morning's trading alone they added another fifty thousand to their store of pounds.

An untaught boy handles his first rifle like a toy. Sean was twenty-two. The power he held was a more deadly weapon than any rifle, and much sweeter, more satisfying to use. It was a game at first with the Witwatersrand as a chessboard, men and gold for pieces. A word or a signature on a slip of paper would set the gold jingling and the men scampering. The consequences were remote and all that mattered was the score, the score chalked up in black figures on a bank statement. Then in that same March he was made to realize that a man wiped off the board could not be laid back in the box with as much compassion as a carved wooden knight.

Karl Lochtkamper, the German with a big laugh and a happy face, laid himself open. He needed money to develop a new property on the east end of the Rand; he borrowed and signed short-term notes on his loans, certain that he could extend them if necessary. He borrowed secretly from men he thought he could trust. He was vulnerable and the sharks smelt him out.

'Where is Lochtkamper getting his money?' asked Max.

'Do you know?' asked Sean.

'No, but I can guess.'

Then the next day Max came back to them again.

'He has eight notes out. Here is the list,' he whispered sadly. 'Mr Hradsky will buy the ones that have a cross against them. Can you handle the rest?'

'Yes,' said Sean.

They closed on Karl on the last day of the quarter; they called the loans and gave him twenty-four hours to meet them. Karl went to each of the three banks in turn.

'I'm sorry, Mr Lochtkamper, we have loaned over our budget for this quarter.'

'Mr Hradsky is holding your notes – I'm sorry.'

'I'm sorry, Mr Lochtkamper, Mr Charleywood is one of our directors.'

Karl Lochtkamper rode back to the Exchange. He walked across the floor and into the lounge for the last time. He stood in the centre of the big room, his face grey, his voice bitter and broken.

'Let Jesus have this much mercy on you when your time comes. Friends! My friends! Sean, how many times haf we drunk together? And you, Duff, was it yesterday you shook my hand?'

Then he went back across the floor, out through the doors. His suite in the Great North Hotel wasn't fifty yards from the Exchange. In the members' lounge they heard the pistol shot quite clearly.

That night Duff and Sean got drunk together in the Victoria rooms.

'Why did he have to do it? Why did he have to kill himself?'

'He didn't,' answered Duff. 'He was a quitter.'

242

'If I'd known he was going to do that — my God, if only I'd known.'

'Damn it, man, he took a chance and lost — it's not our fault. He would have done the same to us.'

'I don't like this — it's dirty. Let's get out, Duff.'

'Someone gets knocked down in the rush and you want to cry "enough! " '

'It's different now somehow, it wasn't like this at the start.'

'Yes, and it'll be different in the morning. Come on, laddie, I know what you need.'

'Where are we going?'

'To the Opera House.'

'What will Candy say?'

'Candy doesn't have to know.'

Duff was right; it was different in the morning. There was the usual hurly-burly of work at the office and some tense action at the Exchange. He thought about Karl only once during the day and somehow it didn't seem to matter so much. They sent him a nice wreath.

He had faced the reality of the game he was playing. He had considered the alternative which was to get out with the fortune he had already made; but to do that would mean giving up the power he held. The addiction was already seated too deeply, he could not deny it. So his subconscious opened, sucked in his conscience and swallowed it deep down into its gut. He could feel it struggling there sometimes, but the longer it stayed swallowed the more feeble those struggles became. Duff comforted him: Duff's words were like a gastric juice that helped to digest that lump in the gut and he had not yet learned that what Duff said and what Duff did were not necessarily what Duff believed.

Play the game without mercy, play to win.

17

Duff stood with his back to the fireplace in Sean's office smoking a cheroot while they waited for the carriage to take them up to the Exchange. The fire behind him silhouetted his slimly tapered legs with the calves encased in polished black leather. He still wore his top coat, for the winter morning was cold. It fell open at his throat to show a diamond that sparkled and glowed in his cravat.

'. . . you get used to a woman somehow,' he was saying. 'I've known Candy four years now and yet it seems I've been with her all my life.'

'She's a fine girl,' Sean agreed absently as he dipped his pen and scribbled his signature on the document in front of him.

'I'm thirty-five now,' Duff went on. 'If I'm ever to have a son of my own . . .'

Sean laid down the pen deliberately and looked up at him; he was starting to grin.

'The man said to me once "They take you into their soft little minds" and again he said "They don't share, they possess". Is this a new tune I hear?'

Duff shifted uneasily from one foot to the other.

'Things change,' he defended himself. 'I'm thirty-five . . .'

'You're repeating yourself,' Sean accused and Duff smiled weakly.

'Well, the truth is . . .'

He never finished the sentence; hooves beat urgently in the street outside and both their faces swung in the direction of the window.

'Big hurry!' said Sean coming quickly to his feet. 'Big trouble!' He crossed to the window. 'It's Curtis, and by his face it's not good news he brings.'

There were voices outside the door raised in agitation and the quick rush of feet, then Timothy Curtis burst into the room without knocking. He wore a miner's overall and splattered gumboots. 'We've hit a mud rush on the ninth level.'

'How bad?' Duff snapped.

'Bad enough – it's flooded right back to number eight.'

'Jesus, that will take two months at least to clear,' Sean exclaimed. 'Does anyone else in town know – have you told anyone?'

'I came straight here – Cronje and five men were up at the face when it blew.'

'Get back there immediately,' ordered Sean, 'but ride quietly, we don't want the whole world to know there's trouble. Don't let a soul off the property. We must have time to sell out.'

'Yes, Mr Courtney.' Curtis hesitated. 'Cronje and five others were hit by the rush. Shall I send word to their wives?'

'Can't you understand English? I don't want a whisper of this to get out before ten o'clock. We've got to have time.'

'But, Mr Courtney – ' Curtis was appalled. He stood staring at Sean and Sean felt the sick little stirring of guilt. Six men drowned in treacle-thick mud . . . He made an irresolute gesture with his hands.

'We can't –' He stopped and Duff cut in.

'They're dead now, and they'll be just as dead when we tell their wives at ten o'clock. Get going, Curtis.'

They sold their shares in the Little Sister within an hour of the start of trading and a week later they bought them back at half the price. Two months later the Little Sister was back on full production again.

18

They split their land at Orange Grove into plots and sold them, all but a hundred acres and on that they started building a house. Into the designing of it they poured their combined energy and imagination. With money Duff seduced the horticulturist of the Capetown Botanical Gardens and brought him up by express coach. They showed him the land.

'Make me a garden,' said Duff.

'The whole hundred acres?'

'Yes.'

'It'll cost a pretty penny.'

'That is no problem.'

The carpets came from Persia, the wood from the Knysna forests and the marble from Italy. On the gates at the entrance to the main drive they engraved the words 'At Xanadu did Kublai Khan a stately pleasure dome decree'. As the gardener had predicted, it all cost a pretty penny. Each afternoon when the Exchange closed they would drive up together and watch the builders at work. One day Candy came with them and they showed it off to her like two small boys.

'This will be the ballroom.' Sean bowed to her. 'May I have the pleasure of this dance?'

'Thank you, sir.' She curtsied, then swept away on his arm across the unsanded boards.

'This will be the staircase,' Duff told her, 'marble – black and white marble – and there on the main landing in a glass case will be Hradsky's head, beautifully mounted with an apple in his mouth.'

They climbed laughing up the rough concrete ramp.

'This is Sean's room – the bed is being made of oak, thick oak to withstand punishment.' They trooped with linked arms down the passage.

'And this is my room – I was thinking of a solid gold bath but the builder says it's too heavy and Sean says it's too vulgar. Look at that view; from here you can see out across the whole valley. I could lie in bed in the mornings and read the prices on the Exchange floor with a telescope.'

'It's lovely,' Candy said dreamily.

'You like it?'

'Oh, yes.'

'It could be your room too.'

Candy started to blush and then her face tightened with annoyance. 'He was right – you are vulgar.'

She started for the door and Sean fumbled for his cigars to cover his embarrassment. With two quick steps Duff caught her and turned her to face him. 'You sweet idiot, that was a proposal.'

'Let me go.' Near to tears she twisted in his hands. 'I don't think you're funny.'

'Candy – I'm serious. Will you marry me?'

The cigar dropped out of Sean's mouth but he caught it before it hit the ground. Candy was standing very still, her eyes fastened on Duff's face.

'Yes or no – will you marry me?'

She nodded once slowly and then twice very fast.

Duff looked at Sean over his shoulder. 'Leave us, laddie.'

On the way back to town Candy had regained her voice. She chattered happily and Duff answered her with his lopsided grin. Sean hunched morosely in one corner of the carriage. His cigar was burning unevenly and he threw it out of the window.

'You'll let me keep the Victoria rooms, I hope, Candy.'

There was a silence.

'What do you mean?' asked Duff.

'Two's company,' Sean answered.

'Oh, no,' Candy exclaimed.

'It's your house as well.' Duff spoke sharply,

'I give it to you – a wedding present.'

'Oh, shut up,' Duff grinned, 'it's big enough for all of us.'

Candy crossed quickly to Sean's seat and put her hand on his shoulder.

'Please – we've been together a long time. We'd be lonely without you.'

Sean grunted.

'Please!'

'He'll come,' said Duff.

'Please.'

'Oh, well –' Sean frowned ungraciously.

19

They went racing at Milnerton. Candy with a hat full of ostrich feathers, Sean and Duff with pearl grey toppers and gold heads on their canes.

'You can pay for your wedding gown by putting fifty guineas on Trade Wind! She can't lose –' Duff told Candy.

'What about Mr Hradsky's new filly? I've heard she's a good bet,' Candy asked and Duff frowned.

'You want to go over to the enemy?'

'I thought you and Hradsky were almost partners.' Candy twirled her parasol. 'From the rumours I've heard you work with him all the time.'

Mbejane slowed the carriage as they ran into the crush of pedestrians and coaches outside the Turf Club gates.

'Well you've heard wrong both times. His Sun Dancer will never hold Trade Wind over the distance, she's bred too light in the legs. Frenchified with Huguenot blood; she'll fade within the mile. And as far as Hradsky being our partner, we throw him an occasional bone. Isn't that right, Sean?'

Sean was watching Mbejane's back. The Zulu, in loin clothes only and his spears laid carefully on the boards at his feet, was handling the horses with an easy familiarity. They cocked their ears back to catch his voice, deep and soft, as he talked to them.

'Isn't that right, Sean?' Duff repeated.

'Of course,' agreed Sean vaguely. 'You know – I think I'll get Mbejane a livery. He looks out of place in those skins.'

'Well, some of the other horses from the same stud were stayers. Sun Honey won the Cape Derby twice and Eclipse showed up the English stock in the Metropolitan Handicap last year,' Candy argued.

'Huh,' Duff smiled his superiority, 'well, you can take my word for it that Trade Wind will walk the main race today and he'll be back in his stable before Sun Dancer sees the finishing post.'

'Maroon and gold – the same as our racing colours,' Sean muttered thoughtfully. 'That would go very well with his black skin, perhaps a turban with an ostrich feather in it.'

'What the hell are you talking about?' complained Duff.

'Mbejane's livery.'

They left the carriage in the reserved area and went through to the members' grandstand, Candy sailing prettily between her escorts.

'Well, Duff, we've got the nicest looking woman here today.'

'Thank you.' Candy smiled up at Sean.

'Is that why you keep trying to look down the front of her dress?' challenged Duff.

'You filthy-minded beast.' Sean was shocked.

'Don't deny, it,' Candy teased, 'but I find it very flattering – you're welcome.'

They moved through the throng of butterfly-coloured dresses and stiffly-suited men. A ripple of greetings moved with them.

'Morning, Mr Courtney.' The accent was on the 'Mister'. 'How's your Trade Wind for the big race?'

'Put your pants on him.'

'Hello, Duff, congratulations on your engagement.'

'Thanks, Jock, it's time you took the plunge as well.'

They were rich, they were young, they were handsome and all the world admired them. Sean felt good, with a pretty girl on his arm and a friend walking beside him.

'There's Hradsky – let's go across and engage in a little hog-baiting,' Duff suggested.

'Why do you hate him so much?' Candy asked softly.

'Look at him and answer your own question. Have you ever seen anything more pompous, joyless and unlovable?'

'Oh, leave him alone, Duff, don't spoil the day. Let's go down to the paddock.'

'Come on!' Duff steered them across to where Hradsky and Max were standing alone by the rail of the track.

'Salome, Norman, and peace to you also, Maximilian.'

Hradsky nodded and Max murmured sadly; his lashes touched his cheeks as he blinked.

'I noticed you two chatting away and thought I would come across and listen to your stimulating repartee.'

He received no answer and went on. 'I saw your new filly exercising on the practice track yesterday evening and I said to myself, Norman's got a girl friend – that's what it is – he's bought a hack for his lady. But now they tell me you are going to race her. Oh, Norman, I wish you'd consult me before you do these silly things. You're an impetuous little devil at times.'

'Mr Hradsky is confident that Sun Dancer will make a reasonable showing today,' Max murmured.

'I was about to offer you a side bet, but being a naturally kindhearted person, I feel it would be taking an unfair advantage.'

A small crowd had gathered round them listening with anticipation. Candy tugged gently at Duff's elbow trying to lead him away.

'I thought five hundred guineas would be acceptable to Norman.' Duff shrugged. 'But let's forget it.'

Hradsky made a fierce little sign with his hands and Max interpreted smoothly. 'Mr Hradsky suggests a thousand.'

'Rash, Norman, extremely rash.' Duff sighed. 'But I suppose I must accommodate you.'

They walked down to the refreshment pavilion. Candy was quiet awhile, then she said, 'An enemy like Mr Hradsky is a luxury that even you two gods can't afford. Why don't you leave him alone?'

'It's a hobby of Duff's,' explained Sean as they found seats at one of the tables. 'Waiter – bring us a bottle of Pol Roger.'

Before the big race they went down to the paddock. A steward opened the wicket gate for them and they passed into the ring of circling horses. A gnome in silk of maroon and gold came to meet them and touched his cap then stood awkwardly, fingering his whip.

'He looks good this morning, sir.' The little man nodded at Trade Wind. There was a dark patch of sweat on the horse's shoulder and he mouthed the snaffle, lifting his feet delicately. Once he snorted and rolled his eyes in mock terror.

'He's got an edge on him, sir, eager kind of – if you follow me.'

'I want you to win, Harry,' said Duff.

'So do I, sir, I'll do my best.'

'There's a thousand guineas for you if you do.'

'A thousand –' the jockey repeated on an outgoing breath.

Duff looked across to where Hradsky and Max were standing

talking to their trainer. He caught Hradsky's eye, glanced significantly at Hradsky's honey-coloured filly and shook his head sympathetically.

'Win for me, Harry,' he said softly.

'That I will, sir!'

The groom led the big stallion across to them and Sean flicked the jockey up into the saddle.

'Good luck.'

Harry settled his cap and gathered up the reins; he winked at Sean, his hobgoblin face wrinkling in a grin.

'There's no better luck than a thousand guineas, sir, if you follow me.'

'Come on.' Duff caught Candy's arm. 'Let's get a place at the rail.'

They hustled her out of the paddock and across the members' enclosure. The rail was crowded but a place opened for them respectfully and no one jostled them.

'I can't understand you two,' Candy laughed breathlessly. 'You make an extravagant bet, then you fix it so you can get nothing even if you win.'

'Money's not the problem,' Duff assured her.

'He won that much from me at Klabejas last night,' Sean commented. 'If Trade Wind beats the filly his prize will be the look on Hradsky's face – the loss of a thousand guineas will hurt him like a kick between the legs.'

The horses came parading past, stepping high next to the grooms who held them, then they turned free and cantered back, dancing sideways, throwing their heads, shining in the sunlight like the bright silk upon their backs. They moved away round the curve of the track.

The crowd rustled with excitement, a bookmaker's voice carried over the buzz.

'Twenty-to-one bar two. Sun Dancer at fives. Trade Wind even money.'

Duff showed his teeth as he smiled. 'That's right, you tell the people.'

Candy twisted her gloves nervously and looked up at Sean.

'You there in the grandstand – can you see what they're doing?'

'They're in line now, moving up together – it looks as though they'll get away first time,' Sean told her without taking his binoculars from his eyes. 'Yes, there they go – they're away!'

'Tell me, tell me,' commanded Candy, pounding Sean's shoulder.

'Harry's showing in front already – can you see the filly, Duff?'

'I saw a flash of green in the pack – yes, there she is lying sixth or seventh.'

'What horse is that next to Trade Wind?'

'That's Hamilton's gelding, don't worry about him, he won't last to the turn.'

The frieze of horses, their heads going like hammers and the dust lifting pale and thin behind them, were framed by the guide rail and the white mine dumps beyond them. Like a string of dark beads they moved up the back stretch and then bunched in the straight.

'Trade Wind's still there – I think he's making ground – the gelding's finished and no sign of the filly yet.'

'Yes! There she is, Duff, wide on the outside. She's moving up.'

'Come on, my darling –' Duff half whispered. 'Let's see you foot it now.'

'She's clear of the pack – she's coming up, Duff, she's coming up fast,' Sean warned.

'Come on, Trade Wind, hold her off,' Duff pleaded. 'Keep her there, boy.'

The pounding of the hooves reached them now, a sound like distant surf, but rising sharply. The colours showed, emerald green above a honey skin and maroon and gold leading on the bay.

'Trade Wind – come on Trade Wind,' shrieked Candy. Her hat flopped over her eyes as she hopped; she ripped it off impatiently and her hair tumbled to her shoulders.

'She's catching him, Duff!'

'Give him the whip, Harry, for Christ's sake – the whip, man.'

The hoof beats crescendoed, thundered up to them, then passed. The filly's nose was at Harry's boot, creeping steadily forward, now level with Trade Wind's heaving shoulder.

'The whip, God damn you,' screamed Duff, 'give him the whip.'

Harry's right arm moved, fast as a mamba – crack, crack; they heard the whip above the howling crowd, above the drumming of hooves and the bay jumped at its sting. Like a pair in harness the two horses swept over the finishing line.

'Who won?' Candy asked as though she were in pain.

'I couldn't see, damn it,' Duff answered.

'Nor could I –' Sean took out his handkerchief and wiped his forehead. 'That didn't do my heart any good – as Francois would say. Have a cigar, Duff.'

'Thanks – I need one.'

Everyone in the crowd was turned to face the board above the judges' box and an uneasy silence held them.

'Why do they take such a long time to make up their minds?' complained Candy. 'I'm so upset that I can only last a minute before I visit the Ladies' Room.'

'The numbers are going up,' shouted Sean.

'Who is it?' Candy jumped to try and see over the heads of the crowd then stopped hurriedly with an expression of alarm on her face.

'Number Sixteen,' bellowed Duff and Sean together, 'it's Trade Wind!'

Sean punched Duff in the chest and Duff leaned over and snapped Sean's cigar in half. Then they caught Candy between them and hugged her. She let out a careful shriek and fought her way out of their arms. 'Excuse me,' she said and fled.

'Let me buy you a drink.' Sean lit the mutilated stump of his cigar.

'No, it's my honour, I insist.' Duff took his arm and they walked with big satisfied grins towards the pavilion. Hradsky was sitting at one of the tables with Max. Duff walked up behind him, lifted his top hat off his head with one hand and with the other ruffled Hradsky's few remaining hairs.

'Never mind, Norman, you can't win all the time.'

Hradsky turned slowly. He retrieved his hat and smoothed back his hair, his eyes glittered yellow.

'He's going to talk,' whispered Duff excitedly.

'I agree with you, Mr Charleywood, you can't win all the time,' said Norman Hradsky. It came out quite clearly with only a small catch on the 'c's' – they were always difficult letters for him. He stood up, put his hat back on his head and walked away.

'I will have a cheque delivered to your office early on Monday morning,' Max told them quietly without taking his eyes off the table. Then he stood up and followed Hradsky.

20

Sean came through from the bathroom, his beard in wild disorder and a bath-towel round his waist.

> 'The famous Duke of York
> He had ten thousand men
> He marched them up to the top of the hill
> And he marched them down again.'

He sang as he poured bay rum from a cut-glass bottle into his cupped hands and rubbed it into his hair. Duff sat in one of the gilt chairs watching him. Sean combed his hair carefully then smiled at himself in the mirror.

'You magnificent creature,' Sean told his reflection.

'You're getting fat,' Duff grunted.

Sean looked hurt. 'It's muscle.'

'You've got a backside on you like a hippopotamus.'

Sean removed his towel and turned his back to the mirror; he surveyed it over his shoulder.

'I need a heavy hammer to drive a long nail,' he protested.

'Oh, no,' groaned Duff. 'Your wit at this time of the morning is like pork for breakfast, heavy on the stomach.'

Sean took a silk shirt out of his drawer, held it like a toreador's cape, made two passes and swirled it onto his back with a half veronica.

'Olé!' applauded Duff wryly. Sean pulled on his trousers and sat to fit his boots.

'You're in a nice mood this morning,' he told Duff.

'I've just come through an emotional hurricane!'

'What's the trouble?'

'Candy wants a church wedding.'

'Is that bad?'

'Well, it's not good.'

'Why?'

255

'Is your memory so short?'

'Oh, you mean your other wife.'

'That's right, my other wife.'

'Have you told Candy about her?'

'Good God, no.' Duff looked horrified.

'Yes, I see your problem – what about Candy's husband? Doesn't that even the score between you?'

'No, he has gone to his reward.'

'Well, that's convenient. Does anyone else know you're married already?' Duff shook his head.

'What about Francois?'

'No, I never told him.'

'Well, what's your problem – take her down to the church and marry her.'

Duff looked uncomfortable.

'I don't mind marrying a second time in a magistrate's court, it would only be a couple of old Dutchmen I'd be cheating, but to go into a church –' Duff shook his head.

'I'd be the only one who'd know,' said Sean.

'You and the headman.'

'Duff,' Sean beamed at him. 'Duff, my boy, you have scruples – this is amazing!'

Duff squirmed a little in his chair.

'Let me think.' Sean held his forehead dramatically. 'Yes, yes, it's coming to me – that's it.'

'Come on, tell me.' Duff sat on the edge of his chair.

'Go to Candy and tell her it's all fixed, not only are you prepared to marry her in a church but you're even going to build your own church.'

'That's wonderful,' Duff murmured sarcastically, 'that's the way out of my difficulties all right.'

'Let me finish.' Sean started filling his silver cigar case. 'You also tell her that you want a civil ceremony as well – I believe that's what royalty do. Tell her that, it should win her over.'

'I still don't follow you.'

'Then you build your own chapel up at Xanadu – we can find a distinguished-looking character, dress him up in a dog collar and teach him the right words. That keeps Candy happy. Immediately after the service the priest takes the coach for Capetown. You take Candy down to the magistrate's office and that keeps you happy.'

Duff looked stunned then slowly his face broke into a great happy smile. 'Genius – pure inspired genius.'

Sean buttoned his waistcoat. 'Think nothing of it. And now if you'll excuse me I'll go and do some work – one of us has to make sufficient to allow you to indulge these strange fancies of yours.'

Sean shrugged on his coat, picked up his cane and swung it. The gold head gave it a balance like a hand-made shotgun. The silk next to his skin and the halo of bay rum round his head made him feel good.

He went down the stairs. Mbejane had the carriage waiting for him in the Hotel yard. The body tilted slightly at Sean's weight and the leather upholstery welcomed him with a yeilding softness. He lit his first cigar of the day and Mbejane smiled at him.

'I see you, Nkosi.'

'I see you also, Mbejane, what is that lump on the side of your head?'

'Nkosi, I was a little drunk, otherwise that ape of Basuto would never have touched me with his fighting stick.'

Mbejane rolled the carriage smoothly out of the yard and into the street.

'What were you fighting about?'

Mbejane shrugged. 'Must a man have a reason to fight?'

'It is usual.'

'It is in my memory that there was a woman,' said Mbejane.

'That is also usual – who won this fight?'

'The man bled a little, his friends took him away. The woman, when I left, was smiling in her sleep.'

Sean laughed, then ran his eyes over the undulating plain of Mbejane's bare back. It was definitely not in keeping. He hoped his secretary had remembered to speak to the tailor. They pulled up in front of his offices. One of his clerks hurried down off the veranda and opened the door of the carriage.

'Good morning, Mr Courtney.'

Sean went up the stairs with his clerk running ahead of him like a hunting dog.

'Good morning, Mr Courtney,' another polite chorus from the row of desks in the main office. Sean waved his cane at them and went through into his own office. His portrait leered at him from above the fireplace and he winked at it.

'What have we this morning, Johnson?'

'These requisitions, sir, and the pay cheques, sir, and development reports from the engineers, sir, and . . .'

Johnson was a greasy-haired little man in a greasy-looking alpaca coat; with each 'sir' he made a greasy little bow. He was efficient so Sean hired him, but that didn't mean he liked him.

'You got a stomach ache, Johnson?'

'No, sir.'

'Well, for God's sake, stand up straight, man.'

Johnson shot to attention.

'Now let's have them one at a time.'

Sean dropped into his chair. At this time of the day came the grind. He hated the paper work and so he tackled it with grim concentration, making random checks on the long rows of figures, trying to associate names with faces and querying requisitions that appeared exorbitant until finally he wrote his signature between the last of Johnson's carefully pencilled crosses and threw his pen onto the desk.

'What else is there?'

'Meeting with Mr Maxwell from the Bank at twelve-thirty, sir.'

'And then?'

'The agent for Brooke Bros. at one, and immediately after that Mr MacDougal, sir, then you're expected up at the Candy Deep mine.'

'Thank you, Johnson, I'll be at the Exchange as usual this morning if anything out of the ordinary comes up.'

'Very good, Mr Courtney. Just one other thing.' Johnson pointed at the brown paper parcel on the couch across the room. 'From your tailor.'

'Ah!' Sean smiled. 'Send my servant in here.' He walked across and opened the parcel. Within a few minutes Mbejane filled the doorway.

'Nkosi?'

'Mbejane – your new uniform.' Sean pointed at the clothes laid out on the couch. Mbejane's eyes switched to the gold and maroon finery, his expression suddenly dead.

'Put it on – come on, let's see how you look.'

Mbejane crossed to the couch and picked up the jacket. 'These are for me?'

'Yes, come on, put it on.' Sean laughed.

Mbejane hesitated, then slowly he loosened his loin cloth and let it drop. Sean watched him impatiently as he buttoned on the jacket and pantaloons, then he walked in a critical circle around the Zulu.

'Not bad,' he muttered, and then in Zulu, 'Is it not beautiful?'

Mbejane wriggled his shoulders against the unfamiliar feel of the cloth and said nothing.

'Well, Mbejane, do you like it?'

'When I was a child I went with my father to trade cattle at Port Natal. There was a man who went about the town with a monkey on a chair, the monkey danced and the people laughed and threw money to it. That monkey had such a suit as this. Nkosi, I do not think he was a very happy monkey.'

The smile slipped off Sean's face. 'You would rather wear your skins?'

'What I wear is the dress of a warrior of Zululand.'

There was still no expression on Mbejane's face. Sean opened his mouth to argue with him but before he could speak he lost his temper.

'You'll wear that uniform,' he shouted. 'You'll wear what I tell you to wear and you'll do it with a smile, do you hear me?'

'Nkosi, I hear you.' Mbejane picked up his loin cloth of leopard tails and left the office. When Sean went out to the carriage Mbejane was sitting on the driver's seat in his new livery. All the way to the Exchange his back was stiff with protest and neither of them spoke. Sean glared at the doorman of the Exchange, drank four brandies during the morning, rode back to his office again at noon scowling at Mbejane's still protesting back, shouted at Johnson, snapped at the bank manager, routed the representative from Brooke Bros. and drove out to the Candy Deep in a high old rage. But Mbejane's silence was impenetrable and Sean couldn't re-open the argument without sacrifice of pride. He burst into the new administrative building of the Candy Deep and threw the staff into confusion.

'Where's Mr du Toit?' he roared.

'He's down the Number Three shaft, Mr Courtney.'

'What the hell is he doing down there? He's supposed to be waiting for me here.'

'He didn't expect you for another hour, sir.'

'Well, get me some overalls and a mining helmet, don't just stand there.'

He clapped the tin hat on his head and stamped his heavy gumboots across to the Number Three shaft. The skip dropped him smoothly five hundred feet into the earth and he climbed out at the tenth level.

'Where's Mr du Toit?' he demanded of the shift boss at the lift station.

'He's up at the face, sir.'

The floor of the drive was rough and muddy; his gumboots squelched as he set off down the tunnel. His carbide lamp lit the uneven rock walls with a flat white light and he felt himself starting to sweat. Two natives pushing a cocopan back along the railway lines forced him to flatten himself against one wall to allow them to pass and while he waited he felt inside his overalls for his cigar case. As he pulled it out it slipped from his hand and plunked into the mud. The cocopan was gone by that time so he stooped to pick up the case. His ear came within an inch of the wall and a puzzled expression replaced his frown of annoyance. The rock was squeaking. He laid his ear against it. It sounded like someone grinding his teeth. He listened to it for a while trying to guess the cause; it wasn't the echo of shovels or drills, it wasn't water. He walked another thirty yards or so down the drive and listened again. Not so loud here but now the grinding noise was punctuated with an occasional metallic snap like the breaking of a knife blade. Strange, very strange; he had never heard anything like it before. He walked on down the drive, his bad mood lost in his preoccupation with this new problem. Before be reached the face he met Francois.

'Hello, Mr Courtney.' Sean had long since given up trying to stop Francois calling him that. '*Gott*, I'm sorry I wasn't there to meet you. I thought you were coming at three.'

'That's all right, Francois, how are you?'

'My rheumatism's been giving me blazes, Mr Courtney, but otherwise I'm all right. How's Mr Charleywood?'

'He's fine.' Sean couldn't restrain his curiosity any longer. 'Tell me something, Franz, just now I put my ear against the wall of the drive and I heard an odd noise, I couldn't make out what it was.'

'What kind of noise?'

'A sort of grinding, like – like . . .' Sean searched for words to describe it, 'like two pieces of glass being rubbed together.'

Francois's eyes flew wide open and then began to bulge, the colour of his face changed to grey and he caught Sean's arm.

'Where?'

'Back along the drive.'

The breath jammed in Francois's throat and he struggled to speak through it, shaking Sean's arm desperately.

'Cave-in!' he croaked. 'Cave-in, man!'

He started to run but Sean grabbed him. Francois struggled wildly.

'Francois, how many men up at the face?'

'Cave-in.' Francois's voice was now hysterically shrill. 'Cave-in.' He broke Sean's grip and raced away towards the lift station, the mud flying from his gumboots. His terror infected Sean and he ran a dozen paces after Francois before he stopped himself. For precious seconds he wavered with fear slithering round like a reptile in his stomach; go back to call the others and perhaps die with them or follow Francois and live. Then the fear in his belly found a mate, a thing just as slimy and cold; its name was shame, and shame it was that drove him back towards the face. There were five blacks and a white man there, bare-chested and shiny with sweat in the heat. Sean shouted those two words at them and they reacted the way bathers do when someone on the beach shouts 'shark'. The same moment of paralysed horror, then the panic. They came stampeding back along the tunnel. Sean ran with them, the mud sucked at his heavy boots and his legs were weak with easy living and riding in carriages. One by one the others passed him.

'Wait for me,' he wanted to scream. 'Wait for me.' He slipped on the greasy footing, scraping his shoulder on the rough wall as he fell, and dragged himself up again, mud plastered in his beard, the blood humming in his ears. Alone now he blundered on down the tunnel. With a crack like a rifle shot one of the thick shoring timbers broke under the pressure of the moving rock and dust smoked from the roof of the tunnel in front of him. He staggered on and all around him the earth was talking, groaning, protesting, with little muffled shrieks. The timbers joined in again, crackling and snapping, and as slowly as a theatre curtain the rock sagged down from above him. The tunnel was thick with dust that smothered the beam of his lamp and rasped his throat. He knew then that he wasn't going to make it but he ran on with the loose rock starting to fall about him. A lump hit his mining helmet and jarred him so that he nearly fell. Blinded by the swirling dust fog he crashed at full run into the abandoned cocopan that blocked the tunnel, he sprawled over the metal body of the trolley with his thighs bruised from the collision.

'Now I'm finished,' he thought, but instinctively he pulled himself up and started to grope his way around the cocopan to continue his flight. With a roar the tunnel in front of him collapsed. He dropped on his knees and crawled between the wheels of the cocopan, wriggling under the sturdy steel body just an instant before the roof above him collapsed also. The noise of the fall around him seemed to last for ever, but then it was over and the rustling and grating of the rock as it settled down was almost silence in comparison. His lamp was lost and the darkness pressed as heavily on him as the earth squeezed down on his tiny shelter. The air was solid with dust and he coughed; he coughed until his chest ached and he tasted salty blood in his mouth. There was hardly room to move, the steel body of the trolley was six inches above him, but he struggled until he managed to open the front of his overalls and tear a piece off the tail of his shirt. He held the silk like a surgical mask across his mouth and nose. It strained the dust out of the air so he could breathe. The dust settled; his coughing slowed and finally stopped. He felt surprise that he was still alive and cautiously he started exploring. He tried to straighten out his legs but his feet touched rock. He felt with his hands, six inches of head room and perhaps twelve inches on either side, warm mud underneath him and rock and steel all around. He took off his helmet and used it as a pillow. He was in a steel coffin buried five hundred feet deep, He felt the first flutter of panic. 'Keep your mind busy, think of something, think of anything but the rock around you, count your assets,' he told himself. He started to search his pockets, moving with difficulty in the cramped space.

'One silver cigar case with two Havanas.' He laid it down next to him.

'One box of matches, wet.' He placed it on top of the case.

'One pocket watch.'

'One handkerchief, Irish linen, monogrammed.'

'One comb, tortoiseshell – a man is judged by his appearance.' He started to comb his beard but found immediately that though this occupied his hands it left his mind free. He put the comb down next to his matches.

'Twenty-five pounds in gold sovereigns –' He counted them carefully, 'yes, twenty-five. I shall order a bottle of good champagne.' The dust was chalky in his mouth so he went on hurriedly, 'and a Malay girl from the Opera. No, why be mean – ten Malay girls. I'll have them dance for me, that'll pass the time. I'll promise them a sovereign each to bolster their enthusiasm.'

He continued the search, but there was nothing else. 'Gumboots, socks, well-cut trousers, shirt torn I'm afraid, overalls, a tin hat, and that's all.'

With his possessions laid out carefully beside him and his cell explored he had to start thinking. First he thought about his thirst. The mud in which he lay was too thick to yield water. He tried straining it through his shirt without success, and then he thought about air. It seemed quite fresh and he decided that sufficient was filtering in from the loosely packed rock around him to keep him alive.

To keep him alive – alive until the thirst killed. Until he died curled up like a foetus in the warm womb of the earth. He laughed, a worm in a dark warm womb. He laughed again and recognized it as the beginnings of panic, he thrust his fist into his mouth to stop himself, biting down hard on his knuckles. It was very quiet, the rock had stopped moving.

'How long will it take? Tell me, Doctor. How long have I got?'

'Well, you are sweating. You'll lose moisture quite rapidly. I'd say about four days,' he answered himself.

'What about hunger, Doctor?'

'Oh, no, don't worry about that, you'll be hungry, of course, but the thirst will kill you.'

'And typhoid, or is it typhus, I can never remember. What about that, Doctor?'

'If there were dead men trapped in here with you there'd be a good chance, but you're alone, you know.'

'Do you think I'll go mad, Doctor, not immediately, of course, but in a few days?'

'Yes, you'll go mad.'

'I've never been mad before, not that I know of anyway, but I think it will help to go mad now, don't you?'

'If you mean, will it make it easier, well, I don't know.'

'Ah! now you're being obscure – but I follow you. You mean

263

in that sleep of madness what dreams will come? You mean, will madness be more real than reality? You mean, will dying mad be worse than dying thirsty? But then I may beat the madness. This cocopan might buckle under the strain, after all there must be thousands of tons of rock bearing down on it. That's quite clever, you know, Doctor; as a medical man you should appreciate it. Mother Earth was saved but, alas, the child was stillborn, she bore down too hard.' Sean had spoken aloud, and now he felt foolish. He picked up a piece of stone and tapped the cocopan with it.

'It sounds firm enough. A most pleasing noise, really.' He beat harder on the metal body – one, two, three, one, two, three – then dropped the stone. Soft as an echo, distant as the moon, he heard his taps repeated. His whole body stiffened at the sound, and he started to shiver with excitement. He snatched up the stone: three times he rapped, and three times the answer came back to him.

'They heard me, sweet merciful Christ, they heard me.' He laughed breathlessly. 'Dear Mother Earth, don't bear down, please don't bear down. Just be patient. Wait a few days and by Caesarian they'll take this child out of your womb.'

Mbejane waited until Sean disappeared down the Number Three shaft before he took off his new jacket. He folded it carefully on the driver's seat next to him. He sat and enjoyed the feel of the sun on his skin for a while, then he climbed off the carriage and went to the horses. He took them one at a time to the trough for water then returned them to their harnesses, buckling them in loosely. He picked up his spears from the footboard and moved across to a patch of short grass next to the administrative building. He sat down and went to work on the blade, humming softly to himself as he honed. At last he ran an expert thumb along each edge, grunted, shaved a few hairs off his forearm, smiled contentedly and laid his spears beside him in the grass. He lay back and the sun warmed him to sleep.

The shouting woke him. He sat up and automatically checked the height of the sun. He had slept an hour or more. Duff was shouting and Francois, mud-splattered and frightened-looking, was answering him. They were standing together in front of the administrative building. Duff's horse was sweating. Mbejane stood up and went across to them; he listened closely, trying to understand their staccato voices. They went too fast for him, but something was wrong, that much he knew.

'It's caved in almost to the Number Ten lift station,' Francois said.

'You left him in there,' accused Duff.

'I thought he was following me, but he turned back.'

'What for – why did he turn back?'

'To call the others –'

'Have you started clearing the drive?'

'No, I was waiting for you.'

'You stupid bloody idiot, he might be alive in there . . . every minute is vital.'

'But he hasn't a chance, Mr Charleywood, he must be dead.'

'Shut up, damn you.'

Duff swung away from him and started running towards the shaft. There was a crowd gathered beneath the high steel structure of the head gear, and suddenly Mbejane knew it was Sean. He caught up with Duff before he reached the shaft.

'Is it the Nkosi?'

'Yes.'

'What has happened?'

'The rock has fallen on him.'

Mbejane pushed his way into the skip next to Duff and neither of them spoke again until they reached the tenth level. They went down the drive, only a short way before they reached the end. There were men there with crowbars and shovels standing undecided, waiting for orders, and Mbejane shouldered a path through them. He and Duff stood together in front of the new wall of broken rock that sealed the tunnel, and the silence went on and on. Then Duff turned on the white shift-boss.

'Were you at the face?'

'Yes.'

'He went back to call you, didn't he?'

'Yes.'

'And you left him there?'

The man couldn't look at Duff.

'I thought he was following us,' he muttered.

'You thought only of your own miserable skin,' Duff told him, 'you filthy little coward, you slimy yellow bastard, you . . .'

265

Mbejane caught Duff's arm and Duff stopped his tirade. They all heard it then – clink, clink, clink.

'It's him – it must be him,' whispered Duff, 'he's alive!' He snatched a crowbar from one of the natives and knocked against the side of the tunnel. They waited, their breathing the only sound, until the answer came back to them louder and sharper than before. Mbejane took the crowbar out of Duff's hands. He thrust it into a crack in the rock jam and his back muscles bunched as he heaved. The bar bent like a liquorice stick, he threw it away and went at the stone with his bare hands.

'You!' Duff snapped at the shift-boss. 'We'll need timber to shore up as we clear the fall – get it.' He turned to the natives. 'Four of you working on the face at one time – the rest of you carry the stone away as we loosen it.'

'Do you want any dynamite?' asked the shift-boss.

'And bring the rock down a second time? Use your brains, man. Go and get that timber and call Mr du Toit while you're at the surface.'

In four hours they cleared fifteen feet of tunnel, breaking the larger slabs of stone with sledge hammers and prising the pieces out of the jam. Duff's body ached and his hands were raw. He had to rest. He walked slowly back to the lift station and there he found blankets and a huge dish of soup.

'Where did this come from?'

'Candy's Hotel, sir. Half Johannesburg is waiting at the head of the shaft.'

Duff huddled into a blanket and drank a little of the soup. 'Where's du Toit?'

'I couldn't find him, sir.'

Up at the face Mbejane worked on. The first four natives came back to rest and fresh men took their place. Mbejane led them, grunting an order occasionally but otherwise reserving his strength for the assault on the rock. For an hour Duff rested and when he returned to the head of the tunnel Mbejane was still there. Duff watched him curl his arms round a piece of stone the size of a beer keg, brace his legs and tear the stone out of the jam. Earth and loose rock followed it burying Mbejane's legs to the knees and Duff jumped forward to help him.

Another two hours and Duff had to rest again. This time he led Mbejane back with him, gave him a blanket and made him drink a little soup. They sat next to each other with their backs against the wall of the tunnel and blankets over their shoulders. The shift-boss came to Duff.

'Mrs Rautenbach sent this down for you, sir.'

It was a half-bottle of brandy.

'Tell her, thank you.' Duff pulled the cork with his teeth and swallowed twice. It brought the tears into his eyes – he offered the bottle to Mbejane.

'It is not fitting,' Mbejane demurred.

'Drink.'

Mbejane drank, wiped the mouth of the bottle carefully on his blanket and handed it back. Duff took another swallow and offered it again but Mbejane shook his head.

'A little of that is strength, too much is weakness. There is work to do now.'

Duff corked the bottle.

'How long before we reach him?' asked Mbejane.

'Another day, maybe two.'

'A man can die in two days,' mused the Zulu.

'Not one with a body like a bull and a temper like a devil,' Duff assured him. Mbejane smiled and Duff went on groping for his words in Zulu.

'You love him, Mbejane?'

'Love is a woman's word.'

Mbejane inspected one of his thumbs; the nail was torn loose, standing up like a tombstone; he took it between his teeth, pulled it off and spat it onto the floor of the drive. Duff shuddered as he watched.

'Those baboons will not work unless they are driven.' Mbejane stood up. 'Are you rested?'

'Yes,' lied Duff, and they went back to the face.

Sean lay in the mud with his head on the hard pillow of the helmet. The darkness was as solid as the rock around him. He tried to imagine where the one ended and the other began – by doing that he could stop himself feeling his thirst so strongly. He could hear the ring of hammer on stone and the rattle of rock falling free but it never seemed to come any closer. The whole side of his body was stiff and sore but he could not turn over, his knees caught on the cocopan every time he tried and the air in his little cave was starting to taste stale – his head ached. He moved again, restlessly, and his hand brushed the small pile of sovereigns. He struck at them, scattering them into the mud. They were the bait that had led him into this trap. Now he would give them, and all the millions of others, for just the feel of the wind in his beard and the sun in his face. The darkness clung to him, thick and cloying as black treacle; it seemed to fill his nose, his throat and eyes, smothering him. He groped and found the matchbox. For a few seconds of light he would burn up most of the precious oxygen in his cave and call it fair exchange – but the box was sodden. He struck match after match but the wet heads crumbled without a spark and he threw them away and clenched his eyelids to keep the darkness out. Bright colours formed in front of his closed eyes, moving and rearranging themselves until suddenly and very clearly they formed a picture of Garrick's face. He hadn't thought about his family for months, he had been too busy reaping the golden harvest, but now memories crowded back. There were so many things he had forgotten. Everything else had become unimportant when compared with power and gold – even lives, men's lives, had meant nothing. But now it was his own life, teetering on the edge of the black cliff.

The sound of the sledge-hammers broke into his thoughts again. There were men on the other side of the blocked tunnel trying to save him, working their way into the treacherous rock pile which might collapse again at any minute. People were more valuable than the poisonous metal, the little gold discs that lay smugly beside him in the mud while men struggled to save him.

He thought of Garry, crippled by his careless shotgun, father to the bastard he had sired, of Ada whom he had left without a word of goodbye, of Karl Lochtkamper with the pistol in his hand and half his head splattered across the floor of his bedroom, of other nameless men dead or broken because of him.

Sean ran his tongue across his lips and listened to the hammers; he was certain they were nearer now.

'If I get out of here, it'll be different. I swear it.'

Mbejane rested for four hours in the next thirty-six. Duff

watched the flesh melt off him in sweat. He was killing himself. Duff was worn out; he could no longer work with his hands but he was directing the teams who were shoring up the reclaimed tunnel. By the second evening they had cleared a hundred feet of the drive. Duff paced it out and when he reached the face he spoke to Mbejane.

'How long since you last signalled to him?'

Mbejane stepped back with a sledge-hammer in his tattered hands; its shaft was sticky and brown with blood.

'An hour ago and even then it sounded as though there were but the length of a spear between us.'

Duff took a crowbar from one of the other natives and tapped the rock. The answer came immediately.

'He's hitting something made of iron,' Duff said. 'It sounds as though he's only a few feet away. Mbejane, let these other men take over. If you wish you can stay and watch but you must rest again now.'

For answer Mbejane lifted the hammer and swung it against the face. The rock he hit cracked and two of the natives stepped up and levered it loose with their crowbars. At the back of the hole it left in the wall they could see the corner of the cocopan. Everyone stared at it, then Duff shouted.

'Sean, Sean, can you hear me?'

'Stop talking and get me out of here.' Sean's voice was hoarse with thirst and dust, and muffled by the rock.

'He's under the cocopan.'

'It's him.'

'Nkosi, are you all right?'

'We've found him.'

The shouts were picked up by the men working behind them in the drive and passed back to those waiting at the lift station.

'They've found him – he's all right – they've found him.'

Duff and Mbejane jumped forward together, their exhaustion completely forgotten. They cleared the last few lumps of rock and with their shoulders touching knelt and peered under the cocopan.

'Nkosi, I see you.'

'I see you also, Mbejane, what took you so long?'

'Nkosi, there were a few small stones in the way.'

Mbejane reached under the cocopan and with his hands under Sean's armpits pulled him out.

'What a hell of a place you chose to go to ground in, laddie. How are you feeling?'

'Give me some water and I'll be all right.'

'Water – bring water,' shouted Duff.

Sean gulped it, trying to drink the whole mug in one mouthful. He coughed and it shot out of his nose.

'Easy, laddie, easy.' Duff thumped his back. Sean drank the next mugful more slowly and finished panting from the effort.

'That was good.'

'Come on, we've got a doctor waiting up on top.' Duff draped a blanket over his shoulders. Mbejane picked Sean up across his chest.

'Put me down, damn you, I haven't forgotten how to walk.'

Mbejane set him down gently, but his legs buckled like those of a man just out of bed from a long illness and he clutched at Mbejane's arm. Mbejane picked him up again and carried him down to the lift station. They rode up in the skip into the open.

'The moon's shining. And the stars – my God, they're beautiful.' There was wonder in Sean's voice; he sucked the night air into his lungs but it was too rich for him and he started coughing again. There were people waiting at the head of the shaft and they crowded round them as they stepped out of the skip.

'How is he?'

'Are you all right, Sean?'

'Doc Symmonds is waiting in the office.'

'Quickly, Mbejane,' said Duff, 'get him out of the cold.'

One on either side of him they hurried Sean across to the administrative building and laid him on the couch in Francois's office. Symmonds checked him over, looked down his throat and felt his pulse.

'Have you got a closed carriage here?'

'Yes,' Duff answered.

'Well, wrap him up warmly and get him home to bed. With the dust and bad air he's been breathing there's serious danger of pneumonia. I'll come down with you and give him a sedative.'

'I won't need one, Doc,' Sean grinned at him.

'I think I know what's best for you, Mr Courtney.' Doctor Symmonds was a young man. He was the fashionable doctor among the rich of Johannesburg and he took it very seriously.

'Now if you please, we'll get you to your hotel.' He started to pack his instruments back into his valise.

'You're the doctor,' Sean agreed, 'but before we go will you have a look at my servant's hands, they're in a hell of a mess. There's hardly any meat left on them.'

Doctor Symmonds did not look up from what he was doing. 'I have no Kaffir practice, Mr Courtney, I'm sure you'll find some other doctor to attend to him when we get back to town.'

Sean sat up slowly, he let the blankets slip off his shoulders. He walked across to Doctor Symmonds and held him by the throat against the wall. The doctor had a fine pair of waxed moustaches and Sean took one of them between the thumb and forefinger of his free hand: he plucked it out like feathers from the carcass of a dead fowl and Doctor Symmonds squealed.

'Starting now, Doctor, you have a Kaffir practice,' Sean told him. He pulled the handkerchief out of Symmonds' top pocket and dabbed at the little drops of blood on the doctor's bare upper lip.

'Be a good fellow – see to my servant.'

21

When Sean woke the next morning the hands of the grandfather clock across the bedroom pointed at the top of their dial. Candy was in the room opening the curtains and with her were two waiters, each with a loaded tray.

'Good morning, how is our hero this morning?' The waiters put down their trays and went out as she came across to Sean's bed.

Sean blinked the sleep out of his eyes. 'My throat feels as though I've just finished a meal of broken glass.'

'That's the dust,' Candy told him and laid her hands on his forehead. Sean's hand sneaked round behind her and she squeaked as he pinched her. Standing well away from the bed she rubbed her bottom and made a face at him.

'There's nothing wrong with you!'

'Good, then I'll get up.' Sean started to pull back the bed-clothes.

'Not until the doctor's had a look at you, you won't.'

'Candy, if that bastard puts one foot in this room I'll punch him so hard in the mouth his teeth will march out of his backside like soldiers.'

Candy turned to the breakfast trays to cover her smile. 'That's no way to talk in front of a lady. But don't worry, it isn't Symmonds.'

'Where's Duff?' Sean asked.

'He's having a bath, then he's coming to eat breakfast with you.'

'I'll wait for him, but give me a cup of coffee in the meantime, there's a sweetheart.'

She brought the coffee to him. 'Your savage has been camping on my trail all morning, he wants to see you. I've just about had to put an armed guard on this room to keep him out.'

Sean laughed. 'Will you send him in, Candy?'

She went to the door and stopped with a hand on the latch.

'It's nice to have you back, Sean, don't do anything silly like that again, will you?'

'That's a promise,' Sean assured her.

Mbejane came quickly and stood in the doorway. 'Nkosi, is it well with you?'

Sean looked at the iodine-stained bandages on his hands and the maroon and gold livery without answering. Then he rolled on his back and stared at the ceiling. 'I sent for my servant and instead there comes a monkey on a chain.'

Mbejane stood still, his face expressionless but for the hurt in his eyes.

'Go – find my servant. You will know him by his dress which is that of a warrior of Zululand.'

It took a few seconds for the laughter to start rolling around in Mbejane's belly; it shook his shoulders and creased the corners of his mouth. He closed the door very softly behind him and when he came back in his loin cloth Sean grinned at him.

'Ah! I see you, Mbejane.'

'And I see you also.'

He stood by the bed and they talked. They spoke little of the cave-in and not at all of Mbejane's part in the rescue. Between them it was understood, words could only damage it. Perhaps they would talk of it later, but not now.

'Tomorrow, will you need the carriage?' Mbejane asked at last.

'Yes – go now. Eat and sleep.' Sean reached out and touched Mbejane's arm. Just that small physical contact – that almost guilty touching – and Mbejane left him.

Then Duff came in in a silk dressing-gown and they ate eggs and steak from the trays and Duff sent down for a bottle of wine just to rinse the dust out of their throats once more.

'They tell me Francois is still down at the Bright Angels – he's been on the drunk ever since he got out of that shaft. When he sobers up he can come to the office and collect his pay packet.'

Sean sat up. 'You're going to fire him?'

'I'm going to fire him so high he'll only touch ground when he reaches Capetown.'

'What the hell for?' demanded Sean.

'What for?' Duff echoed. 'What for? For running – that's what for.'

'Duff, he was in a cave-in at Kimberley, wasn't he?'

'Yes.'

'Broke his legs, didn't you say?'

'Yes.'

'Shall I tell you something? If it were to happen to me a second time I'd run as well.'

Duff filled his wine glass without answering.

'Send down to the Bright Angels, tell him alcohol is bad for the liver – that should sober him – tell him unless he's back at work by tomorrow morning we'll dock it off his pay,' Sean said. Duff looked at him with a puzzled expression. 'What is this?'

'I had some time to think while I was down in that hole. I decided that to get to the top you don't have to stamp on everyone you meet.'

'Ah, I understand.' Duff gave his lopsided grin. 'A good resolution – New Year in August. Well, that's all right, you had me worried there, I thought a rock had fallen on your head. I also make good resolutions.'

'Duff, I don't want Francois fired.'

'All right, all right – he stays on. If you like we can open a soup kitchen at the office and turn Xanadu into a home for the aged.'

'Oh, go and burst. I just don't think it's necessary to fire Francois, that's all.'

'Who's arguing? I agreed with you, didn't I? I have deep respect for good resolutions. I make them all the time.'

Duff pulled his chair up to the bed, 'Quite by chance I happen to have a pack of cards with me.' He took them out of his dressing-gown pocket. 'Would you care for a game of Klabejas?'

Sean lost fifty pounds before he was saved by the arrival of the new doctor. The doctor tapped his chest and tut-tutted, looked down his throat and tut-tutted, wrote out a prescription and confined him to bed for the rest of the day. He was just leaving when Jock and Trevor Heyns arrived. Jock had a bunch of flowers which he presented to Sean in an embarrassed fashion.

Then the room began to fill in earnest: the rest of the crowd from the Exchange arrived, someone had brought a case of champagne, a poker game started in one corner and a political meeting in another.

'Who does this Kruger think he is, anyway – God or something? You know what he said last time we went to see him about getting the vote, he said "Protest, protest – I have the guns and you have not! " '

'Three Kings wins – you *are* holding cards!'

' – you wait and see. Consolidated Wits. will hit thirty shillings by the end of the month.'

' – and the taxes – they're putting another twenty per cent on dynamite.'

' – a new piece at the Opera, Jock's got a season ticket on her – no one else has had a look in yet.'

'All right, you two – stop that. If you want to fight go outside – this is a sick room.'

'This bottle's empty – break open a new one, Duff.'

Sean lost another hundred to Duff and then a little after five Candy came in. She was horrified. 'Out, all of you, out!'

The room emptied as quickly as it had filled and Candy wandered around picking up cigar butts and empty glasses.

'The vandals! Someone's burnt a hole in the carpet and look at this – champagne spilt all over the table.'

Duff coughed and started pouring himself another drink.

'Don't you think you've had enough of that, Dufford?'

Duff put down his glass. 'And it's time you went and changed for dinner.' Duff winked sheepishly at Sean, but he went.

Duff and Candy came back to his room after supper and had a liqueur with him.

'Now to sleep,' Candy commanded and went across to draw the curtains.

'It's still early,' protested Duff with no effect. Candy blew the lamp out.

Sean was not tired, he had lain in bed all day and now his brain was overactive. He lit a cigar and smoked, listening to the street noises below his window and it was past midnight before he finally drifted off. When he woke, he woke screaming, for the darkness was on him again and the blankets pressed down on him suffocating him. He fought them off and stumbled blindly across the room. He had to have air and light. He ran into the thick velvet curtains and they closed around his face; he tore himself free and hit the french windows with his shoulder; they burst open and he was out on the balcony, out in the cold air with the moon fat and yellow in the sky above him. His gasping slowed until he was breathing normally again. He went back inside and lit the lamp, then he went through to Duff's empty bedroom. There was a copy of *Twelfth Night* on the bedside table and he took it back to his own room. He sat with the lamp at his elbow and forced his eyes to follow the printed words even though they made no sense. He read until the dawn showed grey through the open windows, then he put down the book. He shaved, dressed and went down the back stairs into the hotel yard. He found Mbejane in the stables.

'Put a saddle on the grey.'

'Where are you going, Nkosi?'

'To kill a devil.'

'Then I will come with you.'

'No, I will be back before midday.'

He rode up to the Candy Deep and tied his horse outside the administration buildings. There was a sleepy clerk in the front offices.

'Good morning, Mr Courtney. Can I help you?'

'Yes. Get me overalls and a helmet.'

Sean went to the Number Three shaft. There was a frost on the ground that crunched as he walked on it and the sun had just cleared the eastern ridge of the Witwatersrand. Sean stopped at the hoist shed and spoke to the driver.

'Has the new shift gone on yet?'

'Half an hour ago, sir.' The man was obviously surprised to see him. 'The night shift finished blasting at five o'clock.'

'Good – drop me down to the fourteenth level.'

'The fourteenth is abandoned now, Mr Courtney, there's no one working there.'

'Yes, I know.'

Sean walked across to the head of the shaft. He lit his carbide lamp and while he waited for the skip he looked out across the valley. The air was clear and the sun threw long shadows. Everything stood out in sharp relief. He had not been up this early in the morning for many months and he had almost forgotten how fresh and delicately coloured a new day was. The skip stopped in front of him. He took a deep breath and stepped into it. When he reached the fourteenth level he got out and pushed the recall signal for the skip and he was alone in the earth again. He walked up the tunnel and the echo of his footsteps went with him. He was sweating and a muscle in his cheek started to jerk; he reached the face and set the carbide lamp down on a ledge of rock. He checked to make sure his matches were in his pocket, then he blew out the lamp. The darkness came squeezing down on him. The first half hour was the worst. Twice he had the matches in his hand ready to strike but he stopped himself. The sweat formed cold wet patches under his arms and the darkness filled his open mouth and choked him. He had to fight for each lungful of air, suck in, hold it, breathe out. First he regulated his breathing and then slowly, slowly his mind came under control and he knew he had won. He waited another ten minutes breathing easily and sitting relaxed with his back against the side of the tunnel, then he lit the lamp. He was smiling as he went back to the lift station and signalled for the skip. When he reached the surface he stepped out and lit a cigar; he flicked the match into the square black opening of the shaft.

'So much for you, little hole.'

He walked back towards the administration building. What he could not know was that the Number Three shaft of the Candy Deep was to take something from him just as valuable as his courage and that, next time, what it took it would not give back. But that was many years ahead.

22

By October Xanadu was nearly finished. The three of them drove
out to it as usual one Saturday afternoon.

'The builder is only six months behind schedule – now he
says he'll be finished by Christmas and I haven't found the
courage yet to ask him which Christmas,' Sean remarked.

'It's all the alterations Candy has thought up,' Duff said. 'She's
got the poor man so confused he doesn't know whether he's a
boy or a girl.'

'Well, if you'd consulted me in the first place it would have
saved a lot of trouble,' Candy told them.

The carriage turned in through the marble gates and they
looked around them. Already the lawns were smooth and green
and the jacaranda trees lining the drive were shoulder high.

'I think it's going to live up to its name – that gardener's doing
a good job,' Sean spoke with satisfaction.

'Don't you call him a gardener to his face or we'll have a strike
on our hands. He's a horticulturist,' Duff smiled across at him.

'Talking about names,' Candy interrupted, 'don't you think
Xanadu is – well, a bit outlandish?'

'No, I do not,' Sean said. 'I picked it myself. I think it's a
damn good name.'

'It's not dignified – why don't we call it Fair Oaks?'

'Firstly, because there isn't an oak tree within fifty miles and
secondly because it's already called Xanadu.'

'Don't get cross, it was just a suggestion.'

The builder met them at the top of the drive and they began
the tour of the house. That took an hour, then they left the
builder and went out into the garden. They found the gardener
with a gang of natives near the north boundary.

'How's it going, Joubert?' Duff greeted him.

'Not bad, Mr Charleywood, but it takes time you know.'

'You've done a damn fine job so far.'

278

'It's kind of you to say so, sir.'

'When are you going to start laying out my maze?'

The gardener looked surprised; he glanced at Candy, opened his mouth, closed it again and looked once more at Candy.

'Oh, I told Joubert not to worry about the maze.'

'Why did you do that? I wanted a maze – ever since I visited Hampton Court as a child I've wanted my own maze.'

'They're silly things,' Candy told him. 'They just take up a lot of space and they're not even nice to look at.'

Sean thought Duff was going to argue, but he didn't. They talked to the gardener a little longer, then they walked back across the lawns in front of the house towards the chapel.

'Dufford, I've left my parasol in the carriage, would you mind getting it for me?' Candy asked.

When Duff was gone Candy took Sean's arm.

'It's going to be a lovely home. We're going to be very happy here.'

'Have you two decided on a date yet?' Sean asked.

'We want the house finished first so we can move straight in. I think we'll make it some time in February next year.'

They reached the chapel and stopped in front of it.

'It's a sweet little church.' Candy spoke dreamily. 'And such a nice idea of Dufford's – a special church of our own.'

Sean shuffled uncomfortably. 'Yes,' he agreed, 'it's a very romantic idea.' He glanced over his shoulder and saw Duff coming back with the parasol.

'Candy – it's none of my business. I don't know anything about marriage, but I know about training horses – you break them to the halter before you put the saddle on their backs.'

'I don't follow you.' Candy looked puzzled. 'What are you trying to say?'

'Nothing – just forget it. Here comes Duff.'

When they got back to the hotel there was a note at the reception desk for Sean. They went through into the main lounge and Candy went off to check the menu for dinner. Sean opened the envelope and read the note:

'I should like to meet you and Mr Charleywood to discuss a matter of some importance. I will be at my hotel after dinner this evening and hope that it will be convenient for you to call on me then. N. Hradsky.'

Sean passed the note across to Duff.

'What do you suppose he wants?'

'He has heard of your deadly skill as a Klabejas player. He wants to take lessons,' Duff answered.

'Shall we go?'

'Of course. You know I can't resist Norman's exhilarating company.'

It was a superb dinner. The crayfish, packed in ice, had come up from Capetown by express coach.

'Candy – Sean and I are going across to see Hradsky. We might be back a little late,' Duff told her when they were finished.

'As long as it's Hradsky,' Candy smiled at him. 'Don't get lost – I have my spies at the Opera House you know.'

'Shall we take the carriage?' Duff asked Sean, and Sean noticed that he hadn't laughed at Candy's joke.

'It's only two blocks, we might as well walk.'

They walked in silence. Sean felt his dinner settling down comfortably inside him, he belched softly and took another puff from his cigar. When they had almost reached the Grand National Hotel Duff spoke.

'Sean. . .' He stopped.

'Yes?' Sean prompted him.

'About Candy. . .' He stopped again.

'She's a fine girl,' Sean prompted again.

'Yes, she's a fine girl.'

'Is that all you wanted to say?'

'Well – oh! never mind. Let's go and see what Saul and David want.'

Max met them at the door of Hradsky's suite.

'Good evening, gentlemen, I am so pleased you could come.'

'Hello, Max.' Duff went past him to where Hradsky was standing in front of the fireplace.

'Norman, my dear fellow, how are you?'

Hradsky nodded an acknowledgement and Duff took hold of the lapels of Hradsky's coat and adjusted them carefully; then he picked an imaginary piece of fluff off his shoulder.

'You have a way with clothes, Norman. Don't you agree that Norman has a way with clothes, Sean? I know of no one else who can put on a twenty-guinea suit and make it look like a half-filled bag of oranges.' He patted Hradsky's arm affectionately. 'Yes, thank you – I will have a drink.' He went across to the liquor cabinet and poured one for himself. 'Now, what can you gentlemen do for me?'

Max glanced at Hradsky and Hradsky nodded.

'I will come to the point immediately,' said Max. 'Our two groups of companies are the largest on the Witwatersrand.'

Duff put his glass back on top of the cabinet and dropped his grin. Sean sat down in one of the armchairs, his expression also serious; both of them could guess what was coming.

'In the past,' continued Max, 'we have worked together on numerous occasions and we have both benefited from it. The next logical step, of course, is to combine our strength, pool our resources and go on together to new greatness.'

'I take it that you are proposing a merger?'

'Precisely, Mr Courtney, a merger of these two vast financial ventures.'

Sean leaned back in his chair and started to whistle softly. Duff picked up his glass again and took a sip.

'Well, gentlemen, what are your feelings on the subject?' asked Max.

'Have you got a proposal worked out, Max, something definite for us to think about?'

'Yes, Mr Courtney, I have.' Max went to the stinkwood desk which filled one corner of the room and picked up a sheaf of papers. He carried it across to Sean. Sean scanned through it.

'You've done quite a bit of work here, Max. It's going to take us a day or two to work out exactly what you are offering.'

'I appreciate that, Mr Courtney. Take as long as you wish. We have worked for a month to draw up that scheme and I hope our labours have not been in vain. I think you will find our offer very generous.'

Sean stood up.

'We'll contact you again in the next few days, Max. Shall we go, Duff ?'

Duff finished his drink.

'Goodnight, Max, look after Norman. He's very precious to us, you know.'

They went to their building on Eloff Street. Sean let them in through one of the side doors, lit the lamps in his office and Duff pulled up an extra chair to the desk. By two o'clock the following morning they understood the essentials of Hradsky's offer. Sean stood up and went to open one of the windows, for the room was thick with cigar smoke. He came back and flopped onto the couch, arranged a cushion behind his head and looked at Duff.

'Let's hear what you've got to say.'

Duff tapped his teeth with a pencil while he arranged his words.

'Let's decide first if we want to join with him.'

'If he makes it worth our while, we do,' Sean answered.

'I agree with you – but only if he makes it worth our while.' Duff laid back in his chair. 'Now the next point. Tell me, laddie, what is the first thing that strikes you about this scheme of Norman's?'

'We get nice-sounding titles and fat cash payments and Hradsky gets control,' Sean answered.

'You have laid your finger on the heart of it – Norman wants control. More than money, Norman wants control, so that he can sit at the top of the pile, look down on everyone else and say, "All right, you bastards, what if I do stutter?" '

Duff stood up, he walked round the desk and stopped in front of Sean's couch.

'Now for my next question. Do we give him control?'

'If he pays our price, then we give him control,' Sean answered. Duff turned away and went across to the open window.

'You know I rather like the feeling of being top man myself,' he said thoughtfully.

'Listen, Duff, we came here to make money. If we go in with Hradsky we'll make more,' Sean said.

'Laddie, we've got so much now that we could fill this room waist deep in sovereigns. We've got more than we'll ever be able to spend and I like being top man.'

'Hradsky's more powerful than we are – let's face up to that. He's got his diamond interests as well, so you're not top man even now. If we join him you still won't be top man but you'll be a damn sight richer.'

'Unassailable logic,' Duff nodded. 'I agree with you then. Hradsky gets control but he pays for it; we'll put him through the wringer until he's dry.'

Sean swung his legs off the couch. 'Agreed – now let's take this scheme of his by the throat, tear it to pieces and build it up again to suit ourselves.'

Duff looked at his watch. 'It's after two o'clock. We'll leave it now and start on it when we're fresh in the morning.'

They had their lunch brought down to the office the next day, and ate it at the desk. Johnson, who had been sent up to the Stock Exchange with instructions to keep an eye on prices and call them immediately anything out of the ordinary happened, reported back after high change.

'It's been as quiet as a graveyard all day, sir, there's all sorts of rumours flying about. Seems someone saw the lights burning in this office at two o'clock this morning. Then when you didn't come to the Exchange but sent me instead – well, I can tell you, sir, there were a lot of questions asked.' Johnson hesitated, then his curiosity got the better of him.

'Can I help you at all, sir?' He started sidling across towards the desk.

'I think we can manage on our own, Johnson. Shut the door as you go out, please.'

At half-past seven they decided it was enough for one day and they went back to the hotel. As they walked into the lobby Sean saw Trevor Heyns disappear into the lounge and heard his voice.

'Here they are!'

Almost immediately Trevor appeared again with his brother.

'Hello, boys,' Jock appeared surprised to see them. 'What are you doing here?'

'We live here,' said Duff.

'Oh, yes, of course. Well, come and have a drink with us.' Jock smiled expansively.

'And then you can pump us and find out what we've been doing all day,' Duff suggested.

Jock looked embarrassed. 'I don't know what you mean, I just thought we'd have a drink together, that's all.'

'Thanks all the same, Jock, we've had a hard day. I think we'll just go on up to bed,' Duff said. They were halfway across the lobby before Duff turned back to where the two brothers were standing.

'I'll tell you boys something,' he said in a stage whisper. 'This is really big – it's so big it takes a while for the mind to grasp it. When you two realize that it's been right there under your noses all the time, you're going to kick yourselves.'

They left the Heyns brothers in the lobby staring after them and went up the stairs.

'That wasn't very kind,' Sean laughed. 'They won't sleep for a week.'

23

When neither Sean nor Duff put in an appearance at the Exchange the next morning, the rumours surged round the members' lounge and the prices started running amok. Reliable information that Sean and Duff had struck a rich new goldfield across the vaal sent the prices up like rocketing snipe; then twenty minutes later the denial came in and clipped fifteen shillings a share off the Courtney–Charleywood stock. Johnson ran backwards and forwards between the office and the Exchange all morning. By eleven he was so tired he could hardly talk.

'Don't worry any more, Johnson,' Sean told him. 'Here's a sovereign – go down to the Grand National and buy yourself a drink, you've had a hard morning.'

One of Jock Heyns's men, who had been detailed off to watch the Courtney–Charleywood offices, followed Johnson down to the Grand National and heard him place his order with the barman. He raced back to the Exchange and reported to Jock.

'Their head clerk has just gone and ordered himself a bottle of French champagne,' he panted.

'Good God!' Jock nearly jumped out of his chair and beside him Trevor signalled frantically for his clerk.

'Buy,' he whispered in the man's ear. 'Buy every scrap of their script you can lay your hands on.'

Across the lounge Hradsky settled down a little further in his chair; he clasped his hands contentedly over the front of his stomach and he very nearly smiled.

By midnight Sean and Duff had completed their counterproposal to Hradsky's offer.

'How do you think Norman will react to it?' asked Sean.

'I hope his heart is strong enough to stand the shock,' Duff grinned. 'The only reason that his jaw won't hit the floor is that his great gut will be in the way.'

'Shall we go down to his hotel now and show him?' suggested Sean.

'Laddie, laddie.' Duff shook his head sorrowfully. 'After all the time I've spent on your education, and you still haven't learned.'

'What do we do then?'

'We send for him, laddie, we make him come to us. We play him on the home ground.'

'How does that help?' Sean asked.

'It gives us an advantage immediately – it makes him remember that he's the one doing the asking.'

Hradsky came down to their office at ten o'clock the next morning; he came in state driven behind a four-in-hand and attended by Max and two secretaries. Johnson met them at the front door and ushered them into Sean's office.

'Norman, dear old Norman, I'm delighted to see you,' Duff greeted him and, fully aware of the fact that Hradsky never smoked, Duff thrust a cheroot between his lips. When everyone was seated Sean opened the meeting.

'Gentlemen, we have spent some time examining your proposition and in the main we find it just, fair and equitable.'

'Hear, hear,' Duff agreed politely.

'At the outset I want to make it quite clear,' Sean went on, 'that Mr Charleywood and myself feel strongly that the union of our two ventures is desirable – nay! essential. If you will forgive the quotation, *"ex unitate vires".*'

'Hear, hear – hear, hear:' Duff lit his cigar.

'As I was saying, we have examined your proposition and we accept it readily and happily, with the exception of a few minor details which we have listed.' Sean picked up the thick pile of paper. 'Perhaps you would care to glance through it and then we can proceed to the drawing-up of a formal agreement.'

Max accepted the sheaf gingerly. 'If you want privacy, Mr Charleywood's office which adjoins this room is at your disposal.'

Hradsky took his band next door and an hour later when he led them back again they looked like a party of pallbearers. Max was on the verge of tears, he cleared the lump from his throat.

'I think we should examine each item separately,' he said sadly, and three days later they shook hands on the deal.

Duff poured the drinks and gave each man a glass. 'To the

new company, Central Rand Consolidated. It has been a long confinement, gentlemen, but I think we have given birth to a child of which we can be proud.'

Hradsky had control, but it had cost him dearly.

Central Rand Consolidated had its christening party on the main floor of the Johannesburg Stock Exchange; ten per cent of the shares were put out for sale to the public. Before the day's dealings began the crowd had overflowed the Stock Exchange building and jammed in the street for a block in each direction. The President of the Exchange read the prospectus of Central Rand Consolidated; in the cathedral hush his every word carried clearly to the members' lounge. The bell rang and still the hush persisted. Hradsky's authorized clerk broke the silence timidly. 'I sell C.R.C.'s.'

It was nearly a massacre; two hundred men were trying to buy shares from him simultaneously. First his jacket and then his shirt disintegrated beneath the clutching hands; he lost his spectacles, crushed to powdered glass beneath the trampling feet. Ten minutes later he managed to fight his way out of the crowd and report to his masters, 'I was able to sell them, gentlemen.'

Sean and Duff laughed. They had reason to laugh, for in those ten minutes their thirty per cent holding in C.R.C. had appreciated in value by half a million pounds.

24

That year Christmas dinner at Candy's Hotel was considerably better than it had been five years previously. Seventy-five people sat down to it at one table and by three o'clock, when it ended, only half of them were able to stand up. Sean used the banisters to get up the stairs and at the top he told Candy and Duff solemnly, 'I love you – I love you both desperately – but now I must sleep.' He left them and set off down the corridor bouncing against the walls like a trick billiard shot until he ricocheted through the door into his suite.

'You'd better make sure he's all right, Dufford.'

'A case of the blind drunk leading the blind drunk,' said Duff indistinctly, and also employing the wall to wall route followed Sean down the corridor. Sean was sitting on the edge of his bed wrestling with one of his boots.

'What you trying to do, laddie, break your ankle?'

Sean looked up and smiled beatifically. 'Come in, come in – all four of you. Have a drink.'

'Thanks, I brought my own.'

Duff closed the door behind him like a conspirator and produced a bottle from under his coat, 'She didn't see me – she didn't know her little Dufford had a big beautiful bottle in his inside pocket.'

'Would you mind helping me with this damn boot?' Sean asked.

'That's a very good question,' said Duff seriously as he set a course across the room for one of the armchairs. 'I'm glad you asked it.' He reached the chair and dropped into it. 'The answer, of course, is, Yes! I would mind.'

Sean let his foot drop and lay back on the bed.

'Laddie, I want to talk to you,' Duff said.

'Talk's free – help yourself.'

'Sean, what do you think of Candy?'

'Lovely pair of titties,' Sean opined.

'Sure, but a man cannot live by titties alone.'

'No, but I suppose she's also got the other basic equipment,' Sean said drowsily.

'Laddie, I'm being serious now – I want your help. Do you think I am doing the right thing – this marriage business, I mean.'

'Don't know much about marriage.' Sean rolled over on his face.

'She's calling me Dufford already – did you notice that, laddie? That's an omen, that's an omen of the most frightful portent. Did you notice, hey?' Duff waited a second for an answer which he didn't receive. 'That's what the other one used to call me. "Dufford," she'd say – I can hear it now – "Dufford, you're a pig".'

Duff looked hard at the bed. 'Are you still with me?'

No answer.

'Sean, laddie, I need your help.'

Sean snored softly.

'Oh, you drunken oaf,' said Duff miserably.

25

Xanadu was finished by the end of January and the wedding was set for the twentieth of February. Duff sent the Commandant and the entire police force of Johannesburg an invitation: in return they put a twenty-four hour a day guard on the ballroom of Xanadu where the wedding gifts were laid out on long trestle tables. Sean drove up with Duff and Candy on the afternoon of the tenth, as Duff put it, to make the latest count of the booty. Sean gave the constable on duty a cigar and then they went through into the ballroom.

'Look, oh look,' squealed Candy. 'There's a whole lot of new presents!'

'This one's from Jock and Trevor,' Sean read the card.

'Open quickly, please, Dufford, let's see what they've given us.'

Duff prised the lid off the case and Sean whistled softly,

'A solid gold dinner service,' gasped Candy. She picked up one of the plates and hugged it to her chest, 'Oh, I just don't know what to say.'

Sean examined the other boxes. 'Hey, Duff, this one will make you specially happy — "Best wishes, N. Hradsky".'

'This I must see,' said Duff with the first enthusiasm he had shown in a month. He unwrapped the parcel.

'A dozen of them!' Duff hooted gleefully. 'Norman, you priceless little Israelite, a whole dozen dish towels.'

'It's the thought that counts,' laughed Sean.

'Dear old Norman, how it must have hurt him to shell out for them! I'll have him autograph them and I'll frame them and hang them in the front hall.'

They left Candy to arrange the presents and they went out into the garden.

'Have you got this mock priest organized?' asked Duff.

'Yes, he's at a hotel in Pretoria. He's in training now — he'll be able to rattle through the service like an old hand when the time comes.'

'You don't think that faking it is just as bad as doing it properly?' asked Duff dubiously.

'It's a hell of a time to think of that now,' said Sean.

'Yes, I suppose it is.'

'Where are you going for the honeymoon?' Sean asked.

'We'll coach down to Capetown and take the mail boat to London, then a month or so on the Continent. Be back here about June.'

'You should have a good time.'

'Why don't you get married as well?'

'What for?' Sean looked surprised.

'Well, don't you feel as though you're letting the old firm down a bit – me going into this alone?'

'No,' said Sean. 'Anyway, who is there to marry?'

'What about that lass you brought to the races last Saturday; she's a lovely piece of work.'

Sean raised an eyebrow. 'Did you hear her giggle?'

'Yes, I did,' admitted Duff. 'You couldn't very well miss it.'

'Can you imagine that giggle coming at you across the breakfast table?' Sean asked.

Duff shuddered. 'Yes, I see your point. But as soon as we get back I'll have Candy start picking you out a suitable female.'

'I've got a better idea, you let Candy run your life and I'll run my own.'

'That, laddie, is what I'm very much afraid is going to happen.'

Hradsky reluctantly agreed that the activities of the group – the mines, the workshops, the transport companies, all of them – should be suspended on the twentieth to allow their employees to attend Duff's nuptials. This meant that half the businesses on the Witwatersrand would shut down for the day. Consequently, most of the independent companies decided to close as well. On the eighteenth the wagons carrying the food and liquor started caravanning up the hill to Xanadu. Sean in a burst of benevolence that night invited the entire company from the Opera House to the wedding. He remembered it vaguely the next morning and went down to cancel the invitation but Blue Bessie told him that most of the girls had already gone into town to buy new dresses.

'The hell with it then – let them come. I just hope Candy doesn't guess who they are, that's all.'

On the night of the nineteenth Candy gave them the use of the dining-room and all the downstairs lounges of the Hotel for Duff's bachelor party. Francois arrived with a masterpiece made up in the mine workshops – an enormous ball and chain. This was formally locked onto Duff's leg and the party began.

Afterwards there was a school of thought that maintained that the building contractor commissioned to repair the damage to the Hotel was a bandit and that the bill for just under a thousand pounds that he presented was nothing short of robbery. However, none of them could deny that the Bok-Bok game in the dining-room, played by a hundred men, had done a certain amount of damage to the furniture and fittings; nor that the chandelier had not been able to support Mr Courtney's weight and on the third swing had come adrift from the ceiling and knocked a moderately large hole through the floor. Neither did anyone dispute the fact that after Jock Heyns had tried unsuccessfully for half an hour to shoot a glass off the top of his brother's head with champagne corks, the resulting ankle-deep lake of wine in the one lounge made it necessary for the floor to be relaid. Nevertheless they felt that a thousand was a little bit steep. On one point, however, everyone agreed – it was a memorable party.

At the beginning Sean was worried that Duff's heart wasn't in it for Duff stood by the bar with the metal ball under one arm listening to the lewd comment, with a lopsided grin fixed on his face. After seven or eight drinks Sean stopped worrying about him and went off to have his way with the chandelier. At midnight Duff talked Francois into releasing him from his chains and he slipped out of the room. No one – least of all Sean – noticed him go.

Sean could never remember how he got up to bed that night but next morning he was tactfully awakened by a waiter with a coffee tray and a note.

'What time is it?' asked Sean as he unfolded the note.

'Eight o'clock, baas.'

'No need to shout,' muttered Sean. His eyes focused with difficulty for the pain in his head was pushing them out of their sockets.

'Dear Best Man,

This serves as a reminder that you and Duff have an appointment at eleven o'clock. I am relying on you to get him there, whole or in pieces. Love Candy.'

The brandy fumes in the back of his throat tasted like chloroform, he washed them out with coffee and lit a cigar which started him coughing, and every cough nearly took the top off his head. He stubbed out the cigar and went to the bathroom. Half an hour later he felt strong enough to wake Duff. He went across the sitting-room and pushed open Duff's door; the curtains in the room were still drawn. He pulled them open and was nearly blinded by the sunlight that poured in through them. He turned to the bed and frowned with surprise. He walked slowly across and sat on the edge of it.

'He must have slept in Candy's room,' Sean muttered as he looked at the unused pillows and neatly tucked blankets. It took a few seconds for him to find the fault in his reasoning.

'Then why did she write that note?' He stood up, feeling the first twinge of alarm. A picture of Duff, drunk and helpless lying out in the yard or knocked over the head by one of the busy Johannesburg footpads came very clearly to mind. He ran across the bedroom and into the sitting-room. Halfway to the door he saw the envelope propped up on the mantelpiece and he took it down.

'What is this, a meeting of the authors' guild?' he muttered. 'The place is thick with letters.'

'The paper crackled as he opened it and he recognized Duff's back sloping hand.

'The first the worst, the second the same. I'm not going through with it. You're the best man so make my excuses to all the nice people. I'll be back when the dust has settled a little. D.'

Sean sat down in one of the armchairs, he read through it twice more. Then he exploded.

'Damn you, Charleywood – "make my excuses". You craven bastard. Walk out and leave me to sweep up the mess.'

He rushed across the room with his dressing-gown flapping furiously round his legs. 'You'll make your own damned excuses – even if I have to drag you back on the end of a rope.'

Sean ran down the back stairs. Mbejane was in the stable yard talking to three of the grooms.

'Where is Nkosi Duff?' Sean roared.

They stared at him blankly.

'Where is he?' Sean's beard bristled.

'The baas took a horse and went for a ride,' answered one of the grooms nervously.

'When?' bellowed Sean.

'In the night – perhaps seven, eight hours ago. He should be back soon.'

Sean stared at the groom, breathing heavily. 'Which way did he go?'

'Baas, he did not say.'

Eight hours ago – he could be fifty miles away by now. Sean turned and went back to his room. He threw himself on the bed and poured another cup of coffee.

'This is going to break her up badly –' He imagined the tears and the chaos of undisciplined grief.

'Oh, hell – damn you to hell, Charleywood.' He sipped the coffee and thought about going as well – taking a horse and getting as far away as possible. 'It's no mess of my making – I want no part of it.' He finished the coffee and started dressing. He looked in the mirror to comb his hair and saw Candy standing alone in the chapel, waiting while the silence turned to murmuring and then to laughter.

'Charleywood, you pig,' Sean scowled. 'I can't let her go up there – it'll be bad enough without that. I'll have to tell her.'

He picked up his watch from the dressing-table, it was past nine.

'Damn you, Charleywood.'

He went down the passage and stopped outside Candy's door. He could hear women's voices inside and he knocked before he went in. There were two of Candy's friends and the coloured girl Martha. They stared at him.

'Where's Candy?'

'In the bedroom – but you mustn't go in. It's bad luck.'

'It's the worst bloody luck in the world,' agreed Sean. He knocked on the bedroom door.

'Who is it?'

'Sean.'

'You can't come in – what do you want?'

'Are you decent?'

'Yes, but you mustn't come in.'

He opened the door and looked in on a confusion of squealing females.

'Get out of here' – he said harshly – 'I have to speak to Candy alone.'

They fled and Sean closed the door behind them. Candy was in a dressing-gown. Her face was quick with anticipation; her hair was pulled back and hung shiny and soft. She was beautiful, Sean realized. He looked at the frothy pile of her wedding-dress on the bed.

'Candy, bad news – I'm afraid. Can you take it?' He spoke almost roughly – hating it, hating every second of it.

He saw the bloom on her face wither until her expression was dead – blank and dead as a statue.

'He's gone,' said Sean. 'He's run out on you.'

Candy picked up a brush from her dressing-table and started stroking it listlessly through her hair. It was very quiet in the room.

'I'm sorry, Candy.'

She nodded without looking at him; instead she was looking down the lonely corridor of the future. It was worse than tears would have been, that silent acceptance. Sean scratched the side of his nose – hating it.

'I'm sorry – I wish I could do something about it.' He turned to the door.

'Sean, thank you for coming and telling me.' There was no emotion in her voice; like her face it was dead.

'That's all right,' Sean said gruffly.

He rode up to Xanadu. There were people clustered about the marquees on the lawn; by the quality of their laughter he could tell they were drinking already. The sun was bright and as yet not too hot, the band was playing from the wide veranda of the mansion, the women's dresses were gay against the green of the lawns. 'Gala day' fluttered the flags above the tents. 'Gala day' shouted the laughter.

Sean rode up the drive, lifting his hand in brief acknowledgement of the greetings that were shouted to him. From the vantage point of his horse's back he spotted Francois and Martin Curtis, glasses in hand, standing near the house talking to two of the Opera girls. He gave his horse to one of the native grooms and strode across towards them.

'Hello, boss,' called Curtis. 'Why so glum – you're not the one getting married.' They all laughed.

'Francois, Martin, come with me please.'

'What's the trouble, Mr Courtney?' Francois asked as he led them aside.

'The party's over,' Sean said grimly. 'There'll be no wedding.' They gaped at him.

'Go around and tell everybody. Tell them they'll get their presents back.'

He turned to leave them.

'What's happened, boss?' Curtis asked.

'Just tell them that Candy and Duff changed their minds.'

'Do you want us to send them home?'

Sean hesitated. 'Oh, the hell with it – let them stay – let them all get sick drunk. Just tell them there'll be no wedding.'

He went up to the house. He found the pseudo-priest waiting nervously in the downstairs study. The man's adam's apple had been rubbed raw by the starch-stiff dog collar.

'We won't need you,' Sean told him.

He took out his cheque book, sat down at the desk and filled in a cheque form.

'That's for your trouble. Now get out of town.'

'Thank you, Mr Courtney, thank you very much.' The man looked mightily relieved; he started for the door.

'My friend,' Sean stopped him. 'If you ever breathe a word about what we planned to do today, I'll kill you. Do I make myself clear?'

Sean went through to the ballroom, he slipped a small stack of sovereigns into the constable's hand.

'Get all these people out of here.' He gestured with his head at the crowds that were wandering among the tables looking at the gifts. 'Then lock the doors.'

He found the chef in the kitchen. 'Take all this food outside – give it to them now. Then lock up the kitchens.'

He went round the house closing the doors and drawing the curtains. When he walked into the study there was a couple on the big leather couch and the man's hand was under the girl's skirts; she was giggling.

'This isn't a whore house,' Sean shouted at them and they left hurriedly. He sank into one of the chairs. He could hear the voices and the laughter from outside on the lawn, the band was playing a Strauss waltz. It irritated him and he scowled at the marble fireplace. His head was aching again and the skin of his face felt dry and tight from the night's debauch.

'What a mess – what a bloody mess,' he said aloud. After an hour he went out and found his horse. He rode out along the Pretoria Road until he had passed the last houses, then he turned off into the veld. He cantered into the sea of grass with his hat pushed back on his head so the sun and the wind could find his face. He sat relaxed and loose in the saddle and let his horse pick its own way. In the late afternoon he came back to Johannesburg and left his horse with Mbejane in the stableyard. He felt better; the exercise and the fresh air had cleared his head and helped him to see things in truer perspective. He ran himself a deep hot bath, climbed into it and while he soaked the last of his anger at Duff smoothed out. He had control of himself again. He got out of the bath and towelled, then he slipped on his gown and went through to the bedroom. Candy was sitting on his bed.

'Hello, Sean.' She smiled at him, a brittle smile. Her hair was a little tangled now, her face was pale and unrouged. She had not changed from the dressing-gown he had seen her in that morning.

'Hello, Candy.' He picked up the cut-glass bottle of bay rum and rubbed some into his hair and beard.

'You don't mind me coming to see you, do you?'

'No, of course not.' He started combing his hair. 'I was about to come and see you myself.'

She drew her legs up under her in the double-jointed manner of women that is impossible for a man to copy.

'Can I have a drink, please?'

'I'm sorry – I thought you never touched the stuff.'

'Oh, today is special.' She laughed too gaily. 'It's my wedding day, you know.'

He poured the brandy without looking at her. He hated this suffering and he felt his anger at Duff coming back strongly. Candy took the drink and sipped it. She pulled a face. 'It tastes awful.'

'It'll do you good.'

'To the bride,' she said and drank it down quickly.

'Another one?' asked Sean.

'No thanks.' She stood up and went across to the window. 'It's getting dark now – I hate the darkness. Darkness distorts things so; what is bad in the daylight is unbearable at night.'

'I'm sorry, Candy, I wish I could help you.'

She whirled and came to him, her arms circled tight round his neck and her face pale and frightened pressed to his chest.

'Oh, Sean, please hold me – I'm so afraid.'

He held her awkwardly.

'I don't want to think about it. Not now, not now in the darkness,' she whispered. 'Please help me. Please help me not to think about it.'

'I'll stay with you. Don't get yourself upset. Come and sit down. I'll get you another drink.'

'No, no,' she clung to him desperately. 'I don't want to be alone. I don't want to think. Please help me.'

'I can't help you – I'll stay with you but that's all I can do.' Anger and pity mixed together in Sean like charcoal and salt-petre; his fingers tightened hard on her shoulders, digging into the flesh until they met bone.

'Yes, hurt me. That way I'll forget for a while. Take me to the bed and hurt me, Sean, hurt me deep.'

Sean caught his breath. 'You don't know what you're saying, that's crazy talk.'

'It's what I want – to forget for a little. Please, Sean, please.'

'I can't do that, Candy, Duff's my friend.'

'He's finished with me and I with him. I'm your friend too. Oh, God, I'm so alone. Don't you leave me too. Help me, Sean, please help me.'

Sean felt his anger slide down from his chest and flare up, cobra-headed, from his thighs. She felt it also.

'Yes, oh please, yes.'

He picked her up and carried her to the bed. He stood over her while he tore off his gown. She moved on the bed shedding her clothing and spreading herself to meet him, to take him in and let him fill the emptiness. He covered her quickly bayonet-ing through the soft veil and into the warmth of her body. There was no desire in it, it was cruel and hard drawn out to the frontiers of endurance. For him an expression of anger and pity; for her an act of renunciation. Once was not enough. Again and yet again he took her, until there were brown smudges on the bedclothes from his bleeding back, until her body ached and they lay entwined, wet and tired from the fury of it. In the quiescence of after-passion Sean spoke softly. 'It didn't help, did it?'

'Yes, it did.' Physical exhaustion had weakened the barriers that held back her grief. Still holding onto him, she started to cry.

A street lamp outside the room threw a silver square of light on the ceiling. Sean laid on his back and watched it, listening to Candy's sobs. He recognized the moment they reached their climax and followed their decline into silence. They slept then and later before the day woke together as if by arrangement.

'You are the only one who can help him now,' Candy said.

'Help him do what?' asked Sean.

'Find what he is looking for. Peace, himself – whatever you want to call it. He's lost, you know, Sean. He's lost and lonely, almost as lonely as I am. I could have helped him, I'm sure I could.'

'Duff lost?' Sean asked cynically. 'You must be mad!'

'Don't be so blind, Sean, don't be misled by the big talk and the grand manner. Look at the other things.'

'Like what?' asked Sean.

She didn't answer for a while. 'He hated his father, you know.'

'I guessed as much from the little he told me.'

'The way he revolts at any discipline. His attitude to Hradsky, to women, to life. Think about it, Sean, and then tell me if he acts like a happy man.'

'Hradsky did him a disservice once – he just doesn't like him,' Sean defended Duff.

'Oh, no – it's much deeper than that. In a way Hradsky is an image of his father. He's so broken up inside, Sean, that's why he clings to you. You can help him.'

Sean laughed outright. 'Candy, my dear, we like each other that's all, there are no deep and dark motives in our friendship. Don't you start getting jealous of me now.'

Candy sat up and the blankets slipped down to her waist. She leaned towards Sean and her breasts swung forward, heavy, round and silver-white in the half light.

'There's a strength in you, Sean, a kind of solid sureness in you that you haven't discovered yet. Duff has recognized it and so will other unhappy people. He needs you, he needs you very badly. Look after him for me, help him to find what he seeks.'

'Nonsense, Candy,' Sean muttered with embarrassment.

'Promise me you'll help him.'

'It's time you went back to your room,' Sean told her. 'People will start talking.'

'Promise me, Sean.'

'All right, I promise.'

Candy slipped out of the bed. She dressed quickly. 'Thank you, Sean, goodnight.'

26

For Sean, Johannesburg was poorer without Duff: the streets were not so busy, the Rand Club was drearier and the thrills at the Stock Exchange not so intense. However, there was work to do; his share and Duff's as well.

It was late every evening when the conferences with Hradsky and Max ended and he went back to the Hotel. In the reaction from the day's tension, when his brain was numb and his eyes burned, there was little energy to spare for regret. Yet he was lonely. He went to the Opera House and drank champagne with the crowd there. One of the girls did the Can-Can on the big table in the centre of the room and when she stopped in front of Sean and Trevor Heyns, with her forehead touching her knees and her petticoats hanging forward over her shoulders, Sean let Trevor whip her pants down – a week before he would have punched Trevor in the nose rather than concede the honour. It wasn't so much fun any more. He went home early.

The following Saturday noon Curtis and Francois came into the office for the weekly progress meeting. When they had finished and Hradsky had left, Sean suggested, 'Come along with me, we'll go and have a pot or twelve at the Grand National Bar, baptize the weekend so to speak.'

Curtis and Francois fidgeted in their chairs.

'We had arranged to meet some of the other boys down at the Bright Angels, boss.'

'That's fine, I'll come along with you,' said Sean eagerly, the prospect of being with ordinary men again was suddenly very attractive to him. He felt sickened of the company of those who shook his hand and smiled at him while they waited for a chance to wipe him off the board. It would be good to go along with these two and talk mining and not stocks and shares, to laugh with men who didn't give a damn if C.R.C.'s hit sixty shillings on Monday. He'd get a little drunk with Francois and Curtis;

later on perhaps he'd have a fight – an honest, snorting, stand-up fight. God, yes, it would be good to be with men who were clean inside – even if there was dirt under their nails and the armpits of their shirts were stained with sweat.

Curtis glanced quickly at Francois. 'There'll be just a crowd of roughnecks down there, boss, all the diggers come in on a Saturday.'

'That's fine,' said Sean. 'Let's go.'

He stood up and buttoned his dove-grey coat; the lapels were edged in black watered silk and matched the black pearl pin in his tie. He picked up his cane from the desk.

'Come on – let's get moving.'

They ran into the noise from the Bright Angels a block before they reached the building. Sean grinned and quickened his step like an old gun dog with the scent of the bird in its nostrils again. Francois and Curtis hurried along on either side of him. There was a big digger standing on the bar counter. Sean recognized him as one of his men from the Little Sister Mine; the man's body was tilted back to balance the weight of the demijohn he held to his lips and his throat jerked regularly as he swallowed. The crowd around his feet were chanting:

'Drink it, down, down, down, down, down.'

The digger finished, he threw the bottle against the far wall and belched like an air-locked geyser. He bowed to acknowledge the applause and then he caught sight of Sean standing in the doorway. He wiped his mouth guiltily with the back of his hand and jumped down off the counter. The other men in the crowd turned and saw Sean and the noise tapered off. They spread out along the bar in silence. Sean led Francois and Curtis into the room. He placed a pile of sovereigns on the counter.

'Set them up, barman, take the orders. Today is Saturday and it's time to tie the dog loose.'

'Cheers, Mr Courtney.'

'Good luck, sir.'

'*Gezondheid*, Mr Courtney.'

Their voices were subdued with respect.

'Drink up, man, there's plenty more where that came from.' Sean stood with Francois and Curtis at the bar. They laughed at his jokes. His voice was loud with good fellowship and his face flushed with happiness. He bought more drinks. After a while his bladder started making its presence felt and he went through the back door into the washrooms. There were men talking in there; he stopped before he rounded the edge of the screen into the room. ' . . . what's he want to come here for, hey? This isn't the mucking Rand Club.'

'Shh! He'll hear you, man, do you want to lose your job?'

'I don't give a damn. Who does he think he is – "Drink up, boys, there's plenty more where that came from – I'm the boss, boys, do as you're told, boys, kiss my arse, boys." ' Sean stood paralysed.

'Pipe down, Frank, he'll go just now.'

'The sooner the better, say I, the big dandy bastard with his ten-guinea boots and gold cane. Let him go back where he belongs.'

'You're drunk, man, don't talk so loud.'

'Sure I'm drunk, drunk enough to go in there and tell him to his face. . .'

Sean backed out through the door and walked slowly across the bar to Francois and Curtis.

'I hope you'll excuse me; I've just remembered there's something I've got to do this afternoon.'

'That's too bad, boss.' Curtis looked relieved. 'Perhaps some other time, hey?'

'Yes, perhaps some other time.'

They were pleased to see him when he went up to the Rand Club. Three men nearly fought one another to buy him a drink.

27

He had dinner with Candy that night and over the liqueurs he told her about it. She listened without interruption until he finished.

'They didn't want me there, I don't see what I've done to them that they should dislike me that way.'

'And it worries you?' she asked.

'Yes, it worries me. I've never had people feel like that towards me before.'

'I'm glad it worries you.' She smiled gently at him. 'One day you're going to grow into quite a nice person.'

'But why do they hate me?' Sean followed his original line of thought.

'They're jealous of you – you say this man said, "ten-guinea boots and gold cane" – that is what's behind it. You're different from them now, you're rich. You can't expect them to accept that.'

'But I've never done anything to them,' he protested.

'You don't have to. One thing I've found in this life – for everything you get you have to pay a price. This is part of the payment you have to make for success.'

'Hell, I wish Duff was here,' said Sean.

'Then Duff would explain to you that it doesn't matter, wouldn't he?' said Candy. ' "Who gives a damn for them, laddie, the unwashed herd? We can do without them," ' she mimicked. Sean scratched the side of his nose and looked down at the table.

'Please, Sean, don't ever let Duff teach you that people don't matter. He doesn't believe it himself – but he's so convincing. People are important. They are more important than gold or places or – or anything.'

Sean looked up at her. 'I realized that once; when I was trapped in the Candy Deep. I saw it very clearly then in the darkness and the mud. I made a resolution.' He grinned sheepishly. 'I told

304

myself I'd never hurt anyone again if I could help it. I really meant it, Candy. I felt it so strongly at the time – but, but . . .'

'Yes, I think I understand. That's a big resolution to make and a much bigger one to keep. I don't think any single experience is enough to change a person's way of thinking. It's like building a wall brick by brick. You add to it a little at a time until at last it's finished. I've told you before, Sean, that you have a strength in you. I think one day you'll finish building your wall – and when you do, it will have no weak spots.'

28

The next Tuesday Sean rode up to Xanadu for the first time since Duff had left. Johnson and four of the clerks from the office were at work in the ballroom, packing and labelling the presents.

'Nearly finished, Johnson?'

'Just about, Mr Courtney, I'll send a couple of wagons up tomorrow morning to fetch this lot.'

'Yes, do that. I don't want them lying around here any longer.'

He went up the marble staircase and stood on the top landing. The house had a dead feeling to it: new and sterile, it was waiting for people to come into it and bring it to life. He went down the corridor, stopping to look at the paintings that Candy had chosen. They were oils in soft pastels, woman's colours.

'We can do without these – I'll get some with fire in them, scarlets and blacks and bright blues.'

He pushed open the door to his own bedroom. This was better: vivid Persian rugs on the floor, walls panelled in dark satiny wood and a bed like a polo field. He lay on the bed and looked up at the scrolled ornate plaster ceiling.

'I wish Duff were back – we can do some real living in this house.' He went downstairs again.

Johnson was waiting at the foot of the stairs. 'All finished, sir.'

'Good man! Off you go, then.'

He went through into the study and walked across to the gun rack. He took down a Purdey shotgun, carried it to the french windows and looked at it in the light. His nostrils flared a little at the nostalgic smell of gun oil. He brought the gun up to his shoulder, felt the true exciting balance of it and enjoyed it. He swung the barrels in an arc across the room, following the flight of an imaginary bird, and suddenly Duff's face was in his sights.

Sean was taken so by surprise that he stood with the gun trained at Duff's head.

'Don't shoot, I'll come quietly,' said Duff solemnly.

Sean lowered the shotgun and carried it back to the rack.

'Hello.'

'Hello,' Duff answered, still standing in the doorway. Sean made a pretence of fitting the gun into the rack with his back to Duff.

'How are you, laddie?'

'Fine! Fine!'

'How's everybody else?'

'To whom do you refer, in particular?' Sean asked.

'Candy, for one.'

Sean considered the question. 'Well, you could have damaged her more by feeding her into a stamp mill.'

'Bad, hey?'

'Bad,' agreed Sean.

They stood in silence for a while.

'I take it that you are not very well disposed towards me either,' Duff said at last.

Sean shrugged his shoulders and moved across to the fireplace.

'Dufford, you're a pig,' he said conversationally.

Duff winced. 'Well, it was nice knowing you, laddie. I suppose from here on our paths diverge?'

'Don't drivel, Duff, you're wasting time. Pour the drinks and then you can tell me what it feels like being a pig. Also I want to discuss with you those paintings Candy has plastered along the upstairs corridor. I don't know whether to give them away or burn them.'

Duff straightened up from leaning against the door jamb; he tried to stop the relief showing on his face but Sean went on quickly, 'Before we close the lid on the subject and bury it, I want to tell you this. I don't like what you did. I can see why you did it, but I don't like it. That's my piece said. Have you got anything to add to it?'

'No,' said Duff.

'All right then. I think you'll find a bottle of Courvoisier right at the back of the cabinet behind the whisky decanter.'

*

Sean went down to Candy's Hotel that evening and found Candy in her office.

'He's back, Candy.'

'Oh!' Candy caught her breath. 'How is he, Sean?'

'A little chastened, but not much.'

'I didn't mean that – I meant is he well?'

'The same as ever. He had the grace to ask how you were,' said Sean.

'What did you tell him?' asked Candy.

Sean shrugged and sat down in the chair next to her desk. He looked at the tall stacks of sovereigns that Candy was counting.

'Is that last night's bar takings?' he asked, avoiding her question.

'Yes,' she answered absently.

'You're rich – will you marry me?' he smiled.

Candy stood up and walked across to the window.

'I suppose you two will be moving up to Xanadu now,' she said. Sean grunted and she went on quickly. 'The Heyns brothers will take over the Victoria rooms – they've spoken to me about it already, so don't worry about that. You'll have fun up there, it will be marvellous for you. I bet you'll have parties every night and crowds of people. I don't mind, I've gotten used to the idea now.'

Sean stood up and went to her, he took her gently by the elbow and turned her to face him. He gave her the silk handkerchief out of his top pocket to blow her nose.

'Do you want to see him again, Candy?'

She shook her head, not trusting her voice.

'I'll look after him like I promised.' He gave her a hug and turned to go.

'Sean,' she called after him. He looked back. 'You'll come to see me sometimes. We could have dinner and talk a little. You'll still be my friend, won't you?'

'Of course, Candy, of course, my dear.'

She smiled damply. 'If you pack your things and Duff's I'll have them sent up to Xanadu for you.'

29

Sean looked across the boardroom table at Duff, seeking his support. Duff blew a thick ring of cigar smoke. It spun and expanded like a ripple in a pond before it hit the table top and disintegrated. Duff wasn't going to back him up, Sean realized bitterly. They had argued half the previous night. He had hoped that Duff might still change his mind. Now he knew he wouldn't. He made one last appeal.

'They have asked for a ten per cent wage increase. I believe they need it – prices have soared in this town, but wages have remained the same. These men have wives and children, gentlemen, can't we take that into account?'

Duff blew another smoke ring and Hradsky pulled his watch from his pocket and looked at it pointedly. Max coughed and interrupted. 'I think we've been over that before, Mr Courtney. Could we put it to the vote now?'

Sean watched Hradsky's hand go up against him. He didn't want to look at Duff. He didn't want to see him vote with Hradsky, but he forced himself to turn his head. Duff's hands were on the table in front of him. He blew another smoke ring and watched it hit the table top.

'Those in favour of the motion?' asked Max, and Duff and Sean raised their right hands together. Sean realized then how much it would have meant if Duff had voted against him. Duff winked at him and he couldn't help grinning.

'That is thirty votes for, and sixty against,' declared Max. 'Therefore Mr Courtney's motion falls to the ground. I will inform the Mineworkers' Union of the decision. Now is there any other business before we close the meeting?'

Sean walked with Duff back to his own office.

'The only reason I supported you was because I knew Hradsky would win anyway,' said Duff pleasantly. Sean snorted.

'He's right, of course,' Duff went on unperturbed as he held open the door to Sean's office. 'A ten per cent wage increase would jump the group working costs up ten thousand a month.'

Sean kicked the door closed behind them and didn't answer.

'For God's sake, Sean, don't carry this goodwill-towards-men attitude to absurdity. Hradsky's right – Kruger is likely to slap another one of his taxes on us at any moment and we've got to finance all that new development on the East Rand. We can't let production costs creep up now.'

'All right,' gruffed Sean. 'It's all settled. I just hope we don't have a strike on our hands.'

'There are ways of dealing with strikes. Hradsky has got the police on our side and we can have a couple of hundred men up from Kimberley in no time at all,' Duff told him.

'Damn it, Duff, it's wrong. You know it's wrong. That grotesque Buddha with the little eyes knows it's wrong. But what can I do? Damn it, what can I do?' Sean exploded. 'I feel so bloody helpless.'

'Well, you're the one who wanted to give him control.' Duff laughed at him. 'Stop trying to change the world and let's go home.'

Max was waiting for them in the outer office. He looked nervous. 'Excuse me, gentlemen, could I have a word with you?'

'Who's talking,' Sean asked abruptly, 'you or Hradsky?'

'It's a private matter, Mr Courtney.' Max dropped his voice.

'Can't it wait until tomorrow?' Sean pushed past him and kept going for the door.

'Please, Mr Courtney, it's of the utmost importance.'

Max plucked desperately at Sean's arm.

'What is it, Max?' Duff asked.

'I have to speak to you alone,' Max dropped his voice again and glanced unhappily at the street door.

'Well, speak then,' Duff encouraged him. 'We're alone now.'

'Not here. Can you meet me later?'

Duff raised an eyebrow. 'What is this, Maximilian, don't tell me you are selling dirty pictures.'

'Mr Hradsky is waiting for me at the hotel. I told him I was coming to find some papers, he'll get suspicious if I don't go back immediately.' Max was nearly in tears; his Adam's apple played hide-and-seek behind his high collar, bobbing out and disappearing again. Duff was suddenly very interested in what Max had to say.

'You don't want Norman to know about this?' he asked.

'My goodness, no.' Max came closer to tears.

'When do you want to meet us?'

'Tonight, after ten o'clock when Mr Hradsky has retired.'

'Where?' asked Duff.

'There's a side road round the east end of the Little Sister Mine dump. It's not used any more.'

'I know it,' said Duff. 'We'll ride along there about half past ten.'

'Thank you, Mr Charleywood, you won't regret it.' Max scampered for the door and disappeared.

Duff adjusted his beaver at the correct angle, then he prodded Sean in the belly with the point of his cane.

'Smell it – suck it in.' Duff sniffed appreciatively and Sean did the same.

'I don't smell a thing,' Sean declared.

'The air is thick with it,' Duff told him. 'The sweet smell of treachery.'

They left Xanadu just after half past nine. Duff insisted on wearing a black opera cloak.

'Atmosphere is vital, laddie, you can't go to a rendezvous like this dressed in dirty khaki pants and *veldschoen*. It would ruin the whole thing.'

'Well, I'm damned if I'm going to get into fancy dress. This is a very good suit. It will have to do.'

'Can't I persuade you to wear a pistol in your belt?' asked Duff wistfully.

'No,' laughed Sean.

'No?' Duff shook his head. 'You're a barbarian, laddie. No taste, that's your trouble.'

They avoided the main streets on their way through Johannesburg and met the Cape road half a mile beyond the town. There was only a minute slice of moon left in the dark bowl of the sky. The stars, however, were big and by their light the white mine dumps, each the size of a large hill, stood out like pustules on the earth's face.

Despite himself, Sean felt a little breathless with excitement – Duff's zest was always infectious. They cantered with their stirrups almost touching, Duff's cloak billowing out behind him and the breeze of their passage fanning the tip of Sean's cigar to a fierce red spark.

'Slow down, Duff, the turning's just about here somewhere. It's overgrown, we'll miss it.'

They reined to a walk.

'What's the time?' asked Duff.

Sean drew on his cigar and held his watch close to the glow. 'A quarter after ten. We're early.'

'My bet is Maximilian will be there before us – here's the road.' Duff turned his horse onto it and Sean followed him. The Little Sister Mine dump rose up next to them, steep and white in the starlight. They skirted it but its bulk threw a shadow over them. Duff's horse snorted and shied and Sean gripped with his knees as his own horse danced sideways. Max had stepped out from a scraggy cluster of bushes next to the road.

'Well met by moonlight, Maximilian,' Duff greeted him.

'Please bring your horses off the road, gentlemen.' Max was still showing signs of the afternoon's agitation. They tied their horses next to Max's among the bushes and walked across to join him.

'Well, Max, what's new? How are the folks?' Duff asked.

'Before we go any further in this matter, I want you gentlemen to give me your word of honour that, whether anything comes of it or not, you will never say a word to anybody of what I tell you tonight.' Max was very pale, Sean thought, or perhaps it was just the starlight.

'I agree to that,' said Sean.

'Cross my heart,' said Duff.

Max opened the front of his coat and brought out a long envelope. 'I think if I show you these first it will make it easier to explain my proposition.'

Sean took the envelope from him. 'What are they, Max?'

'The latest statements from all four banks at which Mr Hradsky deals.'

'Matches, Sean, give us a light, laddie,' said Duff eagerly.

'I have a lantern with me,' Max said and he squatted down to light it. Sean and Duff squatted with him and spread the bank statements in the circle of yellow light. They examined them in silence until at last Sean rocked back on his heels and lit another cigar.

'Well, I am glad I don't owe that much money,' Sean announced. Sean folded up the sheets and put them back in the envelope. He slapped the envelope into the palm of his free hand

and started chuckling. Max reached across, took it from him and placed it carefully back inside his coat.

'All right, Max, spell it out for us,' said Sean. Max leaned forward and blew out the lantern. What he had to say was easier said in darkness.

'The large cash payment that Mr Hradsky had to make to you gentlemen and the limitation of output from his diamond mines in terms of the new cartel agreements in the diamond industry have forced him to borrow heavily on all his banks.' Max stopped and cleared his throat. 'The extent of this borrowing you have seen. Of course, the banks demanded security for the loans and Mr Hradsky has given them his entire holding of C.R.C. shares. The banks have set a limit on the shares of thirty-five shillings each. As you know C.R.C.'s are currently quoted at ninety shillings, which leaves a wide margin of safety. However, if the shares were to suffer a setback and fall in price to thirty-five shillings the banks would sell. They would dump every single share that Mr Hradsky owns in C.R.C.'s onto the market.'

'Go on, Max,' said Duff. 'I'm beginning to like the sound of your voice.'

'It occurred to me that if Mr Hradsky were temporarily absent from Johannesburg – say if he went on a trip to England to buy new machinery or something of that nature – it would be possible for you gentlemen to force the price of C.R.C.'s down to thirty-five shillings. Done correctly it would only take three or four days to accomplish. You could sell short and start rumours that the Leader Reef had pinched out at depth. Mr Hradsky would not be here to defend his interests and as soon as C.R.C.'s hit thirty-five shillings the banks would off-load his shares. The price would crash and you, with ready cash available, would be in a position to buy up C.R.C. shares at a fraction of their actual value. There is no reason why you shouldn't gain control of the group and make a couple of million to boot.'

There was another silence. It lasted a long time before Sean asked, 'What do you get out of it, Max?'

'Your cheque for one hundred thousand pounds, Mr Courtney.'

'Wages are going up,' remarked Sean. 'I thought the standard pay for this type of work was thirty pieces of silver. The rate, I believe, was set by a countryman of yours.'

'Shut up,' snapped Duff, then more pleasantly to Max, 'Mr Courtney likes his little jokes. Tell me, Max, is that all you want – just the money? I'll be frank with you – it doesn't ring true. You must be a moderately rich man as it is.'

Max stood up quickly and started towards the horses. He hadn't reached them before he swung around. His face was in darkness but his voice was naked as he screamed at them.

'Do you think I don't know what they call me – "The Court Jester", "Hradsky's tongue", "Lick-arse". Do you think I like it? Do you think I enjoy crawling to him every minute of every day? I want to be free again. I want to be a man again.' His voice choked off and his hands came up and covered his face. He was sobbing. Sean couldn't watch him and even Duff looked down at the ground in embarrassment. When Max spoke again it was in his usual soft and sad voice.

'Mr Courtney, if you wear your yellow waistcoat to the office tomorrow, I will take it as a sign that you intend to follow my suggestion and that my terms are acceptable to you. I will then make the necessary arrangements to ensure Mr Hradsky's absence from the country.' He untied his horse, mounted and rode away down the track towards the Cape Road. Neither Sean nor Duff moved to stand up. They listened to the hoof-beats of Max's horse fade into the darkness, before Duff spoke. 'Those bank statements were genuine – I had a good look at the seals.'

'And even more genuine was Max's emotion.' Sean flicked his cigar away into the bushes. 'No one could act that well. It made me feel quite sick listening to him. Hell, how can a man so cold-bloodedly betray his trust?'

'Laddie, let's not turn this into a discussion of Max's morals. Let's concern ourselves with the facts. Norman has been delivered into our hands, neatly trussed, spiced with garlic and with a sprig of parsley behind each ear. I say let's cook him and eat him.'

Sean smiled at him. 'Give me a few good reasons. I want you to convince me. The way I feel towards him after that meeting this afternoon, I shouldn't be surprised if I convince easily.'

'One,' Duff held up a finger. 'Norman deserves it.'

Sean nodded.

'Two,' another of Duff's fingers came up. 'If we gain control we can run things the way we want. You can indulge your good resolution and give everybody a pay rise and I'll be top man again.'

'Yes!' Sean tugged at his moustache thoughtfully.

'Three. We came here to make money, we'll never get another opportunity like this. And my last reason, but the most potent – you look so beautiful in that yellow waistcoat, laddie, I wouldn't miss seeing you in it tomorrow morning, not for a thousand C.R.C. shares.'

'It is rather natty,' admitted Sean. 'But listen, Duff, I don't want another Lochtkamper business. Messy, you know.'

Duff stood up.

'Norman's a big boy, he wouldn't do that. Anyway, he'll still be rich – he's got his diamond mines. We'll only be relieving him of his responsibilities on the Witwatersrand.'

They walked across to the horses. Sean had his foot in the stirrup when he stiffened and exclaimed, 'My God, I can't do it. It's all off.'

'Why?' Duff was alarmed.

'I spilt gravy on that waistcoat – I can't possibly wear it tomorrow. My tailor would murder me.'

30

There was no problem in arranging for Hradsky's absence – someone had to go to London. There was machinery to buy for the new areas on the East Rand and they had to select two engineers from the hundred or so applicants waiting in England. Not ungraciously, Hradsky allowed himself to be elected for the job.

'We'll give him a farewell party,' Duff suggested to Sean during dinner that night. 'Well, not really a farewell party – but a wake.'

Sean started whistling the 'Dead March' and Duff tapped it out on the table with the handle of his knife.

'We'll have it at Candy's Hot –' Duff cut himself short. 'We'll have it here. We'll really lay it on for poor old Norman so afterwards he'll be able to say, "the bastards may have cleaned me out, but they certainly gave me a grand party".'

'He doesn't like parties,' said Sean.

'That's an excellent reason why we should give him one,' agreed Duff.

A week later when Hradsky and Max left on the morning coach for Port Natal there were fifty members of the Johannesburg Stock Exchange still in full evening dress from the night's party to wave him goodbye. Duff made a touching, if somewhat slurred, little speech and presented Hradsky with a bouquet of roses. Nervous of the crowd that milled about them, the horses bolted when the driver cracked his whip and Max and Hradsky were thrown together in an undignified heap on the rear seat of the coach. The crowd cheered them out of sight. With an arm around his shoulder Sean led Duff across the street to the office and deposited him in one of the deep leather armchairs.

'Are you sober enough to talk sense?' Sean asked dubiously.

'Sure. Always at your service as the lady said to the customer.'

'I managed to have a word with Max last night,' Sean told him. 'He will send us a telegram from Port Natal when he and

Hradsky are safely on the mailboat. We won't start anything until we receive it.'

'Very wise – you're the wisest chap I know,' Duff grinned happily.

'You'd better go to bed,' Sean told him.

'Too far,' said Duff. 'I'll sleep here.'

It was another ten days before Max's telegram arrived. Sean and Duff were eating lunch in the Rand Club when it was delivered to their table. Sean slit open the envelope and read the message to Duff.

'Sailing four o'clock this afternoon. Good luck. Max.'

'I'll drink to that,' Duff lifted his wine glass.

'Tomorrow,' said Sean, 'I'll go up to the Candy Deep and tell Francois to pull all the men out of the bottom levels of the mine. No one's to be allowed in.'

'Put a guard at the fourteenth level,' suggested Duff. 'That'll make it more impressive.'

'Good idea,' agreed Sean. He looked up as someone passed their table and suddenly he started to smile. 'Duff, do you know who that is?'

'Who are you talking about?' Duff looked bewildered.

'That chap who's just gone out into the lounge – there he is, going into the lavatories.'

'Isn't that Elliott, the newspaper fellow?'

'Editor of the *Rand Mail*,' nodded Sean. 'Come with me, Duff.'

'Where are we going?'

'To get a bit of cheap publicity.'

Duff followed Sean out of the dining-room, across the lounge and into the men's lavatories. The door of one of the closets was closed and as they walked in someone farted softly behind it. Sean winked at Duff and went across to the urinal. As he addressed himself to it he said, 'Well, all we can hope for now, Duff, is that Norman will be able to work a miracle in England. Otherwise – ' He shrugged his shoulder. Duff picked up his cue.

'We're taking a hell of a chance relying on that. I still say we should sell out now. C.R.C.'s were at ninety-one shillings this morning so it's obvious that the story hasn't leaked out yet. But when it does you won't be able to give the bloody shares away. I say we should get out while the going's good.'

'No,' Sean disagreed. 'Let's wait until we hear from Norman. It's taking a bit of a chance, I know, but we have a responsibility to the men working for us.' Sean took Duff's arm and led him out of the lavatory again; at the door he added the cherry to the top of the pie. 'If and when C.R.C. collapses there are going to be thousands of men out of work – do you realize that?'

Sean closed the door behind them and they grinned delightedly at each other.

'You're a genius, laddie,' whispered Duff.

'I'm happy to say I agree with you,' Sean whispered back.

The next morning Sean woke with the knowledge that something exciting was going to happen that day. He lay and savoured the feeling before he sent his mind out to hunt for the reason. Then he sat up suddenly and reached for the newspaper that lay folded on the coffee tray beside his bed. He shook it open and found what he was looking for on the front page, big headlines: *Is all well with the Central Rand Consolidated? Norman Hradsky's mystery journey.* The story itself was a masterpiece of journalistic evasion. Seldom had Sean seen anyone write so fluently or convincingly on a subject about which he knew nothing. 'It is suggested', 'Usually reliable sources report' and 'There is reason to believe' – all the old phrases of no significance. Sean groped for his slippers and padded down the corridor to Duff's room.

Duff had all the blankets and most of the bed; the girl was curled up like a pink anchovy on the outskirts. Duff was snoring and the girl whimpered a little in her sleep. Sean tickled Duff's lips with the tassel of his dressing-gown cord, Duff's nose twitched and his snores gurgled into silence. The girl sat up and looked at Sean with eyes wide but vacant from sleep.

'Quickly, run,' Sean shouted at her, 'the rebels are coming.'

She leapt straight into the air and landed three feet from the bed quivering with panic. Sean ran a critical eye over her. A pretty filly, he decided, and made a mental note to take her for a trot just as soon as Duff put her out to grass.

'All right,' he reassured her, 'they've gone away now.'

She became aware of her nakedness and Sean's frank appraisal of it. She tried to cover it with hands too small for the task. Sean picked up Duff's gown from the foot of the bed and handed it to her.

'Go and have a bath or something, sweetheart, I want to talk to Mr Charleywood.'

With the gown on she recovered her composure and told him severely, 'I didn't have any clothes on, Mr Courtney.'

'I would never have guessed,' said Sean politely.

'It's not nice.'

'You are too modest – I thought it was better than average. Off you go now, there's a good girl.' With a saucy flick of her head she disappeared into the bathroom and Sean transferred his attention to Duff. Duff had held grimly onto the threads of sleep throughout the exchange but he let go when Sean whacked him across the backside with the folded newspaper. Like a tortoise coming out of its shell his head emerged from the blankets. Sean handed him the paper and sat down on the edge of the bed. He watched Duff's face crease into laughter lines before he spoke.

'You better get down to the Editor's office and shout at him a little – just to confirm his suspicions. I'll go up to the Candy Deep and close all the bottom levels. I'll meet you back at the Exchange at opening time and don't forget to clean that grin off your face before you show it round town. Try and look haggard, it shouldn't be difficult for you.'

When Sean arrived at the Stock Exchange building the crowd had filled the street outside. Mbejane eased the landau into it and it opened to give them a passage. Sean scowled straight ahead and ignored the questions which were shouted at him from all around. Mbejane stopped the carriage outside the main entrance and four police constables held back the mob while Sean hurried across the pavement and through the double doors. Duff was there ahead of him, the centre of a turbulent circle of members and brokers. He saw Sean and waved frantically over the heads of his inquisitors. That was sufficient to switch their attention from Duff to Sean and they flocked to him, ringing him in with anxious angry faces. Sean's hat was knocked forward over his eyes and a button popped off his coat as one of them caught hold of his lapels.

'Is it true?' the man shouted, spittle flying from his lips into Sean's face. 'We've got a right to know if it's true.'

Sean swung his cane in a full overarm stroke onto the man's head and sent him tottering backwards into the arms of those behind him.

'Back, you bastards,' he roared at them using both the point and the edge of his cane to beat them away, scattering them across the floor until he stood alone, glowering at them with the cane still twitching restlessly in his hand.

'I'll make a statement later on. Until then, behave yourselves.' He adjusted his hat, picked the loose thread where the button had been from his coat and stalked across to join Duff. He could see Duff's grin starting to lift the corner of his mouth and he cautioned him silently with his eyes. Grim-faced they walked through into the members' lounge.

'How's it going your end?' Duff kept his voice low.

'Couldn't be better.' Sean contrived a worried expression. 'I've got an armed guard on the fourteenth level. When this bunch hear about that, they'll really start frothing at the mouth.'

'When you make your statement, let it ring with obvious false confidence,' Duff instructed. 'If it goes on like this we'll have the shares down to thirty-five shillings within an hour of opening.'

Five minutes before opening time Sean stood in the President's box and made his address to his fellow members, Duff listened to him with mounting admiration. Sean's hearty reassurances and verbal side-stepping were enough to strike despair into the souls of the most hardened optimists. Sean finished his speech and climbed down from the box amid a gloomy lack of applause. The bell rang and the brokers stood singly or in small disconsolate groups about the floor. The first tentative offer was made. 'I sell C.R.C.'

But there was no rush to buy. Ten minutes later there was a sale recorded at eighty-five shillings, six shillings lower than the previous day's closing price. Duff leaned across to Sean. 'We'll have to start selling some of our own shares to get things moving, otherwise everybody's going to keep sitting on the fence.'

'That's all right,' Sean nodded, 'we'll buy them back later at a quarter of the price. But wait until the news about the Candy Deep gets out.'

It was just before ten o'clock when that happened. The reaction was sharp. In one quick burst of selling C.R.C.'s dropped to sixty shillings. But there they hung, fluctuating nervously in the chaos of hope and doubt.

'We'll have to sell now,' whispered Duff, 'they are short of script. We'll have to give it to them otherwise the price will stick here.'

Sean felt his hands trembling and he clenched them in his

pockets. Duff was showing signs of the strain as well, there was a nerve jumping in his cheek and his eyes had receded into their sockets a little. This was a game with high stakes.

'Don't overdo it – sell thirty thousand.'

The price of C.R.C.'s sagged under the weight but levelled out at forty-five shillings. There was still another hour until high change and Sean's whole body was screwed up tight with tension. He felt the cold patches of sweat under his arms.

'Sell another thirty thousand,' he ordered his clerk and even to himself his voice sounded wheezy. He stubbed out his cigar in the copper ashtray next to his chair; it was already half full of butts. It was no longer necessary for either of them to act worried. This time the price stuck at forty shillings and the sale of sixty thousand more of their shares failed to move it down more than a few shillings.

'Someone's buying up,' muttered Sean uneasily.

'It looks like it,' agreed Duff. 'I'll lay odds it's that bloody Greek Efthyvoulos. It looks as if we'll have to sell enough to glut him before they'll drop any further.'

By high change Duff and Sean had sold three-quarters of their holdings in C.R.C.'s and the price still stood stubbornly at thirty-seven and sixpence. So tantalizingly close to the magic figure that would release a flood of Hradsky's shares onto the unprepared market, but now they were nearing the stage when they would no longer have any shares with which to force the price down that last two and sixpence.

The market closed and left Duff and Sean sitting limply in their armchairs, shaken and tired as prizefighters at the end of the fifteenth round. Slowly the lounge emptied but still they sat on. Sean leaned across and put his hand on Duff's shoulder. 'It's going to be all right,' he said. 'Tomorrow it will be all right.'

They looked at each other and they exchanged strength, each of them drawing it from the other until they were both smiling. Sean stood up. 'Come on, let's go home.'

Sean went to bed early and alone. Although he felt drained of energy, sleep was a long time coming to him and when it did it was full of confused dreams and punctuated with sharp jerks back into wakefulness. It was almost a relief to see the dawn define the windows as grey squares and to be released from his unrewarding rest. At breakfast he drank a cup of coffee and found that his stomach was unable to accept the plateful of steak and eggs that was offered it for it was already screwing up tight in anticipation of the day ahead. Duff was edgy and tired-looking as well; they spoke only a little during the meal and not at all in the carriage when Mbejane drove them down to the Exchange.

The crowd was outside the Stock Exchange again. They forced their way through it and into the building; they took their seats in the lounge and Sean looked round at the faces of his fellow members. In each of them were the marks of worry, the same darkness round the eyes and the jerkiness in movement. He watched Jock Heyns yawn extravagantly and had to do the same; he lifted his hand to cover his mouth and found it was trembling again. He laid the hand on the arm of his chair and kept it still. Across the lounge Bonzo Barnes caught Sean's eye and looked away quickly, then he also gaped into a cavernous yawn. It was the tension. In the years ahead Sean would see men yawn like that while they waited for the dawn to send them against the Boer guns. Duff leaned across to him and broke his line of thought.

'As soon as the trading starts, we'll sell. Try and panic them. Do you agree?'

'Sudden death,' Sean nodded. He couldn't face another morning of that mental agony. 'Couldn't we offer shares at thirty-two shillings and sixpence and get it over with?' he asked.

Duff grinned at him. 'We can't do that, it's too obvious – we'll just have to go on offering to sell at best and let the price fall on its own.'

'I suppose you're right – but we'll play our high cards now and dump the rest of our shares as soon as the market opens. I don't see how the price can possibly hold after that.'

Duff nodded. He beckoned to their authorized clerk who was waiting patiently at the door of the lounge and when the man came up to them he told him, 'Sell one hundred thousand C.R.C.'s at best.'

The clerk blinked but he jotted the order down on his pad and went out onto the main floor where the other brokers were gathering. It was a few minutes from the bell.

'What if it doesn't work?' Sean asked. The tightness in his belly was nauseating him.

'It must work – it's got to work,' Duff whispered as much to himself as to Sean. He was twisting his fingers round the head of his cane and chewing against clenched teeth. They sat and waited for the bell and when it rang Sean jumped then reached sheepishly for his cigar case. He heard their clerk's voice, raised sharply, 'I sell C.R.C.'s,' and then the confused mumble of voices as the trading started. Through the lounge door he saw the recorder chalk up the first sale. 'Thirty-seven shillings.'

He drew hard on his cigar and lay back in his chair forcing himself to relax, ignoring the restless tapping of Duff's fingers on the arm of the chair next to him. The recorder wiped out the figures and wrote again. 'Thirty-six shillings.'

Sean blew out cigar smoke in a long jet. 'It's moving,' he whispered and Duff's hand clenched on the arm of the chair, his knuckles paling from the pressure of his grip.

'Thirty-five.' The elusive number at last. Sean heard Duff sigh next to him and his voice, 'Now! watch it go, laddie, now the banks will come on. Get ready, laddie, get ready now.'

'Thirty-four and six,' wrote the recorder.

'They must come in now,' said Duff again. 'Get ready to get rich, laddie.'

Their clerk was coming back across the floor and into the lounge. He stopped in front of their chairs. 'I managed to sell them, sir.'

Sean straightened up quickly. 'So soon?' he asked.

'Yes, sir, three big sales and I got rid of them all. I'm afraid the last was only at thirty-four and sixpence.'

Sean stared back at the board. The figure was still at thirty-four and sixpence.

'Duff, something's going on here. Why haven't the banks come in yet?'

'We'll force them to off-load.' Duff's voice was unnaturally hoarse. 'We'll force the bastards.' He pulled himself half out of his chair and snarled at the clerk.

'Sell another one hundred thousand at thirty shillings.' The man's face went slack with surprise. 'Hurry, man, do you hear me? What are you waiting for?' The clerk backed away from Duff, then he turned and scurried out of the lounge.

'Duff, for God's sake.' Sean grabbed his arm. 'Have you gone mad?'

'We'll force them,' muttered Duff. 'They'll have to sell.'

'We haven't got another hundred thousand shares.' Sean jumped up. 'I'm going to stop him.' He ran across the lounge but before he reached the door he saw the sale being chalked up on the board at thirty shillings. He pushed his way across the crowded floor until he reached his clerk. 'Don't sell any more,' he whispered.

The man looked surprised. 'I've sold them already, sir.'

'The whole hundred thousand?' There was horrified disbelief in Sean's voice.

'Yes, sir, someone took the lot in one batch.'

Sean walked back across the floor in a daze. He sank into the chair beside Duff.

'They're sold already.' He spoke as though he didn't believe himself.

'We'll force them, we'll force them to sell,' muttered Duff again and Sean turned to him with alarm. Duff was sweating in little dewdrops across his forehead and his eyes were very bright.

'Duff, for God's sake,' Sean whispered to him, 'steady, man.' Sean knew that they were watched by everybody in the lounge. The watching faces seemed as large as those seen through a telescope and the buzz of their voices echoed strangely in his ears. Sean felt confused: everything seemed to be in slow motion like a bad dream. He looked through into the trading floor and saw the crude number thirty still chalked accusingly against C.R.C. Where were the banks? Why weren't they selling?

'We'll force them, we'll force the bastards,' Duff said again. Sean tried to answer him but the words wouldn't come. He looked back across the trading floor and now he knew it was a bad dream for Hradsky and Max were there, walking across the floor towards the members' lounge. Men were crowding around them and Hradsky was smiling and holding up his hands as if to fend off their questions. They came through into the lounge and Hradsky went to his chair by the fireplace. He lowered himself into it with his shoulders sagging forward and his waist-coat wrinkled tightly around the full bag of his belly. He was still smiling and Sean thought that his smile was one of the most unnerving things he had ever seen. He watched it with flesh-crawling fascination and beside him Duff was just as still and stricken. Max spoke quickly to Hradsky and then he stood up and walked across to Sean and Duff. He stopped in front of them.

'The clerk informs us that you have contracted to sell to Mr Hradsky five hundred thousand shares in C.R.C.'s at an average price of thirty-six shillings.' Max's lashes drooped sadly onto his cheeks. 'The total issue of C.R.C.'s, as you know, is one million shares. During the last two days Mr Hradsky was able to purchase another seventy-five thousand shares apart from the ones you sold to him. This makes his total holdings of C.R.C.'s almost six hundred thousand shares. It seems therefore that you have sold shares that don't exist. Mr Hradsky foresees that you will have some difficulty in fulfilling your contract.'

Sean and Duff went on staring at him. He turned to leave them and Duff blurted out. 'But the banks – why didn't the banks sell?'

Max smiled a mournful little smile. 'The day he reached Port Natal Mr Hradsky transferred sufficient funds from his accounts there to liquidate his overdrafts in Johannesburg. He sent you that telegram and returned here immediately. We only arrived an hour ago.'

'But – but, you lied to us. You tricked us!'

Max inclined his head. 'Mr Charleywood, I will not discuss honesty with a man who does not understand the meaning of the word.' He went back to Hradsky's side. Everyone in the lounge had heard him and while Duff and Sean went on sitting amongst the ruins of their fortune the struggle to buy C.R.C. shares started on the main floor. In five minutes the price was over ninety shillings and still climbing. When it reached one hundred shillings, Sean touched Duff's arm.

'Let's go.' They stood up together and started for the door of the members' lounge. As they passed Hradsky's chair he spoke.

'Yes, Mr Charleywood, you can't win all the time.' It came out quite clearly with only a slight catch on the 'c's' – they were always difficult letters for Norman Hradsky.

Duff stopped, he turned to face Hradsky, his mouth open as he struggled to find a reply. His lips moved, groping, groping for words – but there were none. His shoulders drooped, he shook his head and turned away. He stumbled once at the edge of the floor. Sean held his arm and guided him through the excited jabber of brokers. No one took any notice of the two of them. They were bumped and jostled before they were through the crush and out onto the pavement. Sean signalled Mbejane to bring the carriage. They climbed into it and Mbejane drove them up to Xanadu.

They went through into the drawing-room.

'Get me a drink, please, Sean.' Duff's face was grey and crumpled-looking. Sean poured two tumblers half full of brandy and carried one across to Duff. Duff drank and then sat staring into the empty glass.

'I'm sorry – I lost my head. I thought we'd be able to buy those shares for dirt, when the banks started selling.'

'It doesn't matter,' Sean's voice was tired. 'We were smashed before that happened. Christ! What a well-laid trap it was!'

'We couldn't have known. It was so damn cunning, we couldn't have guessed, could we, Sean?' Duff was trying to excuse himself.

Sean kicked off his boots and loosened his collar. 'That night up at the mine dump – I would have staked my life Max wasn't lying.' He lay back in the chair and stirred his brandy with a circular movement of his hand, 'Christ, how they must have laughed to see us stampede into the pitfall!'

'But we aren't finished, Sean, we aren't completely finished, are we?' Duff was pleading with him, begging for a peg to hang his hope on. 'We'll come out of this all right, you know we will, don't you? We'll save enough out of the wreckage to start again. We'll build it all up again, won't we, Sean?'

'Sure,' Sean laughed brutally. 'You can get a job down at the Bright Angels cleaning out the spittoons and I'll get one at the Opera House playing the piano.'

'But – but – there'll be something left. A couple of thousand even. We could sell this house.'

'Don't dream, Duff, this house belongs to Hradsky. Everything belongs to him.' Sean flicked the brandy that was left in his glass into his mouth and swallowed it. He stood up quickly and went across to the liquor cabinet. 'I'll explain it to you. We owe Hradsky a hundred thousand shares that don't exist. The only way we can deliver them is to buy them from him first and he can set his own price on them. We're finished, Duff, do you know what that means? Smashed! Broken!' Sean poured brandy into his glass, slopping a little on the sideboard. 'Have another drink on Hradsky, it's his brandy now.' Sean swept his arm round the room, pointing at the rich furniture and heavy curtains. 'Take a last look at this lot. Tomorrow the Sheriff will be here to attach it; then through the due processes of the law it will be handed to its rightful owner – Mr Norman Hradsky.' Sean started back towards his chair and then he stopped.

'The due processes of the law,' he repeated softly. 'I wonder – it might just work.'

Duff sat up eagerly in his chair. 'You've got an idea?'

Sean nodded. 'Well, half an idea anyway. Listen, Duff, if I can save a couple of thousand out of this do you agree that we get out of here?'

'Where to – where will we go?'

'We were facing north when we started. It's as good a direction as any. They say there's gold and ivory beyond the Limpopo for those who want it.'

'But, why can't we stay here?' We could play the stock market.' Duff looked uncertain, almost afraid.

'Damn it, Duff, we're finished here. It's a different story playing the market when you are paying the fiddler and calling the tune, but with a mere thousand or so we'd be among the dogs fighting for the scraps under Hradsky's table. Let's get out and start again. We'll go north, hunt ivory and prospect for a new reef. We'll take a couple of wagons and find another fortune. I bet you've forgotten how it feels to sit on a horse and handle a rifle, to have the wind in your face and not a whore or a stockbroker within five hundred miles.'

'But it means leaving everything we've worked for,' Duff groaned.

'Sweet merciful heavens, man, are you blind or just plain stupid?' Sean stormed at him. 'You don't own anything, so how the hell can you leave something you haven't got? I'm going down to see Hradsky and try to make a deal with him. Are you coming?'

Duff looked at him without seeing him, his lips were trembling and he was shaking his head. At last he was realizing the position they were in and the impact of it had dazed him. The higher you ride the further there is to fall.

'All right,' said Sean. 'Wait for me here.'

Hradsky's suite was full of talking, laughing men. Sean recognized most of them as the courtiers who used to cluster round the throne on which he and Duff had sat. The King is dead, long live the King! They saw him standing in the doorway and the laughter and loud voices fizzled out. He saw Max take two quick steps to the stinkwood desk in the corner, pull open the top drawer and drop his hand into it. He stood like that watching Sean. One by one the courtiers picked up their hats and canes and hurried out of the room. Some of them mumbled embarrassed greetings as they brushed passed Sean. Then there were only the three of them left: Sean standing quietly in the doorway, Max behind the desk with his hand on the pistol and Hradsky in the chair by the fireplace watching through yellow, half-hooded eyes.

'Aren't you going to invite me in, Max?' Sean asked and Max glanced quickly at Hradsky, saw his barely perceptible nod and looked back at Sean. 'Come in, please, Mr Courtney.'

Sean pushed the door shut behind him. 'You won't need the gun, Max, the game is over.'

'And the score is in our favour, is it not, Mr Courtney?'

Sean nodded. 'Yes, you've won. We are prepared to make over to you all the C.R.C. shares we hold.'

Max shook his head unhappily. 'I'm afraid it's not quite as easy as that. You have undertaken to sell us a certain number of shares and we must insist upon delivery in full.'

'Just where do you suggest we get them?' Sean asked.

'You could buy them on the Stock Exchange.'

'From you?'

Max shrugged but made no reply.

'So you are going to twist the knife, are you?'

'You put it very poetically, Mr Courtney,' agreed Max.

'Have you considered the consequences of forcing us into bankruptcy?'

'I will admit freely that the consequences to you do not concern us.'

Sean smiled. 'That was not very nice, Max, but I was talking about it from your point of view. Sequestration orders, creditors' meetings – you can rest assured that the liquidator appointed will be a member of the *Volksraad* or a relative of one. There will be court actions and counter actions, enforced sale of the shares in the estate and costs to pay. A liquidator with any sense at all could string it out for three or four years, all the time drawing a handsome commission. Have you thought about that, Max?'

The narrowing of Max's eyes showed that he hadn't. He looked at Hradsky with a trace of helplessness in his face, and Sean took a little comfort from that look.

'Now what I suggest is this – you let us draw ten thousand, take our horses and personal belongings. We in exchange will give you the rest. Shares, bank accounts, property, everything. You cannot possibly get more out of it if you force us into bankruptcy.'

Hradsky gave Max a message in their private facial code and Max interpreted it to Sean.

'Would you mind waiting outside, please, while we discuss this offer of yours.'

'I'll go down and have a drink in the bar,' said Sean. He pulled his watch from his waistcoat pocket and checked the time. 'Will twenty minutes be enough?'

'Ample, thank you, Mr Courtney.'

Sean had his drink by himself although the bar was nowhere near empty. This was not an arrangement of his own choosing, but he was flying the fever flag of failure and so he had to take an isolation berth at one end of the bar while all the other ships steered wide of him. No one looked in his direction and the conversation that went on round him was carefully arranged so as to exclude him. While he waited out the twenty minutes he amused himself by imagining the reactions of these his friends if he were to ask them for a loan. This helped to take the sting out of their snubs but still he felt it rankling. He looked at his watch again. The twenty minutes were up. Sean walked back along the counter towards the door. Jock and Trevor Heyns saw him coming, they turned away abruptly and immediately became absorbed in staring at the bottle-lined shelves behind the bar counter. Sean stopped level with Jock and cleared his throat deferentially. 'Jock, could you spare a minute?'

Jock turned slowly. 'Ah, Sean. Yes, what is it?'

'Duff and I are leaving the Rand. I have something for you, just something to remember us by. I know Duff would want you to have it too.'

Jock reddened with embarrassment. 'That's not necessary,' he said and started to turn back to his drink.

'Please, Jock.'

'Oh, all right,' Jock's voice was irritable. 'What is it?'

'This,' Sean said and stepped forward, moving his weight behind the fist. Jock's large and whisky-flushed nose was a target to dream about. It was not one of Sean's best punches, he was out of training, but it was good enough to send Jock in a spectacular back-somersault over the counter. Dreamily Sean picked up Jock's glass and emptied it over Trevor's head.

'Next time you meet me smile and say "Hello",' he told Trevor. 'Until then – stay out of mischief.'

He went up the stairs to Hradsky's suite in much better spirits. They were waiting for him.

'Give me the word, Max,' Sean could even grin at him.

'Mr Hradsky has very generously –'

'How much?' Sean cut him short.

'Mr Hradsky will allow you to take fifteen hundred and your personal effects. As part of the agreement you will give an undertaking not to embark on any business venture on the Witwatersrand for a period of three years.'

'That will be too soon,' said Sean. 'Make it two thousand and you've got a deal.'

'The offer is not open to discussion.'

Sean could see they meant it. They didn't have to bargain; it was a statement.

'All right, I accept.'

'Mr Hradsky has sent for his lawyer to draw up the agreement. Would you mind waiting, Mr Courtney?'

'Not at all, Max, you forget I am a gentleman of leisure now.'

31

Sean found Duff still sitting in the chair where he had left him in the drawing-room of Xanadu. The bottle clutched in his hand was empty and he was unconscious. He had spilt brandy down the front of his waistcoat and three of the buttons were undone. Huddled in the big chair, his body seemed to have shrunk and the curly hair hanging onto his forehead softened the gaunt lines of his face. Sean loosened his fingers from the neck of the bottle and Duff moved restlessly, muttering and twisting his head.

'Bedtime for small boys,' said Sean. He lifted him out of the chair and hung him over one shoulder.

Duff sicked up copiously.

'That's the way, show Hradsky what you think of his bloody carpet,' Sean encouraged him. 'Give him another one for luck, but not on my boots.'

Duff did as he was bid and, chuckling, Sean carried him up the stairs. At the top he stopped and with Duff still bundled over one shoulder tried to analyse his own feelings. Damn it, he felt happy. It was ridiculous to feel so happy in the midst of disaster. He went on down the passage still wondering at himself and into Duff's room. He dropped Duff on the bed and stripped his clothes off, then he rolled him under the blankets. He brought the enamel wash basin from the bathroom and placed it next to the bed.

'You may need this – sleep well. There's a long ride ahead of us tomorrow.'

He stopped again at the top of the stairs and looked down their marble slope into the splendour of the lobby. He was leaving all of it and that was nothing to feel happy about. He laughed aloud. Perhaps it was because he had faced complete annihilation and at the last instant had changed it into something less; by avoiding the worst he had made defeat into a victory. A pathetic little victory to be sure, but at least they were no worse off now than they had been when they had arrived on the Rand. Was that the reason? Sean thought about it and found that it wasn't the whole truth. There was also a feeling of release. That was another part of it. To go on his way: north to a new land. He felt the tingle of anticipation.

'Not a whore or a stockbroker within five hundred miles,' he said aloud and grinned. He gave up trying to find words for his feeling. Emotion was so damned elusive: as soon as you cornered it, it changed its shape and the net of words which you had ready to throw over it was no longer suitable. He let it go free to range through his body, accepting and enjoying it. He ran down the stairs, out through the kitchens and into the stable yard.

'Mbejane!' he shouted, 'where the hell are you?'

The clatter of a stool overturning in the servants' quarters and the door of one of the rooms burst open.

'Nkosi – what is it?' The urgency of Sean's voice had alarmed Mbejane.

'Which are the six best horses we have?'

Mbejane named them, making no attempt to hide his curiosity.

'Are they all salted against the Nagana?'*

'All of them, Nkosi.'

'Good – have them ready before tomorrow's light. Two with saddles, the others to carry the packs.'

Mbejane turned on his smile. 'Could it be we are going hunting, Nkosi?'

'It could easily be,' Sean agreed.

'How long will we be gone, Nkosi?'

'How long is for ever? Take leave of all your women, bring your kaross and your spears and we will see where the road leads.'

Sean went back to his bedroom. It took him half an hour to pack. The pile of discarded clothing in the centre of the room grew steadily and what he kept made only half a horseload. He crammed it into two leather valises. He found his sheepskin coat in the back of one of the closets and threw it over a chair with his leather breeches and slouch hat, ready to wear in the

---

* Sleeping sickness. Salting involved deliberate exposure to the sting of the tsetse fly. Animals that recovered were then immune.

morning. He went down to the study and made his selection from the gun rack, ignoring the fancy doubles and obscure calibres. He took down a pair of shotguns and four Mannlichers.

Then he went to tell Candy goodbye. She was in her suite but she opened quickly to his knock.

'Have you heard?' he asked her.

'Yes, the whole town knows. Oh! Sean, I'm so sorry – please come in.' She held the door open for him. 'How is Duff?'

'He'll be all right – right now he's both drunk and asleep.'

'I'll go to him,' she said quickly. 'He'll need me now.'

For answer Sean raised an eyebrow and looked at her until she dropped her eyes.

'No, you're right, I suppose. Perhaps later, when he's got over the first shock.' She looked up at Sean and smiled. 'I suppose you need a drink. It must have been hell for you as well.' She went across to the cabinet. She had on a blue gown and it clung to the womanish thrust of her hips and did not go high enough to cover the cleft of her breasts. Sean watched her pour his drink and bring it to him. She was lovely, he thought.

'Till we meet again, Candy,' Sean lifted his glass.

Her eyes went wide and very blue. 'I don't understand. Why do you say that?'

'We're going, Candy, first thing tomorrow.'

'No, Sean – you're joking.' But she knew he wasn't. There wasn't much to say after that. He finished his drink and they talked for a while, then he kissed her.

'Be happy, please,' he ordered her.

'I'll try. Come back one day soon.'

'Only if you promise to marry me,' he smiled at her and she caught hold of his beard and tugged his head from side to side.

'Get away with you – before I hold you to that.' He left her then because he knew she was going to weep and he didn't want to watch it.

The next morning Duff packed his gear under Sean's direction. He followed each instruction with a dazed obedience, answering when Sean spoke but otherwise withdrawn in a protective shell of silence. When he had finished Sean made him pick up his bags and marched him down to where the horses waited in the chill gloom of not-yet day. With the horses were men, four shapes in the darkness. Sean hesitated before going out into the yard.

'Mbejane,' he called. 'Who are these with you?'

They came forward into the light that poured through the doorway and Sean chuckled.

'Hlubi, of the noble belly! Nonga! And is it you, Kandhla?' Men who had worked beside him in the trenches of the Candy Deep, had plied the spades that had uncovered his fortune, had plied the spears that protected it from the first predators. Happy at his recognition of them, for it had been many years, they crowded forward smiling as widely and whitely as only a Zulu can.

'What brings you three rogues together so early in the day?' Sean asked, and Hlubi answered for them.

'Nkosi, we heard talk of a trek and our feet burned, we heard talk of hunting and we could not sleep.'

'There is no money for wages,' Sean spoke gruffly to cover the sudden rush of affection he felt for them.

'We made no talk of wages,' Hlubi answered with dignity. Sean nodded, it was the reply he had expected. He cleared his throat and went on.

'You would come with me when you know that I have the Tagathi on me?' He used the Zulu word for witchcraft. 'You would follow me knowing that behind me I leave a spoor of dead men and sorrow?'

'Nkosi,' Hlubi was grave as he answered. 'Something always dies when the lion feeds – and yet there is meat for those that follow him.'

'I hear the chatter of old women at a beer drink,' Mbejane observed drily. 'There is no more to say and the horses grow restless.'

They rode down the driveway of Xanadu between the jacaranda trees and the smooth wide lawns. Behind them the mansion was grey and unlighted in the half darkness. They took the Pretoria road, climbed to the ridge and checked their horses at the crest. Sean and Duff looked back across the valley. The valley was filled with early morning mist, and the mine headgears probed up out of it. They watched the mists turn to gold as the low sun touched them and a mine hooter howled dismally.

'Couldn't we stay for just a week longer – perhaps we could work something out?' Duff asked softly.

Sean sat silently staring at the golden mist. It was beautiful. It hid the scarred earth and it hid the mills – it was a most appropriate cloak for that evil, greedy city. Sean turned his horse away towards Pretoria and slapped the loose end of his reins across its neck.

Part III

The Wilderness

Part III

THE Wilderness

I

They stayed five days in Pretoria, just long enough to buy the wagons and commission them, and when they left on the morning of the sixth day they went north on the Hunters Road. The wagons moved in column urged on by the Zulus and a dozen new servants that Sean had hired. They were followed by a mixed bag of black and white urchins and stray dogs; men called good luck after them and women waved from the verandas of the houses which lined the road. Then the town was behind them and they were out into the veld with only a dozen of the more adventurous mongrels still following them.

They made fifteen miles the first day and when they camped that night beside the ford of a small stream, Sean's back and legs ached from his first full day in the saddle in over five years. They drank a little brandy and ate steaks grilled over wood embers, then they let the fire die and sat and looked at the night. The sky was a curtain at which a barrel of grape-shot had been fired, riddling it with the holes through which the stars shone. The voices of the servants made a hive murmur as a background to the wailing of a jackal in the darkness beyond the firelight. They went to their living wagon early and for Sean the feel of rough blankets instead of silk sheets and the hardness of a straw mattress were not sufficient to keep him long from sleep.

From an early start the following morning they put another twenty miles behind them before outspan that night and twenty more the next day. The push and urgent drive were habits Sean had acquired on the Rand when every minute was vital and the loss of a day was a disaster. They were habits that stuck, and he pushed the caravan northward as impatiently as he would have chivvied the men on the Candy Deep who were cutting a drive to intersect the Reef. Then one morning, when they were inspanning the oxen at the usual hour of dawn, Mbejane asked him, 'Do we go to meet someone, Nkosi?'

'No. Why do you ask?'

'When a man moves fast there is usually a reason. I was seeking the reason for our haste.'

'The reason is –' Sean stopped. He looked around him quickly as if to find it, then he cleared his throat and scratched the side of his nose, '– outspan an hour before high sun,' he finished abruptly and went to his horse. He and Duff rode out a mile or two ahead of the wagons that day, then instead of keeping to the track or hurrying back to chase up the caravan Sean suggested, 'Let's ride across to that kopje over there. We'll leave the horses at the bottom and climb up to the top.'

'What for?' asked Duff.

'For the hell of it – come on.'

They hobbled the horses and set off up the steep side of the kopje, picking their way over the tumbled boulders and through the tangle of tree trunks. They were sweating and blowing hard when they came out on the summit and found a place with shade and a flat rock ledge on which to sit. Sean gave Duff a cheroot and they smoked and looked out across the land that was spread like a map below them.

Here the grasslands of the high veld were starting to blend into the forests and hilly country of the bushveld. There were vleis open as wheatfields, ending suddenly against a hill or bounded by haphazard plantations of tall trees. From the height at which they sat they could trace the courses of underground rivers by the dark green and superior height of the trees that grew above them. Everything else was the colour of Africa – brown, a thousand different shades of brown. Pale brown grass on red brown soil, with twisted, chocolate-brown tree trunks reaching up to the moving masses of brown leaves at their tips. Flickering indefinite brown were the herds of springbok that fed amongst the trees and on the slopes of the bare bulging brown hills, and the brown land reached away vast and unhurried into immeasurable distance, unmarred by the scratchings of man: tranquil and dignified in its immensity.

'It makes me feel small, but sort of safe – as though no one will notice me here,' said Duff, then laughed self-consciously.

'I know what you mean,' Sean answered him. He saw that for the first time since they had left the Rand the strain was gone from Duff's face. They smiled at each other and leaned back against the rock face behind them. They watched their wagons, far below them, coil into the tight circle of the laager and the cattle turned free move out to graze. The sun sank and the shadows stretched out longer and longer across the land. At last they went down the hill and found their horses. That night they stayed later than usual next to the fire and though they talked little there was the old feeling between them again. They had discovered a new reef that was rich with the precious elements of space and time. Out here there was more of those two treasures than a man could use in a dozen lifetimes. Space to move, to ride or to fire a rifle; space spread with sunlight and wind, grass and trees, but not filled with them. There was also time. This was where time began: it was a quiet river, moving but not changed by movement; draw on it as much as you would and still it was always full. It was measured by the seasons but not restricted by them, for the summer that was now standing back to let autumn pass was the same summer that had flamed a thousand years before and would flame again a thousand years hence. In the presence of so much space and time all striving was futile.

From then on their lives took their tempo from the leisurely turning of wagon-wheels. Sean's eyes which had been pointing straight ahead along the line of travel now turned aside to look about him. Each morning he and Duff would leave the wagons and wander out into the bush. Sometimes they would spend the day panning for gold in the sands of a stream, another day they would search for the first signs of elephant, but mostly they just rode and talked or lay hidden and watched the herds of game that daily became more numerous. They killed just enough to feed themselves, their servants and the pack of dogs that had followed them when they left Pretoria. They passed the little Boer settlement at Pietersburg and then the Zoutpansberg climbed up over the horizon, its sheer sides dark with rain forest and high rock cliffs. Here under the mountains they spent a week at Louis Trichardt, the most northerly permanent habitation of white men.

In the town they spoke with men who had hunted to the north of the mountains, across the Limpopo. These were taciturn brown-faced Boers with tobacco-stained beards – big men with the peace of the bush in their eyes. In their courteous, unhurried speech Sean sensed a fierce possessive love of the animals that they hunted and the land through which they moved so freely.

They were a different breed from the Natal Afrikanders and those he had met on the Witwatersrand, and he conceived the respect for them that would grow stronger in the years ahead when he would have to fight them.

There was no way through the mountains, they told him, but wagons could pass around them. The western passage skirted the edge of the Kalahari desert and this was bad country where the wagon wheels sank into the sandy soil and the marches between water became successively longer. To the east there was good rich forest land, well watered and stocked with game: low country, hotter the nearer one went to the coast, but the true bushveld where a man could find elephant.

So Sean and Duff turned east and, holding the mountains always in sight at their left hand, they went down into the wilderness.

2

Within a week's trek they saw elephant sign: trees broken and stripped of their bark. Although it was months old – the trees already dried out – nevertheless Sean felt the thrill of it and that night spent an hour cleaning and oiling his rifles. The forest thickened until the wagons had to weave continually between the trunks of the trees. But there were clearings in the forest – open vleis filled with grass where buffalo grazed like herds of domestic cattle and white tick birds squawked about them. This country was well watered with streams as clear and merry as a Scottish trout stream, but the water was blood-warm and the banks thick with bush. Along the rivers, in the forest and in the open were the herds of game: impala twisting and leaping away at the first approach with their crumpled horns laid back, kudu with big ears and soft eyes, black sable antelope with white bellies and horns curved like a naval cutlass, zebra trotting with the dignity of fat ponies, while about them frolicked their companions, the gnu, waterbuck, nyala, roan antelope and – at last – elephant.

Sean and Mbejane were ranging a mile ahead of the wagons when they found the spoor. It was fresh, so fresh that sap still oozed from the mahoba-hoba tree where the bark had been prised loose with the tip of a tusk and then stripped off. The wood beneath was naked and white.

'Three bulls,' said Mbejane. 'One very big.'

'Wait here,' Sean spun his horse and galloped back to the column. Duff lay on the driver's seat of the first wagon rocking gently to its motion, his hat covering his face and his hands behind his head.

'Elephant! Duff,' Sean yelled. 'Not an hour ahead of us. Get saddled up, man!'

Duff was ready in five minutes. Mbejane was waiting for them; he had already worked the spoor a short distance and picked up the run of it and now he went away on it, They followed him, riding slowly side by side.

'You've hunted elephant before, laddie?' asked Duff.

'Never,' said Sean.

'Good grief!' Duff looked alarmed. 'I thought you were an expert. I think I'll go back and finish my sleep, you can call me when you've had a little more experience.'

'Don't worry,' Sean laughed with excitement. 'I know all about it; I was raised on elephant stories.'

'That sets my heart at ease,' Duff murmured sarcastically and Mbejane glanced over his shoulder at them, not trying to conceal his irritation.

'Nkosi, it is not wise to talk now for we will soon come up with them.'

So they went on in silence: passing a knee-high pile of yellow dung that looked like the contents of a coir mattress, following the oval pad marks in the dust and the trail of torn branches.

It was a good hunt, this first one. The small breeze held steadily into their faces and the spoor ran straight and hot. They closed in, each minute strengthening the certainty of the kill. Sean sat stiff and eager in the saddle with his rifle across his lap, his eyes restlessly moving over the frieze of bush ahead of him. Mbejane stopped suddenly and came back to Sean's stirrup.

'Here they halted for the first time. The sun is hot and they will rest but this place was not to their liking and they have moved on. We will find them soon now.'

'The bush becomes too thick,' Sean grunted; he eyed the untidy tangle of catbush into which the spoor had led them. 'We will leave the horses here with Hlubi and go in on foot.'

'Laddie,' Duff demurred. 'I can run much faster on horseback.'

'Off!' said Sean and nodded to Mbejane to lead. They moved forward again. Sean was sweating and the drops clung heavily to his eyebrows and trickled down his cheeks; he brushed them away. The excitement was an indigestible ball in his stomach and a dryness in his throat.

Duff sauntered casually next to Sean with that small half smile on his face, but there was a quickness in his breathing. Mbejane cautioned them with a gesture of his hand and they stopped. Minutes passed slowly and then Mbejane's hand moved again, pink-palmed eloquence.

'It was nothing,' said the hand. 'Follow me.'

They went on again. There were Mopani flies swarming at the corners of Sean's eyes, drinking the moisture, and he blinked them away. Their buzzing was so loud in his ears that he thought it must carry to their quarry. His every sense was tuned to its limit: hearing magnified, vision sharp and even his sense of smell so clear that he could pick up the taint of dust, the scent of a wild flower and Mbejane's faintly musky body-smell.

Suddenly in front of him Mbejane was still; his hand moved again gently, unmistakably.

'They are here,' said the hand.

Sean and Duff crouched behind him, searching with eyes that could see only brown bush and grey shadows. The tension coarsened their breathing and Duff was no longer smiling. Mbejane's hand came up slowly and pointed at the wall of vegetation in front of them. The seconds strung together like beads on the string of time and still they searched.

An ear flapped lazily and instantly the picture jumped into focus. Bull elephant, big and very close, grey among grey shadow. Sean touched Mbejane's arm. 'I had seen it,' said that touch.

Slowly Mbejane's hand swivelled and pointed again. Another wait, another searching and then a belly rumbled, a great grey belly filled with half-digested leaves. It was a sound so ridiculous in the silence that Sean wanted to laugh – a gurgling sloshy sound – and Sean saw the other bull. It was standing in shadow also, with long yellow ivory and small eyes tight-closed. Sean put his lips to Duff's ear.

'This one is yours,' he whispered. 'Wait until I get into position for the other,' and he began moving out to the side, each step exposing a little more of the second bull's flank until the shoulder was open to him and he could see the point of the elbow beneath the baggy, wrinkled skin. The angle was right; from here he could reach the heart. He nodded at Duff, brought his rifle up – leaning forward against the recoil, aiming close behind the massive shoulder – and he fired.

The gunfire was shockingly loud in the confined thorn bush; dust flew in a spurt from the bull's shoulder and it staggered from the strike of the bullet. Beyond it the third elephant burst from sleep into flight and Sean's hands moved neatly on his weapon, ejecting and reloading, swinging up and firing again. He saw the bullet hit and he knew it was a mortal wound. The two bulls ran together and the bush opened to them and swallowed them: they were gone, crashing away wounded, trumpeting in pain. Sean ran after them, dodging through the catbush, oblivious to the sting of the thorns that snatched at him as he passed.

'This way, Nkosi,' Mbejane shouted beside him. 'Quickly or we will lose them.' They sprinted after the sounds of flight – a hundred yards, two hundred, panting now and sweating in the heat. Suddenly the catbush ended and in front of them was a wide riverbed with steep banks. The river sand was blindingly white and in the middle was a sluggish trickle of water. One of the bulls was dead, lying in the stream with the blood washing off him in a pale brown stain. The other bull was trying to climb the far bank; it was too steep for him and he slid back wearily. The blood dripped from the tip of his trunk, and he swung his head to look at Sean and Mbejane. His ears cocked back defiantly and he began his charge, blundering towards them through the soft river sand.

Sean watched him come and there was sadness in him as he brought up his rifle, but it was the proud regret that a man feels when he watches hopeless courage. Sean killed with a brain shot, quickly.

They climbed down the bank into the riverbed and went to the elephant; it knelt with its legs folded under it and its tusks driven deep into the sand with the force of its fall. The flies were already clustering at the little red mouths of the bullet wounds. Mbejane touched one of the tusks and then he looked up at Sean.

'It is a good elephant.' He said no more, for this was not the time to talk. Sean leaned his rifle against the bull's shoulder; he felt in his top pocket for a cheroot and stood with it unlit between his teeth. He would kill more elephant, he knew, but always this would be the one he would remember. He stroked his hand over the rough skin and the bristles were stiff and sharp.

'Where is Nkosi Duff?' Sean remembered him suddenly. 'Did he also kill?'

'He did not shoot,' answered Mbejane.

'What!' Sean turned quickly to Mbejane. 'Why not?'

Mbejane sniffed a pinch of snuff and sneezed, then he shrugged his shoulders.

'It is a good elephant,' he said again, looking down at it.

'We must go back and find him.' Sean snatched up his rifle

346

and Mbejane followed him. They found Duff sitting alone in the catbush with his rifle propped beside him and a water-bottle to his lips. He lowered the bottle as Sean came up and saluted him with it.

'Hail! the conquering hero comes.' There was something in his eyes that Sean could not read.

'Did you miss yours?' Sean asked.

'Yes,' said Duff, 'I missed mine.' He lifted the bottle and drank again. Suddenly and sickeningly Sean was ashamed for him. He dropped his eyes, not wanting to acknowledge Duff's cowardice.

'Let's get back to the wagons,' he said. 'Mbejane can come with packhorses for the tusks.'

They did not ride together on the way home.

3

It was almost dark when they arrived back at the laager. They gave their horses to one of the servants and washed in the basin that Kandhla had ready for them, then they went to sit by the fire. Sean poured the drinks, fussing over the glasses to avoid looking at Duff. He felt awkward. They'd have to talk about it and he searched his brain for a way to bring it into the open. Duff had shown craven and Sean started to find excuses for him – he may have had a misfire or he may have been unsighted by Sean's shot. At all events Sean determined not to let it stay like this, sour and brooding between them. They'd talk it out then forget it. He carried Duff's glass to him and smiled at him.

'That's right, try and cover it with a grin,' Duff lifted his glass. 'To our big brave hunter. Dammit, laddie, how could you do it?'

Sean stared at Duff. 'What do you mean?'

'You know what I mean, you're so damned guilty you can't even look me in the face. How could you kill those bloody great animals – but even worse how could you *enjoy* doing it?'

Sean subsided weakly into his chair. He couldn't tell which of his emotions was uppermost – relief or surprise. Duff went on quickly.

'I know what you're going to say, I've heard the arguments before – from my dear father. He explained it to me one evening after we'd ridden down a fox. When I say "we", I mean twenty horsemen and forty hounds.'

Sean had not yet rallied from the shock of finding himself in the dock after preparing himself to play the role of prosecutor.

'Don't you like hunting?' he asked incredulously. The way he might have asked, 'don't you like eating?'.

'I'd forgotten what it was like. I was carried away by your exitement, but when you started to kill them it all came back to me.' Duff sipped his brandy and stared into the fire. 'They never had a chance. One minute they were sleeping and the next you were ripping them with bullets the way the hounds ripped that fox. They didn't have a chance.'

'But, Duff, it wasn't meant to be a contest.'

'Yes, I know, my father explained that to me. It's a ritual – a sacred rite to Diana. He should have explained it to the fox as well.'

Sean was getting angry now. 'We came out here to hunt ivory – and that's what I'm doing.'

'Tell me that you killed those elephant only for their teeth, laddie, and I'll call you a liar. You loved it. Christ! You should have seen your face and the face of your damned heathen.'

'All right! I like hunting and the only other man I ever met who didn't was a coward,' Sean shouted at him.

Duff's face paled and he looked up at Sean. 'What are you trying to say?' he whispered. They stared at each other and in the silence Sean had to choose between letting his temper run or keeping Duff's friendship, for the words that would spoil it for ever were crowding into his mouth. He made his hands relax their grip on the arms of his chair.

'I didn't mean that,' he said.

'I hoped you didn't,' Duff's grin came precariously back onto his face. 'Tell me why you like hunting, laddie. I'll try and understand but don't expect me to hunt with you again.'

It was like explaining colour to a blind man, describing the lust of the hunter to someone who was born without it. Duff listened in agonized silence as Sean tried to find the words for the excitement that makes a man's blood sing through his body, that heightens his senses and allows him to lose himself in an emotion as old as the urge to mate. Sean tried to show him how the nobler and more beautiful was the quarry, the stronger was the compulsion to hunt and kill it, that it had no conscious cruelty in it but was rather an expression of love: a fierce possessive love. A devouring love that needed the complete and irrevocable act of death for its consummation. By destroying something, a man could have it always as his own: selfish perhaps, but then instinct knows no ethics. It was all very clear to Sean, so much a part of him that he had never tried to voice it before and now he stumbled over the words, gesticulating in helpless inarticulateness, repeating himself, coming at last to the end and knowing by the look on Duff's face that he had failed to show it to him.

'And you were the gentleman who fought Hradsky for the rights of man,' Duff said softly, 'the one who always talked about not hurting people.'

Sean opened his mouth to protest but Duff went on. 'You get ivory for us and I'll look for gold – each of us to what he is best suited. I'll forgive you your elephants as you forgave me my Candy – still equal partners. Agreed?'

Sean nodded and Duff held up his glass.

'It's empty,' he said. 'Do me a favour, laddie.'

4

There was never any after-taste to their disputes, no rankling of unspoken words or lingering of doubt. What they had in common they enjoyed, where there were differences they accepted them. So when after each hunt the packhorses brought the tusks into the camp there was no trace of censure in Duff's face or voice; there was only the genuine pleasure of having Sean back from the bush. Sometimes it was a good day and Sean would cut the spoor, follow, kill and be back in the laager the same night. But more often, when the herd was moving fast or the ground was hard or he could not kill at the first approach, he would be gone for a week or more. Each time he returned they celebrated, drinking and laughing far into the night, lying late in bed the next morning, playing Klabejas on the floor of the wagon between their cots or reading aloud out of the books that Duff had brought with him from Pretoria. Then a day or two later Sean would be gone again, with his dogs and his gunboys trotting behind him.

This was a different Sean from the one who had whored it up at the Opera House and presided over the panelled offices in Eloff Street. His beard, no longer groomed and shaped by a barber, curled onto his chest. The doughy colour of his face and arms had been turned by the sun to the rich brown of a newly-baked loaf. The seat of his pants that had been stretched to danger point across his rump now hung loosely; his arms were thicker and the soft swell of fat had given way to the flatness and bulge of hard muscle. He walked straighter, moved quicker and laughed more easily.

In Duff the change was less noticeable. He was lean and gaunt-faced as ever, but now there was less of the restlessness in his eyes. His speech and movements were slower and the golden beard he was growing had the strange effect of making him appear younger. Each morning he left the wagons, taking one of the servant's with him, and spent the days wandering in the bush, tapping with his prospecting hammer at the occasional outcrops of rock or squatting beside a stream and spinning the gravel in his pan. Every evening he came back to camp and analysed the bag of rock samples he had collected during the day; then he threw them away, bathed and set out a bottle and two glasses on the table beside the fire. While he ate his supper he listened and waited for the dogs to bark, for the sound of horses in the darkness and Sean's voice. If the night remained silent he put the bottle away and climbed up into his wagon. He was lonely then, not with a deep loneliness but just enough to add relish to Sean's return.

Always they moved east, until gradually the silhouette of the Zoutpansberg softened as the mountains became less steep and began to fade into the tail of the range. Scouting along their edge Sean found a pass and they took the wagons up and over and down into the Limpopo valley beyond. Here the country changed character again; it became flat, the monotony of thorn scrub relieved only by the baobab trees with their great, swollen trunks crowned in a little halo of branches. Water was scarce and Sean rode ahead from each camp to find the next waterhole before they moved. However, the hunting was good for the game was concentrated on the isolated drinking places, and before they were halfway from the mountains to the Limpopo Sean had filled another wagon with ivory.

'We'll be coming back this way, I suppose?' Duff asked.

'I suppose so,' agreed Sean.

'Well then, I don't see any point in carrying a ton of ivory with us. Let's bury it and we can pick it up on our way back.'

Sean looked at him thoughtfully. 'About once in every year you come up with a good idea – we'll do exactly that.'

The next camp was a good one. There was water – an acre of muddy liquid not as heavily salted with elephant urine as some of the previous ones had been; there was shade provided by a grove of wild fig trees and the grazing was of a quality that promised to restore the condition that the oxen had lost since crossing the mountains. They decided to make it a rest camp: bury the ivory, do some repairs and maintenance on the wagons and let the servants and animals fatten up a little. The first task was to dig a hole large enough to contain all the hundred-odd tusks they had accumulated and it was evening on the third day before they finished.

5

Sean and Duff sat together inside the laager and watched the sun go down, bleeding below the land, and after it had gone the clouds were oyster and lilac-coloured in the brief twilight. Kandhla threw wood on the fire and it burnt up fiercely. They ate grilled kudu liver, and thick steaks with a rind of yellow fat on them, and they drank brandy with their coffee. The conversation lagged into contented silence for they were both tired. They sat staring into the fire, too lazy to make the effort required for bed. Sean watched the fire pictures form in the coals, the faces and the phantoms flickering and fading. He saw a tiny temple have its columns pulled out from under it by a fiery Samson and collapse in a shower of sparks – a burning horse changed magically into a dragon of blue flame. He looked away to rest his eyes and when he turned back there was a small black scorpion scuttling out from under the loose bark on one of the logs. It lifted its tail like the arm of a flamenco dancer and the flames that ringed it shone on its glossy body armour. Duff was also watching it, leaning forward with his elbows on his knees.

'Will he sting himself to death before the flames reach him?' he asked softly. 'I have heard that they do.'

'No,' said Sean.

'Why not?'

'Only man has the intelligence to end the inevitable; in all other creatures the instinct of survival is too strong,' Sean answered him, and the scorpion crabbed sideways from the nearest flames and stopped again with its raised sting jerking slightly. 'Besides he's immune to his own poison so he has no choice.'

'He could jump down into the fire and get it over with,' murmured Duff, subdued by the little tragedy.

The scorpion started its last desperate circuit of the closing ring. Its tail drooped and the grip of its claws was unsteady on the rough bark; it was shrivelling with the heat, its legs curling up and its tail subsiding. The flames caressed it with swift yellow hands and smeared its shiny body with the dullness of death. The log tipped sideways and the speck was gone.

'Would you?' asked Sean. 'Would you have jumped?'

Duff sighed softly, 'I don't know,' he said and stood up. 'I'm going to pump out my bilges and crawl into bed.' He walked away and went to stand at the edge of the circle of firelight.

Since they had left Pretoria the small voices of the jackals had yapped discreetly around each outspan – they were so much a part of the African night that they went unnoticed – but now suddenly there was a difference. Only one jackal spoke, and with a voice that stammered shrilly – a sound of pain, a crazy hysterical shrieking that made Sean's skin prickle. He scrambled to his feet and stood staring undecided into the darkness. The jackal was coming towards the camp, coming fast – and suddenly Sean knew what was happening.

'Duff!' he called. 'Come back here! Run, man, run!'

Duff looked back at Sean helplessly, his hands held low in front of him and his water arcing down, curving silver in the firelight from his body to the ground.

'Duff!' Sean's voice was a shout. 'It's a rabid jackal. Run, damn you, run!' The jackal was close now, very close, but at last Duff started to move. He was halfway back to the fire before he tripped. He fell and rolled over and brought his feet up under his body to rise. His head turned to face the darkness from which it would come. Then Sean saw it. It flitted out of the shadows like a grey moth in the bad light and went straight for where Duff knelt. Sean saw him try to cover his face with his hands as the jackal sprang at him. One of the dogs twisted out of Mbejane's hand and brushed past Sean's legs. Sean snatched up a piece of firewood and sprinted after it, but already Duff was on his back, his arms flailing frantically as he tried to push away the terrier-sized animal that was slashing at his face and hands. The dog caught it and dragged it off, worrying it, growling through locked jaws. Sean hit the jackal with the club – breaking its back. He swung again and again, beating its body, into shapelessness before he turned to Duff. Duff was on his feet now. He had unwound the scarf from his neck and was mopping with it at his face but the blood dribbled down his chin and blotched the front of his shirt. His hands were trembling. Sean led him close to the fire, pulled Duff's hands down and examined the bites. His nose was torn and the flesh of one cheek hung open in a flap.

'Sit down!'

Duff obeyed, holding the scarf to his face again. Sean went quickly to the fire: with a stick he raked embers into a pile, then he drew his hunting-knife and thrust the blade into the coals.

'Mbejane,' he called, without taking his eyes off the knife. 'Throw that jackal onto the fire. Put on plenty of wood. Do not touch its body with your hands. When you have done that tie up that dog and keep the others away from it.' Sean turned the knife in the fire. 'Duff, drink as much of that brandy as you can.'

'What are you going to do?'

'You know what I've got to do.'

'He bit my wrist as well.' Duff held up his hand for Sean to see the punctures, black holes from which the blood oozed watery and slow.

'Drink.' Sean pointed at the brandy bottle. For a second they looked at each other and Sean saw the horror moving in Duff's eyes: horror of the hot knife and horror of the germs which had been injected into him. The germs that must be burnt out before they escaped into his blood, to breed and ferment there until they ate into his brain and rode him to a screaming, gibbering death.

'Drink,' said Sean again. Duff took up the bottle and lifted it to his mouth. Sean stooped and pulled the knife out of the fire. He held the blade an inch from the back of his hand. It was not hot enough. He thrust it back into the coals.

'Mbejane, Hlubi, stand on each side of the Nkosi's chair. Be ready to hold him.' Sean loosened his belt, doubled the thick leather and handed it to Duff. 'Bite on this.'

He turned back to the fire and this time when he drew the knife its blade was pale pink. 'Are you ready?'

'The work you are about to do will break the hearts of a million maids.' A last hoarse attempt at humour from Duff.

'Hold him,' said Sean.

Duff gasped at the touch of the knife — a great shuddering gasp — and his back arched, but the two Zulus held him down remorselessly. The edges of the wound blackened and hissed as

Sean ran the blade in deeper. The stink of burning brought the vomit into his throat. He clenched his teeth. When he stepped back Duff hung slackly in the Zulus' hands, sweat had soaked his shirt and wet his hair. Sean heated the knife again and cleaned the bites in Duff's wrist while Duff moaned and writhed weakly in the chair. He smeared axle grease over the burns and bandaged the wrist loosely with strips torn from a clean shirt. They lifted Duff into the wagon and laid him on his cot. Sean went out to where Mbejane had tied the dog. He found scratches beneath the hair on its shoulder. They put a sack over its head to stop it biting and Sean cauterized its wounds also.

'Tie it to the far wagon, do not let the other dogs near it, see it has food and water,' he told Mbejane.

Then he went back to Duff. Delirious with pain and brandy Duff did not sleep at all that night and Sean stayed by his cot until the morning.

6

About fifty yards from the laager under one of the wild fig trees the servants built Duff a hut. The framework was of poles and over it they stretched a tarpaulin. They made a bed for him and brought his mattress and blankets from the wagon. Sean joined four trekchains together, forging new links and hammering them closed. He passed one end of the chain round the base of the fig tree and riveted it back up on itself. Duff sat in the shade of a wagon and watched them work. His hurt hand was in a sling and his face was swollen, the wound crusty-looking and edged in angry red. When he was finished with the chain, Sean walked across to him.

'I'm sorry, Duff, we have to do it.'

'They abolished the slave trade some time ago – just in case you didn't know.' Duff tried to grin with his distorted face. He stood up and followed Sean to the hut. Sean looped the loose end of the chain round Duff's waist. He locked it with a bolt through two of the links then flattened the end of the bolt with a dozen strokes of the hammer.

'That should hold you.'

'An excellent fit,' Duff commended him. 'Now let us inspect my new quarters.'

Sean followed him into the hut. Duff lay down on the bed. He looked very tired and sick.

'How long will it take before we know?' he asked quietly.

Sean shook his head. 'I'm not sure. I think you should stay here at least a month – after that we'll allow you back into society.'

'A month – it's going to be fun. Lying here expecting any minute to start barking like a dog and lifting my leg against the nearest tree.'

Sean didn't laugh. 'I did a thorough job with the knife. It's a thousand to one you'll be all right. This is just a precaution.'

'The odds are attractive – I'll put a fiver on it.' Duff crossed his ankles and stared up at the roof. Sean sat down on the edge of the bed. It was a long time before Duff ended the silence.

'What will it be like, Sean, have you ever seen someone with rabies?'

'No.'

'But you've heard about it, haven't you? Tell me what you've heard about it,' Duff persisted.

'For Chrissake, Duff, you're not going to get it.'

'Tell me, Sean, tell me what you know about it.' Duff sat up and caught hold of Sean's arm.

Sean looked steadily at him for a moment before he answered. 'You saw that jackal, didn't you?'

Duff sank back onto his pillows. 'Oh, my God!' he whispered.

Together they started the long wait. They used another tarpaulin to make an open shelter next to the hut and under it they spent the days that followed.

In the beginning it was very bad. Sean tried to pull Duff out of the black despair into which he had slumped, but Duff sat for hours at a time gazing out into the bush, fingering the scabs on his face and only occasionally smiling at the banquet of choice stories that Sean spread for him. But at last Sean's efforts were rewarded – Duff began to talk. He spoke of things he had never mentioned before and listening to him Sean learned more about him than he had in the previous five years. Sometimes Duff paced up and down in front of Sean's chair with the chain hanging down behind him like a tail; at other times he sat quietly, his voice filled with longing for the mother he had never known.

' – there was a portrait of her in the upper gallery, I used to spend whole afternoons in front of it. It was the kindest face I had ever seen –'

Then it hardened again as he remembered his father, 'that old bastard'.

He talked of his daughter. '– she had a fat chuckle that would break your heart. The snow on her grave made it look like a big sugar-iced cake, she would have liked that –'

At other times his voice was puzzled as he examined some past action of his, angry as he remembered a mistake or a missed opportunity. Then he would break off and grin self-consciously. 'I say, I am talking a lot of drivel.'

359

The scabs on his face began to dry up and come away, and more often now his old gaiety bubbled to the surface.

On one of the poles that supported the tarpaulin roof he started a calendar, cutting a notch for each day. It became a daily ceremony. He cut each notch with the concentration of a sculptor carving marble and when he had finished he would stand back and count them aloud as if by doing so he could force them to add up to thirty, the number that would allow him to shed his chain.

There were eighteen notches on the pole when the dog went mad. It was in the afternoon. They were playing Klabejas. Sean had just dealt the cards when the dog started screaming from among the wagons. Sean knocked over his chair as he jumped up. He snatched his rifle from where it leant against the wall and ran down to the laager. He disappeared behind the wagon to which the dog was tied and almost immediately Duff heard the shot. In the abrupt and complete stillness that followed, Duff slowly lowered his face into his hands.

It was nearly an hour before Sean came back. He picked up his chair, set it to the table and sat down.

'It's you to call – are you going to take on?' he asked as he picked up his cards. They played with grim intensity, fixing their attention on the cards, but both of them knew that there was a third person at the table now.

'Promise you'll never do that to me,' Duff blurted out at last.

Sean looked up at him. 'That I'll never do what to you?'

'What you did to that dog.'

The dog! The bloody dog. He should never have taken a chance with it, he should have destroyed it that first night,

'Just because the dog got it doesn't mean that you – '

'Swear to me,' Duff interrupted fiercely, 'swear you won't bring the rifle to me.'

'Duff, you don't know what you're asking. Once you've got it – ' Sean stopped; anything he said would make it worse.

'Promise me,' Duff repeated.

'All right, I swear it then.'

7

It was worse now than it had been in the beginning. Duff abandoned his calendar and with it the hope that had been slowly growing stronger. If the days were bad then the nights were hell, for Duff had a dream. It came to him every night – sometimes two or three times. He tried to keep awake after Sean had left, reading by the light of a lantern; or he lay and listened to the night noises, the splash and snort of buffalo drinking down at the waterhole, the liquid half-warble of night birds or the deep drumming of a lion. But in the end he would have to sleep and then he dreamed.

He was on horseback riding across a flat brown plain: no hills, no trees, nothing but lawnlike grass stretching away on all sides to the horizon. His horse threw no shadow – he always looked for a shadow and it worried him that there never was one. Then he would find the pool – clear water, blue and strangely shiny. The pool frightened him but he could not stop himself going to it. He would kneel beside it and look into the water; the reflection of his own face looked up at him – animal-snouted, shaggy-brown with wolf teeth, white and long. He would wake then and the horror of that face would last until morning.

Nearly desperate with his own utter helplessness, Sean tried to help him. Because of the accord they had established over the years and because they were so close to each other, Sean had to suffer with him. He tried to shut himself off from it; sometimes he succeeded for an hour or even half a morning, but then it came back with a stomach-swooping shock. Duff was going to die – Duff was going to die an unspeakable death. Was it a mistake to let someone get too deep inside you, so that you must share his agony in every excruciating detail? Didn't a man have enough of his own that he must share the full measure of another's suffering?

By then the October winds had started, the heralds of the rain:

361

hot winds full of dust, winds that dried the sweat on a man's body before it had time to cool him, thirsty winds that during daylight brought the game to the waterhole in full view of the camp.

Sean had half a case of wine hoarded under his cot. That last evening he cooled four bottles, wrapping them in wet sacking. He took them up to Duff's shelter just before supper and set them on the table. Duff watched him. The scars on his face were almost completely healed now, glassy red marks on his pale skin.

'Chateau Olivier,' said Sean and Duff nodded.

'It's a good wine – most probably travel-sick.'

'Well, if you don't want it, I'll take it away again,' said Sean.

'I'm sorry, laddie,' Duff spoke quickly. 'I didn't mean to be ungrateful. This wine suits my mood tonight. Did you know that wine is a sad drink?'

'Nonsense!' Sean disagreed as he twisted the corkscrew into the first cork. 'Wine is gay.' He poured a little into Duff's glass and Duff picked it up and held it towards the fire so the light shone through it.

'You see only the surface, Sean. A good wine has the elements of tragedy within it. The better the wine the more sad it is.'

Sean snorted. 'Explain yourself,' he invited.

Duff put his glass down on the table again and stared at it. 'How long do you suppose this wine has taken to reach its present perfection?'

'Ten or fifteen years, I suppose,' Sean answered.

Duff nodded. 'And now all that remains is to drink it – the work of years destroyed in an instant. Don't you think that is sad?' Duff asked softly.

'My God, Duff, don't be so damned morbid.'

But Duff wasn't listening to him. 'Wine and mankind have this in common. They can find perfection only in age, in a lifetime of seeking. Yet in the finding they find also their own destruction.'

'So you think that if a man lives long enough he will reach perfection?' Sean challenged him, and Duff answered him still staring at the glass.

'Some grapes grew in the wrong soil, some were diseased before they went to the press and some were spoiled by a careless vintner – not all grapes make good wine.' Duff picked up his glass and tasted from it, then he went on. 'A man takes longer and he must find it not within the quiet confines of the cask but in the cauldron of life; therefore his is the greater tragedy.'

'Yes, but no one can live for ever,' Sean protested.

'So you think that makes it less sad?' Duff shook his head. 'You're wrong, of course. It does not detract from it, it enhances it. If only there were some escape, some way of ensuring that what is good could endure instead of this complete hopelessness.'

Duff lay back in his chair, his face pale and gaunt-looking. 'Even that I could accept, if only they had given me more time.'

'I've had enough of this talk. Let's discuss something else. I don't know what you're worrying about. You're not fit to drink yet, you've got another twenty or thirty years to go,' Sean said gruffly and Duff looked up at him for the first time.

'Have I, Sean?'

Sean couldn't meet his eyes. He knew Duff was going to die. Duff grinned his lopsided grin and looked down again at his glass. Slowly the grin disappeared and he spoke again.

'If only I had more time, I could have done it. I could have found the weak places and fortified them. I could have seen the answers.' His voice rose higher. 'I could have! I know I could have! Oh God, I'm not ready yet. I need more time.' His voice was shrill and his eyes wild and haunted. 'It's too soon – it's too soon!'

Sean couldn't stand it, he jumped up and caught Duff's shoulders and shook him.

'Shut up, God damn you, shut up,' he shouted at him. Duff was panting, his lips were parted and quivering. He touched them with the tips of his fingers as though to stop them.

'I'm sorry, laddie, I didn't mean to let go like that.' Sean dropped his hands from Duff's shoulders.

'Both of us are too damned edgy,' he said. 'It's going to be all right, you wait and see.'

'Yes – it will be all right.' Duff ran his fingers through his hair, combing it back from his eyes. 'Open another bottle, laddie.'

8

That night after Sean had gone to bed, Duff had his dream again. The wine he had drunk slowed him down and prevented him from waking. He was trapped in his fancy, struggling to escape into wakefulness but only reaching the surface before he sank back to dream that dream again.

Sean went up to Duff's shelter the next morning early. Although the night's coolness still lingered under the spreading branches of the wild figs the rising day promised to blow dry and burn hot. The animals could sense it. The trek oxen were clustered among the trees and a small herd of eland was moving from the waterhole. The bull, with his short thick horns and the dark tuft on his forehead, was leading his cows away to find shade. Sean stood in the doorway of the hut and waited while his eyes adjusted themselves to its gloom. Duff was awake.

'Get out of bed or you'll have bed sores to add to your happiness.'

Duff swung his feet off the litter and groaned.

'What did you put in that wine last night?' He massaged his temples gently. 'I've got a hundred hobgoblins doing a Cossack dance around the roof of my skull.'

Sean felt the first twinge of alarm. He put his hand on Duff's shoulder feeling for the heat of fever, but Duff was quite cool. He relaxed.

'Breakfast's ready,' said Sean. Duff played with his porridge and barely tasted the grilled eland liver. He kept screwing his eyes up against the glare of the sun and when they had finished their coffee he pushed back his chair.

'I'm going to take my tender head to bed.'

'All right.' Sean stood up as well. 'We're a bit short of meat. I'll go and see if I can get a buck.'

'No, stay and talk to me,' Duff said quickly. 'We can have a few hands of cards.'

They hadn't played in days and Sean agreed readily. He sat on the end of Duff's bed and within half an hour he had won thirty-two pounds from him.

'You must let me teach you this game sometime,' he gloated.

Petulantly, Duff threw his hand in. 'I don't feel like playing any more.' He pressed his fingers to his closed eyelids. 'I can't concentrate with this headache.'

'Do you want to sleep?' Sean gathered up the cards and put them in their box.

'No. Why don't you read to me?'

Duff picked up a leather-bound copy of *Bleak House* from the table beside the bed and tossed it into Sean's lap.

'Where shall I start?' Sean asked.

'It doesn't matter, I know it almost by heart.' Duff lay back and closed his eyes. 'Start anywhere.'

Sean read aloud. He stumbled on for half an hour with his tongue never quite catching the rhythm of the words. Once or twice he glanced up at Duff, but Duff lay still with a faint sheen of sweat on his face and the scars very noticeable. He was breathing easily. Dickens is a powerful sleeping-draught for a hot morning and Sean's eyelids sagged down and his voice slowed and finally stopped. The book slid off his lap.

The small tinkle of Duff's chain disturbed him; he awoke and looked at the bed. Duff crouched apelike. The madness was a fire in his eyes and his cheeks twitched. A yellowish froth coated his teeth and formed a thin line of scum along his lips.

'Duff – ' Sean said, and Duff lunged at him with fingers hooked and a noise in his throat that was not human nor yet animal. It was a sound that jellied Sean's stomach and took the strength from his legs.

'Don't!' screamed Sean, and the chain caught on one of the posts of the bed, jerking Duff back sprawling onto the bed before he could sink his teeth into Sean's paralysed body.

Sean ran. He ran out of the hut and into the bush. He ran with terror trembling in his legs and choking his breath. He ran with his heart taking its beat from his racing feet and his lungs pumping in disordered panic. A branch ripped across his cheek and the sting of it served to steady him. His feet slowed – he stopped and stood gasping, staring back towards the camp. He waited while his body settled and he forced his terror down until it was only a sickening sensation in his stomach. Then he circled

365

through the thorn bush and approached the laager from the side farthest away from Duff's shelter. The camp was empty, the servants had fled in the same terror that had driven Sean. He remembered that his rifle was still in the hut beside Duff's bed. He slipped into his wagon and quickly opened the case of unused rifles. His hands were unsteady again as he fumbled with the locks, for the chain might have parted and at every second he expected to hear that inhuman sound behind him. He found his bandolier hanging on the end of his cot and he took cartridges from it. He loaded the rifle and cocked it. The weight of steel and wood in his hands gave him comfort. It made him a man again.

He jumped down out of the wagon and with the rifle held ready he went cautiously out of the circle of wagons. The chain had held. Duff stood in the shade of the wild fig plucking at it. He was making a sound like a new-born puppy. His back was turned to Sean and he was naked, his torn clothing scattered about him. Sean walked slowly towards him. He stopped outside the reach of the chain.

'Duff!' Sean called uncertainly. Duff spun and crouched, the froth was thick in his golden beard; he looked at Sean and his teeth bared. Then he charged screaming until the chain caught him and threw him onto his back once more. He scrambled to his feet and fought the chain, his eyes fastened hungrily on Sean. Sean backed away. He brought up the rifle and aimed between Duff's eyes.

Swear to me. Swear to me you won't bring the rifle to me.

Sean's aim wavered. He kept moving backwards. Duff was bleeding now. The steel links had smeared the skin off his hips, but still he pulled against them fighting to get at Sean – and Sean was shackled just as effectively by his promise. He could not end it. He lowered the rifle and watched in impotent pity.

Mbejane came to him at last.

'Come away, Nkosi. If you will not end it, come away. He no longer has need of you. The sight of you inflames him.'

Duff still struggled and screamed against his chain. From his torn waist the blood trickled down and clung in the hair of his legs with the stickiness of molten chocolate. With each jerk of his head the froth sprayed from his mouth and splattered his chest and arms.

Mbejane led Sean back into the laager. The other servants were there and Sean roused himself to give orders.

'I want everyone away from here. Take blankets and food – go camp on the far side of the water. I will send for you when it is over.' He waited until they had gathered their belongings and as they were leaving he called Mbejane back. 'What must I do?' he asked.

'If a horse breaks a leg?' Mbejane answered him with a question.

'I gave him my word,' Sean shook his head desperately, still facing towards the sound of Duff's raving.

'Only a rogue and a brave man can break an oath,' Mbejane answered simply. 'We will wait for you.' He turned and followed the others. When they were gone Sean hid in one of the wagons and through a tear in the canvas he watched Duff. He saw the idiotic shaking of his head, the curious shambling gait as he moved around the circle of the chain. He watched when the pain made him roll on the ground and claw at his head, tearing out tufts of hair and leaving long scratches down his face. He listened to the sounds of insanity: the bewildered bellows of pain, the senseless giggling and that growl, that terrible growl.

A dozen times he sighted along the rifle barrel, holding his aim until the sweat ran into his eyes and blurred them and he had to take the butt from his shoulder and turn away.

Out there on the end of the chain, its exposed flesh reddening in the sun a piece of Sean was dying. Some of his youth, some of his laughter, some of his carefree love of life – so he had to creep back to the hole in the canvas and watch.

The sun reached its peak and started down again and the thing on the chain grew weaker. It fell and was a long time crawling on its hands and knees before it regained its feet again.

An hour before sunset Duff had his first convulsion. He was standing facing Sean's wagon, swinging his head from side to side, his mouth working silently. The convulsion took him and he stiffened; his lips pulled up grinning, showing his teeth, his eyes rolled back and disappeared leaving only the whites, and his body started to bend backwards. That beautiful body, still slim as a boy's with the long moulded legs, bending tighter and tighter until with a brittle crack the spine snapped and he fell. He lay wriggling, moaning softly and his trunk was twisted at an impossible angle from the broken spine.

Sean jumped from the wagon and ran to him: standing over him he shot Duff in the head and turned away. He flung his rifle from him and heard it clatter on the hard earth. He walked back to his wagon and took a blanket off Duff's cot. He came back and wrapped Duff in it, averting his eyes from the mutilated head. He carried him to the shelter and laid him on the bed. The blood soaked through the blanket, spreading on the cloth, like ink spilled on blotting-paper. Sean sank down on the chair beside the bed.

Outside the darkness gathered and became complete. Once in the night a hyena came and snuffled at the blood outside on the earth, then it moved away. There was a pride of lions hunting in the bush beyond the waterhole; they killed two hours before dawn and Sean sat in the darkness and listened to their jubilant roaring.

In the morning, Sean stood up stiffly from his chair and went down to the wagons. Mbejane was waiting beside the fire in the laager.

'Where are the others?' Sean asked.

Mbejane stood up. 'They wait where you sent them. I came alone – knowing you would need me.'

'Yes,' said Sean. 'Get two axes from the wagon.'

They gathered wood, a mountain of dry wood, and packed it around Duff's bed – then Sean put fire to it. Mbejane saddled a horse for Sean and he mounted up and looked down at the Zulu.

'Bring the wagons on to the next waterhole. I will meet you there.'

Sean rode out of the laager. He looked back only once and saw that the breeze had spread the smoke from the pyre in a mile long smudge across the tops of the thorn trees.

9

Like a bag of pus at the root of an infected tooth the guilt and grief rotted in Sean's mind. His guilt was double-edged. He had betrayed Duff's trust, and he had lacked the courage to make the betrayal worthwhile. He had waited too long. He should have done it at the beginning, cleanly and quickly, or he should not have done it at all. He longed with every fibre of his body to be given the chance to do it again, but this time the right way. He would gladly have lived once more through all that horror to clear his conscience and clean the stain from the memory of their friendship.

His grief was a thing of emptiness, an aching void – so immense that he was lost in it. Where before there had been Duff's laughter, his twisted grin and his infectious zest there was now only a grey nothingness. No glimmer of sun penetrated it and there were no solid shapes in it.

The next waterhole was shallow soup in the centre of a flat expanse of dry mud the size of a polo field. The mud was cracked in an irregular chequered pattern forming small brickettes, each the size of a hand. A man could have jumped across the water without wetting his feet. Scattered thickly round its circumference were the droppings of the animals that had drunk there. Back and forth across its surface, changing direction as the wind veered, a few loose feathers sailed. The water was brackish and dirty. It was a bad camp. On the third day Mbejane went to Sean's wagon. Sean lay in his cot. He had not changed his clothes since leaving Duff. His beard was beginning to mat, sticky with sweat for it was hot as an oven under the wagon canvas.

'Nkosi, will you come and look at the water. I do not think we should stay here.'

'What is wrong with it?' Sean asked without interest.

'It is dirty, I think we should go on towards the big river.'

'Do whatever you think is right.' Sean rolled away from him, his face towards the side of the wagon.

So Mbejane took the wagon-train down towards the Limpopo. It was two days later that they found the ribbon of dark green trees that lined the banks. Sean stayed in his cot throughout the trek, jolting over the rough ground, sweating in the heat but oblivious to all discomfort. Mbejane put the wagons into laager on the bank above the riverbed, then he and all the other servants waited for Sean to come to life again. Their talk round the fire at nights was baited with worry and they looked often towards Sean's living wagon, where it stood unlit by lantern, dark as the mood of the man that lay within.

Like a bear coming out of its cave at the end of winter, Sean came out of the wagon at last. His clothes were filthy. The dogs hurried to meet him, crowding round his knees, begging for attention and he did not notice them. Vaguely he answered the greetings of his servants. He wandered down the bank into the river bed.

The summer had shrunk the Limpopo into a sparse line of pools strung out down the centre of the watercourse. The pools were dark olive green. The sand around them was white, glaring snowfield white, and the boulders that choked the barely moving river were black and polished smooth. The banks were steep, half a mile apart and walled in with trees. Sean walked through the sand, sinking to his ankles with each step. He reached the water and sat down at the edge, he dabbled his hand in it and found it warm as blood. In the sand next to him was the long slither mark of a crocodile, and a troop of monkeys were shaking the branches of a tree on the far bank and chattering at him. A pair of Sean's dogs splashed across the narrow neck between two pools and went off to chase the monkeys. They went half-heartedly with their tongues flapping at the corners of their mouths for it was very hot in the whiteness of the riverbed. Sean stared into the green water. It was lonely without Duff; he had only his guilt and his sorrow for company. One of the dogs that had stayed with him touched his cheek with its cold nose. Sean put his arm round its neck and the dog leaned against him. He heard footsteps in the sand behind him, he turned and looked up. It was Mbejane.

'Nkosi, Hlubi has found elephant not an hour's march up stream. He has counted twenty who show good ivory.'

Sean looked back at the water. 'Go away,' he said.

Mbejane squatted down beside him with his elbows on his knees. 'For whom do you mourn?' he asked.

'Go away, Mbejane, leave me alone.'

'Nkosi Duff does not need your sorrow – therefore I think that you mourn for yourself.' Mbejane picked up a pebble and tossed it into the pool.

'When a traveller gets a thorn in his foot,' Mbejane went on softly, 'and he is wise he plucks it out – and he is a fool who leaves it and says "I will keep this thorn to prick me so that I will always remember the road upon which I have travelled." Nkosi, it is better to remember with pleasure than with pain.' Mbejane lobbed another pebble into the pool, then he stood up and walked back to the camp. When Sean followed him ten minutes later he found a saddle on his horse, his rifle in the scabbard and Mbejane and Hlubi waiting with their spears. Kandhla handed him his hat, he held it by the brim, turning it in his hands. Then he clapped it onto his head and swung up onto the horse.

'Lead,' he ordered.

During the next weeks Sean hunted with a single-mindedness that left no time for brooding. His returns to the wagons were short and intermittent; his only reasons for returning at all were to bring in the ivory and change his horse. At the end of one of these brief visits to camp and as Sean was about to mount up for another hunt, even Mbejane complained. 'Nkosi, there are better ways to die than working too hard.'

'You look well enough,' Sean assured him, although Mbejane was now as lean as a greyhound and his skin shone like washed anthracite.

'Perhaps all men look healthy to a man on horseback,' Mbejane suggested and Sean stopped with one foot in the stirrup. He looked at Mbejane thoughtfully, then he lowered his leg again. 'We hunt on foot now, Mbejane, and the first to ask for mercy earns the right to be called "woman" by the other.'

Mbejane grinned; the challenge was to his liking. They crossed the river and found spoor before midday – a small herd of young bulls. They followed it until nightfall and slept huddled together under one blanket, then they went on again next morning. On the third day they lost the spoor in rocky ground and they cast back towards the river. They picked up another herd within ten

371

miles of the wagons, went after them and killed that evening – three fine bulls, not a tusk between them under fifty pounds weight. A night march back to the wagons, four hours' sleep and they were away again. Sean was limping a little now and on the second day out, during one of their infrequent halts, he pulled off his boot. The blister on his heel had burst and his sock was stiff with dried blood. Mbejane looked at him expressionlessly. 'How far are we from the wagons?' asked Sean.

'We can be back before dark, Nkosi.' Mbejane carried Sean's rifle for him on the return. Not once did his mask of solemnity slip. Back in camp Kandhla brought a basin of hot water and set it in front of Sean's chair. While Sean soaked his feet in it his entire following squatted in a circle about him. Every face wore an expression of studied concern and the silence was broken only by the clucking sounds of Bantu sympathy. They were loving every minute of it and Mbejane with the timing of a natural actor was building up the effect, playing to his audience. Sean puffed at a cheroot, scowling to stop himself laughing. Mbejane cleared his throat and spat into the fire. Every eye was on him; they waited breathlessly.

'Nkosi,' said Mbejane, 'I would set fifty head of oxen as your marriage price – if you were my daughter.'

One instant more of silence, then a shout of laughter. Sean laughed with them at first, but after a while when Hlubi had nearly staggered into the fire and Nonga was sobbing loudly on Mbejane's shoulder with tears of mirth streaming down his cheeks, Sean's own laughter stopped. It wasn't *that* funny.

He looked at them sourly – at their wide open pink mouths and their white teeth, at their shaking shoulders and heaving chests and suddenly it came to him very clearly that they were no longer laughing at him. They were laughing for the joy of it. They were laughing because they were alive. A chuckle rattled up Sean's throat and escaped before he could stop it, another one bounced around inside his chest and he lay back in his chair, opened his mouth and let it come. The hell with it, he was alive, too.

In the morning when he climbed out of his wagon and limped across to see what Kandhla was cooking for breakfast, there was a faint excitement in him again, the excitement of a new day. He felt good. Duff's memory was still with him, it always would be, but now it was not a sickening ache. He had plucked out the thorn.

10

They moved camp three times in November, keeping to the south bank of the river, following it back towards the west. Slowly the wagons which they had emptied of ivory beside the waterhole began to fill again, for the game was concentrated along the river. The rest of the land was dry but now each day there was promise of relief.

The clouds that had been scattered across the sky began to crowd together, gathering into rounded dark-edged masses or rearing proudly into thunderheads. All of nature seemed impressed by their growing importance. In the evenings the sun dressed them in royal purple and during the day the whirlwinds did dervish dances for their entertainment. The rains were coming. Sean had to make a decision, cross the Limpopo and cut himself off from the south when the river flooded, or stay where he was and leave the land beyond undisturbed. It wasn't a difficult decision. They found a place where the banks flattened out a little on both sides of the river. They unloaded the first wagon and double-teamed it; then with everybody shouting encouragement the oxen galloped down the steep slope into the riverbed. The wagon bounced behind them until it hit the sand where it came to a halt, tilted at an abandoned angle, with its wheels sunk axle-deep into the sand.

'Onto the spokes,' shouted Sean. 'They flung themselves on the wheels and strained to keep them turning, but half the oxen were down on their knees, powerless in the loose footing.

'Damn it to hell.' Sean glared at the wagon. 'Outspan the oxen and take them back. Get out the axes.'

It took them three days to lay a bridge of corduroyed branches across the river and another two to get all the wagons and ivory to the far bank. Sean declared a holiday when the last wagon was manhandled into the laager and the whole camp slept late the next morning. The sun was high by the time Sean descended from his wagon. He was still muzzy and a little liverish from lying abed. He yawned wide and stretched like a crucifix. He ran his tongue round his mouth and grimaced at the taste, then he scratched his chest and the hair rasped under his fingers.

'Kandhla, where's the coffee? Don't you care that I am near dead from thirst?'

'Nkosi, the water will boil very soon.'

Sean grunted and walked across to where Mbejane squatted with the other servants by the fire watching Kandhla.

'This is a good camp, Mbejane.' Sean looked up at the roof of leaves above them. It was a place of green shade, cool in the late morning heat. Christmas beetles were squealing in the wide stretched branches.

'There is good grazing for the cattle,' Mbejane agreed; he stretched out his hand towards Sean.

'I found this in the grass – someone else has camped here.' Sean took it from him and examined it, a piece of broken china with a blue fig-leaf pattern. It was a shock to Sean, that little fragment of civilization in the wilderness; he turned it in his fingers and Mbejane went on. 'There are the ashes of an old fire there against the shuma tree and I found the ruts where wagons climbed the bank at the same place as ours.'

'How long ago?'

Mbejane shrugged. 'A year perhaps. Grass has grown in the wagon tracks.'

Sean sat down in his chair, he felt disturbed. He thought about it and grinned as he realized he was jealous; there were strangers here in the land he was coming to regard as his own, those year-old tracks gave him a feeling of being in a crowd. Also there was the opposite feeling, that of longing for the company of his own kind. The sneaking desire to see a white face again. It was strange that he could resent something and yet wish for it simultaneously.

'Kandhla, am I to have coffee now or at supper tonight?'

'Nkosi, it is done.' Kandhla poured a little brown sugar into the mug, stirred it with a stick and handed it to him. Sean held the mug in both hands, blowing to cool it, then sipping and sighing with each mouthful. The talk of his Zulus passed back and forth about the circle and the snuff-boxes followed it, each remark of worth being greeted with a solemn chorus of 'It is true, it is true,' and the taking of snuff. Small arguments jumped

375

up and fell back again into the leisurely stream of conversation. Sean listened to them, occasionally joining in or contributing a story until his stomach told him it was time to eat. Kandhla started to cook, under the critical supervision and with the helpful suggestions of those whom idleness had made garrulous. He had almost succeeded in grilling the carcass of a guinea-fowl to the satisfaction of the entire company, although Mbejane felt that he should have added a pinch more salt, when Nonga sitting across the fire from him jumped to his feet and pointed out towards the north. Sean shaded his eyes and looked.

'For Chrissake,' said Sean.

'Ah! ah! ah!' said his servants.

A white man rode towards them through the trees; he cantered with long stirrups, slouched comfortably, close enough already for Sean to make out the great ginger beard that masked the bottom half of his face. He was a big man; the sleeves of his shirt rolled high around thick arms.

'Hello,' shouted Sean and went eagerly to meet him. The rider reined in at the edge of the laager. He climbed stiffly out of the saddle and grabbed Sean's outstretched hand. Sean felt his finger-bones creak in the grip.

'Hello, man! How goes it?' He spoke in Afrikaans. His voice matched the size of his body and his eyes were on a level with Sean's. They pumped each other's arms mercilessly, laughing, putting sincerity into the usual inanities of greeting.

'Kandhla – get out the brandy bottle,' Sean called over his shoulder, then to the Boer, 'Come in, you're just in time for lunch. We'll have a dram to celebrate. Hell, it's good to see a white man again!'

'You're on your own, then?'

'Yes – come in, man, sit down.'

Sean poured drinks and the Boer took one up.

'What's your name?' he asked.

'Courtney – Sean Courtney.'

'I'm Jan Paulus Leroux – glad to meet you, meneer.'

'Good health, meneer,' Sean answered him and they drank. Jan Paulus wiped his whiskers on the palm of his hand and breathed out heavily, blowing the taste of the brandy back into his mouth.

'That was good,' he said and held out his mug. They talked excitedly, tongues loose from loneliness, trying to say everything and ask all the questions at once – meetings in the bush are always like this. Meanwhile the tide was going out in the bottle and the level dropped quickly.

'Tell me, where are your wagons?' Sean asked.

'An hour or two behind. I came ahead to find the river.'

'How many in your party?' Sean watched his face, talking just for the sound of it.

'Ma and Pa, my little sister and my wife – which reminds me – you had better move your wagons.'

'What?' Sean looked puzzled.

'This is my outspan place,' the Boer explained to him. 'See, there are the marks of my fire – this is my camp.'

The smile went out of Sean's voice. 'Look around you, Boer, there is the whole of Africa. Take your pick – anywhere except where I am sitting.'

'But this is my place.' Jan Paulus flushed a little. 'I always camp at the same place when I return along a spoor.'

The whole temper of their meeting had changed in a few seconds. Jan Paulus stood abruptly and went to his horse. He stooped and tightened the girth, hauling so savagely on the strap that the animal staggered off balance. He flung himself onto its back and looked down at Sean.

'Move your wagons,' he said, 'I camp here tonight.'

'Would you like to bet on that?' Sean asked grimly.

'We'll see!' Jan Paulus flashed back.

'We certainly shall,' agreed Sean.

The Boer wheeled his horse and rode away. Sean watched his back disappear among the trees and only then did he let his anger slip. He rampaged through the laager working himself into a fury, pacing out frustrated circles, stopping now and then to glare out in the direction from which the Boer's wagons would come – but under all the external signs of indignation was his unholy anticipation of a fight. Kandhla brought him food, hurrying along behind him with the plate. Sean waved him away impatiently and continued his pugnacious patrol. At last a trek whip popped in the distance and an ox lowed faintly, to be answered immediately by Sean's cattle. The dogs started barking and Sean crossed to one of the wagons on the north side of the laager and leaned against it with assumed nonchalance. The long line of wagons wound out of the trees towards him. There were bright blobs of colour on the high box seat of the lead wagon.

Women's dresses! Ordinarily they would have made Sean's nostrils flare like those of a stud stallion, but now his whole attention was concentrated on the larger of the two outriders. Jan Paulus cantered ahead of his father, and Sean, with his fists clenched into bony hammers at his sides, watched him come. Jan Paulus sat straight in the saddle; he stopped his horse a dozen paces from Sean and shoved his hat onto the back of his head with a thumb as thick and as brown as a fried sausage; he tickled his horse a little with his spurs to make it dance and he asked with mock surprise, 'What, *Rooi Nek*, still here?'

Sean's dogs had rushed forward to meet the other pack and now they milled about in a restrained frenzy of mutual bottom-smelling, stiff-limbed with tension, backs abristle and legs cocking in the formal act of urination.

'Why don't you go and climb a tree? You'll feel more at home there,' Sean suggested mildly.

'Ah! so?' Jan Paulus reared in his stirrups. He kicked loose his right foot, swung it back over his horse's rump to dismount and Sean jumped at him. The horse skittered nervously, throwing the Boer off balance and he clutched at the saddle. Sean reached up, took a double handful of his ginger beard and leaned back on it with all his weight. Jan Paulus came over backwards with his arms windmilling, his foot caught in the stirrup and he hung suspended like a hammock, held at one end to the plunging horse and at the other by his chin to Sean's hands. Sean dug his heels in, revelling in the Boer's bellows.

Galvanized into action by Sean's example, the dogs cut short the ceremony and went at each other in a snarling, snapping shambles; the fur flew like sand in a Kalahari dust-storm.

The stirrup-leather snapped; Sean fell backwards and rolled to his feet just in time to meet Jan Paulus's charge. He smothered the punch that the Boer bowled overarm at him, but the power behind it shocked him; then they were chest to chest and Sean felt his own strength matched. They strained silently with their beards touching and their eyes inches apart. Sean shifted his weight quickly and tried for a fall, but smoothly as a dancer Jan Paulus met and held him. Then it was his turn; he twisted in Sean's arms and Sean sobbed with the effort required to stop him. Oupa Leroux joined in by driving his horse at them, scattering the dogs, his hippo-hide sjambok hissing as he swung it.

'Let it stand! you thunders, give over – hey! Enough, let it stand!'

Sean shouted with pain as the lash cut across his back and at the next stroke Jan Paulus howled as loudly. They let go of each other and massaging their whip-weals retreated before the skinny old white-beard on the horse.

The first of the wagons had come up now and two hundred pounds of woman, all in one package, called out from the box seat, 'Why did you stop them, Oupa?'

'No sense in letting them kill each other.'

'Shame on you – so you must spoil the boys' fun. Don't you remember how you loved to fight? Or are you now so old you forget the pleasures of your youth? Leave them alone!'

Oupa hesitated, swinging the sjambok and looking from Sean to Jan Paulus.

'Come away from there, you old busybody,' his wife ordered him. She was solid as a granite kopje, her blouse packed full of bosom and her bare arms brown and thick as a man's. The wide brim of her bonnet shaded her face but Sean could see it was pink and pudding-shaped, the kind of face that smiles more easily than it frowns. There were two girls on the seat beside her but there was no time to look at them. Oupa had pulled his horse out of the way and Jan Paulus was moving down on him. Sean went up on his toes, crouching a little, preoccupied with the taste he had just had of the other's strength, watching Jan Paulus close in for the main course and not too certain he was going to be able to chew this mouthful.

Jan Paulus tested Sean with a long right-hander but Sean rolled his head with it and the thick pad of his beard cushioned the blow; he hooked Jan Paulus in the ribs under his raised arm and Jan Paulus grunted and circled away.

Forgetting his scruples, Oupa Leroux watched them with rising delight. It was going to be a good fight. They were well matched – both big men, under thirty, quick and smooth on their feet. Both had fought before and that often; you could tell it by the way they felt each other out, turning just out of reach, moving in to offer an opening that a less experienced man might have attempted and regretted, then dropping back.

The fluid, almost leisurely pattern of movement exploded. Jan Paulus jumped in, moving left, changed direction like the recoil of a whip lash and used his right hand again; Sean ducked under

379

it and laid himself open to Jan Paulus's left. He staggered back from its kick, bleeding where it had split the flesh across his cheek-bone, and Jan Paulus followed him eagerly, his hands held ready, searching for the opening. Sean kept clear, instinct moving his feet until the blackness faded inside his head and he felt the strength in his arms again. He saw Jan Paulus following him and he let his legs stay rubbery; he dropped his hands and waited for Jan Paulus to commit himself. Too late Jan Paulus caught the cunning in Sean's eyes and tried to break from the trap, but clenched bone raked his face. He staggered away and now he was bleeding also.

They fought through the wagons with the advantage changing hands a dozen times. They came together and used their heads and their knees, they broke and used their fists again. Then locked chest to chest once more they rolled down the steep bank into the river bed of the Limpopo. They fought in the soft sand and it held their legs, it filled their mouths when they fell and clung like white icing-sugar to their hair and beards. They splashed into one of the pools and they fought in the water, coughing with the agony of it in their lungs, floundering like a pair of bull hippos, their movements slowing down until they knelt facing each other, no longer able to rise, the water running from them and the only sound their gasping for air.

Not sure whether the darkness was actuality or a fantasy of fatigue, for the sun had set by the time they were finished, Sean watched Jan Paulus starting to puke, retching with a tearing noise to bring up a small splash of yellow bile. Sean crawled to the edge of the pool and lay with his face in the sand. There were voices echoing in his ears and the light of a lantern – the light was red – filtered through the blood that had trickled into his eyes. His servants lifted him and he hardly felt them. The light and the voices faded into blackness as he slipped over the edge of consciousness.

The sting of iodine woke him and he struggled to sit up but hands pushed him down.

'Gently, gently, the fight is over.' Sean focused his one eye to find the voice. The pinkness of Ouma Leroux hung over him. Her hands touched his face and the antiseptic stung him again. He exclaimed through puffed lips.

'So! Just like a man,' Ouma chuckled. 'Your head nearly

knocked off without a murmur but one touch of medicine and you cry like a baby.'

Sean ran his tongue round inside his mouth; one tooth loose but all the others miraculously present. He started to lift his hand to touch his closed eye but Ouma slapped it down impatiently and went on working over him.

'Glory, what a fight!' She shook her head happily. 'You were good, *kerel*, you were very good.'

Sean looked beyond her and saw the girl. She was standing in shadow, a silhouette against the pale canvas. She was holding a basin. Ouma turned and dipped the cloth in it, washing out the blood before she came back to his face. The wagon rocked under her weight and the lantern that hung from the roof swung, lighting the girl's face from the side. Sean's legs straightened on his cot and he moved his head slightly to see her better.

'Be still, *jong*,' Ouma commanded. Sean looked past her at the girl at the full serene line of her lips and the curve of her cheek. He saw the pile of her hair fluff up in happy disarray and then, suddenly – penitent, slide down behind her neck, curl over her shoulder and hang to her waist in a plait as thick as his wrist.

'Katrina, do you expect me to reach right across to the basin each time? Stand closer, girl.'

She stepped into the light and looked at Sean. Green, laughing, almost bubbling green was the colour of her eyes. Then she dropped them to the basin. Sean stared at her, not wanting to miss the moment when she would look up again.

'My big bear,' Ouma spoke with grudging approval. 'Steal our camp site, fight my son and ogle my daughter. If you go on like this I might have to knock the thunder out of you myself. Glory, but you are a dangerous one! Katrina, you had better go back to our wagons and help Henrietta see to your brother. Leave the basin on the chest there.'

She looked at Sean once more before she left. There were secret shadows in the green – she didn't have to smile with her mouth.

II

Sean woke to the realization that something was wrong. He started to sit up but the pain checked him: the stiffness of bruised muscle and the catch of half-dried scab. He groaned and the movement hurt his lips. Slowly he swung his legs off the cot and roused himself to take stock of the damage. Dark through the hair of his chest showed a heel imprint of Jan Paulus's boot. Sean prodded round it gently, feeling for the give of a broken rib; then, satisfied with that area, he went on to inspect the raw graze that wrapped round onto his back, holding his left arm high and peering closely at the broken skin. He picked a bit of blanket fluff from the scab. He stood up, only to freeze as a torn muscle in his shoulder knifed him. He started to swear then softly, monotonously, and he kept it up all through the painful business of climbing down out of the wagon.

His entire following watched his descent – even the dogs looked worried. Sean reached the ground and started to shout.

'What the hell –' He stopped hurriedly as he felt his lip crack open again and start to bleed.

'What the hell' – he said again, keeping his lips still – 'are you doing standing round like a bunch of women at a beer drink – is there no work here? Hlubi, I thought I sent you out to look for elephant.' Hlubi went. 'Kandhla, where's breakfast? Mbejane, get me a basin of water and my shaving-mirror.' Sean sat in his chair and morosely inspected his face in the mirror.

'If a herd of buffalo had stampeded across it they would have done less damage.'

'Nkosi, it is nothing compared to his face,' Mbejane assured him.

'Is he bad?' Sean looked up.

'I have spoken to one of his servants. He has not left his bed yet and he lies there, growling like a wounded lion in a thicket; but his eyes are as tightly closed as those of a new cub.'

'Tell me more, Mbejane. Say truly, was it a good fight?'

Mbejane squatted down next to Sean's chair. He was silent a moment as he gathered his words.

'When the sky sends its cloud impis against the peaks of the Drakensberg, with thunder and the spears of lightning, it is a thing to thrill a man. When two bull elephants fight unto death there is no braver show in all the veld. Is this not so?'

Sean nodded, his eyes twinkling.

'Nkosi, hear me when I tell you these things were as the play of little children beside this fight.'

Sean listened to the praises. Mbejane was well versed in the oldest art of Zululand and when he had finished he looked at Sean's face. It was happy. Mbejane smiled and took a fold of paper out of his loin cloth. 'A servant from the other camp brought this while you slept.'

Sean read the note. It was written in a big round schoolgirl hand and worded in High Dutch. He liked that writing. It was an invitation to dinner.

'Kandhla, get out my suit and my number one boots.' He picked up the mirror again. There wasn't very much he could do about his face – trim the beard, perhaps, but that was all. He laid the mirror down and looked up stream to where the Leroux wagons were half hidden among the trees.

Mbejane carried a lantern in front of Sean. They walked slowly to enable Sean to limp with dignity. When they reached the other laager, Jan Paulus climbed stiffly out of his chair and nodded an equally stiff greeting. Mbejane had lied – except for a missing tooth there was little to choose between their faces. Oupa slapped Sean's back and pressed a tumbler of brandy into his hand. He was a tall man, but twenty thousand suns had burnt away his flesh and left only stringy muscle, had faded his eyes to a pale green and toughened his skin to the texture of a turkey's neck. His beard was yellowish-white with still a touch of ginger round the mouth. He asked Sean three questions without giving him time to answer the first, then he led him to a chair.

Oupa talked, Sean listened and Jan Paulus sulked. Oupa talked of cattle and hunting and the land to the north. After a few minutes Sean realized that he was not expected to take part in the conversation: his few tentative efforts were crushed under Oupa's verbal avalanche. So Sean listened half to him and half to the whisper of women's voices from the cooking fires behind the laager. Once he heard her laugh. He knew it was her for it was the rich sound of the thing that he had seen in her eyes. At last the women's business with food and pots was finished and Ouma led the girls to where the men sat. Sean stood up and saw that Katrina was tall, with shoulders like a boy. As she walked towards him the movement pressed her skirt against her legs – they were long but her feet were small. Her hair was red-black and tied behind her head in an enormous bun.

'Ah, my battling bear,' Ouma took Sean's arm, 'let me present my daughter-in-law, Henrietta – here is the man that nearly killed your husband.' Jan Paulus snorted from his chair and Ouma laughed, her bosom wobbling merrily. Henrietta was a small dark-eyed girl. *She doesn't like me,* Sean guessed instantly. He bowed slightly and took her hand. She pulled it away.

'This is my youngest daughter, Katrina. You met her last night.'

She does like me. Her fingers were long and square-tipped in his. Sean risked his lips with a smile.

'Without her ministrations I might have bled to death,' he said. She smiled straight back at him but not with her mouth.

'You wear your wounds well, maneer, the blue eye has an air of distinction.'

'That will be enough from you, girl,' Oupa spoke sharply. 'Go and sit by your mother.' He turned to Sean. 'I was telling you about this horse – I said to the fellow, "He's not worth five pounds let alone fifteen, look at those hocks, thin as sticks." So he says to me, trying to get me away, you follow, he says, "Come and look at the saddle." But I can see he's worried –'

The thin cotton of the girl's blouse could hardly contain the impatient push of her breasts, Sean thought that he had never seen anything so wonderful.

There was a trestle-table next to the cooking fire; they went to it at last. Oupa said grace. Sean watched him through his lashes. Oupa's beard waggled as he spoke and at one point he thumped the table to emphasize the point he was making to the Almighty. His 'amen' had such an impressive resonance that Sean had to make an effort to stop himself applauding and Oupa fell back spent.

'Amen,' said Ouma and ladled stew from a pot the size of a bucket. Henrietta added pumpkin fritters and Katrina stacked slices of fresh mealie bread on each plate. A silence fell on the table, spoiled only by the clank of metal on china and the sound of Oupa breathing through his nose.

'Mevrouw Leroux, I have waited a long time to taste food like this again.' Sean mopped up the last bit of gravy with a piece of mealie bread. Ouma beamed.

'There's plenty more, meneer. I love to see a man eat. Oupa used to be a great trencherman. My father made him take me away for he could not afford to feed him every time he came courting.' She took Sean's plate and filled it. 'You look to me like a man who can eat.'

'I think I'll hold my own in most company,' Sean agreed.

'So?' Jan Paulus spoke for the first time. He passed his plate to Ouma. 'Fill it up, please, Mother, tonight I am hungry.'

Sean's eyes narrowed, he waited until Jan Paulus had his plate back in front of him, then he took up his fork deliberately. Jan Paulus did the same.

'Glory,' said Ouma happily. 'Here we go again. Oupa, you may have to go out and shoot a couple of buffalo before dinner is finished tonight.'

'I will bet one sovereign on Jan Paulus,' Oupa challenged his wife. 'He is like an army of termites. I swear that if there was nothing else he'd eat the canvas off the wagons.'

'All right,' agreed Ouma. 'I've never seen the Bear eat before, but it seems to me he has plenty of room to put it.'

'Your woollen shawl against my green bonnet that Jan Paulus gives up first,' Katrina whispered to her sister-in-law.

'When Jannie has finished the stew he'll eat the Englishman,' Henrietta giggled. 'But it's a pretty bonnet – I'll take the wager.'

Plateful for plateful, Ouma measuring out each ladle with scrupulous fairness, they ate against each other. The talk round the table dwindled and halted.

'More?' asked Ouma each time the plates were clean, and each time they looked at each other and nodded. At last the ladle scraped the bottom of the pot.

'That's the end of it, my children, we will have to call it another draw.'

The silence went on after she had spoken. Sean and Jan Paulus sat very still looking at their respective plates. Jan Paulus hiccupped, his expression changed. He stood up and went into the darkness.

'Ah! listen! listen!' crowed Ouma. They, waited and then she exploded into laughter. 'The ungrateful wretch, is that what he thinks of my food? Where's your sovereign, Oupa?'

'Wait, you greedy old woman, the game's not finished yet.' He turned and stared at Sean. 'To me it looks as though your horse is nearly blown.'

Sean closed his eyes. The sounds of Jan Paulus's distress came to him very clearly.

'Thank you for a – ' He didn't have time to finish. He wanted to get far away so the girl couldn't hear him.

12

The following morning during breakfast Sean thought about his next move. He would write an invitation to dinner and then he would deliver it himself. They would have to ask him to stay for coffee and then, if he waited, there would be a chance. Even Oupa would have to stop talking sometime and Ouma might relax her vigilance. He was sure there'd be a chance to talk to the girl. He didn't know what he would say to her but he'd worry about that when the time came. He climbed into the wagon and found pencil and paper in his chest. He went back to the table and spread the paper in front of him. He chewed the end of the pencil and stared out into the bush. Something moved against the trees. Sean put the pencil down and stood up. The dogs barked then stopped as they recognized Hlubi. He was coming at a trot – he was coming with news. Sean waited for him.

'A big herd, Nkosi, with many showing ivory. I saw them drink at the river and then go back into the bush, feeding quietly.'

'When?' asked Sean to gain time. He was searching for a plausible excuse to stay in camp – it would have to be good to satisfy Mbejane who was already saddling one of the horses.

'Before the sun this morning,' answered Hlubi and Sean was trying to remember which was his sore shoulder – he couldn't hunt with a sore shoulder. Mbejane led the horse into the laager. Sean scratched the side of his nose and coughed.

'The tracker from the other camp follows close behind me, Nkosi, he too has seen the herd and brings the news to his master. But I, being as swift as a springbok when I run, have outdistanced him,' Hlubi ended modestly.

'Is that so?' For Sean it changed the whole problem, he couldn't leave the herd to that red-headed Dutchman. He ran across to

387

the wagon and snatched his bandolier from the foot of the cot. His rifle was already in the scabbard.

'Are you tired, Hlubi?' Sean buckled the heavy ammunition belt across his chest. The sweat had run in oily streaks down the Zulu's body; his breathing was deep and quick.

'No, Nkosi.'

'Well, then, lead us to these elephant of yours, my fleet-footed springbok.' Sean swung up onto his horse He looked over his shoulder at the other camp. She would still be there when he came back.

Sean was limited to the speed of Hlubi's feet while the two Leroux had only to gallop along the easy spoor left by Sean's party and they caught up with him before he had gone two miles.

'Good morning to you,' Oupa greeted him as he drew level and pulled his horse in to a trot. 'Out for a morning's ride, I see.'

Sean made the best of it with a grin. 'If we are all to hunt then we must hunt together. Do you agree?'

'Of course, meneer.'

'And we must share the bag equally, one third to each man.'

'That is always the way.' Oupa nodded.

'Do you agree?' Sean turned in his saddle towards Jan Paulus. Jan Paulus grunted. He showed little inclination to open his mouth since he had lost his tooth.

They found the spoor within an hour. The herd had wrecked a road through the thick bush along the river. They had stripped the bark from the saplings and left them naked and bleeding. They had knocked down bigger trees to reach the tender top leaves and they had dropped their great piles of dung in the grass.

'We need no trackers to follow this.' Jan Paulus had the first excitement on him. Sean looked at him and wondered how many elephant had died in front of his rifle. A thousand perhaps, and yet the excitement was on him again now.

'Tell your servants to follow us. We'll go ahead. We'll catch them within an hour.' He smiled at Sean, gap-toothed, and Sean felt the excitement lift the hair on his own forearms. He smiled back.

They cantered in a rough line abreast, slack-reined to let the horses pick their own way among the fallen trees. The river bush thinned out as they moved north and soon they were into parkland. The grass brushed their stirrups and the ground beneath it was firm and smooth.

They rode without talking, leaning forward in their saddles, looking ahead. The rhythmic beat of hooves was a war drum. Sean ran his fingers along the row of bullets strapped across his chest, then he drew his rifle, checked the load and thrust it back into its scabbard.

'There!' said Oupa and Sean saw the herd. It was massed among a grove of fever trees a quarter of a mile ahead.

'Name of a name,' Paulus whistled. 'There must be two hundred at least.'

Sean heard the first pig-squeal of alarm, saw ears fan out and trunks lift. Then the herd bunched together and ran with their backs humped, a thin screen of dust trailing behind them.

'Paulus take the right flank. You, meneer, in the middle and I'll ride left,' shouted Oupa.

Sean jammed his hat down over his ears and his horse jumped under him as he hit it with his heels. Like a thrown trident the three horsemen hurled themselves at the herd. Sean rode into the dust. He picked an old cow elephant from the moving mountain range in front of him and pressed his horse so close upon her that he could see the bristles in her tail tuft and the erosion of her skin, wrinkled as an old man's scrotum. He touched his hand to his horse's neck and it plunged – from full gallop to standstill in half a dozen strides. Sean threw his feet free of the stirrups and hit the ground, loose-kneed to ride the shock. The cow's spine was a line of lumps beneath the grey skin – Sean broke it with his first bullet and she dropped, sliding on her hindquarters like a dog with worms. His horse started to run again before he was properly in the saddle and everything became movement and noise, dust and the smell of burnt powder. Chase them, coughing in the dust. Close with them. Off the horse and shoot. Wet blood on grey skin. Slam, slam of the rifle – its barrel hot, recoiling savagely. Sweat in the eyes, stinging. Ride. Shoot again. Two more down, screaming, anchored by paralysed legs. Blood-red as a flag. Load, cramming cartridges into the rifle. Ride. Chase them, shoot again and again. The bullets striking on flesh with a hollow sound, then up and ride again. Ride – until the horse could no longer keep up with them and he had to let them go. He stood holding his horse's head, the dust and the thirst closed his throat. He could not swallow. His hands trembled in reaction. His shoulder was aching again. He untied his silk scarf, wiped his face with it and blew the mud out of his nose, then he drank from his water-bottle. The water tasted sweet.

The hunt had led from parkland into mopani bush. It was very thick, shiny green leaves hanging to the ground and pressing close around him. The air was still and warm to breathe. He turned back along the line of the chase. He found them by their squealing. When they saw him they tried to charge, dragging themselves towards him – using the front legs only and groping with their trunks. They sagged into stillness after the head shot. This was the bad part. Sean worked quickly. He could hear the other rifles in the mopani forest around him and when he came to one of the long clearings among the trees he saw Jan Paulus walking towards him, leading his horse.

'How many?' called Sean.

'*Gott*, man, I didn't count. What a killing, hey? Have you got a drink for me? I dropped my water-bottle somewhere.'

Jan Paulus's rifle was in its saddle scabbard. The reins were slung over his shoulder and his horse followed him with its head drooping from exhaustion. The clearing was walled in with the dense mopani trees and a wounded elephant broke into the open. It was lung shot – the side of its chest painted with froth – and when it squealed the blood sprayed in a pink spout from the end of its trunk. It went for Jan Paulus, streaming the black battle ensigns of its ears. His horse reared, the reins snapped, it turned free and galloped away, leaving him full in the path of the charge. Sean went up onto his horse's back without touching stirrups. His horse threw its head, dancing in a tight circle, but he dragged it around and drove it to intercept the charge.

'Don't run, for God's sake, don't run!' he shouted as he cleared his rifle from the scabbard. Jan Paulus heard him. He stood with his hands at his sides, his feet apart and his body braced. The elephant heard Sean shout also and it swung its head and Sean saw the first hesitation in its run. He fired, not trying to pick his shot, hoping only to hurt it, to bring it away from Jan Paulus. The bullet slapped into it with the sound of a wet towel flicked against a wall. The elephant turned, clumsy with the weakness of its shattered lungs. Sean gathered his horse beneath him and wheeled it away and the elephant followed him.

Sean fumbled as he reloaded, his hands were slippery with

sweat. One of the brass shells slipped through his fingers, tapped against his knee and dropped into the grass under his horse's hooves. The elephant gained on him. He loosened his bed-roll from the saddle and let it fall – they would sometimes stop to savage even a fallen hat, but not this one. He turned in the saddle and fired into it. It squealed again so close upon him that the blown blood splattered into his face. His horse was almost finished; he could feel its legs flopping with every stride and they were nearly at the end of the clearing racing towards the solid wall of green mopani. He pushed another round into the breech of his rifle and swung his body across the saddle. He slid down until his feet touched the ground and he was running next to his horse. He let go and was flung forward, but he fought to keep his balance, his body jarring with the force of his run. Then, still on his feet, he turned for his first steady shot. The elephant was coming in fast, almost on top of him, hanging over him like a cliff. Its trunk coiled on its chest and the curves of its ivory were lifted high.

It's too close, much too close, I can't hit the brain from here.

He aimed at the hollow in its forehead just above the level of its eyes. He fired and the elephant's legs folded up; its brain burst like an overripe tomato within the bone castle of its skull.

Sean tried to jump aside as the massive body came skidding down upon him, but one of its legs hit him and threw him face down into the grass. He lay there. He felt sick, for his stomach was still full of warm oily fear.

After a while he sat up and looked at the elephant. One of its tusks had snapped off flush with the lip. Jan Paulus came, panting from his run. He stopped next to the elephant and touched the wound in its forehead, then he wiped his fingers on his shirt.

'Are you all right, man?'

He took Sean's arm and helped him to his feet; then he picked up Sean's hat and dusted it carefully before handing it to him.

13

In the three-sided shelter formed by the belly and out-thrust legs of one of the dead elephants they made their camp that night. They drank coffee together and Sean sat between the two Leroux with his back against the rough skin of the elephant's belly. The silhouettes of the tree against the night sky were deformed by the shapes of the vultures that clustered in them and the darkness was ugly with the giggling of hyena. They had set a feast for the scavengers. They spoke little for they were tired, but Sean could feel the gratitude of the men who sat beside him and before they rolled into their blankets Jan Paulus said gruffly, 'Thank you, *kerel*.'

'You might be able to do the same for me one day.'

'I hope so, *ja*! I hope so.'

In the morning Oupa said, 'It's going to take us three or four days to cut out all this ivory.' He looked up at the sky. 'I don't like these clouds. One of us had better ride back to camp to fetch more men and wagons to carry the ivory.'

'I'll go.' Sean stood up quickly.

'I was thinking of going myself.' But Sean was already calling to Mbejane to saddle his horse and Oupa couldn't really argue with him, not after yesterday.

'Tell Ouma to take the wagons across the river,' he acquiesced. 'We don't want to be caught on this side when the river floods. Perhaps you wouldn't mind helping her.'

'No,' Sean assured him. 'I don't mind at all.'

His horse was still tired from the previous day's hunt and it was three hours before he reached the river.

He tied his horse on the bank and went down to one of the pools. He stripped off his clothes and lowered himself into the water. He scrubbed himself with handfuls of the coarse sand and when he waded out of the pool and dried on his shirt his skin was tingling. He rode along the bank and the temptation to gallop his horse was almost unbearable. He laughed to himself a little.

'The field's almost clear, though I wouldn't put it past that suspicious old Dutchman to follow me.'

He laughed again and thought about the colour of her eyes, green as *crème-de-menthe* in a crystal glass, and the shape of her bosom. The muscles in his legs tightened and the horse lengthened its stride in response to the pressure of his knees. 'All right, run then,' Sean encouraged it, 'I don't insist on it, but I would be grateful.'

He went to his own wagons first and changed his sweaty shirt for a fresh one, his leather breeches for clean calico and his scuffed boots for soft polished leather. He scrubbed his teeth with salt and dragged a comb through his hair and beard. He saw in the mirror that the battle damage to his face was fading and he winked at his image. 'How can she resist you?' He gave his moustache one more twirl, climbed out of the wagon and was immediately aware of a most uncomfortable feeling in his stomach. He walked towards the Leroux laager thinking about it, and he recognized it as the same feeling he used to have when Waite Courtney called him to the study to do penance for his boyhood sins.

'That's odd,' he muttered. 'Why should I feel like that?' His confidence faded and he stopped. 'I wonder if my breath smells – I think I'd better go back and get some cloves.' He turned with relief, knew it as cowardice and stopped again. 'Get a grip on yourself. She's only a girl, an uneducated little Dutch girl. You've had fifty finer women.'

'Name me two,' he shot back at himself.

'Well, there was – Oh! for Chrissake, come on.' Resolutely he set off for the Leroux' laager again.

She was sitting in the sun within the circle of wagons. She was leaning forward on the stool and her newly-washed hair fell thickly over her face almost to the ground. With each stroke of the brush it leapt like a live thing and the sun sparkled the red lights in it. Sean wanted to touch it – he wanted to twist fistfuls of it round his hands and he wanted to smell it, it would smell warm and slightly milky like a puppy's fur. He stepped softly towards her but before he reached her she took the shiny mass with both hands and threw it back over her shoulders – a startled flash of green eyes, one despairing wail, 'Oh, no! not with my hair like this.' A swirl of skirts that sent the stool flying and she was gone into her wagon. Sean scratched the side of his nose and stood awkwardly.

'Why are you back so soon, meneer?' she called through the canvas. 'Where are the others? Is everything all right?'

'Yes, they're both fine. I left them and came to fetch wagons to carry the ivory.'

'Oh, that's good.' Sean tried to interpret the inflection of her voice: was it good that they were fine, or good that he had left them? So far the indications were favourable; her confusion at seeing him boded well.

'What's wrong?' Ouma bellowed from one of the other wagons. 'It's not Oupa, don't tell me something has happened to him?' The wagon rocked wildly and her pink face, puckered with sleep, popped out of the opening. Sean's reassurances were smothered by her voice.

'Oh, I knew this would happen. I had a feeling. I shouldn't have let him go.'

'Paulus, oh, Jan Paulus – I must go to him. Where is he?'

Henrietta came running from the cooking fire behind the wagons and then the dogs started barking and the servants added their chatter to the confusion. Sean tried to shout them all down and watch Katrina emerging from her wagon at the same time. She had disciplined her hair now – it had a green ribbon in it and hung down her back. She was laughing and she helped him to quieten Ouma and Henrietta.

They brought him coffee, then they sat round him and listened to the story of the hunt. Sean went into detail on the rescue of Jan Paulus and was rewarded by a softening of the dislike in Henrietta's eyes. By the time Sean had finished talking it was too late to start moving the wagons across the river. So he talked some more, it was most agreeable to have three women as an attentive audience, and then they ate supper.

With ostentatious tact Ouma and Henrietta retired early to their respective living wagons and left Sean and Katrina sitting by the fire. At carefully-spaced intervals there was a stage cough from Ouma's wagon, a reminder that they were not entirely alone. Sean lit a cheroot and frowned into the fire searching desperately for something intelligent to say, but all his brain could dredge up was, 'Thank God, Oupa isn't here.' He sneaked a glance at Katrina: she was staring into the fire as well and she was blushing. Instantly Sean felt his own cheeks starting to heat up. He opened his mouth to talk and made a squawking noise. He shut it again.

'We can speak in English if you like, meneer.'

'You speak English?' Sean's surprise brought his voice back.

'I practise every night – I read aloud out of my books.'

Sean grinned at her delightedly – it was suddenly very important that she could speak his language. The dam, holding back all the questions that there were to ask and all the things there were to say, burst and the words came pouring out over each other. Katrina fluttered her hands when she couldn't find the word she wanted and then lapsed back into Afrikaans. They killed the short taut silences with a simultaneous rush of words, then laughed together in confusion. They sat on the edges of their chairs and watched each other's faces as they talked. The moon came up, a red rain moon, and the fire faded into a puddle of ashes.

'Katrina, it's long past the time decent people were asleep. I'm sure Meneer Courtney is tired.'

They dropped their voices to a whisper, drawing out the last minutes.

'In just one minute, girl, I'm coming out to fetch you to bed.'

They walked to her wagon and with each step her skirts brushed against his leg. She stopped with one hand on the wagon step. She wasn't as tall as he'd imagined, the top of her head came to his chin. The seconds slid by as he hesitated, reluctant to touch, strangely frightened to test the delicate thread they had spun together lest he destroy it before it became strong. Slowly he swayed towards her and something surged up inside him as he saw her chin lift slightly and the lashes fall over her eyes.

'Goodnight, Meneer Courtney.' Ouma's voice again, loud and with an edge to it. Sean started guiltily.

'Goodnight, mevrouw.'

Katrina touched his arm just above the elbow, her fingers were warm.

'Goodnight, meneer, I shall see you in the morning.'

She rustled up the steps and slipped through the opening of the canvas. Sean scowled at Ouma's wagon.

'Thanks very much – and if there is ever anything I can do for you, please don't hesitate to ask.'

14

They started moving the wagons early next morning. There was no time to talk to Katrina in the bustle of inspanning and working the wagons across the corduroy bridge. Sean spent most of the morning in the riverbed and the white sand bounced the heat up at him. He threw off his shirt and sweated like a wrestler. He trotted beside Katrina's wagon when they ran it through the riverbed. She looked once at his naked chest and arms; her cheeks darkened in the shadow of her bonnet and she dropped her eyes and didn't look at him again. With only the two wagons that were going back to fetch the ivory still on the north bank and the rest safely across, Sean could relax. He washed in one of the pools, put on his shirt and went across to the south bank looking forward to a long afternoon of Katrina's company.

Ouma met him. 'Thank you, my bear, the girls have made you a parcel of cold meat and a bottle of coffee to eat on your way.' Sean's face went slack. He had forgotten all about that stinking ivory; as far as he was concerned Oupa and Paulus could keep the lot of it.

'Don't worry about us any more now, maneer. I know how it is with a man who is a man. When there's work to do everything else comes after.'

Katrina put the food in his hands. Sean looked for a sign from her. One sign and he'd defy even Ouma.

'Don't be too long,' she whispered. The thought that he might shirk work had obviously not even occurred to her. Sean was glad he hadn't suggested it.

It was a long ride back to the elephant.

'You've taken your time, haven't you?' Oupa greeted him with sour suspicion. 'You'd better get to work if you don't want to lose some of your share.'

Taking out the tusks was a delicate task: a slip of the axe would scar the ivory and halve its value. They worked in the

396

heat with a blue haze of flies around their faces, settling on their lips and crawling into their nostrils and eyes. The carcases had started to rot and the gases ballooned their bellies and escaped in posthumous belches. They sweated as they worked and the blood caked their arms to the elbows, but each hour the wagons filled higher until on the third day they loaded the last tusk. Sean reckoned his share at twelve hundred pounds, the equivalent of a satisfactory day on the Stock Exchange.

He was in a good mood on the morning that they started back to the camp, but it deteriorated as the day wore on and they struggled with the heavily-loaded wagons. The rain seemed to have made up its mind at last and now the sky's belly hung down as heavily as that of a pregnant sow. The clouds trapped the heat beneath them and the men panted and the oxen complained mournfully. At mid-afternoon they heard the first far thunder.

'It will be on us before we pass the river,' fretted Oupa. 'See if you can't get some pace out of those oxen.'

They reached Sean's camp an hour after dark and threw his share of the ivory out of the wagons almost without stopping; then they went down to the river and across the bridge to the south bank.

'My mother will have food ready,' Jan Paulus called back to Sean. 'When you have washed come across and eat with us.'

Sean had supper with the Leroux, but his attempts to get Katrina by herself were neatly countered by Oupa whose suspicions were now confirmed. The old man played his trump card immediately after supper and ordered Katrina to bed. Sean could only shrug helplessly in reply to Katrina's appealing little glance. When she had gone Sean went back to his own camp. He was dizzy, with fatigue and he fell onto his cot without bothering to undress.

The rains opened their annual offensive with a midnight broadside of thunder. It startled Sean to his feet before he was awake. He pulled open the front of the wagon and heard the wind coming.

'Mbejane, get the cattle into the laager. Make sure all the canvas is secure.'

'It is done already, Nkosi, I have lashed the wagons together so the oxen cannot stampede and I have –' Then the wind whipped his voice away.

It came out of the east and it frightened the trees so they thrashed their branches in panic; it drummed on the wagon canvas and filled the air with dust and dry leaves. The oxen turned restlessly within the laager. Then came the rain: stinging like hail, drowning the wind and turning the air to water. It swamped the sloping ground that could not drain It fast enough, it blinded and it deafened. Sean went back to his cot and listened to its fury. It made him feel drowsy. He pulled the blankets up to his chin and slept.

In the morning he found his oilskins in the chest at the foot of his cot. They crackled as he pulled them on. He climbed out of the wagon. The cattle had churned the inside of the laager to calf-deep mud and there was no chance of a fire for breakfast. Although the rain was still falling the noise was out of proportion to its strength. Sean paused in his inspection of the camp; he thought about it and suddenly he knew that it was the flood voice of the Limpopo that he heard. Sliding in the mud, he ran out of the laager and stood on the bank of the river. He stared at the mad water. It was so thick with mud it looked solid and it raced so fast it appeared to be standing still. It humped up over piles of submerged rock, gullied through the deeps and hissed in static waves through the shallows. The branches and tree trunks in it whisked past so swiftly that they did little to dispel the illusion that the river was frozen in this brown convulsion.

Reluctantly Sean lifted his eyes to the far bank. The Leroux' wagons were gone.

'Katrina,' he said with the sadness of the might-have-been, then again, 'Katrina,' with the sense of his loss melting in the flame of his anger; and he knew that his wanting was not just the itch that is easily scratched and forgotten, but that it was the true ache, the one that gets into your hands and your head and your heart as well as your loins. He couldn't let her go. He ran back to his wagon and threw his clothes onto the cot.

'I'll marry her,' he said and the words startled him. He stood naked, with an awed expression on his face.

'I'll marry her,' he said again; it was an original thought and it frightened him a little. He took a pair of shorts out of his chest and put his legs into them; he pulled them up and buttoned the fly.

'I'll marry her!' He grinned at his own daring. 'I'm damned if

398

I won't!' He buckled his belt on and tied a pair of *veldschoen* to it by their laces. He jumped down into the mud. The rain was cold on his bare back and he shivered briefly. Then he saw Mbejane coming out of one of the other wagons and he ran.

'Nkosi, Nkosi, what are you doing?' Sean put his head down and ran faster with Mbejane chasing him out onto the bank of the river.

'It's madness . . . let us talk about it first,' Mbejane shouted. 'Please, Nkosi, please.' Sean slipped in the mud and slithered down the bank. Mbejane jumped down after and caught him at the edge of the water, but the mud had coated Sean's body like grease and Mbejane couldn't hold him. Sean twisted out of his hands and sprang far out. He hit the water flat and swam on his back trying to avoid the undertow. The river swept him away. A wave slapped into his mouth and he doubled up to cough; immediately the river caught him by the heels and pulled him under the surface. It let him go again, just long enough to snatch air then it stirred him in a whirlpool and sucked him under once more. He came up beating at the water with his arms, then it tumbled him over a cascade and he knew by the pain in his chest that he was drowning. He swooped down a chute of swift water between rocks and it didn't matter anymore. He was too tired. Something scraped against his chest and he put out his hand to protect himself; his fingers closed round a branch and his head lifted out of the water. He drank air and then he was clinging to the branch, still alive and wanting to live. He started kicking, edging across the current, riding the river with his arms around the log.

One of the eddies beneath the south bank swung the log in, under the branches of a tree. He reached up, caught them and dragged himself out. He knelt in the mud and water came gushing up out of him, half through his mouth and half through his nose. He had lost his *veldschoen*. He belched painfully and looked at the river. How fast was it moving, how long had he been in the water? He must be fifteen miles below the wagons. He wiped his face with his hand. It was still raining. He stood shakily and faced upstream.

It took him three hours to reach the spot opposite his wagons. Mbejane and the others waved in wild relief when they saw him, but their shouts could not carry across the river. Sean was cold now and his feet were sore. The tracks of the Leroux wagons were dissolving in the rain. He followed them and at last the pain in his feet healed as he saw the flash of canvas in the rain mist ahead of him.

'Name of a name,' shouted Jan Paulus. 'How did you cross the river?'

'I flew, how else?' said Sean. 'Where's Katrina?'

Paulus started to laugh, leaning back in the saddle. 'So that's it then, you haven't come all this way to say goodbye to me.'

Sean flushed. 'All right, laughing boy. That's enough merriment for today . . . Where is she?'

Oupa came galloping back towards them. He asked his first question when he was fifty yards away and his fifth as he arrived. From experience Sean knew there was no point in trying to answer them. He looked beyond the two Leroux and saw her coming. She was running back from the lead wagon, her bonnet hanging from its ribbon around her throat and her hair bouncing loosely with each step. She held her skirts out of the mud, her cheeks flushed darker than the brown of her face and her eyes were very green. Sean ducked under the neck of Oupa's horse and went wet, muddy and eager to meet her.

Then the shyness stopped them and they stood paces apart. 'Katrina, will you marry me?'

She went pale. She stared at him then turned away, she was crying and Sean felt the bottom drop out of his stomach.

'No,' shouted Oupa furiously. 'She won't marry you. Leave her alone, you big baboon. You've made her cry. Get out of here. She's only a baby. Get out of here.' He forced his horse between them.

'You hold your mouth, you old busybody.' Ouma came panting back to join the discussion. 'What do you know about it anyway? Just because she's crying doesn't mean she doesn't want him.'

'I thought he was going to let me go,' sobbed Katrina, 'I thought he didn't care.'

Sean whooped and tried to dodge around Oupa's horse.

'You leave her alone,' shouted Oupa desperately, manoeuvring his horse to cut Sean off. 'You made her cry. I tell you she's crying.'

Katrina was undoubtedly crying. She was also trying to get around Oupa's horse.

'*Vat haar*,' shouted Jan Paulus. 'Get her, man, go and get her!'

Ouma caught the horse by the reins and dragged it away: she was a powerful woman. Sean and Katrina collided and held tight.

'Hey, that's it, man,' Jan Paulus jumped off his horse and pounded Sean's back from behind. Unable to protect himself Sean was driven forward a pace with each blow.

Much later Oupa muttered sulkily. 'She can have two wagons for her dowry.'

'Three!' said Katrina.

'Four!' said Ouma.

'Very well, four. Take your hands off him, girl. Haven't you any shame?' Hastily Katrina dropped her arm from Sean's waist. Sean had borrowed a suit of clothing from Paulus and they were all standing round the fire. It had stopped raining but the low clouds were prematurely bringing on the night.

'And four of the horses,' Ouma prompted her husband.

'Do you want to beggar me, woman?'

'Four horses,' repeated Ouma.

'All right, all right . . . four horses.' Oupa looked at Katrina, his eyes were stricken. 'She's only a baby, man, she's only fifteen years.'

'Sixteen,' said Ouma.

'Nearly seventeen,' said Katrina, 'and anyway you've promised, Pa, you can't go back on your word now.'

Oupa sighed; then he looked at Sean and his face hardened.

'Paulus, get the Bible out of my wagon. This big baboon is going to swear an oath.'

Jan Paulus put the Bible on the tailboard of the wagon. It was thick and the cover was of black leather, dull with use.

'Come here,' Oupa said to Sean. 'Put your hand on the book . . . don't look at me. Look up, man, look up. Now say after me, "I do most solemnly swear to look after this woman" – don't gobble, speak slower – "until I can find a priest to say the proper words. Should I fail in this then I ask you, God, to blast me with lightning, sting me with serpents, burn me in eternal fire –"'
Oupa completed the list of atrocities, then he grunted with satisfaction and tucked the Bible under his arm. 'He won't have a chance to do all that to you . . . I'll get you first.'

Sean shared Jan Paulus's wagon that night; he wasn't in a mood for sleep and anyway Jan Paulus snored. It was raining again in the morning, depressing weather for farewells. Jan

Paulus laughed, Henrietta cried and Ouma did both. Oupa kissed his daughter.

'Be a woman like your mother,' he said, then he scowled at Sean.

'Remember, just you remember!'

Sean and Katrina stood together and watched the trees and the curtain of rain hide the wagon train. Sean held Katrina's hand. He could feel the sadness on her; he put his arm round her and her dress was damp and cold. The last wagon disappeared and they were alone in a land as vast as solitude. Katrina shivered and looked up at the man beside her. He was so big and over-poweringly male; he was a stranger. Suddenly she was fright-ened. She wanted to hear her mother's laugh and see her brother and father riding ahead of her wagon, the way it had always been.

'Oh, please, I want . . .' she pulled out from his arm. She never finished that sentence, for she looked at his mouth and his lips were full and burnt dark by the sun – they were smiling. Then she looked at his eyes and her panic smoothed away. With those eyes watching over her she was never to feel frightened again, not until the very end and that was a long time away. Going into his love was like going into a castle, a thick-walled place. A safe place where no one else could enter. The first feeling of it was so strong that she could only stand quietly and let the warmth wrap her.

15

That evening they outspanned Katrina's wagons back at the south bank of the river. It was still raining. Sean's servants waved and signalled to them, but the brown water bellowed down between them cutting off all sound and hope of passage. Katrina looked at the water. 'Did you really swim that, meneer?'

'So fast that I hardly got wet.'

'Thank you,' she said.

Despite the rain and smoky fire Katrina served up a meal as good as one of Ouma's. They ate it in the shelter of the tarpaulin beside her wagon. The wind guttered the hurricane lamp, flogged the canvas and blew a fine haze of rain in on them. It was so uncomfortable that when Sean suggested that they go into the wagon Katrina barely hesitated before agreeing. She sat on the edge of her cot and Sean sat on the chest opposite her. From an awkward start their conversation was soon running as fast as the river outside the wagon.

'My hair is still wet,' Katrina exclaimed at last. 'Do you mind if I dry it while we talk?'

'Of course not.'

'Then let me get my towel out of the chest.'

They stood up at the same time. There was very little space in the wagon. They touched. They were on the cot. The movement of his mouth on hers, the warm taste of it, the strong pleading of his fingers at the nape of her neck and along her spine – all these things were strangely confusing. She responded slowly at first, then faster with bewildered movements of her own body and little graspings at his arms and shoulders. She did not understand and she did not care. The confusion spread through her whole body and she could not stop it, she did not want to. She reached up and her fingers went into his hair. She pulled his face down on hers. His teeth crushed her lips – sweet, exciting pain. His hand came round from her back and enclosed a fat round breast. Through the thin cotton he found the erectness of her nipple and rolled it gently between his fingers. She reacted like a filly feeling the whip for the first time. One instant she lay under the shock of his touch and then her convulsive heave caught him by surprise. He went backwards off the cot and his head cracked against the wooden chest. He sat on the floor and stared up at her, too surprised even to rub the lump on his head. Her face was flushed and she pushed the hair back from her forehead with both hands. She was shaking her head wildly in her effort to speak through her gasping. 'You must go now, meneer – the servants have made a bed for you in one of the other wagons.'

Sean scrambled to his feet. 'But, I thought . . . surely we are . . . well, I mean.'

'Keep away from me,' she warned anxiously. 'If you touch me again tonight, I'll . . . I'll bite you.'

'But, Katrina, please, I can't sleep in the other wagon.' The thought appalled him.

'I'll cook your food, mend your clothes . . . everything! But until you find a priest . . .' She didn't go on, but Sean got the idea. He started to argue. It was his introduction to Boer immovability and at last he went to find his own bed. One of Katrina's dogs was there before him – a three-quarters-grown brindle hound. Sean's attempts to persuade it to leave were as ill-fated as had been his previous arguments with its mistress. They shared the bed. During the night a difference of opinion arose between them as to what constituted a half-share of the blankets. From it the dog earned its name – Thief.

16

Sean determined to show Katrina just how strongly he resented her attitude. He would be polite but distant. Five minutes after they had sat down to breakfast the next morning this demonstration of disapproval had deteriorated to the stage where he was unable to take his eyes off her face and he was talking so much that breakfast lasted an hour.

The rain held steady for three more days and then it stopped. The sun came back, as welcome as an old friend, but it was another ten days before the river regained its sanity. Time, rain or river meant very little to the two of them. They wandered out into the bush together to pick mushrooms; they sat in camp and when Katrina was working Sean followed her around. Then, of course, they talked. She listened to him. She laughed at the right places and gasped with wonder when she was meant to. She was a good listener. As for Sean, if she had repeated the same word over and over the sound of her voice alone would have held him entranced. The evenings were difficult. Sean would start getting restless and make excuses to touch her. She wanted him to, but she was frightened of the confusion that had so nearly trapped her the first night. So she drew up a set of rules and put them to him. 'Do you promise not to do anything more than kiss me?'

'Not unless you say I can,' Sean agreed readily.

'No.' She saw the catch in that.

'You mean, I must never do anything but kiss you even if you say I can?'

She started to blush. 'If I say so in the daytime, that's different . . . but anything I say at night doesn't count, and if you break your promise I'll never let you touch me again.'

Katrina's rules stood unchanged by the time the river had dropped enough for the wagons to be taken across to the north bank. The rains were resting, gathering their strength, but soon they would set in once more. The river was full but no longer murderous. Now was the time to cross. Sean took the oxen across first, swimming them in a herd. Holding on to one of their tails he had a Nantucket sleigh-ride across the river and when he reached the north bank there was a joyous welcome awaiting him.

They took six thick coils of unused rope from the stores wagon and joined them together. With the end of the rope round his waist Sean made one of his horses tow him back across the river, Mbejane paying out the line to him as he went. Then Sean supervised Katrina's servants as they emptied all the water barrels and lashed them to the sides of the first wagon to serve as floats. They ran the wagon into the water, tied on the rope and adjusted the barrels so that the wagon floated level. Sean signalled to Mbejane and waited until he had made the other end of the rope fast to a tree on the north bank. Then they pushed the wagon into the current and watched anxiously as it swung across the river like a pendulum, the current driving it but the tree anchoring it. It hit the north bank a distance the exact width of the river downstream of the tree, and Sean's party cheered as Mbejane and the other servants ran down the bank to retrieve it. Mbejane had a team of oxen standing ready and they dragged it out. Sean's horse towed him across the river again to fetch the rope.

Sean, Katrina and all her servants rode across on the last wagon. Sean stood behind Katrina with his arms round her waist, ostensibly to steady her, and the servants shouted and chattered like children on a picnic.

The water piled up brown against the side of the wagon, tilting it and making it roll, and with an exhilarating swoop they shot across the river and crashed into the far bank. The impact tumbled them overboard, throwing them into the knee-deep water beside the bank. They scrambled ashore. The water streamed out of Katrina's dress, her hair melted wetly over her face; she had mud on one cheek and she was gasping with laughter. Her sodden petticoats clung to her legs, tripping her, and Sean picked her up and carried her to his own laager. His servants shouted loud encouragement after him and Katrina shrieked genteelly to be put down, but held tight round his neck with both arms.

17

Now that the rains had changed every irregularity in the land into a waterhole and sowed new green grass where before had been dust and dry earth, the game scattered away from the river. Every few days Sean's trackers came into camp to report that there were no elephant. Sean condoled with them and sent them out again. He was well satisfied; there was a new quarry now, more elusive and therefore more satisfying than an old bull elephant with a hundred and fifty pounds of ivory on each side of his face. Yet to call Katrina his quarry was a lie. She was much more than that.

She was a new world – a place of endless mysteries and unexpected delights, an enchanting mixture of woman and child. She supervised the domestic routine with deceptive lack of fuss. With her there, suddenly his clothes were clean and had their full complement of buttons; the stew of boots and books and unwashed socks in his wagon vanished. There were fresh bread and fruit preserves on the table; Kandhla's eternal grilled steaks gave way to a variety of dishes. Each day she showed a new accomplishment. She could ride astride, though Sean had to turn his back when she mounted and dismounted. She cut Sean's hair and made as good a job of it as his barber in Johannesburg. She had a medicine chest in her wagon from which she produced remedies for every ailing man or beast in the company. She handled a rifle like a man and could strip and clean Sean's Mannlicher. She helped him load cartridges, measuring the charges with a practised eye. She could discuss birth and procreation with a clinical objectivity and a minute later blush all over when he looked at her that way. She was as stubborn as a mule, haughty when it suited her, serene and inscrutable at times and at others a little girl. She would push a handful of grass down the back of his shirt and run for him to chase her, giggle for minutes at a secret thought, play long imaginative games in which the dogs were her children and she talked to them and answered for them. Sometimes she was so naive that Sean thought she was joking until he remembered how young she was. She could drive him from happiness to spitting anger and back again within the space of an hour. But, once he had won her confidence and she knew that he would play to the rules, she responded to his caresses with a violence that startled them both. Sean was completely absorbed in her. She was the most wonderful thing he had ever found and, best of all, he could talk to her. He told her about Duff. She saw the extra cot in his wagon and found clothing that was obviously too small for him. She asked about it and he told her all of it and she understood.

The days became weeks. The cattle grew fat, their skins sleek and tight. Katrina planted a small vegetable garden and reaped a crop from it. Christmas came and Katrina baked a cake. Sean gave her a kaross of monkey skins that Mbejane had worked on in secret. Katrina gave Sean hand-sewn shirts, each with his initials embroidered on the top pocket, and she relaxed the rules a fraction.

Then when the new year had begun and Sean hadn't killed an elephant in six weeks, Mbejane headed a deputation from the gunboys. The question he had to ask, though tactfully disguised, was simply, 'Did we come here to hunt, or what?'

They broke camp and moved north again and the strain was showing on Sean at last. He tried to sweat it out by long days of hunting but this didn't help for conditions were so bad that they added to his irritability. The grass in most places was higher than a mounted man's head, its sharp edges cut as he passed through it. But the grass seeds were the worst: half an inch long and barbed like an arrow they worked their way quickly through clothing and into the skin. In the humid heat the small wounds they made festered within hours. Then there were the flies. Hippo-flies, greenheaded flies, sand-flies all with one thing in common – they stung. The soft skin behind the ears was their favourite place. They'd creep upon him, settle so lightly he wouldn't feel it – then, ping with the red-hot needle. Always wet, sometimes with sweat, other times with rain, Sean would close with a herd of elephant. He would hear them moving in the long grass around him and see the white canopy of egrets fluttering over them, but it was seldom he could get a shot at them. If he did he had to stand in the centre of a storm of blundering bodies. Often they would be following a herd, almost upon them, when Sean would lose interest and they'd all go back to camp. He couldn't keep away.

He was miserable, his servants were miserable, and Katrina was happy as a bird at daybreak. She had a man, she was mistress of a household which she ran with confidence and, because her senses were not yet as seasoned as Sean's, she was physically content. Even with Sean's strict adherence to the rules, their evenings in her wagon would end for her with a sigh and a shudder and she would go dreamy-eyed to bed and leave Sean with a burning devil inside of him. The only person Sean could complain to was Thief. He would lie with his snout buried in Sean's armpit, with at least his share of the blankets over him, and listen quietly.

The Zulus could see what the trouble was but they didn't understand it. They didn't discuss it, of course, but if one of them spread his hands expressively or coughed in a certain way the others knew what he meant. Mbejane came closest to actually putting it into words. Sean had just thrown a tantrum. It was a matter of a lost axe and who was responsible. Sean lined them up and expressed doubts as to their ancestry, present worth and future prospects, then he stormed off to his wagon. There was a long silence and Hlubi offered his snuff-box to Mbejane.

Mbejane took a pinch and said, 'It's a stupid stallion that doesn't know how to kick down a fence.'

'It is true, it is true,' they agreed, and there the matter rested.

18

A week later they reached the Sabi river. The mountains on the far side were blue-grey with distance and the river was full — brown and full.

The next morning was fresh and cool from the night's rain. The camp smelt of wood-smoke, cattle and wild mimosa. From one of the ostrich eggs that Mbejane had found the day before, Katrina made an omelette the size of a soup-plate. It was flavoured with nutmeg and chunks of mushroom, yellow and rich. Afterwards there were scones and wild honey, coffee and a cheroot for Sean.

'Are you going out today?' Katrina asked.

'Uh huh.'

'Oh!'

'Don't you want me to?'

'You haven't stayed in camp for a week.'

'Don't you want me to go?'

She stood up quickly and started clearing the table. 'Anyway you won't find any elephant . . . you haven't found anything for ages.'

'Do you want me to stay?'

'It's such a lovely day.' She signed to Kandhla to take the plates away.

'If you want me to stay, ask me properly.'

'We could look for mushrooms.'

'Say it,' said Sean.

'All right then, please!'

'Mbejane! Take the saddle off that horse, I won't be using him.'

Katrina laughed. She ran to her wagon, skirts swirling around her legs, calling to the dogs. She came back with her bonnet on and a basket in her hand. The dogs crowded round them, jumping up and barking.

'Go on . . . seek up then,' Sean told them and they raced ahead, circling back barking, chasing one another. Sean and Katrina walked holding hands. The brim of Katrina's bonnet kept her face in shadow, but even then her eyes when she looked at him were bright green. They picked the new mushrooms, round and hard, brown and slightly sticky on top, fluted underneath delicately as a lady's fan. In an hour they had filled the basket and they stopped under a marula tree. Sean lay on his back. Katrina broke off a blade of grass and tickled his face with it until he caught her wrist and pulled her down onto his chest. The dogs watched them, sitting around them in a circle, their tongues hanging out pink and wet.

'There's a place in the Cape, just outside Paarl. The mountains stand over it and there's a river . . . the water's very clear, you can see the fish lying on the bottom,' said Katrina. Her ear was against his chest and she was listening to his heart. 'Will you buy me a farm there one day?'

'Yes,' said Sean.

'We'll build a house with a wide veranda and on Sundays we'll drive to church with the girls and the little ones in the back and the bigger boys riding next to the buggy.'

'How many will there be?' asked Sean. He lifted the side of her bonnet and looked at her ear. It was a very pretty ear, in the sunlight he could see the fine fur on the lobe.

'Oh lots . . . boys mostly, but a few girls.'

'Ten?' suggested Sean.

'More than that.'

'Fifteen?'

'Yes, fifteen.'

They lay and thought about it. To Sean it seemed a fairly well-rounded number.

'And I'll keep chickens, I want lots of chickens.'

'All right,' said Sean.

'You don't mind?'

'Should I?'

'Some people mind chickens, some people don't like them at all,' said Katrina. 'I'm glad you don't mind them. I've always wanted them.'

Stealthily Sean advanced his mouth towards her ear but she felt him move and sat up.

'What are you doing?'

'This,' said Sean and his arm shot out.

'No, Sean, they're watching us.' She waved her hand at the dogs.

'They'll understand,' said Sean and then they were both quiet for a long time.

The dogs burst out together in full hunting chorus. Katrina sat up and Sean turned his head and saw the leopard. It stood fifty yards away on the edge of the thick bush along the river bank watching them, poised elegantly in tights of black and gold, long and small-bellied. It moved then, blurring with speed, touching the ground as lightly as a swallow touches the water when it drinks in flight. The dogs went after it in a pack, Thief leading them, his voice cracking with excitement.

'Back, come back,' shouted Sean. 'Leave it, damn you, come back.'

'Stop them, Sean, go after them. We'll lose them all.'

'Wait here,' Sean told her.

He ran after the sound of the pack. Not shouting, saving his wind. He knew what would happen and he listened for it. He heard the tone of the hunt change – sharper now. Sean stopped and stood panting, peering ahead. The dogs were not moving. The sound of their barking was steady in volume.

'The swine has stopped; he's going to take them.'

He started running again and almost immediately heard the first dog scream. He kept running. He found the dog lying where the leopard had flung it – the old bitch with white ears, her stomach was stripped out. Sean went on. The tan ridgeback next, disembowelled, still alive and crawling to meet him. He ran on; always the hunt was out of sight ahead of him but he kept after it. He no longer stopped to help the dogs that had been mauled. Most of them were dead before he reached them. The saliva thickened in his mouth, his heart jumped against his ribs and he reeled as he ran.

Suddenly he was in the open and the hunt was spread out before him. There were three dogs left. One of them was Thief. They were circling the leopard, belling him, darting in at his back legs, snapping, then jumping back as the leopard spun snarling. The grass was short and green in the clearing. The sun was directly overhead: it threw no shadow, it lit everything with a flat, even light. Sean tried to shout but his throat wouldn't let the sound out. The leopard dropped onto its back and lay with the sprawled grace of a sleeping cat, its legs open and its belly exposed. The dogs hung back, hesitating. Sean shouted again but his voice still would not carry. That creamy yellow belly, soft and fluffy, was too much temptation. One of the dogs went for it, dipping its head, its mouth open. The leopard closed on it like a spring trap. It caught and held the dog with its front paws and its back legs worked quickly. The dog yammered at the swift surgeon strokes and then it was thrown aside, its bowels hanging out. The leopard relaxed again to show the yellow bait of its belly. Sean was close now and this time the two dogs heard his shout. The leopard heard it also. It flashed to its feet and tried to break, but the instant it turned Thief was at it, slashing at its back legs forcing it to swing and crouch.

'Here, boy, leave him! Here, Thief, come here!'

Thief took Sean's shout as encouragement. He danced just out of reach of the flicking paws, shrilly taunting the leopard. The hunt was finely balanced now. Sean knew if he could get the dogs to slacken their attack the leopard would run. He went forward a pace, stooped to pick up a stone to throw at Thief and his movement tipped the balance. When he straightened up the leopard was watching him and he felt the eel of fear move in his stomach. It was going to come for him. He knew it by the way its ears flattened against its head and its shoulders bunched like loaded springs. Sean dropped the stone and reached for the knife on his belt.

The leopard's lips peeled back. Its teeth were yellow, its head with the ears flattened was like a snake's. It came fast and low against the ground, brushing the dogs aside. Its run was long-reaching, smoothly beautiful. It snaked towards him, fast over the short grass. It came into the air, lifting high, very fast and very smoothly. Sean felt the shock and the pain together. The shock threw him backwards and the pain sucked the breath from his lungs. Its claws hooked into his chest, he felt them scrape his ribs. He held its mouth from his face, his forearm against its throat and he smelt the overripe grave smell of its breath. They rolled together in the grass, its front claws still holding in the flesh of his chest, and he felt its back legs coming up to rake his stomach. He twisted desperately to keep clear of them, using his knife at the same time, slipping the blade into its back. The leopard screamed, its back legs came up again; he felt the claws go into his hip and tear down his thigh. The pain

413

was deep and strong and he knew he was badly hurt. The legs came up again. This time they would kill him.

Thief locked his teeth in the leopard's leg before the claws could catch in Sean's flesh, he dragged back, digging in with his front feet, holding the leopard stretched out across Sean's body. Sean's vision was dissolving into blackness and bright lights. He pushed the knife into the leopard's back, close to the spine and pulled it down between the ribs the way a butcher cuts a chop. The leopard screamed again with its body shuddering and its claws curling in Sean's flesh. Sean cut again, deep and long – and again, then again. Tearing at it, mad with the pain, its blood gushed out and mixed with his and he rolled away from it. The dogs were worrying it, growling. It was dead. Sean let the knife slip out of his hand and touched the tears in his leg. The blood was dark red, pouring with the thickness of treacle, much blood. He was looking down a funnel of darkness. The leg was far away, not his – not his leg.

'Garry,' he whispered. 'Garry, oh God! I'm sorry. I slipped, I didn't mean it, I slipped.' The funnel closed and there was no leg – only darkness. Time was a liquid thing, all the world was liquid, moving in darkness. The sun was dark and only the pain was steady, steady as a rock in the dark moving sea. He saw Katrina's face indistinct in the darkness. He tried to tell her how sorry he was. He tried to tell her it was an accident, but the pain stopped him. She was crying. He knew she would understand so he went back into the dark sea. Then the surface of the sea boiled and he choked in the heat, but always the pain was there like a rock to hold onto. The steam from the sea coiled up around him and it hardened into the shape of a woman and he thought it was Katrina, then he saw its head was a leopard's head and its breath stank like the rotting of a gangrenous leg.

'I don't want you – I know who you are,' he shouted at it. 'I don't want you. It's not my child,' and the thing broke into steam, twisting grey steam, and came back gibbering at him on a chain that tinkled, frothing yellow from the grey misty mouth, and terror came with it. He twisted and covered his face, holding onto the pain for the pain was real and steady.

Then after a thousand years the sea froze and he walked on it and the white ice stretched away wherever he looked. It was cold and lonely on the ice. There was a small wind, a cold small wind, the wind whispered across the ice and its whispering was a sad sound, and Sean held his pain, hugging it close to him for he was lonely and only the pain was real. Then there were other figures moving around him on the ice, dark figures all hurrying one way, crowding him, pushing him along with them and he lost his pain, lost it in the desperate hurrying press. And though they had no faces, some of the figures wept and others laughed and they hurried forward until they came to the place where the crevasse split across the ice in front of them. The crevasse was wide and deep and its sides were white, then pale-green shading to blue and at last to infinite blackness, and some of the figures threw themselves joyfully into it singing as they fell. Others clung to edges, their formless faces full of fear, and still others stepped off into the void, tiredly, like travellers at the end of a long journey. When Sean saw the crevasse he began to fight, throwing himself back against the crowd that bore him forward, carrying him to the edge of the pit, and his feet slid over the edge. He clawed with his fingers at the slippery edge of the ice. He fought and he shouted as he fought for the dark drop sucked at his legs. Then he lay quietly and the crevasse had closed and he was alone. He was tired – wasted and terribly tired. He closed his eyes and the pain came back to him, throbbing softly in his leg.

He opened his eyes and he saw Katrina's face. She was pale and her eyes were big and heavily underscored in blue. He tried to lift his hand to touch her face but he couldn't move.

'Katrina,' he said. He saw her eyes go green with surprise and happiness.

'You've come back. Oh, thank God. You've come back.'

Sean rolled his head and looked at the canvas of the wagon tent.

'How long?' he asked. His voice was a whisper.

'Five days . . . Don't talk – please, don't talk.'

Sean closed his eyes. He was very tired so he slept.

19

Katrina washed him when he woke. Mbejane helped her lift
and turn him, his big pink-palmed hands very gentle as he
handled the leg. They washed the smell of fever off him and
changed the dressings. Sean watched Katrina as she worked and
every time she looked up they smiled at each other. Once he
used a little of his strength to ask Mbejane, 'Where were you
when I needed you?'

'I slept in the sun, Nkosi, like an old woman,' Mbejane half-
laughed, half-apologized. Katrina brought him food and when he
smelt it he was hungry. He ate it all and then he slept again.

Mbejane built a shelter with open sides and a roof of thatch.
He sited it in the shade on the bank of the Sabi. Then he made
a bed of poles and laced leather thongs. They carried Sean from
the wagon, Katrina fussing around them until they had laid him
in the shelter. Katrina went back to the wagon for pillows and
when she returned she found Thief and Sean settling down
comfortably.

'Sean, get that monster out of there – those blankets have just
been washed.'

Thief flattened his body and hid his head in Sean's armpit.

'It's all right, he's quite clean,' Sean protected him.

'He smells.'

'He does not.' Sean sniffed at Thief. 'Well, not much anyway.'

'You two!' She put the pillows under Sean's head and went
round to his leg. 'How does it feel?'

'It's fine,' said Sean. Thief inched himself up the bed until he
reached the pillows.

In the slow slide of days Sean's body healed and the well of
his strength filled. The moving air under the shelter dried the
scabs off his chest and leg, but there would be scars. In the
mornings, after breakfast, Sean held court from his couch.
Katrina sat on the end of the bed and his servants squatted

around him. First they talked over domestic matters – the health of the oxen, mentioning them by name, discussing their eyes, hooves and stomachs. There was a tear in the canvas of one wagon. The single remaining bitch was in season – was Thief man enough for the job yet? There was meat to kill – perhaps the Nkosikaze would take the rifle later today. Hlubi had caught four barbel of medium size in his fish trap, and here the talk turned to the bush around them. A lion had killed a buffalo below the first bend in the river – there you could see the vultures. During the night a herd of cow elephant had drunk a mile upstream. Each item was considered by the meeting. Everyone felt free to comment or argue against any view which conflicted with his own. When everything had been said Sean gave them their tasks for the day and sent them away. Then he and Katrina could be alone.

From the shelter they could see the full sweep of the river, with the crocodiles lying on the white sandbars and the kingfishers plopping into the shallows. They sat close to each other and they talked of the farm they would have. Sean would grow grapes and breed horses and Katrina would keep chickens. By the next rainy season they would have filled all the wagons; one more trip after that and they would have enough to buy the farm.

Katrina kept him in bed long after he was strong enough to leave it. She mothered him and he loved it. Shamelessly, in the fashion of the male, he accepted her attentions and even exaggerated his injuries a little. Finally but reluctantly Katrina let him up. He stayed in camp a week more, until his legs stopped wobbling, then one evening he took his rifle and went with Mbejane to shoot fresh meat. They went slowly, Sean favouring his leg, and he shot a young eland not far from the laager. Sean sat against a msasa tree and smoked a cheroot while Mbejane went back to fetch servants to carry the meat. Sean watched them butcher the carcass; there were slabs of white fat on the meat. They slung it on poles and carried it between them, two men to a pole, and when they got back to camp Sean found Katrina in one of her inscrutable moods. When he talked to her at supper she answered him from far away and afterwards by the fire she sat detached from him. She was very lovely and Sean was puzzled and a little resentful. At last he stood up.

'It's time for bed – I'll see you to your wagon.'

'You go. I'll sit a little longer.'

Sean hesitated. 'Is there something wrong? Have I done something wrong?'

'No,' she said quickly. 'No. I'm all right. You go to bed.'

He kissed her cheek. 'If you need me I'll be close. Goodnight, sleep sweet.'

He straightened up. 'Come on, Thief,' he said. 'Time for bed.'

'Leave Thief with me, please.' Katrina caught the skin at the back of the dog's neck and restrained him.

'Why?'

'I just feel like company.'

'Then I'll stay as well,' Sean moved to sit down again.

'No, you go to bed.' She sounded desperate and Sean looked hard at her.

'Are you sure you're all right?'

'Yes, please go.'

He went to his wagon and looked back at her. She was sitting very straight, holding the dog. He climbed into the wagon. The lamp was lit and he stopped in surprise when he saw his cot. There were sheets on it, not just the rough blankets. He ran his hand over the smooth fabric; it was crisp from new ironing. He sat on the cot and pulled off his boots. He undid his shirt and threw it onto the chest, then he lay back and looked up at the lamp.

'There's something bloody funny going on here,' he said.

'Sean' – her voice just outside the wagon. Sean jumped up and opened the flap. 'Can I come in?'

'Yes, of course.' He gave her his hand and lifted her into the wagon. He looked at her face. She was frightened.

'There *is* something wrong,' he said.

'No, don't touch me. There's something I've got to tell you. Sit down on the cot.'

Sean watched her face. He was worried.

'I thought I loved you when I came away with you. I thought we had for ever to be together.' She swallowed painfully. 'Then I found you there in the grass – torn and dead. Before our life together had begun you were dead.'

Sean saw the pain come back into her eyes; she was living it again. He put out his hand to her but she held his wrist.

'No, wait . . . please let me finish. I have to explain to you. It's very important.'

Sean dropped his hand and she went on speaking quickly.

'You were dead and I, too, was dying inside. I felt empty. There was nothing left. Nothing . . . just the hollowness inside and the dry dead feeling on the outside. I touched your face and you looked at me. I prayed then, Sean, and I prayed through the days when you fought the rotting of your body.'

She knelt in front of him and held him around the waist.

'Now we are alive and together again, but I know that it cannot be for ever. A day more, a year, if we are lucky, twenty. But not for ever. I see how small I have been to us. I want to be your wife.'

He bent to her quickly but she pulled away and stood up. She slipped the buttons and her clothing fell away. She loosed her hair and let it drop shiny bright down the whiteness of her body.

'Look at me, Sean, I want you to look at me. This and my love I can give you . . . is it enough?'

There was smoothness, hollow and swell, hair like black fire and soft light on soft skin. He saw the flush from her cheeks spread onto her breasts until they glowed, pink and shy but proud in their perfection. He looked no further. He took her to him and covered her nakedness with his big body. She was trembling and he put her between the sheets and gentled her with his voice until the trembling stopped and she lay with her face pressed up under his beard into his neck.

'Show me how . . . I want to give everything to you. Please show me how,' she whispered.

So they married each other and their marriage was a co-mingling of many things. There was the softness of the wind in it and wanting, the way the baked earth wants the rain. There was pain sharp and swift, movement like running horses, sound low as voices in the night but glad as a greeting, joy climbing on eagles' wings, the triumphant surge and burst of wild water on a rock shore and then there was stillness and warmth within and the snuggling of drowsy puppies, and sleep. Yet it did not end in the sleep, it went on to another seeking and finding, another union and a stranger mystery in the secret depths of her body.

20

In the morning she brought her Bible to him.

'Hey, hey,' protested Sean, 'I've already sworn one oath.'
Katrina laughed at him, the memory of the night still warm and
happy inside her. She opened the book at its fly leaf.

'You've got to write your name in it . . . here, next to mine.'

She watched him, standing next to his chair with her hip
touching his shoulder.

'And your date of birth,' she said.

Sean wrote: 'Ninth Jan. 1862.' Then he said: 'What's this "date
of death" . . . do you want me to fill that in as well?'

'Don't talk like that,' she said quickly and touched the wooden
table.

Sean was sorry he'd said it. He tried to cover up. 'There's only
space for six children.'

'We can write the others in the margin. That's what Ma did . . .
hers even go over onto the first page of Genesis. Do you think
we'll get that far, Sean?'

Sean smiled at her. 'The way I feel now we should reach the
New Testament without much trouble.'

They had made a good start. By June the rains were over and
Katrina walked with her shoulders back to balance her load.
There was a good feeling in the camp. Katrina was more woman
than child now. She was big and radiant, pleased with the awe
her condition inspired in Sean. She sang to herself often and
sometimes in the night she would let him share in it. She would
let him pull the nightdress back from the mound of her stomach
and lay his ear against the tight-stretched, blue-veined skin. He
listened to the suck and gurgle and felt the movement against
his cheek. When he sat up his eyes would be full of the wonder
of it and she would smile proudly at him and take his head on
her shoulder and they would lie together quietly. In the daytime

things were right as well. Sean laughed with the servants and hunted without the intensity of before.

They moved north along the Sabi river. Sometimes they camped for a month at one place. The game came back to the rivers as the veld dried out and once more the ivory started piling up in the wagons.

One afternoon in September Sean and Katrina left the camp and walked along the bank. The land was brown again and smelt of dry grass. The river was pools and white sand.

'Hell, it's hot.' Sean took off his hat and wiped the sweat off his forehead. 'You must be cooking under all those clothes.'

'No, I'm all right.' Katrina was holding his arm.

'Let's have a swim.'

'You mean with no clothes on?' Katrina looked shocked.

'Yes, why not?'

'It's rude.'

'Come on.' He took her down the bank protesting every step and at a place where boulders screened the water he prised her out of her dress. She was laughing and gasping and blushing all at the same time. He carried her into the pool and she sat down thankfully with the water up to her chin.

'How's that feel?' Sean asked.

She let her hair down and it floated out round her, she wriggled her toes in the sand and her stomach showed through the water like the back of a white whale.

'It's nice,' she admitted. 'It feels like silk underwear against my skin.'

Sean stood over her with only his hat on. She looked at him.

'Sit down,' she said uncomfortably and looked away from him.

'Why?' he asked.

'You know why . . . you're rude, that's why.'

Sean sat down beside her.

'You should be used to me by now.'

'Well, I'm not.'

Sean put his arm round her under the water.

'You're lovely,' he said. 'You're my fancy.'

She let him kiss her ear.

'What's it going to be?' He touched the ripe swelling. 'Boy or girl?' This was currently the favourite topic of conversation.

'Boy.' She was very definite.

'What shall we call him?'

'Well, if you don't find a *predikant* soon we'll have to call him the name you're always giving to the servants.'

Sean stared at her. 'What do you mean?'

'You know what you call them when you're cross.'

'Bastard,' said Sean, then really concerned, 'Hell, I hadn't thought of that! We'll have to find a priest. No child of mine will be a bastard. We'll have to go back to Louis Trichardt.'

'You've got about a month,' Katrina warned him.

'My God, we'll never make it. We've left it too late.' Sean's face was ghastly. 'Wait, I've got it. There are Portuguese settlements across the mountains on the coast.'

'Oh, Sean, but they're Roman Catholics.'

'They all work for the same boss.'

'How long will it take to cross the mountains?' Katrina asked doubtfully.

'I don't know. Perhaps two weeks to reach the coast on horseback.'

'On horseback?' Katrina looked still more doubtfully.

'Oh hell ... you can't ride!' Sean scratched the side of his nose. 'I'll have to go and fetch one. Will you stay on your own? I'll leave Mbejane to look after you.'

'Yes, I'll be all right.'

'I won't go if you don't want me to. It's not that important.'

'It is important, you know it is. I'll be all right, truly I will.'

Before he left the next morning Sean took Mbejane aside. 'You know why you're not coming with me, don't you?'

Mbejane nodded, but Sean answered his own question. 'Because there is more important work for you to do here.'

'At night,' said Mbejane, 'I will sleep beneath the Nkosikazi's wagon.'

'You'll sleep?' asked Sean threateningly.

'Only once in a while and then very lightly,' Mbejane grinned.

'That's better,' said Sean.

·

21

Sean said goodbye to Katrina. There were no tears, she understood necessity and helped him to a quiet acceptance of it. They stood a long while beside their wagon, holding each other, their lips almost touching as they whispered together and then Sean called for his horse. Hlubi followed him leading the packhorse when he crossed the Sabi and when Sean reached the far bank he turned and looked back. Katrina was still standing by their wagon and behind her hovered Mbejane. In her bonnet and green dress she looked very young. Sean waved his hat over his head and then set off towards the mountains.

The forests dwindled into grassland as they climbed and each night was colder than the last. Then, in its turn the grassland conceded to the sheer bluffs and misty gorges of the mountain back. Sean and Hlubi struggled upwards, following the game trails, losing them, turning back from impassable cliffs, scouting for a pass, leading the horses over the steep pitches and at night sitting close to the fire and listening to the baboons barking in the kranses around them. Then suddenly, in the middle of a morning that was bright as a cut diamond, they were at the top. To the west the land lay spread out like a map and the distance they had travelled in a week was pathetically small. By straining his eyes and his imagination Sean could make out the dark-green belt of the Sabi watercourse. To the cast the land merged with a blueness that was not the sky and for a while he failed to recognize it. Then – 'the sea,' he shouted and Hlubi laughed with him for it was a godlike feeling to stand above the world. They found an easier route down the eastern slopes and followed it onto the coastal plain. At the bottom of the mountains they came to a native village. To see cultivated lands and human dwellings again was a small shock to Sean. He had come to accept the fact that he and his retinue were the only people left on earth.

The entire population of the village fled when they saw him. Mothers snatched up a child in each hand and ran as fast as their menfolk – memories of the slave-traders still persisted in this part of Africa. Within two minutes of his arrival Sean again had the feeling that he was the only person left on earth. With the contempt of the Zulu for every other tribe in Africa, Hlubi shook his head sadly.

'Monkeys,' he said.

They dismounted and tied their horses under the big tree that was the centre of the village. They sat in the shade and waited. The huts were grass beehives, their roofs blackened with smoke, and a few chickens picked and scratched at the bare earth between them. Half an hour later Sean saw a black face watching him from the edge of the bush and he ignored it. Slowly the face emerged, followed closely by a reluctant body. With a twig, Sean went on drawing patterns in the dust between his feet. Out of the corner of his eye he watched the hesitant approach. It was an old man with stork thin legs and one eye glazed into a white jelly by tropical ophthalmia. Sean concluded that his fellows had picked him to act as ambassador on the grounds that of all their number he would be the least loss.

Sean looked up and gave him a radiant smile. The old man froze and then his lips twitched into a sickly grin of relief. Sean stood up, dusted his hands on the sides of his breeches and went to shake the old man's hand. Immediately the bush around them swarmed with people, they poured back into the village jabbering and laughing: they crowded round Sean and felt his clothing, peered into his face and exclaimed delightedly. It was obvious that most of them had never seen a white man before. Sean was trying to shake off One-Eye, who still had a possessive hold on Sean's right hand, and Hlubi leaned disdainfully against the tree, taking no part in the welcome. One-Eye ended the confusion by screeching at them in a voice rusty with age. The courage he had displayed earlier now earned its reward. At his command a dozen of the younger women scampered off and came back with a carved wooden stool and six earthenware pots of native beer. By the hand, on which he had not for an instant relaxed his grip, One-Eye led Sean to the stool and made him sit; the rest of the villagers squatted in a circle round him and one of the girls brought the biggest beer-pot to Sean. The beer was yellow and it bubbled sullenly. Sean's stomach shied at the sight of it. He glanced at One-Eye who was watching him anxiously, he lifted the pot and sipped. Then he smiled with surprise; it was creamy and pleasantly tart.

'Good,' he said.

'Goot,' chorused the villagers.

'Your health,' said Sean.

' 'ealt,' said the village as one man, and Sean drank deep. One of the girls took another beer-pot to Hlubi. She knelt in front of him and shyly offered it. She had a plaited-grass string around her waist from which a small kilt hung down in front, but her stern was completely exposed and her bosoms were the size and shape of ripe melons. Hlubi looked at them until the girl hung her head, then he lifted the beer-pot.

Sean wanted a guide to the nearest Portuguese settlement. He looked at One-Eye and said, 'Town? Portagee?'

One-Eye was almost overcome by Sean's attention. He grabbed Sean's hand again before he could pull it away and shook it vigorously.

'Stop that, you bloody fool,' said Sean irritably and One-Eye grinned and nodded, then without releasing Sean's hand he began an impassioned speech to the other villagers. Sean meanwhile was searching his memory for the name of one of the Portuguese ports on this coast.

'Nova Sofala,' he shouted as he got it.

One-Eye broke off his speech abruptly and stared at Sean.

'Nova Sofala,' said Sean again pointing vaguely towards the east and One-Eye showed his gums in his biggest grin yet.

'Nova Sofala,' he agreed pointing with authority and then it was only a matter of minutes before it was understood between them that he would act as guide. Hlubi saddled the horses, One-Eye fetched a grass sleeping mat and a battle-axe from one of the huts. Sean mounted and looked at Hlubi to do the same but Hlubi was acting strangely.

'Yes?' Sean asked with resignation. 'What is it?'

'Nkosi.' Hlubi was looking at the branches of the tree above them. 'The Old One could lead the packhorse.'

'You can take it in turns,' said Sean.

Hlubi coughed and transferred his eyes to the fingernails of his left hand.

'Nkosi, is it possible that you will return to this village on the way back from the sea?'

425

'Yes, of course,' said Sean, 'we'll have to leave the Old One here. Why do you ask?'

'I have a thorn in my foot, Nkosi, it gives me pain. If you do not require me I will wait here for you. Perhaps the thorn wound will have healed by then.' Hlubi looked up at the tree again and shuffled his feet with embarrassment. Sean had not noticed him limping and he was puzzled as to why Hlubi should start malingering now. Then Hlubi could not stop himself from glancing at where the girl stood in the circle of villagers. Her kilt was very small and from the sides gave her no cover at all. Understanding came to Sean and he chuckled.

'The thorn you have is painful, but it's not in your foot.' Hlubi shuffled his feet again. 'You said they were monkeys . . . have you changed your mind?' Sean asked.

'Nkosi, they are indeed monkeys,' Hlubi sighed. 'But very friendly monkeys.'

'Stay then . . . but do not weaken yourself too much. We have mountains to cross on the way home.'

22

One-Eye led the packhorse – this made him very proud. Through tall grass, mangrove swamp and thick hot jungle, then through white coral sand and the curving stems of palm trees, they came at last to the sea. Nova Sofala was a fort with brass cannon and thick walls. The sea beyond it was muddy brown from the estuary that flowed into it.

The sentry at the gates said, *'Madre de Dio'* when he saw Sean, and took him to the Commandant. The Commandant was a small man with fever-yellowed face and a tired, sweat-darkened tunic. The Commandant said, *'Madre de Dio,'* and shot his chair back from his desk. It took some time for him to realize that contrary to appearance this dirty, bearded giant was not dangerous. The Commandant could speak English and Sean laid his problem before him.

For a certainty he could be of assistance. There were three Jesuit missionaries in the fort, freshly arrived from Portugal and eager for employment. Sean could take his pick but first he must bath, eat dinner with the Commandant and help him sample the wines that had arrived on the same boat as the missionaries. Sean thought that was a good idea.

At dinner he met the missionaries. They were young men, pink-faced still, for Africa had not yet had a chance to mark them. All three of them were willing to go with him and Sean selected the youngest – not for his appearance but rather for his name. 'Father Alphonso' had a heroic ring to it. The Jesuits went early to bed and left the Commandant, the four junior officers and Sean to the port. They drank toasts to Queen Victoria and her family and to the King of Portugal and his family. This made them thirsty so they drank to absent friends, then to each other. The Commandant and Sean swore a mutual oath of friendship and loyalty and this made the Commandant very sad, he cried and Sean patted his shoulder and offered to dance the Dashing

White Sergeant for him, The Commandant said that he would esteem it as a very great honour and furthermore he would be delighted. He himself did not know this dance but perhaps Sean would instruct him. They danced on the table. The Commandant was doing very well until in his enthusiasm he misjudged the size of the table. Sean helped the junior officers put him to bed and in the morning Sean, Father Alphonso and One-Eye started back towards the mountains.

Sean was impatient of any delay now; he wanted to get back to Katrina. Father Alphonso's English was on a par with Sean's Portuguese. This made conversation difficult, so Alphonso solved the problem by doing all the talking. At first Sean listened but when he decided that the good father was trying to convert him he no longer bothered. Alphonso did not seem put out – he just went on talking and clinging to the horse with both hands while his cassock flapped about his legs and his face sweated in the shade of his wide-brimmed hat. One-Eye followed them like an ancient stork.

It took them two days back to One-Eye's village and their entry was a triumphal procession. Father Alphonso's face lit up when he saw so many prospective converts. Sean could see him mentally rubbing his hands together, and he decided to keep going before Alphonso forgot the main object of the expedition. He gave One-Eye a hunting-knife in payment for his services. One-Eye sat down under the big tree in the centre of the village, his own thin legs no longer able to support his weight and the knife clutched to his chest.

'Hlubi, you've had enough of that . . . come on now!' Sean had not dismounted and was restlessly waiting for Hlubi to say his farewells to three of the village girls. Hlubi had displayed traditional Zulu taste – all three of them were big-breasted, big-bottomed and young. They were also crying.

'Come on, Hlubi . . . what's the trouble?'

'Nkosi, they believe that I have taken them for my wives.'

'What made them think that?'

'Nkosi, I do not know.' Hlubi broke the armhold that the plumpest and youngest had around his neck, he snatched up his spears and fled. Sean and Alphonso galloped after him. The villagers shouted farewells and Sean looked back and saw One-Eye still sitting at the base of the big tree.

The pace which Sean set was at last telling on Alphonso.

His verbal spring-tides slackened and he showed a measure of reluctance to let his backside touch the saddle; he rode crouched forward on his horse's neck with his buttocks in the air. They crossed the mountains and went down the other side; the ground levelled out into the Sabi Valley and they rode into the forest. On the ninth day out from Nova Sofala they reached the Sabi river. It was late afternoon. Flocks of guinea-fowl were drinking in the riverbed, they went up in a blue haze of whirling wings as Sean led his party down the bank. While the horses watered Sean spoke with Hlubi.

'Do you recognize this part of the river?'

'Yes, Nkosi, we are two hours' march upstream from the wagons . . . we held too far to the north coming through the forest.'

Sean looked at the sun, it was on the tree-tops.

'Half an hour's light left . . . and there's no moon tonight.'

'We could wait until morning,' Hlubi suggested hopefully. Sean ignored him and motioned to Alphonso to mount up. Alphonso was prepared to debate the advisability of moving on. Sean took a handful of his cassock and helped him into the saddle.

23

In the darkness the lantern burning in Katrina's wagon glowed through the canvas and guided them the last half mile into camp. Thief bayed them welcome and Mbejane ran out at the head of the other servants to take Sean's horse. His voice was loud with worry and relief.

'Nkosi, there is little time . . . it has begun.'

Sean jumped off his horse and ran to the wagon. He tore open the canvas flap.

'Sean.' She sat up. Her eyes were very green in the lantern light, but they were dark-ringed. 'Thank God, you've come.'

Sean knelt beside her cot and held her. He said certain things to her and she clung to him and moved her lips across his face. The world receded and left one wagon standing in darkness, lit by a single lamp and the love of two people.

Suddenly she stiffened in his arms and gasped. Sean held her, his face suddenly helpless and his big hands timid and uncertain on her shoulders.

'What can I do, my fancy? How can I help you?'

Her body relaxed slowly and she whispered, 'Did you find a priest?'

'The priest!' Sean had forgotten about him. Still holding onto her he turned his head and bellowed, 'Alphonso . . . Alphonso. Hurry, man.'

Father Alphonso's face in the opening of the wagon was pale with fatigue and grimy with dust.

'Marry us,' said Sean. 'Quickly, man, che-cha, chop-chop . . . you savvy?'

Alphonso climbed into the wagon. The skirts of his cassock were torn and his knees were white and bony through the holes. He stood over them and opened his book. 'Ring?' he asked in Portuguese.

430

'I do,' said Sean.

'No! No! Ring?' Alphonso held up a finger and made an encircling gesture. 'Ring?'

'I think he wants a wedding ring,' whispered Katrina.

'Oh, my God,' said Sean. 'I'd forgotten about that.' He looked round desperately. 'What can we use? Haven't you got one in your chest or something?'

Katrina shook her head, opened her lips to answer but closed them again as another pain took her. Sean held her while it lasted and when she relaxed he looked up angrily at Alphonso.

'Marry us . . . damn you. Don't you see there's no time for all the trimmings?'

'Ring?' said Alphonso again. He looked very unhappy.

'All right, I'll get you a ring.' Sean leapt out of the wagon and shouted at Mbejane.

'Bring my rifle, quickly.'

If Sean wanted to shoot the Portuguese that was his business and Mbejane's duty was to help him. He brought Sean the rifle. Sean found a gold sovereign in the pouch on his belt, he threw it on the ground and held the muzzle of the rifle on it. The bullet punched a ragged hole through it. He tossed the rifle back to Mbejane, picked up the small gold circle and scrambled back into the wagon.

Three times during the service the pains made Katrina gasp and each time Sean held her tight and Alphonso increased the speed of his delivery. Sean put the punctured sovereign on Katrina's finger and kissed her. Alphonso gabbled out the last line of Latin and Katrina said, 'Oh, Sean, it's coming.'

'Get out,' Sean told Alphonso and made an expressive gesture towards the door – thankfully Alphonso went.

It did not take long then, but to Sean it was an eternity – like that time when they had taken Garrick's leg. Then in a slippery rush it was finished. Katrina lay very quiet and pale, while on the cot below her, still linked to her, purple-blotched and bloody lay the child that they had made.

'It's dead,' croaked Sean. He was sweating and he had backed away against the far wall of the wagon.

'No,' Katrina struggled up fiercely. 'No, it's not . . . Sean, you must help me.'

She told him what to do and at last the child cried.

'It's a boy,' said Katrina softly. 'Oh, Sean . . . it's a boy.' She was more beautiful than he had ever seen her before; pale and tired and beautiful.

24

Sean's protests were in vain – Katrina left her bed the next morning and squeezed into one of her old dresses. Sean hovered between her and the child on the cot.

'I'm still so *fat*,' she lamented.

'Fancy, please stay in bed another day or two.'

She pulled a face at him and went on struggling with the lacing of her bodice.

'Who's going to look after the baby?'

'I will!' said Sean earnestly. 'You can tell me what to do.'

Arguing with Katrina was like trying to pick up quicksilver with your fingers, not worth the effort. She finished dressing and took up the child.

'You can help me down the steps.' She smiled at him. Sean and Alphonso set a chair for her in the shade of one of the big shuma trees and the servants came to see the child. Katrina held him in her lap and Sean stood over them in uncertain possession. For Sean it seemed unreal yet ... too much for his mind to digest in so short a time. He grinned dazedly at the steady stream of comment from his servants and his arm was limp when Alphonso shook his hand for the twentieth time that morning.

'Hold your child ... Nkosi. Let us see you with him on your arm,' called Mbejane and the other Zulus took up the cry. Sean's expression changed slowly to one of apprehension.

'Pick him up, Nkosi.'

Katrina proffered the bundle and a hunted look came into Sean's eyes.

'Have no fear, Nkosi, he has no teeth, he cannot harm you,' Hlubi encouraged him. Sean held his first-born awkwardly and assumed the hunchbacked posture of the new father. The Zulus cheered him and slowly Sean's face relaxed and his smile was a glow of pride.

'Mbejane, is he not beautiful?'

433

'As beautiful as his father,' Mbejane agreed.

'Your words are a blade with two edges,' laughed Sean. He looked at the child closely. It wore a cap of dark hair, its nose was flat as a bulldog's, its eyes were milky-grey and its legs were long, skinny and red,

'How will you name him?' asked Hlubi. Sean looked at Katrina.

'Tell them,' he said.

'He shall be called Dirk,' she said in Zulu.

'What is the meaning?' asked Hlubi, and Sean answered him.

'It means a dagger . . . a sharp knife.'

There was immediate nodded approval from all the servants. Hiubi produced his snuff-box and passed it among them and Mbejane took a pinch.

'That,' he said, 'is a good name.'

25

Paternity, the subtle alchemist, transformed Sean's attitude to life within twelve hours. Never before had anything been so utterly dependent upon him, so completely vulnerable. That first evening in their wagon he watched Katrina sitting cross-legged on her cot, stooping forward over the child to give it her breast. Her hair hung in a soft wing across one cheek, her face was fuller, more matronly and the child in her lap fed with a red face and small wheezings. She looked up at him and smiled and the child tugged her breast with its tiny fists and hunting mouth.

Sean crossed to the cot, sat beside them and put his arm around them. Katrina rubbed her cheek against his chest and her hair smelt warm and clean. The boy went on feeding noisily. Sean felt vaguely excited as though he were on the threshold of a new adventure.

A week later, when the first rain clouds built up in the sky, Sean took the wagons across the Sabi and onto the slopes of the mountains to escape the heat of the plains. There was a valley he had noticed when he and Hlubi had made their journey to the coast. The valley bottom was covered with short sweet grass and cedar trees grew along a stream of clean water. Sean took them to this place.

Here they would wait out the rainy season and when it was finished and the baby was strong enough to travel they could take the ivory south and sell it in Pretoria. It was a happy camp. The oxen spread out along the valley, filling it with movement and the contented sound of their lowing; there was laughter among the wagons and at night when the mist slumped down off the mountains the camp fire was bright and friendly. Father Alphonso stayed with them for nearly two weeks. He was a pleasant young man and although he and Sean never understood what the other was saying yet they managed well enough with sign language. He left at last with Hlubi and one of the other servants to escort him back over the mountains, but before he did he managed to embarrass Sean by kissing him goodbye. Sean and Katrina were sorry to see him go. They had grown to like him and Katrina had almost forgiven him his religion.

The rains came with the usual flourish and fury. Weeks drifted into months. Happy months, with life centring around Dirk's cot. Mbejane had made the cot for him out of cedarwood and one of Katrina's chests produced the sheets and blankets for it. The child grew quickly: each day he seemed to occupy more of his cot, his legs filled out, his skin lost its blotchy-purple look and his eyes were no longer a vague milky-blue. There was green in them now – they would be the same colour as his mother's.

To fill the long lazy days Sean started to build a cabin beside the stream. The servants joined in and from a modest first plan it grew into a thing of sturdy plastered walls and neatly thatched roof with a stone fireplace at one end. When it was finished Sean and Katrina moved into it. After their wagon with its thin canvas walls, the cabin gave a feeling of permanence to their love. One night, when the rain hissed down in darkness outside and the wind whined at the door like a dog wanting to be let in, they spread a mattress in front of the fireplace and there in the moving firelight they started another baby.

Christmas came, and after it the New Year. The rains stuttered and stopped and still they stayed on in their valley. Then at last they had to go, for their supplies of basic stores – powder, salt, medicines, cloth – were nearly finished. They loaded the wagons, inspanned and left in the early morning. As the line of wagons wound down the valley towards the plains Katrina sat on the box-seat of the lead wagon holding Dirk on her lap and Sean rode beside her. She looked back – the roof of their cabin showed brown through the branches of the cedar trees. It seemed forlorn and lonely.

'We must come back one day, we've been so happy here,' she said softly. Sean leaned out of the saddle towards her and touched her arm.

'Happiness isn't a place, my fancy, we aren't leaving it here, we're taking it with us.'

She smiled at him. The second baby was starting to show already.

26

They reached the Limpopo river at the end of July and found a place to cross. It took three days to unload the wagons, work them through the soft sand and then carry the ivory and stores across. They finished in the late afternoon of the third day and by then everyone was exhausted. They ate an early supper and an hour after sunset the Zulus were rolled in their blankets, and Sean and Katrina were sleeping arms-around and head-on-chest in the wagon. In the morning Katrina was quiet and a little pale. Sean didn't notice it until she told him that she felt tired and was going to lie down – immediately he was all attentive. He helped her into the wagon and settled the pillows under her head.

'Are you sure you're all right?' he kept asking.

'Yes . . . it's nothing, I'm just a bit tired. I'll be all right,' she assured him. She appreciated his concern but was relieved when finally he went to see to the business of reloading the wagons for Sean's ministrations were always a little clumsy. She wanted to be left alone, she felt tired and cold.

By midday the wagons were loaded to Sean's satisfaction. He went to Katrina's wagon, lifted the canvas and peeped in. He expected her to be asleep. She was lying on the cot with her eyes open and two of the thick grey blankets wrapped around her. Her face was as pale as a two-day corpse. Sean felt the first leap of alarm, he scrambled into the wagon.

'My dear, you look ghastly. Are you sick?' He put his hand on her shoulder and she was shivering. She didn't answer him, instead her eyes moved from his face to the floor near the foot of the bed and Sean's eyes followed hers. Katrina's luxury was her chamberpot; it was a massive china thing with red roses hand-painted on it. She loved it dearly and Sean used to tease her when she was perched on top of it. Now the pot stood near the foot of the bed and when Sean saw what was in it his breathing stopped. It was half full of a liquid the colour of milk stout. 'Oh, my God,' he whispered. He went on staring at it, standing very still while a gruesome snatch of doggerel he remembered hearing sung in the canteens of the Witwatersrand began trotting through his brain like an undertaker's hack.

> Black as the Angel,
> Black as disgrace
> When the fever waters flow
> They're as black as the ace.
>
> Roll him in a blanket
> Feed him on quinine
> But all of us we know
> It's the end of the line.
>
> Black as the Angel
> Black as disgrace
> Soon we'll lay him down below
> And chuck dirt in his face.

He raised his head and looked steadily at her, searching for the signs of fear. But just as steadily she looked back at him.

'Sean, it's blackwater.'

'Yes . . . I know,' Sean said, for there was nothing to be gained by denial, no room for extravagant hope. It was blackwater fever: malaria in its most malignant form, attacking the kidneys and turning them to fragile sacks of black blood that the slightest movement could rupture. Sean knelt by her cot. 'You must lie very still.' He touched her forehead lightly with the tips of his fingers and felt the heat of her skin.

'Yes,' she answered him, but already the expression in her eyes was blurring and she made the first restless movement of delirium. Sean put his arm across her chest to hold her from struggling.

By nightfall Katrina was deep in the nightmare of malaria. She laughed, she screamed in senseless terror, she shook her head and fought him when he tried to make her drink. But she had to drink, it was her one chance, to flush out her kidneys that she might live. Sean held her head and forced her.

Dirk started crying, hungry and frightened by the sight of his mother.

'Mbejane!' shouted Sean, his voice pitched high with desperation. Mbejane had waited all afternoon at the entrance of the wagon.

'Nkosi, what can I do?'

'The child ... can you care for him?'

Mbejane picked up the cot with Dirk still in it. 'Do not worry about him again. I will take him to the other wagon.'

Sean turned his whole attention back to Katrina. The fever built up steadily within her. Her body was a furnace, her skin was dry and with every hour she was wilder and her movements more difficult to control.

An hour after dark Kandhla came to the wagon with a pot of steaming liquid and a cup. Sean's nose wrinkled as he caught the smell of it.

'What the hell is that?'

'I have stewed the bark from a maiden's breast tree ... the Nkosikazi must drink it.'

It had the same musty smell as boiling hops and Sean hesitated. He knew the tree. It grew on high ground, it had a diseased-looking lumpy bark and each lump was the size and shape of a breast surmounted by a thorn.

'Where did you get it? I have seen none of these trees near the river.' Sean was marking time while he decided whether to make Katrina drink the brew. He knew these Zulu remedies, what they didn't kill they sometimes cured.

'Hlubi went back to the hills where we camped four days ago ... he brought the bark into the camp an hour ago.'

A thirty-mile round journey in something under six hours – even in his distress Sean could smile.

'Tell Hlubi the Nkosikazi will drink his medicine.'

Kandhla held her head and Sean forced the evil-smelling liquid between her lips – he made her finish the whole potful. The juice of the bark seemed to relieve the congestion of her kidneys; four times before morning she passed frothy black water. Each time Sean held her gently, cushioning her body from any movement that might have killed her. Gradually her delirium became coma; she lay huddled and still in the cot, shaken only by the brief fits of shivering. When the morning sun hit the wagon canvas and lit the interior, Sean saw her face, and he knew that she was dying. Her skin was an opaque yellowish white, her hair had lost its glow and was lifeless as dry grass. Kandhla brought another pot of the medicine and they fed it to her. When the pot was empty Kandhla said, 'Nkosi, let me lay a mattress on the floor beside the Nkosikazi's bed. You must sleep and I will stay here with you and wake you if the Nkosikazi stirs.'

Sean looked at him with haunted eyes. 'There will be time to sleep later, my friend.' He looked down at Katrina and went on softly. 'Perhaps, very soon there will be time.'

Suddenly Katrina's body stiffened and Sean dropped on his knees beside her cot. Kandhla hovered anxiously behind him. It took Sean a while to understand what was happening and then he looked up at Kandhla.

'Go! go quickly!' he said and the suffering in his voice sent Kandhla stumbling blindly from the wagon. Sean's second son was born that morning and while Kandhla watched over Katrina Sean wrapped the child in a blanket, took him into the veld and buried him. Then he went back to Katrina and stayed with her while days and nights blended together into a hopeless muddle of grief. As near as Katrina was to death, that near was Sean to insanity. He never moved out of the wagon, he squatted on the mattress next to her cot, wiping the perspiration from her face, holding a cup to her lips or just sitting and watching her. He had lost his child and before his eyes Katrina was turning into a wasted yellow skeleton. Dirk saved him. Mbejane brought the boy to him and he romped on the mattress, crawling into Sean's lap and pulling his beard. It was the one small glimmer of light in the darkness.

27

Katrina survived. She came back slowly from the motionless coma that precedes death and with her hesitant return Sean's despair changed to hope and then to a wonderful relief. Her water was no longer black but dark pink and thick with sediment. She was aware of him now and, although she was so weak that she could not lift her head off the pillow, her eyes followed him as he moved about the wagon. It was another week before she learned about the baby. She asked him, her voice a tired whisper, and Sean told her with all the gentleness of which he was capable. She did not have the strength for any great show of emotion; she laid quietly staring up at the canvas above her head and her tears slid down across her yellow cheeks.

The damage that the fever had done to her body was hardly credible. Her limbs were so thin that Sean could completely encircle her thigh with one hand. Her skin hung in loose yellow folds from her face and body and pink blood still stained her water. This was not all: the fever had sucked all the strength from her mind. She had nothing left to resist the sorrow of her baby's death, and the sorrow encased her in a shell through which neither Sean nor Dirk could reach her. Sean struggled to bring her back to life, to repair the terrible damage to her mind and body. Every minute of his time he employed in her service.

He and the servants scoured the veld for thirty miles around the laager to find delicacies to tempt her appetite, wild fruits, honey, giraffe marrows, the flesh of a dozen animals: kabobs of elephant heart and duiker liver, roasted iguana lizard as white and tender as a plump pullet, golden fillets of the yellow-mouthed bream from the river. Katrina picked at them listlessly then turned away and lay staring at the canvas wall of the cot.

Sean sat beside her and talked about the farm they would buy, trying vainly to draw her into a discussion of the house they would build. He read to her from Duff's books and the only reaction he received was a small quivering of her lips when he read the words 'death' or 'child'. He talked about the days on the Witwatersrand, searching his mind for stories that might amuse her. He brought Dirk to her and let him play about the wagon. Dirk was walking now, his dark hair had started to curl and his eyes were green. Dirk, however, could not be too long confined in the wagon. There was too much to do, too much to explore. Before long he would stagger to the entrance and issue the imperial summons: 'Bejaan! Bejaan!'

Almost immediately Mbejane's head would appear in the opening and he would glance at Sean for permission.

'All right, take him out then . . . but tell Kandhla not to stuff him full of food.'

Quickly, before Sean changed his mind, Mbejane would lift Dirk down and lead him away. Dirk had nearly two dozen Zulus to spoil him. They competed hotly for his affections, no effort was too much – dignified Mbejane down on his hands and knees being ridden mercilessly in and out among the wagons, Hlubi scratching himself under the arms and gibbering insanely in his celebrated imitation of a baboon while Dirk squealed with delight, fat Kandhla raiding Katrina's store of fruit preserves to make sure Dirk was properly fed and the others keeping in the background, anxious to join the worship but fearful of incurring the jealousy of Mbejane and Hlubi. Sean knew what was happening but he was powerless to prevent it. His time was completely devoted to Katrina.

For the first time in his life Sean was giving more than just a superficial part of himself to another human being. It was not an isolated sacrifice: it went on throughout the months it took for Katrina to regain sufficient of her strength to enable her to sit up in bed without assistance; it continued through the months that she needed before Sean judged it safe to resume the trek towards the south. They built a litter for her – Sean would not risk the jarring of the wagon – and the first day's trek lasted two hours. Four of the servants carried the litter and Katrina lay in it, protected from the sun by a strip of canvas spread above her head. Despite the gentleness with which the Zulus handled her, at the end of the two hours Katrina was exhausted. Her back ached and she was sweating in small beads from her yellow skin. The next week they travelled two hours daily and then gradually increased the time until they were making a full day's journey.

They were halfway to the Magaliesberg, camped at a muddy waterhole in the thorn flats, when Mbejane came to Sean.

'There is still one wagon empty of ivory, Nkosi.'

'The others are full,' Sean pointed out.

'Four hours' march from this place there is enough ivory buried to fill those wagons.'

Sean's mouth twisted with pain. He looked away towards the south-east and he spoke softly. 'Mbejane, I am still a young man and yet already I have stored up enough ugly memories to make my old age sad. Would you have me steal from a friend not only his life but his share of ivory also?'

Mbejane shook his head. 'I asked, that is all.'

'And I have answered, Mbejane. It is his . . . let it lie.'

28

They crossed the Magaliesberg and turned west along the mountain range. Then, two months after they had left the Limpopo river, they reached the Boer settlement at Louis Trichardt. Sean left Mbejane to outspan the wagons on the open square in front of the church and he went to search for a doctor. There was only one in the district, Sean found him in his surgery above the general dealer's store and took him to the wagons. Sean carried his bag for him and the doctor, a greybeard and unused to such hardships, trotted to keep up with Sean. He was panting and pouring sweat by the time they arrived. Sean waited outside while the doctor completed his examination and when he finally made his descent from the wagon Sean fell on him impatiently. 'What do you think, man?'

'I think, meneer, that you should give hourly thanks to your Maker.' The doctor shook his head in amazement. 'It seems hardly possible that your wife could have survived both the fever and the loss of the child.'

'She is safe then, there's no chance of a relapse?' Sean asked.

'She is safe now . . . but she is still a very sick woman. It may take a year before her body is fully mended. There is no medicine I can give you. She must be kept quiet, feed her well and wait for time to cure her.' The doctor hesitated. 'There is other damage –' he tapped his forehead with his forefinger. 'Grief is a terrible destroyer. She will need love and gentleness and after another six months she will need a baby to fill the emptiness left by the one she lost. Give her those three things, meneer, but most of all give her love.' The doctor hauled his watch from his waistcoat and looked at it. 'Time! there is so little time. I must go, there are others who need me.' He held out his hand to Sean. 'Go with God, meneer.'

Sean shook his hand. 'How much do I owe you?'

The doctor smiled, he had a brown face and his eyes were pale blue; when he smiled he looked like a boy. 'I make no charge for words. I wish I could have done more.' He hurried away across the square and when he walked you could see that his smile lied, he was an old man.

'Mbejane,' said Sean. 'Get a big tusk out of the wagon and take it to the doctor's room above the store.'

Katrina and Sean went to the morning service in the church next day. Katrina could not stand through the hymns. She sat quietly in her pew, watching the altar, her lips forming the words of the hymn and her eyes full of her sorrow.

They stayed on for three more days in Louis Trichardt and they were made welcome. Men came to drink coffee with them and see the ivory and the women brought them eggs and fresh vegetables, but Sean was anxious to move south. So on the third day they started the last stage of their trek.

Katrina regained her strength rapidly now. She took over the management of Dirk from the servants, to their ill-concealed disappointment, and soon she left her litter and rode on the box seat of the lead wagon again. Her body filled out and there was colour showing once more through the yellow skin of her cheeks. Despite the improvement to her body the depression of her mind still persisted and there was nothing that Sean could do to lift it.

A month before the Christmas of 1895 Sean's wagon train climbed the low range of hills above the city and they looked down into Pretoria. The jacaranda trees that filled every garden were in bloom – masses of purple – and the busy streets spoke well of the prosperity of the Transvaal Republic. Sean outspanned on the outskirts of the city, simply pulling the wagons off the road and camping beside it, and once the camp was established and Sean had made certain that Katrina no longer needed his help he put on his one good suit and called for his horse. His suit had been cut to the fashion of four years previously and had been made to encompass the belly he had acquired on the Witwatersrand. Now it hung loosely down his body but bunched tightly around his thickened arms. His face was burnt black by the sun and his beard bushed down onto his chest and concealed the fact that the stiff collar of his shirt could no longer close around his neck. His boots were scuffed almost through the uppers, there was not a suspicion of polish on them and they had completely lost their shape. Sweat had soaked through his hat around the level of the band and left dark greasy marks; the brim drooped down over his eyes so he had to wear it pushed onto the back of his head. There was, therefore, some excuse for the curious glances that followed him that afternoon as he rode down Church Street with a great muscular savage trotting at his one stirrup and an overgrown brindle hound at the other. They pushed their way between the wagons that cluttered the wide street; they passed the Raadsaal of the Republican Parliament, passed the houses standing back from the road in their spacious purple and green gardens and came at last to the business area of the city that crowded round the railway station. Sean and Duff had bought their supplies at a certain general dealer's stores and now Sean went back to it. It was hardly changed – the signboard in front had faded a little but still declared that I. Goldberg, Importer & Exporter, Dealer in Mining Machinery, Merchant & Wholesaler, was prepared to consider the purchase of gold, precious stone, hides and skins, ivory and other natural produce. Sean swung down from the saddle and tossed his reins to Mbejane. 'Unsaddle, Mbejane. This may take time.'

Sean stepped up onto the sidewalk, lifted his hat to two passing ladies and went through into the building where Mr Goldberg conducted his diverse activities. One of the assistants hurried to meet him, but Sean shook his head and the man went back behind the counter. He had seen Mr Goldberg with two customers at the far end of the store. He was content to wait. He browsed around among the loaded shelves of merchandise, feeling the quality of a shirt, sniffing at a box of cigars, examining an axe, lifting a rifle down off the rack and sighting at a spot on the wall, until Mr Goldberg bowed his customers through the door and turned to Sean. Mr Goldberg was short and fat. His hair was cropped short and his neck bulged over the top of his collar. He looked at Sean and his eyes were expressionless while he rifled through the index cards of his memory for the name. Then he beamed like a brilliant burst of sunlight. 'Mr Courtney, isn't it?'

Sean grinned. 'That's right. How are you, Izzy?' They shook hands. 'How's business?'

Mr Goldberg's face fell. 'Terrible, terrible, Mr Courtney. I'm a worried man.'

'You look well enough on it,' Sean prodded his stomach. 'You've put on weight.'

'You can joke, Mr Courtney, but I'm telling you it's terrible. Taxes and worry, taxes and worry.' Mr Goldberg sighed, 'and now there's talk of war.'

'What's this?' Sean frowned.

'War, Mr Courtney, war between Britain and the Republic.'

Sean's frown dissolved and he laughed. 'Nonsense, man, not even Kruger could be such a bloody fool! Get me a cup of coffee and a cigar and we'll go through to your office and talk business.'

Mr Goldberg's face went blank and his eyelids drooped almost sleepily.

'Business, Mr Courtney?'

'That's right, Izzy, this time I'm selling and you're buying.'

'What are you selling, Mr Courtney?'

'Ivory!'

'Ivory?'

'Twelve wagon loads of it.'

Mr Goldberg sighed sadly. 'Ivory's no good now, the bottom's fallen out of it. You can hardly give it away.' It was very well done; if Sean had not been told the ruling prices two days before he might have been convinced.

'I'm sorry to hear that,' he said. 'If you're not interested, I'll see if I can find someone else.'

'Come along to my office anyway,' said Mr Goldberg. 'We can talk about it. Talk costs nothing.'

Two days later they were still talking about it. Sean had fetched his wagons and had off-loaded the ivory in the back yard of the store. Mr Goldberg had personally weighed each tusk and written the weights down on a sheet of paper. He and Sean had added the columns of figures and agreed on the total. Now they were in the last stages of agreeing the price.

'Come on, Izzy, we've wasted two days already. That's a fair price and you know it . . . let's get it over with,' Sean growled.

'I'll lose money on this,' protested Mr Goldberg. 'I've got to make a living, every man's got to live.'

'Come on,' Sean held out his right hand. 'Let's call it a deal.'

Mr Goldberg hesitated a second longer, then he put his pudgy hand in Sean's fist and they grinned at each other, both well satisfied. One of Mr Goldberg's assistants counted out the sovereigns, stacking them in piles of fifty along the counter, then

447

Sean and Mr Goldberg checked them and agreed once more. Sean filled two canvas bags with the gold, slapped Mr Goldberg's back, helped himself to another cigar and headed heavily laden for the bank.

'When are you going into the veld again?' Mr Goldberg called after him.

'Soon!' said Sean.

'Don't forget to get your supplies here.'

'I'll be back,' Sean assured him.

Mbejane carried one of the bags and Sean the other. Sean was smiling and streamers of cigar smoke swirled back from his head as he strode along the sidewalk. There's something in the weight of a sack of gold that makes the man who holds it stand eight feet tall.

That night as they lay together in the darkness of the wagon Katrina asked him.

'Have we enough money to buy the farm yet, Sean?'

'Yes,' said Sean. 'We've got enough for the finest farm in the whole Cape peninsular . . . and, after one more trip, we'll have enough to build the house and the barns, buy the cattle, lay out the vineyard and still have some left over.'

Katrina was silent for a moment then, 'So we are going back into the bushveld again?'

'One more trip,' said Sean. 'Another two years and then we'll go down to the Cape.' He gave her a hug. 'You don't mind, do you?'

'No,' she said. 'I think I'd like that. When will we leave?'

'Not just yet awhile,' Sean laughed. 'First we're going to have some fun.' He hugged her again, her body was still painfully thin; he could feel the bones of her hips pressed against him.

'Some pretty clothes for you, my fancy, and a suit for me that doesn't look like a fancy dress. Then we'll go out and see what this burg has to offer in the way of entertainment –' He stopped as the idea swelled up in his mind. 'Damn it! I know what we'll do. We'll hire a carriage and go across to Jo'burg. We'll take a suite at the Grand National Hotel and do some living. Bath in a china bath, sleep in a real bed; you can have your hair prettied-up and I'll have my beard trimmed by a barber. We'll eat crayfish and penguin eggs . . . I can't remember when I last tasted pork or mutton . . . we'll wash it down with the old bubbling wine and waltz to a good band –' Sean raced on and when he stopped

448

for breath Katrina asked softly, 'Isn't the waltz a very sinful dance, Sean?'

Sean smiled in the darkness. 'It certainly is!'

'I'd like to be sinful just once . . . not too much, just a little with you to see what it's like.'

'We will be' – said Sean – 'as wicked as hell.'

29

The next day Sean took Katrina to the most exclusive ladies' shop in Pretoria. He chose the material of half a dozen dresses. One of them was to be a ball gown in canary-yellow silk. It was extravagance and he knew it, but he didn't care once he saw the flash of guilty delight in Katrina's cheeks and the old green sparkle in her eyes. For the first time since the fever she was living again. He spilled out his sovereigns with thankful abandon. The sales girls were delighted with him, they crowded round him with trays of feminine accessories.

'A dozen of those,' said Sean and, 'yes, those will do.' Then a flash of green on the racks across the room caught his eye – it was Katrina's green.

'What's that?' He pointed and two sales girls nearly knocked each other down in the rush to get it for him. The winner carried the shawl back to him and Sean took it and placed it around Katrina's shoulders. It was a beautiful thing.

'We'll take it,' said Sean and Katrina's lips quivered – then suddenly she was crying, sobbing brokenly. The excitement had been too much. There was immediate consternation among the shop assistants, they flapped around Sean like hens at feeding time while he picked Katrina up and carried her out to the hired carriage. At the door he paused and spoke over his shoulder.

'I want those dresses finished by tomorrow evening. Can you do it?'

'They'll be ready, Mr Courtney, even if my girls have to work all night on them.'

He took Katrina back to the wagons and laid her on her cot.

'Please forgive me, Sean, I've never done that in my life before.'

'It's all right, my fancy, I understand. Now you just go to sleep.'

The following day Katrina stayed at the camp resting, while Sean went to see Mr Goldberg again and buy from him the stores they would need for the next expedition. It took another day to load the wagons and by then Katrina seemed well enough to make the trip to Johannesburg.

They left in the early afternoon. Mbejane driving, Sean and Katrina sitting close together on the back seat holding hands under the travelling rug and Dirk bouncing round the interior of the carriage, pausing now and then to flatten his face against a window and keeping up a flow of comment in the peculiar mixture of English, Dutch and Zulu that Sean called Dirkese. They reached Johannesburg long before Sean expected to. In four years the town had doubled its size and had spread out into the veld to meet them. They followed the main road through the new areas and came to the centre. There were changes here as well but it was, in the main, the way he remembered it. They threaded their way through the babble of Eloff Street, and around them, mingling with the crowds on the sidewalks, were the ghosts of the past. He heard Duff laugh and twisted quickly in his seat to place the sound; a dandy in a boater hat with gold fillings in his teeth laughed again from a passing carriage and Sean heard that it was not Duff's laugh. Very close, but not the same. All of it was like that – similar but subtly changed, nostalgic but sad with the knowledge of loss. The past was lost – and he knew then that you can never go back. Nothing is the same, for reality can exist at one time only and in one place only. Then it dies and you have lost it and you must go on to find it at another time and in another place.

They took a suite at the Grand National, with a sitting-room and two bedrooms, a private bathroom and a balcony that looked out over the street – over the rooftops to where the headgears and white dumps stood along the ridge. Katrina was exhausted. They had supper sent up to the room early and when they had eaten Katrina went to bed and Sean went down alone to drink a nightcap at the bar. The bar-room was crowded. Sean found a seat in the corner and sat silently in the jabber of conversation. In it, but no longer a part of it.

They had changed the picture above the bar – it used to be a hunting print; but now it was a red-coated general, impressively splattered with blood, taking leave of his staff in the middle of a battlefield. The staff looked bored. Sean let his eyes wander on along the dark panelled walls. He remembered – there was so much to remember! Suddenly he blinked. Near the side door was a star-shaped crack in the wooden panelling. Sean started to grin and put down his glass and massaged the knuckles of his right hand. If Oakie Henderson hadn't ducked under that punch it would have taken his head off.

Sean signalled to the barman. 'Another brandy, please.' While the man was pouring, Sean asked, 'What happened to that panel near the door?'

The man glanced up and then back at the bottle. 'Some fellow put his fist through it in the old days. Boss left it like that, sort of souvenir, you know.'

'He must have been quite a fellow ... that wood's an inch thick. Who was he?' Sean asked expectantly.

The man shrugged. 'One of the drifters. They come and they go. Make a few pounds, piss it against the wall and then go back where they came from.' He looked at Sean with bored eyes. 'That'll be half a dollar, mate.' Sean drank the brandy slowly, turning the glass in his hands between sips and watching the liquor cling to its sides like thin oil. By a cracked panel in a bar-room they shall remember you.

And now I shall go to bed, he decided, this is no longer my world. My world is upstairs sleeping – I hope! He smiled a little to himself and finished the brandy in his glass.

'Sean' – a voice at his ear and a hand on his shoulder as he turned to leave. 'My God, Sean, is it really you?'

Sean stared at the man beside him. He did not recognize the neatly clipped beard and the big sun-burned nose with the skin peeling off the tip, but suddenly he knew the eyes.

'Dennis, you old rogue. Dennis Petersen from Ladyburg. That's right isn't it?'

'You didn't recognize me!' laughed Dennis. 'So much for our friendship – you disappear without a word and ten years later you don't even know me!'

Now they were both laughing.

'I thought they would have hanged you long ago –' Sean defended himself. 'What on earth are you doing in Johannesburg?'

'Selling beef – I'm on the committee of the Beef Growers' Association.' There was pride in Dennis's voice. 'I have been up here negotiating the renewal of our contracts.'

'When are you going back?'

'My train leaves in an hour.'

'Well, there's time for a drink before you go – what will it be?'

'I'll have a small brandy, thanks.'

Sean ordered the drinks and they took them up and stood, suddenly awkward in the awareness that ten years were between their once complete accord.

'So, what have you been doing with yourself?' Dennis ended the pause.

'This and that, you know – a bit of mining, just come back from the bushveld. Nothing very exciting.'

'Well, it's good to see you again anyway. Your health.'

'And yours,' said Sean, and then suddenly he realized that here was news of his family – news he had been without for many years.

'How's everyone at Ladyburg – your sisters?'

'Both married – so am I, with four sons,' and the pride was in Dennis's voice again.

'Anyone I know?' asked Sean.

'Audrey – you know old Pye's daughter.'

'No!' Sean ripped out the word, and then quickly, 'That's wonderful, Dennis. I'm pleased for you – she was a lovely girl.'

'The best,' agreed Dennis complacently. He had the sleek well-fed, well-cared for look of a married man, fatter in the face and his stomach starting to show. I wonder if I have it yet, Sean thought. 'Of course, old man Pye's dead now – that's one creditor he couldn't buy off. Ronnie's taken over the bank and the store.'

'The bat-eared bush rat,' said Sean and knew immediately that he had said the wrong thing. Dennis frowned slightly. 'He's family now, Sean. A very decent chap really – and a clever business man.'

'I'm sorry, I was joking. How's my mother?' Sean changed the subject by asking the question that had been in the forefront of his mind and he had picked the right topic. Dennis's expression softened immediately – you could see the warmth in his eyes.

'The same as ever. She's got a dress shop now, next door to Ronnie's store. It's a gold mine – no one would think of buying anywhere else but at Aunt Ada's. She's godmother to my two eldest, I guess she's godmother to half the kids in the district,' and then his expression hardened again, 'The least you could have done was write to her sometime, Sean. You can't imagine the pain you have caused her.'

'There were circumstances.' Sean dropped his eyes to his glass.

'That's no excuse – you have a duty which you neglected. There is no excuse for it.'

You little man, Sean lifted his head and looked at him without trying to disguise his annoyance. You pompous, preaching little man peering out at the world one-eyed through the keyhole of your own self-importance. Dennis had not noticed Sean's reaction and he continued. 'That's a lesson a man must learn before he grows up – we all have our responsibilities and our duties. A man grows up when he faces those duties, when he accepts the burdens that society places on him. Take my own case: despite the vast amount of work I have on the farms – I now own Mahoba's Kloof as well – and despite the demands made on me by my family, yet I have time to represent the district on the committee of the Beef Growers' Association, I am a member of the Church Council and the village management board, and I have every reason to believe that next month I will be asked to accept the office of mayor.' Then he looked steadily at Sean, 'What have *you* done with your life so far?'

'I've lived it,' Sean answered, and Dennis looked a little perplexed – then he gathered himself.

'Are you married yet?'

'I was – but I sold her to the Arab slavers up north.'

'You did what?'

'Well,' grinned Sean, 'she was an old wife and the price was good.'

'That's a joke, hey? Ha, ha!' You couldn't fool good old Dennis – Sean laughed out loud. This unbelievable little man!

'Have a drink, Dennis,' he suggested.

'Two is my limit, thanks Sean.' Dennis pulled the gold hunter from his waistcoat pocket and inspected it. 'Time to go – I'm afraid. Nice seeing you again.'

'Wait,' Sean stopped him. 'My brother – how's Garry?'

'Poor old Garry.' Dennis shook his head solemnly.

'What's wrong with him?' Sean's voice was sharp with his sense of dread.

'Nothing –' Dennis reassured him quickly. 'Well, I mean nothing more than ever was.'

'Why did you say "poor old Garry" then?'

'I don't really know – except that everybody says it. It's habit,

454

I suppose – he's just one of those people you say *poor old* in front of.'

Sean suppressed his irritation, he wanted to know. He had to know.

'You haven't answered me – how is he?'

Dennis made a significant gesture with his right hand. 'Looking into the bottle quite a bit these days – not that I blame him with that woman he married. You were well out of it there if I may say so, Sean.'

'You may,' Sean acquiesced, 'but is he well? How are things at Theunis Kraal?'

'We all took a bit of a beating with the rindepest* but Garry – well, he lost over half of his herds. Poor old Garry, everything happens to him.'

'My God – fifty per cent!'

'Yes – but, of course, Ronnie helped him out. Gave him a mortgage on the farm to tide him over.'

'Theunis Kraal bonded again,' groaned Sean. 'Oh Garry, Garry.'

'Yes – well,' Dennis coughed uneasily. 'Well, I think I'd better be going. *Totsiens*, Sean.' He held out his hand. 'Shall I tell them I saw you?'

'No,' said Sean quickly. 'Just leave it stand.'

'Very well then.' Dennis hesitated. 'Are you all right, Sean? I mean' – he coughed again – 'are you all right for money?'

Sean felt his unhappiness dissolve a little; this pompous little man was going to offer him a loan. 'That's very good of you, Dennis. But I've got a couple of pounds saved up – enough to eat on for a few days,' he spoke seriously.

'All right then.' Dennis looked mightily relieved. 'All right then – *totsiens*, Sean,' and he turned and walked quickly out of the bar. As he left the room so he went out of Sean's mind, and Sean was thinking of his brother again.

Then suddenly Sean decided. I will go back to Ladyburg when this next trip is over. The dream farm outside Paarl would not lose anything in being transplanted to Natal – and he suddenly longed to sit in the panelled study at Theunis Kraal again, and to feel the mist come cold down the escarpment in the mornings, and see the spray blowing off the white falls in the wind. He

* An epidemic cattle disease.

wanted to hear Ada's voice again and to explain to her, knowing she would understand and forgive.

But more, much more it was Garry – poor old Garry. I must go back to him – ten years is a long time and he will have lost the bitterness. I must go back to him – for his sake and for Theunis Kraal. With the decision made, Sean finished his drink and went up the stairs to his suite.

Katrina was breathing softly in her sleep, the dark mass of her hair spread out on the pillow. While he undressed he watched her and slowly the melancholy dissolved. Gently he pulled back the blankets on his side of the bed and just then Dirk whimpered from the next room. Sean went through to him. 'All right, what's the trouble?'

Dirk blinked owlishly and searched for an excuse, then the relief flooded into his face and he produced the one that creaked with age. 'I want a drink a water.'

The delay while Sean went through to the bathroom gave Dirk an opportunity to rally his forces and when Sean came back he opened the offensive in earnest.

'Tell me a story, Daddy.' He was sitting up now, bright-eyed.

'I'll tell you a story about Jack and a Nory –' said Sean.

'Not that one –' protested Dirk. The saga of Jack and his brother lasted five seconds and Dirk knew it. Sean sat down on the edge of the bed and held the glass for him.

'How about this one? There once was a king who had everything in the world . . . but when he lost it he found out that he had never had anything and that he now had more than he ever had before.'

Dirk looked stunned.

'That's not a very good one,' he gave his opinion at last.

'No,' said Sean. 'It isn't . . . is it? But I think we should be charitable and admit that it's not too bad for this time of night.'

30

Sean woke feeling happy. Katrina was sitting up in bed filling cups from a pewter coffee pot and Dirk was hammering at the door to be let in. Katrina smiled at him. 'Good morning, meneer.'

Sean sat up and kissed her. 'How did you sleep, fancy?'

'Well, thank you,' but there were dark rings under her eyes. Sean went across to the bedroom door.

'Prepare to receive cavalry,' he said and swung it open. Dirk's charge carried him onto the bed and Sean dived after him. When two men are evenly matched, weight will usually decide and within seconds Dirk had straddled Sean's chest, pinning him helplessly and Sean was pleading for quarter.

After breakfast Mbejane brought the carriage round to the front of the hotel. When the three of them were settled in it, Sean opened the small window behind the driver's seat and told Mbejane, 'To the office first. Then we have to be at the Exchange by ten o'clock.'

Mbejane grinned at him. 'Yes, Nkosi, then lunch at the Big House.' Mbejane had never been able to master the word Xanadu.

They went to all the old places. Sean and Mbejane laughing and reminiscing at each other through the window. There was a panic at the Exchange, crowds on the pavement outside. The offices on Eloff Street had been refaced and a brass plate beside the front door carried the roll of the subsidiaries of Central Rand Consolidated. Mbejane stopped the carriage outside and Sean boasted to Katrina. She sat silently and listened to him, suddenly feeling inadequate for a man who had done so much. She misinterpreted Sean's enthusiasm and thought he regrett-the past and wished he were back.

'Mbejane, take us up to the Candy Deep,' Sean called at last. 'Let's see what's happening there.'

The last five hundred yards of the road was overgrown and pitted with disuse. The administration block had been demolished and grass grew thick over the foundations. There were new buildings and headgears half a mile farther along the ridge, but here the reef had been worked out and abandoned. Mbejane pulled up the horses in the circular drive in front of where the offices had stood. He jumped down and held their heads while Sean helped Katrina out of the carriage. Sean lifted Dirk and sat him on his shoulder and they picked their way through the waist-high grass and piles of bricks and rubbish towards the Candy Deep Number Three Shaft.

The bare white concrete blocks that had held the machinery formed a neat geometrical pattern in the grass. Beyond them reared the white mine dump; some mineral in the powdered rock had leaked out in long yellow stains down its sides. Duff had once had the mineral identified. It was of little commercial value, used occasionally in the ceramics industry. Sean had forgotten the name of it; it sounded like the name of a star – Uranus perhaps.

They came to the shaft. The edges of it had crumbled and the grass hung into it, the way an unkempt moustache hangs into an old man's mouth. The headgear was gone and only a rusty barbed-wire fence ringed the shaft. Sean bent his knees: keeping his back straight for Dirk still sat on his shoulder, he picked up a lump of rock the size of a man's fist and tossed it over the fence. They stood quietly and listened to it clatter against the sides as it fell. It fell for a long time and when at last it hit the bottom the echo rang faintly up from a thousand feet below.

'Throw more!' commanded Dirk, but Katrina stopped him.

'No, Sean, let's go. It's an evil place.' She shuddered slightly. 'It looks like a grave.'

'It very nearly was,' said Sean softly, remembering the darkness and the rock pressing down upon him.

'Let's go,' she said again, and they went back to where Mbejane waited with the carriage.

Sean was gay at lunch, he drank a small bottle of wine, but Katrina was tired and more miserable than she had been since they left Louis Trichardt. She had begun to realize the type of life he had led before she met him and she was frightened that now he wanted to return to it. She had only known the bush and the life of the Trek-Boer, she knew she could never learn to live like this. She watched as he laughed and joked during the meal, she watched the easy assurance with which he commanded the white head waiter, the way he picked his way through the maze of cutlery that was spread out on the table before them and at last she could hold it in no longer.

'Let's go away, let's go back into the bush.'

Sean stopped with a loaded fork halfway to his mouth. 'What?'

'Please, Sean, the sooner we go the sooner we'll be able to buy the farm.'

Sean chuckled. 'A day or two more won't make any difference. We're starting to have fun. Tonight I'll take you dancing – we were going to be sinful, remember?'

'Who will look after Dirk?' she asked weakly.

'Mbejane will –' Sean looked at her closely. 'You have a good sleep this afternoon and tonight we'll go out and tie the dog loose.' He grinned at the memories that expression invoked.

When Katrina woke from her rest that evening she found the other part of the reason for her depression. For the first time since the baby her periodic bleeding had started again, the tides of her body and mind were at their lowest ebb. She said nothing to Sean, but bathed and put on the yellow gown. She brushed her hair furiously, dragging the brush through it until her scalp tingled, but still it hung dull and lifeless – as dull as the eyes that looked back at her out of the yellow face in the mirror.

Sean came up behind her and leaned over her to kiss her cheek. 'You look,' said he, 'like a stack of gold bars five-and-a-half feet high.' But he realized that the yellow gown had been a mistake: it matched too closely the fever colour of her skin. Mbejane was waiting in the sitting-room when they went through.

'It may be late before we return,' Sean told him.

'That is of no account, Nkosi,' Mbejane's face was as impassive as ever, but Sean caught a sparkle of anticipation in his eyes and realized that Mbejane could hardly wait to get Dirk to himself.

'You are not to go into his room,' Sean warned.

'What if he cries, Nkosi?'

'He won't . . . but if he does see what he wants, give it to him then leave him to sleep.'

Mbejane's face registered his protest.

'I'm warning you, Mbejane, if I come home at midnight and find him riding you round the room I'll have both your hides for a kaross.'

459

'His sleep shall be unspoiled, Nkosi,' lied Mbejane.

In the hotel lobby Sean spoke to the receptionist. 'Where can we find the best food in this town?' he asked.

'Two blocks down, sir, the Golden Guinea. You can't miss it.'

'It sounds like a gin palace,' Sean was dubious.

'I assure you, sir, that you'll have no complaint when you get there. Everyone goes there. Mr Rhodes dines there when he's in town, Mr Barnato, Mr Hradsky –'

'Dick Turpin, Cesare Borgia, Benedict Arnold,' Sean continued for him. 'All right, you have convinced me. I'll take a chance on having my throat cut.'

Sean went out through the front entrance with Katrina on his arm. The splendour of the Golden Guinea subdued even Sean a little. A waiter with a uniform like a major-general's led them down a marble staircase, across the wide meadow of carpet between the group of elegant men and women to a table that even in the soft light dazzled with its bright silver and snowy linen. Chandeliers of crystal hung from the vaulted ceiling, the band was good, and the air was rich with the fragrance of perfume and expensive cigars.

Katrina stared helplessly at the menu until Sean came to her rescue and ordered the meal in a French accent that impressed her but not the waiter. The wine came and with it Sean's high spirits returned. Katrina sat quietly opposite him and listened. She tried to think of something witty to answer him with; in their wagon or alone in the veld they could talk for hours at a time but here she was dumb.

'Shall we dance?' Sean leaned across the table and squeezed her hand. She shook her head.

'Sean, I couldn't. Not with all these people watching. I'd only make a fool of myself.'

'Come on, I'll show you how . . . it's easy.'

'No, I couldn't, truly I couldn't.'

And to himself Sean had to admit that the dance floor of the Golden Guinea on a Saturday night was not the best place for a waltz lesson. The waiter brought the food, great steaming dishes of it. Sean addressed himself to it and the one-sided conversation wilted. Katrina watched him, picking at the too rich food herself, acutely conscious of the laughter and voices around them, feeling out of place and desperately miserable.

'Come on, Katrina,' Sean smiled at her. 'You've hardly touched your glass. Be a devil and get a little of that in you to warm you up.'

Obediently she sipped the champagne. She didn't like the taste. Sean finished the last of his crayfish thermidor and leaning back in his chair glowing with wine and good food said, 'Man . . . I only pray the chef can keep the rest of the meal up to that standard.' He belched softly behind his fingers and ran his eyes contentedly round the room. 'Duff used to say that a well-cooked crayfish was proof that –'

Sean stopped abruptly. He was staring at the head of the marble staircase – a party of three had appeared there. Two men in evening dress hovering attentively on each side of a woman. The woman was Candy Rautenbach. Candy with her blonde hair piled on top of her head. Candy with diamonds in her ears and at her throat, her bosom overflowing her gown as white as the frothy head on a beer tankard. Candy with bright blue eyes above a red mouth, Candy poised and lovely. Laughing, she glanced towards him and her eyes met his across the room. She stared in open disbelief, the laughter frozen on her lips, then suddenly her poise was gone and she was running down the stairs towards him, holding her skirts up to her knees, her escorts cantering after her in alarm, waiters scattering out of her path and every head in the room turning to watch her. Sean pushed back his chair, stood up to meet her and Candy reached him and jumped up to throw her arms around his neck. There was a long incoherent exchange of greetings and at last Sean prised her loose from his neck and turned her to face Katrina. Candy was flushed and panting with excitement; with every breath her bosom threatened to spring out of her bodice, and she was still holding on to Sean's arm.

'Candy, I want you to meet my wife, Katrina. My dear, this is Candy Rautenbach.'

'How do you do.' Katrina smiled uncertainly and Candy said the wrong thing.

'Sean, you're joking! You married?'

Katrina's smile faded. Candy noticed the change and went on quickly, 'But I must applaud your choice. I am so pleased to meet you, Katrina. We must get together sometime and I'll tell you all about Sean's terrible past.'

Candy was still holding Sean's arm and Katrina was watching her hand – the long tapered fingers against the dark cloth of

Sean's suit. Sean saw the direction of Katrina's eyes and tried tactfully to disengage himself but Candy held on. 'Sean, these are my two current beaux.' They were standing to heel behind her like well-trained gundogs. 'They are both so nice I can't make up my mind about them. Harry Lategaan and Derek Goodman. Boys, this is Sean Courtney. You've heard lots about him.'

They shook hands all round.

'Do you mind if we join you?' asked Derek Goodman.

'I'd be upset if you didn't!' said Sean. The men spread out to find chairs while Candy and Katrina studied each other. 'Is this your first visit to Johannesburg, Mrs Courtney?' Candy smiled sweetly. *I wonder where Sean found her, she's thin as a stick and that complexion! – that accent! he could have done better for himself – he could have had his pick.*

'Yes, we won't be here very long though.' *She's a harlot. She must be – her breasts half-naked and the paint on her face and they way she touches Sean. She must have been his mistress. If she touches him again I'll – I'll kill her.*

Sean came back to the table carrying a chair and set it down for Candy. 'Candy's one of my old friends, my dear, I'm sure you two will like each other.'

'I'm sure we will,' said Candy but Katrina didn't answer and Candy turned back to him. 'Sean, how wonderful it is to see you again. You look so well . . . as sunburnt and handsome as the first time I met you. Do you remember that day you and Duff came to eat at the Hotel?'

A shadow fell across Sean's face at the mention of Duff's name. 'Yes, I remember.' He looked round and snapped his fingers for the waiter. 'Let's have some more champagne.'

'I'll get it,' Candy's escorts cut in simultaneously and then started wrangling good-naturedly as to whose turn it was.

'Is Duff with you tonight, Sean?' Candy asked.

'Candy, didn't Derek get the drinks last time? It's my turn now.' Harry sought her support. Candy ignored them and looked at Sean for a reply but he turned and went round the table to the seat beside Katrina.

'I say, old girl, can I have the first dance?' asked Derek.

'I'll spin you for it, Derek, winner pays but gets first dance,' Harry suggested.

'You're on.'

'Sean, I said is Duff here tonight?' Candy looked at him across the table,

'No, he's not. Listen, you two, how about letting me in on this.' Sean avoided her eyes and joined in the haggle with Harry and Derek. Candy bit her lip – she wanted to press Sean further. She wanted to know about Duff – then suddenly she turned on her smile again. She wasn't going to plead with him.

'What is this?' She tapped Harry's shoulder with her fan. 'Am I going to be the prize in a game of chance? Derek will pay for the wine and Sean gets first dance.'

'I say old girl, that's a bit rough, you know.' But Candy was already standing up.

'Come on, Sean, let's see if you can still tread a stately measure.'

Sean glanced at Katrina. 'You don't mind, do you . . . just one dance?'

Katrina shook her head.

I hate her. She's a harlot. Katrina had never in her life spoken the word out loud, she had seen it only in her Bible, but now it gave her a fierce pleasure to think it. She watched Sean and Candy walk arm-in-arm to the dance floor.

'Would you care to dance, Mrs Courtney?' said Derek. Katrina shook her head again without looking at him. She was staring at Sean and Candy. She saw Sean take her in his arms and a cold lump settled in her stomach. Candy was looking up into Sean's face, laughing at him, her arm on his shoulder, her hand in his.

She's a harlot. Katrina felt her tears very near the surface and thinking that word held them back. Sean swirled Candy into a turn – Katrina stiffened in her chair, her hands clenching in her lap – their legs were touching, she saw Candy arch her back slightly and press her thighs against Sean. Katrina felt as though she were suffocating, jealousy had spread up cold and tight through her chest.

I could go and pull him away, she thought. *I could stop him doing that. He has no right. It's as though the two of them are doing – doing it together. I know they have before, I know it now – Oh God, make them stop it. Please make them stop.*

At last Sean and Candy came back to the table. They were laughing together and when he reached her chair Sean dropped his hand on Katrina's shoulder, She moved away from it but

Sean seemed not to notice. Everybody was having a good time. Everybody except Katrina. Harry and Derek were jostling for position. Sean's big laugh kept booming out and Candy was sparkling like the diamonds she wore. Every few minutes Sean turned to Katrina and tried to draw her into the conversation but Katrina stubbornly refused to be drawn. She sat there hating them all. Hating even Sean – for the first time she was unsure of him, jealous and frightened for him. She stared down at her hands on the tablecloth in front of her and saw how bony they were, chapped and reddened by the sun and wind, ugly compared to Candy's. She pulled them quickly into her lap and leaned across towards Sean. 'Please, I want to go back to the hotel. I don't feel well.'

Sean stopped in the middle of a story and looked at her with a mixture of concern and dismay. He didn't want to leave and yet he knew she was still sick. He hesitated one second and then he said, 'Of course, my fancy, I'm sorry. I didn't realize –' He turned to the others. 'We'll have to be going ... my wife's not too strong ... she's just had one hell of a go of blackwater.'

'Oh, Sean, must you?' Candy couldn't hide her disappointment. 'There's still so much to talk about.'

'I'm afraid so. We'll get together another night.'

'Yes,' agreed Katrina quickly, 'next time we come to Johannesburg we'll see you.'

'Oh, I don't know ... perhaps before we go,' Sean demurred. 'Some night next week. How about Monday?'

Before Candy could answer Katrina interrupted. 'Please, Sean, can we go now. I'm very tired.' She started towards the stairs but looked back to see Candy jump up and take Sean's arm, hold her lips close to his ear and whisper a question. Sean answered her tersely and Candy turned back to the table and sat down. When they were out on the street Katrina asked, 'What did she say to you?'

'She just said goodbye,' muttered Sean and Katrina knew he was lying. They didn't talk again on the way back to the hotel. Katrina was preoccupied with her jealousy and Sean was thinking about what Candy had asked and what he had answered.

'Sean, where's Duff? You must tell me.'

'He's dead, Candy.'

The second before she turned back to the table Sean had seen her eyes.

31

Sean woke with a headache and Dirk's jumping on his chest did not help to ease it at all. Sean had to bribe him off with the promise of sweets. Dirk, sensing his advantage, raised his price to a packet of bull's eyes and two lollipops, the kind with red stripes, before he allowed Katrina to lead him away to the bathroom. Sean sighed and settled back under the blankets. The pain moved up and crouched just behind his eyes. He could taste stale champagne on his own breath and his skin smelt of cigar smoke. He drowsed back in half sleep and the ache faded a little.

'Sean, it's Sunday you know. Are you coming to church with us?' Katrina asked coldly from the bedroom door. Sean squeezed his eyelids tighter closed.

'Sean!' No answer.

'Sean!' He opened one eye.

'Are you going to get up?'

'I don't feel very well,' he croaked. 'I think I have a touch of malaria.'

'Are you coming?' Katrina demanded remorselessly. Her feelings towards him had not softened during the night.

'I don't feel up to it this morning, truly I don't. I'm sure the Good Lord will understand.'

'Thou shalt not take the Lord's name in vain,' Katrina warned him with ice in her voice.

'I'm sorry.' Sean pulled the blankets up to his chin defensively. 'But truly, fancy, I can't get up for another couple of hours. My head would burst.'

Katrina turned back into the sitting-room and Sean heard her speak to Dirk in a voice purposely pitched to reach him.

'Your father's not coming with us. We will have to go down to breakfast by ourselves. Then we will have to go to church on our own.'

'But,' Dirk pointed out, 'he's going to buy me a packet of bull's

465

eyes and *two* lollipops with red stripes.' In Dirk's opinion that levelled the score. Sean heard the door of the suite close and Dirk's voice receded down the passage. Sean relaxed slowly and waited for the ache behind his eyes to diminish. After a while he became aware of the coffee tray on the table beside the bed and he weighed the additional pain that the effort of sitting up would involve against the beneficial effect of a large cup of coffee. It was a difficult decision but in the end he carefully raised his body to a sitting position and poured a cupful. There was a small jug of fresh cream on the tray, he took it in his right hand and was just about to add a little to the cup when there was a knock on the sitting-room door.

'Come in!' called Sean. He supposed it was the waiter coming to collect the tray. Sean searched his mind for a really scathing remark to send him on his way. He heard the sitting-room door open.

'Who is it?' he asked. There were quick footsteps and then Sean started so violently that the cream slopped out of the jug onto his sheets and his new nightshirt.

'Good God, Candy, you shouldn't have come here.' Sean was in a frenzy of agitation. He put the jug back on the tray with nervous haste and wiped ineffectually at the mess on his night-shirt with his hands. 'If my wife . . . Did anyone see you? You mustn't stay. If Katrina knows you've been here she'll . . . well I mean, she won't understand.'

Candy's eyes were puffy and rimmed with red. She looked as though she hadn't slept. 'It's all right, Sean, I waited across the street until I saw your wife leave. One of my servants followed her, she went to the Dutch church on Commissioner Street and there the service lasts about fifty years.' She came into the room and sat down on the edge of his bed.

'I had to talk to you alone. I couldn't let you go without knowing about Duff. I want you to tell me about it . . . everything about it. I promise not to cry, I know how you hate it.'

'Candy, let's not torture ourselves with it. He's dead. Let's remember him alive.' Sean had forgotten his headache for its place had been taken by pity for her and worry at the position in which she had placed him.

'Tell me, please. I must know. I'd never rest again if I didn't,' she said quietly.

'Candy, don't you see that it doesn't matter? The way in

466

which he went is not important. All that you need to know is he's gone.' Sean's voice faded but went on softly, almost to himself, 'He's gone, that is the only thing that matters, he's gone and left us richer for knowing him and a little poorer for having lost him.'

'Tell me,' she said again and they looked at each other, their emotions locked behind expressionless faces. Then Sean told her, his words limping at first, then faster and stronger as the horror of it came back to him. When he had finished she said nothing. She sat on the edge of the bed staring down at the patterned carpet. Sean moved closer to her and put his arm around her.

'There is nothing we can do. That's the thing about death, there is nothing you can do to make it change its mind.'

She leaned against him, against the comfort of his big body and they sat silently until suddenly Candy pulled away from him and smiled her gay brittle smile.

'And now tell me about you. Are you happy? Was that your son with Katrina? He's a lovely child.'

With relief Sean followed her away from the memory of Duff. They talked about each other, filling in the blanks from the time they had last met until suddenly Sean returned to reality.

'Good God, Candy, we've been talking for ages. Katrina will be back at any moment. You had better run.'

At the door she turned, buried her fingers in his beard and tugged his head from side to side. 'If she ever throws you out, you magnificent brute, here's somebody who'll have a place for you.'

She stood up on her toes and kissed him. 'Be happy,' she commanded and the door closed softly behind her.

Sean rubbed his chin, then he pulled off his nightshirt, screwed it into a ball, tossed it through the open door of the bedroom and went to the bathroom. He was towelling himself and whistling the waltz that the band had played the night before, sweating a little in the steamy warmth of the bathroom when he heard the front door open. 'Is that you, Fancy?'

'Daddy! Daddy! Mummy got sweets for me.' Dirk hammered on the bathroom door, and Sean wrapped the towel round his waist before opening it.

'Look! Look at all my sweets,' gloated Dirk. 'Do you want one, Pa?'

'Thank you, Dirk,' Sean put one of the huge striped humbugs in his mouth, moved it to one side and spoke around it.

'Where's your Mummy?'

'There.' Dirk pointed at the bedroom. He closed the sweet packet carefully. 'I'll keep some for Bejaan,' he announced.

'He'll like that,' Sean said and went across to the bedroom. Katrina lay on the bed; as soon as he saw her he knew something was desperately wrong. She lay staring up at the ceiling, her eyes unseeing, her face as yellow and set as that of a corpse. Two quick strides carried him to her. He touched her cheek with his fingers and the sense of dread settled on him again, heavily, darkly.

'Katrina?' There was no response. She lay still without a flicker of life in her eyes. Sean swung round and ran out of the suite, down the corridor to the head of the stairs. There were people in the lobby below him and he yelled over their heads to the clerk behind the desk.

'Get a doctor, man, as fast as you can . . . my wife's dying.'

The man stared up at him blankly. He had a neck too thin for his high stiff collar and his black hair was parted down the centre and polished with grease.

'Hurry, you stupid bastard, get moving,' roared Sean. Everybody in the lobby was looking at him. He still wore only a small towel around his waist and, heavy with water, his hair hung down over his forehead.

'Move, man! Move!' Sean was dancing with impatience. There was a heavy stone vase on the banister at Sean's side, he picked it up threateningly and the clerk jerked out of his trance and scuttled for the front door. Sean ran back to the suite.

Dirk was standing by Katrina's bed, his face distorted by the humbug it contained and his eyes large with curiosity. Sean snatched him up, carried him through to the other bedroom and locked the door on his outraged howls. Dirk was unused to being handled in that manner. Sean went back to Katrina and knelt beside her bed. He was still kneeling there when the doctor arrived. Tersely Sean explained about the blackwater, and the doctor listened then sent him to wait in the sitting-room. It was a long wait before the doctor came through to him and Sean sensed that behind his professional poker face the man was puzzled.

'Is it a relapse?' Sean demanded.

'No, I don't think so. I've given her a sedative.'

'What's wrong with her? What is it?' Sean pursued him and the doctor hedged.

'Has your wife had some sort of shock . . . some bad news, something that could have alarmed her? Has she been under nervous strain?'

'No . . . she's just come back from church. Why? What's wrong?' Sean caught the doctor's lapels and shook him in his agitation.

'It appears to be some sort of paralytic hysteria. I've given her laudanum. She'll sleep now and I'll come back to see her this evening.'

The doctor was trying to loosen Sean's hands from his jacket. Sean let him go and pushed past him to the bedroom.

The doctor called again just before dark, Sean had undressed Katrina and put her into the bed, but apart from that she had not moved. Her breathing was shallow and fast despite the drug she had been given. The doctor was baffled.

'I can't understand it, Mr Courtney. There is nothing I can find wrong with her apart from her general run-down condition. I think we'll just have to wait and see, I don't want to give her any more drugs.'

Sean knew the man could be of no more help to him and he hardly noticed when he left with a promise to come again in the morning. Mbejane gave Dirk his bath, fed him and put him to bed and then he slipped quietly out of the suite and left Sean alone with Katrina. The afternoon of worry had tired Sean. He left the gas burning in the sitting-room and stretched out on his own bed. After a while he slept.

When the rhythm of his breathing changed Katrina looked across at him. Sean lay fully clothed on top of his blankets, one thickly-muscled arm thrown above his head and his tension betrayed by the twitching of his lips and the frown that puckered his face. Katrina stood up and moved across to stand over him, lonely as she had never been in the solitude of the bush, hurt beyond the limits of physical pain and with everything that she believed in destroyed in those few minutes that it had taken for her to discover the truth.

She looked down at Sean and with surprise realized that she still loved him, but now the security that she had found with him was gone. The walls of her castle had proved paper. She had felt the first cold draughts blowing in through them as she watched him reliving his past and regretting it. She had felt the walls tremble and the wind howl stronger outside when he danced with that woman – then, they had collapsed into ruin around her. Standing in the half-darkened room, watching the man she trusted so completely and who just as completely had betrayed her, she went carefully over the ground again to make sure there was no mistake.

That morning, she and Dirk had stopped at the sweet shop on the way back from church. It was almost opposite the hotel. It had taken Dirk a long time to select his tuppenny worth. The profusion of wares on display unmanned him and reduced him to a state of dithering indecision. Finally, with the assistance of the proprietor and a little prompting from Katrina his purchases were made and packed into a brown paper bag. They were just about to go when Katrina looked out through the large front window of the shop and saw Candy Rautenbach leaving the hotel. She came quickly down the front steps, glanced about her, crossed the street to a waiting carriage and her coachman whisked her away. Katrina had stopped the instant she caught sight of her. A pang of last night's jealousy returned, for Candy looked very lovely even in the morning sunlight. It was not until Candy's carriage disappeared that Katrina began to question her presence at their hotel at eleven o'clock on a Sunday morning. Her jealousy was a bayonet thrust up under her ribs: it made her catch her breath. Vividly she remembered Candy's whispered question as they left the Golden Guinea the previous night. She remembered the way Sean had answered and the way he had lied about it afterwards. Sean knew that Katrina would go to church that morning. How simple it all was! Sean had arranged to meet her, he had refused to accompany Katrina and while Katrina was out of the way that harlot had gone to him.

'Mummy, you're hurting me.' Unconsciously she had tightened her grip on Dirk's hand. She hurried out of the shop, dragging Dirk with her. She almost ran across the hotel lobby, up the stairs and along the passage. The door was closed. She opened it and the smell of Candy's perfume met her. Her nostrils flared at it. There was no mistaking it, she remembered it from the previous evening – the smell of fresh violets. She heard Sean call from the bathroom, Dirk ran across the room and hammered on the door.

470

'Daddy! Daddy! Mummy got sweets for me.'

She put her Bible down on top of the writing desk and moved across the thick carpet with the smell of violets all around her. She stood in the doorway of the bedroom. Sean's nightshirt lay on the floor, there were still damp stains on it. She felt her legs begin to tremble. She looked up and saw the stains on the bed, grey on the white sheets. She felt giddy, her cheeks burned; she only just managed to reach her own bed.

32

She knew there was no mistake. Sean had taken that woman in such a casually blatant manner – in their own bedroom, almost before her eyes, that his rejection of her could hardly have been more final if he had slapped her face and thrown her into the street. Weakened by fever, depressed by the loss of her child and the phase of her cycle, she had not the resilience to fight against it. She had loved him but she had proved insufficient for him. She could not stay with him: the stubborn pride of her race would not allow it. There was only one alternative.

Timidly she bent over him and as she kissed him she smelt the warm man-smell of his body and felt his beard brush her cheek. Her determination wavered; she wanted to throw herself across his chest, lock her arms around his neck and plead with him. She wanted to ask for another chance. If he could tell her how she had failed him she could try to change, if only he could show her what she had done wrong. Perhaps if they went back into the bush again – She dragged herself away from his bed. She pressed her knuckles hard against her lips. It was no use. He had decided and even if she begged him to take her back there would always be this thing between them. She had lived in a castle and she would not change it now for a mud hut. Driven by the trek whip of her pride she moved quickly across to the wardrobe. She put on a coat and buttoned it – it reached to her ankles and covered her nightdress; she spread the green shawl over her head, winding the loose end around her throat. Once more she looked across at Sean. He slept with his big body sprawled and the frown still on his face.

In the sitting-room she stopped beside the writing desk. Her Bible lay where she had left it. She opened the front cover, dipped the pen and wrote. She closed the book and went to the door. There she hesitated once more and looked back at Dirk's bedroom. She could not trust herself to see him again. She lifted

an end of the shawl to cover her mouth, then she went out into
the passage and closed the door softly behind her.

33

Sean was surprised to find himself fully dressed and lying on top of his bed when he woke next morning. It was still half dark outside the hotel windows and the room was cold. He propped himself up on one elbow and rubbed at his eyes with the back of a clenched fist. Then he remembered and he swung his legs off the bed and looked at Katrina's bed. The blankets were thrown back and it was empty. Sean's first feeling was relief, she had recovered enough to get up on her own. He went through to the bathroom, stumbling a little from the stiffness of uneasy sleep. He tapped on the closed door.

'Katrina?' he questioned and then again louder. 'Katrina, are you in there?'

The handle turned when he tried it and the door swung open without resistance. He blinked at the empty room, white tiles reflecting the uncertain light, a towel thrown across a chair where he had left it. He felt the first twinge of alarm. Dirk's room – the door was still locked, the key on the outside. He flung it open. Dirk sat up in bed, his face flushed, his curls standing up like the leaves of a sisal bush. Sean ran out into the passage, along it and looked down into the lobby. There was a light burning behind the reception desk. The clerk slept with his head on his arms, sitting forward on his chair snoring, Sean went down the stairs three at a time. He shook the clerk.

'Has anybody been out through here during the night?' Sean demanded.

'I . . . I don't know.'

'Is that door locked?' Sean pointed at the front door.

'No, sir, there's a night latch on it. You can get out but not in.'

Sean ran out onto the pavement. Which way, which way to search for her? Which way had she gone? Back to Pretoria to the wagons? Sean thought not. She would need transport and she had no money to hire it. Why should she leave without waking him, leave Dirk, leave her clothing and disappear into the night. She must have been unbalanced by the drugs the doctor had given her. Perhaps there was something in his theory that she had suffered a shock, perhaps she was wandering in her night-dress through the streets with no memory, perhaps – Sean stood in the cold grey Transvaal morning, the city starting to murmur into wakefulness around him, the questions crowding into his head and finding there no answers with which to mate.

He turned and ran back through the hotel, out of the rear door into the stable yard.

'Mbejane,' he shouted, 'Mbejane, where the hell are you?'

Mbejane appeared quickly from the stall where he was curry-ing one of the hired horses.

'Nkosi.'

'Have you seen the Nkosikazi?'

Mbejane's face creased into a puzzled frown. 'Yesterday –' 'No, man,' shouted Sean. 'Today, last night . . . have you seen her?'

Mbejane's expression was sufficient reply.

Sean brushed impatiently past him and ran into the stable. He snatched a saddle off the rack and threw it onto the back of the nearest horse. While he clinched the girth and forced a bit between its teeth he spoke to Mbejane.

'The Nkosikazi is sick. She has left during the night. It is possible that she walks as one who still sleeps. Go quickly among your friends and tell them to search for her, tell them that there's ten pounds in gold for the one who finds her. Then come back here and care for Dirk until I return.'

Sean led the horse from the stable and Mbejane hurried off to spread the word. Sean knew that within minutes half the Zulus in Johannesburg would be looking for Katrina – tribal loyalty and ten pounds in gold were strong incentives. He swung up onto the horse and galloped out of the yard. He tried the Pretoria road first. Three miles out of town a native herd boy grazing sheep beside the road convinced him that Katrina hid not passed that way. He turned back. He paid a visit to the police station at Marshal Square. The Kommandant remembered him from the old days; Sean could rely on his co-operation. Sean left him and rode fast through the streets that were starting to fill with the bustle of a working day. He hitched his horse outside the hotel and took the front steps three at a time. The clerk had no news for him. He ran up the stairs and along the passage to his suite. Mbejane was feeding Dirk his breakfast. Dirk beamed at Sean through a faceful of egg and spread his arms to be picked up but Sean had no time for him.

'Has she come back?'

Mbejane shook his head. 'They will find her, Nkosi. Fifty men are searching for her now.'

'Stay with the child,' said Sean and went down to his horse. He stood beside it ready to mount but not knowing which way to go. 'Where the hell has she got to?' he demanded aloud. In her night clothes with no money, where the hell had she gone?

He mounted and rode with aimless urgency through the streets, searching the faces of the people along the sidewalks, turning down the sanitary lanes and peering into backyards and vacant plots. By midday he had tired his horse and worked himself into a ferment of worry and bad temper. He had searched every street in Johannesburg, made a nuisance of himself at the police station and sworn at the hotel clerk, but there was still no sign of Katrina. He was riding down Jeppe Street for the fifth time when the imposing double-storey of Candy's Hotel registered through his preoccupation.

'Candy,' he whispered. 'She can help.'

He found her in her office among Persian rugs and gilt furniture, walls covered with pink and blue patterned wallpaper, a mirrored ceiling hung with six crystal waterfalls of chandeliers and a desk with an Indian mosaic top. Sean pushed aside the little man in the black alpaca coat who tried to stop him entering and burst into the room. Candy looked up and her small frown of annoyance smoothed as she saw who it was.

'Sean . . . oh, how nice to see you.' She came round from behind the desk, the bell tent of her skirts covering the movement of her legs so she seemed to float. Her skin was smooth white and her eyes were happy blue. She held out her hand to him, but hesitated as she saw his face. 'What is it, Sean?'

He told her in a rush and she listened and when he had finished she rang the bell on her desk.

'There's brandy in the cabinet by the fireplace,' she said, 'I expect you are in need of one.'

The little man in the alpaca coat came quickly to the bell. Sean poured himself a large brandy and listened to Candy giving orders.

'Check the railway station. Telegraph the coach stages on each of the main roads. Send someone up to the hospital. Check the registers of every hotel and boarding-house in town.'

'Very well, madame.' The little man bobbed his head as he acknowledged each instruction and then he was gone.

Candy turned back to Sean.

'You can pour a drink for me also and then sit down and simmer down. You're behaving just the way she wanted you to.'

'What do you mean?' demanded Sean.

'You are being given a little bit of wifely discipline, my dear. Surely you have been married long enough to recognize that?'

Sean carried the glass across to her and Candy patted the sofa next to her.

'Sit down,' she said. 'We'll find your little Cinderella for you.'

'What do you mean . . . wifely discipline?' he demanded again.

'Punishment for bad behaviour. You may have eaten with your mouth open, answered back, taken more than your share of the blankets, not said good morning with the right inflection or committed one of the other mortal sins of matrimony, but –' Candy sipped her drink and gasped slightly, I see that time has not given you a lighter hand with the brandy bottle. One Courtney tot always did equal an imperial gallon . . . but, as I was saying, my guess is that little Katy is having an acute attack of jealousy. Probably her first, seeing that the two of you have spent your whole married life out in the deep sticks and she has never had an opportunity of watching the Courtney charm work on any other female before.'

'Nonsense,' said Sean. 'Who's she got to be jealous of?'

'Me,' said Candy. 'Every time she looked at me the other night I felt as though I'd been hit in the chest with an axe.' Candy touched her magnificent bosom with her fingertips, skilfully drawing Sean's attention to it. Sean looked at it. It was deeply cleft and smelt of fresh violets. He shifted restlessly and looked away.

'Nonsense,' he said again. 'We're just old friends, almost like –' he hesitated.

'I hope, my dear, that you weren't going to say "brother and sister" . . . I'll not be party to any incestuous relationship . . . or had you forgotten about that?'

Sean had not forgotten. Every detail of it was still clear. He blushed and stood up.

'I'd better be going,' he said. 'I'm going to keep looking for her. Thanks for your help, Candy, and for the drink.'

'Whatever I have is yours, m'sieur,' she murmured, lifting an eyebrow at him, enjoying the way he blushed. 'I'll let you know as soon as we hear anything.'

The assurance that Candy had given him wore thinner as the afternoon went by with no news of Katrina. By nightfall Sean was again wild with worry, it had completely swamped his bad temper and even anaesthetized his fatigue. One by one Mbejane's tribesmen came in to report a blank score, one by one the avenues Candy's men were exploring proved empty, and long before midnight Sean was the only hunter left. He rode hunched in the saddle, a lantern in his hand, riding the ground that had already been covered a dozen times, visiting the mining camps along the ridge, stopping to question late travellers he met along the network of roads between the mines. But the answer was always the same. Some thought he was joking: they laughed until they saw that his face was haunted and dark-eyed in the lantern light, then they stopped laughing and moved hurriedly on. Others had heard about the missing woman; they started to question him, but as soon as Sean realized they could not help him, he pushed past them and went on searching. At dawn he was back at the hotel. Mbejane was waiting for him.

'Nkosi, I have had food ready for you since last night. Eat now and sleep a little. I will send the men out to search again today, they will find her.'

'Tell them, I will give one hundred pounds to the one who finds her.' Sean passed his hand wearily across his face. 'Tell them to hunt the open veld beyond the ridges, she may not have followed a road.'

'I will tell them . . . but now you must eat.'

Sean blinked his eyes, they were red-veined and each had a little lump of yellow mucus in the corner.

'Dirk?' he asked.

'He is well, Nkosi, I have stayed with him all the while.'

Mbejane took Sean firmly by the arm. 'There is food ready. You must eat.'

'Saddle me another horse,' said Sean. 'I will eat while you do it.'

Without sleep, unsteady in the saddle as the day wore on, Sean widened the circle of his search until he was out into the treeless veld and the mine headgears were small spidery triangles on the horizon.

A dozen times he met Zulus from the city, big black men in loin cloths, moving at their businesslike trot, hunting the ground like hounds. There was a concealed sympathy behind their greetings.

'Mbejane has told us, Nkosi. We will find her.' And Sean left them and rode on alone, more alone than he had ever been in his life before. After dark he rode back into Johannesburg, the faint flutter of hope inside him stilled as he limped stiffly into the gas-lit lobby, of the hotel and saw the pity in the reception clerk's face.

'No word, I'm afraid, Mr Courtney.'

Sean nodded. 'Thanks anyway. Is my son all right?'

'Your servant has taken good care of him, sir. I sent dinner up to him an hour ago.'

The stairs seemed endless as he climbed them. By God, he was tired – sick-tired and sick with worry. He pushed open the door of his suite and Candy stood up from a chair across the room. The hope flared up in him again.'

'Have you –' he started eagerly.

'No,' she said quickly. 'No, Sean, I'm sorry.' He flopped into one of the chairs and Candy poured a drink for him from a decanter that was waiting on the writing desk. He smiled his thanks and took a big gulp at the glass. Candy lifted his legs one at a time and pulled off his boots, ignoring his faint protest. Then she took up her own glass and went to sit across the room from him.

'I'm sorry I joked yesterday,' she apologized softly. 'I don't think I realized how much you love her.' She lifted her glass to him. 'Here's a speedy end to the search.'

Sean drank again, half a glass at a swallow.

'You do love her, don't you?' Candy asked.

Sean answered her sharply. 'She's my wife.'

'But it's not only that,' Candy went on recklessly, knowing his anger was just below the surface of his fatigue.

'Yes, I love her. I'm just learning how much, I love her as I'll never be able to love again.' He drained his glass and stared at it, his face grey under the brown and his eyes dark with unhappiness. 'Love,' he said. 'Love,' mouthing the word, weighing it. 'They've dirtied that word . . . they sell love at the Opera

479

House . . . they have used that word so much that now when I want to say "I love Katrina" it doesn't sound what I mean.' Sean hurled the glass against the far wall, it shattered with a crack and a tingle and Dirk stirred in the bedroom. Sean dropped his voice to a fierce whisper. 'I love her so it screws my gut, I love her so that to think of losing her now is like thinking of dying.'

He clenched his fists and leaned forward in his chair. 'I'll not lose her now, by Christ, I'll find her and when I do I'll tell her this. I'll tell her just like I'm telling you.' He stopped and frowned. 'I don't think I've ever said to her "I love you." I've never liked using that word. I've said "Marry me" and "You're my fancy," but I've never said it straight before.'

'Perhaps that's part of the reason she ran away, Sean, perhaps because you never said it she thought you never felt it.' Candy was watching him with a strange expression – pity and understanding and a little yearning.

'I'll find her,' said Sean, 'and this time I'll tell her . . . if it's not too late.'

'You'll find her and it won't be too late. The earth can't have swallowed her, and she'll be glad to hear you say it.' Candy stood up. 'You must rest now, you have a hard day ahead of you.'

Sean slept fully dressed in the chair in the sitting-room. He slept brokenly, his mind struggling and kicking him back to half wakefulness every few minutes. Candy had turned the gas low before she left and its light fell in a soft pool onto the writing desk beneath it. Katrina's Bible lay where she had left it and each time Sean started awake the fat, leather-covered book caught his eye. Some time before dawn he woke for the last time and knew he could not sleep again.

He stood up and his body still ached and his eyes felt gritty. He moved across to the gas lamp and turned it up high, he let his hand drop from the lamp onto the Bible. Its leather was cool and softly polished beneath his fingers. He opened the front cover and caught his breath with a hiss.

Beneath Katrina's name, in her carefully rounded writing, the ink still freshly blue, *she had filled in the date of death.*

The page magnified slowly in front of his eyes until it filled the whole field of his vision. There was a rushing sound in his ears, the sound of a river in flood, but above it he heard voices, different voices.

'Let's go, Sean, it looks like a grave.'

'But more than anything she needs love.'

'The earth can't have swallowed her.'

And his own voice, 'If it's not too late, if it's not too late.'

The morning light was gathering strength as he reached the ruins of the old Candy Deep office block. He left his horse and ran through the grass towards the mine dump. The wind was small and cold; it moved the tops of the grass and went on to where Katrina's green shawl was caught on the barbed wire fence that ringed the shaft. In the wind the shawl flapped its wings like a big green bird of prey.

Sean reached the fence and looked down into the mouth of the shaft. At one place the grass had been torn away from the edge as though someone had snatched at it as they fell.

Sean loosed the shawl from the spikes of the barbed wire, he balled the heavy material in his fists, then he held it out over the shaft and let it drop. It spread out as it floated down into the blackness, and it was the bright green of Katrina's eyes.

'Why?' whispered Sean. 'Why have you done this to us, my fancy?' He turned away and walked back to his horse, stumbling carelessly in the rough footing.

Mbejane was waiting for him in the hotel suite.

'Get the carriage,' Sean told him.

'The Nkosikazi –?'

'Get the carriage,' Sean repeated.

Sean carried Dirk downstairs. He paid his bill at the reception desk and went out to where Mbejane had the carriage ready. He climbed up into it and held Dirk on his lap.

'Drive back to Pretoria,' Sean said.

'Where's Mummy?' Dirk demanded.

'She's not coming with us.'

'Are we going alone?' Dirk insisted and Sean nodded wearily.

'Yes, Dirk, we are going alone.'

'Is Mummy coming just now?'

'No, Dirk. No, she's not.'

It was finished, Sean thought. It was all over – all the dreams and the laughter and the love, He was too numbed to feel the pain yet – it would come later.

'Why are you squeezing me so hard, Daddy?'

Sean slackened his grip and looked down at the child on his lap. It was not finished, he realized; it was only a new beginning.

But first I must have time for this to heal: time – and a quiet place to lie up with this wound. The wagons are waiting and I must go back into the wilderness.

Perhaps after another year I will have healed sufficiently to start again, to go back to Ladyburg with my son, back to Ladyburg, and to Ada and to Garry – he thought. Then suddenly and sickeningly he felt the pain again, and the deep raw ache of it frightened him. *Please God*, prayed Sean who had never prayed before, *please God give me the strength to endure it.*

'Are you going to cry, Daddy? You look like you're going to cry.' Dirk was watching Sean's face with solemn curiosity. Sean pulled the child's head gently against his shoulder and held it there.

If tears could pay both our debts, thought Sean, if with my tears I could buy for you an indulgence from all pain, if by weeping now I could do all your weeping for you – then I would cry until my eyes were washed away.

'No, Dirk,' he answered. 'I am not going to cry – crying never helps very much.'

And Mbejane took them to where the wagons waited at Pretoria.

The Sound of Thunder

This book is for my children –
Shaun and Lawrence
and Christian Laurie

I

Four years of travel in the roadless wilderness had battered the wagons. Many of the wheel-spokes and *disselbooms* had been replaced with raw native timber; the canopies were patched until little of the original canvas was visible; the teams were reduced from eighteen to ten oxen each, for there had been predators and sickness to weed them out. But this exhausted little caravan carried the teeth of five hundred elephant; ten tons of ivory; the harvest of Sean Courtney's rifle; ivory that he would convert into nearly fifteen thousand gold sovereigns once he reached Pretoria.

Once more Sean was a rich man. His clothing was stained and baggy, crudely mended; his boots were worn almost through the uppers and clumsily resoled with raw buffalo hide; a great untrimmed beard covered half his chest and a mane of black hair curled down his neck to where it had been hacked away with blunt scissors above the collar of his coat. But despite his appearance he was rich in ivory, also in gold held for him in the vaults of the Volkskaas Bank in Pretoria.

On a rise of ground beside the road he sat his horse and watched the leisurely plodding approach of his wagons. It is time now for the farm, he thought with satisfaction. Thirty-seven years old, no longer a young man, and it was time to buy the farm. He knew the one he wanted and he knew exactly where he would build the homestead – site it close to the lip of the escarpment so that in the evenings he could sit on the wide stoep and look out across the plain to the Tugela River in the blue distance.

'Tomorrow early we will reach Pretoria.' The voice beside him interrupted his dreaming, and Sean moved in the saddle and looked down at the Zulu who squatted beside his horse.

'It has been a good hunt, Mbejane.'

'Nkosi, we have killed many elephant.' Mbejane nodded and

487

Sean noticed for the first time the strands of silver in the woolly cap of his hair. No longer a young man either.

'And made many marches,' Sean went on and Mbejane inclined his head again in grave agreement.

'A man grows weary of the trek,' Sean mused aloud. 'There is a time when he longs to sleep two nights at the same place.'

'And to hear the singing of his wives as they work the fields.' Mbejane carried it further. 'And to watch his cattle come into the kraal at dusk with his sons driving them.'

'That time has come for both of us, my friend. We are going home to Ladyburg.'

The spears rattled against his raw-hide shield as Mbejane stood up, muscles moved beneath the black velvet of his skin and he lifted his head to Sean and smiled. It was a thing of white teeth and radiance, that smile. Sean had to return it and they grinned at each other like two small boys in a successful bit of mischief.

'If we push the oxen hard this last day we can reach Pretoria tonight, Nkosi.'

'Let us make the attempt.' Sean encouraged him and walked his horse down the slope to intercept the caravan.

As it toiled slowly towards them through the flat white glare of the African morning a commotion started at its rear and spread quickly along the line, the dogs clamoured and the servants shouted encouragement to the rider who raced past them towards the head of the caravan. He lay forward in the saddle, driving the pony with elbows and heels, hat hanging from the leather thong about his neck and black hair ruffled with the speed of his run.

'That cub roars louder than the lion that sired him,' grunted Mbejane, but there was a fondness in his expression as he watched the rider reach the leading wagon and drag the pony from full run down on to his haunches.

'Also he spoils the mouth of every horse he rides.' Sean's voice was as harsh as Mbejane's, but there was the same fond expression in his eyes as he watched his son cut loose the brown body of a springbok from the pommel of his saddle and let it drop into the road beside the wagon. Two of the wagon drivers hurried to retrieve it, and Dirk Courtney kicked his pony and galloped down to where Sean and Mbejane waited beside the road.

'Only one?' Sean asked as Dirk checked the pony and circled back to fall in beside him.

'Oh, no. I got three – three with three shots. The gunboys are bringing the others.' Offhanded, taking as natural that at nine years of age he should be providing meat for the whole company, Dirk slouched down comfortably in the saddle, holding the reins in one hand and the other resting negligently on his hip in faithful imitation of his father.

Scowling a little to cover the strength of his pride and his love, Sean examined him surreptitiously. The beauty of this boy's face was almost indecent, the innocence of the eyes and faultless skin should have belonged to a girl. The sun struck ruby sparks from the mass of dark curls, his eyes spaced wide apart were framed with long black lashes and overscored by the delicate lines of the brow. His eyes were emerald and his skin was gold and there were rubies in his hair – a face fashioned by a jewelsmith. Then Sean looked at the mouth and experienced a twinge of uneasiness. The mouth was too big, the lips too wide and soft. The shape of it was wrong – as though it were about to sulk or whine.

'We are making a full day's trek today, Dirk. No *outspan* until we reach Pretoria. Ride back and tell the drivers.'

'Send Mbejane. He's doing nothing.'

'I told *you* to go.'

'Hell, Dad! I've done enough today.'

'Go, damn you!' Sean roared with unnecessary violence.

'I've only just come back, it's not fair that – ' Dirk started, but Sean did not let him finish.

'Every time I ask you to do something I get a mouthful of argument. Now do what I tell you.' They held each other's eyes; Sean glaring and Dirk resentful, sulky. Sean recognized that expression with dismay. This was going to be another of those tests of will that were becoming more frequent between them. Would this end as most of the others had? Must he admit defeat and use the *sjambok* again? When was the last time – two weeks ago – when Sean had reprimanded Dirk on some trivial point concerning the care of his pony. Dirk had stood sullenly until Sean was finished, and then he had walked away among the wagons. Dropping the subject from his mind, Sean was chatting with Mbejane when suddenly there was a squeal of pain from the laager and Sean ran towards it.

In the centre of the ring of wagons stood Dirk. His face still darkly flushed with temper, and at his feet the tiny body of one of the unweaned puppies flopped and whimpered with its ribs stoved in from Dirk's kick.

In anger Sean had beaten Dirk, but even in his anger he had used a length of rope and not the viciously tapered *sjambok* of hippo hide. Then he had ordered Dirk to his living-wagon.

At noon he had sent for him and demanded an apology – and Dirk, uncrying, with lips and jaw set grimly, had refused it.

Sean beat him again, with the rope, but this time coldly – not for the sake of retribution. Dirk did not break.

Finally, in desperation Sean took the *sjambok* to him. For ten hissing strokes, each of which ended with a wicked snap across his buttocks, Dirk lay silently under the whip. His body convulsed slightly at each lash but he would not speak, and Sean beat him with a sickness in his own stomach and the sweat of shame and guilt running into his eyes, swinging the *sjambok* mechanically with his fingers clawed around the butt of it, and his mouth full of the slimy saliva of self-hatred.

When at last Dirk screamed, Sean dropped the *sjambok*, reeled back against the side of the wagon and leaned there gasping – fighting down the nausea which flooded acid-tasting up his throat.

Dirk screamed again and again, and Sean caught him up and held him to his chest.

'I'm sorry, Pa! I'm sorry. I'll never do it again, I promise you. I love you, I love you best of all – and I'll never do it again,' screamed Dirk, and they clung to each other.

For days thereafter not one of the servants had smiled at Sean nor spoken to him other than to acknowledge an order. For there was not one of them, including Mbejane, who would not steal and cheat and lie to ensure that Dirk Courtney had whatever he desired at the exact moment he desired it. They could hate anyone, including Sean, who denied it to him.

That was two weeks ago. And now, thought Sean watching that ugly mouth, do we do it all again?

Then suddenly Dirk smiled. It was one of those changes of mood that left Sean slightly bewildered, for when Dirk smiled his mouth came right. It was irresistible.

'I'll go, Dad.' Cheerfully, as though he were volunteering, he prodded the pony and trotted back towards the wagons.

'Cheeky little bugger!' gruffed Sean for Mbejane's benefit, but silently he queried his share of the blame. He had raised the boy with a wagon as his home and the veld as his schoolroom, grown men his companions and authority over them as his undisputed right of birth.

Since his mother had died five years before he had not known the gentling influence of a woman. No wonder he was a wild one.

Sean shied away from the memory of Dirk's mother. There was guilt there also, guilt that had taken him many years to reconcile. She was dead now. There was no profit in torturing himself. He pushed away the gloom that was swamping the happiness of a few minutes before, slapped the loose end of the reins against his horse's neck and urged it out on to the road – south towards the low line of hills upon the horizon, south towards Pretoria.

He's a wild one. But once we reach Ladyburg he'll be all right, Sean assured himself. They'll knock the nonsense out of him at school, and I'll knock manners into him at home. No, he'll be all right.

That evening, the third of December, 1899, Sean led his wagons down the hills and laagered them beside the Apies River. After they had eaten, Sean sent Dirk to his cot in the living-wagon. Then he climbed alone to the crest of the hills and looked back across the land to the north. It was silver-grey in the moonlight, stretching away silent and immeasurable. That was the old life and abruptly he turned his back upon it and walked down towards the lights of the city which beckoned to him from the valley below.

2

There had been a little unpleasantness when he had ordered
Dirk to stay with the wagons; in consequence Sean was in an
evil mood as he crossed the bridge on the Apies and rode into
the city the following morning. Beside him Mbejane ran to keep
pace with his horse.

Deep in his own thoughts Sean turned into Church Street
before he noticed the unusual activity about him. A column of
horsemen forced him to rein his horse to the side of the road.
As they passed Sean examined them with interest.

Burghers in a motley of homespun and store clothes, riding in
a formation which might imaginatively have been called a
column of fours. But what excited Sean's curiosity was their
numbers – By God! there must be two thousand of them at
least, from lads to greybeards each of them was festooned with
bandoliers of ammunition and beside each left knee the butt of
a bolt-action Mauser rifle stuck up from its scabbard. Blanket-
rolls tied to the saddles, canteens and cooking-pots clattering,
they filed past. There was no doubting it. This was a war commando.

From the sidewalk women and a few men called comment at
them.

'*Geluk hoor*! Shoot straight.'

'*Spoedige terugkoms.*'

And the commandos laughed and shouted back. Sean stooped
to a pretty girl who stood beside his horse. She was waving a
red scarf and suddenly Sean saw that though she smiled her
eyelashes were loaded with tears like dew on a blade of grass.

'Where are they going?' Sean raised his voice above the uproar.

She lifted her head and the movement loosed a tear; it dropped
down her cheek, slid from her chin and left a tiny damp spot on
her blouse.

'To the train, of course.'

492

'The train? Which train?'

'Look, here come the guns.'

In consternation Sean looked up as the guns rumbled past, two of them. Uniformed gunners in blue, frogged with gold, sitting stiffly to attention on the carriages, the horses leaning forward against the immense weight of the guns. Tall wheels shod with steel, bronze glittering on the breeches in contrast to the sombre grey of the barrels.

'My God!' breathed Sean. Then turning back to the girl he grasped her shoulder and shook it in his agitation. 'Where are they going? Tell me quickly – where?'

'*Menheer*!' She bridled at his touch and wriggled away from it.

'Please. I'm sorry – you must tell me.' Sean called after her as she disappeared into the crowd.

A minute longer Sean sat stupefied, then his brain began to work again.

It was war, then. But where and against whom?

Surely no tribal rising would call out this array of strength. Those guns were the most modern weapons Sean could conceive.

No, this was a white man's war.

Against the Orange Republic? Impossible, they were brothers.

Against the British, then? The idea appalled him. And yet – and yet five years ago there had been rumours. It had happened before. He remembered 1895, and the Jameson Raid. Anything could have happened during the years he had been cut off from civilization – and now he had stumbled innocently into the midst of it.

Quickly he considered his own position. He was British. Born in Natal under the Union Jack. He looked like a burgher, spoke like one, rode like one, he was born in Africa and had never left it – but technically he was just as much an Englishman as if he had been born within sound of Bow bells.

Just supposing it was war between the Republic and Britain, and just supposing the Boers caught him – what would they do with him?

Confiscate his wagons and his ivory certainly, throw him into prison perhaps, shoot him as a spy possibly!

'I've got to get the hell out of here,' he mumbled, and then to Mbejane, 'Come on. Back to the wagons, quickly.' Before they reached the bridge he changed his mind. He had to learn with certainty what was happening. There was one person he could go to, and he must take the risk.

'Mbejane, go back to the camp. Find Nkosizana Dirk and keep him there – even if you have to tie him. Speak to no man and, as you value your life, let Dirk speak with no man. It is understood?'

'It is understood, Nkosi.'

And Sean, to all appearances another burgher among thousands of burghers, worked his way slowly through the crowds and the press of wagons towards a general dealer's store at the top end of the town near the railway station.

Since Sean had last seen it the sign above the entrance had been freshly painted in red and gold. 'I. Goldberg. Importer & Exporter, Dealing in Mining Machinery, Merchant & Wholesaler, Purchasing Agent: gold, precious stones, hides and skins, ivory and natural produce.'

Despite this war, or because of it, Mr Goldberg's emporium was doing good business. It was crowded and Sean drifted unnoticed among the customers, searching quietly for the proprietor.

He found him selling a bag of coffee beans to a gentleman who was plainly sceptical of its quality. The discussion of the merits of Mr Goldberg's coffee beans as opposed to those of his competitor across the street was becoming involved and technical.

Sean leaned against a shelf full of merchandise, packed his pipe, lit it and while he waited he watched Mr Goldberg in action. The man should have been a barrister, his argument was strong enough to convince first Sean and finally the customer. The latter paid, slung the bag over his shoulder and grumbled his way out of the shop, leaving Mr Goldberg glowing pink and perspiring in the flush of achievement.

'You haven't lost any weight, Izzy,' Sean greeted him.

Goldberg peered at him uncertainly over his gold-framed spectacles, beginning to smile until suddenly he recognized Sean. He blinked with shock, jerked his head in a gesture of invitation so his jowls wobbled, and disappeared into the back office. Sean followed him.

'Are you mad, Mr Courtney?' Goldberg was waiting for him, quivering with agitation. 'If they catch you . . . '

'Listen, Izzy. I arrived last night. I haven't spoken to a white man in four years. What the hell is going on here?'

'You haven't heard?'

'No, damn it, I haven't.'

'It's war, Mr Courtney.'

'I can see that. But where? Against whom?'

'On all the borders – Natal, the Cape.'

'Against?'

'The British Empire.' Goldberg shook his head as though he did not believe his own statement. 'We've taken on the whole British Empire.'

'We?' Sean asked sharply.

'The Transvaal Republic and the Orange Free State. Already we have won great victories – Ladysmith is besieged, Kimberley, Mafeking –'

'You, personally?'

'I was born here in Pretoria. I am a burgher.'

'Are you going to turn me in?'

'No, of course not. You've been a good customer of mine for years.'

'Thanks, Izzy. Look, I've got to get out of here as fast as I can.'

'It would be wise.'

'What about my money at the Volkskaas – can I get it out?' Izzy shook his head sadly. 'They've frozen all enemy accounts.'

'Damn it, God damn it!' Sean swore bitterly, and then, 'Izzy, I've got twenty wagons and ten tons of ivory parked out there on the edge of town – are you interested?'

'How much?'

'Ten thousand for the lot; oxen, wagons, ivory – the lot.'

'It would not be patriotic, Mr Courtney,' Goldberg decided reluctantly. 'Trading with the enemy – besides I have only your word that it's ten tons.'

'Hell, Izzy, I'm not the British Army – that lot is worth twenty thousand quid.'

'You want me to buy sight unseen – no questions asked? All right. I'll give you four thousand – gold.'

'Seven.'

'Four and a half,' countered Izzy.

'You bastard.'

'Four and a half.'

'No, damn you. Five!' growled Sean.

'Five?'

'Five!'

'All right, five.'

'Thanks Izzy.'

'Pleasure, Mr Courtney.'

Sean described the location of his laager hurriedly.

'You can send someone out to pick it up. I am going to run for the Natal border as soon as it's dark.'

'Keep off the roads and well clear of the railway. Joubert has thirty thousand men in Northern Natal, massed around Ladysmith and along the Tugela heights.' Goldberg went to the safe and fetched five small canvas bags from it. 'Do you want to check?'

'I'll trust you as you trusted me. Good-bye, Izzy.' Sean dropped the heavy bags down the front of his shirt and settled them under his belt.

'Good luck, Mr Courtney.'

3

There were two hours of daylight left when Sean finished paying his servants. He pushed the tiny pile of sovereigns across the tailboard of the wagon towards the last man and went with him through the complicated ritual of farewell, the hand-clapping and clasping, the repetition of the formal phrases – then he stood up from his chair and looked around the circle. They squatted patiently, watching him with wooden black faces – but reflected back from them he could sense his own sorrow at this parting. Men with whom he had lived and worked and shared a hundred hardships. It was not easy to leave them now.

'It is finished,' he said.

'*Yebho*, it is finished.' They agreed in chorus and no one moved.

'Go, damn you.'

Slowly one of them stood and gathered the bundle of his possessions, a *kaross* (or skin blanket), two spears, a cast-off shirt that Sean had given him. He balanced the bundle on his head and looked at Sean.

'Nkosi!' he said and lifted a clenched fist in salute.

'Nonga,' Sean replied. The man turned away and trudged out of the laager.

'Nkosi!'

'Hlubi.'

'Nkosi!'

'Zama.'

A roll call of loyalty – Sean spoke their names for the last time, and singly they left the laager. Sean stood and watched them walk away in the dusk. Not one of them looked back and no two men walked together. It was finished.

Wearily Sean turned back to the laager. The horses were ready. Three with saddles, two carrying packs.

'We will eat first, Mbejane.'

'It is ready, Nkosi. Hlubi cooked before he went.'

'Come on, Dirk. Dinner.'

Dirk was the only one who spoke during the meal. He chattered gaily, wrought up with excitement by this new adventure, while Sean and Mbejane shovelled fat Hlubi's stew and hardly tasted it.

Out in the gathering darkness a jackal yelped, a lonely sound on the evening wind, fitting the mood of a man who had lost friends and fortune.

'It is time.' Sean shrugged into his sheepskin jacket and buttoned it as he stood to kick out the fire, but suddenly he froze and stood with his head cocked as he listened. There was a new sound on the wind.

'Horses!' Mbejane confirmed it.

'Quickly, Mbejane, my rifle.' The Zulu leapt up, ran to the horses and slipped Sean's rifle from its scabbard.

'Get out of the light and keep your mouth shut,' Sean ordered as he hustled Dirk into the shadows between the wagons. He grabbed the rifle from Mbejane and levered a cartridge into the breech and the three of them crouched and waited.

The click and roll of pebbles under hooves, the soft sound of a branch brushed aside.

'One only,' whispered Mbejane. A pack-horse whickered softly and was answered immediately from the darkness. Then silence, a long silence broken at last by the jingle of a bridle as the rider dismounted.

Sean saw him then, a slim figure emerging slowly out of the night and he swung the rifle to cover his approach. There was something unusual in the way the stranger moved, gracefully but with a sway from the hips, long-legged like a colt and Sean knew that he was young, very young to judge by his height.

With relief Sean straightened up from his crouch and examined him as he stopped uncertainly beside the fire and peered into the shadows. The lad wore a peaked cloth cap pulled down over his ears and his jacket was an expensive, honey-coloured chamois. His riding breeches were beautifully tailored and hugged his buttocks snugly. Sean decided that his backside was too big and out of proportion to the small feet clad in polished English hunting boots. A regular dandy, and the scorn was in Sean's tone as he called out.

'Stay where you are, friend, and state your business!'

The effect of Sean's challenge was unexpected. The lad jumped, the soles of his glossy boots cleared the ground by at least six inches, and when he landed again he was facing Sean.

'Talk up. I haven't got all night.'

The lad opened his mouth, closed it again, licked his lips and spoke.

'I was told you were going to Natal.' The voice was low and husky.

'Who told you that?' demanded Sean.

'My uncle.'

'Who is your uncle?'

'Isaac Goldberg.'

Sean digested this intelligence and while he did so he examined the face before him. Cleanshaven, pale, big dark eyes and a laughing kind of mouth that was now pursed with fright.

'And if I am?' Sean demanded.

'I want to go with you.'

'Forget it. Get back on your horse and go home.'

'I'll pay you – I'll pay you well.'

Was it the voice or the posture of the lad, Sean pondered, there was something very odd about him. He stood with a flat leather pouch held in both hands across the front of his hips – in an attitude of defence, as though he were protecting – protecting what? And suddenly Sean knew what it was.

'Take off your cap,' he ordered.

'No.'

'Take it off.'

A second longer the lad hesitated, then in a gesture that was almost defiance he jerked off the cap and two thick black braids of hair, shiny in the firelight, dropped and hung down almost to his waist and transformed him instantly from gawky masculinity into stunning womanhood.

Although he had guessed it, Sean was unprepared for the shock of this revelation. It was not so much her beauty, but her attire that caused the shock. Never in his life had Sean seen a woman in breeches, and now he gasped. Breeches, by God, she might as well be naked from the waist down – even that would be less indecent.

'Two hundred pounds –' She was coming towards him now, offering the pouch. At each step the cloth of the breeches tightened across her thighs and Sean dragged his eyes guiltily back to her face.

'Keep your money, lady.' Her eyes were grey, smoky grey.

'Two hundred on account, and as much again when we reach Natal.'

'I'm not interested.' But he was, those soft lips starting to quiver.

'How much then? Name your price.'

'Look, lady. I'm not heading a procession. There are three of us already – one a child. There is hard riding ahead, plenty of it, and an army of Boers in between. Our chances are slim enough as it is. Another member to the party, and a woman at that, will make them prohibitive. I don't want your money, all I want is to get my son to safety. Go home and sit this war out – it won't last long.'

'I'm going to Natal.'

'Good. You go then – but not with us.' Sean could not trust himself longer to resist the appeal of those grey eyes and he turned to Mbejane. 'Horses,' he snapped and walked away from her. She stood watching him quietly as they mounted up, making no protest. She seemed very small and alone as Sean looked down at her from the saddle.

'I'm sorry,' he growled. 'Go home now like a good girl,' and quickly he wheeled away and trotted out into the night.

All night they rode, east through the open moonlit land. Once they passed a darkened homestead and a dog barked, but they sheered away and then turned east again and held the great crucifix of the Southern Cross at their right-hand. When Dirk fell asleep in the saddle and slipped sideways, Sean caught him before he hit the ground, pulled him across into his lap and held him there for the rest of the night.

Before dawn they found a clump of bush on the bank of a stream, hobbled the horses and made camp. Mbejane had the billycan boiling over a small well-screened fire and Sean had rolled Dirk unconscious into his blankets when the girl rode into camp and jumped down from her horse.

'I nearly lost you twice.' She laughed and pulled off the cap. 'Gave me a horrible fright.' She shook down the shiny braids. 'Coffee! Oh good, I'm famished.'

Menacingly Sean climbed to his feet and with clenched fists

he glared at her, but undismayed she hobbled her horse and turned it loose before acknowledging him again.

'Don't stand on ceremony, please be seated.' And she grinned at him with such devilment in her grey eyes, aping so faithfully his stance with hands on those indecent hips, that Sean suddenly found himself smiling. He tried to stop it for he knew it was an admission of surrender, but his effort was so unsuccessful that she burst into delighted laughter.

'How's your cooking?' he demanded.

'So, so.'

'You'd better brush up on it because from now on you're working your passage.'

Later, when he had sampled it for the first time, he admitted grudgingly:

'Not bad – in the circumstances,' and wiped the plate with a crust of bread.

'You are too kind, sir.' She thanked him and lugged her blanketroll into the shade, spread it, pulled off her boots, wriggled her toes and lay back with a sigh.

Sean positioned his own bedroll with care so that, when he opened his eyes, without turning his head he could watch her from under the brim of the hat that covered his face.

He woke at midday and saw that she slept with one cheek in her open hand, the lashes of her eyes meshed together and a few loose strands of dark hair across a face that was damp and flushed in the drowsy heat. He watched her for a long time before silently rising and crossing to his saddle-bags. When he went down to the stream he took with him his flat canvas toilet-bag, the remaining pair of breeches that were neither patched nor too badly stained and a clean silk shirt.

Sitting on a rock beside the water, naked and freshly scrubbed, he regarded his face in the polished steel mirror.

'A big job.' He sighed and started snipping at the great bush of beard which had not felt the scissors in three years.

At dusk, self-conscious as a girl in her first party dress, Sean walked back into the camp. They were all awake. Dirk and the girl sat together on her blanket in such earnest conversation that neither of them noticed his arrival. Mbejane was busy at the fire; he rocked back on his heels and examined Sean without change of expression.

'We'd better eat and get going.'

Dirk and the girl looked up. Her eyes narrowed and then widened thoughtfully.

Dirk gaped at him, and then, 'Your beard's all funny –' he announced, and the girl tried desperately to quell her laughter.

'Get your blankets rolled up, boy.'

Sean tried to break Dirk's grip on the subject, but like a bulldog Dirk held on relentlessly.

'– and why are you wearing your best clothes, Dad?'

4

They rode three abreast in the darkness, Dirk between them and Mbejane trailing behind with the pack-horses. The land rose and fell beneath them like the swells of an endless sea and the way in which the grass moved with the night wind heightened the illusion of waves. Islands in the sea were the dark bulks of the kopjes they passed, and the yelp of a jackal was the voice of a seabird.

'Aren't we holding too far east?' The girl broke the silence and her voice blended with the soft sound of the wind.

'Intentionally,' Sean answered. 'I want to cross the tail of the Drakensberg well clear of the Boer concentrations around Ladysmith and the line of rail,' and he looked over Dirk's head at her. She rode with her face lifted to the sky.

'You know the stars?' he asked.

'A little.'

'So do I. I know them all.' Dirk accepted the challenge and swivelled towards the south. 'That's the Cross with the pointers, and that's Orion with his sword on his belt, and that's the Milky Way.'

'Tell me some others,' the girl invited.

'The others are just ordinary ones – they don't count. They haven't even got names.'

'Oh, but they have and most of them have got a story.'

There was a pause. Dirk was now in an invidious position; either he had to admit ignorance, and Dirk's pride was too large to swallow with ease, or else he would forgo what promised to be a choice series of stories. Large as was his pride, his appetite for stories was even larger.

'Tell me some,' he conceded.

'You see that little clump there underneath the big bright one? They are called the Seven Sisters. Well, once upon a time –'

Within minutes Dirk was completely absorbed. These were

even better than Mbejane's stories – probably because they were new, while Dirk could recite from memory Mbejane's entire repertoire. He fell upon any weakness in the plot like a prosecuting attorney.

'But why didn't they just shoot the old witch?'

'They didn't have guns in those days.'

'They coulda used a bow and arrow.'

'You can't kill a witch with a bow and arrow. The arrow just goes – psst – straight through her without hurting her.'

'Hangs teeth!' That was really impressive, but before accepting it Dirk found it necessary to corroborate with expert opinion. He checked with Mbejane, translating the problem to the Zulu. When Mbejane supported the girl Dirk was convinced, for Mbejane was a celebrated authority on the supernatural.

That night Dirk did not fall asleep in the saddle and when they camped before dawn the girl's voice was hoarse with overwork, but her conquest of Dirk was complete and that of Sean was well advanced.

All night while he listened to her voice and the husky bursts of laughter that punctuated it Sean had felt the seed that was planted at their first meeting sinking its roots down into his lower belly and loins, spreading its tendrils up through his chest. He wanted this woman so violently that in her presence his wits failed him. Many times during the night he had attempted to join the discussions, but each time Dirk had brushed his efforts aside with contempt and turned avidly back to the girl. By morning he had made the disturbing discovery that he was jealous of his own son – jealous of the attention Dirk was getting, and for which he hungered so strongly.

While they drank coffee after the morning meal lying on their blankets beneath a grove of syringa trees, Sean remarked:

'You haven't told us your name yet.' And of course it was Dirk that answered.

'She told me. Your name's Ruth – isn't it?'

'That's right, Dirk.'

With an effort Sean clamped down on the senseless anger that boiled up through him, but when he spoke his voice carried traces of it.

'We've heard enough from you for one night, my boy. Now get your head down, close your eyes and your mouth and keep them that way.'

504

'I'm not sleepy, Dad.'

'Do what I tell you.' Sean jumped up and strode out of the camp. He climbed the small kopje above them. By now it was full daylight and he searched the veld to the horizon on all sides. There was no trace of habitation or human. He climbed down again and fussed with the hobbles of the horses before returning to the grove of syringas.

Despite his protestations Dirk was curled like a sleeping puppy and, near the fire from a large bundle of blankets issued the unmistakable snoring of Mbejane. Ruth lay a little apart from them, a blanket thrown over her legs, her eyes closed and the front of her shirt rising and falling in a manner that gave Sean two good reasons for not sleeping. He lay propped on one elbow and fed his eyes and his imagination on her.

These four years past he had not seen a white woman, four years without the sound of a woman's voice or the comfort of her body. In the beginning it had worried him – the restlessness, the undirected fits of depression, and sudden bursts of temper. But gradually in the long days of hunting and riding, in the endless struggle with drought and storm, with beasts and the elements, he had brought his body under control. Women had faded into unreality, vague phantoms that plagued him only in the night so he twisted and sweated and cried out in his sleep until nature gave him release and the phantoms dispersed for a while to gather strength for their next visitation.

But this was no phantom that lay beside him now. By stretching out a hand he could stroke the faint down on her cheek and feel the blood-warm silk of her skin.

She opened her eyes, they were milky grey with sleep, slowly focusing until they levelled with his and returned his scrutiny.

Because of what she read there, she lifted her left hand from the blanket and held it out towards him. Her riding gloves were off. For the first time he noticed the slender gold ring that encircled her third finger.

'I see,' he muttered dully, and then in protest: 'But you are too young – you're too young to be married.'

'I'm twenty-two years old,' she told him softly.

'Your husband – where is he?' Perhaps the bastard was dead, his one last hope.

'I am going to him now. When war seemed inevitable he went to Natal, to Durban, to find a job and a home for us there. I was to follow him – but the war came earlier than we expected. I was stranded.'

'I see.' I am taking you to another man, he thought with bitterness, and put it in different words. 'So he is sitting in Durban waiting for you to make your own way through the lines.'

'He is with the army of Natal. A week ago he got a message through to me. He wanted me to stay on in Johannesburg and wait until the British capture the city. He says that with so great a force they will be in Johannesburg within three months.'

'Why didn't you wait, then?'

She shrugged. 'Patience is not one of my virtues,' and then the devilment was in her eyes again. 'Besides, I thought it would be fun to run away – it was so terribly dull in Johannesburg.'

'Do you love him?' he demanded suddenly. The question startled her and the smile died on her lips.

'He's my husband.'

'That doesn't answer my question.'

'It was a question you had no right to ask.' She was angry now.

'You have to tell me.'

'Do you love your wife?' she snapped at him.

'I did. She's been dead five years.' And her anger flickered out as swiftly as it had blazed.

'Oh, I'm sorry. I didn't know.'

'Forget it. Forget I ever asked.'

'Yes, that's best. We are getting into an awful tangle.' Her hand with the ring upon it was still held out towards him, lying between them on the soft carpet of fallen leaves. He reached out and lifted it. It was a small hand.

'Mr Courtney – Sean, it's best if – we mustn't – I think we'd better sleep now.' And she withdrew the hand and rolled away from him.

The wind woke them in the middle of the afternoon, it roared in from the east, flattening the grass on the hills and thrashing the branches above their heads.

Sean looked up at the sky with the wind fluttering his shirt and ruffling his beard. He leaned forward against it, towering over Ruth so that suddenly she realized how big he was. He looked like a god of the storm, with long powerful legs braced apart and the muscles of his chest and arms standing out proudly beneath the white silk of his shirt.

'Clouds building up,' Sean shouted above the rush of the wind. 'No moon tonight.'

She stood up quickly and a sudden violent gust threw her off balance. She staggered against him and his arms closed about her. For a moment she was pressed to his chest, could feel the lean, rubbery resilience of his body and smell the man smell of it. It was a shock for both of them, this unexpectedly intimate contact and when she broke away her eyes were wide and grey with fear of the thing she had felt stir within her.

'I'm sorry,' she whispered. 'That was an accident.' And the wind caught her hair and streamed it across her face in a dancing, snapping black tangle.

'We'll upsaddle and ride with the daylight that is left,' Sean decided. 'We won't be able to move tonight.'

The clouds rolled in on the wind, spreading upon themselves, changing shape and dropping closer to the earth. Clouds the colour of smoke and bruises, heavy with the rain they carried.

The night came early, but still the wind roared and buffeted them in the gloom.

'It will drop in an hour or so, then we'll get the rain. We'll try and find shelter while there's still light enough to see.'

On the reverse slope of a kopje they found an overhang of rock and offloaded the packs beneath it. While Sean pegged the horses out on their head ropes to prevent them walking away before the storm, Mbejane cut grass and piled it into a mattress on the rock floor beneath the overhang. Huddled in their oilskins they ate biltong and cold mealie bread and afterwards Mbejane withdrew discreetly to the far end of the shelter and disappeared under his blankets. He had that animal knack of being able to sleep instantly and completely even under the most adverse conditions.

'All right, boy. Get into your blankets.'

'Can't I just . . . ' Dirk began his nightly protest.

'No, you can't.'

'I'll sing for you,' Ruth offered.

'What for?' Dirk was puzzled.

'A sleepy-time song – haven't you ever had a lullaby?'

507

'No.' But Dirk was intrigued. 'What you going to sing?'

'Into your blankets first.'

Sitting beside Sean in the darkness, very conscious of his bulk and the touch of his shoulder against hers, the muted roar of the wind as her accompaniment – Ruth sang.

First the old Dutch folksongs, 'Nooi, Nooi' and 'Jannie met die Hoepel been', then other old favourites like 'Frère Jacques'. Her voice meant something to each of them.

Mbejane woke to the sound of it and it made him remember the wind on the hills of Zululand and the singing of the young girls in the fields at harvest-time. It made him glad he was going home.

To Dirk it was the voice of the mother he had hardly known. A safe sound – and soon he slept.

'Don't stop,' whispered Sean.

So she sang for him alone. A love-song from two thousand years ago, filled with all the suffering of her people, but with joy in it also. The wind died away while she sang and her voice died away with it into the vast silence of the night.

The storm broke. The first thunder crashed and the lightning forked jagged-blue through the clouds. Dirk whimpered a little but slept on.

In the stark, blue light Sean saw that Ruth's cheeks were wet with tears and when the darkness closed around them again she started to tremble against him. He reached out for her and she clung to him, small and warm against his chest, and he could taste the salt of her tears on his lips.

'Sean, we mustn't.'

But he lifted her and held her across his chest as he walked out into the night. The lightning blazed again and lit the land with startling brilliance so he could see the horses huddling heads down, and the crisp outline of the kopje above them.

The first raindrops splashed against his shoulders and into his face. The rain was warm and he walked on carrying Ruth. Then the air was filled with rain, an encompassing pearly mist of it in the next flash of lightning, and the night was filled with the odour of rain on dry earth – a clean warm smell.

5

In a still morning, washed so clean by the rain that they could see the mountains, blue and sharp on the southern horizon, they stood together on the crest of the kopje.

'That's the tail of the Drakensberg, we've cleared it by twenty miles. There's very little chance of a Boer patrol this far out. We can ride by day now. Soon we'll be able to work in again and meet the railway beyond the battle lines.'

Because of the beauty of the morning, of the land that dripped away into the great, grassy bowl that was Natal, and of the woman that stood beside him, Sean was gay.

Because of the promise of an end to the journey and the promise of a new one with this woman as his companion, he was content.

When he spoke she turned slowly to look up at him, her chin lifting in acknowledgement of his superior height. For the first time Sean realized that his own mood was not reflected in her eyes.

'You are very lovely,' he said, and still she remained silent, but now he could recognize the shadows in her eyes as sorrow or something even stronger.

'Ruth, you'll come with me?'

'No.' She shook her head slowly, regretfully. The fat black python of hair rolled across her shoulder and hung down against the honey chamois leather of her jacket.

'You must.'

'I cannot.'

'But, last night.'

'Last night was madness . . . the storm.'

'It was right. You know that.'

'No. It was the storm.' She looked away from him towards the sky. 'And now the storm is ended.'

'It was more than that. You know it. It was from the first moment of our meeting.'

'It was a madness based upon deceit. Something that I will have to cover with lies – the way we had to cover it with darkness at the time.'

'Ruth. My God, don't talk about it like that.'

'Very well, I won't. I won't talk about it again, ever.'

'We can't leave it now. You know we can't.'

And in answer she held up her left hand so that the gold upon it caught the sun.

'We'll say good-bye here on a mountain in the sunlight. Though we'll ride together a little farther – it's here we'll say good-bye.'

'Ruth . . . ' he started, but she placed the hand across his mouth and he felt the metal of the ring on his lips and it seemed to him that the ring was as cold as his dread of the loss she was about to inflict upon him.

'No,' she whispered. 'Kiss me once more and then let me go.'

6

Mbejane saw it first and spoke quietly to Sean, perhaps two miles out on their flank, like a smudge of brown smoke rising beyond the fold of the nearest ridge, so faint that Sean had to search a moment before he found it. Then he swivelled away from it and hunted frantically for cover. The nearest was an outcrop of red stone half a mile away, much too far.

'What is it, Sean?' Ruth noticed his agitation.

'Dust,' he told her. 'Horsemen. Coming this way.'

'Boers?'

'Probably.'

'What are we to do?'

'Nothing.'

'Nothing?'

'When they show on the ridge I'll ride to meet them. Try to bluff our way through.' He turned to Mbejane and spoke in Zulu. 'I will go to them. Watch me carefully, but keep moving away. If I lift my arm let the pack-horses go and ride. I will hold them as long as I can, but when I lift my arm then it is finished.' Quickly he unbuckled the saddle-bag which held the gold and handed it to the Zulu. 'With a good start you should be able to hold them off until nightfall. Take the Nkosikazi where she wishes to go and then with Dirk return to my mother at Lady-burg.'

He looked again at the ridge just in time to see two horsemen appear upon it. Sean lifted the binoculars from his chest; in the round field of the glasses the two riders stood broadside, their faces turned towards him so he could make out the shape of their helmets. He saw the burnished sparkle of their accoutrements, the size of their mounts and their distinctive saddlery and he yelled with relief.

'Soldiers!'

As if in confirmation a squadron of cavalry in two neat ranks broke over the skyline with the pennants fluttering gaily on the forest of their lances.

Dirk hooting with excitement, Ruth laughing beside him and Mbejane dragging the pack-horses after them, Sean galloped standing in the stirrups and waving his hat above his head to meet them.

Unaffected by the enthusiasm of the welcome the lancers sat stolidly and watched them come and the subaltern at their head greeted Sean suspiciously as he arrived.

'Who are you, sir?' But he seemed less interested in Sean's reply than in Ruth's breeches and what they contained. During the explanations that followed Sean conceived for the man a growing dislike. Although the smooth, sun-reddened skin and the fluffy, yellow moustache aggravated this feeling, the central cause was the pair of pale blue eyes. Perhaps they always popped out that way, but Sean doubted it. They focused steadily on Sean only during the short period when Sean reported that he had made no contact with the Boer, then they swivelled back to Ruth.

'We'll not detain you longer, Lieutenant,' Sean grunted and gathered his reins to turn away.

'You are still ten miles from the Tugela River, Mr Courtney. Theoretically this area is held by the Boers and although we are well out on the flank of their main army it would be much safer if you entered the British lines under our protection.'

'Thank you, no. I want to avoid both armies and reach Pietermaritzburg as soon as possible.' The subaltern shrugged. 'The choice is yours. But if it were my wife and child . . . ' He did not finish, but turned in the saddle to signal the column forward.

'Come on, Ruth.' Sean caught her eye, but she did not move.

'I'm not going with you.' There was a flat quality in her voice and she looked away from him.

'Don't be silly.' It shocked him and gave his reply a harshness that lit sparks of anger in her eyes.

'May I travel with you?' she demanded of the subaltern.

'Well, ma'am.' He hesitated, glancing quickly at Sean before he went on. 'If your husband . . . '

'He's not my husband. I hardly know him.' She cut in and ignored the exclamation of protest from Sean. 'My husband is with your army. I want you to take me with you, please.'

'Well, now . . . ! That's a horse of another colour,' the officer drawled, but the lazy arrogance of his tone barely concealed his pleasure at the prospect of Ruth's company. 'I'd be delighted to escort you, ma'am.'

With her knees Ruth backed her mount and fell in beside the subaltern. This small manoeuvre placed her directly facing Sean – as though she were on the far side of a barrier.

'Ruth, please. Let me talk to you about this. Just a few minutes.'

'No.' There was no expression in her voice, nor in her face.

'Just to say good-bye,' he pleaded.

'We've said good-bye.' She glanced from Sean to Dirk and then away.

The subaltern raised his clenched first high and lifted his voice. 'Column! Column, Forward!' and as his big, glossy hunter started he grinned maliciously at Sean and touched the brim of his helmet in ironical salute.

'Ruth!'

But she was no longer looking at Sean. Her eyes were fixed ahead and as she swept away at the head of the column her chin was up, that smiling type of mouth was drawn into two straight lips and the thick braid of hair thumped against her back with each thrust of the horse beneath her.

'Rough luck, matey!' called a trooper from the rear rank and then they were past.

Hunched in the saddle Sean stared after them.

'Is she coming back, Pa?' Dirk inquired.

'No, she's not coming back.'

'Why not?'

Sean did not hear the question. He was watching, waiting for Ruth to look back at him. But he waited in vain, for suddenly she was gone over and beyond the next fold in the land and a few seconds later the column had followed her. Afterwards there was only the vast emptiness of the land and the sky above – as vast as the emptiness within him.

7

Sean rode ahead. Ten yards behind they followed, Mbejane restraining Dirk from a closer approach for he understood that Sean must now be left alone. Many times in the years they had been together Mbejane and Sean had travelled in this formation – Sean riding ahead with his sorrow or his shame and Mbejane trailing him patiently, waiting for Sean's shoulders to straighten and his chin to lift from where it drooped forward on his chest.

There was no coherence in Sean's thoughts, the only pattern was the rise and swoop of alternate anger and despair.

Anger at the woman, anger almost becoming hatred before the plunge of despair as he remembered she was gone. Then anger building up towards madness, this time directed at himself for letting her go. Again the sickening drop as he realized that there was no means by which he could have held her. What could he have offered her? Himself? Two hundred pounds of muscle and bones and scars supporting a face like a granite cliff? Poor value! His worldly goods? A small sack of sovereigns and another woman's child – By God, that was all he had. After thirty-seven years that was all he had to show! Once more his anger flared. A week ago he had been rich – and his anger found a new target. There was at least somewhere he could seek vengeance, there was a tangible enemy to strike, to kill. The Boer. The Boer had robbed him of his wagons and his gold, had sent him scurrying for safety; because of them the woman had come into his life and because of them she had been snatched away from him.

So be it, he thought angrily, this then is the promise of the future. War!

He straightened in the saddle, his shoulders seemed to fill out wide and square. He lifted his head and saw the shiny snake of a river in the valley below. They had reached the Tugela. Without pause Sean pushed his horse over the lip of the escarpment.

On its haunches, loose rock rolling and slithering beneath its hooves, they began the descent.

Impatiently Sean followed the river downstream, searching for a drift. But between the sheer banks it ran smooth and swift and deep, twenty yards wide and still discoloured with mud from the storm.

At the first place where the far bank flattened sufficiently to promise an easy exit from the water, Sean checked his horse and spoke brusquely.

'We'll swim.'

In reply Mbejane glanced significantly at Dirk.

'He's done this before,' Sean answered him as he dismounted and began to shed his clothing, then to the boy, 'Come on, Dirk. Get undressed.'

They drove the pack-horses in first, forcing them to jump from the steep bank and watched anxiously until their heads reappeared above the surface and they struck out for the far bank. Then all three of them naked, their clothing wrapped in oilskins and lashed to the saddles, they remounted.

'You first, Mbejane.'

A splash that rose above the bank.

'Off you go, Dirk. Remember to hang on to the saddle.'

Another high splash, and Sean flogged his mount as it baulked and danced sideways along the bank. A sudden lunge outwards and the long drop before the water closed over them.

Snorting water, they surfaced and with relief Sean saw Dirk's head bobbing beside that of his horse and heard his shouted excitement. Moments later they stood on the far bank, water streaming from their naked bodies, and laughed together at the fun of it.

Abruptly the laughter was strangled to death in Sean's throat. Lining the bank above them, grinning with the infection of merriment but with Mauser rifles held ready, stood a dozen men. Big men, bearded, festooned with bandoliers of ammunition, dressed in rough clothing and a selection of hats that included a brown derby and a tall beaver.

In imitation of Sean, both Mbejane and Dirk stopped laughing

515

and stared up at the frieze of armed men along the bank. A complete silence fell on the gathering.

It was broken at last by the man in the brown derby as he pointed at Sean with the barrel of his Mauser.

'*Magtig*! But you'd need a sharp axe to cut through that branch.'

'Don't anger him,' warned the gentleman in the beaver. 'If he hits you over the head with it, it will crack your skull!' and they all laughed.

It was hard for Sean to decide which was the more discomforting; the intimate discussion of his nudity, or the fact that the discussion was conducted in the Taal (or Cape Dutch). In his impatience he had walked, or rather swum, into the arms of a Boer patrol. There was just a forlorn hope that he might be able to bluff his way through, and he opened his mouth to make the attempt. But Dirk forestalled him.

'Who are they, Pa, and why are they laughing?' he asked in clear piping English, and Sean's hope died as abruptly as did the Boer laughter when they heard that hated language.

'Oh, So!' growled the man in the beaver, and gestured eloquently with his Mauser. 'Hands up please, my friend.'

'Will you allow me to put my trousers on first?' Sean asked politely.

'Where are they taking us?' For once Dirk was subdued and there was a quiver in his voice that touched Beaver, who rode beside him. He answered for Sean.

'Now don't you worry, you're going to see a general. A real live general.' Beaver's English was intelligible and Dirk studied him with interest.

'Will he have medals and things?'

'*Nee*, man. We don't use such rubbish.' And Dirk lost interest. He turned back to Sean.

'Pa, I'm hungry.'

Again Beaver intervened. He pulled a long black stick of biltong, dried meat, from his pocket and offered it to Dirk.

'Sharpen your teeth on that, *Kerel*.'

With his mouth full Dirk was taken care of and Sean could concentrate on the other Boers. They were convinced they had caught a spy, and were discussing the impending execution. In a friendly manner Sean was admitted to the argument, and they listened with respectful attention to his defence. This was interrupted while they forded the Tugela and climbed the escarpment once more, but Sean continued it while they rode in a bunch along the crest. Finally, he convinced them of his innocence – which they accepted with relief, as none of them were really looking forward to shooting him.

Thereafter the talk turned to more pleasant topics. It was a glorious day, sunshine lit the valley in gold and green. Below them the river twisted and sparkled, working its devious way down from the smoky blue wall of the Drakensberg that stood along the far horizon. A few fat clouds dawdled across the sky, and a light breeze took the edge off the heat.

The youngsters in the party listened avidly as Sean spoke of elephant beyond the Limpopo, and of the wide land that waited for men to claim it.

'After the war . . . ' they said, and laughed in the sun. Then a change in the wind and a freak lie of the hills brought a faint but ugly sound down to them and the laughter died.

'The guns,' said one of them.

'Ladysmith.'

Now it was Sean's turn to ask the questions. They told him how the commandos had raced down on the town of Ladysmith and rolled up the force that stood to oppose them. Bitterly they remembered how old Joubert had held his horsemen and watched while the broken English army streamed back into the town.

'Almighty! Had he loosed us on them then! We would sweep them into the sea.'

'If Oom Paul had commanded instead of old Joubert, the war would be finished already – but instead we sit and wait.'

Gradually Sean filled in the picture of the war in Natal. Ladysmith was invested. General George White's army was bottled and corked within the town. Half the Boer army had moved forward along the railway and taken up a defensive line straddling the Escarpment, overlooking the river and the tiny village of Colenso.

Below them on the great plain of the Tugela, General Buller was massing his army for the breakthrough to relieve Ladysmith.

'But let him try – Oom Paul is waiting for him.'

'Who is Oom Paul – Surely not Kruger?' Sean was puzzled. Oom Paul was the affectionate nickname of the President of the South African Republic.

'*Nee*, man! This is another Oom Paul. This one is Vecht-General Jan Paulus Leroux of the Wynberg commando.' And Sean caught his breath.

'Is he a big man with red hair and a temper to go with it?'

Laughter, and then. '*Ja*! that's the one. Do you know him?'

'Yes. I know him.'

So my brother-in-law is now a general, Sean grinned to himself, and then asked:

'Is this the general we are going to visit?'

'If we can find him.'

Young Dirk will meet his uncle at last – and Sean found himself anticipating the reunion with a tingle of pleasure.

8

The canvas of the tent did little to moderate the volume of the voice within. It carried clearly to where Sean waited with his escort.

'Must I drink coffee and shake hands with every *rooinek* we catch? Have I not already enough work for ten men, but you must bring me more? Send him to one of the Field-Cornets! Send him to Pretoria and let them lock him up! Do whatever you like with him if he is a spy – but, in the name of a merciful providence, don't bring him to me.'

Sean smiled happily. Jan Paulus certainly hadn't lost his voice. There was an interval of comparative quiet while Beaver's voice mumbled within the tent. Then again the muted bellow.

'No! I will not! Take him away.'

Sean filled his lungs, cupped his hands about his mouth and shouted at the tent.

'Hey, you bloody Dutchman! Are you afraid to meet me again? You think I'll knock your teeth out like I did last time.'

A few moments of appalling stillness, then the clattering of an overturned stool and the flap of the tent was thrown open. Into the sunlight, blinking in the glare, but scowling, the red hair that fringed his bald pate burning like a bush-fire, and his shoulders hunched aggressively, came Jan Paulus. His face turned from side to side as he searched for the source of the insult.

'Here,' called Sean, and Jan Paulus stopped dead. Uncertainly he peered at Sean.

'You!' He took a pace forward and then, 'It is you, isn't it. Sean!' And he began to laugh. His right hand that had been clenched into a huge fist unfolded and was thrust forward.

'Sean! Hell, man! Sean!'

They gripped hands and grinned at each other.

'Come into the tent. Come on in, man.'

Once they were inside, Jan Paulus's first question was:

'Where's Katrina? Where is my little sister?' and immediately the smile was gone from Sean's face. He sat down heavily on the *reimpje* stool and took off his hat before he answered.

'She's dead, Paulus. She's been dead these last four years.'

Slowly the expression on Jan Paulus's face changed until it was bleak and hard.

'How?' he asked.

And what can I answer him, thought Sean. Can I tell him she killed herself for some reason that no one will ever know.

'Fever,' he said. 'Blackwater fever.'

'You did not send word to us.'

'I did not know where to find you. Your parents –'

'They too are dead,' Jan Paulus interrupted brusquely and turned away from Sean to stare at the white canvas wall of the tent. There was silence between them then as they remembered the dead in sorrow, made more poignant by its utter helplessness. At last Sean stood up and went to the entrance of the tent.

'Dirk. Come here.'

Mbejane pushed him forward and he crossed to Sean and took his hand. Sean led him into the tent.

'Katrina's son,' he said and Jan Paulus looked down at him.

'Come here, boy.' Hesitantly Dirk went to him. Suddenly Jan Paulus dropped into a squat so that his eyes were on a level with those of the child. He took Dirk's face between the palms of his hands and studied it carefully.

'Yes,' he said. 'This is the type of son she would breed. The eyes –' His voice stumbled and stopped. A second longer he looked into Dirk's eyes. Then he spoke again.

'Be proud,' he said and stood up. Sean motioned at the flap of the tent, and thankfully Dirk scampered out to where Mbejane waited.

'And now?' Jan Paulus asked.

'I want passage through the lines.'

'You are going over to the English?'

'I am English,' said Sean. Frowning a little, Jan Paulus considered this before he asked:

'You will give me your word not to take up arms with them?'

'No,' answered Sean and Jan Paulus nodded, it as the answer he had expected.

'There is a debt between us,' he decided. 'I have not forgotten the time of the elephant. This is full payment of that debt.' He crossed to the portable desk and dipped a pen. Still standing he wrote rapidly, fanned the paper dry and proffered it to Sean.

'Go,' he said. 'And I hope we do not meet again, for next time I will kill you.'

'Or I you,' Sean answered him.

9

That afternoon Sean led his party across the steel railway bridge over the Tugela, on through the deserted village of Colenso and out again across the plain. Far ahead, sown on the grass plain like a field of white daisies, were the tents of the great British encampment at Chievely Siding. But long before he reached it Sean came to a guard post manned by a sergeant and four men of an illustrious Yorkshire regiment.

"'Ullo, Piet. And where the hell do you think you're off to?'

'I am a British subject,' Sean informed them. The sergeant ran an eye over Sean's beard and patched coat. He glanced at the shaggy pony he rode, and then considered the direction from which Sean had approached.

'Say that again,' he invited.

'I am a British subject,' Sean repeated obligingly in an accent that fell heavily on the Yorkshireman's ear.

'And I'm a ruddy Japanee,' agreed the sergeant cheerfully. 'Let's have your rifle, mate.'

Two days Sean languished in the barbed-wire prison compound while the Intelligence Department cabled the Registrar of Births at Ladyburg and waited for his reply. Two long days during which Sean brooded incessantly, not on the indignities which had been inflicted on him, but on the woman he had found and loved and lost again so quickly. These two days of enforced inactivity came at precisely the worst moment. By repeating over and over in his imagination each word that had passed between them, by feeling again each contact of their hands and bodies, by forming her face in his mind's eye and gloating over every detail of it – Sean burned her memory so deeply into himself that it was there for all time. Although he did not even know her surname, he would never forget her.

By the time he was released with apologies and given back his horses, rifle, moneybag and packs – Sean had driven himself into a mood of such overpowering depression that it could only be alleviated by liquor or physical violence.

The village of Frere, which was the first station south on the line to the coast, promised both of these.

'Take Dirk with you,' instructed Sean, 'beyond the town find a camp beside the road and make a big fire, so I can find you in the dark.'

'What will you do, Nkosi?'

Sean started towards the dingy little canteen that catered for the thirsty of Frere.

'I'm going there,' he answered.

'Come, Nkosizana.' As he and Dirk continued on down the street Mbejane was deciding how long he should give Sean before coming to fetch him. It was many years since the Nkosi had headed for a bar in such a determined fashion, but then there had been much to distress him these last few days. He will need until midnight, Mbejane decided, then he will be in a condition conducive to sleep.

From the door Sean surveyed the interior of the canteen. A single large room with a trestle bar counter along the back wall, and the room was comfortably full of warmth and men and the smell of liquor and cigars. Still standing in the entrance, Sean slipped his hand into the pocket of his trousers and surreptitiously counted his money— ten sovereigns he had allowed himself, more than sufficient for the purchase of the liquor he intended to consume.

As he worked his way through the crowd towards the bar, he looked at the men about him. Soldiers mostly, from a dozen different regiments. Colonials and Imperial troops, other ranks predominating, although a party of junior officers sat at a table against the far wall. Then there were a few civilians whom he judged to be transport drivers, contractors and business men, two women with the officers whose profession was never in doubt, and a dozen black waiters.

'What will it be, ducks?' the large woman behind the counter asked as he reached it and Sean regarded her moustache and her term of address with disfavour.

'Brandy.' He was in no mood for the niceties.

'You want the bottle, ducks?' She had recognized his need.

'That will do for a start,' he agreed.

He drank three large brandies, and with a faint dismay knew

523

that they were having no effect – apart from sharpening his imagination to the point where he could clearly see Ruth's face before his eyes, complete in every detail down to the little black beauty spot high on her cheek and the way the corners of her eyes slanted upwards as she smiled. He would have to make a more active approach to forgetfulness.

Leaning back with both elbows on the counter and the glass clutched in his right hand, he studied the men about him once more. Evaluating each of them as a source of distraction and then discarding and moving his attention on, he was finally left with the small group around the gaming-table.

Seven players, the game draw poker, and from what he could see the stakes were modest. He picked up his bottle, crossed the room to join the circle of spectators and took up his position behind a sergeant of yeomanry who was receiving a battering from the cards. A few hands later the sergeant drew one to fill his flush, missed and pushed the bluff – raising twice until he was called by two pairs across the table. He threw his hand in and blew through his lips in disgust.

'That cleans me out.' He gathered the few coins left on the table in front of him and stood up.

'Rough luck, Jack. Anyone care to take his place?' The winner looked around the circle of spectators. 'Nice friendly little game, table stakes.'

'Deal me in.' Sean sat down, placed his glass and bottle strategically at his right hand and stacked five gold sovereigns in front of him.

'The man's got gold! Welcome.'

Sean ducked the first hand, lost two pounds to three queens on the next, and won five pounds on the third. The pattern of his luck was set, he played with cold single-mindedness – and when he wanted cards it seemed he had only to wish for them.

What was the old adage? – 'Unlucky in love, and the cards turn hot.' Sean grinned without amusement and filled a small straight with the five of hearts, beat down the three sevens that came against him and drew the pot towards him to swell the pile of his winnings. Up about thirty or forty pounds. He was enjoying himself now.

'A small school, gentlemen.' Three players had dropped out in the last hour leaving four of them at the table. 'How about giving the losers a chance to recoup?'

'You want to raise the stakes?' Sean asked the speaker. He was the only other winner, a big man with a red face and the smell of horses about him. Transport rider, probably.

'Yes, if everyone agrees. Make the minimum bet five pounds.'

'Suits me,' grunted Sean, and there was a murmur of agreement round the table. With heavy money out an air of caution prevailed at first, but slowly the game opened up. Sean's luck cooled a little, but an hour later he had built up his kitty on a series of small wins to a total of seventy-five pounds. Then Sean dealt a strange hand.

The first caller on Sean's left raised before the draw, and was raised in turn by the gentleman with the horsy smell, number three called and Sean fanned his cards open.

With a gentle elation he found the seven, eight, nine and ten of Clubs – with a Diamond six. A pretty little straight dealt pat.

'Call your twenty, and raise it twenty,' he offered, and there was a small stir of excitement among the onlookers.

'Call.' Number one was short of cash.

'Call,' echoed Horse Odour and his gold clinked into the pot.

'I'm dropping.' Number three closed his cards and pushed them away. Sean turned back to number one.

'How many cards?'

'I'll play with these.' Sean felt the first premonition of disaster.

'And you?' he asked Horse Odour.

'I'm also happy with what I have.'

Two pat hands against his small straight; and from the suit distribution, Sean's four Clubs, one of them would certainly be a flush. With a queasy feeling in his stomach Sean knew he was in trouble, knew his hand to be a loser.

Break the straight and go for the other Club, still not a certain winner, but the only thing worth trying.

'I'll draw one.' He tossed the six of Diamonds into the welter of discards, and dealt to himself from the top of the pack.

'My bet.' Number one's face was glowing with confidence. 'I'll raise the maximum – another forty. Cost you eighty pounds to look at me, boys. Let's see the colour of your money.'

'I'd like to push you – but that's the limit. I'll call.' Horse Odour's expression was completely neutral but he was sweating in a light sheen across his forehead.

'Let me go to the books.' Sean picked up his cards and, from behind the other four, pressed out the corner of the card he had drawn. It was black, he opened it a little more – a black six. Slowly he felt the pressure build up within him like a freshly fired boiler. He drew a long breath and opened the card fully.

'I'll call also.' He spoke on a gusty outgoing breath.

'Full house,' shouted number one. 'Queen's full – beat that, you bastards!'

Horse Odour slapped his cards down viciously, his red face crumbling in disappointment. 'Goddam it – of all the filthy luck. I had an ace-high flush.' Number one giggled with excitement and reached for the money.

'Wait for it, friend,' Sean advised him, and spread his cards face up upon the table.

'It's a flush. My full house beats you,' protested number one.

'Count the pips –' Sean touched each card as he named them, 'six, seven, eight, nine and the ten – all Clubs. Straight flush! You come second by a day's march.' He lifted number one's hands off the money, pulled it towards him and began stacking it in columns of twenty.

'Pretty hot run of luck you're having,' Horse Odour gave his opinion, his face still twisted with disappointment.

'Yes,' agreed Sean. Two hundred and sixty-eight pounds. Very pretty.

'Funny how it comes to you on the big hands,' Horse Odour went on. 'And especially when you're dealing. What did you say your profession was?'

Without looking up Sean began transferring the stacks of sovereigns to his pockets. He was smiling a little. The end to a perfect evening, he decided.

Satisfied that the money was secure Sean looked up at Horse Odour and turned that smile full upon him.

'Come along then, laddie,' he said.

'It will be a pleasure.' Horse Odour shoved his chair back and stood up.

'It will indeed,' agreed Sean.

Horse Odour led down the back-stairs into the yard, followed by Sean and the entire clientele of the canteen. At the bottom he paused, judging Sean's footstep on the wooden stairs behind him – then he spun and hit, swinging his body into the punch.

Sean rolled his head, but it caught him on the temple and he went over backwards into the crowd behind him. As he fell he saw Horse Odour jerk back the tail of his jacket and bring out the knife. It shone dull silver in the light from the canteen windows – skinning knife, curved, eight inches of blade.

The crowd scattered leaving Sean lying on the stairs, and Horse Odour came in to kill him, making an ugly sound, bringing the knife arching down from overhead, a clumsy, unprofessional blow.

Only slightly stunned, Sean followed the silver sweep of the knife with ease and the man's wrist slapped loudly into Sean's open left hand.

For a long moment the man lay on top of Sean, his knife-arm helpless in Sean's grip, while Sean assessed his strength – and with regret realized it was no match. Horse Odour was big enough, but the belly pressed against Sean's was flabby and large, and the wrist in Sean's hands was bony without the hard rubbery give of sinew and muscle.

Horse Odour started to struggle, trying to wrestle his knife-arm free, the sweat dewed on his face and then began to drip – it had an oily, unpleasant smell like rancid butter that blended poorly with the odour of horses.

Sean tightened his grip on the man's wrist, at first using only the strength of his forearm.

'Aah!' Horse Odour stopped struggling. Sean brought in the power of his whole arm, so he could feel his shoulder muscles bunching and writhing.

'Jesus Christ!' Shrieking, as bone cracked in his wrist, Horse Odour's fingers sprang open and the knife thumped on to the wooden stairs.

Still holding him, Sean sat up, then came slowly to his feet.

'Leave us, friend.' Sean flung him backwards into the dust of the yard. He was breathing easily, still feeling cold and detached as he looked down and watched Horse Odour scrabbling to his knees, nursing his broken wrist.

Perhaps it was the man's first movement towards flight that triggered Sean – or perhaps it was the liquor he had drunk that twisted his emotions, aggravated his sense of loss and frustration and channelled it into this insane outburst of hatred.

Suddenly it seemed to Sean that here before him on the ground was the source of all his ills – this was the man who had taken Ruth from him.

'You bastard!' he growled. The man sensed the change in Sean and scrambled to his feet, his face turning desperately from side to side as he sought an avenue of escape.

'You filthy bastard!' Sean's voice rose, shrill with the strength of this new emotion. For the first time in his life Sean craved to kill. He advanced upon the man slowly, his fists opening and closing, his face contorted and the words that spilled from his mouth no longer making sense.

A great stillness had fallen upon the yard. In the shadows the watchers stood, chilled with the dreadful fascination of it. The man was frozen also, only his head moved and no sound came from his open lips – and Sean closed in with the weaving motion of a cobra in erection.

At the last moment the man tried to run, but his legs were slack and heavy with fear – and Sean hit him in the chest with a sound like an axe swung against a tree-trunk.

As he fell Sean went in after him, straddling his chest, roaring incoherently with only a single word recognizable – the name of the woman he loved. In his madness he felt the man's face breaking up under his fists, felt the warm splatter of blood thrown into his own face and on to his arms, and heard the shouts of the crowd.

'He'll kill him!'

'Get him off!'

'For Chrissake give me a hand – he's as strong as a bloody ox.'

Their hands upon him, an arm locked around his throat from behind, the shock as someone hit him with a bottle, the press of their bodies as they swarmed over him.

With men clinging to him, two of them riding his back and a dozen others on his arms and legs, Sean came to his feet.

'Pull his legs out from under him.'

'Get him down, man. Get him down.'

With a convulsive heave Sean swung the men on his arms into violent collision with each other. They released him.

He kicked his right leg free, and those on his other leg let go and scattered. Reaching over his shoulders he plucked the men off his back and stood alone, his chest swelling and subsiding as he breathed, the blood from the bottle gash in his scalp trickling down his face and soaking into his beard.

'Get a gun!' someone shouted.

'There's a shotgun under the bar.' But no one left the circle that ringed him in, and Sean glared around at them his eyes staring wildly from the plain of glistening blood that was his face.

'You've killed him!' a voice accused him. And the words reached Sean through the madness, his body relaxed slightly and he tried to wipe away the blood with the open palm of his hand. They saw the change in him.

'Cool down, mate. Fun's fun but the hell with murder.'

'Easy, now. Let's have a look what you've done to him.'

Sean looked down on the body, and he was confused and then suddenly afraid. The man was dead – he was certain of it.

'Oh, my God!' he whispered, backing away, wiping at his eyes ineffectually and smearing blood.

'He pulled a knife. Don't worry, mate, you've got witnesses.' The temper of the crowd had changed.

'No,' Sean mumbled; they didn't understand. For the first time in his life he had abused his strength, had used it to kill without purpose. To kill for the pleasure of it, to kill in the manner in which a leopard kills.

Then the man moved slightly, he rolled his head and one of his legs flexed and straightened. Sean felt hope leap within him.

'He's alive!'

'Get a doctor.'

Fearfully Sean approached and knelt beside the man, he unknotted the scarf from around his own throat and cleaned the bloody mouth and nostrils.

'He'll be all right – leave him to the Doc.'

The doctor came, a lean and laconic man chewing tobacco. In the yellow light of a hurricane lamp he examined and prodded while they crowded close about him craning to see over his shoulders. At last the doctor stood up.

'All right. He can be moved. Carry him up to my surgery.' Then he looked at Sean. 'Did you do it?'

Sean nodded.

'Remind me not to annoy you.'

'I didn't mean to – it just sort of happened.'

'Is that so?' The doctor shot a stream of yellow tobacco juice into the dust of the yard. 'Let's have a look at your head.' He pulled Sean's head down to his own level and parted the sodden black hair.

'Nicked a vein. Doesn't need a stitch. Wash it and a little iodine.'

'How much, Doc, for the other fellow?' Sean asked.

'You paying?' The doctor looked at him quizzically.

'Yes.'

'Broken jaw, broken collar-bone, about two dozen stitches and a few days in bed for concussion,' he mused, adding it up. 'Say two guineas.'

Sean gave him five. 'Look after him, Doc.'

'That's my job.' And he followed the men who were carrying Horse Odour out of the yard.

'Guess you need a drink, mister. I'll buy you one,' someone offered. The whole world loves a winner.

'Yes,' agreed Sean. 'I need a drink.'

Sean had more than one drink. When Mbejane came to fetch him at midnight he had a deal of difficulty getting Sean up on to the back of the horse. Half-way to the camp Sean slid off and subsided into the road, so Mbejane loaded him sideways – head and arms hanging over to port and legs dangling starboard.

'It is possible that tomorrow you will regret this,' Mbejane told him primly as he unloaded him beside the fire and rolled him still booted and bloody into his blanket.

He was correct.

10

In the dawn as Sean cleaned his face with a cloth dipped in a mug of hot water, regarding its reflection in the small metal mirror, the only fact that gave him the faintest satisfaction was the two hundred-odd sovereigns he had salvaged from the night's debauch.

'Are you sick, Pa?' Dirk's ghoulish interest in Sean's condition added substantially to his evil temper.

'Eat your breakfast.' Sean's tone was calculated by its sheer malevolence to dry up further questioning.

'There is no food.' Mbejane fell into the familiar role of protector.

'Why not?' Sean focused his bloodshot eyes upon him.

'There is one among us who considers the purchase of strong drink, and other things, more important than food for his son.'

From the pocket of his jacket Sean drew a handful of sovereigns. 'Go!' he ordered. 'Buy food and fresh horses. Go quickly so that in my grave illness I may not be afflicted with the wisdom of your counsel. Take Dirk with you.'

Mbejane examined the money, and grinned.

'The night was not wasted.'

When they had gone back to Frere, Dirk trotting beside the huge half-naked Zulu and his voice only fading at a distance of a hundred yards, Sean poured himself another mug of coffee and cupping it in his hands he sat staring into the ash and pink coals of the fire. He could trust Mbejane to use the money with care, he had the bargaining patience peculiar to his race that could if necessary devote two days to the purchase of a single ox. These things did not concern Sean now. Instead he went over the events of the previous night. Still sickened by his display of murderous rage, he tried to justify it. Taking into account the loss of nearly all he owned, the accumulation of years of hard work that had been stripped from him in a single day; the hardship and uncertainty that had followed. And finally he had reached the flash point when liquor and poker-tensed nerves had snapped the last reserve in him and translated it all into that violent outburst.

But that was not all, he knew he had avoided the main issue. *Ruth.* As he came back to her a wave of hopeless longing overwhelmed him, a tender despair such as he had never experienced before. He groaned aloud, and lifted his eyes to the morning star which was fading on the pink horizon as the sun came up behind.

For a while longer he wallowed in the softness of his love, remembering the way she walked, the dark serenity of her eyes and her mouth when she smiled and her voice when she sang – until it threatened to smother him in its softness.

Then he sprang to his feet and paced restlessly in the grass beside the fire. We must leave this place, ride away from it – go quickly. I must find something to do, some way to keep from thinking of it, something to fill my hands which ache now from the need to hold her.

Along the road, going north to Colenso, a long column of infantry filed past him in the dawn. He stopped his pacing and watched them. Each man leaned forward against his pack and the rifles stood up behind their shoulders.

Yes, he thought, I will go with them. Perhaps at the place to which they march I can find what I could not find last night. We will go home to Ladyburg, riding hard on fresh horses. I will leave Dirk with my mother, then come back to this war.

He began to pace again impatiently. Where the hell was Mbejane?

From the heights above, Sean looked down on Ladyburg. The village spread in a neat circle around the spire of the church. He remembered the spire as beacon-bright in its cladding of new copper, but nineteen years of weather had dulled it to a mellow brown.

Nineteen years. It did not seem that long. There were goods yards around the station now, a new concrete bridge over the Baboon Stroom, the blue gums in the plantation beyond the school were taller, and the flamboyants that had lined the main street were gone.

With a strange reluctance Sean turned his head and looked out to the right, across the Baboon Stroom, close in against the escarpment, to where he had left the sprawling Dutch gabled homestead of Theuniskraal with its roof of combed yellow thatch and the shutters of yellow-wood across the windows.

It was there, but not as he remembered it. Even at this distance he could see the walls were flaking and mottled with patches of dampness; the thatch was shaggy as the coat of an airedale; one of the shutters tilted slightly from a broken hinge; the lawns were brown and ragged where the bare earth showed through. The dairy behind the house had crumbled, its roof gone and the remains of its walls jutted forlornly upwards to the height of a man's shoulder.

'Damn the little bastard!' Sean's anger flared abruptly as he saw the neglect with which his twin brother had treated the lovely old house. 'He's so lazy he wouldn't get out of a bed he'd peed in.'

To Sean it was not just a house. It was the place his father had built, which had sheltered Sean on the day of his birth and through the years of his childhood. When his father died under the Zulu spears at Isandlawana, half the farm and the house had belonged to Sean; he had sat in the study at nights with the logs burning in the stone fireplace and the mounted buffalo head above it throwing distorted, moving shadows up on to the plaster ceiling. Although he had given his share away – yet it was still his home. Garry, his brother, had no right to let it decay and fall apart this way.

'Damn him!' Sean voiced his thoughts out loud – then almost immediately his conscience rebuked him. Garry was a cripple, his lower leg shot away by the blast of a careless shotgun. And Sean had fired that shotgun. Will I never be free of that guilt, how long must my penance continue? He protested at the goad of his conscience.

That is not your only trespass against your brother, his conscience reminded him. Who sired the child he calls his son? Whose loins sowed the seed that became man-child in the belly of Anna, your brother's wife?

'It has been a long time, Nkosi.' Mbejane had seen the expression on his face as Sean looked towards Theuniskraal and remembered those things from the past that were better forgotten.

'Yes.' Sean roused himself, and straightened in the saddle. 'A long road and many years. But now we are home again.'

He looked back towards the village, searching the quarter beyond the main street and the hotel for the roof of that little cottage on Protea Street. As he found it, showing through the tall, fluffy blue gum trees, there was a lift in his mood, a new excitement. Did she live there still? How would she look – a little grey surely; had her fifty years marked her deeply, or had they treated her with the same consideration which she showed all those with whom *she* came in contact? Had she forgiven him for leaving without a farewell? Had she forgiven his long years of silence since then? Did she understand the reasons why he had never written – no word or message, except that anonymous gift of ten thousand pounds he had transferred to her bank account. Ten thousand miserable little pounds, which he had hardly noticed among all the millions he had won and lost in those days long ago when he was one of the lords of the Witwatersrand goldfields.

Again the sense of guilt closed in upon him. As he knew with utter certainty that she *had* understood, that she *had* forgiven. For that was Ada, the woman who was his stepmother – and whom he loved beyond the natural love one owes their own full-blooded mother.

'Let's go down,' he said and kicked his horse to a canter.

'Is this home, Pa?' Dirk shouted as he rode beside him.

'Yes, my boy. This is home.'

'Will Gran'ma be here?'

'I hope so,' Sean answered, and then softly, 'Beyond all other things, I hope that she will.'

Over the bridge above the Baboon Stroom, past the cattle-pens alongside the line of rail, past the old wood and iron station buildings with the sign, white and black faded to grey, 'Ladyburg. Altitude 2,256 ft. above sea level', swinging left into the dusty main street which was wide enough to turn a full span of oxen, and down to Protea Street rode Sean and Dirk, with Mbejane and the pack-mule trailing far behind.

At the corner Sean checked his mount to a walk, drawing out the last few minutes of anticipation until they stopped outside the wicket fence of white that encompassed the cottage. The garden was neat and green, gay with beds of Barberton daisies and blue rhododendrons. The cottage had been enlarged, a new room built on the far side, and it was crisp-looking in a coat of new whitewash. A sign at the gate said in gold letters on a green ground.

> 'Maison Ada.
> High-class Costumier'

Sean grinned. 'The old girl's gone all French, by God.' Then to Dirk, 'Stay here!'

He swung down from his horse, handed the reins to Dirk and went through the gate. At the door he paused self-consciously and adjusted his cravat. He glanced down at the severe dark broadcloth suit and new boots which he had purchased in Pietermaritzburg, slapped the dust from his breeches, stroked his newly trimmed beard into place, gave his moustache a twirl and knocked on the door.

It was opened at last by a young lady. Sean did not recognize her. But the girl reacted immediately, flushing slightly, attempting to pat her hair into place without drawing attention to its disarray, trying to dispose of the sewing in her hands, and exhibiting all the signs of confusion peculiar to the unmarried female who finds herself suddenly and unexpectedly in the presence of a large, well-dressed and attractive male. But Sean felt a twinge of pity as he looked at her scarred face, ugly with the purple cicatrice of acne.

Sean lifted his hat. 'Is Mrs Courtney here?'

'She's in the workroom, sir. Who shall I tell her is calling?'

'Don't tell her anything – it's a surprise,' Sean smiled at her, and she lifted her hands self-consciously in an attempt to mask the ruin of her face.

'Won't you come in, sir?' She turned her head aside, shyly – as though to hide it.

'Who is it, Mary?' Sean started at the voice from the depths of the cottage, it hadn't changed at all – and the years dropped away.

'It's a gentleman, Aunt Ada. He wants to see you.'

'I'm coming. Ask him to sit down, and please bring us coffee, Mary.'

Mary escaped thankfully and left Sean standing alone in the

535

small sitting-room, twisting his hat in big brown hands, staring up at the daguerreotype print of Waite Courtney above the mantel. Although he did not recognize the fact, the face of his father in the picture was almost his own – the same eyes under heavy black brows, the same arrogance about the mouth, even the identical thrust of stubbornness in the jaw beneath the thick spade-shaped beard – and the big, hooked Courtney nose.

The door from the work-room opened and Sean swung quickly to face it. Ada Courtney came through it smiling, until she saw him, then she stopped and the smile died on her lips and she paled. Uncertainly her hand lifted to her throat and she made a small choking sound.

'Dear God,' she whispered.

'Ma.' Sean fidgeted his feet awkwardly. 'Hello, Ma. It's good to see you.'

'Sean.' The colour flooded back into her cheeks. 'For a moment I thought – you're grown so much like your father. Oh, Sean!' And she ran to him. He tossed his hat on to the sofa and caught her around the waist as she came.

'I've waited for you. I knew you'd come.'

Sean scooped her up and kissed her into a confusion of joy and laughter, swinging her while he did it, laughing himself.

'Put me down,' Ada gasped at last, and when he did she clung to him.

'I knew you'd come back. At first there were bits in the newspaper about you, and people told me things – but these last years there has been nothing, nothing at all.'

'I'm sorry.' Sean sobered.

'You're a bad boy.' She was sparkling with excitement, her hair had escaped from its bun and a wisp of it hung down her cheek. 'But it's so good to have you back –' and suddenly she was crying.

'Don't, Ma. Please don't.' He had never seen her cry before.

'It's just that . . . It's the surprise.' She brushed impatiently at her tears. 'It's nothing.'

Desperately Sean sought something to distract her. 'Hey!' he exclaimed with relief, 'I've another surprise for you.'

'Later,' she protested, 'One at a time.'

'This won't wait.' He led her to the door and out on to the front stoep with his arm around her shoulders.

'Dirk,' he shouted. 'Come here.'

He felt her standing very still as they watched Dirk coming up the garden walk.

'This is your Gran'ma.' He introduced them.

'Why is she crying?' Dirk eyed her with frank curiosity.

Later they sat at the table in the kitchen while Ada and Mary plied them with food. Ada Courtney believed that the first thing to do with a man was feed him.

Mary was almost as excited as Ada, she had taken full advantage of the few minutes she had been alone, and now her hair was freshly brushed and she wore a gay new apron, but the powder with which she had tried to cover the terrible disfiguration of the skin served only to call attention to it. In sympathy Sean refrained from looking at her, and Mary noticed. Shyly she devoted herself to winning Dirk's attention. She fussed over him quietly – and Dirk accepted this as the natural order of things.

While they ate Sean filled in the missing years for Ada with a brief outline of his activities, glossing over the death of Dirk's mother, and other things of which he had no reason to be proud. He came to the end of it.

'And so here we are.

> "Home is the sailor, home from the sea,
> And the hunter home from the hill."

Dirk, don't put so much in your mouth and keep it closed when you chew.'

'How long will you stay? Mary, see if there are any cream-puffs in the jar – Dirk is still hungry,' said Ada.

'You'll make him sick. I don't know; not long though – there's a war on.'

'You're going to join?'

'Yes.'

'Oh, Sean. Must you?' Knowing that he must. While he selected a cheroot from his case Sean studied her closely for the first time. There was grey now as he had known there would be, almost as much grey as black; long streaks of it across her temples and the texture of her skin had altered, losing the moisture of youth, drying out so that it creased around the eyes and stretched tight across her hands to show the knuckles more prominently and the blueness of veins beneath it. She was plumper also, her bosom was full and round, each breast having lost its separate identity in the whole.

Yet the other qualities whose memories he had treasured so long ago still persisted, seemed indeed to have grown stronger; the composure which showed in the stillness of her hands and body, yet was given the lie by the humour that hovered around her lips; the eyes whose depths held compassion and a sure understanding of those things they looked upon. But mostly it was the indefinable aura of goodness about her – looking at her, he sensed again that behind those eyes no destructive thought could live for long.

Sean lit the cheroot and spoke while the smoke masked his face.

'Yes, Ma. I must go.'

And Ada, whose husband had ridden to war also, and not ridden home, could not prevent the sadness showing for an instant in her eyes.

'Yes. I suppose you must. Garry has gone already – and Michael has been agitating to follow him.'

'Michael?' Sean fired the question.

'Garry's son – he was born a short while after – after you left Ladyburg. He will be eighteen this winter.'

'What's he like?' Sean's voice was too eager. Michael – so that is what my son is named. My first-born. By God, my first-born, and I didn't even know his name until he was almost fully grown. Ada was looking at him with her own question unasked in her eyes.

'Mary, take Dirk through to the bathroom please. Try and get a little of that food from around his mouth.' When they had gone she answered Sean's question.

'He's a tall boy, tall and lean. Dark like his mother, but a serious lad. He doesn't laugh much. Always top of his class. I like him very much. He comes here often.' She was silent for a moment, then, 'Sean . . .'

Quickly Sean cut in. 'And how is Garry?' He sensed what she was going to ask.

'Garry has not changed very much. He has had a run of bad luck . . . Poor Garry, things have been bad on the farm. The rinder-pest ravaged his herds, he had to borrow money from the bank.' She hesitated an instant. 'And he is drinking a lot these days. I can't be sure of it – he never visits the hotel and I have never seen him take a drink. But it must be that.'

'I'll find out where he is when I go up to Colenso.'

'You'll have no difficulty finding him. Garry is a lieutenant-colonel on the General's staff. He was given promotion from major last week, and he has been awarded the Distinguished Service Order to go with his Victoria Cross. He is in charge of liaison between the Imperial and the Colonial troops.'

'Good God!' Sean was stunned. 'Garry a colonel!'

'General Buller thinks very highly of him. The General is also a holder of the Victoria Cross.'

'But,' Sean protested. 'You know how Garry got that decoration. It was a mistake. If Garry is on the General's staff – then Lord have mercy on the British Army!'

'Sean, you mustn't talk about your brother that way.'

'Colonel Garrick Courtney.' Sean laughed out loud.

'I don't know what there is between you and Garry. But it's something very nasty – and I don't want any of it in this house.' Ada's tone was fierce and Sean stopped laughing.

'I'm sorry.'

'Before we close the subject, I want to warn you. Please be very careful how you handle Garry. Whatever happened between you two – and I don't want to know what it is – Garry still hates you. Once or twice he started talking about you but I stopped him. Yet I know it from Michael – the boy has picked it up from his father. It's almost an obsession with him. Be careful of Garry.'

Ada stood up. 'And now about Dirk. What a lovely child he is, Sean. But I'm afraid you've spoiled him a little.'

'He's a tiger,' Sean admitted.

'What schooling has he been given?'

'Well, he can read a little –'

'You'll leave him here with me. I'll enrol him when the school term begins.'

'I was going to ask. I'll leave money with you.'

'Ten years ago there was a very large and mysterious deposit to my bank account. It wasn't mine – so I placed it out at interest.' She smiled at him and Sean looked guilty. 'We can use that.'

'No,' he said.

'Yes,' she contradicted. 'And now tell me when you are leaving.'

'Soon.'

'How soon?'

'Tomorrow.'

II

Since climbing the World's View road out of Pietermaritzburg, Sean and Mbejane had travelled in sunshine and in companionship. The feelings between them were solid, compacted by time and the pressure of trouble and shared laughter into a shield of affection – so that now they were happy as only men can be together. The jokes were old jokes, and the responses almost automatic – but the excitement between them was new, in the same way that each day's sun is new. For they were riding to war, to another meeting with death, so that everything else lost significance. Sean felt free, the thoughts and relationships with other people which had weighed him down over the past months slipped away. Like a ship clear for action he hurried with a new lightness to meet his chance.

At the same time he could stand aside from himself and grin tolerantly at his own immaturity. By God, we're like a couple of kids sneaking out of school. Then, following the thought further – he was suddenly thankful. Thankful that this was so; thankful that there was still this capacity to forget everything else and approach the moment in childlike anticipation. For a while this new habit of self-appraisal asserted itself; I am no longer young and I have learned much, gathered it brick by brick along the way and trimmed each brick and cemented it into the wall. The fortress of my manhood is not yet completed, but what I have built so far is strong. Yet the purpose of a fortress is to protect and hold safely those things that are precious; if, during the building, a man loses and expends those things which he wishes to protect, then the finished fortress is a mockery. I have not lost it all, a little I have used in barter. I have traded a little faith for the knowledge of evil; exchanged a little laughter for the understanding of death; a measure of freedom for two sons (and this was a good trade) – but I know there is still something left.

At his side Mbejane noticed the change of Sean's mood, and he moved in front of it to turn it once more into the sunshine.

'Nkosi, we must hurry if you wish to reach your drinking-place at Frere.'

With an effort Sean thrust his thoughts aside, and laughed. They rode on into the north, and on the third day they reached Chievely.

Sean remembered his innocent amazement when, as a youth, he had joined Lord Chelmsford's column at Rorke's Drift at the beginning of the Zulu War. He had believed then no greater accumulation of men was possible. Now he looked out across the encampment of the British Army before Colenso and smiled; Chelmsford's little force would have been lost in the artillery and ordnance park, yet beyond that the tents stretched away for two miles. Row upon row of white canvas cones with the horse lines in between – and to the rear the orderly acres of transport vehicles, thousands of them, with the draught animals scattered grazing across the veld almost to the range of the eye.

It was an impressive sight not only in its immensity but also in its neat and businesslike layout; so was the military precision of the blocks of men at drill, the massed glitter of their bayonets as they turned and marched and countermarched.

When Sean wandered into the camp and read the names of the regiments at the head of each row of tents he recognized them as the sound of glory. But the new khaki uniforms and pith helmets had reduced them all to a homogeneous mass. Only the cavalry retained a little of the magic in the pennants that fluttered gaily at their lance-tips. A squadron trotted past him and Sean eyed their mounts with envy. Great shiny beasts, as arrogant as the men upon their backs. Horse and rider given an air of inhuman cruelty by the slender bright-tipped lance they carried.

A dozen times Sean asked his question, 'Where can I find the Guides,' and though the answer was given in the dialects of Manchester and Lancashire, in the barely intelligible accents of Scotland and Ireland, each had a common factor – they were all singularly unhelpful.

Once he stopped to watch a group training with one of the new Maxim machine-guns. Clumsy, he decided, no match against a rifle. Later he would remember this judgement and feel a little foolish.

All morning he trudged through the camp, with Mbejane trailing him, and at noon he was tired and dusty and bad-tempered. The Natal Corps of Guides appeared to be a mythical unit. He stood on the edge of the camp and looked out across the open veld, pondering his next move in the search.

Half a mile out on the grassy plain a thin drift of blue smoke caught his eye. It issued from a line of bush that obviously marked the course of a stream. Whoever had picked that spot to camp certainly knew how to make himself comfortable in the veld. Compared to the bleak surroundings of the main encampment it would be paradise; protected from the wind, close to firewood and water, well away from the attention of senior officers. That was his answer, Sean grinned and set out across the plain.

His guess was proved correct by the swarm of black servants among the trees. These could only be Colonial troops, each with a personal retainer. Also, the wagons were drawn up in the circular formation of the laager. With a feeling of homecoming Sean approached the first white man he saw.

In an enamel hipbath beneath the shade of a mimosa tree this gentleman sat, waist deep, while a servant added hot water from a large black kettle.

'Hello,' Sean greeted him. The man looked up from his book, removed the cheroot from his mouth and returned Sean's greeting.

'I'm looking for the Guides.'

'Your search is ended, my friend. Sit down.' Then to the servant, 'Bring the Nkosi a cup of coffee.'

Thankful, Sean sank into the *reimpje* chair near the bath and stretched his legs out before him. His host laid aside the book and began to lather his hairy chest and armpits while he studied Sean with frank appraisal.

'Who's in charge here?' Sean asked.

'You want to see him?'

'Yes.'

The bather opened his mouth and yelled.

'Hey! Tim!'

'What you want?' The reply came from the nearest wagon.

'Fellow here to see you.'

'What's *he* want?'

'Says he wants to talk to you about his daughter.'

There was a long silence while the man in the wagon digested this, then:

'What's he look like?'

'Big bloke, with a shotgun.'

'You're joking!'

'The hell I am! Says if you don't come out he's coming in to get you.'

The canvas of the wagon canopy was lifted cautiously and an eye showed behind the slit. The ferocious bellow that followed startled Sean to his feet. The canvas was thrown aside and out of the wagon vaulted the Commanding Officer of the Guides. He moved in on Sean with his arms held like a wrestler. For a moment Sean stared at him, then he answered the bellow and dropped into a defensive crouch.

'Yaah!' The man charged and Sean met him chest to chest, locking his arms around him as they closed.

'Tim Curtis, you miserable bastard,' he roared in laughter and in pain as Tim tried to pull his beard out by the roots.

'Sean Courtney, you evil son of a bitch,' breathless as the air was forced from his lungs by Sean's hug.

'Let's have a drink.' Sean punched him.

'Let's have a bottle.' Tim caught his ears and twisted.

At last they broke apart and stood laughing incoherently in the pleasure of meeting again.

The servant returned with Sean's coffee and Tim waved him away disgustedly. 'None of that slop! Get a bottle of brandy out of my chest.'

'You two know each other, I presume.' The man in the bath interrupted them.

'Know each other! Jesus, I worked five years for him!' snorted Tim. 'Digging his dirty gold out of the ground. Worst boss I ever had.'

'Well, now's your chance,' Sean grinned, 'because I've come to work for you.'

'You hear that, Saul? The idiot wants to join.'

'*Mazeltov.*' The bather dunked the tip of his cheroot in his bath water, flicked it away and stood up. He offered Sean a soapy hand.

'Welcome to the legion of the lost. My name's Saul Friedman. I gather yours is Sean Courtney. Now where's that bottle and we'll celebrate your arrival.'

The commotion had summoned the others from their wagons and Sean was introduced to each of them. It seemed the uniform of the Guides was a khaki tunic without insignia or badges of rank, slouch hats and riding breeches. There were ten of them. A tough-looking bunch and Sean found their company to his liking.

Naked except for a towel draped round his waist, Saul did duty as barman, then they all settled down in the shade to a bout of drinking. Tim Curtis entertained them for the first twenty minutes with a biographical and biological account of Sean's career, to which Saul contributed comments that were met with roars of laughter. It was obvious that Saul was the Company wit, a function which he performed with distinction. He was the youngest of them all, perhaps twenty-five years old, and physically the smallest. His body was thin and hairy, and in a pleasant sort of way he was extremely ugly. Sean liked him.

An hour later when the brandy had taken them to the stage of seriousness which precedes wild and undirected hilarity, Sean asked,

'Captain Curtis . . . '

'Lieutenant, and don't forget it,' Tim corrected him.

'Lieutenant, then. What is our job, and when do we do it?'

Tim scowled at his empty glass, then looked across at Saul. 'Tell him,' he instructed.

'As mentioned earlier, we are the legion of the lost. People look on us with pity and a mild embarrassment. They pass us by on the far side of the street, making the sign of the Cross and murmuring a spell to avert the evil eye. We live here in our own little leper colony.'

'Why?'

'Well, first of all, we belong to the most miserable little runt in the entire army of Natal. An officer, who, despite a formidable array of medals, would not inspire confidence in a young ladies' choir. He is chief liaison officer for the Colonial troops on the general staff. Lieutenant-Colonel Garrick Courtney, V.C., D.S.O.' Saul paused and his expression changed. 'No relation of yours, I trust?'

'No,' lied Sean without hesitation.

'Thank God,' Saul continued. 'Anyway, this is why people pity us. The embarrassment arises from the fact that nobody recognizes our official existence. Even the drawing of rations must be preceded by a comic opera dialogue between Tim and the Quartermaster. But because we are called "Guides" everybody expects us to get out there and start doing a bit of guiding. So in some weird fashion the failure of General Buller to advance even one hundred yards in three months is laid at our door.' Saul filled his glass. 'Anyway, we haven't run out of brandy yet.'

'You mean we don't do anything?' Sean asked incredulously.

'We eat, we sleep and we drink.'

'Occasionally we go visiting,' Tim added. 'Now is as good a time as any.'

'Who do we visit?'

'There is a most enterprising woman in the area, not five miles distant. She owns a travelling circus – forty wagons and forty girls. They follow along behind the main army to comfort and encourage it. Let's go and get some comfort and encouragement. If we start now we'll get to the head of the line – first come, first served.'

'I'll leave you to it,' Saul stood up and drifted away.

'He's a good kid,' Tim observed as he watched him leave.

'Is it against his religion?'

'No. But he's married and takes it seriously. How about you?'

'I'm not married.'

'Let's go them.'

Much later they rode home together in the moonlight, both pleasantly melancholy with love and liquor. The girl who had taken Sean to her wagon was a friendly lass with a pair of fat maternal bosoms.

'I like you, mister,' she had told him afterwards.

'I like you also,' he replied truthfully.

Although Sean experienced no more shame or guilt than after satisfying any of his other bodily needs, yet he knew that half an hour with a stranger in a wagon bed was a very poor substitute.

He began to hum the tune that Ruth had sung on the night of the storm.

12

Lieutenant-Colonel Garrick Courtney removed his uniform jacket and hung it carefully on the dumb-valet beside his desk. The way a houseproud wife straightens a picture on her wall, he touched the purple watered silk on which was suspended the heavy, bronze cross, until it hung to his satisfaction. His lips moving, he read the inscription again. 'For Valour', and smiled.

The champagne he had drunk during lunch made his brain feel like a great brilliant diamond set in his skull, sharp and hard and clear.

He sat down, swivelled the chair sideways to the desk and stretched his legs out in front of him.

'Send him in, Orderly!' he shouted, and dropped his eyes to his boots. You couldn't tell the difference, he decided. No one could tell by looking at them which one was flesh and bone beneath the polished leather – or which leg was carved wood with a cunningly articulated ankle.

'Sir.' The voice startled him and he pulled his legs in guiltily, hiding them beneath his chair.

'Curtis!' He looked up at the man who stood before his desk. Tim stood rigidly to attention, staring stolidly over Garry's head, and Garry let him stand. He felt satisfaction that this hulking bastard must use those two powerful legs to pay respect to Garrick Courtney. Let him stand. He waited, watching him, and at last Tim fidgeted slightly and cleared his throat.

'At ease!' There was no doubt now as to who held the power. Garry picked up the paper-knife from his desk and turned it in his hands as he spoke.

'You're wondering why I sent for you.' He smiled expansively. 'Well, the reason is that I have a job for you at last. I lunched with General Buller today.' He paused to let that absorb. 'We discussed the Offensive. He wanted my views on certain plans he has in mind.' Garry caught himself. 'Anyway, that is beside the point. I want you and your men to reconnoitre the river on both sides of Colenso. See here.' Garry spread a map on the desk in front of him. 'There are fords marked here and here.' He jabbed at the map with the paper-knife. 'Find them and mark them well. Check the bridges – both the railway and the road bridge, make certain they are intact. Do it tonight. I want your full report in the morning. You can go.'

'Yes, sir.'

'Oh, Curtis –' Garry stopped him as he stooped in the entrance of the tent. 'Don't fail. Find those fords.' The canvas flap dropped closed behind the American, and Garry opened the drawer of his desk and took out a silver flask set with carnelians. He unscrewed it and sniffed the contents before he drank.

With the dawn, in bedraggled pairs the Guides dribbled into camp. Sean and Saul were the last to return. They dismounted, turned their horses over to the servants and joined the group around the fire.

'Yes?' Tim looked up from where he squatted with a mug of coffee cupped in his hands. His clothing was soaked and steam lifted off it as it dried in the heat from the flames. 'They've blown the rail bridge – but the road bridge is still intact.'

'You're sure?'

'We walked across.'

'That's something anyway,' grunted Tim, and Sean raised a sceptical eyebrow.

'You think so. Hasn't it occurred to you that they've left the bridge because that is where they *want* us to cross?'

No one replied and Sean went on wearily:

'When we checked the bridges, Saul and I did a bit of exploring on the far side. Just beyond the railway bridge there is a series of little kopjes. We crawled around the bottom of them.'

'And?'

'There are more Boers sitting on those kopjes than there are quills on a porcupine's back. Whoever tries to cross those bridges in daylight is going to get the Bejesus shot out of him.'

'Lovely thought!' growled Tim.

'Charming, isn't it? Further contemplation of it will make me puke. What did you find?'

'We found plenty of water.' Tim glanced down at his sodden clothing. 'Deep water.'

'No ford,' Sean anticipated gloomily.

'None. But we found a ferryboat on the bank with the bottom knocked out of it. That could be the excuse for marking a ford on the map.'

'So now you can go and tell our beloved Colonel the glad tidings.' Saul grinned. 'But one gets you five that it has no effect. My guess is that Buller will attack Colenso within the next two days. He might just be able to get a couple of thousand men across that bridge, then we'd have a chance.'

Tim regarded him balefully. 'And the Guides will be the first across. All very well for you. The Rabbi has reduced your target area considerably – but what about us?'

'But it's marked on the map,' protested Lieutenant-Colonel Garrick Courtney. His head was bowed so that Tim could see the pink scalp through the furrows the comb had left in his sandy-brown hair.

'I've seen dragons and sea monsters marked on maps, sir,' Tim answered, and Garry looked up at him coldly with pale blue eyes.

'You're not paid to be a comedian, Curtis.'

'I beg your pardon, sir,' and Garry frowned. Curtis could make the 'sir' sound like an insult.

'Who did you send?' he demanded.

'I went myself, sir.'

'You could have missed it in the dark.'

'If there is a ford there, it would have a road or at least a path leading down to it. I wouldn't have missed that, sir.'

'But in the darkness you could have been mistaken,' insisted Garry. 'You might have missed something that would be obvious in daylight.'

'Well, sir . . . '

'Good.' Briskly Garry went on. 'Now, the bridges. You say these are still intact.'

'Only the road bridge, but . . . '

'But what?'

'The men I sent report that the hills beyond the river are

heavily defended. Almost as though the bridge has been preserved to bait a trap.'

'Curtis.' Deliberately Garry laid his paper-knife upon the map before him. His nose was too large for the space between his eyes and when he pursed his lips this way he looked, Tim thought, like a bird – a sparrow, a little brown sparrow.

'Curtis,' Garry repeated softly. 'It seems to me you have very little enthusiasm for this business. I send you out to do a job and you come back with a long list of excuses. I don't think you realize how important this is.'

Chirp, chirp – little sparrow. Tim smiled secretly and Garry flushed.

'For instance. Who did you send to reconnoitre these bridges – reliable men, I hope?'

'They are, sir.'

'Who?'

'Friedman.'

'Oh! The little Jewish lawyer. A wise choice, Curtis, a commendably wise choice.' Garry sniffed and picked up the paper-knife.

My God! Curtis marvelled. *He's a Jew-baiter as well, this little sparrow has all the virtues.*

'Who else did you send?'

'A new recruit.'

'A new recruit? A new recruit!' Garry dropped the knife and lifted his hands in appeal.

'I happen to have worked for him before the war. I know him well, sir. He's a first-class man. I'd trust him before anyone else you could name. In fact, I was going to ask you to approve his promotion to sergeant.'

'And what is the name of this paragon?'

'Funnily enough it's the same as yours, sir. Although he tells me you're not related. His name is Courtney. Sean Courtney.'

Slowly, very slowly, the expression of Garry's face altered. It became smooth, neutral. Pale also, the lifeless, translucent paleness of a corpse's face. All life died in his eyes as well – they were looking inwards, back into the secret places of long ago. The dark places. They saw a small boy climbing a hill.

He was climbing up through thick bush, young legs strong beneath him. Climbing in deep shade, with the smell of leaf-mould and the soft murmur of insects, sweating in the heat of

550

a Natal summer's morning, eyes straining ahead through the dense green foliage for a glimpse of the bush buck they were hunting, the dog leaning eagerly against the leash and the same eagerness pumping in his own chest.

The dog barked once, and immediately the brush and stir of a big body moving ahead of them, the click of a hoof against rock, then the rush of its run.

The shot, a blunt burst of sound, and the buck bleating wounded as it thrashed through the grass, and Sean's voice high and unbroken: 'I got him. I got him first shot! Garry. Garry! I got him, I got him!'

Into the sunlight, the dog dragging him. Sean wild with excitement, running down the slope towards him with the shotgun. Sean falling, the gun flung from his hands, the roar of the second shot and the blow that knocked Garry's leg out from under him.

Sitting now in the grass and staring at the leg. The little white splinters of bone in the pulped flesh and the blood pumping dark and strong and thick as custard.

'I didn't mean it . . . Oh God, Garry, I didn't mean it. I slipped. Honest, I slipped.'

Garry shuddered, a violent almost sensual spasm of his whole body, and the leg beneath the desk twitched in sympathy.

'Are you all right, sir?' There was an edge of concern on Tim's voice.

'I am perfectly well, thank you, Curtis.' Garry smoothed back the hair from his temples. There were deep bays of baldness there and his hairline was frayed and irregular. 'Please continue.'

'Well, I was saying – it looks like a trap. They've left those bridges because . . . '

'It is your duty to collect information, Curtis. It is the duty of the general staff to evaluate it. I think that completes your report? Good, then you may leave.'

He must have a drink now, already his hand was on the handle of the drawer.

'Oh, Curtis.' His voice croaked with the terrible dryness in his throat, but he spoke on through it. 'That promotion you spoke of is approved. Make the man a sergeant.'

'Very well, sir.'

'Of course, in the event of a frontal assault on the bridges he will act as guide for the first attack.'

'Sir?'

'You see the need for it, don't you?' Tim had never heard this wheedling tone from him before. It was almost as though he wanted Tim's approval. As though he were trying to justify his decision. 'I mean, he knows the bridges. He's been over them. He's the one who knows them, isn't he?'

'Yes, sir.'

'And after all, he's a sergeant. I mean, we should send someone with rank – we can't just send anybody.'

'I could go, sir.'

'No. No. We'll need you at the ford.'

'As you wish.'

'You won't forget, will you? You *will* send him, won't you?' Almost pleading now.

'I'll send him,' agreed Tim and stooped out of the tent. Garry jerked open the drawer and his fingernails scrabbled on the rough wood in their haste to find the flask.

13

To General Sir Redvers Buller, V.C.,
Officer Commanding,
British Expeditionary Army of Natal

At Chievely

December 19th 1899

Sir,
   I have the honour to report that in accordance with orders received a reconnaissance was carried out by officers and men of the Natal Corps of Guides on the night of December 18th. The results of which are set out below:

Ford marked 'A' on attached Map: Although the ford promises passage for a large body of men, it is difficult to locate in darkness and a night crossing is not recommended.

Bridge marked 'B' on attached Map: This is a road bridge of metal construction. At present it is undamaged, probably due to its sturdy construction resisting demolition by the enemy.

Bridge marked 'C' on attached Map: This is a railway bridge also constructed of metal, but has been demolished by the enemy.

General: Limited penetration of the area beyond the Tugela River by elements of the N.C.G. revealed the presence of the enemy on the hills marked 'D' and 'E'. However, no evidence of artillery or excessive force was noted.

Courtney G., Lieutenant-Colonel
Officer Commanding N.C.G.,

In the Field.

EXTRACTS FROM THE BATTLE ORDERS OF GENERAL SIR
REDVERS BULLER V.C. MADE AND SIGNED ON THE
NIGHT OF DECEMBER 19TH 1899.

'. . . The force commanded by Brigadier Lyttelton will advance
on and capture the village of Colenso. Thereafter it will seize
and cross the metal bridge, and drive the enemy from the kopjes
on the far bank. (See attached Map.)'

14

They lay in the grass, side by side, and the dew had soaked through the backs of their tunics. The night was still and silent. No clouds above and the fat stars were very bright. Ahead of them the silver smear of the Milky Way threw the silhouette of the Tugela heights into bold relief, gave it an aspect of brooding menace.

Saul yawned loudly, and immediately Sean was forced to do the same. Though they had not slept that night, it was not the weariness – but the symptom of nerves wound tight at the prospect of going in against the Boer guns . . .

'Another hour and a half until dawn,' Saul whispered, and Sean grunted. There was no profit in counting the hours. At forty-seven minutes past six the sun would rise, and from behind them the British Army would move forward across the brown grass plain.

Once more Sean rose to his knees and swept the ground before them with his eyes, letting them move slowly along the bank of the Tugela, picking up the loom of the steel road bridge a hundred paces ahead of them, accounting for each bush on this bank, that they had not multiplied or moved. Then satisfied, he sank down again.

'My God, it's cold!' He could feel Saul shivering beside him.

'It will warm up quite soon.' Sean grinned in the darkness as he answered. The clear night sky had allowed yesterday's warmth to escape, the grass and their clothing were wet, even the steel of the rifles was painfully cold to touch – but Sean had long ago learned to ignore physical discomfort. He could, when necessary, lie completely motionless while tsetse flies settled on his neck and sank their red-hot needles into the soft skin behind his ears. Nevertheless, it was a relief when the false dawn showed and it was time to move.

'I'll go in now,' he whispered.

'Good luck – I'll have breakfast ready when you come back.'

This was a job for one man. A job that Sean did not relish. They had made certain that there were no enemy on this side of the river, now at the last minute when it was too late for the Boers to alter their dispositions – someone had to cross and find out in what strength they were holding the bridge. A couple of Boer Maxims sited to command the bridge at short range, or even demolition charges set ready to blow, would mean that the chances of success instead of being slim would be non-existent.

Sean slung his rifle across his back and began crawling forward through the grass. Twice he stopped to listen briefly, but there was little time – true dawn in an hour. He reached the bridge and lay in its heavy shadow, staring across at the far bank. Nothing moved. In the starlight the kopjes loomed like the backs of dark whales in the grassy sea. He waited five minutes – long enough for a restless sentry to fidget – still nothing.

'Here we go,' he whispered aloud, and suddenly he was afraid. For an instant he did not recognize the sensation, for he had experienced it only three or four times in his life, but never with so little cause. He crouched beside the steel girders of the bridge, with the weakness in his legs and his belly full of the oiliness. It was only when he caught the taste of it at the back of his throat, a taste a little like that of fish oil mixed with the effluence of something long dead, that he knew what it was.

I'm afraid. His first reaction was of surprise, which changed quickly to alarm.

This was how it happened. He knew it happened to other men. He had heard them talk of it around the camp fires, remembered the words and the pity underlying them.

Ja, his gunboy led him back to camp. He was shaking like a man with fever, and he was crying. I thought he was hurt. "Daniel," I said, "Daniel, what is wrong?"

"'It broke," he said with the tears running into his beard. "It broke there in my head, I heard it break. I threw the gun away and I ran."

"'Did he charge, Daniel?" I asked.

"'No, man. I didn't even see him, just heard him feeding close by in the catbush. Then it broke in my head and I was running."

'He was no coward. I had hunted with him many times, seen him kill an elephant from a charge so that it fell close enough to touch with the gun-barrel. He was good, but he had lived too close to it. Then suddenly it broke in his head. He hasn't hunted again.'

I have accumulated fear the way an old ship collects barnacles and weed below the water-line, now it is ready to break in me also – Sean knew. Knew also that if he ran now, as the old hunter had run, he would never hunt again.

Crouching in the darkness, sweating in the cold of dawn with the iciness of his fear, Sean wanted to vomit. He was physically sick, breathing heavily through his open mouth, the warm oiliness in his belly coming close to venting itself, so weak with it that his legs began to tremble and he caught at one of the iron girders of the bridge for support.

A minute that seemed like all eternity, he stood like that. Then he began to fight it, bearing down on it, stiffening his legs and forcing them to move forward. Consciously he checked the relaxation of his sphincter muscle – that close he had come to the ultimate degradation.

He knew then that the old joke about cowards was true. And that it applied to him also.

He went up on to the bridge; picking up each foot deliberately, swinging it forward, laying it down and moving the weight of his body over it. His breathing was deliberate, each breath taken and expelled at the command of his brain. He couldn't trust his body now to perform even the simplest task – not after it had betrayed him so monstrously.

Had they been waiting at the bridge, the Boers would have killed him that morning. Without caution he paced slowly down the centre of it, big and heavily moving in the starlight and his footsteps rang on the metal.

Under his feet the metal gave way to gravel. He was across. He kept walking, down the middle of the road, following the gentle curve towards the dark hills.

He walked on with his terror and the sound of it roared in his head like the sound of the sea. The sling of his rifle slipped from his shoulder and the weapon clattered into the road. He stood for a full minute before he could gather himself to stoop and pick it up. Then he turned and went back. Pacing slowly, counting his footsteps, measuring them out – one each second – timing them carefully to prevent himself from running. Because if he ran he knew it was finished. He too would never hunt again.

'You all right?' Saul was waiting.

'Yes.' Sean sank down beside him.

'See anything?'

'No.'

Saul was staring at him. 'Are you sure you're all right?'

Sean sighed. Once before he had been afraid. Fear had come to him in a caved-in mineshaft, later he had gone back and left his fear in the same mineshaft, and had walked away from it alone. In the same way he had hoped to leave it now beyond the river, but this time it had followed him back. With a certainty he knew that it would never leave him from now onwards. It would always be near.

I will have to tame it, he thought. I will have to break it to the halter and the curb.

'Yes, I'm all right,' he answered Saul. 'What's the time?'

'Half-past five.'

'I'll send Mbejane back now.'

Sean stood up and went to where Mbejane waited with their horses. He handed Mbejane the small square of green cloth which was the prearranged signal that neither the bridge nor the town was defended in force. The red square he replaced in his breastpocket.

'I will come back,' Mbejane told him.

'No.' Sean shook his head. 'There is nothing for you here.'

Mbejane untied the horses. 'Stay in peace.'

'Go in peace.' Sean was thankful that Mbejane would not be there as witness, should he break under his new-found fear.

But I must not break, he decided grimly. Today will be the test. If I can last out this day, then perhaps I will have tamed it.

He went back to where Saul waited in the darkness, and together they lay and watched the dawn come on.

15

The darkness drew back, each minute enlarging the circle of their vision. Now the upper works of the bridge stood out, a neat geometrical pattern against the dark bulk of the heights. Then he could see the patterns of dark bush against pale grass and rock.

The new light distorted distance, made the high ground seem remote and no longer hostile. A flight of egrets flew in long formation above the course of the river, high enough to catch the sun so that they were birds of bright, glowing gold in a world of shadow. And the dawn brought with it a small cold wind whose voice in the grass blended with the murmur of the river.

Then the sun hit the heights as though to bless the army of the Republic. The mist in the gullies writhed in agony at its warmth, lifted into the wind and smeared away.

The rim of the sun pushed up over the edge of the land, and the day came bright and clean with dew.

Through his glasses Sean studied the crest of the high ground. At a hundred paces there were traces of smoke as the Boer Army brewed coffee.

'You think they'll spot us?' asked Saul.

Sean shook his head without lowering his glasses. Two small bushes and the thin screen of grass they had constructed during the night hid them effectively.

'Are you sure you are all right?' Saul asked once more. From the set of his face Sean seemed to be in pain.

'Stomach gripes,' Sean grunted. Let it start soon, please let it start. The waiting is the worst.

Then the ground trembled under his chest, the faintest vibration, and Sean felt relief flood through him. 'Here come the guns,' he said, and using the cover of one of the bushes, he stood up and looked behind him.

In a single column, following each other at strictly spaced

intervals, the guns were moving into action. They were coming in fast, still tiny with distance but growing as the gunners astride the lead horses of each team urged them on. Closer now so that Sean could see the whip arms rising and falling, he heard the rumble and rattle of the carriages and faintly the shouts of the outriders.

Sixteen guns, one hundred and fifty horses to drag them, and a hundred men to serve them. But in the vastness of the great plain before Colenso the column seemed small and insignificant. Sean looked beyond them and saw the foot soldiers following them, line upon line, like the poles of a fence, thousands of them creeping forward across the plain. Sean felt the old wild elation begin. He knew the army was centred upon the line of markers which he and Saul had laid early the previous night, and that the two of them would be the first across the bridge – the first of all those thousands.

But it was elation of a different quality to anything he had experienced before. It was sharper and more poignant, seasoned by the red pepper of his fear. So that for the first time in his life Sean learned that fear can be a pleasurable sensation.

He watched the patterns of men and guns evolve upon the brown gaming-table – counters thrown down at chance, to be won or irretrievably lost at the fall of the dice of war. Knowing also that he was one of the counters, afraid and strangely jubilant in this knowledge.

The guns were close now. He could make sense of the shouting, see the features of the men and even recognize his own feelings in their faces.

Close, perhaps too close. Uneasily Sean glanced back at the forbidding heights beyond the river and gauged the range. Two thousand yards perhaps, long rifle shot. And still the guns came on.

'Jesus Christ! Are they mad?' Sean asked aloud.

'They must engage now.' Saul also saw the danger. 'They can't come closer.'

And still the guns came on. The sound of their charge was low thunder; dust from the dew-damp earth rose reluctantly behind them; horses with wide mouths throwing froth as they drove against the traces.

'They're in range now. They must stop, they must!' groaned Sean.

560

Then at last the column splayed open, alternate guns wheeling left and right still at full gallop. Swinging broadside to the waiting Boer rifles.

'My God! My God!' Sean mouthed the blasphemy in agony as he watched. 'They'll be massacred.'

Gunners rising in the stirrups, leaning back to check the carriages. The Gun-Captains jumping from their mounts, letting them gallop free as they ran to begin the unhitching and the pointing.

In this helpless moment while men swarmed over the guns, manhandling them to train upon the heights; while the horses still reared and whinnied in hysterical excitement; before the shells could be unloaded and stacked beside their pieces – in that moment the Boer rifles opened together. It was a sound that lacked violence, strangely unwarlike, muted by distance to the popping of a hundred strings of fireworks, and at first there was no effect. The grass was thick enough to hide the strike of the bullets, the dust too lazy with dew to jump and mark their fall.

Then a horse was hit and fell kicking, dragging its mate on to its knees also. Two men ran to cut it loose, but one of them never reached it. He sat down suddenly in the grass with his head bowed. Two more horses dropped, another reared and pawed wildly at the air with one front leg flapping loosely where a bullet had broken the bone above the knee.

'Get out!' roared Sean. 'Pull back while there's still time,' but his voice did not carry to the gun crews, could not carry above the shouting and the screaming of wounded horses.

There was a new sound now which Sean could not identify, a sound like hail on a tin roof, isolated at first then more frequent until it was a hundred hammers clanging together in broken rhythm – and he knew it was the sound of bullets striking the metal of the guns.

He saw:

A gunner fall forward and jam the breech of the piece until he was dragged clear;

A loader drop the shell he was carrying and stumble on with his legs folding until he subsided and lay still;

One of the horses break loose and gallop away across the plain dragging a tangle of torn traces behind it;

A covey of wild pheasant rise together out of the grass near the batteries and curve away along the river before dropping on stiff wings back into cover;

And behind the guns the infantry in neat lines advancing placidly towards the huddle of deserted cottages that was Colenso.

Then, with a crash that made the earth jump, and with sixteen long spurts of blue smoke, the guns came into action.

Sean focused his glasses on the ridge in time to see the first shells burst along the crest. The evil blossoms of greenish-yellow lyddite fumes bloomed quickly in the sunlight, then drifted oily-thick on the wind.

Again the guns crashed, and again – each salvo more ragged than the last until it became a continuous stuttering, hammering roar. Until the stark outline of the ridge was blurred and indefinite in the dust and lyddite fumes. There was smoke also, a fine greyish mist of it banked along the heights – the smoke of thousands of rifles.

Quickly Sean set the rear sight of his Lee-Metford at a thousand yards, wriggled forward on his elbows, hunched down over his rifle and began shooting blindly into the smoke on the heights. Beside him Saul was firing also.

Twice Sean emptied his magazine before looking back at the guns. The tempo of their fire had slackened. Most of the horses were down in the grass. Dead men were draped across the gun carriages, others badly wounded crouched for cover behind the mountings, and where six men had served each piece before, now four or only three carried shell and loaded and fired.

'The fools, the bloody fools,' Sean whispered, and began to shoot again, concentrating his whole attention on the routine of jerking the bolt back, sliding it forward in the same motion, sighting up into the mist of gun smoke, and firing. He did not count the shots and each time the weapon clicked empty he groped for another clip from his bandolier and re-loaded. He was starting to sweat now, could feel it trickling down his armpits, his ears buzzed from the concussion of the rifle and his shoulder was beginning to throb.

Gradually a sense of unreality induced by the clamour of the guns and the smell of burnt powder came over him. It seemed that all he would ever do was lie and shoot at nothing, shoot at smoke. Then reality faded further so that all of existence was the vee and dot of a rifle sight, standing solid in mist. And the mist had no shape. In his ears was the vast buzzing silence that drowned all the other sounds of battle. He was alone and tranquil, heavy and dulled by the hypnotic drift of smoke and the repetitive act of loading and firing.

Abruptly the mood was broken. Over them passed a rustle like giant wings, then a crack as though Satan had slammed the door of hell. Startled he looked up and saw a ball of shimmering white smoke standing in the air above the guns, spinning and spreading, growing in the sky like a flower.

'What the . . . '

'Shrapnel,' grunted Saul. 'Now they're finished.'

Then crack and crack again as the Boer Nordenfeldts planted their cotton flowers of smoke above the plain, flailing the guns and the men who still worked them with a buzzing hissing storm of steel.

Then there were voices. Confused and dazed by the gunfire, it took Sean a minute to place them. He had forgotten the infantry.

'Close up there.'

'Close up on the right. Keep the line!'

'Don't run. Steady, men. Don't run.'

Long lines of men, lines that bulged and lagged and straightened again at the urging of their officers. Evenly spaced, plodding quietly with their rifles held across their chests, they passed the guns. Behind them they left khaki bundles lying on the plain, some of the bundles lay still but others writhed and screamed. As the gaps appeared in the lines they were quickly filled at the chant of 'Close up. Close up there on the flank.'

'They are heading for the railway bridge.' Sean felt the first premonition of disaster. 'Don't they know that it's been destroyed?'

'We'll have to stop them.' Saul scrambled to his feet beside Sean.

'Why didn't the fools follow our markers?' Angrily Sean shouted the question that had no answer. He did it to gain time, to postpone the moment when he must leave the flimsy cover of the grass shelter and go out into the open where the shrapnel and the Mausers swept the ground. Sean's fear came back on him strongly. He didn't want to go out there.

'Come on, Sean. We must stop them.' And Saul started to run. He looked like a skinny little monkey, capering out towards the advancing waves of foot soldiers. Sean sucked in his breath and held it a moment before he followed.

Twenty yards ahead of the leading rank of infantry, carrying a naked sword in one hand and stepping out briskly on long legs, came an officer.

'Hey, you!' Sean shouted at him, waving his hat to catch his attention. He succeeded. The officer fixed him with bright blue eyes like a pair of bayonets and the waxed points of his grey moustache twitched. He strode on towards Sean and Paul.

'You're heading for the wrong bridge,' Sean yelled at him, his voice high-pitched with agitation. 'They've blown the rail bridge, you'll never get across there.'

The officer reached them and checked his stride.

'And who the hell are you, if it's not a rude question?'

'We're the ground scouts . . . ' Sean started, then leapt in the air as a Mauser bullet flicked into the ground between his legs. 'And put that bloody sword away – you'll have every Boer on the Tugela competing for you.'

The officer, a colonel by the crowns on his shoulders, frowned at Sean.

'The correct form of address, Sergeant . . . '

'The hell with that!' Sean roared at him. 'Swing your advance on to the road bridge.' He pointed with agitation at the metal superstructure of the bridge that showed on the left through the thorn trees. 'If you continue as you're going they'll cut you to pieces.'

A moment longer the Colonel fixed Sean with his bayonet eyes, then he lifted a silver whistle to his lips and blew a piercing blast.

'Take cover,' he shouted. 'Take cover!'

And immediately the first rank dropped into the grass. Behind them the other ranks lost their rigidity, as men hesitated.

'Get into the town,' a voice shouted. 'Take cover in the buildings.' And they broke and ran, a thousand men, jostling each other, racing for the security of the cottages of Colenso. Pouring into the single street, diving into doorways and windows. Within thirty seconds they had all gone to ground.

'Now, what's this all about?' demanded the Colonel, turning back to Sean. Impatiently Sean repeated himself, standing out in the open and uncomfortably aware that for absence of other targets the Boers were beginning to take a very active interest in them.

'Are you sure?'

'Dammit! Of course, I'm sure. The bridge is destroyed and they have torn up all the barbed wire fences and thrown them into the river. You'll never get across there.'

'Come along.' The Colonel set off towards the nearest cottage and Sean walked beside him. Afterwards he was never certain how he had managed to cover that hundred yards without running.

'For God's sake, put that sword away,' he growled at the Colonel as they walked with the flit, spang, flit, spang of bullets around them.

'Nervous, Sergeant?' And for the first time the Colonel grinned.

'You're damn right, I am.'

'So am I. But it would never do to let the men see that, would it?' He steadied the scabbard on his hips and ran the sword back into it. 'What's your name, Sergeant?'

'Sean Courtney, Natal Corps of Guides. What's yours?' Sean ducked instinctively as a bullet cracked past his head, and the Colonel smiled again at the familiarity.

'Acheson. John Acheson. 2nd Battalion, Scots Fusiliers.'

And they reached the cottage. No longer able to restrain himself, Sean dived thankfully through the kitchen door and found Saul already there. He handed Sean a cheroot and held a match for him.

'These crazy Souties!' he observed. 'And you're as bad as he is – strolling around in the middle of a battle.'

'Right, Courtney.' Acheson followed him into the kitchen. 'Let's go over the situation.'

He listened quietly while Sean explained in detail. He had to shout to lift his voice above the whistle and crack of the Boer artillery and the roar of a thousand Lee-Metford rifles as they replied from the windows and doorways of the village. Around them the kitchen was being used as a dressing-station and the moan and whimper of wounded men added to the hubbub of battle.

When Sean had finished Acheson turned away and strode to the window. He looked out across the railway tracks, to where the guns stood. They were drawn up in precise parade-ground formation. But now they were silent. Dribbling back towards the shelter of a deep donga – or gully – in the rear, the surviving gunners dragged their wounded with them.

'The poor bastards,' Sean whispered, as he saw one of the retreating gunners killed, shot in the head so that his helmet was thrown spinning upwards in a brief pink cloud of blood.

The sight seemed to rouse Acheson also.

'All right,' he said. 'We'll advance on the road bridge. Come on, Courtney.'

Behind him someone cried out, and Sean heard him fall. But he did not look round. He watched the bridge ahead of him. Although his legs moved mechanically under him it seemed to come no nearer. The thorn trees were thicker here beside the river and they gave a little cover from the merciless marksmen on the far bank. Yet men were falling steadily, and the shrapnel raged and cracked above them.

'Let's get across. Get the best seats on the other side,' Saul shouted beside him.

'Come on, then,' agreed Sean and they ran together. They were first on to the bridge, with Acheson just behind them. Bullets left bright scars on the grey painted metal, and then suddenly, miraculously, they were across. They had crossed the Tugela.

A drainage ditch beside the road and they dived into it, both of them panting. Sean looked back. Over the bridge poured a mass of khaki, all semblance of order gone as they crowded into the bottleneck and the fire from the Boers churned into them.

Once across, the leaders fanned out along the river, crouching below the dip in the bank, while behind them the slaughter on the bridge continued. A struggling mass of cursing, running, angry, frightened and dying men.

'It's a bloody abattoir.' Sean was appalled as he watched it. Dead and wounded men were falling over the low guard rail, splashing into the brown waters of the Tugela to sink or strike out clumsily for the banks. But a steady stream of men was coming across and going to ground in the two-deep drainage ditches, and beneath the angle of the river bank.

It was clear to Sean that the attack was losing its impetus. As the men jumped down into the ditches he saw in their faces and in the way they flattened themselves into shelter that they had lost all stomach for the attack. The ordeal of the bridge had destroyed the discipline that had held their steady advance into those neatly controlled ranks; Officers and men were inextricably mixed into a tired and badly frightened rabble. There was no contact between the different groups in the drainage trenches and those lying in the lee of the river banks – and already there was little cover for the men who were still coming across. The fire from the Boer positions never faltered, and now the bridge was blocked with the bodies of the fallen, so that each new wave had to climb over them, stepping on dead and wounded alike, while the storm of Boer rifle-fire lashed them like wind-driven rain.

Rivulets of fresh bright blood dribbled down the supports of the bridge in ghastly contrast to the grey paint, and the surface of the river was stained by a chocolate-brown cloud of it spreading slowly downstream. Here and there a desperate rallying voice was lifted in the hubbub of incoherent shouts and groans.

'Here the 21st. Form on me the 21st.'

'Independent fire. On the heights. Ten rounds rapid.'

'Stretcher-bearer!'

'Bill. Where are you, Bill?'

'Jesus Christ! Jesus sobbing Christ!'

'Up, you men! Get up!'

'Come on the 21st. Fix bayonets.'

Some of them were head and shoulders out of the ditch returning the Boer fire, a few were drinking from their water-bottles already. A sergeant struggled with a jammed rifle and swore softly without looking up, while beside him a man sat with his back against the wall of the ditch, his legs sprawled open, and watched while the blood pumped from the wound in his belly.

Sean stood and felt the wind of a bullet slap against his cheek, while low in his stomach the slimy reptile of fear coiled itself tighter. Then he scrambled up the side of the ditch.

'Come on!' he roared and started running towards the hills. It was open here, like a meadow, and ahead of him an old barbed-wire fence sagged on rotten poles. He reached it, lifted his foot and kicked with his heel. The fence pole snapped level with the ground, the wire collapsed. He jumped over it.

'They're not coming,' Saul shouted beside him, and Sean stopped. The two of them were alone in the middle of the field – and the Boer rifles were seeking them eagerly.

'Run, Saul!' Sean shouted and snatched off his hat. 'Come on, you bastards.' He waved at the men behind him.

A bullet missed him so narrowly that he staggered in the wind of its passage.

'This way! Follow us! Come on!' Saul had not left him. He was dancing with excitement, and flapping his arms.

'Come back.' Acheson's voice floated across to them. He stood in the drainage ditch, showing clear from the waist up. 'Come back, Courtney!'

The attack was finished. Sean knew it in that instant, and saw the wisdom of Acheson's decision. Further advance over the open meadowland below the heights was suicide. The resolve that had carried him this far collapsed, and his terror snapped the leash he had held upon it. He ran back blindly, sobbing, leaning forward, his elbows pumping in time to his fear-driven feet.

Then suddenly Saul was hit beside him. It took him in the head, threw him forward, his rifle spinning from his hands, squawking hoarsely with pain and surprise as he went down skidding on his belly. And Sean ran on.

'Sean!' Saul's voice left behind him.

'Sean!' A cry of dreadful need, and Sean closed his mind against it and ran on towards the safety of the ditch.

'Sean. Please!' and he checked and stood uncertain with the Mausers barking above and the bullets clipping the grass around him.

Leave him, shrieked Sean's terror. *Leave him. Run! Run!*

Saul crawled towards him, blood on his face and his eyes fastened on Sean's face.

'Sean!'

Leave him. Leave him.

But there was hope in that pitiful blood-smeared face, and the fingers of Saul's hands clawed among the coarse grass roots as he dragged himself forward.

It was beyond all reason. But Sean went back to him.

Beneath the spurs of his terror Sean found the strength to lift him and run with him.

Hating him as he had never hated before, Sean blundered towards the drainage ditch carrying Saul. The acceleration of his brain slowed down the passage of time so that he seemed to run for ever.

'Damn you!' he mouthed at Saul, hating him.

'Damn you to hell!' The words came easily from his mouth, an inarticulate expression of his terror.

Then the ground gave way beneath his feet and he fell. Together they dropped into the drainage ditch and Sean rolled away from him. He lay on his stomach and pressed his face into the earth and shook as a man shakes in high fever.

Slowly he came back from that far place where fear had driven him, and he lifted his head.

Saul sat against the bank of the ditch. His face was streaked with a mixture of blood and dirt.

'How are we doing?' Sean croaked and Saul looked at him dully. It was bright and very hot here in the sun. Sean unscrewed the stopper of his water-bottle and held it to Saul's lips. Saul swallowed painfully and water spilled from the corner of his mouth down his chin and on to his tunic.

Then Sean drank and finished panting with pleasure.

'Let's have a look at your head.'

He lifted Saul's hat from his head, and the blood that had accumulated around the sweat band poured in a fresh flood down Saul's neck. Parting the sodden black hair Sean found the groove in the flesh of his scalp.

'Grazed you,' he grunted and groped for the field dressing in the pocket of Saul's tunic. While he bound an untidy turban round Saul's head he noticed that a strange stillness had fallen on the field, a stillness accentuated rather than broken by the murmur of voices from the men around him and the occasional report of a rifle from the heights above.

The battle was over. At least we got across the river, he thought bitterly. The only problem that now remains is getting back again.

'How's that feel?' He had wet his handkerchief and wiped some of the blood and dust from Saul's face.

'Thank you, Sean.' Suddenly Sean realized that Saul's eyes were full of tears and it embarrassed him. He looked away from them.

'Thank you for . . . for coming back to get me.'

'Forget it.'

'I'll never forget it. Never as long as I live.'

'You'd have done the same.'

'No, I don't think so. I wouldn't have been able to. I was so scared, so afraid, Sean. You'd never know. You'll never know what it's like to be that afraid.'

'Forget it, Saul. Leave it alone.'

'I've got to tell you. I owe it to you – from now on I owe you . . . If you hadn't come back I'd be . . . I'd still be out there. I owe you.'

'Shut up, damn you!' He saw that Saul's eyes were different, the pupils had shrunk to tiny black specks and he was shaking his head in a meaningless idiotic fashion. The bullet had concussed him. But this could not prevent Sean's anger. 'Shut up,' he snarled. 'You think I don't know about fear. I was so scared out there – I hated you. Do you hear that? I hated you!'

And then Sean's voice softened. He had to explain to Saul and himself. He had to tell him about it, to justify it and place it securely in the scheme of things.

Suddenly he felt very old and wise. In his hands he held the key to the whole mystery of life. It was all so clear, for the first time he understood and he could explain it.

They sat close together in the sun, isolated from the men around them, and Sean's voice sank to an urgent whisper as he tried to make Saul understand, tried to pass on to him this knowledge that embraced all truth.

Beside them lay a corporal of the Fusiliers. He lay on his back, dead, and the flies swarmed over his eyes and laid their eggs. They looked like tiny grains of rice clustered in the lashes around his dead open eyes.

Saul leaned heavily against Sean's shoulder, now and then he shook his head in confusion as he listened to Sean. Listened to Sean's voice tripping and stumbling then starting to hurry as his ideas broke up and crumpled, heard the desperation in it as Sean strove to retain just a few grains of all that knowledge which had been his a few moment before. Heard it peter out into silence and sorrow as he found that it was gone.

'I don't know,' Sean admitted at last.

Then Saul spoke, his voice was dull and his eyes would not focus properly as he peered at Sean from beneath the blood-soiled turban of bandages.

'Ruth,' he said. 'You speak like Ruth does. Sometimes in the night when she cannot sleep she tries to tell me. Almost I understand, almost she finds it and then she stops. "I don't know," she says at last. "I just don't know."'

Sean jerked away from him, and stared into his face. 'Ruth?' he asked quietly.

'Ruth – my wife. You'd like her, Sean – she'd like you. So brave – she came to me through the Boer lines. All the way from Pretoria – riding alone. She came to me. I couldn't believe it. All that way. She just walked into camp one day and said, "Hello, Saul. I'm here!" just like that! You'll like her when you meet her, Sean. She's so beautiful, so serene . . . '

In October when the big winds blow they come for the first time on a still day. It has been hot and dry for perhaps a month, then you hear them from far away, roaring softly. The roar mounts quickly, the dust races brown on the wind and the trees lean away from it, threshing and churning their branches. You see it coming but all your preparations are nothing when it hits. The vast roaring and the dust envelope you and you are numbed and blinded by the violence of it.

In the same way Sean saw it coming, he recognized it as the murderous rage which before had nearly killed a man, but still he could not prepare himself. And then it was upon him and the roaring filled his head and narrowed his vision so that all he could see was the face of Saul Friedman. The face was in profile for Saul was staring back across the plain of Colenso towards the English lines.

Sean lifted the dead corporal's rifle and laid it across his lap. With his thumb he slipped off the safety-catch, but Saul did not notice the movement.

'She's in Pietermaritzburg, I had a letter from her last week,' he murmured, and Sean shifted the rifle in his lap so that the muzzle aimed into the side of Saul's chest below the armpit.

'I sent her down to Pietermaritzburg. She's staying with her uncle there.' Saul lifted his hand and touched his head. Sean curled his finger on the trigger. 'I wish you could meet her, Sean. She'd like you.' Now he looked into Sean's face, and there was such pathetic trust in his eyes. 'When I write I am going to tell her about today – about what you did.'

Sean took up the slack in the trigger until he could feel the final resistance.

'We both owe you –' Saul stopped and smiled shyly. 'I just want you to know that I'll never forget it.'

Kill him, roared Sean's head. Kill him now – kill him quickly. Don't let him talk.

It was the first conscious command his instinct had issued. *Now! Do it now!* But his trigger-finger relaxed.

This is all that stands between you and Ruth. Do it, do it now. The roaring in his head abated. The big wind had passed by and he could hear it receding. He lifted the rifle and slowly pushed the safety-catch across.

In the stillness after the wind he knew suddenly that from now on Saul Friedman was his special charge. Because he had come so close to taking it from him, Saul's life had become a debt of honour.

He laid the rifle aside and closed his eyes wearily.

'We'd better think about getting out of here,' he said quietly. 'Otherwise I might never get around to meeting this beauty of yours.'

16

'Hart has got himself into a mess out there!' General Sir Redvers Buller's voice matched the pompous jut of his belly and he leaned back against the weight of the telescope he held to his eye. 'What do you think, Courtney?'

'Well, he certainly hasn't reached the drift, sir. It looks to me as though he's been pinned down in the loop of the river,' Garry agreed.

'Damn the man! My orders were clear,' growled Buller. 'What can you make of the guns – can you see anything there?'

Every telescope in the party of officers swivelled back to the centre, to where the corrugated iron roofs of Colenso showed above the thorn trees, dimly through the dust and the smoke.

'I can't . . .' Garry started, then jumped uncontrollably as the naval 4·7 bellowed from its emplacement beside them. Every time that morning it had fired, Garry had jumped. If only I knew when it was going to, he thought and jumped again as it bellowed.

'They are not being served,' one of the other staff officers interposed and Garry envied him his composure and his calmness of voice. His own hands were trembling so that he must grip hard with both hands to keep his binoculars focused on the town. Each time the naval gun fired the dust of its recoil drifted over them, also the sun was fierce and he was thirsty. He thought of the flask in his saddle-bags and the next bellow of the gun caught him completely off guard. This time both his feet left the ground.

' . . . Do you agree, Courtney?' Buller's voice, he had not heard the beginning of the question.

'I do indeed, sir.'

'Good.' The General turned to his A.D.C. 'Send a rider to Hart. Tell him to pull out of there before he gets badly mauled. Quick as you can, Clery.'

At that moment Garry made a remarkable discovery. Behind the inscrutable mask of his face with its magnificent silver moustache, behind the bulging expressionless eyes – General Sir Redvers Buller was every bit as agitated and uncertain as was Garry Courtney. His continual appeals to Garry for support confirmed this. Of course, Garry did not consider that another reason why Buller addressed his appeals to him, rather than the regular officers of his staff, was because this was the one quarter from which Buller could rely on unquestioning support.

'That takes care of the left flank.' Buller was clearly relieved at his decision as he searched out towards the right, fixing the low round bulk of Hlangwane Kopje in the field of his telescope. 'Dundonald seems to be keeping his end up.' Earlier, there had been desultory rifle and pompom fire from the right flank. Now it was silent.

'But the centre . . . ' As though he had been delaying the moment, Buller at last turned his attention on the holocaust of dust and flame and shrapnel that enveloped Colenso.

'Come along.' He snapped his telescope closed. 'We'd better have a closer look at what they've accomplished there.' And he led his staff back to the horses. Careful that no one should usurp his place at the General's right hand, Garry limped along beside him.

At the headquarters of Lyttelton's Brigade, established in a deep donga half a mile before the first scattered buildings of the town, it took Buller half a minute to find out what had been accomplished. It appalled him.

'We hold the town, sir. And three companies have advanced to the road bridge and seized it. But we cannot hope to hold it. I have sent a runner ordering them to withdraw on the town.'

'But why aren't the guns firing? What's happened to Colonel Long?'

'The guns have been silenced. Long is badly wounded.'

While Buller sat his horse, slowly absorbing this, a sergeant of the Transvaal Staats Artillerie jerked the lanyard of his quick-firing Nordenfeldt and fired the shell which changed a British reverse into a resounding defeat that would echo around the world.

From out of the broken and rocky complex of hills on the north bank the shell arched upwards; over the river with its surface churned to brown by shrapnel and short shell and blood;

high over the deserted guns manned only by corpses; shrieking over the heads of the surviving gunners as they crouched in the rear with their wounded, forcing them to duck as they had ducked a thousand times before; plunging in its descent over the town of Colenso where weary men waited; down across thorn tree and mimosa and brown grass veld littered with dead men; falling at last in a tall jump of dust and smoke in the midst of General Buller's staff.

Beneath him Garry's horse dropped, killed instantly, pinning his leg so that had it been flesh and bone, not carved oak, it would have been crushed. He felt the blood soaking through his tunic and splattered in his face and mouth.

'I've been hit. Help me, God help me, I'm wounded.' And he writhed and struggled in the grass, wiping the blood on his face.

Rough hands freed his leg and dragged him clear of his horse.

'Not your blood. You're all right. Not your blood, it's his.'

On his hands and knees Garry stared in horror at the Surgeon-Major who had stood beside him and who had shielded him from the blast. Shrapnel had cut his head away, and the blood still spouted from his neck as though it were a severed hose.

Around him men fought their panic-stricken horses as they reared and whinnied. Buller was doubled up in the saddle, clutching the side of his chest.

'Sir, sir. Are you all right?' An A.D.C. had the reins and was bringing Buller's horse under control. Two officers ran to Buller and helped him down. He stood between them, his face contorted with pain, and his voice when he spoke was shaky, but hoarse.

'Disengage, Lyttelton! Disengage on your whole front!'

'Sir,' protested the Brigadier. 'We hold the town. Let me cover the guns until nightfall when we can retrieve them at our . . . '

'Damn you, Lyttelton. You heard me. Pull your brigade back immediately. The attack has failed.' Buller's breathing wheezed in his throat and he still clutched the side of his chest with both hands.

'To withdraw now will mean accepting heavier losses than we have suffered already. The enemy artillery is accurately ranged . . . '

'Pull them out, do you hear me!' Buller's voice rose to a shout.

'The guns . . . ' Lyttelton tried again, but Buller had already turned to his A.D.C.

'Send riders to Lord Dundonald's Brigade. He must retire immediately. I give him no latitude of discretion, he is to disengage his force at once and withdraw. Tell him . . . tell him the attack has failed on left and centre, tell him the guns are lost and he is in danger of being surrounded. Go. Ride fast.'

There was a murmur among them, horrified as they listened to these orders. Miserably every eye turned to Lyttelton, silently they pleaded with him, for he was the senior officer present.

'General Buller.' He spoke softly, but with an urgency that caught even Buller's shell-shocked attention. 'At least, let me try to recover the guns. We cannot abandon them. Let me call for volunteers. . . .'

'I'll go, sir. Please let me try.' A young subaltern elbowed Garry aside in his eagerness. Garry knew who he was, all of them did, for apart from being one of the most promising and popular youngsters in Buller's command – he was also the only son of the legendary Lord Roberts.

Assisted by his A.D.C., Buller moved to the shade of a mimosa tree and sank down heavily with his back against the rough bark of the trunk. He looked up at young Roberts, dully, without apparent interest.

'All right, Bobbie, Lyttelton will give you men. Off you go then.' He pronounced the sentence of death upon him, and Roberts laughed excitedly, gaily, and ran to his horse.

'I think we are all in need of refreshment. Will you join me in a sandwich and a glass of champagne, gentlemen?' Buller nodded to his A.D.C., who hurried to bring food and drink from his saddle-bags. A stray shell burst twenty yards away, scattering clods of earth over them. Stolidly Buller brushed a piece of dry grass from his whiskers and selected a smoked salmon sandwich.

17

Sean crawled down the drainage ditch towards the bank of the river. A shell burst on the edge of the ditch and scattered clods of earth over his back. He paused to brush a tangle of grass roots out of his whiskers and then crawled on to where Colonel Acheson squatted on his haunches in earnest conversation with a captain of the Fusiliers.

'Hey, Colonel Acheson. I doubt you'll need me again, will you?' The Captain looked shocked at Sean's term of address, but Acheson grinned briefly.

'A runner just got through. We have been ordered to withdraw.'

'What a pity!' Sean grunted sarcastically. 'Just when we were knocking the daylights out of old brother Boer,' and all three of them ducked as a machine-gun hammered lumps of dirt out of the bank above their heads. Then Sean took up from where he had been interrupted. 'Well, in that case – I'll be leaving you.'

'Where are you going?' the Captain demanded suspiciously.

'Not across that bridge.' Sean removed the stub of his cheroot from his mouth and pointed with it at the grey structure with its gruesome streaks of new paint. 'I've got a wounded man with me. He'll never make it. Have you got a match?'

Automatically the Captain produced a box of wax matches from his breast-pocket. 'Thanks. I'm going to swim him downstream and find a better place to cross.' Sean re-lit his cheroot, blew a cloud of smoke and returned the Captain's matches.

'A pleasure meeting you, Colonel Acheson.'

'You have permission to fall out, Courtney.' A second longer they looked into each other's eyes, and Sean experienced a powerful desire to shake this man's hand but instead he started crawling back along the ditch.

'Courtney!' Sean paused and glanced over his shoulder. 'What's the name of the other Guide?'

'Friedman. Saul Friedman.'

Acheson scribbled briefly in his notebook, then returned it to his pocket.

'You'll hear more about today – good luck.'

'And to you, sir.'

From a tree that hung out over the brown water of the Tugela, Sean hacked a bushy green branch with his bayonet.

'Come on,' and Saul slid down the greasy clay of the bank, waist-deep into the river beside Sean.

'Leave your rifle.' Obediently Saul dropped it into the river.

'What's the bush for?'

'To cover our heads.'

'Why are we waiting?'

'For Acheson to create a diversion when he tries to get back across the bridge.'

At that moment a whistle shrilled on the bank above them. Immediately a fierce covering fire blared out and a party of khaki-clad figures stampeded out on to the bridge.

'Now,' grunted Sean. They sank together into the blood-warm water with only their heads, wreathed in leaves, above the surface. Sean pushed out gently and the current caught them. Neither of them looked back at the shrieking carnage on the bridge as they drifted away.

Twenty minutes later and a half-mile downstream, Sean edged across the current towards the remains of the railway bridge that hung like a broken drawbridge into the river. It offered a perfect access to the south and the embankment of the railway would cover them in their retreat across the plain.

Sean's feet touched mud bottom, then they were under the sagging bridge like chickens under the wing of a hen. He let the branch float away and dragged Saul to the bank between the metal girders.

'Five minutes' rest,' he told him and squatted beside him to rewind the bandage that had come down over Saul's ears. Muddy water streamed from sodden uniforms, and Sean mourned the cheroots in his tunic pocket.

There was another drainage ditch running beside the high gravel embankment of the railway. Along it, walking in a crouch, Sean prodded Saul ahead of him, yelling at him every time he attempted to straighten up and relieve his aching back. Once a sniper on the kopjes behind them thumped a bullet into the gravel near Sean's head, and Sean swore wearily and almost touched his knees with his nose. But Saul did not notice it. With his legs sloppy under him he staggered along in front of Sean, until finally he fell and lay in a sprawling, untidy heap in the bottom of the ditch.

Sean kicked him.

'Get up, damn you!'

'No, Ruth. Don't wake me up yet. It's Sunday. I don't have to work today.' Speaking quite clearly in a reasonable persuasive tone Saul looked up at Sean, but his eyes were matt and the pupils shrunken to black points.

'Get up. Get up!' The use of Ruth's name inflamed Sean. He caught Saul's shoulder and shook him. Saul's head jerked crazily and fresh blood seeped through his bandage. Instantly contrite, Sean laid him back gently.

'Saul, please. You must try. Just a little farther.'

'Glossless,' whispered Saul. 'There is no gloss on it. I don't want it.' And he closed his eyes, his lips bulged open and his breath snored through them in tiny bubbles of spittle.

A suffocating despair drooped down over Sean as he studied Saul's face. The eyes had receded into dark plum-coloured cavities, leaving the skin stretched tight across his cheeks and across the gaunt bony nose.

Not because I nearly killed him, not because I owe it to him. But because – but because? How can you define your feelings for another man. All you can say is – because he is my friend. Then, because he is my friend I cannot leave him here.

Sinking down beside him, Sean lifted his slack body into a sitting position, draped one of Saul's arms around his shoulder and stood up. Saul hung beside him, his head lolled forward on his chest, and Sean looked ahead. He could see the survivors from the bridge struggling back through the village, dragging their wounded with them.

Across the whole breadth of the plain, singly and in twos and threes, harried by shrapnel, beaten, broken, Buller's mighty army was in retreat. And there, not a hundred yards from where Sean crouched in the railway ditch, drawn up neatly in the grass, deserted, forlorn, stood the field guns.

Quickly Sean averted his eyes from them and began plodding away from the river. Over his shoulder he held Saul's wrist, his free arm was wrapped around Saul's waist.

Then slowly he was aware that the Boer fire was crescendoing once more. Shell that had fallen haphazard among the retreating men began to concentrate on an area directly ahead of Sean. Behind him the rifle-fire that had popped spasmodically on the heights now swelled into a fierce, sustained crackle like a bush-fire in green forest.

Leaning against the side of the ditch Sean peered ahead through the mimosa trees and the storm of dust and bursting shell. He saw horses, two teams in harness, men with them racing in through the thorn trees, lifting pale dust in a cloud to mingle with the dust of the shells. Far ahead of them, brandishing his cane, leading them in towards the abandoned guns, galloped a figure on a big shiny bay.

'He's laughing.' In wonder, Sean watched the leading rider disappear behind a column of dust and high explosive, only to emerge again as he swerved his mount like a polo player. His mouth was open and Sean saw the glint of white teeth. 'The fool is laughing his head off!'

And suddenly Sean was cheering wildly.

'Ride, man, Ride!' he shouted and his voice was lost in the shriek and crash of the bombardment.

'They've come to fetch the guns,' howled Sean. 'Saul, they've come for the guns.' Without knowing how he had done it, mad with the excitement of it, Sean found himself out of the ditch, running with new strength, running with Saul's unconscious weight slung over his shoulder, running through the grass towards the guns.

By the time he reached the battery the first team was already there. The men were down struggling to back the horses up to the trail of the Number One gun. Sean slid the inert body from his shoulder and dropped it in the grass. Two of them were trying to lift the trail of the field gun, but this task required four men.

'Get out of the way!' Sean shouted at them and straddled the long wedge-shaped trail of steel. He locked his hands into the grips and heaved upwards, lifting it clear and high.

'Get the carriage.' Quickly they rolled the detachable axle and wheels in under the trail and locked them into position. Sean stepped back panting.

'Well done!' The young officer leaned forward in his saddle as he shouted at Sean. 'Get up on the carriage.'

But Sean turned and ran to Saul, he picked him up and stumbled with him to the carriage.

'Grab him!' he grunted at the two soldiers who were already aboard. Between them they dragged Saul up on to the carriage seat.

'No room for you, cock. Why don't you take Taffy's place on the right-hand wheeler?' one of them shouted down, and Sean saw he was correct. The drivers were mounting up, but one saddle was empty.

'Look after him,' he told the man who held Saul.

'Don't worry, I've got him,' the gunner assured him, and then urgently, 'You'd best grab a seat – we're pulling out.'

'Look after him,' Sean repeated and started forward.

In that moment the luck which had protected him all morning ran out. A shell burst beside him. He felt no pain but his right leg gave under him and he went down on his knees.

He tried to stand but his body would not obey.

'Forward!' shouted the subaltern, and the gun carriage trundled away, gathering speed, beginning to jolt and bounce as the drivers lashed the horses. Sean saw the gunner who held Saul staring back at him from the carriage, his face was contorted with helplessness.

'Look after him!' Sean shouted. 'Promise me you'll look after him.'

The gunner opened his mouth to reply, but another shell burst between them, throwing up a curtain of dust that hid the carriage. This time Sean felt the shrapnel tear into his flesh. It stung like the cut of a razor and he sagged sideways. As he went down he saw that the Subaltern had been hit as well. Saw him throw up his arms and fall backwards over the rump of his horse, rolling from the saddle, hitting the ground with his shoulder, one foot caught in the stirrup so that he dragged over the rough ground until the stirrup leather snapped and left him lying. His horse galloped away in pursuit of the careering gun carriage.

Sean dragged himself after it. 'Look after him,' he shouted. 'For God's sake, look after Saul.' But nobody heard that shout for they were gone away amongst the trees, gone away in the dust with the shellfire escorting them like a troop of brown demons.

Still Sean crawled after them, using one hand to reach ahead and claw into the earth and inch his whole body belly down through the grass. His other arm dragged at his side, and he could feel his right leg slithering after him, until it caught and tethered him. He struggled against it, but his toe had hooked in a tuft of coarse grass and he could not free it. He wriggled on to his side and doubled up with his broken arm beneath him to look back at his leg.

There was much blood, a wet, slippery drag-mark of it across the flattened grass, and still it welled up out of his body. But there was no pain, only a dizziness and a weariness in his head.

His leg twisted at a ridiculous angle from his trunk, and the spur on his boot stood up jauntily. He wanted to laugh at the leg, but somehow the effort was too great and he closed his eyes against the glare of the sun.

Near him he heard somebody groaning and for a while he thought it must be Saul. Then he remembered that Saul was safe, and it was the young subaltern. With his eyes closed Sean lay and listened to him die. It was an ugly sound.

18

Battle-General Jan Paulus Leroux stood upon the heights above the Tugela and removed his Terai hat. His head was bald with a fringe of ginger hair above the ears and thick around the back. The skin of his pate was smooth and creamy white where the hat had protected it from the sun, but his face had been weathered and sculptured by the elements until it looked like a cliff of red-stone.

'Bring my pony, Hennie.' He spoke to the lad who stood beside him.

'*Ja*, Oom Paul.' And he hurried away down the reverse slope to the pony laager.

From the firing trench at Jan Paulus's feet one of his burghers looked up at him.

'God has heard our prayers, Oom Paul. He has given us a great victory.'

Jan Paulus nodded heavily, and his voice as he replied was low and humble, without any trace of jubilation.

'*Ja*, Fredevik. In God's name, a great victory.'

But not as great as I had planned it, he thought.

Out of cannon shot, almost out of range of the naked eye, the last tattered remnants of the British were dwindling into the brown distance.

If only they could have waited, he thought with bitterness. So clearly I explained it to them, and they did not heed me.

His whole strategy had revolved upon the bridge. If only his burghers on the kopje below the heights had held their fire and let them cross. Then God would have delivered the enemy to them in thousands instead of hundreds. Caught in the amphitheatre of the heights with the river at their backs none of them would have escaped when his artillery destroyed the bridge behind them. Sadly he looked down upon the trap he had laid with such infinite care. From above he could see the trenches, each of them, masked and cunningly overlapped so that an unbearable fire could sweep the grassy bowl into which he had hoped to lure the British centre. The trap that would never be sprung, for he knew they would not come again.

Hennie climbed back to him, leading his pony, and Jan Paulus mounted quickly.

'Come, let us go down.'

At forty-two years of age, Jan Paulus Leroux was very young for the command he held. There had been opposition in Pretoria to his appointment when old Joubert retired, but President Kruger had ridden rough-shod over it and forced the Volkraad to accept. Ten minutes before, Jan Paulus had sent him a tele-graphed message which had justified this confidence.

With long stirrup leathers, his massive body loose and relaxed in the saddle, his *sjambok* trailing from his wrist and the wide-brimmed hat shading his face, Jan Paulus went down to gather the harvest of war.

As he reached the kopjes and rode in among them, his burghers rose from their trenches on the slopes and cheered him. Their voices blended in a savage roar that echoed from the heights like the jubilation of lions on a new kill. Impassively Jan Paulus examined their faces as he passed. They were coated with red dust and burned powder, and sweat had run in dark lines through the grime. One man used his rifle as a crutch to balance himself against his wound, and there were harsh lines of pain around his mouth as he cheered. Jan Paulus checked his pony. 'Lie down, don't be a fool, man!' The man grinned painfully and shook his head.

'*Nee*, Oom Paul. I'm going with you to fetch the guns.'

Brusquely Jan Paulus motioned to the men who stood beside the wounded burgher. 'Take him away. Take him to the doctors.' And he trotted on to where Commandant Van Wyk waited for him.

'I told you to hold your men until they crossed,' he greeted him, and Van Wyk's grin faded.

'*Ja*, Oom Paul. I know. But I could not hold them. The young ones started it. When they saw the guns right there under their noses – I could not hold them.' Van Wyk turned and pointed across the river. 'Look how near they were.'

Jan Paulus looked across the river. The guns were standing in the open, so close and so lightly screened by the intervening

thorn scrub that he could count the spokes of the wheels and
see the sparkle of the brass breech fittings.

'It was too much temptation,' Van Wyk ended lamely.

'So! It is done, and we cannot undo it with words.' Grimly
Jan Paulus determined that this man would never command
again. 'Come, we will fetch them.'

At the road bridge Jan Paulus halted the long column of horsemen behind him. Although none of it showed on his face, yet
his stomach heaved with horror at what he saw.

'Move them,' he ordered, and as the thirty burghers dismounted and went forward to clear the bridge he called out after
them. 'Handle them gently, lift them – do not drag them away
like mealie sacks. These were men. Brave men.' Beside him the
boy, Hennie, was crying openly. The tears falling on to his
patched tweed jacket.

'Be still, Jong,' Jan Paulus murmured gently. 'Tears are for
women.' And he urged his pony into the narrow passage between
the dead. It was the dust and the sun and the lyddite fumes
which had irritated his own eyes, he told himself angrily.

Quietly, lacking the triumphant bearing of victors, they came
to the guns and spread out among them. Then a single rifle-shot
cracked out and a burgher staggered and clutched the wheel of
a gun carriage for support.

Whirling his pony, and flattening himself along its neck, Jan
Paulus charged the donga beyond the guns from which the shot
had come. Another shot hissed past his head, but by then Jan
Paulus had reached the donga. Pulling his mount down from
full gallop on to its haunches, he jumped from the saddle and
kicked the rifle out of the British private's hands before dragging
him to his feet.

'We have killed too much already, you fool.' Stumbling over
the English words, his tongue clumsy with rage, he roared into
the soldier's face. 'It is finished. Give up.' And then turning on
the surviving gunners who huddled along the donga. 'Give up,
give up, all of you!' None of them moved for a long minute,
then slowly one at a time they stood up and shuffled out of the
donga.

While a party of Boers led the prisoners away, and the others
went about the business of hitching up the guns and the ammunition wagon, the British stretcher-bearers began filtering
forward through the mimosa trees. Soon khaki figures were

mingled everywhere with the burghers as they searched like bird-dogs for the wounded.

Two of them, dark-skinned Indians of the Medical Corps, had found a man lying out on the left flank. They were having difficulty with him, and Jan Paulus handed the reins of his pony to Hennie and walked across to them.

In semi-delirium the wounded man was cursing horribly and resisting all attempts by the two Indians to fix splints on his leg.

'Leave me alone, you bastards,' and a flying fist knocked one of them sprawling. Jan Paulus, recognizing the voice and the punch, started to run.

'You behave yourself, or I'll klop you one,' he growled as he reached them. Groggily Sean rolled his head and tried to focus on him.

'Who's that? Who are you? Get the hell away from me.'

Jan Paulus did not answer. He was looking at the wounds and they made him want to vomit.

'Give to me.' He took the splints from the shaken bearers and squatted down beside Sean.

'Get away!' Sean screamed at him. 'I know what you're going to do. You're going to cut it off!'

'Sean!' Jan Paulus caught his wrist and held it while Sean writhed and swore.

'I'll kill you, you filthy bastard. I'll kill you if you touch it.'

'Sean! It's me. Look at me!'

And slowly Sean relaxed, his eyes steadied.

'It's you? It's really you?' he whispered. 'Don't let them . . . don't let them take my leg. Not like they did to Garry.'

'Be still, or I'll break your stupid head,' growled Jan Paulus. Like his face, his hands were beefy and red, big hands with fingers like calloused sausages, but now they worked as gently as those of a mother on her child. At last, holding the ankle, he looked at Sean.

'Hold fast, now. I must straighten it.'

Sean tried to grin, but his face was grey beneath the coating of battle filth, and sweat squeezed from his skin like a rash of tiny blisters.

'Don't talk so much, you bloody Dutchman. Do it!'

Bone grated on broken bone deep in the torn flesh and Sean

gasped. Every muscle in his body convulsed and then relaxed again as he fainted.

'Ja,' grunted Jan Paulus. 'That's better,' and for the first time the set of his features betrayed his compassion. He finished with the bandages, and for a few seconds continued to squat beside Sean's unconscious body. Then he whispered so low that the two bearers could not catch the words.

'Sleep well, my brother. May God spare you your leg.'

And he stood, all trace of pity and sorrow locked away behind the red-stone of his face.

'Take him away,' he ordered, and waited while they lifted the stretcher and staggered away with it.

He went to his pony, and his feet dragged a little through the grass. From the saddle he looked once more towards the south but the two bearers had disappeared wth their burden among the mimosa trees. He touched spurs to his pony's flanks and followed the long procession of wagons, prisoners and guns back towards the Tugela. The only sound was the jingle of harness and the melancholy rumble of wheels.

19

Garrick Courtney watched the champagne spilling into the crystal bowl of his glass. The bubbles swirled in golden patterns, catching the lantern light. The mess corporal lifted the bottle, dexterously caught a drop of wine on his napkin and moved behind Garry to fill the glass of Brigadier Lyttelton, who sat beside him.

'No.' Lyttelton placed a hand over his empty glass to prevent him doing so.

'Come, come, Lyttelton.' Sir Redvers Buller leaned forward and looked down the table. 'That's an excellent wine.'

'Thank you, sir, but champagne is for victory – perhaps we should have a case sent across the river.'

Buller flushed slowly and looked down at his own glass. Once more an ugly silence descended on the mess. In an effort to break it Garry spoke up.

'I do think the withdrawal today was made in extremely good order.'

'Oh. I agree most heartily.' From across the table Lord Dundonald's icy sarcasm added to the gaiety. 'But in all fairness, Colonel, we were travelling very light on our return.'

This oblique reference to the guns sent every eye to Buller's face – Dundonald was showing a reckless disregard of that notorious temper. But as a peer of the realm he could take the chance. With a courteous insolence he met Buller's glare, and held it until the pale bulging eyes faded and dropped.

'Gentlemen.' Buller spoke heavily. 'We have had a most trying day, and for all of us there is still work to do.' He glanced at his A.D.C. 'Clery, will you be kind enough to propose the Queen?'

Alone, Garry limped from the huge marquee mess tent. The smaller tents, lit internally, were a vast field of luminous cones, and above them the night was black satin sown with silver stars. The wine that Garry had drunk during dinner hummed in his head so that he did not notice the dejected silence that smothered the encampment as he picked his way through it.

As Garry entered his headquarters a man stood up from the camp chair beside his desk. In the light of the lantern his features were gaunt, and weariness showed in every line of his body.

'Ah! Curtis.'

'Good evening, sir.'

'You've come to make your report?'

'I have, sir. For what it's worth.'

'Tell me, Curtis – how many casualties?' There was an eagerness behind the question which Tim found ghoulish. Speculatively he examined Garry's face before replying.

'We suffered heavily, out of a strength of twenty we had four killed, two missing and five wounded – three of them seriously.'

'Have you made out a list?'

'Not yet.'

'Well, tell me. Who were they?'

'Killed were Booth, Amery . . .'

No longer could Garry hold his impatience, he blurted out suddenly:

'What about that sergeant?'

'You mean Courtney?'

'Yes. *Yes*.' And now with his impatience was mingled a dread that made his stomach feel hollow.

'Wounded, sir.'

And Garry felt a lift of relief so intense that he must close his eyes and suck in his breath to ride it up.

Sean was still alive! Thank God. Thank God for that.

'Where is he now?'

'They've got him down at the railhead hospital. He's being sent out with the first batch of badly wounded.'

'Badly?' Garry's relief changed quickly to concern, and he demanded harshly, 'How badly? *How badly?*'

'That's all they told me. I went down to the hospital but they wouldn't allow me to see him.'

Garry sank into his chair and instinctively reached for the drawer before he checked himself.

'Very well, Curtis. You may go.'

'The rest of my report, sir?'

'Tomorrow. Leave it till tomorrow.'

With the liquor glowing hotly in his belly, Garry set off

through the night towards the hospital. It did not matter now that he had planned and hoped that Sean would die. He no longer reasoned, but hurried through the sprawling camp, driven by his desperate need. Unrecognized but strong within him was the hope that he might again draw comfort and strength from that fountain as he had done so long ago. He started to run, stiffly, so the toe of his boot scuffed in the dust with each pace.

Desperately he searched through the hospital. He hurried along the rows of stretchers examining the faces of the wounded; he saw pain and mutilation and slow creeping death soaking like spilt red ink through the white bandages. He heard the moan and murmur and delirious laughter, he smelt the taint of agony-induced sweat blended with the heavy sweetness of corruption and disinfectant – and he hardly noticed them. One face, one face only, he wanted. And he did not find it.

'Courtney.' The medical orderly examined his list, tilting it to catch the lamplight. 'Ah! Yes. Here it is – let's see. Yes! He's gone already – left on the first train an hour ago . . . I can't say, sir, probably to Pietermaritzburg. They've established a big new hospital there. I can't tell you that either, I'm afraid, but they've got him listed here as *dangerous* . . . that's better than *critical* anyway.'

Wearing his loneliness like a cloak, Garry stumbled back to his quarters.

'Good evening, sir.' His servant was waiting for him. Garry always made them wait up. A new man this, they changed so fast. Never could keep a batman more than a month.

Garrick pushed past him, and half fell against the camp bed.

'Steady on, sir. Let's get you on to the bed, sir.' The man's voice was insidiously servile, the voice men used towards drunks. The touch of his hands infuriated Garry.

'Leave me.' He lashed out with a clenched fist across the man's face, throwing him back. 'Leave me. Get out and leave me!'

The servant rubbed his bruised cheek uncertainly, backing away.

'Get out!' Garry hissed at him.

'But, sir –'

'Get out, damn you. Get out!'

The man went out and closed the tent flap softly behind him. Garry stumbled across to it and laced it closed. Then he stood back. Alone. They can't see me now. They can't laugh now. They can't. Oh God, Sean!

He turned from the flap. The dummy leg caught on the rough floor and he fell. One of the straps parted and the leg twisted under him. On his hands and knees he crawled towards the commode across the tent, and the leg jerked and twisted grotesquely behind him.

Kneeling beside the commode he lifted the china basin from its recess and reached into the space below it and he found the bottle. His fingers were too clumsy for the cork, he pulled it with his teeth and spat it on to the floor. Then he held the bottle to his lips and his throat jerked rhythmically as he swallowed. A little of the brandy spilled on to his tunic and stained the ribbon of the Victoria Cross.

He lowered the bottle and rested, panting from the sting of the liquor. Then he drank again more slowly. The trembling of his hands stilled. His breathing smoothed out. He reached up and took the tumbler from the top of the commode, filled it, then placed the bottle beside him on the floor and wriggled into a more comfortable position against the commode.

In front of him his artificial leg twisted on its broken straps at an unnatural angle below the knee. He contemplated it, sipping the brandy slowly and feeling it numb the taste-buds of his tongue.

The leg was the centre of his existence. Insensate, unmoving, still as the eye of a great storm upon which the whole turmoil of his life revolved. The leg – always the leg. Always and only the leg.

Now under the lulling spell of the liquor he had drunk, from the stillness at the centre where the leg lay, he looked outward at the gigantic shadows of the past, and found them preserved and perfect, not distorted or blurred by time, whole and complete in each detail.

While they paraded through his mind, the night telescoped in upon itself so that time had no significance. The hours endured for a few minutes and were gone while the level in the bottle fell and he sat against the commode sipping at the tumbler and watching while the night wasted away. In the dawn the final act was played out before him.

Himself on a horse in the darkness riding in cold soft rain towards Theuniskraal. One window showing a yellow oblong of lantern light, the rest dark in the greater dark mass of the homestead.

The unaccountable premonition of coming horror closing cold and soft as the rain around him, the silence spoiled only by the crunch of his horse's hooves in the gravel of the drive. The thump of his pegleg as he climbed the front steps and the chill of the brass doorknob in his hand as he turned it and pushed it in upon the silence.

His own voice slurred with drink and dread. 'Hello. Where's everybody? Anna! Anna! I'm back!'

The blue flare of his match and the smell of burnt sulphur and paraffin as he lit the lamp, then the urgent echoing thump of his pegleg along the passage.

'Anna, Anna, where are you?'

Anna, his bride, lay upon the bed in the darkened room, half-naked, turning quickly away from the light, but he had seen the dead-white face with swollen and bruised lips.

The lamp from the table threw bloated shadows on the wall as he stooped over and gently drew down the petticoats to cover the whiteness of her lower body, then turned her to face him. 'My darling, oh Anna, my darling. What's happened?' Through the torn blouse her breasts were engorged and darkly nippled with pregnancy. 'Are you hurt? Who? Tell me who did it?' But she covered her face and broken lips with her hands.

'My darling, my poor darling. Who was it – one of the servants?'

'No.'

'Please tell me, Anna. What happened?'

Suddenly her arms were about his neck and her lips close against his ear. 'You know, Garry! You know who did it.'

'No, I swear I don't. Please tell me.'

Her voice tight and hoarse with hatred, uttering that word, that one unbelievable horrible word. 'Sean!'

'Sean!' he said aloud in his desolation. 'Sean. Oh God!' and then savagely. 'I hate him. I hate him! Let him die – please God, let him die.'

He closed his eyes, losing his grip upon reality, and felt the first dizzy swing of vertigo as the liquor took firm hold upon him.

Too late now to open his eyes and focus them upon the bed across the tent, the giddiness had begun – now he would not be able to hold it down. The warm, acid-sweet taste of brandy welled up into his throat and mouth and nose.

20

When his servant found him it was the middle of the morning. Garry lay fully dressed but asleep upon the bed with his sparse hair ruffled, his uniform stained and grubby, and the leg lying derelict in the centre of the floor.

The servant closed the door softly and studied his master, his nostrils flaring at the sour smell of stale brandy and vomit.

'Had yourself one hell of a bust-out. Hey – Hop, Skip and Jump?' he murmured without sympathy. Then he picked up the bottle and examined the inch of liquor remaining in it. 'Your bloody good health, cock,' he saluted Garry and drained the bottle, patted his lips delicately and spoke again. 'Right! Let's get your sty clean up.'

'Leave me alone,' Garry groaned.

'It's eleven o'clock, sir.'

'Leave me. Get out and leave me.'

'Drink this coffee, sir.'

'I don't want it. Leave me.'

'I've got your bath filled, sir, and a clean uniform laid out for you.'

'What time is it?' Garry sat up unsteadily.

'Eleven o'clock,' the man repeated patiently.

'My leg?' Garry felt naked without it.

'One of the harness makers is stitching the straps, sir. It'll be ready by the time you've bathed.'

Even in a position of rest Garry's hands, laid upon the desk in front of him trembled slightly, and the rims of his eyelids prickled. The skin of his face was stretched like that of a drum over the slow pain that throbbed within his skull.

At last he sighed and picked Lieutenant Curtis's report from the top of the slim sheaf of papers that waited for his attention. Garry skimmed through it dully, few of the names upon it meant anything to him. He saw Sean's name headed the list of wounded, and below him was the little Jewish lawyer. At last satisfied that the report contained nothing to the discredit of Colonel Garrick Courtney, he initialled it and laid it aside.

He picked up the next document. A letter addressed to him as Officer Commanding the Natal Corps of Guides, from a Colonel John Acheson of the Scots Fusiliers. Two pages of neat, pointed handwriting. He was about to discard it and leave it to his Orderly's attention when the name in the body of the text caught his eye. He leaned forward attentively and read quickly from the beginning.

'. . . pleasure in bringing to your attention . . . conduct beyond the call of . . . under intense enemy fire . . . once more, initiated an advance . . . although wounded . . . disregard of personal danger . . . two members of your Guides.

Sergeant Sean Courtney.
Pte. Saul Friedman.
. . . earnestly recommend . . . Distinguished Conduct Medal . . . great gallantry and powers of leadership.'

Garry dropped the letter and leaned back in his chair, staring at it as though it were his own death warrant. For a long while he did not move, while the pain kept beating in his head. Then he picked it up once more. Now his hands trembled so violently that the paper fluttered like the wing of a wounded bird.

'Everything of mine, everything I've ever owned – he's taken it from me,' and he looked down at the ribbons on his breast. 'I've never had . . . Now this, the one thing.'

A drop of moisture fell on to the letter, blurring the ink.

'I hate him,' he whispered and tore the letter across. 'I hope he dies,' and he tore again and again, ripping it to shreds and at last screwing them into a ball in his clenched fist.

'No. You'll not get that from me. It's mine – it's the one thing you'll never have!' He hurled the crumpled ball against the canvas of the tent, and lowered his head on to his arms upon the desk. His shoulders shook as he sobbed:

'Don't die. Please, Sean, don't die.'

21

Simply by putting his shoulder against her and shoving her aside, Dirk Courtney cleared a small girl from the doorway and was first down the steps and out into the sun. Without looking back at the schoolhouse he headed for the hole in the back hedge, the others would be following.

They caught up with him while he was selecting a *klei-lat* from the hedge.

'Hurry up,' Dirk ordered. 'We got to get to the river first else they'll get the best place.'

They spread out along the hedge, small boys chattering like a troop of excited monkeys.

'Lend me your knife, Dirkie.'

'Hey, look at my lat.' Nick Peterson brandished the short rod of Port Jackson Willow he had cut and peeled. It whipped with a satisfying swish.

'It's not a lat,' Dirk informed him. 'It's a Lee-Metford.' He looked round at the rest of his team. 'You remember now – I'm Lord Kitchener, and you got to call me "My Lord".'

'And I'm General French,' announced Nick. This was fair enough, after all, he was Dirk's chief lieutenant. It had taken Dirk a mere two weeks and five bloody fist-fights to reach his position as unchallenged leader.

'And I'm General Methuen!' one of the lesser members yelped.

'And I'm General Buller!'

'And I'm General Gatacre!'

'You can't all be generals.' Dirk glared around. 'Only Nick and I are generals. You are all just privates and things.'

'Gee, man, Dirkie! Why you always got to spoil things?'

'You shut your mouth, Brian.' Dirk sensed mutiny, and quickly he diverted their attention. 'Come on, let's go and get ammo.'

Dirk took the long route down the sanitary lane. This way he

596

was unlikely to meet adults and have any of his force seconded to serve elsewhere at wood chopping or gardening under parental control.

'Peaches are nearly ripe,' Nick commented as they passed the Pye orchard.

'Another week,' Dirk agreed, and crawled through the hedge into the Van Essen plantation that spread down to the Baboon Stroom.

'There they are!' someone shouted as they emerged from the trees.

'Boers, General!'

Out on the right, busy along the bank of the river was another bunch of small figures – sons of the Dutch families in the district.

'I'll go and talk to them,' Dirk said. 'You go for ammo.' They trotted off towards the river and Dirk called after them: 'Hey, Nick, get me a good dollop of clay.'

'All right, My Lord.'

With all the dignity of a general, officer and a peer of the realm, Dirk approached the enemy and stopped a short distance from them.

'Hey, Piet, are you ready yet?' he asked haughtily. Piet Van Essen was his second cousin twice removed. A chunky lad but not as tall as Dirk.

'Ja.'

'The same rules?' Dirk asked.

'Ja, the same rules.'

'No clothes,' Dirk warned him.

'And no throwing with stones,' Piet shot back.

'How many you got?' Dirk began counting the enemy suspiciously.

'Fifteen – same as you.'

'All right then,' Dirk nodded.

'All right then!'

Nick was waiting for him below the bank. Dirk jumped down beside him and accepted the large ball of blue clay that Nick handed him.

'It's just right, Dirkie, not too wet.'

'Good – let's get ready.'

Quickly Dirk stripped off his clothing, pulled the belt from the loops of his pants and buckled it around his waist to hold his spare lats.

'Hide the clothes, Brian,' Dirk ordered and surveyed his naked warriors. Nearly all of them still retained the almost womanly shape of youth; undeveloped chests, protruding stomachs and fat white buttocks.

'They'll come down the river like they do every time,' Dirk said. 'This time we're going to ambush them.' As he spoke he kneaded a handful of clay into a ball and spiked it on to the end of the lat. 'Me and Nick'll wait here – the rest of you on top of the bank in those bushes back there.'

He was looking for a target to practise on, and found it in a water tortoise which was laboriously climbing the far bank.

'Watch that old skilpad.' He interrupted himself; stepped forward with his right hand holding the lat thrown back, then whipped it through in an overhead swing. The ball of clay flew from the end of the rod with a vicious hum and smacked onto the shiny black carapace with a force that left a white starshaped crack upon the shell. The tortoise jerked in its head and limbs and toppled backwards into the stream.

'Good shot!'

'There he is, let me have a shot.'

'That's enough! You'll get plenty shots just now.' Dirk stopped them. 'Now listen to me! When they come me and Nick will hold them here for a bit, then we'll run back along the river and they'll chase us. Wait until they are right underneath you – then give it to them.'

Dirk and Nick crouched side by side, close in against the bank with the water up to their noses. A tuft of reeds hid those parts of their heads still above the surface and within easy reach their loaded clay-lats lay on dry land.

Below water Dirk felt Nick's elbow nudge his ribs, and he nodded carefully. He also had heard the whisper of voices around the bend of the river, and the roll and plop of loose earth dislodged by a careless foot. He turned his head and answered Nick's grin with one just as bloodthirsty, then he peered around the reeds.

Twenty paces in front of him a head appeared cautiously around the angle of the bank and the expression on its face was set and nervous – and Dirk moved his own head back behind the bunch of reeds.

A long silence broken suddenly. 'They're not here.' The voice was squeaky with adolescence and tension. Boetie was a delicate child, small for his age, who insisted on joining the rest of them in games beyond his strength.

Another long silence and then the sound of a wholesale but stealthy approach. Dirk reached out and gripped Nick's arm – the enemy were committed, out in the open – he lifted his mouth above the surface.

'Now!' he whispered and they reached for their lats. The surprise was complete and devastating. As Dirk and Nick rose dripping, with throwing arms cocked, the attackers were bunched in such a way that they could neither run nor return the fire unhampered.

The clay pellets flew into them, slapping loudly on bare flesh, producing howls of anguish and milling, colliding confusion.

'Give it to them,' shouted Dirk, and threw again without picking his man, blindly into the mass of legs and arms and pink backsides. Beside him Nick worked in a silent frenzy of load and throw.

The confusion lasted perhaps fifteen seconds, before the howls of pain became shouts of anger.

'It's only Dirk and Nick.'

'Get them – it's only two of them.'

The first pellet flipped Dirk's ear, the second hit him full in the chest.

'Run!' he gasped through the pain, and floundered to the bank. Bent forward to climb from the stream he was frighteningly vulnerable, and a pellet thrown at point-blank range took him in that portion of his anatomy which he was offering to the enemy. The sting of it propelled him from the water and clouded his vision with tears.

'Chase them!'

'Hit them!'

The pack bayed after them, pellets hissed about them and slapped at them as they pelted back along the stream. Before they reached the next bend their backs and bottoms were dappled with the angry red spots which tomorrow would be bruises.

Without discretion, hot with the chase, shouting and laughing, the attackers poured into the trap and as they rounded the bend it closed upon them.

Dirk and Nick stood poised to meet them, and suddenly the bank above their heads was lined with squealing, dancing, naked savages, who hurled a steady stream of missiles into them.

For a minute they stood it, then completely broken they scrambled out of the river-bed with pellets flailing them and raced panic-stricken for the shelter of the plantation.

One of them remained below the bank, kneeling in the mud, sobbing softly. But according to the unspoken laws that governed them this one was exempt from further punishment.

'It's only Boetie,' Nickie shouted. 'Leave him. Come on! Chase the others!' And he scrambled up the bank and led them after the flight. Yelling and shrilling with excitement they streamed away through the brown grass to where Piet Van Essen was desperately trying to stay the rout on the edge of the plantation, and gather his men to meet the charge.

But another of them remained below the bank – Dirk Courtney.

There were just two of them now. Screened by the bank, completely alone. Boetie looked up and through his tears saw Dirk coming slowly towards him. He saw the lat in Dirk's hand and the expression on his face. He knew he was alone with Dirk.

'Please, Dirk,' he whispered. 'I give up. Please. I give up.'

Dirk grinned. Deliberately he moulded the clay pellet onto his lat.

'I'll give you all my lunch tomorrow,' pleaded Boetie. 'Not just the sweets, I'll give you all of it.'

Dirk hurled the clay. Boetie's shriek thrilled his whole body. He began to tremble with the pleasure of it.

'I'll give you my new pocket-knife.' Boetie's voice was muffled by sobs and his arms which he had crossed over his face.

Dirk loaded the lat, slowly so he could savour this feeling of power.

'Please, Dirkie. Please, man, I'll give you anything you –' and Boetie shrieked again.

'Take your hands off your face, Boetie.' Dirk's voice was strangled, thick with pleasure.

'No, Dirkie. Please no!'

'Take your hands away, and I'll stop.'

'You promise, Dirkie. You promise you'll stop.'

'I promise,' whispered Dirk.

Slowly Boetie lowered his arms, they were thin and very white, for he always wore long sleeves against the sun.

'You promised, didn't you. I did what you –' and the clay hit him across the bridge of his nose, spreading as it struck, jerking his head back. Immediately there was blood from both nostrils.

Boetie clawed at his face, smearing blood on to his cheeks.

'You promised,' he whimpered. 'You *promised*!' But Dirk was already moulding the next pellet.

Dirkie walked home alone. He walked slowly, smiling a little, with soft hair falling forward on to his forehead and a smear of blue clay on one cheek.

Mary was waiting for him in the kitchen of the cottage on Protea Street. She watched from the window while he slipped through the hedge and crossed the yard. As he came towards the door she noticed the smile on his face. There was hardly sufficient room in her chest for what she felt as she looked at the innocent beauty of his face. She opened the door for him.

'Hello, darling.'

'Hello, Mary,' Dirk greeted her, and his little smile became a thing of such radiance that Mary had to reach for him.

'My goodness, you're covered in mud. Let's get you bathed before your gran'ma gets home.'

Dirk extricated himself from her embrace and moved in on the biscuit-tin.

'I'm hungry.'

'Just one,' Mary agreed, and Dirk took a handful. 'Then I've got a surprise for you.'

'What is it?' Dirk was more interested in the biscuits. Mary had a surprise for him every evening and usually it was something silly like a new pair of socks she had knitted.

'I'll tell you when you're in the bath.'

'Oh, all right.' Still munching Dirk set off for the bathroom. He began to disrobe along the passage dropping first his shirt and then his pants for Mary to retrieve as she followed.

'What is the surprise?'

'Oh Dirk, you've been playing that horrible game again.' Mary knelt beside the tub and gently passed the soapy flannel down his bruised back and buttocks. 'Please promise me you'll never play it again.'

'All right.' It was a very simple matter to extract a promise from Dirk, he had made this particular one before. 'Now, what's your surprise?'

'Guess.' Mary was smiling now, a secret knowing smile which immediately caught Dirk's attention. He studied her scarred face, her ugly loving face.

'Sweets?' he hazarded, and she shook her head and caressed his naked body with the flannel.

'Not socks!'

'No.' She dropped the flannel into the soap-scummed water and clasped him to her chest. 'No, not socks,' she whispered.

He knew then.

'Is it . . . ? Is it . . . '

'Yes, Dirkie, it's about your father.'

Instantly he began to struggle.

'Where is he, Mary? Where is he?'

'Into your nightshirt first.'

'Is he here? Has he come home?'

'No, Dirk. He isn't here yet. He's in Pietermaritzburg. But you're going to see him soon. Very soon. Gran'ma has gone now to make reservations on the train. You're going to see him tomorrow.'

His hot, wet body began to tremble in her arms, quivering with excitement.

22

'In some respects, Mrs Courtney, it was possibly all to the good that we were unable to contact you before.' The Surgeon-Major tamped tobacco into his pipe, and began methodically searching all his pockets.

'Your matches are on the desk.' Ada came to his assistance.

'Oh! Thank you.' He got the pipe drawing, and continued, 'You see, your son was attached to an irregular unit – there was no record of next-of-kin, and when he came to us from Colenso six weeks ago he was, shall we say, in no condition to inform us of your address.'

'Can we see Pa now?' Dirk could no longer contain himself, for the past five minutes he had wriggled and fidgeted on the couch beside Ada.

'You'll see your father in a few minutes, young man.' And the surgeon turned back to Ada. 'As it so happens, Mrs Courtney, you have been spared a great deal of anxiety. At first there were grave doubts that we would be able to save your son's life, let alone his right leg. Four weeks it hung in the balance, so to speak. But now' – and he beamed at Ada with justifiable pride – 'well, you'll see for yourself.'

'He's well?' Quickly, anxiously she asked.

'What a formidable constitution your son has, all muscle and determination.' He nodded, still smiling. 'Yes, he's well on the road to recovery. There may be a slight limp in the right leg – but when you weigh that against what might have been . . . ' He spread his hands eloquently. 'Now the sister will take you through to him.'

'When can he come home?' Ada asked from the doorway.

'Soon – another month, perhaps.'

*

A deep veranda, cool with shade and the breeze that came in across the hospital lawns. A hundred high metal beds along the wall, a hundred men in grey flannel nightshirts propped against white pillows. Some of them slept, a few were reading, others talked quietly or played chess and cards on boards set between the beds. But one lay withdrawn, staring at, but not seeing, the pair of fiscal shrikes which squabbled raucously over a frog on the lawn.

The beard was gone, removed while he was too weak to protest on the orders of the ward sister who considered it unhygienic, and the result was a definite improvement that even Sean secretly admitted. Shielded for so long, the skin on the lower half of his face was smooth and white like that of a boy; fifteen years had been shaved away with that coarse black matt. Now emphasis was placed on the heavy brows which, in turn, directed attention to his eyes, dark blue, like cloud shadow on mountain lakes. Darker blue at this moment as he considered the contents of the letter he held in his right hand.

The letter was three weeks old, and already the cheap paper was splitting along the creases from constant refolding. It was a long letter, much of it devoted to detailed description of the clumsy sparring along the Tugela River in which Buller's army was now engaged. There was one reference to the headaches from which the writer periodically suffered as a result of his wound which was now externally healed, and many more to the deep gratitude that Saul felt for him. These embarrassed Sean to such an extent that when re-reading the letter he scowled and skipped each one as he came to it.

But there was one paragraph to which Sean returned each time, and read slowly, whispering it to himself so that he could savour each word:

> I remember telling you about Ruth, my wife. As you know, she escaped from Pretoria and is in Pietermaritz- burg staying with relatives of hers. Yesterday I had a letter from her that contained the most wonderful tid- ings. We have been married four years this coming June, and now at last as a result of our brief meeting when she arrived in Natal – I am to become a father! Ruth tells me she has determined on a daughter (though I am certain it will be a son!) and she has

selected a name. It is a most unusual name, to be charitable – I can see that it will require a great deal of diplomacy on my part to make her change her mind. (Among her many virtues is an obstinacy reminiscent of the rock of ages.) She wants to name the poor waif 'Storm' – Storm Friedman – and the prospect appals me!

Although our faiths differ, I have written to Ruth asking her to agree to your election as 'Sandek' – which is the equivalent of godfather. I can foresee no objection from Ruth (especially in view of the debt which we both owe you) and it needs now only your consent. Will you give it?

At the same time I have explained to Ruth your present situation and address (c/o Greys Hospital!) and asked her to visit you there so that she can thank you personally. I warn you in advance that she knows as much about you as I do – I am not one to hide my enthusiasms!

Lying with the letter clutched in his hand, Sean stared out across the lawns into the sunlight. Beneath the bedclothes, swelling up like a pregnant belly, was the wicker basket that cradled his leg. 'Storm!' he whispered, remembering the lightning playing blue and blinding white upon her body.

'Why doesn't she come?' Three weeks he had waited for her. 'She knows that I am here, why doesn't she come to me?'

'Visitors for you.' The sister paused beside him and straightened the bedclothes.

'Who?' He struggled up on to his good elbow, with the other arm still in its sling across his chest.

'A lady.' And he felt it surge through him. 'And a small boy.' The cold backwash of disappointment, as he realized it was not her. Then immediately guilt – Ada and Dirk, how could he hope it was someone else?

Without the beard Dirk did not recognize him until he was ten paces away. Then he charged, his cap flew from his head and his dark hair, despite the bonds of brilliantine, sprang up into curls as he ran. He was squeaking incoherently as he reached the bed, clambered up on to Sean's chest to lock both arms around his neck.

It was some time before Sean could prise him loose and look at him.

'Well, boy,' he said, and then again, 'well, my boy.' Unable to trust himself not to lay his love for the child bare for all to see – there were a hundred men watching and grinning – Sean sought diversion by turning to Ada.

She waited quietly, as she had spent half her life waiting, but when he looked at her the tenderness showed in her smile.

'Sean.' She stooped to kiss him. 'What happened to your beard? You look so young.'

They stayed for an hour, most of which was taken up by a monologue from Dirk. In the intervals while he regained his breath Ada and Sean were able to exchange all their accumulated news. Finally, Ada stood up from the chair beside Sean's bed.

'The train leaves in half an hour, and Dirk has school tomorrow. We'll come up from Ladyburg each week-end until you are ready to return home.'

Getting Dirk out of the hospital was like evicting an unruly drunk from a bar. Alone Ada could not manage it and she enlisted a male hospital orderly to the cause. Kicking and struggling in tantrum, Dirk was carried down the veranda with his screams ringing back to Sean long after he had disappeared from view.

'I want my Dad. I want to stay with my Dad.'

23

Benjamin Goldberg was the executor of his brother's estate. This estate consisted of a forty-per-cent shareholding in Goldberg Bros. Ltd., a company which listed among its assets a brewery, four small hotels and a very large one situated on the Marine Parade at Durban, sixteen butcher shops, and a factory devoted to the manufacture of polony, pork sausages, bacon and smoked ham. The last products caused Benjamin some embarrassment, but their manufacture was too profitable to be discontinued. Benjamin was also the Chairman of the Board of Goldberg Bros., and a sixty-per-cent shareholder. The presence of an army of twenty-five thousand hungry and thirsty men in Natal had increased the consumption of beer and bacon in a manner that caused Benjamin further embarrassment, for he was a peaceable man. The huge profits forced upon him by the hostilities both troubled and delighted him.

These same two emotions were evoked by the presence in his household of his neice. Benjamin had four sons and not a single daughter, his brother Aaron had left one daughter for whom Benjamin would gladly have traded all four of his own sons. Not that the boys weren't doing very well, all of them settled into the business very nicely. One of them running the Port Natal Hotel, the eldest managing the brewery and the two others in the meat section. But – and here Benjamin sighed – but Ruth! There was a girl for a man's old age. He looked at her across the polished stinkwood breakfast table with its encrustation of silver and exquisite bone china, and he sighed again.

'Now, Uncle Ben, don't start again. Please.' Ruth buttered her toast firmly.

'So all I'm saying is that we need him here. Is that so bad?'

'Saul is a lawyer.'

'*Nu!* Is that so bad. He's a lawyer, but we need a lawyer with us. The fees I pay out to those other *schmoks!*'

'He doesn't want to come into the Company.'

'All right. We know he doesn't want charity. We know he doesn't want your money working for him. We know all about his pride – but now he's got responsibilities. Already he should be thinking about you – and the baby – not so much about what he wants.'

At the mention of the baby, Ruth frowned slightly. Benjamin noticed it, there were few things he did not notice. Young people! If only you could tell them. He sighed again.

'All right. We'll leave it until Saul comes back on leave,' he agreed heavily.

Ruth, who had never mentioned her uncle's offers of employment to Saul, had a momentary vision of living in Pietermaritzburg – close enough to be drowned in the tidal waves of affection that emanated from her Uncle Benjamin, caught like a tiny insect in the suffocating web of family ties and duties. She flashed at him in horror.

'You even mention it to Saul and I'll never speak to you again.'

Her cheeks flushed wondrously and fire burned in her eyes. Even the heavy braid of dark hair seemed to come alive like the tail of an angry lioness, flicking as she moved her head.

Oi Yoi Yoi! Benjamin hid his delight behind hooded lids. *What a temper! What a woman! She could keep a man young for ever.*

Ruth jumped up from the table. For the first time he noticed that she wore riding habit.

'Where are you going? Ruth, you're not riding again today.'

'Yes I am.'

'The baby!'

'Uncle Ben, why did you never learn to mind your own business?' And she marched out of the room. Her waist was not yet thickened with pregnancy and she moved with a grace that played a wild discord on the old man's heart strings.

'You should not let her treat you that way, Benjamin.' Mildly, the way she did everything, his wife spoke from across the table.

'There's something troubling that girl.' Carefully Benjamin wiped egg from his moustache, laid the napkin on the table, consulted the gold fob watch he drew from his waistcoat, and stood up. 'Something big. You mark my words.'

*

It was Friday, strange how Friday had become the pivot on which the whole week turned. Ruth urged the chestnut stallion, and he lengthened his stride under her, surging forward with such power that she had to check him a little and bring him down into an easy canter.

She was early and waited ten impatient minutes in the oak-lined lane behind Greys Hospital before, like a conspirator, the little nurse slipped out through the hedge.

'Have you got it?' Ruth demanded. The girl nodded, glanced around quickly and took an envelope out of her grey nursing cloak. Ruth exchanged it for a gold sovereign. Clutching the coin the nurse started back for the hedge.

'Wait.' Ruth stopped her. This was her only physical contact and she was reluctant to break it so soon. 'How is he?'

'It's all there, m'am.'

'I know – but tell me how he looks. What he does and says,' Ruth insisted.

'Oh, he's looking fine now. He's been up and about on his sticks all week, with that big black savage helping him. The first day he fell and you should have heard him swear. Lordy!' They both laughed together.

'He's a real card, that one. He and sister had another tiff yesterday when she wanted to wash him. He called her a shameless strumpet. She gave him what for all right. But you could see she was ever so pleased and she went around telling everybody about it.'

She burbled on and Ruth listened enchanted, until:

'Then yesterday, you know what he did when I was changing his dressing?' She blushed coyly. 'He gave me a pinch behind!'

Ruth felt a hot flood of anger wash over her. Suddenly she realized that the girl was pretty in an insipid fashion.

'And he said . . .'

'Thank you!' Ruth had to restrain the hand that held her riding-crop. 'I have to go now.' Usually the long skirts of her habit hampered her in mounting, but this time she found herself in the saddle without effort.

'Next week, m'am?'

'Yes,' and she hit the stallion across his shoulder. He lunged forward so violently that she had to clutch at the pommel of the saddle. She rode him as she had never ridden a horse before, driving him with whip and spur until dark patches of sweat showed on his flanks and froth spattered back along his shoulders, so that by the time she reached a secluded spot on the bank of the Umgeni River far out of town her jealousy had abated and she felt ashamed of herself. She loosened the stallion's girth and petted him a little before leaving him tethered to one of the weeping willows, and picking her way down the bank to her favourite log on the water's edge.

There she settled herself and opened the envelope. If only Sean could have known that his temperature chart, progress report, house-doctor's recommendations, and the sucrose content of his urine were being so avidly studied, he would probably have added a ruptured spleen to his other ills.

At last Ruth folded the pages into their envelope and tucked it away in the jacket of her habit. He must look so different without his beard. She stared into the pool below her and it seemed as though his face formed in the green water and looked back at her. She touched the surface with the toe of her riding-boot so that the ripples spread and shattered the image.

She was left with only the feeling of loneliness.

'I must not go to him,' she whispered, steeling the resolve which had kept her from him these past weeks since she had known he was there. So close – so terribly near.

Determinedly she looked down again into the pool and tried to conjure up the face of her husband. All she saw was a yellowfish, gliding quietly across the sandy bottom with the pattern of its scales showing like the teeth of a file along its sides. She dropped a pebble into the water and the fish darted away.

Saul. Merry little Saul with his monkey face, who made her laugh the way a mother laughs at her child. *I love him*, she thought. And it was true, she loved him. But love has many shapes, and some are the shapes of mountains – tall and jagged and big. While others are the shape of clouds – which have no shape, no sharp outline, soft they blow against the mountain and change and stream away but the mountain stands untouched by them. The mountain stands for ever.

'My mountain,' she murmured, and she saw him again so vividly, standing tall above her in the storm.

'Storm,' she whispered and clasped her open hands across her belly that was still flat and hard.

'Storm,' she whispered and felt the warmth within her. It spread outwards from her womb, the heat rising with it until it was a burning madness she could no longer control. With her skirts flying about her legs she ran to the stallion, her hands trembled on the straps of the girth.

'Just once,' she promised herself. 'Just this once more.' Desperately she clawed up into the saddle.

'Just this once, I swear it!' and then brokenly, 'I can't help myself. I've tried – oh God, how I've tried!'

An appreciative stirring and hum of comment from the beds along the wall followed her as she swept down the hospital veranda. There was urgent grace in the way she held her skirts gathered in one hand, in the crisp staccato tap of her pointed boots along the cement floor and the veiled swing of her hips above. There was unrestrained eagerness in the sparkle in her eyes and the forward thrust of her breasts beneath the wine-coloured jacket. The wild ride which brought her here had flushed her cheeks and tumbled her hair glossy black down her temple and on to her forehead.

Those sick and lonely men reacted as though a goddess had passed them by, thrilled by her beauty, yet saddened because she was unattainable. She did not notice them, she did not feel their hungry eyes upon her nor hear the aching whisper of their voices – for she had seen Sean.

He came slowly across the lawns towards the veranda, using the stick awkwardly to balance the drag of his leg. His eyes were downcast and he frowned in thought. Her breath caught in her throat as she saw how wasted was his body. She had not remembered him so tall with shoulders gaunt and wide like the cross-tree of a gallows. Never before had she seen the bony thrust of his jawline, nor the pale smoothness of his skin faintly blue with new-shaved beard. But she remembered the eyes heavily overscored with black brows, and his great beaky nose above the wide sensuality of his mouth.

On the edge of the lawn he stopped with feet apart, set the point of the cane between them with both hands clasped over the head of it, and he lifted his eyes and looked at her.

For many seconds neither of them moved. He stood balancing on the cane with his shoulders hunched and his chin raised as he stared at her. She in the shadow of the veranda, her skirts still held in one hand – but the other at her throat, fingers trying to still the emotions that fluttered there.

Gradually his shoulders straightened until he stood tall. He hurled the cane aside and reached both hands open towards her.

Suddenly she was running over the smooth, green lawn. Into his arms, trembling in silent intensity, while he held her.

With both arms around his waist and her face pressed against his chest she could smell the man smell of him and feel the hard muscle of his arms as he enfolded her – and she knew she was safe. As long as she stayed like this – nothing, nobody could touch her.

24

On the slope of the table-topped mountain that crouches over the town of Pietermaritzburg there is a glade among the wattle trees. It is a secret place where even the timid little blue buck come out to graze in daylight. On a still day you can hear very faintly the pop of the wagon whips on the road below, or farther off the steam whistle of a train. But that is all that intrudes in this wild place.

A butterfly crossed the glade in uncertain wobbling flight, it came out of the sunlight into the dappled, moving shade along the edge, and settled.

'That's good luck,' Sean murmured lazily and Ruth lifted her head from the plaid rug on which they lay. As the butterfly moved its wings, fanning them gently, the iridescent green and yellow markings sparkled in the speck of sunlight that pierced the roof of leaves above them and fell upon it like a spotlight.

'It tickles,' she said, and the insect moved like a living jewel across the smooth white field of her belly. It reached her navel and paused. Then the tiny tendril of its tongue uncurled and dabbed at the fine sheen of moisture that their loving had left upon her skin.

'He's come to bless the baby.'

The butterfly skirted the deep, delicately chiselled pit and moved on downwards.

'Don't you think he's being just a little forward – he doesn't have to bless that as well?' Ruth asked.

'He certainly seems to know his way around,' Sean admitted dubiously.

The butterfly found its road southwards blocked by a forest of dark curls, so laboriously it turned and retraced its steps towards the north. Once more it detoured round her navel and then headed unerringly for the pass between her breasts.

'Keep right on, friend,' Sean cautioned, but it turned suddenly and climbed the steep slope until at last it sat triumphant on the peak.

Sean watched it throbbing its wings, blazing in oriental splendour upon her nipple, and he felt himself stirred once more.

'Ruth.' His voice was husky again. She rolled her head to look into his eyes.

'Go away, little butterfly,' and she brushed it from her breast.

Later, after they had slept a little, Ruth woke him and they sat facing each other on the rug with the open hamper between them.

While Sean uncorked the wine she worked over the hamper with the dedication of a priestess preparing a sacrifice. He watched her split the bread rolls and fill them with salty, yellow butter, then open the screw-topped jars of soused beans and pickled onions and beetroot. A heart of young lettuce rustled crisply as she plucked its leaves into a wooden bowl, and poured dressing over them.

Her hair, released from its braid, broke like a black wave over the marble of her shoulders, then rippled and swung with the small movements of her body. With the back of her hand she brushed it from her forehead, then looked up at him and smiled.

'Don't stare. It's bad manners.' She took the glass he offered her and sipped the cool yellow wine, set it aside and went on to dismember the fat-breasted chicken. Pretending to ignore his eyes upon her body, she began to sing, softly, the love-song she had sung on the night of the storm and shyly her breasts peeped at him through the black curtain of her hair.

She wiped her fingers carefully on a linen napkin, took up the wineglass again and with elbows on her knees leaned forward slightly and returned his scrutiny with equal frankness.

'Eat,' she said.

'And you?'

'In a little while. I want to watch you.'

Then he was hungry.

'You eat the way you make love – as though tomorrow you die.'

'I'm taking no chances.'

'You're covered with scars, like an old tom-cat who fights too much,' and she leaned forward and touched his chest with one finger. 'What happened there?'

'Leopard.'

'And there?' She touched his arm.

'Knife.'

'And there?' his wrist.

'Burst shotgun.'

She dropped her hand and caressed the fresh purple cicatrice that twined around his leg like some grotesque parasitic vine.

'This one I know,' she whispered and her eyes were sad as she touched it.

Quickly, to change her mood, he spoke.

'Now it's my turn to ask the questions.' He reached across and laid his open hand upon her stomach where the first faint bulge pressed warmly into his palm.

'What happened there?' he demanded, and she giggled before she replied. 'Burst shotgun – or was it a cannon?'

When she had repacked the hamper she knelt beside him. He lay flat on his back with a long black cheroot between his teeth.

'Have you had sufficient?' she asked.

'My God, yes,' and he sighed happily.

'Well, I haven't.' She leaned over him, took the cheroot from his mouth and flicked it into the brambles.

With the first faint flush of evening in the sky a small breeze came down from the mountain and rustled the leaves above them. The fine hairs upon her forearms came erect, each on its tiny pimple of gooseflesh, and her nipples stood out dark and hard.

'You must not be late back to the hospital on the very first day they've let you out.' She rolled away from him and reached for her clothing. 'Matron will have me hung, drawn and quartered.' Sean agreed. They dressed quickly, and she was remote from him. All the laughter gone from her voice and her face cold and expressionless.

He stood behind her to lace the whalebone corset. He hated to cage that lovely body and was about to say so.

'Saul is coming tomorrow. A month's leave.' Her voice was harsh. His hands stilled and they stood without moving. It was the first time either of them had referred to Saul since that morning a month ago when she had come to him at the hospital.

'Why didn't you tell me sooner?' His voice also was harsh.

'I didn't want to spoil today.' She had not turned towards him, but stood staring out across the glade to the far hills beyond the town.

'We must decide what we are going to tell him.'

'There is nothing to tell him,' she answered flatly.

'But what are we going to do?' Now his voice was ugly with mingled dread and guilt.

'Do, Sean?' She turned slowly and her face was still cold and expressionless. 'We are going to do nothing – nothing at all.'

'But you belong to me!' he cried in protest.

'No,' she answered.

'The child – it's mine!'

At his words her eyes narrowed and the sweet line of her lips hardened in anger.

'No, damn you, it isn't! Not yours – although you sired it.' She flamed at him. It was the first time she had unleashed her temper at him. It startled Sean. 'The child belongs to Saul – and I belong to Saul. We owe you nothing.'

He stared at her. 'You don't mean that,' and the flames of her anger faded. Quickly he tried to press his advantage.

'We'll go away together.'

'*Run away* – you mean. *Sneak away* like a pair of thieves. What would we take with us, Sean? The happiness of a man who loves and trusts us both – that, and our own guilt. You'd never forgive me, nor I you. Even now when we talk of it you cannot meet my eyes. Already you are beginning to hate me a little'

'No! No!'

'And I would hate you,' she whispered. 'Call for my horse, please.'

'You don't love him.' The agonized accusal was wrung from him, but it was as though he had not spoken. She went on dressing.

'He'll want to see you. Half of every letter he writes is about you. I've told him that I've visited you at the hospital.'

'I'm going to tell him,' Sean shouted. 'I'll tell him everything.'

'No, you won't.' She answered him calmly. 'You did not save him at Colenso to destroy him now. You would destroy him – and us. Please call for my horse.'

Sean whistled and they stood together, not touching, not talking, not even looking at each other. Until Mbejane emerged from the bush below the glade leading the horses.

Sean lifted her into the saddle.

'When?' he asked quietly.

'Perhaps never,' she answered and swung the horse away. She did not look back so Sean never saw the tears that streamed down her face. The muffled drum of hooves drowned her sobs and she held her back and her shoulders stiff so that he would not know.

25

The War Council ended long after dark and when his commandants had unsaddled and ridden away to their laagers among the
hills, Jan Paulus sat alone beside the fire.

He was tired, as though his brain was the cold, flabby body of
an octopus and its tentacles spread out to every extremity of his
body. He was lonely. Now at the head of five thousand men he
was alone as he had never been in the vast solitude of the open
veld.

Because of the loneliness and because of the companionship
she had given him these past twenty years his thoughts turned
to Henrietta, and he smiled in the darkness and felt the longing
blunt the edge of his determination.

I would like to go back to the farm, for a week only. Just to
see that they are all well. I would like to read to them from the
Book and watch the faces of the children in the lamplight. I
would like to sit with my sons on the stoep and hear the voices
of Henrietta and the girls as they work in the kitchen. I would
like . . .

Abruptly he stood up from beside the fire. Ja, you would like
this and you would like that! Go, then! Give yourself leave of
absence as you have refused it to so many others. He clenched
his jaw, biting into the stem of his pipe. Or else, sit here and
dream like an old woman while twenty-five thousand English-
men pour across the river.

He strode out of the laager, and the earth tilted upwards
beneath his feet as he headed for the ridge. Tomorrow, he
thought. Tomorrow.

God has been merciful that they did not rush the ridge two
days ago when I had three hundred men to hold it. But now I
have five thousand to their twenty-five – so let them come!

Suddenly, as he reached the crest, the valley of the Tugela lay
below him. Soft with moonlight so that the river was a black

gash in the land. He scowled as he saw the field of bivouac fires that straddled the drift at Trichardts farm.

They have crossed. May God forgive me that I had to let them cross, but I could not meet and hold them with three hundred. Two days I have waited in agony for my columns to cover the twenty miles from Colenso. Two days while the cannon bogged down in the mud. Two days while I watched their cavalry and their foot soldiers and their wagons crossing the drift and I could not stop them.

Now they are ready. Tomorrow they will come up to us. This is where they will come, to try at any other place is madness, a stupidity far beyond any they have shown before.

They cannot try the right, for to reach it they must march across our front. With little cover and the river fencing them in they would expose their flank to us at two thousand yards. No, they cannot try the right – not even Buller will try the right.

Slowly he turned his head and looked out to the left where the tall peaks rose sheer out of the heights. The formation of the ground resembled the back of a gigantic fish. Jan Paulus stood upon its head, on the relatively smooth slope of Tabanyama – but on his left rose the dorsal fin of the fish. This was a series of peaks – Vaalkrans, Brakfontein, Twin Peaks, Conical Hill and, the highest and the most imposing of all, Spion Kop.

Once again, he experienced the nagging prickle of doubt. Surely no man, not even Buller, would throw any army against that line of natural fortresses. It would be senseless as the sea hurling its surf at a line of granite cliffs. Yet the doubt remained.

Perhaps Buller, that pedestrian and completely predictable man; Buller who seemed eternally committed to the theory of frontal assault, perhaps this time he would know that the slopes of Tabanyama were *too* logically the only point at which he could break through. Perhaps he would know that the whole of the Boer Army waited for him there with all their guns. Perhaps he would guess that only twenty burghers guarded each of the peaks on the left flank – that Jan Paulus had not dared to spread his line so thin, and had risked everything on Tabanyama.

Jan Paulus sighed. Now it was past the time for doubt. He had made the choice and tomorrow they would know. Tomorrow, *van more*.

Heavily he turned away and started down towards the laager. The moon was setting behind the black massif of Spion Kop, and its shadow hid the path. Loose rock rolled under his feet. Jan Paulus stumbled and almost fell.

'*Wies Daar?*' The challenge from an outcrop of granite beside the path.

'A friend.' Jan Paulus saw the man now, he leaned against the rock with a Mauser held low across his hips.

'Tell me – what commando are you with?'

'The Wynbergers under Leroux.'

'So! Do you know Leroux?' the sentry asked.

'Yes.'

'What colour is his beard?'

'Red – red as the flames of hell.'

The sentry laughed.

'Tell Oom Paul from me I'll tie a knot in it next time I see him.'

'Best you shave before you try – he might do the same for you,' Jan Paulus warned him.

'Are you his friend?'

'And his kinsman too.'

'The hell with you then also.' The sentry laughed again. 'Will you drink coffee with us?'

It was an ideal opportunity for Jan Paulus to mingle with his men and gauge their temper for tomorrow. '*Dankie.*' He accepted the invitation.

'Good.' The sentry straightened up and Jan Paulus saw he was a big man, made taller by the homburg hat he wore. 'Karl, is there any coffee left in the pot?' He yelled into the darkness beyond the rocks and was answered immediately.

'In the name of God, must you bellow? This is a battlefield, not a political meeting.'

'The English are as loud. I've heard them all night.'

'The English are fools. Must you be the same?'

'For you, only for you.' The sentry dropped his voice to a sepulchral whisper, and then roared again suddenly: 'But what about that damned coffee?'

This one is not short of stomach, Jan Paulus grinned to himself, as the man, still chuckling happily, placed an arm about his shoulder and led him to the screened fire among the rocks. Three burghers squatted about it with blankets draped over their shoulders. They were talking among themselves as the sentry and Jan Paulus approached.

620

'The moon will be down in half an hour,' one of them said.
'Ja. I will not be happy to see it gone. If the English plan a night attack, then they will come in the dark of the moon.'

'Who is with you?' Karl asked as they came towards the fire.

'A friend,' the sentry replied.

'From what commando?'

'The Wynbergers,' Jan Paulus answered for himself, and Karl nodded and lifted the battered enamel coffee-pot from the fire.

'So, you are with Oom Paul. And what does he think of our chances for tomorrow?'

'That of a man with one bullet left in thick catbush with a lungshot buffalo coming down in full charge.'

'And does it worry him?'

'Only a madman knows no fear. Oom Paul is afraid. But he tries not to show it, for fear spreads among men like the white sore throat diphtheria,' Jan Paulus replied as he accepted the mug of coffee and settled down against a rock out of the firelight so they would not recognize his face nor the colour of his beard.

'Show it or not,' grunted the sentry as he filled his mug. 'But I reckon he'd give one of his eyeballs to be back on his farm at Wynberg with his wife beside him in the double bed.'

Jan Paulus felt the glow of anger in his belly and his voice as he replied was harsh.

'You think him a coward?'

'I think I would rather stand on a hill a mile behind the fighting and send other men in to die,' the sentry chuckled again, but there was a sardonic note in it.

'I've heard him swear that tomorrow he will be in front wherever the fight is fiercest,' growled Jan Paulus.

'Oh, he said so? So that we fight more cheerfully? But when the Lee-Metfords rip your belly open – how will you know where Oom Paul is?'

'I have told you he is my kin. When you insult him you insult me.' Anger had closed Jan Paulus's throat so that his voice was hoarse.

'Good!' The sentry stood up quickly. 'Let us settle it now.'

'Be still, you fools.' Karl spoke irritably. 'Save your anger for the English,' and then more softly, 'all of us are restless, knowing what tomorrow will bring. Let your quarrel stand.'

'He is right,' Jan Paulus agreed, still choked with anger. 'But when I meet you again . . . !'

'How will you know me?' the sentry demanded.

'Here!' Jan Paulus jerked the wide-brimmed Terai hat from his head and flung it at the man's feet. 'Wear that and give me yours in exchange.'

'Why?' The sentry stood puzzled.

'Then if ever a man comes up to me and says, "You're wearing my hat", he will be saying, "Jan Paulus Leroux is a coward!"'

The man grinned so that his teeth glittered in the firelight, then he dropped his own black homburg into Jan Paulus's lap and stooped to pick up the Terai. In that instant, faintly on the wind, soft as the crackle of dried twigs, they heard the rifle-fire.

'Mausers!' shouted Karl and he leapt to his feet sending the coffee-pot flying.

'On the left,' moaned Jan Paulus in anguish. 'Oh, God help us! They've tried the left.'

The chorus of rifle-fire rose, swelling urgently; and now blending with the crisp crackle of the Mausers was the deep belling of the Lee-Metfords.

'Spion Kop! They're on Spion Kop,' and Jan Paulus ran, hurling himself down the path towards the laager with the black homburg jammed down over his ears.

26

The mist lay heavily on the peak of Spion Kop that morning, so that the dawn was a thing of liquid, pearly light. A soft uncertain thing that swirled about them and condensed in tiny drops upon the metal of their rifles.

Colonel John Acheson was breakfasting on ham sandwiches spread thickly with Gentleman's Relish. He sat on a boulder with his uniform cloak draped over his shoulders and chewed morosely.

'No sign of the jolly old Boer yet,' the captain beside him announced cheerfully.

'That trench is not deep enough.' Acheson glowered at the shallow ditch which had been scraped in the stony soil and which was now filled to capacity with men in all the various attitudes of relaxation.

'I know, sir. But there's not much we can do about it. We're down to bedrock and it would need a wagon-load of dynamite to sink another foot.' The captain selected a sandwich and upended the Relish bottle over it. 'Anyway, all the enemy fire will be from below and the parapets will cover that.' Along the front edge of the trench clods of earth and loose rock had been piled to a height of two feet. Pathetic cover for two thousand men.

'Have you ever been on this mountain before?' Acheson asked politely.

'No, sir. Of course not.'

'Well, what makes you so bloody certain how the land lies. You can't see a thing in this mist.'

'Well, sir, we *are* on the crest, and it *is* the highest . . . ' But Acheson interrupted him irritably. 'Where are those damned scouts? Haven't they come in yet?' He jumped up and with his cloak swirling about him strode along the trench. 'You men. Can't you get that parapet higher there!'

At his feet a few of them stirred and began half-heartedly piling stone. They were exhausted by the long night climb and the skirmish which had driven the Boer garrison from the mountain, and Acheson heard them muttering sullenly behind him as he walked on.

'Acheson!' Out of the mist ahead of him loomed the figure of General Woodgate followed closely by his staff.

'Sir!' Acheson hurried to meet him.

'Are your men entrenched?'

'As best they can.'

'Good. What of the enemy? Have your scouts reported back yet?'

'No. They're still out there in the mist.' And Acheson pointed into the smoky billows that limited the range of their vision to fifty feet.

'Well, we should be able to hold until we are reinforced. Let me know the moment . . . ' A small commotion in the mist behind them, and Woodgate paused. 'What is it?'

'My scouts, sir.'

Saul Friedman began delivering his report from a range of twenty feet. His face was working with excitement as he scurried out of the mist.

'False crest! We're on the false crest. The true summit is two hundred yards ahead and there's a rise of ground out on our right flank, like a little knoll all covered with aloes, that enfilades our whole position. There are Boers everywhere. The whole bloody mountain is crawling with them.'

'Good God, man! Are you certain?'

'Colonel Acheson,' snapped Woodgate, 'turn your right flank to face the knoll,' and as Acheson strode away he added under his breath, 'if you have time!' and he felt the agitated swirl of the mist as it was swept away before the wind.

27

Jan Paulus stood beside his pony. The mist had dewed in his beard and set it a-sparkle in red-gold. Across both shoulders heavy bandoliers of ammunition drooped, and the Mauser rifle seemed like a child's toy in his huge hairy hands. His jaw was thrust forward in thought as he reviewed his dispositions. All night he had flogged his pony from laager to laager, all night he had roared and bullied and driven men up the slopes of Spion Kop. And now around him the mountain rustled and murmured with five thousand waiting burghers, and in an arc of 120 degrees behind it stood his guns. From Green Hill in the north-west to the reverse slopes of the Twin Peaks in the east, his gunners crouched beside their creusots and their Nordenfeldts, ready to range in upon the crest of Spion Kop.

All things are ready and now I must earn the right to wear this hat. He grinned and settled the homburg more firmly over his ears.

'Hennie, take my horse back to the laager.'

The boy led it away and he started up the last slope towards the summit. The light strengthened as he climbed and the burghers among the rocks recognized the flaming beacon of his beard.

'*Goeie Jag*, Oom Paul,' and, '*Kom saam om die Rooi Nekke te skiet*,' they called. Then two burghers ran down to meet him.

'Oom Paul. We've just been forward to Aloe Knoll. There are no English on it!'

'Are you sure?' It seemed too generous a gift of fortune.

'*Ja*, man. They are all on the back of the mountain. We heard them digging and talking there.'

'What commando are you?' Jan Paulus demanded of the men massed around him in the mist.

'The Carolina commando,' voices answered.

'Come,' ordered Jan Paulus. 'Come, all of you. We are going to Aloe Knoll.'

They followed. Skirting the summit, with the brush, brush, brush of hundreds of feet through the grass, hurrying so that their breathing steamed in the moist air. Until abruptly ahead of them humped the dark mound of Aloe Knoll and they swarmed over it and disappeared among the rocks and crevices like a column of ants returning to their nest.

Lying on his belly Jan Paulus lit his pipe and tamped down on the glowing tobacco with a fire-calloused thumb, sucked the smoke into his mouth and peered into the solid white curtain of mist. In the eerie silence that had fallen upon the mountain his stomach rumbled loudly and he remembered that he had not eaten since the previous noon. There was a stick of biltong in his coat pocket.

A lion hunts best on an empty stomach, he thought and drew again on his pipe.

'Here comes the wind,' a voice whispered near him, and he heard the rising sibilance of it through the aloes above his head. The aloes stood tall as a man, multi-headed, green candelabra tipped in crimson and gold, nodding slightly in the morning wind.

'*Ja.*' Jan Paulus felt it stirring deep in his chest, that blend of fear and exhilaration that drowned his fatigue. 'Here it comes.' He knocked out his pipe, stuffed it still hot into his pocket and lifted his rifle from the rock in front of him.

Dramatically, as though unveiling a monument, the wind stripped the mists away. Beneath a sky of cobalt blue, soft golden brown in the early sunshine, lay the rounded peak of Spion Kop. A long uneven scar of red earth five hundred yards long was slashed across it.

'*Almagtig!*' Jan Paulus gasped. 'Now we have them.'

Above the crude parapet of the trench, like birds on a fence rail, so close that he could see the chinstraps and the button on each crown, the light khaki helmets contrasted clearly with the darker earth and grass. While beyond the trench, completely exposed from boots to helmets, standing in the open or moving leisurely forward with ammunition and water canteens, were hundreds of English soldiers.

For long seconds the silence persisted, as though the burghers who stared over their rifles at this unbelievable target could not bring themselves to press the triggers on which their fingers rested. The English were too close, too vulnerable. A universal reluctance held the Mausers silent.

'Shoot!' roared Jan Paulus. '*Skiet, Kerels, Skiet,*' and his voice carried to the English behind the trenches. He saw all movement among them suddenly paralysed, white faces turn to stare in his direction – and he sighted carefully into the chest of one of them. The rifle jumped against his shoulder, and the man went down into the grass.

That single shot broke the spell. Gunfire crackled in hysterical unison and the frieze of khaki figures along the trench exploded into violent movement as the bullets thudded amongst them. At that range most of Jan Paulus's burghers could be trusted to knock down four running springbok with five shots. In the few seconds that it took the English to dive into the trench, at least fifty of them went down, dead or wounded, and lay sprawled against the red earth.

Now there were only the helmets and heads above the parapet to shoot at and these were never still. They ducked and weaved and bobbed as Woodgate's men fired and reloaded, and seventeen hundred Lee-Metford rifles added their voices to the pandemonium.

Then the first shell, lobbed from a field gun on the reverse slope of Conical Hill, shrieked over the heads of the burghers and burst in a leap of smoke and red dust fifty feet in front of the English trench. A lull while Jan Paulus's heliograph team below the crest signalled the range correction to the battery, then the next shell burst beyond the trench; another lull and the third fell full upon the trench. A human body was thrown high, legs and arms spinning like the spokes of a wagon wheel. When the dust cleared there was a gap in the parapet and half a dozen men frantically trying to plug it with loose rock.

Together all the Boer guns opened. The constant shriek of big shells was punctuated by the vicious whine of the quick-firing pompoms. And once again a mist covered the peak, this time a thin sluggish mist of dust and lyddite fume which diluted the sunlight and clogged the nostrils and eyes and mouths of men for whom a long, long day had begun.

28

Lieutenant-Colonel Garrick Courtney was damnably uncomfortable. It was hot in the sun. Sweat trickled down under his tunic and moistened his stump so that already it was chafed. His fieldglasses magnified the glare as he looked out across the Tugela River to the great hump of the mountain four miles away. The glare aggravated the ache behind his eyes, which was a memorial to last night's drinking.

'Woodgate seems to be holding very well. His reinforcements should be up to him soon enough.'

Sir Redvers Buller appeared to be satisfied, and none of his staff had any comment to add. Stolidly they stood and stared through their glasses at the peak which was now faintly blurred with the dust and smoke of battle.

Garrick was puzzling once more the devious lines of authority which Buller had established for the attack on Spion Kop. Commanding the actual assault was General Woodgate, who was now 'holding very well' on the peak, yet Woodgate was responsible not to Buller but to General Charles Warren, who had his headquarters beyond Trichardts Drift where the column had crossed. Warren was in turn responsible to Buller, who was well back behind the river, standing on a pleasant little hill called Mount Alice.

Everyone on the staff was aware that Buller hated Warren. Garrick was certain that Warren had been given command of an operation which Buller considered very risky, so that in the event it failed Warren would be discredited and goaded into resigning. Of course, if he succeeded, Sir Redvers Buller was still supreme Commander and the credit would therefore accrue to him.

It was a line of reasoning Garrick found easy to follow, in fact, had he been in Buller's position he would have done exactly the same thing. This secret knowledge gave Garry a deal of satisfaction, and standing beside Buller on the slope of Mount Alice he felt very much in tune with him. He found himself hoping that Spion Kop would soon be a bloody slaughter-house, and that Warren would retreat across the river in disgrace. He remembered the occasion in the mess when Sir Charles had referred to him as an 'irregular, and a damned *colonial* irregular – at that!' Garry's fingers tightened on his field-glasses and he glared out at the mountain. He was so deep in his resentment that he hardly noticed the signaller who came running from the mule wagon that housed the field telegraph which connected Buller's headquarters with those of Warren beyond the river.

'Sir! Sir! A message from General Warren.' The urgency of the man's tone caught all their attentions. As one man the entire general staff lowered their glasses and turned to him.

'Let's have it then, my man!' Buller snatched the sheet of notepaper and read it slowly. Then he looked up at Garry and there was something in those pale, bulging eyes, a pleasure, a conspiratorial gleam that made Garry almost grin.

'What do you make of that, Courtney?' He handed the sheet across and waited while Garry read it.

'Message from Colonel Crofton on the Spion Kop. *Reinforce at once or all is lost. General Woodgate dead. What do you suggest. Warren.*'

'It seems to me, sir,' Garry spoke slowly, trying to mask the fierce jubilation he felt, 'that Sir Charles Warren is on the verge of panic.'

'Yes, that's the way it looks.' Buller was openly gloating now.

'I would suggest sending him a message that will stiffen him, sir.'

'Yes, I agree.' Buller turned to the signaller and began to dictate. 'The mountain must be held at all costs. No withdrawal. I repeat no withdrawal. Reinforce with Middlesex and Dorset regiments.' Then he hesitated and looked around his staff. 'What do you know of this fellow Crofton. Is he the right man to command on the peak?'

There were non-committal sounds of negation from them until A'Court, Buller's A.D.C., spoke up.

'Sir. There is one excellent man up there – Acheson – Colonel John Acheson. You remember his showing at Colenso?'

Buller nodded thoughtfully and turning back to the signaller he went on with his dictation. 'You must put some really good hard fighting man in command on the peak. Suggest you promote Acheson to Major-General.'

29

In front of the trench the grass was flattened by the repeated counter-attacks that had swept across it, stained by the blood of those who had dragged themselves back from the Boer positions along the crest, and littered with the twisted corpses of those who had not. Every few seconds a shell exploded along the British line, so there was a continual moving forest of bursts, and the shrapnel hissed like the flails of threshing giants.

John Acheson forced himself to his feet and climbed on to the parapet and shouted, 'Come on, lads. This time they'll not stop us!' In the trench below him the dead and the wounded lay upon each other two and three deep, all of them coated with a layer of red dust. The same red dust coated the faces that looked up at him as he shouted again.

'Bugler, sound the charge. Come, lads, forward. Take the bayonet to them.'

The bugle started to sing, brassy and urgent. Acheson hopped like a gaunt, old stork from the parapet and flapped his sword. Behind him he heard laughter from a dozen throats, not the laughter of ordinary men, but the chilling discord of insanity.

'Follow me, the Lancs! Follow me!' His voice rose to a shriek and they scrambled from the trench behind him. Dusty spectres with bloodshot eyes, smeared with dust and their own sweat. Their laughter and their curses blended with the babbling of the wounded, outstripped it and climbed into a chorus of wild cheers. Without form, spreading like spilled oil, the charge flowed out towards the crest. Four hundred men staggering through the dust-storm of shell-fire and the tempest of the Mausers.

Acheson stumbled over a corpse and fell. His ankle twisted with a shock of pain that jolted his dulled senses. He recovered his sword, dragged himself up and limped grimly on towards the rampart of boulders that marked the crest. But this time they did not reach it to be thrown back as they had before. This time the charge withered before it had covered half the distance. In vain Acheson waved them forward, yelling until his voice was a hoarse croak. They slowed and wavered, then at last they broke and streamed back down the open bullet-swept slope to the trench. Tears of frustrated anger streaking his dusty cheeks, Acheson hobbled after them. He fell over the parapet and lay face down on the corpses that lined the trench.

A hand shaking his shoulder roused him and he sat up quickly and tried to control the breathing that shuddered up his throat. Dimly he recognized the man who crouched beside him.

'What is it, Friedman?' he gasped. But the reply was drowned in the arrival of another shell, and the delirious shrieks of a man wounded in the belly in the trench beside them.

'Speak up, man!'

'Heliograph message from Sir Charles Warren,' shouted Saul. 'You have been promoted General. You are in command of the peak.' And then with a dusty sweat-streaked grin he added: 'Well done, sir.'

Acheson stared at him aghast. 'What about General Woodgate?'

'He was shot through the head two hours ago.'

'I didn't know.' Since morning Acheson had known nothing that was happening outside his own small section of the line. His whole existence had closed down to a hundred yards of shrapnel-and-bullet-swept earth. Now he peered out at the holocaust around him and whispered, 'In command! No man commands here! The devil is directing this battle.'

'Sir Charles is sending up three more battalions to reinforce us,' Saul shouted into his ear.

'We can well use them,' Acheson grunted, and then, 'Friedman, I've sprained my ankle. I want you to lace up my boot as tight as you can – I'm going to need this foot again before the day is done.'

Saul knelt without argument and began working over his foot. One of the riflemen at the parapet beside him was thrown sideways. He fell across Acheson's lap, and from the wound in his temple the contents of his skull splattered them both. With an exclamation of surprise and disgust Saul pulled back and wiped his face, then he reached forward to drag the body from Acheson's legs.

'Leave him.' Acheson prevented him sharply. 'See to that boot.' While Saul obeyed, Acheson unwound the silk scarf from around his own neck and covered the mutilated head. It was a wound he had seen repeated a hundred times that day, all of them shot through the right side of the head.

'Aloe Knoll,' he whispered fiercely. 'If only we'd taken Aloe Knoll.' Then his tone dulled. 'My poor lads.' And gently he eased the shattered head from his lap.

30

'They are ripe now, let us pluck them!' With five hundred of his
burghers Jan Paulus had left the shelter of Aloe Knoll and worked
his way forward, crawling belly down through the jumble of
rocks, until now they were crouched in a line along a fold of
dead ground below the false crest. Twenty yards ahead of them
was the right-hand extremity of the English trench. They could
not see it, but clearly they heard the incoherent cries of the
wounded; the shouts of 'Stretcher-bearer! Stretcher-bearer!' and
'Ammunition boys, here!' and above the splutter of musketry,
the continuous metallic rattle of breech bolts reloading.

'You must signal to the guns, Oom Paul.' The burgher next
to him reminded him.

'*Ja*,' Jan Paulus removed the homburg from his head and waved
with it at the fat mound at Aloe Knoll behind them. He saw his
signal briefly acknowledged and knew that the order to cease
fire was being flashed by heliograph to the batteries.

They waited, tense to charge, a long line of men. Jan Paulus
glanced along them and saw that each man stared ahead fixedly.
Most of their faces masked by beards of fifty different hues, but
here and there a lad too young for this work, too young to hide
his fear. Thank God my eldest is not yet twelve, or he would
be here. He stopped that train of thought guiltily, and concentrated his whole attention on the volume of shell-fire that raged
just ahead of them. Abruptly it ceased, and in the comparative
silence the rifle-fire sounded strangely subdued. Jan Paulus let
the slow seconds pass, counting silently to ten, before he filled
his lungs and roared:

'*Vrystaat!* Come on the Free Staters!'

Echoing his cry, yelling wildly, his burghers surged forward
over the crest on to the English flank. They came from so close
in, seeming to appear as a solid wall from under the English
parapet, that the momentum of their charge carried them

instantly into the depleted line of shell-shocked, thirst-tormented and dazed Lancashires. Hardly a shot was fired, and though a few individual scuffles rippled the smooth onward flow of the charge – most of the English responded immediately to the shouts of 'Hands Op! Hands Op!' by throwing down their rifles and climbing wearily to their feet with hands held high. They were surrounded by jubilant burghers and hustled over the parapet and down the slope towards Aloe Knoll. A great milling throng of burghers and soldiers spread over fifty yards of the trench.

'Quickly!' Jan Paulus shouted above the hubbub. 'Catch them and take them away.' He was well aware that this was only a very localized victory, involving perhaps a tenth of the enemy. Already cries of 'The Lancs are giving in!', 'Where are the officers?', 'Back, you men', were spreading along the English line. He had planted the germ of defeat among them, now he must spread it through them before he could carry the entire position. Frantically he signalled for reinforcements from the Boer positions along the crest, hundreds of his burghers were already running forward from Aloe Knoll. Another five minutes and complete victory would emerge from the confusion.

'Damn you, sir! What do you think you're doing!' The voice behind him was impregnated with authority, unmistakably that of a high-ranking officer. Jan Paulus wheeled to face a tall and enraged old gentleman, whose pointed grey whiskers quivered with fury. The apoplectic crimson of his countenance clashed horribly with its coating of red dust.

'I am taking your men hands-up away.' Jan Paulus struggled gutturally with the foreign words.

'I'll be damned if you are, sir.' Leaning heavily on the shoulder of a skinny little dark-haired man who supported him, the officer reached forward and shook a finger in Jan Paulus's face. 'There will be no surrender on this hill. Kindly remove your rabble from my trench!'

'Rabble, is it!' roared Jan Paulus. Around them the Boers and the British had ceased all activity and were watching with interest. Jan Paulus turned to the nearest burghers: '*Vat hulle weg!* Take them away!' His gesture that accompanied the order was unmistakable.

'We'll have none of that, sir!' Acheson glared at him before issuing his own order. 'You men, fall back and re-form on the Devonshires. Hurry it up, now. Come along. Come along.'

'Hey!' Jan Paulus held up his hand. 'These are my . . .' He groped for the word. 'My captures.'

'Sir.' Acheson released his grip on Saul's shoulder, drew himself up to his full height and glared up into Jan Paulus's face. 'I will give you five minutes to vacate this trench – otherwise you will become my prisoner. Good day to you.' And he hobbled away through the grass. Jan Paulus stared in disbelief when fifty paces away Acheson turned, folded his arms across his chest, and waited grimly for the expiry of the five minutes. About him he had gathered a handful of battle-stained soldiers and it was clearly his intention to implement his threat with this pitiful little band. Jan Paulus wanted to laugh with frustration – the skinny old goat. But he realized with dismay that most of his prisoners were filtering away and hurrying to join Acheson. He must do something, but what? The whole position was deteriorating into a farce.

'Stop them!' he shouted at his burghers. 'Hold those men – they went hands-up. They cannot change their minds now.'

Then abruptly the whole position altered. Over the skyline behind Acheson and his tiny party poured a solid phalanx of fresh khaki-clad figures. The three battalions of reinforcements sent up from the foot of the mountain by Sir Charles Warren had at last arrived. Acheson glanced over his shoulder and saw them swarming forward. The brown parchment of his face tore laterally in a wide and wicked grin.

'Fix bayonets!' he shrieked, and drew his sword. 'Buglers sound the charge. Charge, men! Charge!'

Hopping and stumbling like a stork with a broken leg, he led them. Behind him, the glittering crest of a wave, a line of bayonets raced down on the trench. Jan Paulus's burghers hated naked steel. There were five hundred of them against two thousand. They broke and blew away like smoke on a high wind. Their prisoners ran with them.

Jan Paulus reached the crest and dropped behind a boulder that already sheltered three men.

'Stop them! Here they come!' he panted.

While the British wave slowed and expended itself against the reef of hidden Mausers, while they fell back with the shrapnel scourging them once more – Jan Paulus knew that he would not stand in the British trench again that day.

He could sense the despondency among his burghers. He knew that already the faint-hearted were slipping away to where their ponies waited at the foot of the mountain. He knew with sickened acceptance that he had lost Spion Kop. Oh! The English had paid a heavy price all right, there must be fifteen hundred of their dead and wounded strewn upon the peak, but they had torn a gap in his line. He had lost Spion Kop and through this breach would pour twenty-five thousand men to relieve Ladysmith, and to drive his burghers out of Natal and into the Transvaal. They had lost. It was finished.

John Acheson tried desperately to ignore the agony of his bloated foot, he tried to shut out the shrill chorus of the wounded pleading for water. There was no water on the peak. He turned his gaze away from the trench where men, drugged with exhaustion, oblivious to the thunder of the bombardment that still raged about them, lay in sleep upon the bodies of their dead and dying comrades.

He looked instead at the sun, that great, bloody orb lightly screened with long streamers of cloud. In an hour it would be dark – and he knew he had lost. The message he held in his hands admitted it, the grotesque piles of dead men that clogged the trench proved it. He re-read the message with difficulty for his vision jerked and swam giddily.

'If you cannot hold until tomorrow, retire at your discretion. Buller.'

Tomorrow. What would tomorrow bring, if not a repetition of today's horror? They had lost. They were going down from this mountain. They had lost.

He closed his eyes and leaned back against the rough stone of the parapet. A nerve in his eyelid began to twitch insistently, he could not stop it.

31

How many are there left? Half, perhaps. I do not know. Half my men gone, all night I heard their ponies galloping away, and the crack and rumble of their wagons, and I could not hold them.

Jan Paulus stared up at the mountain in the dawn.

'Spion Kop.' He mouthed the name with loathing, but its outline was blurred for his eyes could not focus. They were rimmed with angry red and in each corner was a lump of yellow mucus. His body seemed to have shrunk, dried out like that of an ancient mummy. He slumped wearily in the saddle, every muscle and nerve in his body screamed for rest. To sleep a while. Oh God, to sleep.

With a dozen of his loyal commandants he had tried all night to staunch the dribble of deserters that was bleeding his army to death. He had ridden from laager to laager, blustering, pleading, trying to shame them. With many he had succeeded, but with many he had not – and once he had himself been shamed. He remembered the old man with the long white beard straggling from his yellow, wizened face, his eyes glistening with tears in the firelight.

'Three sons I have given you today, Jan Paulus Leroux. My brothers have gone up your accursed mountain to beg for their bodies from the English. Three sons! Three fine sons! What more do you want from me?' From where he sat against the wheel of his wagon the old man struggled to his feet hugging the blanket around his shoulders, 'You call me coward, Leroux. You say I am afraid.' He stopped and struggled with his breathing, and when he went on his voice was a croak. 'I am seventy-eight years old and you are the first man to ever call me that – if God is merciful you'll be the last.' He stopped again. 'Seventy-eight years. Seventy-eight! and you call me that! Look, Leroux. Look well!' He let the blanket fall away and Jan Paulus stiffened in the saddle as he saw the bloody mess of bandages that swathed the old man's chest. 'Tomorrow morning I will be with my sons. I wait for them now. Write on our grave, Leroux! Write *"Cowards"* on our grave!' And through the old lips burst a froth of pink bubbles.

Now with red eyes Jan Paulus stared up at the mountain. The lines of fatigue and shame and defeat were etched deep beside his nostrils and around his mouth. When the mists cleared they would see the English on the crest and with half his men he would go back. He touched the pony with his spurs and started him up the slope.

The sun gilded the mountain mist, it swirled golden and began to dissipate.

Faintly on the morning wind he heard the cheering and he frowned. *The English cheer too soon*, he thought. *Do they think we will not come again?* He urged his pony upward, but as it scrambled over loose rock and scree he reeled drunkenly in the saddle and was forced to cling to the pommel.

The volume of cheering mounted, and he peered uncomprehendingly at the crest above him. The skyline was dotted with figures who danced and waved their hats, and suddenly there were voices all around him.

'They've gone.'

'The mountain is ours.'

'We've won! Praise God, we've won. The English have gone.'

Men crowded about his pony, and dragged him from the saddle. He felt his legs buckle under him, but rough hands were there to support him, and half dragging, half carrying him, they bore him up towards the peak.

Jan Paulus sat upon a boulder and watched them harvest the rich crop of battle. He could not sleep yet, not until this was done. He had allowed the English stretcher-bearers to come up his mountain and they were at work along the trench while his own burghers gleaned their dead from along the crest.

Four of them approached Jan Paulus, each holding the corner of a grey woollen blanket as though it were a hammock. They staggered under the load, until they reached the neat line of corpses already laid out on the grass.

'Who knows this man?' one of them called, but there was no reply from the group of silent men who waited with Jan Paulus.

They lifted the body out of the blanket and laid it with the others. One of the burghers who had carried him removed from his clutching, dead fingers a wide Terai hat and placed it over his face. Then he straightened and asked:

'Who claims him?' Unless a friend or a kinsman claimed the corpse it would be buried in a communal grave.

Jan Paulus stood up and walked across to stand over the body. He lifted the hat and replaced it with the homburg from his own head.

'*Ja*. I claim him,' he said heavily.

'Is he kin or friend, Oom Paul?'

'He is a friend.'

'What is his name?'

'I do not know his name. He is just a friend.'

32

Saul Friedman fidgeted impatiently. In his eagerness he had arrived half an hour before visiting-time began and for this he was doing penance in the bleak little waiting-room of Greys Hospital. He sat forward on the straight-backed chair, twisted his helmet between his fingers and stared at the large sign on the opposite wall.

'Gentlemen are requested *Not* to smoke'.

He had asked Ruth to come with him, but she had pleaded a headache. In a sneaking fashion Saul was glad. He knew that her presence would inhibit his reunion with Sean Courtney. He didn't want polite conversation about the weather and how was he feeling now, and he must come round to dinner some evening. It would have been difficult not to be able to swear if they wanted – it would have been even more difficult in view of Ruth's attitude.

Yesterday, the first day of his leave, he had spoken of Sean with enthusiasm. How many times had she visited him? How was he? Did he limp badly? Didn't Ruth think he was a wonderful person? Twice she replied and, well, no not badly, yes he was very nice. Just about then Saul perceived the truth. Ruth did not like Sean. At first he could hardly believe it. He tried to continue the conversation. But each of her monosyllabic replies confirmed his first suspicion. Of course, she had not said so, but it was so obvious. For some reason she had taken a dislike to Sean which was close to loathing.

Now Saul sat and pondered the reason. He discounted the possibility that Sean had offended her. If that were the case Sean would have received as good as he gave and afterwards Ruth would have related the whole tale with glee and relish.

No, Saul decided, it was something else. Like a swimmer about to dive into icy water, Saul drew a metaphorical deep breath and plunged into the uncharted sea of feminine thought processes. Was Sean's masculinity so overpowering as to be offensive? Had his attention to her been below average (Ruth was accustomed to extravagant reactions to her beauty)? Could it be that . . . ? Or, on the other hand, did Sean . . . ? Saul was floundering heavily when suddenly, as a shipwrecked victim surfacing for the last time finds a tall ship close alongside with lifeboats being lowered from every derrick, the solution came to him.

Ruth was jealous!

Saul leaned back in the chair, astounded at the depth of his own perception.

His lovely, hot-tempered wife was jealous of the friendship between Sean and himself!

Chuckling tenderly, Saul laid plans to appease Ruth. He'd have to be less fulsome in his praises of Sean. He must get them together and in Sean's presence pay special attention to Ruth. He must . . .

Then his thoughts ricocheted off in another direction and he began to think about Ruth. As always when he thought too intensely about her, he experienced a feeling of bemusement similar to what a poor man feels on winning a large lottery.

He had met her at the Johannesburg Turf Club during the big Summer Meeting, and he had fallen in love at a range of fifty paces, so that when he was presented to her, his usually nimble tongue lay like a lump of heavy metal in his mouth and he squirmed and was silent. The friendly smile she bestowed upon him licked across his face like a blow torch, heating it until he felt the skin would blister.

That night, alone in his lodging, he planned his campaign. To its conduct he allocated the sum of five hundred guineas, which was exactly half his savings. The following morning he began his intelligence work, and a week later he had collected a mass-ive volume of information.

She was eighteen years old and was on a visit to relations in Johannesburg, a visit scheduled to last a further six weeks. She came from a rich Natal family of brewers and hotel-keepers, but she was an orphan and a ward of her uncle. While in Johannes-burg she rode every day, visited the theatre or danced every night with an assortment of escorts, except Fridays when she attended the Old Synagogue in Jeppe Street.

His opening manoeuvre was the hire of a horse and he waylaid her as she rode out with her cousin. She did not remember him and would have ridden on, but at last his tongue, which was sharpened by three years of practice at the Johannesburg Bar, came to life. Within two minutes she was laughing and an hour later she invited him back to tea with her relatives.

The following evening he called for her in a splendid carriage and they dined at Candy's Hotel and went on to the Ballet in company with a party of Saul's friends.

Two nights later she went with him to the Bar Association Ball and found that he was a superb dancer. Resplendent in brand-new evening dress, with an ugly yet mobile and expressive face, an inch taller than her five feet six, with wit and intelligence that had earned him a wide circle of friends – he was the perfect foil for her own beauty. When he returned her home Ruth had a thoughtful but dreamy look in her eye.

The following day she attended Court and listened to him successfully defend a gentleman accused of assault with intent to do grievous bodily harm. She was impressed by his display and decided that in time he would reach the heights of his profession.

A week later Saul again proved his command of the spoken word in an impassioned declaration of love. His suit was judged and found worthy, and after that it was merely a case of informing the families and sending out the invitations.

Now, at last, four years later they were to have their first child. Saul grinned happily as he thought about it. Tomorrow he would begin his attempt to discourage the adoption of the name 'Storm'. It would be a difficult case to win, one worthy of his talents. In the preceding four years Saul had learned that once Ruth set her small white teeth into something she had a bulldog grip. A great deal of finesse was needed to loosen that grip without invoking her wrath. Saul had an awesome respect for his wife's wrath.

'It's four o'clock.' The little blonde nurse poked her head around the waiting-room door and smiled at him. 'You may go in now. You'll find him out on the veranda.'

Saul's eagerness returned in full flood and he had to restrain himself from bouncing too boisterously down the veranda.

He recognized Sean's bulk, clad in uniform khaki, reclining elegantly in a cane-backed chair and chatting to the men in the row of beds in front of him. He came up behind the chair.

'Don't stand up, Sergeant. Just toss me a salute from where you are.'

'Saul!' Lugging himself out of the chair and pivoting easily on his game leg, Sean gripped both Saul's shoulders in the old show of affection. The pleasure that fired Sean's expression was genuine and that was enough for Saul.

'Good to see you, you old bastard.' He returned Sean's grip, grinning happily. He did not notice how swiftly Sean's pleasure faded, and was replaced by a shifty, nervous smile.

'Have a drink.' They were the first words that came into Sean's mind. He must have time to feel his way. Had Ruth said anything to Saul, had he guessed?

'Water?' Saul grimaced.

'Gin,' whispered Sean, guilt making him garrulous and he went on in a clumsy attempt at humour. 'Water carafe is full of gin. For God's sake don't tell Matron. I smuggle it in. Argue with the nurse whenever she tries to change it – she says "Water stale, must change!" I say, "Like stale water, raised on stale water, stale water strongly indicated in all cases of leg injury!"'

'Give me stale water too,' laughed Saul.

While he poured Sean introduced Saul to the gentleman in the next bed, a Scotsman who agreed with them that stale water was a sovereign therapeutic for shrapnel wound in the chest – a complaint from which he was currently suffering. The three of them settled down to a course of intensive treatment.

At Sean's prodding Saul embarked on a long account of the battle of Spion Kop. He made it seem very funny. Then he went on to describe the final break through at Hlangwane, Buller's eventual relief of Ladysmith, and his cautious pursuit of Leroux's army which was now in full retreat into the Transvaal.

They discussed Lord Roberts's offensive that had driven up from the Cape, relieved Kimberley, swept on to take Bloemfontein and was now poised for the final thrust up through the belly of the Transvaal to Pretoria which was the heart.

'It will all be over in three months.' The Scotsman gave his opinion.

'You think so?' Sean sneered at him a little, and succeeded in provoking an argument whose flames were fed with gin.

As the level in the carafe fell the time for sober and serious discussion passed and they became sentimental. Tenderly Saul inquired after their injuries.

The Scotsman was being shipped home across the sea, and at the thought of parting they became sad.

Sean was returning the following day to Ladyburg for convalescent leave. At the end of which, if the doctors were satisfied that the pieces of shrapnel in his leg were satisfactorily encysted (two words which Sean had difficulty enunciating) he would be returned to duty.

The word 'duty' aroused their patriotism and Sean and Saul with arms around each other's shoulders swore a mighty oath that together, comrades in arms, brothers in blood, they would see this war out. Never counting the cost in hardship and danger, together they would ride against the foe.

Suitable music was needed for their mood, and the Scotsman gave them 'The Wild Colonial Boy'. His eyes were moist and his voice quavered with emotion.

Deeply touching, but not entirely appropriate to the occasion, Sean and Saul did 'Hearts of Oak' as a duet, then all three launched into a lively rendition of 'Are you awake, Johnny Cope?'

The Matron arrived in the middle of the third chorus, by which time Johnny Cope and anybody else within a hundred yards could not possibly have been sleeping.

'Gentlemen, visiting hour ended at five o'clock.' She was a fearsome woman with a voice like a cavalry charge, but Saul who had pleaded before hanging judges rose undaunted to the defence.

'Madam.' He opened his address with a bow. 'These men – nay, let me speak with truth – these heroes have made great sacrifice in the name of freedom. Their blood has flowed like gin in defence of that glorious ideal – Freedom! All I ask is that a little of that precious stuff be granted unto them. Madam. In the name of honour, of fairness, and of gratitude I appeal to you.' He ended with one fist clenched above his heart and his head tragically bowed.

'Hoots, mon!'

'Oh good! Very good!'

The two heroes burst into spontaneous and heartwarming applause, but over the Matron's features descended a frosty veil of suspicion. She elevated her nose a little and sniffed.

'You're drunk!' she accused grimly.

'Oh, foul libel! Oh, monstrous untruth.' Saul backed hurriedly out of range.

'All right, Sergeant.' She turned grimly on Sean. 'Where is it?'

'What?' Sean was all helpless innocence.

'The bottle!' She lifted the bedclothes and began her search. Saul picked up his helmet, saluted them behind her back and tiptoed down the veranda.

33

Sean's leave in Ladyburg passed quickly, much too quickly. Mbejane had disappeared on a mysterious errand into Zululand. Sean guessed that it related to the two wives and their offspring that Mbejane had cheerfully sent to the kraals of their parents when he and Sean had left Ladyburg so many years before.

Dirk was incarcerated each morning in the schoolhouse, and so Sean was free to roam alone upon the hills and over the veld that surrounded the town. Most of his time he spent covering the huge derelict ranch called Lion Kop which spread above the escarpment. After a month he knew the course of every stream and each fold and slope of the land. His leg strengthened with the exercise. It no longer pained him and the scar lost its purple shine and dulled down to a closer match with his skin colour.

But as his strength returned and flesh filled out his shoulders and padded the gaunt bones of his face, so restlessness came back to him. His daily pilgrimage to Lion Kop Ranch became an obsession. He wandered through the bare rooms of the old homestead and saw them as they could be with the thatched roof replaced to keep out the rain and the flaking plaster renewed and freshly painted. He stood before the empty, smoke-blackened fireplace and imagined the glow and the warmth it could give. Stamping across the dusty floors he judged the yellow-wood planking as sound as the massive beams that supported the roof. Then he wandered out across the land, stooping now and then to take up a handful of earth and feel its rich loamy texture.

In the May of 1900 he went to the Deeds Registry at the Magistrate's office and surreptitiously inspected the title. He found that the fifteen thousand acres of Lion Kop Ranch had been purchased from the estate of the late Stephanus Johannes Erasmus by the Ladyburg Banking & Trust Co. Ltd. Transfer had been signed by Ronald Pye, Esq., in his capacity as Chairman of the Bank. Sean grinned. Ronny Pye was his most cherished childhood enemy. This could be very amusing.

Sean settled himself in the deep, soft nest of polished leather formed by the arm-chair and glanced curiously around the pan-elled office.

'A few changes since you were last here. Hey, Sean?' Ronny Pye interpreted his thoughts accurately.

'A few.' The Ladyburg Banking & Trust Co. was doing very prettily, judging by the furnishings. Some of its prosperity showed on the figure of its Chairman. Plenty of flesh under the solid gold watch-chain, dark but expensive jacket to offset the extravagant waistcoat, fifteen-guinea hand-made boots. Very nice until you looked at the face; pale so that the freckles showed like irregular gold coins, greedy eyes, ears like the handles of a shaving-mug – that much hadn't changed. But although Ronny was just two years Sean's senior, there was plenty of grey in his ginger sideburns and little wrinkles of worry around his eyes.

'Been out to Theuniskraal to visit your sister-in-law yet?' There was a sly expression in Ronny's face as he asked.

'No.'

'No, of course you wouldn't,' Ronny nodded understandingly and managed to convey that the scandal, though old, was by no means dead. Sean felt a repugnance that made him shift in his chair. The little ginger moustache heightened Ronny's resem-blance to a bush rat. Now Sean wanted to end the business and get out into the fresh air again.

'Listen, Ronny. I've searched title on Lion Kop. You own it,' he began abruptly.

'Lion Kop?' The previous morning the clerk from the Registry had hurried down to Mr Pye with news that earned him a sover-eign. There had been many others calling with the news that Sean had visited the ranch every day for a month. But now Ronny had to search his memory to place the name. 'Lion Kop? Ah, yes! The old Erasmus place. Yes, I do believe we picked it up from the estate. Paid too much for it, I'm afraid.' Here he sighed with resignation. 'But we can hold on to it for another ten years or so and get our money back. No hurry to sell.'

'I want it.' Sean cut short the preliminaries and Ronny laughed easily.

'You're in good company. Half the farmers in Natal want it – but not enough to meet our price.'

'How much?'

The established price of grazing land in the Ladyburg area was one shilling and sixpence an acre. Ten minutes before Ronny had set himself to ask two shillings. But now he was looking into Sean's eyes and remembering a fist crushing his nose and the taste of his own blood. He heard again Sean's arrogant laughter rejecting his overtures of friendship. No, he thought with hatred. No, you big cocky bastard, now you pay for those.

'Three shillings,' he said.

Sean nodded thoughtfully. He understood. Then suddenly he grinned. 'My God, Ronny, I heard you were a pretty sharp business man. But I must have heard wrong. If you paid three shillings for Lion Kop they really caught you with your skirts up.' And Ronny flushed. Sean had probed deep into his pride.

'I paid ninepence,' he snapped. 'I'm selling for three shillings.'

'Make out the deed of sale for £2,250. I'll take it.'

Damn it! Damn it to hell! Ronny swore silently. *He would have paid five.*

'That's for the land only. An extra £1,000 for the improvements.'

'Anything else?' Sean inquired.

'No.'

Sean calculated quickly, with transfer tax he could meet the price with a few hundred spare.

'I'll still take it.'

Ronny stared at him while his brain wriggled like a snake. *I didn't realize he wanted it that badly – I could have had his soul!*

'Of course, my Board will have to approve the sale. It depends on them really.' Ronny's Board of Directors consisted of himself, his little sister Audrey, and her husband Dennis Petersen. Ronny held eighty per cent of the shares, and Sean knew this. He had examined the Company's Articles that were lodged with the Registrar.

'Listen to me, dear friend of my youth.' Sean leaned forward across the stinkwood desk and picked up a heavy silver cigar-box. 'You made an offer. I accepted it. I'll be here at four o'clock this afternoon with the money. Please have the documents ready.' Sean lifted the cigar-box in one fist and started to squeeze. The muscles in his forearm writhed like mating pythons and the box crumpled and burst open at the seams. Sean placed the distorted lump of metal on the blotter in front of Ronny.

'Don't misunderstand me, Sean.' Ronny grinned nervously and dragged his eyes away from the box. 'I'm certain I'll be able to convince my Board.'

34

The following day was a Saturday. No school for Dirk and Sean took him along on the daily ride out to the ranch. Almost beside himself with joy at being alone with his god, Dirkie raced his pony ahead and then circled at full gallop to fall in beside Sean once more. Laughing with excitement, chattering ecstatically for a while, then he could no longer contain his high spirits and he galloped ahead. Before Sean reached the cross-roads below the escarpment he met a small caravan of travellers coming in the opposite direction.

Sean greeted the leader solemnly. 'I see you, Mbejane.' Mbejane had the jaded and slightly sheepish look of a tom-cat returning from a busy night out. 'I see you also, Nkosi.'

There was a long, embarrassed silence while Mbejane took a pinch of snuff and stared fixedly at the sky above Sean's head. Sean was studying Mbejane's travelling companions. There were two in their middle age, which is about thirty-five years old for a Zulu woman. Both of them wore the tall head-dress of clay which denotes matronhood. Though they retained the proud, erect carriage, their breasts were pendulous and empty and the skin of their bellies above the brief aprons was wrinkled with the marks of child-bearing. There were also two girls just beyond puberty, moon-faced, skins glowing with youth, straight and well-muscled, buttocks like ripe melons and firm, round breasts. They hung their heads and giggled shyly.

'Perhaps it will rain tonight,' Mbejane remarked.

'Perhaps.'

'It will be good for the grazing.' Mbejane ploughed on doggedly.

'Who the hell are these women?' Sean could contain his curiosity no longer and Mbejane frowned at this breach of etiquette. Observations on the weather and the grazing should have continued another five minutes.

'Nkosi, these two are my wives.' He gestured at the matrons.

'The other two your daughters?'

'No.' Mbejane paused, then went on gravely: 'It is not fitting that a man of my years should have but two women who are old for work and the bearing of children. I have purchased two younger wives.'

'I see,' said Sean, and kept the grin off his face. Mbejane had invested a large percentage of his capital. 'And what do you propose doing with all your wives, you know we must soon return again to fight?'

'When the time comes they will go to the kraals of their fathers and wait for me there.' Mbejane hesitated delicately. 'I bring them with me until I am certain that I have trodden on the moon of each of them.'

Treading on a woman's moon was the Zulu expression for interrupting her menstrual cycle. Mbejane was making sure his investment bore interest.

'There is a farm upon the hills up there.' Sean seemed to be changing the subject.

'Many time, Nkosi, you and I have spoken of it.' But Mbejane understood and there was an anticipatory gleam in his eyes.

'It is a good farm?' Sean held him a little longer in suspense.

'It is truly an excellent and beautiful farm. The water is sweeter than the juice of the sugar-cane, the earth is richer than the flesh of a young ox, the grass upon it as thick and as full of promise as the hair on a woman's pudendum.' Now Mbejane's eyes were shining with happiness. In his book a farm was a place where a man sat in the sun with a pot of millet beer beside him and listened to his wives singing in the fields. It meant cattle, the only true wealth, and many small sons to herd them. It meant the end of a long weary road.

'Take your wives with you and select the place where you wish to build your kraal.'

'Nkosi.' There is no Zulu equivalent of *thank you*. He could say *I praise you*, but that was not what Mbejane felt. At last he found the word. '*Bayete! Nkosi, Bayete!*' The salute to a King.

Dirk's pony was tethered to the hitching-post in front of the homestead. Using a charred stick Dirk was writing his name in big crude capitals on the wall of the front veranda.

Although the entire house would be replastered and painted Sean found himself quivering with anger. He jumped from his horse roaring and brandishing his *sjambok* and Dirk disappeared round the corner of the house. By the time Sean had regained self-control and was sitting on the veranda wall revelling in the pride of ownership, Mbejane arrived. They chatted a while and then Mbejane led his women away. Sean could trust him to build the beehive huts of his kraal on the richest earth of Lion Kop.

The last girl in the line was Mbejane's youngest and prettiest wife. Balancing the large bundle on her head, her back straight, her buttocks bare except for the strip of cloth that covered the cleft, she walked away with such unconsciously regal grace that Sean was instantly and forcibly reminded of Ruth.

His elation subsided. He stood up and walked away from the old building. Without Ruth in it, this house would not be a home.

He sat alone on the slope of the hills. Again he was reminded of Ruth. This place was so much like their secret glade. Except, of course, there were no wattle trees here.

35

'Wattle!' exclaimed Ronny Pye and glared at his sister and his brother-in-law. 'He's planting wattle.'

'What for?' Dennis Petersen asked.

'For the bark, man. The bark! There's a fortune in it. Twenty pounds a ton!'

'What do they use it for?'

'The extract is used in tanning leather.'

'If it's so good why haven't other people –' Dennis began, but Ronny brushed him aside impatiently.

'I've gone into it thoroughly. Lion Kop is ideal wattle ground, high and misty. The only other really good ground in the district is Mahobo's Kloof Ranch and Theuniskraal. Thank God you own Mahobo's Kloof! Because that's where we're going to plant our own wattle.' He looked at Dennis but without seeing him as he went on. 'I've spoken to Jackson at Natal Wattle Company. He'll sell us the saplings on the same terms as he's supplying that bastard Courtney, and he'll buy our bark – every scrap of it at a guaranteed twenty pounds a ton. I've hired two men to supervise the planting. Labour will be our big problem, Sean has grabbed every native within twenty miles. He's got an army of them up there.' Suddenly Ronny stopped. He had seen the expression on Dennis's face. 'What's wrong with you?'

'Mahobo's Kloof!' Dennis moaned. 'Oh God! Oh my God!'

'What do you mean?'

'He came to see me last week. Sean . . . He wanted an option to purchase. A five years' option.'

'You didn't give it to him!' Ronny screamed.

'He offered three shillings an acre – that's six times as much as I paid for it. How could I refuse.'

'You fool! You blithering bloody idiot! In five years that land will be worth . . . ' Ronny gulped, 'It will be worth at least ten pounds!'

'But nobody told me!' Dennis wailed the age-old cry of the might-have-been, the lament of those that never quite succeed.

'Nobody told Sean either.' Audrey spoke softly for the first time and there was that in her voice that made Ronny turn savagely on his handsome sister.

'All right – we all know about you and Sean. But he didn't stay around long enough for you to get your hooks into him, did he?' Ronny stopped himself and glanced guiltily at Dennis. It was years before Audrey had abandoned all hope of Sean's return to Ladyburg and succumbed to Dennis's gentle but persistent courtship. Now Dennis coughed awkwardly and looked at his hands on the desk in front of him.

'Well, anyway,' he murmured, 'Sean's got it and there's nothing we can do about it.'

'Isn't there – hell!' Ronny pulled a notebook towards him and opened it. 'This is how I see it. He's borrowed that ten thousand from his mother – you know the money we tried to get her to invest in the Burley deal.' They all remembered the Burley deal and looked a little ashamed. Ronny hurried on. 'And he's borrowed another five thousand from Natal Wattle – Jackson let it slip out.' Ronny went on with his calculations. When he finished he was smiling again. 'Mr Sean Courtney is stretched about as thin as he can get without breaking. Just one slip, one little slip and – Pow!' He made a chopping motion with his open hand. 'We can wait!'

He selected a cigar from the leather box which had replaced the silver one and lit it before he spoke again. 'By the way – did you know he hasn't been discharged from the army yet? The way the war is going they certainly need good fighting men. That leg of his looks all right to me. Perhaps a word in the right ear – a little pressure somewhere.' Ronny was positively grinning now. His cigar tasted delicious.

36

The doctors at Greys Hospital had given Sean his final examination a week before Christmas. They had judged his disability as roughly one per cent, a slight limp when he was physically tired. This disqualified him from a war wound pension and had made him available for immediate return to duty.

A week after New Year's Day of 1901 the first letter from the army arrived. He was to report immediately to the Officer Commanding the Natal Mounted Rifles – the regiment which had now swallowed up the old Natal Corps of Guides.

The war in South Africa had entered a new phase. Throughout the Transvaal and Orange Free State the Boers had begun a campaign of guerilla warfare alarming in its magnitude. The war was far from over and Sean's presence was urgently required to swell the army of a quarter of a million British troops already in the field.

He had written begging for an extension of his leave, and had received in reply a threat to treat him as a deserter if he wasn't in Johannesburg by February 1st.

The last two weeks had been filled with frantic activity. He had managed to finish the planting of ten thousand acres of wattle begun the previous May. He had arranged a further large loan from Natal Wattle to pay for the tending of his trees. The repairs and renovation of the Homestead on Lion Kop were completed and Ada had moved from the cottage in Protea Street to act as caretaker and manager of the estate during his absence.

Now, as he rode alone over his land in a gesture of farewell, he had an opportunity to think of other things. The main one of these was his daughter. His first and only daughter. She was two months old now. Her name was Storm and he had never seen her. Saul Friedman had written a long, joyous letter from the front where Sean was soon to join him. Sean had sent hearty congratulations and then tried once again to contact Ruth. He had written her without result and, finally, had abandoned his work on Lion Kop and gone up to Pietermaritzburg. Four days he waited, calling morning and afternoon at the Goldberg mansion – and each time Ruth was either out or indisposed. He had left a bitter little note for her and gone home.

Deep in gloom he rode through his plantations. Great blocks of young trees, row upon endless row, covered the hills of Lion Kop. The older wattle planted ten months before had started to come away. Already it was waist high with fluffy green tops. It was an achievement of almost superhuman proportion, ten months of ceaseless gruelling labour by two thousand native labourers. Now it was done. He had retained a gang of fifty Zulus, who would work under Ada's supervision, clearing the undergrowth between the rows and guarding against fire. That was all there was to it; four years of waiting until the trees reached maturity and were ready for stripping.

But now he was so completely absorbed in thought that he passed over the boundary of Lion Kop without noticing, and rode on along the foot of the escarpment. He crossed the road and the railway line. From ahead the murmur of the White Falls blended with the wind whisper in the grass, and he glimpsed the flash of water cascading down from the high rock in the sunshine. The acacia trees were in bloom, covered with the golden mist of their flowers above, gloomy with shadows beneath.

He crossed the river below the pool of the falls. The escarpment rose steeply above him, striped with dark dense bush in the gulleys, a thousand feet high so it blocked out the sunlight. The pool was a place of fern and green moss, and the rocks were black and slippery with the spray. A cold place, out of the sun – and the water roared as it fell in a white, moving veil like smoke.

Sean shivered and rode on, ambling up the slope of the escarpment. Then he knew that instinct had directed him. In his distress he had come back to the first home he had ever known. This was Courtney land beneath his feet, and spreading down and out towards the Tugela. The nostalgia came upon him more strongly as he climbed, until at last he reached the rim and stood looking down upon the whole of Theuniskraal.

He picked out the landmarks below him; the homestead with the stables and the servants' quarters behind it; the paddocks with the horses grazing heads down and tails swinging; the dip-tanks among the trees – and each of them had some special memory attached to it.

Sean dismounted and sat down in the grass. He lit a cheroot, while his mind went back and picked over the scrap-heap of the past. An hour, and then another, passed before he came back to the present, pulled his watch from the front pocket of his waist-coat and checked the time.

'After one!' he exclaimed, and stood to dust the seat of his pants and settle his hat on to his head before beginning the descent of the escarpment. Instead of crossing the river at the pool, he stayed on Theuniskraal and keeping to higher ground aimed to intersect the road on this side of the bridge. Occasion-ally he found cattle feeding together in herds of less than a dozen; they were all in condition, fat on the new grass, for the land was not carrying nearly its fully capacity. As he passed they lifted their heads and watched him with vacant, bovine expressions of unsurprise.

The forest thickened, then abruptly ended and before him lay one of the small swampy depressions that bellied out from the river. From his look-out on the escarpment this area had been screened by trees, so now for the first time Sean noticed the saddled horse tethered on the far edge of the swamp. Quickly Sean searched for its rider, and found him in the swamp – only his head visible above the bright poisonous green field of papyrus grass. The man's head disappeared again and there was a com-motion in the grass; a wild thrashing and the sudden panic-ridden bellow of a beast.

Sean worked his way quickly round the edge of the swamp until he reached the horse. The head and shoulders of the man in the swamp reappeared and Sean could see that he was splatt-ered with mud.

'What's the trouble?' Sean shouted, and the head turned towards him.

'There's a beast bogged down here.'

'Hold on, I'll give you a hand.' Sean stripped his jacket, waist-coat and shirt and hung them with his hat on a branch before going in. Ploughing knee-deep through ooze that bubbled and belched gas as he disturbed it, using both arms to part the coarse tangle of reeds and march grass, Sean finally reached them.

The beast was an old black cow; her hindquarters completely

submerged in a mudhole and her front legs twisted helplessly under her chest.

'She's just about finished,' said the man. Sean looked at him and saw he was not a man but a youth. Tall for his age, but lightly built. Dark hair, cropped short and the big nose to show he was a Courtney.

With an unnatural tightness in his gut and a shortening of his breath, Sean knew that he was looking at his son.

'Don't just stand there,' snapped the boy. He was covered from the chest down in a glistening evil-smelling coat of mud, sweat pouring down his face and dissolving the spots of mud on his forehead and cheeks, breathing heavily through open mouth, crouching over the animal to hold its head above the surface.

'Have to roll her,' said Sean. 'Keep her head up.' He waded to the hindquarters and the mud bubbled greasily up around his waist. He thrust his arms down through it – groping for the trapped legs.

Sean's hands could only just encompass the thick bone and sinew of the hock. He settled his grip and leaned back against it, straining upwards, gradually bringing the full strength of his body into the pull until he knew that something in his belly was on the point of tearing. He held like that, his whole face contorted, mouth wide open so that his breathing rattled hoarsely up his throat, the great muscles of his chest and arms locked in an iron convulsion.

A minute, two minutes, he held the stance while the boy watched him with a mingled expression of alarm and wonder. Then suddenly there was a squelching popping escape of swamp gas around Sean's chest, and the beast began to move. Slowly at first, reluctantly up through the ooze showed the swell of its rump – then faster, as the mud lost its hold, until, with a final belch and sigh, it yielded and Sean came to his feet holding the legs above the surface – the cow lying exhausted on her side.

'Hell's teeth!' breathed the boy in open admiration. For a moment the beast lay quiescent, then realizing that its legs were free, it began to struggle, thrashing wildly to regain them.

'Hold the head,' shouted Sean, and blundered sideways until he could grab its tail and prevent it from attempting to stand. When the animal was quiet again he began to drag it, moving backwards, towards the firm ground. Like a bobsleigh the carcass slid easily over the carpet of mud and flattened reeds until it grounded. Then Sean jumped clear while she struggled up, stood a moment and then lumbered unsteadily away into the trees.

Sean and his son stood together, gasping, covered with filth, still ankle-deep in mud, watching the cow disappear.

'Thanks. I'd never have done it on my own, sir.' The form of address and the boy's tone touched something deep in Sean.

'It needed two of us,' he agreed. 'What's your name?'

'Courtney, sir. Michael Courtney.' He held out his hand towards Sean.

'Nice to meet you, Mike.' Sean took the hand.

'I know you, don't I, sir? I'm sure I've seen you before – it's been worrying me.'

'I don't think so.' With an effort Sean kept his feelings from showing in his voice and face.

'I'd . . . I'd count it an honour to know *your* name.' As Michael spoke a shyness came upon them both.

What can I tell him? thought Sean. For I must not lie – and yet I cannot tell him the truth.

'My God, what a bloody mess,' he laughed instead. 'We stink like we've been dead ten days.'

Michael seemed to notice their condition for the first time. 'Ma will have a hernia when she sees me,' he laughed also, then, 'Come up to the house. It's not far from here. Have lunch with us and you can clean up – the servants will wash your clothes for you.'

'No.' Sean shook his head. 'I must get back to Ladyburg.'

'Please. I'd like you to meet my mother. My father's not here – he's at the war. But, please come home with me.'

He really wants me to. As Sean looked into his son's eyes the warm feeling that he had been struggling to suppress flooded up from his chest and he felt his face flush with the pleasure of it.

'Mike,' he spoke slowly, groping for the right words. 'Things are a bit difficult right now. I can't take you up on the invitation. But I'd like to see you again and I'll be through this way one day. Shall we leave it until then?'

'Oh!' Michael made no attempt to hide his disappointment. 'Anyway, I'll ride with you as far as the bridge.'

'Good.' Sean picked up his shirt and wiped off the surplus mud, while Michael unhitched their horses.

They rode slowly, in silence at first with the shyness still on them. Then they started to talk, and quickly the barriers

660

between them crumbled. With a feeling of pride that was ridiculous in the circumstances, Sean became aware of the quickness of Michael's brain, the ease of expression unusual in one so young, and the maturity of his views.

They spoke of Theuniskraal.

'It's a good farm.' There was pride in Michael's voice. 'My family has owned it since 1867.'

'You're not running much stock,' Sean grunted.

'Pa has had a run of bad luck. The rinderpest hit us but we'll build it up again – you wait and see.' He was silent a moment, then, 'Pa's not really a cattleman, instead of putting money into stocks he spends it on horses – like Beauty here.'He patted the neck of his magnificent golden mare. 'I've tried to argue with him, but –' Then he realized that he was steering close to the leeshore of disloyalty, and he checked himself then went on hurriedly: 'Don't misunderstand me, my father is an unusual man. Right now he's on the army staff – a colonel, and one of General Buller's right-hand men. He is a holder of the Victoria Cross for bravery, and he has been awarded the D.S.O. for the job he is doing now.'

Yes, thought Sean, I have defended Garry also; many times, as often as you will by the time you reach my age. In understanding he changed the direction of the conversation.

They spoke of the future:

'So you want to be a farmer, then?'

'I love this place. I was born here. To me it is not just a piece of land and a house. It is part of a tradition to which I belong – built by men of whom I am proud. After Pa, I will be the only one left to continue it. I won't fail that trust. But . . . '

They had reached the rise above the road, and Michael stopped and looked at Sean as though trying to make up his mind how much he should tell this stranger.

'But?' Sean prompted him gently. For a moment longer Michael stared at him, trying to account for his certainty in this man – for the conviction he had that he could trust him beyond all other men on earth. He felt that he had known him all his life, and between them was something so strong – so good and strong as to be almost tangible.

'But,' he jerked himself back to their conversation, 'that is not all. I want something beyond just land and cattle. It's so difficult to explain. My grandfather was a big man; he worked with people as well as animals. He had . . . you do understand me, don't you?'

'I think so,' Sean nodded 'You feel you'd like to make a place for yourself in the scheme of things.'

'Yes, that's it. I'd like to make decisions other than when to cull and when to brand, or where to build a new dip-tank.'

'What are you going to do about it then?'

'Well, I'm at Cape Town University. This is my third year – I'll have my degree by Christmas.'

'Then what?'

'I don't know, but I'll find something.' Then Michael smiled. 'There's a lot to learn first. Sometimes when I realize how much it frightens me a little.'

They walked their horses down towards the road, so completely absorbed in each other that neither of them noticed the buggy coming towards them from the direction of Ladyburg until it was almost on them.

Then Michael glanced up. 'Hey! Here comes my mother. Now you can meet her.'

With a sense of dread numbing him, Sean realized he was trapped. There was no escape – the buggy was less than fifty yards away, and he could see Anna sitting up behind the coloured driver staring at them.

Michael shouted, 'Hello, Ma!'

'Michael! Whatever have you been doing? Look at you!' There was a shrewishness in her voice now. The years had treated Anna in the manner she deserved, had sharpened her features and exaggerated the catlike set of her eyes. She turned those eyes on Sean and she frowned. The frown cut deep grooves in her forehead and showed the heavy lines of flesh beneath her chin.

'Who's that with you?' she asked Michael.

'A friend. He helped me free a bogged animal. You should have seen him, Ma. He lifted it clean out of the mud.'

Sean saw that she was expensively dressed, ostentatiously so for a farmer's wife on a working day. Velvet and ostrich feathers – those pearls must have cost Garry a small fortune. The rig was new, polished black lacquer picked out with scarlet, and brass fittings – another few hundred pounds' worth. Sean ran his eyes over the horses, matched bays, blood stock – Jesus! he thought.

Anna was still frowning at him, recognition and doubt mixed in her expression. She was starting to flush, her lips trembling.

'Hello, Anna.'

'Sean!' She spat the word.

'It's been a long time. How are you?'

Her eyes slanted venomously. She hardly moved her lips as she snapped at Michael, 'Get away from that man!'

'But . . . ' The bewildered look on Michael's face hurt Sean like a spear thrust.

'Do as your mother says, Michael,' Sean told him.

'Are you . . . are *you* my Uncle Sean?'

'Yes.'

'Get away from him,' shrilled Anna. 'Don't you ever speak to him again. Do you hear me, Michael? He's evil – evil! Don't ever let him near you. He'll destroy you.' Anna was panting, shaking with rage and hatred, babbling like a madwoman. 'Get off our land, Sean Courtney. Get off Theuniskraal and don't come on again.'

'Very well, Anna. I'm going.'

'Michael. Get on your horse!' she screamed at him. 'Hurry. Come away from him.'

Michael swung up into the saddle.

'Drive on. Drive quickly,' she ordered the coloured coachman. At the touch of the whip the big bays jumped forward and Anna was thrown back against the padded seat. 'Come on, Michael. Come home immediately.'

Michael looked across at Sean. He was bewildered, uncertain. 'I don't . . . I don't believe that you . . . '

'We'll talk again some other time, Mike.'

And suddenly Michael's expression changed, the corners of his mouth drooped and his eyes were dark with regret at having found, and lost, so soon.

'No,' he said, lifted his hand in a gesture of farewell, and wheeled his horse. Crouched forward on its neck he drove in savage pursuit of the buggy.

'Michael,' Sean called after him, but he did not seem to hear.

37

And so Sean went back to war. The farewell was an ordeal. Ada was so brave about it that Sean wanted to shake her and shoud, 'Cry, damn you! Get it over with!' Dirk threw one of his more spectacular fits. He clung to Sean and yelled until he almost suffocated himself. By the time the train pulled out Sean was in a towering rage that lasted until they reached Pietermaritzburg four hours later.

He took his anger into the saloon on the station and sedated it with half a dozen brandies. Then, with Mbejane carrying his luggage, he worked his way through the crowd on the platform, searching for an empty compartment on the northbound express. As all traffic was on military permit only, his fellow-travellers were exclusively clad in khaki. A vast, drab throng speckled with gay spots of colour, women who were sending men to war and not very happy about it. The sound of weeping blended with the roar of loud voices, men's laughter and the occasional squeal of a child. Suddenly, above it all Sean heard his name called. He peered about and saw an arm waving frantically above the heads of the crowd.

'Sean! Hey, Sean!' Saul's head bobbed into view and then disappeared as he hopped up and down. Sean fought his way through to him and they shook hands delightedly.

'What the hell are you doing here?' Saul demanded.

'Heading back to duty – and you?'

'A week's leave just ended. Came down to see the baby. My God, what luck I spotted you!'

'Is Ruth here?' Sean could not contain the question.

'She's waiting in the carriage outside.'

'I'd like to have a look at this infant.'

'Of course. Let's find a couple of seats first and dump our luggage, then we've got twenty minutes before the train leaves.'

Sean saw her as they came out on to the front steps of the

station building. She sat in an open carriage while a coloured coachboy held a parasol over her. She was dressed in dove-grey with big leg-o'-mutton sleeves slashed with pink and a huge hat piled with pink roses. Her face was in profile as she leaned forward over the bundle of white lace on her lap. Sean felt the leap in his chest as he looked at the calm lines of her face. He stopped and whispered,

'My God, she's lovely,' and beside him Saul laughed with pleasure.

'Wait until you meet my daughter!'

She did not see them approach the carriage, she was too intent on her child.

'Ruth, I've a surprise for you,' bubbled Saul. She looked up and Sean was watching her. She went rigid with shock, staring at him while all colour drained away from her face.

'Hello, Ruth.'

She did not reply immediately. Sean saw her mask her face with a pale impassivity.

'Hello, Sean. You startled me.'

Saul had missed the interplay of their emotions. He was climbing up into the carriage beside her.

'Come, have a look.' Now he was opening the lace shawl, leaning over the infant, his face alight with pride.

Silently Sean climbed up into the carriage and sat opposite them.

'Let Sean hold her, Ruth.' Saul laughed. 'Let him get a good look at the loveliest girl in the world.' And he did not notice the way in which Ruth froze again and hugged the child to her protectively.

'Take her, Sean. I promise she'll not wet you too badly, though she might sick up a little,' Saul went on happily.

Sean held out his hands for the infant, watching Ruth's face. It was defiant, but afraid.

'Please,' he said. The colour of her eyes seemed to change a darker bluer grey. The hard lines around her mouth dissolved and her lips quivered pink and moist. She leaned forward and placed her daughter in his arms.

38

It was a long, slow journey up to Johannesburg – a journey broken by interminable halts. At every siding there was a delay, sometimes of half an hour but usually of three times that length. Occasionally, without apparent reason, they groaned to a stop in the middle of the veld.

'What the hell is the trouble now?'

'Somebody shoot the driver.'

'Not again!'

Protest and comment were shouted by the angry heads that protruded from the windows of every coach. And when the guard trotted up along the gravelled embankment towards the front of the train, he was followed by a chorus of catcalls and hooting.

'Please be patient, gentlemen. We have to check the culverts and bridges.'

'The war's over.'

'What are you worried about?'

'The jolly old Boer is running so hard he hasn't got time to worry about bridges.'

Men climbed down beside the tracks, and stood in small impatient groups until the whistle blew and they scrambled aboard as the train jolted and began crawling forward again.

Sean and Saul sat together in a corner of a crowded compartment and played Klabrias. Because the majority regarded the cold clean highveld air with the same horror as if it had been a deadly cyanide gas, the windows were tightly closed. The compartment was blue with pipe-smoke and fetid with the smell of a dozen unwashed bodies. The conversation was inevitable. Confine a number of men in a small space and they'll get round to it in under ten minutes.

This company had a vast experience in matters pornographic.

A sergeant had served three years in Bangkok, but it took him two hours to convince his companions that what rumour placed horizontally, nature, in fact, had maintained at the vertical. He carried his point only after an expedition down the corridor from which he returned with another old China hand. This expert produced photographic evidence which was studied minutely and deemed conclusive.

It served also to remind a corporal who had done a tour of duty in India of his visit to the Temple of Konarak. A subject which was good for another hour and paved the way for a smooth entry into a discussion of the famous Elephant House in Shanghai.

They kept it up from noon until nightfall.

In the meantime, Saul had lost interest in the cards and taken a book from his bag and started reading. Sean was bored. He cleaned his rifle. Then he picked his teeth with a match and stared out of the window at the small herds of springbok that grazed along the line of rail. He listened to a detailed account of the pleasures provided by the proprietress of the Elephant House, and decided to give it a wide berth if he ever visited Shanghai.

'What are you reading?' he demanded of Saul at last.

'Huh?' Saul looked up vaguely and Sean repeated the question. '*The Westminster System of Government*'. Saul held the book so that Sean could see the title.

'Jesus!' grunted Sean. 'What do you read that stuff for?'

'I am interested in politics,' Saul explained defensively and returned to reading.

Sean watched him for a while then, 'Have you got any other books with you?'

Saul opened his bag again. 'Try this.'

'*The Wealth of Nations*'. Sean handled the book dubiously. 'What's it about?' But Saul was reading again.

Sean opened the heavy volume and glanced idly at the first page. He sighed with resignation for it was a long time since he had read anything but a letter or a bank statement – then his eyes started moving back and forth across the page like the shuttle of a loom. Without knowing it, they were weaving the first threads into a fabric that would cover a part of his soul which until now had been naked.

After an hour Saul looked across. 'What do you make of it?' he asked.

Sean grunted without looking up. He was completely

absorbed. This was important. The language of Adam Smith had a certain majestic clarity. With some of his conclusions Sean did not agree but the reasoning evoked a train of thought in Sean's own brain, stimulating it to race ahead and anticipate – sometimes correctly, but often reaching a point wide of where the author was aimed.

He read quickly, knowing that he would go back and read it all again for this was only a scouting party into the unknown territory of economics. With his eyes still fixed on the pages, he groped in the pockets of his tunic, found a stub of pencil and underlined a passage to which he wanted to return. Then he left it and went on. Now he used the pencil frequently.

'No!' he wrote in the margin at one place.

'Good,' at another.

Saul looked up again and frowned as he realized Sean was defacing the book. Then he noticed Sean's expression, saw its scowling concentration and his own face relaxed. He watched Sean from under lowered eyelashes. His feeling for this man of muscle and moods and unexpectedly soft places had passed affection and now reached the borders of adulation. He did not know why Sean had placed protecting wings above him, nor did he care. But it was good to sit quietly, no longer reading, and watch the face of this big man who was more than just a friend.

Alone in the midst of a multitude they sat together. The train snaked northwards across the grassland, spreading a long trail of silver-grey smoke behind it and the sun sank exhausted to the earth and bled on to the clouds. After it was gone the darkness came quickly.

They ate canned meat spread on coarse bread with the blade of a bayonet. There was no lighting in the compartment, so after they had eaten they sat together wrapped in their blankets and talked in darkness. Around them all other conversation died and was replaced by the sounds of sleep. Sean opened one of the windows and the cold sweet air cleaned their minds and sharpened them so that they talked in quietly suppressed excitement.

They talked of men and land and the welding of the two into a nation; and how that nation should be governed. They spoke a little of war and much of the peace that would follow it; of the rebuilding of that which had been destroyed into something stronger.

They saw the bitterness ahead that would flourish like an evil weed nourished on blood and the corpses of the dead, and they discussed the means by which it should be rooted out before it strangled the tender growth of a land that could be great.

They had never spoken like this before. Saul hugged his blankets about his shoulders and listened to Sean's voice in the darkness. Like most of his race his perception had been sensitized and sharpened so that he could pick up a new quality, a new sense of direction in this man.

I have had a hand in this, he thought, with a stirring of pride. He is a bull, a wild bull, charging anything that moves; charging without purpose, then breaking his run and swinging on to something new; using his strength to destroy because he had never learned to use it in any other way; confused and angry, roaring at the barbs in his shoulders; chasing everything and as a consequence catching nothing. Perhaps I can help him, show him a purpose and a way out of the arena.

And so they talked on into the night. The darkness added another dimension to their existence. Unseen, their physical forms no longer limited them and it seemed that their minds were freed to move out and meet in the darkness, to combine into a cushion of words that carried each idea forward. Until abruptly, the whole delicate pattern was shattered and lost in the concussion of dynamite and the shriek of escaping steam, the roar of breaking timber and glass, and the confusion of equipment and sleeping bodies thrown violently together as the train reared and twisted and plunged from the tracks. Almost immediately a further sound blended into it all – the crackling of musketry at close range and the steady hammering beat of a Maxim machine-gun.

Sean was pinned helplessly in the complete darkness, unable to breathe under an immense weight. He struggled wildly, tearing at the men and baggage above him, his legs bound by loose blankets. The weight eased enough for him to drag air into his lungs, but a knee was driven into his face with such force that his lip burst open and the blood oozed saltily into his mouth. He lashed out and felt the stinging rake of broken glass along his arm.

In the darkness men screamed in terror and in pain, leading the hideous chorus of groans and oaths and gunfire.

Sean dragged his body free of the press, felt men thrashing under him as he stood.

Now he could hear the repeated splintering thud of bullets into woodwork much louder than the guns that fired them.

Someone reeled against him and Sean caught him.

'Saul?'

'Leave me, let me go.' A stranger, Sean released him.

'Saul. Saul. Where are you?'

'Sean.'

'Are you hurt?'

'No.'

'Let's get out of here.'

'My rifle.'

'Bugger your rifle.'

'Where's the window?'

'Blocked.'

At last Sean was able to get some idea of their situation. The coach was on its side with the windows against the earth and the whole welter of dead and broken men piled upon them. The door was high above them, probably jammed.

'We'll have to break out through the roof.' He groped blindly, then swore and jerked his hand back as a splinter of wood knifed up under a fingernail, but he felt a draught of cold air on his face.

'There's a hole.' He reached out again eagerly and felt the torn timber. 'One of the planks is sprung.'

Immediately there was a rush of bodies in the darkness, hands clawed at him as half a dozen men fought to find the opening.

'Get back, you bastards.' Sean struck out with both fists and felt them connect. He was panting and he could feel the sweat sliding down his back. The air was heavy with the body warmth and breath of terrified men.

'Get back. I'll work on it.' He forced his hands into the crack and tore the loose plank out. For an instant he struggled with the temptation to press his face to the narrow opening and suck in the clean air. Then he locked his hands on to the next plank, braced his legs against the roof and heaved back with all his strength. It wouldn't budge. He felt the panic mounting in him once more.

'Find me a rifle, somebody,' he shouted above the uproar.

'Here.' Saul's voice, and the rifle was thrust into his hands. He ran the barrel into the opening and using it as a lever flung his weight on to it. He felt wood tearing, moved the barrel and pulled again. It gave and he cleared the plank and started on the next.

'All right. One at a time. Saul, you first.' With his panic just below the surface, Sean shoved each man unceremoniously through the jagged opening. A fat one stuck and Sean put a boot behind him and pushed. The man squeaked and went out like a champagne cork.

'Is there anyone else?' he shouted in the darkness.

'Sean,' Saul's voice from outside. 'Get out of there.'

'You get under cover,' Sean roared back at him.

The Boer fire still flailed the wrecked train. Then he asked again, 'Is there anyone else?' and a man groaned at Sean's feet.

Quickly Sean found him. Hurt badly, his head twisted. Sean cleared the tangle of baggage from above his body and straightened him out. Can't move him, he decided, safer here until the medicos come. He left him and stumbled over another.

'Damn them,' he sobbed in his dreadful anxiety to get out. This one was dead. He could feel the reptilian clamminess of death on his skin, and he left him and scrabbled his way out into the open night.

After the utter blackness of the compartment, the stars lit the land with a pearly light and he saw the fog of steam hanging above the locomotive in a high, hissing bank, and the leading coaches telescoped into each other, and the others jack-knifed and twisted into a weird sculpture of destruction. At intervals along the chain a few rifles winked a feeble reply to the Boer fire that poured down upon them.

'Sean,' Saul called from where he was crouched beside the overturned coach. Sean ran to him and lifted his voice above the clamour.

'Stay here. I'm going back to look for Mbejane.'

'You'll never find him in this lot. He was with the horses – listen to them.'

From the horse-boxes at the rear of the train came such a sound that Sean hoped never to hear again. Two hundred trapped and frenzied animals – it was far worse than the sound of those men still in the wreckage.

'My God!' whispered Sean. Then his anger rose higher than his fear. 'The bastards,' he grated and looked up at the high ground above them.

The Boers had chosen a place where the line curved along the bank of a river. The watercourse cut off escape on that side, and on the other the ground rose steeply in a double fold that commanded the full length of the railway line.

Along the first fold lay their riflemen, two hundred of them at least, judging by the intensity of their fire, while from above them on the summit ridge the muzzle flashes of the Maxim gun faded and flared as it traversed relentlessly back and forth along the train. Sean watched it hungrily for a moment, then he lifted the rifle that he still carried and emptied the magazine, firing at the Maxim. Immediately the flashes grew brighter as it came questing back to find him, and around Sean's head the air was filled with the swishing crack of a hundred whips.

Sean ducked down while he reloaded, then stood up again to shoot.

'You bastards,' he shouted at them, and his voice must have carried for now the riflemen up there were helping the Maxim to search him out. They were getting very close.

Sean crouched down once more, and beside him Saul was firing also.

'Where did you get the rifle?'

'I went back for it.' Saul punctuated his reply with gunfire and Sean grinned as his fingers fumbled with the reload. 'You're going to get hurt one day,' he said.

'You taught me how to go about it,' Saul retorted.

Once more Sean emptied his magazine to no effect, except that the recoil of the rifle invoked the old high madness in him. It needed only Mbejane's voice beside him to trigger it completely.

'Nkosi.'

'Where the hell have you been?' Sean demanded.

'My spears were lost. I spent much time finding them in the darkness.'

Sean was silent for a moment while he peered up at the ridge. Out on the left there was a gap in the line of riflemen where a narrow donga ran through them and down towards the railway. A small party might be able to go up that gully and pass through the rear of the Boer firing-line. From there the solitary Maxim on the ridge would be very vulnerable.

'Bring your spears, Mbejane.'

'Where are you going?' Saul asked.

'I'm going to try for that machine-gun. Stay here and keep these gentlemen's minds on other things.'

Sean started off along the train towards the outlet of the donga. He covered fifty yards before he realized that not only Mbejane but Saul was with him.

'Where do you think you're going?'

'With you.'

'The hell you are!'

'Watch me.' There was that peculiar note of obstinacy in Saul's voice that Sean had come to recognize, and there was no time to argue. He ran on until he was opposite the donga where again he sought shelter in the lee of an overturned coach while he made his final assessment of the position.

The donga looked narrow but deep, and the scrub-bush that filled it would give them cover to the top where there was a definite gap in the Boer line.

'It'll do,' he decided aloud, and then to the other two, 'I'll go first, then you follow me, Saul, and watch those big feet of yours.'

He was vaguely aware that some show of resistance was being organized among the survivors of the wreck. He could hear the officers rallying them and now a hundred rifles were returning the Boer fire.

'All right. I'm off.' Sean stood up. 'Follow me as soon as I get across.'

At that moment a new voice hailed them. 'What are you men up to?'

'What's it to you?' Sean flashed impatiently.

'I'm an officer,' and then Sean recognized the voice and the lanky figure with a bared sabre in one hand. 'Acheson!'

A second's hesitation before Acheson recognized him. 'Courtney. What are you doing?'

'I'm going up that donga to attack the Maxim.'

'Think you can reach it?'

'I can try.'

'Good fellow – off you go then. We'll be ready to support you if you make it.'

'See you at the top,' said Sean and ran out towards the mouth of the donga.

They moved quietly in single file upwards and the guns and the shouting cloaked the soft sounds of their advance. Sean

673

could hear the voices of the burghers above them growing closer and louder as they approached – very close now – on the side of the donga just above their heads – then behind them, and they were through.

The donga was shallower here, starting to flatten out as it neared the crest. Sean lifted his head above the side and looked out. Below him he could just make out the lumpy shapes of the Boers in the grass but their rifles threw long orange spouts of flames when seen from above – while the British replies were mere pinpricks of light from around the dark tangle of coaches.

Then Sean's attention focused on the Maxim and he could see why the rifle-fire from below had made no effect on it. Sited just below the crest of the ridge on a forward bulge of the slope, it was protected by a scharnz of rock and earth that had been thrown up in front of it. The thick water-jacketed barrel protruded through a narrow opening and the three men that served it crouched low behind the wall.

'Come on,' whispered Sean, and wriggled up out of the donga on to his belly to begin the stalk.

One of the gunners saw him when he was a few yards from the gun. *'Magtig! Pasop, daars 'n –'* and Sean went in with the rifle clubbed in both hands and the man never finished his warning. Mbejane and Saul followed him in, and for a few seconds the emplacement was filled with a struggling mass of bodies. Then it was over and the three of them panted heavily in the stillness.

'Do you know how to work this thing, Saul?'

'No.'

'Nor do I.' Sean squatted behind the gun and settled his hands on to the twin grips, his thumbs automatically resting on the firing-button.

'Wat makeer julle daar bo? Skiet, man, skiet!' a Boer shouted from below, and Sean shouted back, *'Wag maar 'n oomblik – dan skiet ek bedonderd.'*

'Wie's dar? Who's that?' the Boer demanded and Sean depressed the gun.

It was too dark to use the sights, so he took a vague aim over the barrel and thrust his thumbs down on the button. Immediately his shoulders shook like those of a man using a jack hammer and he was deafened by the harsh beat of the gun, but he swung the barrel in a low, sweeping arc across the ridge below him.

A storm of shouts and cries of protest broke out along the Boer line, and Sean laughed with savage delight. The Boer fire upon the train withered miraculously as men jumped up and scattered beneath the spray of bullets. Most of them streamed back to where their horses waited behind the crest, keeping well out on the flanks of the Maxim, while a line of cheering British infantry followed them up from the train – giving the support that Acheson had promised.

Only a tiny but determined group of Boers came up the slope towards Sean, yelling angrily and shooting as they came. There was dead ground directly below the emplacement where Sean could not reach them with the Maxim.

'Get out of here. Run out to the sides,' Sean shouted back at Saul and Mbejane as he hoisted the heavy gun on to the rock wall in front of him to improve its field of fire. But the movement twisted the belt of ammunition and after the first burst the gun jammed hopelessly. Sean lifted it above his head, stood like that for an instant and then hurled it among the men below him. It knocked two of them down into the grass. Sean snatched up a pumpkin-sized rock from the top of the wall and sent it after the gun – and another, and another. Howling with the laughter of fear and excitement, he rained rocks upon them. And they broke. Most of them veered out to the sides and joined the general rush for the horses.

Only one man kept coming, a big man who climbed quickly and silently. Sean missed him with three rocks, and suddenly he was too close – not ten feet away. There he paused and lifted his rifle. Even in the dark, at that range, the Boer could hardly miss and Sean sprang from the top of the wall. For an instant he dropped free, and then with a shock that knocked the wind from both of them, he drove into the burgher's chest. They rolled down the slope, kicking and grappling, bouncing over the rocky ground, until a small thorn bush held them.

'Now, you bloody Dutchman!' rasped Sean. He knew there was only one possible outcome to this encounter. With supreme confidence in his own strength Sean reached for the man's throat, and with a sense of disbelief felt his wrist held in a grip that made the bone creak.

'*Kom, ons slaat aan,*' the burgher's mouth was an inch from Sean's ear, and the voice was unmistakable.

'Jan Paulus!'

'Sean!' The shock of recognition eased his grip for an instant, and Sean broke his hand loose.

Only once in his life had Sean met a man whose strength matched his own – and now again they were pitted against each other. He drove the heel of his right hand up under Jan Paulus's chin, forcing his head back against the encircling left arm. It should have broken Jan Paulus's neck. Instead he locked his arms around Sean's chest below the level of his armpits – and squeezed. Within seconds Sean felt his face swelling and congesting with blood, his mouth opened and his tongue came out between his teeth.

Without breath, yet he maintained the pressure on Jan Paulus's neck, felt it give fractionally – and knew that another inch of movement would snap the vertebrae.

The earth seemed to tilt and turn beneath him, he knew he was going for his vision was blotched with moving patches of deeper darkness – the knowledge gave him a little more strength. He flung it all on to Jan Paulus's neck. It moved. Jan Paulus gave a wild muffled cry and his grip on Sean's chest eased a fraction.

Again, Sean told himself, again. And he gathered all of what was left for the final effort.

Before he could make it, Jan Paulus moved quickly under him, changing his grip, lifting Sean clear of his chest. Then his knees came up under Sean's pelvis and with a convulsive heave drove Sean's lower body forward and over – cartwheeling him so that he was forced to release Jan Paulus's neck and use his hands to break his own fall.

A rock caught him in the small of the back and agony flared in him like sheet lightning in a summer sky. Dimly through it he heard the shouts of the British infantry very near, saw Jan Paulus scramble up and glance down the slope at the starlight on the bayonets, and saw him take off up the slope.

Sean dragged himself to his feet and tried to follow him but the pain in his back was an effective hobble and Jan Paulus reached the crest ten paces ahead of him. But as he ran, another dark shape closed on his flank the way a good dog will quarter on a running rybuck. It was Mbejane and Sean could see the long steel in his hand as he lifted it above Jan Paulus's back.

'No!' shouted Sean. 'No, Mbejane! Leave him! Leave him!'

Mbejane hesitated, slowed his run, stopped and looked back at Sean.

Sean stood beside him, his hands clasped to his back and his breathing hissing in his throat. Below them from the dark rear slope of the ridge came the hoof-beats of a single running pony.

The sounds of Jan Paulus's flight dwindled, and they were engulfed in the advance of the lines of the bayonet men from the train. Sean turned and limped back through them.

39

Two days later, on the relief train, they reached Johannesburg.

'I suppose we should report to somebody,' Saul suggested as the three of them stood together on the station platform beside the small pile of luggage they had been able to salvage from the train wreck.

'You go and report, if that's what you want,' Sean answered him. 'Me, I'm going to look around.'

'We've got no billets,' Saul protested.

'Follow your Uncle Sean.'

Johannesburg is an evil city, sired by Greed out of a dam named Gold. But it has about it an air of gaiety, of brittle excitement and bustle. When you are away from it you can hate it – but when you return you are immediately re-infected. As Sean was now.

He led them through the portals of the railway building into Eloff Street and grinned as he looked up that well-remembered thoroughfare. It was crowded. The carriages jostled for position with the horse-drawn trams. On the sidewalks beneath the tall three- and four-storeyed buildings the uniforms of a dozen different regiments set off the butterfly colours of the women's dresses.

Sean paused on the station steps and lit a cigar. At that moment the sounds of carriage wheels and human voices were drowned by the plaintive wail of a mine hooter and immediately others joined in signalling the noon. Automatically Sean reached for his pocket-watch to check the time, and noticed the same general movement in the crowded street. He grinned again.

Jo'burg hasn't changed much – still the old habits, the same feeling about it. The mine dumps higher than he remembered them, a few new buildings, a little older and a little smarter – but still the same heartless bitch beneath it all.

And there on the corner of Commissioner Street, ornate as a

wedding-cake with its fancy ironwork and corniced roof, stood Candy's Hotel.

With rifle and pack slung over each shoulder, Sean pushed his way through the press on the sidewalk with Saul and Mbejane in his wake. He reached the hotel and went in through the revolving glass doors.

'Very grand.' He looked about the lobby as he dumped his pack on the thick pile of the carpet. Crystal chandeliers, velvet curtains roped with silver, palms and bronze urns, marble tables, fat plush chairs.

'What do you think, Saul. Shall we give this flophouse a try?' His voice carried across the lobby and stilled the murmuring of polite conversation.

'Don't talk so loudly,' Saul cautioned.

A general officer in one of the plush chairs hoisted himself and slowly turned his head to train a monocled stare upon them, while his aide-de-camp leaned across and whispered, '*Colonials*'.

Sean winked at him and moved across to the reception desk.

'Good afternoon, sir.' The clerk regarded them frostily.

'You have reservations for my chief of staff and myself.'

'What name, sir?'

'I'm sorry, I can't answer that question. We are travelling incognito,' Sean told him seriously, and a helpless expression appeared on the man's face. Sean dropped his voice to conspiratory level. 'Have you seen a man come in here carrying a bomb?'

'No.' The man's eyes glazed a little. 'No, sir. No, I haven't.'

'Good.' Sean appeared relieved. 'In that case we'll take the Victoria Suite. Have our luggage sent up.'

'General Caithness has the Victoria Suite, sir.' The clerk was becoming desperate.

'What?' Sean roared. 'How dare you!'

'I didn't . . . We had no . . . ' Stuttering, the clerk backed away from him.

'Call the owner,' ordered Sean.

'Yes, sir.' And the clerk disappeared through a door marked 'Private'.

'Have you gone mad?' Saul was fidgeting with embarrassment. 'We can't afford to stay at this place. Let's get out of here.' Under the concentrated scrutiny of every guest in the lobby he was very conscious of their grubby travel-stained uniforms.

Before Sean could answer a woman came through the 'Private'

doorway, a very lovely but very angry woman with eyes that blazed like the blue sapphires at her throat.

'I am Mrs Rautenbach – the owner. You asked to see me.'

Sean just smiled at her, and her anger withered slowly as she began to recognize him beneath the creased ill-fitting tunic and without the beard.

'Do you still love me, Candy?'

'Sean?' She was still uncertain.

'Who else?'

'Sean!' And she came to him on the run. Half an hour later General Caithness had been evicted and Sean and Saul were settling comfortably into the Victoria Suite.

Freshly bathed, with only a towel round his waist, Sean lay back in his chair while the barber scraped away his three-day growth of beard.

'Some more champagne?' Candy had not taken her eyes off him for the last ten minutes.

'Thanks.'

She filled his glass, replaced it at his right hand and then touched the thick muscles of his upper arm. 'Still hard,' she murmured. 'You've kept ahead of the years.' Her fingers moved on to his chest. 'Just a little grey here and there – but it suits you,' and then to the barber, 'Haven't you finished yet?'

'One moment more, madam.' He again scissored along the line of Sean's temple, stood back and studied his masterpiece – then, with modest pride, held the mirror for Sean's approval.

'Excellent. Thank you.'

'You may go now. See to the gentleman next door.' Candy had waited long enough. As the door closed behind the barber she turned the key. Sean stood up from the chair and they faced each other across the room.

'My God, but you're big.' Her voice was husky, unashamedly hungry.

'My God, but you're beautiful,' Sean answered her, and they moved slowly to meet in the centre of the floor.

Later, they lay quietly while the darkness gathered in the room as evening fell. Then Candy moved her mouth across his shoulder and, the way a cat cleans its kittens, she began gently to lick the long red scratches upon his neck.

When the room was truly dark Candy lit one of the shaded

gas-lights and sent down for biscuits and a bottle of champagne. They sat together upon the rumpled bed and talked.

At first there was a shyness between them because of what they had done together – but soon it passed – and they sat up far into the night.

Rare it is for a man to have a friend as well as a lover in one woman – but with Candy this was possible. And to her he released all those things that had been bottled and fomenting within him.

He told her of Michael, and the strange bond between them.

He told her of Dirk, and hinted at his misgivings for the boy.

He spoke of the war and of what he would do when it finished.

He told her of Lion Kop and his wattle.

But one thing he could not tell her. He could not speak of Ruth or the man who was her husband.

40

During the next few days Sean and Saul reported to the headquarters of the Regional Commander and were assigned neither billets nor duties. Now that they had arrived no one seemed very interested in them. They were told to report daily, and turned loose again. They returned to Candy's Hotel and spent most of the days playing billiards or cards and most of the evenings eating and drinking and talking.

A week of this and Sean was getting bored. He began to feel like a stud stallion. Even a solid diet of heavenly manna begins to pall after a while – so when Candy asked him to escort her to a reception and dinner with which Lord Kitchener was celebrating his promotion to Supreme Command of the Army in South Africa, Sean accepted with relief.

'You look like some sort of god,' Candy told him as he entered her suite through the concealed doorway which connected it with his own bedroom in the Victoria rooms. When she had shown him this discreet little panel and demonstrated how at a touch it slid silently aside, Sean had thrust down the temptation of asking how many others had used it. It was senseless to resent the nameless host who had passed through the panel to teach Candy all those little tricks with which she now delighted him.

'You don't look too bad yourself.' She was dressed in blue silk, the colour of her eyes, and she wore diamonds at her throat.

'How gallant you are!' She came to him and stroked the silk lapels of his newly tailored evening jacket. 'I wish you'd wear your medals.'

'I haven't any medals.'

'Oh Sean! You must have! With all those bullet holes in you, you must have medals.'

'I'm sorry, Candy.' Sean grinned. At times she was so far from being the glittering sophisticated woman of the world. Although she was a year older than he was, time had not destroyed that fragile quality of skin and hair that most women lose so quickly. There was no thickening of her body, no coarsening of her features.

'Never mind – even without medals, you'll be the handsomest man there tonight.'

'And you the loveliest girl.'

As the carriage rolled down Commissioner Street towards the Grand National Hotel, Sean lay back against the yielding support of soft polished leather. His cigar was drawing evenly with an inch of firm grey ash, the single brandy he had drunk before leaving glowed beneath the starched front of his dress-shirt, a faint aura of bay rum clung and hovered around him – and Candy's hand lay lightly upon his leg.

All these things induced in him a mood of deep contentment. He laughed easily at Candy's chatter and let the smoke of his cigar trickle through his lips – tasting it with an almost childlike pleasure. When the carriage stopped before the entrance to the hotel and rocked gently on its superb springing, he climbed down and stood by the big rear-wheel to guard Candy's skirt as she descended.

Then, with her fingers on his forearm, he guided her up the front steps and through the glass doors into the lobby of the hotel. The splendour of the place did not equal Candy's own establishment. But it was impressive enough – and so was the reception line that awaited them. While they took their places among those waiting to meet the Commander-in-Chief, Sean spoke quietly to an aide-de-camp.

'My Lord, may I present Mr Courtney and Mrs Rautenbach.'

Lord Kitchener had a formidable presence. His hand was cold and hard and he stood as tall as Sean. The eyes that stared for an instant into Sean's held a disquieting ridigity of purpose. Then he turned to Candy and his expression softened momentarily as he bowed over her hand.

'Very kind of you to come, madam.'

Then they were past and into the gaudy of uniforms and velvet and silk. The whole was dominated by dress scarlet of the Guards and Fusiliers, but there was also the gold-frogged blue of the Hussars, the green of the Foresters, kilts of half a dozen Highland regiments, so that Sean's black dress suit was conspicuously conservative. Among the glitter of orders and decorations shone the jewellery and white skins of the women.

Here assembled were the prize blooms of the huge tree that was the British Empire. A tree grown strong above the rest of the forest. Two centuries of victory in war had nurtured it, two hundred million persons were its roots that sucked in the treasures of half the world and sent them up along the shipping lanes to that grey city astride the Thames that was its heart. And there this rich sap was digested and transmuted into men. These were the men whose lazy speech and careful nonchalance reflected the smugness and arrogance which made them hated and feared by even the trunk of the great tree that gave them flower. While the lesser trees crowded closer and sent their own roots out to divert a little of its sustenance to themselves, the first disease had already eaten into the wood beneath the bark of the giant. America, India, Afghanistan, and South Africa, had started the dry rot that one day would bring it crashing down with a force that would shatter its bulk into so many pieces as to prove it not teak but soft pine.

Watching them now, Sean felt himself apart from them, closer in spirit and purpose to those shaggy men whose Mausers still shouted desperate defiance at them from the vast brown veld.

These thoughts threatened to spoil his mood and he thrust them down, exchanged his empty glass for another filled with bubbling yellow wine and attempted to join the banter of the young officers who surrounded Candy. He succeeded only in conceiving a burning desire to punch one of them between his downy moustaches. He was savouring the idea with increasing relish when a touch on his arm turned him.

'Hello, Courtney. Seem to find you everywhere there is either a fight or a free drink.' Startled, Sean turned to look into the austere face and incongruously twinkling eyes of Major-General John Acheson.

'Hello, General. I notice you frequent the same areas.' Sean grinned at him.

'Bloody awful champagne. Old K. must be economizing.' Then he ran his eyes over Sean's immaculate evening dress. 'A bit difficult to tell whether you have received the awards for which I recommended you.'

Sean shook his head. 'Still a sergeant. I didn't want to embarrass the General Staff by appearing in my chevrons.'

'Ah!' Acheson's eyes narrowed slightly. 'Must be some hold up. I'll look into it.'

'I assure you I'm quite happy this way.'

Acheson nodded and changed the subject. 'You haven't met my wife?' This was patronage on the grand scale. Sean was not to know that Acheson considered him his personal good luck charm. His own rapid promotion dated from their first meeting. Sean blinked in surprise before answering,

'I haven't yet had the honour.'

'Come along them.'

Sean excused himself from Candy, who dismissed him with a tap of her fan and Acheson steered him through the press towards a group at the end of the room. A dozen paces from it Sean stopped abruptly.

'Something wrong?' Acheson asked.

'No. Nothing.' Sean started forward again, but now his eyes were fastened with fascination on one of the men who was a part of the group towards which they were headed.

A slim figure in the dark blue dress uniform of the Natal Mounted Rifles. Sandy brown hair brushed straight back from his high forehead, nose too big for the mouth and the chin beneath it, slightly round-shouldered but with the highest reward for bravery showing purple and bronze beside the striped ribbon of the Distinguished Service Order on his chest, while on his shoulders the silver crowns and lace proclaimed him a colonel.

Slowly, with a new awakening of his guilt, Sean let his eyes move down to this man's legs. With incomprehension he saw them perfectly matched, booted in polished black leather. Only when the man moved slightly, shifting his weight, Sean saw the leadenness in one of them and understood.

'My dear – I would like to present Mr Courtney. I think you have heard me speak of him. He was with me at Colenso, and on the train a few weeks ago.'

'Indeed. Mr Courtney, this is a great pleasure.' She was plump and friendly but Sean was hardly able to murmur the correct response so conscious was he of the other eyes upon his face.

'And this is Major Peterson of my staff.'

Sean nodded.

'Colonel Courtney you will probably know – seeing that you bear the same name, and not to mention the fact that he is your Commanding Officer.'

For the first time in nineteen years Sean looked into the face of the man he had crippled.

'Hello, Garry,' he said and held out his hand. He stood with it out and waited.

Garry Courtney's lips moved. He hunched his shoulders and his head swung slightly from side to side.

Take it, Garry. Please take my hand. Sean tried silently to urge him. Realizing the forbidding setf of his own countenance, Sean forced his lips into a smile. It was an uncertain thing that smile, it trembled a little at the corners of his mouth.

In response Garry's own lips relaxed and for a moment Sean saw the terrible longing in his brother's eyes.

'It's been a long time, Garry. Much too long.' Sean prodded forward with his open right hand. *Take it. Oh God, please make him take it.*

Then Garry straightened. As he did so the toe of his right book scraped softly, awkwardly on the marble floor. The naked longing in his eyes was glazed over, the corners of his mouth lifted upwards in something close to a sneer.

'Sergeant,' his voice was too loud, too high. 'Sergeant, you are incorrectly dressed!' Then he turned, pivoting on the dead leg, and limped slowly away through the throng.

Sean stood with his hand still out and the smile frozen on his mouth.

You shouldn't have done that to us. We both wanted – I know you wanted it as much as I.

Sean let his hand fall empty to his side and balled it into a fist.

'You know him?' Acheson asked softly.

'My brother.'

'I see,' Acheson murmured. He saw many things – and one of them was the reason why Sean Courtney was still a sergeant.

Major Peterson coughed and lit a cigar. Mrs Acheson touched the General's arm. 'My dear, Daphne Langford arrived yesterday. There she is with John – we must have them to dinner.'

'Of course, my dear. I will ask them this evening.'

They turned their attention on each other, giving Sean the respite he needed to recover from his snubbing.

'Your glass is empty and so is mine, Courtney. I suggest we go on to something more substantial than K's cooking champagne.'

Brandy, fiery Cape brandy, very different from that soapy

liquor they make in France. A dangerous spirit to take in his present mood. And only one mood was possible for Sean after what Garry had done to him – cold, murderous rage.

His face was impassive, politely he responded to Mrs Acheson's charm, once he smiled at Candy across the room, but always he sent brandy after brandy down to feed the rage that seethed in his belly; his eyes followed the figure in dark blue as it limped from group to group.

The aide-de-camp who arranged the dinner seating could never have known that Sean was a mere sergeant. As Mrs Rautenbach's guest he believed him to be an influential civilian and placed him high at the long table, between Candy and Mrs Acheson, with Major Peterson below him and a brigadier and two colonels opposite. One of the colonels was Garrick Courtney.

Beneath the almost uninterrupted stare which Sean fastened on him, Garry became nervously garrulous. Never once meeting Sean's eyes, he aimed his remarks higher up the table, and that bronze cross suspended on he ribbon of shot purple silk that bumped against his chest each time he leaned forward gave a weight to his opinions that was evident in the attention they received from the officers of general rank.

The food was excellent. Rock lobster that had run the gauntlet of Boer blockade from the Cape, plump young pheasant, venison, four assorted sauces – even the quality of the champagne had improved. But Sean ate little, instead he gave permanent employment to the wine steward who hovered behind his chair.

'And so,' said Garrick as he selected a cigar from the cedarwood box that was offered him, 'I cannot see hostilities continuing another three months at the outside.'

'I agree with you, sir,' Major Peterson nodded. 'We'll be back in London for the season.'

'Poppycock!' Sean made his first contribution to the discussion. It was a word he had learned only recently – but he liked it. Besides, there were ladies present.

Peterson's face chameleoned to a creditable match with the scarlet of his dress coat, Acheson started to smile then changed his mind, Candy wriggled in anticipation for she had reached the edge of boredom, and a chilly stillness fell over that area of the table.

'I beg your pardon?' Garry looked at him for the first time.

'Poppycock,' Sean repeated, and the wine steward stepped forward to cascade champagne into the crystal bowl of his glass, an operation which he had repeated at least a dozen times during the course of the evening – but this time it commanded the attention of the entire company.

'You don't agree with me?' Garry challenged.

'No.'

'Why not?'

'Because there are still eighteen thousand Boers in the field, because they are still an organized army, because not once have they had a decisive defeat inflicted on them – but mainly because of the character of these eighteen thousand that are left.'

'You don't –' Garry's voice was petulant, but Acheson interrupted smoothly. 'Excuse me, Colonel Courtney.' Then he turned to Sean. 'I believe you know these people –' he hesitated and then went on, 'you are even related through marriage.'

'My brother-in-law leads the Wynberg commando,' Sean affirmed. The old boy knew more of his past than he suspected – must have made a few inquiries. Sean was flattered and the harshness gone from his voice.

'What, in your opinion, will be their course of action from now on?' Acheson pursued the subject and Sean tasted his champagne while he considered his reply.

'They will scatter – break up into their traditional fighting units, the commando.' Acheson nodded, from his position on the General Staff he knew this had already happened.

'In so doing they will avoid the necessity of dragging a supply column with them. Once the rainy season begins these small units will find grazing less of a problem for their horses.'

'Yes.' Sean saw they were all listening now. He thought quickly, cursing the wine that had dulled his brain. 'They will avoid battle, run from it and swing round to jab at the flanks, then run again.'

'Supplies?' asked the Brigadier.

'The veld is their storeroom, each farm upon it a haven.'

'Ammunition, weapons, clothing?' persisted the Brigadier.

'Every British soldier they capture or kill will provide a brand-new Lee-Metford rifle and a hundred rounds of ammunition.'

'But how long can they live like that?' Garry spoke indulgently, as though to a child. 'How far can they run?' He glanced around at the others seeking their support, but everyone was watching Sean.

'How wide is the veld – that is how far they can run.' Sean turned on him, stung by the tone of his voice. 'My God, you know them. Hardship is a way of life with them. Pride, the watchword that will carry them on.'

'You paint a pretty picture.' Garry smiled easily. 'It is unusual to find such appreciation of grand strategy among the rank and file.' Then he looked higher up the table once more with an emphasis that excluded Sean from the conversation. 'As I was saying, General Acheson, I believe –'

'One moment please, Colonel.' Acheson in turn excluded him and put his question to Sean. 'If you had the running of it, what plan of action would you adopt?'

Across the table Garrick Courtney coughed in a manner intended to inform the company that his brother was about to make a fool of himself.

It was not lost on Sean. 'The problem revolves around one single fact. The mobility of the enemy,' he stated grimly.

'Your perception does you great credit,' murmured Garry.

'Our first problem is to contain him and then to wear him down,' Sean went on, trying to ignore the taunts of his brother.

'Contain him?' The Brigadier fired the question.

'Hold him into a limited area,' Sean explained.

'How?'

'Say, by a series of set fortifications,' Sean suggested.

'Correct me if I'm wrong – but you propose to divide the whole of the highveld into paddocks and farm the enemy as one would dairy cattle?' Garry was still smiling.

'The new blockhouse lines along the line of rail are proving effective. It should be possible to extend them across the open veld – every time the enemy had to pass through them he would be subjected to a mauling by the garrisons and his position would immediately be pin-pointed.'

'The cost would be enormous,' Acheson pointed out.

'Not as great as supporting an army of a quarter of a million men in the field for another five years,' Sean brushed his objection aside, he was well set on his run of ideas. 'Then, within the defined areas small well-mounted bodies of men, unimpeded by supply wagons and artillery, could be used to raid the commandos – hitting them in an unrelenting series of raids and ambushes. Driving them on to the blockhouse lines, wearing down their horses, giving them no chance to rest, employing exactly their tactics of skirmishing. Against the commandos use counter-commandos.'

Acheson nodded thoughtfully. 'Go on,' he said.

'Then, clear out the farms,' Sean went on recklessly. 'Bring in the women and old men whose crops keep the commandos fed. Force them to operate in a vacuum.'

In the years ahead Sean was to regret the impulse that made him say it. Perhaps Kitchener would have scorched the land without Sean's suggestion, perhaps he had no hand in the formation of the concentration camps that bred bitterness Sean would spend the rest of his life trying to sweeten. But he could never be certain. He was drunk and angry – but later this knowledge would not comfort him.

Now suddenly he felt empty as though in a premonition of the monstrous seed he had sown and he sank into brooding silence while the others passed his ideas back and forth, building on them, already beginning to plan.

When the dinner party broke up and they drifted through to drink coffee, Sean made one more attempt to tear down the barrier between his brother and himself. He went to him with his pride in his hands and offered it. 'I was in Ladyburg last month. All's well there. Ada writes to say –'

'I receive a weekly letter not only from my wife but from my stepmother and my son. I am fully aware of the latest news from home. Thank you.' Garry stared over Sean's shoulder as he replied.

'Garry . . .'

'Excuse me.' Garry nodded briefly and limped away to speak to a brother officer. He kept his back towards Sean.

'Let's go home, Candy.'

'But, Sean . . .'

'Come on.'

Sean slept very little that night.

41

The Headquarters of the General Officer Commanding the eastern sector were tastefully situated in the offices of a brewery company in Plein Street. Major Peterson was waiting for Garry when he arrived.

'I sent for you two hours ago, sir.'

'I was indisposed,' Garry told him.

'Old Ach is not in a very good mood today – we'd better not keep him waiting any longer. Come along.'

Down the passage, where orderlies bustled, Peterson led him, and to a door at the far end. He knocked once and then opened it. Acheson looked up from his paperwork.

'Colonel Courtney is here, sir.'

'Thank you, Peterson. Come in, Courtney.'

Peterson closed the door and left Garry standing alone on the thick Persian rug in front of Acheson's desk.

'I sent for you two hours ago, Courtney.' Acheson used the same reprimand, and Garry shifted his leg uncomfortably.

'I wasn't too well this morning, sir. Had to get the doctor in.'

Acheson fingered his white moustache as he examined the dark circles beneath Garry's eyes, and the chalky colour of his face. 'Sit down,' he ordered.

Acheson was silent, watching him. Bur Garry avoided his eyes. He felt brittle from the previous night's drinking, his skin dry and sensitive, and he fidgeted in the chair, clasping and unclasping the hand that lay in his lap.

'I want one of your men,' Acheson spoke at last.

'Of course, sir,' Garry nodded.

'That sergeant – Courtney. I want to give him an independent command.'

Garry sat very still.

'You know who I mean?' Acheson persisted.

'Yes, sir.'

691

'You should,' Acheson murmured dryly. 'I have personally recommended him to you on two occasions for recognition.' He flicked through the sheaf of papers in front of him.

'Yes, sir.' Garry's right hand was opening and closing again.

'I notice you took no action on either of my recommendations.'

'No, sir.'

'May I ask why?'

'I didn't have . . . I didn't think the occasions merited further action.'

'You thought that my judgement was in error?' Acheson asked politely.

'No, sir. Of course not, sir.' Garry answered quickly.

'Well, then?' Acheson's eyes were pale blue, but cold.

'I spoke to the man. Congratulated him. After Colenso I gave him leave.'

'Very decent of you – in view of the wounds he received there.'

'I didn't want to . . . You see – he's my brother. It was difficult – favouritism. I couldn't really do much.' Garry wriggled sideways in his chair, his hands came up pawing the air as though to pluck words from it.

'Your brother?' Acheson demanded.

'Yes. My brother. I know him, I know him – you don't. You can't have any idea.' Garry could feel the pattern of his thoughts disintegrating, his voice sounded shrill in his own ear. He had to explain, he had to tell Acheson. 'My leg,' he shrilled, 'my leg. You see it. look at it! He did that. he took my leg. You don't know him. He's evil. He's evil, evil. I tell you he's evil.'

Acheson's expression had not changed, but his eyes were colder, more watchful. Garry had to reach him and make him understand.

'Anna.' Garry's lips were wet and blubbery. 'My wife,, Anna. He did that to her. Everything he touches – you can't know how he is. I know. He's evil. I tried, I hoped at Colenso – but you can't destroy him. He is the destroyer.'

'Colonel Courtney!' Acheson's voice cut into his tirade, and Garry jerked at the crack of it. He covered his lips with his fingers and slowly he subsided into the chair.

'I just want to explain. You don't understand.'

'I think I do,' Acheson clipped the words short and harsh. 'I am granting you indefinite leave on grounds of ill-health.'

'You can't do that – I won't resign my commission.'

'I have not asked you to,' Acheson snapped. 'I will send the papers to your hotel this afternoon. You can take tomorrow's train south.'

'But – but, sir –'

'That will be all, Courtney. Thank you.'

Acheson turned his attention once more to his papers.

42

That afternoon Sean spent two hours with Acheson, then he returned to Candy's Hotel and found Saul in the billiard room. Sean selected a cue. Saul laid both balls against the far cushion and straightened.

'Well?' he asked, as Sean chalked his stick.

'You'll never believe it.'

'Tell me, and let me be the judge.'

Grinning secretly Sean cannoned twice and then sank the red.

'From sergeant without portfolio, to a full-blown major and an independent command,' he announced.

'*You*?'

'Me.' Sean chuckled and missed a cannon.

'They must be crazy.'

'Crazy or not. From now on you will stand in my presence, adopt a respectful tone of speech – and miss that shot.'

Saul missed.

'If you're an officer and a gentleman why don't you behave like one and keep your mouth shut when I'm making a play.'

'You also have changed your status.'

'How?'

'You're now a lieutenant,' Sean informed him.

'No!'

'With a gong.'

'A gong?'

'A medal, you fool.'

'I'm overcome. I am speechless.' At last Saul broke down and began to laugh. It was a sound which Sean enjoyed. 'What kind of a gong – and what for?'

'Distinguished Conduct Medal – for the night of the train.'

'But, Sean, you . . . '

Sean interrupted. 'Yes, they gave me one also. Old Acheson got quite carried away. He started hanging medals and promotions on everything that moved, with the same dedicated fervour as a bill-poster putting up advertisements for Bovril. He damned nearly pinned a medal on the orderly who brought in the coffee.'

'He gave you coffee?'

'And a cigar,' Sean answered. 'He counted not the cost. It was like two lovers on an assignation. Repeatedly he addressed me as *My dear fellow.*'

'And what is this command he gave you?'

Sean racked his cue and stopped laughing.

'You and I are to head one of the first counter-commandos. Small, lightly equipped units to ride in and ginger up the Boer. Harass him, wear him down, chase the guts out of his horses and keep him moving until he runs on to one of the big columns.'

The following morning they rode out with Major Peterson to inspect the band of volunteers he had assembled for them.

'A mixed bag I'm afraid, Courtney. We've scratched together three hundred and fifteen.' Peterson was gloating a little behind the apology. He had not forgotten that *poppycock.*

'It must have been difficult,' Sean agreed. 'You only had a quarter of a million to choose from. What about officers?'

'Sorry. Only Friedman here. But I have got you an absolute gem. Sergeant-major. Snaffled him from the Dorsets. Fellow by the name of Eccles. First-class, absolutely first-class.'

'And Tim Curtis – the one I asked for?'

'Sorry again. They've reopened the gold mines. All engineers are being pulled out and sent back to work.'

'Damn it, I wanted him. What about machine-guns?'

'Four Maxims. Bloody lucky to get them.'

'Horses?'

'A bit of a struggle – but you can go down to remount and take your pick.'

Sean went on relentlessly with his demands and questions during the ride out towards Randfontein. His excitement for the challenge of this venture rose steadily as they argued and talked. At last he was taking it seriously. He asked the final and crucial question as they trotted past the sentries into the great army camp on the outskirts of Johannesburg.

'Has Acheson decided in which area I will be operating?'

'Yes.' Peterson dropped his voice. 'South-east Transvaal.'

'That's where Leroux is!'

'That's right. The gentleman who met your train the other day.'

Jan Paulus again!

'Here you are, Courtney.'

A little apart from the main camp stood three lines of white canvas tents. A field kitchen smoked at the far end and around it were clustered Sean's warriors.

'My God, Peterson. You said a mixed bag! You've robbed the army of cooks and batmen. And what are those – *sailors*, Bejesus!'

Peterson smiled thinly and shifted in the saddle.

'Press-ganged them,' he admitted. 'Gunnery detail from *Repulse*. Ah, here comes your sergeant-major.'

Eccles approached in column of fours; bull-built, black moustache, a few inches over six feet and all of it held stiffly erect. Peterson introduced them and they appraised each other.

'A right scruffy lot we got here, sir.'

'We've got a bit of work to do, Eccles.'

'That we 'ave, sir.'

'Let's get started than.' And they glowered at each other in mutual respect and liking.

A week later they were ready to go. Saul had named them 'Courtney's Fighting Scouts'. They were all well mounted, although there were some interesting styles of horsemanship evident – especially among the delegates from the Royal Navy. By bullying the quartermaster Sean had arrived at a standard uniform similar to that of the Imperial Light Horse; slouch hats, khaki tunics and riding breeches, bandoliers, puttees and issue boots. They had forty fat and healthy pack-mules, four Maxim machine-guns and Eccles had trained teams to serve them.

Acheson had approved Sean's request to use Charlestown as a base. He had arranged rail transport south to this tiny village near the Natal border, promised support from the big flying columns in the area, and informed Sean that he was expecting *big things* from him. He made it sound like a threat.

43

'But, darling, you haven't even been given a real uniform. You look so drab.' Candy, who was watching him dress from the double bed, held very definite views on what constituted a real uniform. It had gold lace and frogging with, say a Star of the Garter on a rich scarlet ground. 'Look at those buttons – they're not even shiny.'

'Boers like shiny things – makes for good shooting in the sun.' Sean glanced over his shoulder at her. Her hair was fluffed into golden disorder and the blue gown was arranged to provoke rather than conceal. Hastily Sean returned his eyes to his own reflection in the full-length mirror and brushed the hair back along his temples. A touch of grey in it now. Quite dignified, he decided. Pity about the nose. He took it between his fingers and straightened it, a hell of a nose, but when he released his grip it returned immediately to a half-cock position.

'Well, I'll be leaving you now,' he said, and she stood up quickly and the laughter was gone from her lips, they trembled a little.

'I'll come down with you.' She rearranged the gown quickly.

'No.'

'Yes, I have a farewell present for you.'

In the hotel yard, hitched behind four fat mules, was a scotch cart. She led him to it and lifted the tarpaulin cover.

'A few things I thought you might need.'

Against the cold she had provided a sheepskin coat, six fine woollen blankets and a silk eiderdown, two feather pillows and a mattress; a case of Courvoisier brandy and a case of Veuve Clicquot champagne. Against starvation there was potted salmon, strawberry jam, caviar in little glass jars, tinned delicacies all carefully packed in wooden boxes. For his health a medicine chest complete with a set of surgical instruments. Against the Boer there was a Toledo steel sabre in a leather scabbard worked with silver and a matched pair of Colt revolvers in a mahogany presentation case.

'Candy . . . ' Sean stumbled. 'I don't know what to say.'

She smiled a little and took his arm, hugging it. 'There's something else also.' She nodded to one of the grooms, who disappeared into the stables and led out a full-blooded Arab stallion with an English hunting saddle on its back.

'My God!' exclaimed Sean, and the stallion danced sideways so that the early sun glowed on the sheen of its coat. It flared the great pink pits of its nostrils and rolled its eyes before rearing high and dragging the groom off his feet.

'Candy, my dear,' Sean repeated.

'Good-bye, Sean.' She lifted her lips for his kiss and then broke away and almost ran back to the hotel.

While Saul shouted ribald encouragement, Mbejane and the groom held its head. Sean mounted the stallion, then they turned it loose and Sean fought to quieten it. At last he brought it under a semblance of control and, crabbing and prancing with arched neck and dainty high-stepping gait, persuaded it to head off in the general direction of Johannesburg railway station.

Eccles watched his approach impassively.

'What the hell are you laughing at, Sergeant-Major?'

'I wasn't laughing, sir.'

Sean dismounted and, with relief, gave the stallion into the care of two of his troopers.

'Nice bit of horseflesh, sir."

'What do you think he'll fetch?'

'You're going to sell him, sir?' Eccles could not hide his relief.

'You're damn right, I am. But it's a gift, so no sale here in Johannesburg.'

'Well, Colonel Jordan at Charlestown is usually in the market for a good nag. I should be able to get you a price, sir. We'll see what we can do.'

Colonel Jordan purchased not only the stallion but the pistols and the sabre as well. The secretary of the Charlestown garrison officers' mess frothed at the mouth with excitement when Eccles drew back the tarpaulin cover from the scotchcart.

When Sean's column rode out into the brown open winter grassland towards the jagged line of the Drakensberg, the little scotchcart trotted behind with the Maxims and a dozen ammunition cases making a full load.

44

There was cold that first night, and the stars were brilliant, clear and very far away. In the morning the land lay white and brittle in the grip of frost; each blade of grass, each twig and fallen leaf transformed into a white-jewelled wonder. A thin scum of ice covered the pool beside which the column had camped.

Mbejane and Sean squatted together. Mbejane with his monkey-skin kaross draped over his shoulders and Sean with the sheepskin coat buttoned to the throat.

'Tonight we will camp below that mountain.' Sean pointed away towards the west at the blue cone that stood out against the lighter blue of the dawn sky. 'You will find us there.'

'Nkosi,' Mbejane nodded over his snuffbox.

'These others.' Sean pointed with his chin at the group of four natives who waited quietly with the spears beside the pool. 'Are they men?'

Mbejane shrugged. 'I know little of them. The best of those I spoke with, perhaps. But they work for gold – and of their hearts I do not know.' Before going on, he regarded their clothing; tattered European cast-offs which were everywhere replacing the traditional tribal costume. 'They dress without dignity. But beneath the rags it is possible that they are men.'

'They are all we have so we must use them. Yet I wish we had those others who now grow fat in the company of their women.'

Mbejane smiled. A week before he had put the message into the grapevine and he knew that both Hlubi and Nonga were at that moment dissipating their accumulations of fat as they trotted north from their kraals along the Umfolozi River. They would be here soon.

'This is the way we will hunt,' Sean told him. 'Your men will spread out ahead of us and search for sign. The horses of those we seek will carry no steel on their hooves. If you find it fresh, then follow it until the run and direction of it is clear. Then return to me in haste.'

Mbejane nodded and sniffed a pinch from his snuffbox.

'While you search, stop at the kraals you find along the way. Speak with the people there, clearly, if the Mabune are here these people will know of it.'

'It will be as you say, Nkosi.'

'The sun comes.' Sean looked up at the glow of it upon the high places while the valleys were blue with shadow. 'Go in peace, Mbejane.'

Mbejane folded his kaross and tied it with a strip of leather. He picked up his stabbing spear and slung the great oval war shield on his shoulder. 'Go in peace, Nkosi.'

Sean watched while he talked with the other trackers, listening to the sonorous rise and fall of his voice. Then they scattered, trotting away into the veld, dwindled and were gone.

'Eccles.'

'Sir.'

'Finished breakfast?'

'Yes, sir.'

The men stood to their horses, blanket-rolls and carbines on the saddles, slouch hats pulled well down and the collars of their greatcoats turned up against the cold. Some were still eating with their bayonets from the cans of shredded beef.

'Let's go, then.'

The column closd up, riding four abreast, the pack-mules and the scotchcart in the centre, the outriders fanning out ahead to screen the advance. It was a tiny command, not a hundred and fifty paces long even with the pack animals, and Saul smiled as he remembered the massive fifteen-mile column that had marched from Colenso to Spion Kop.

Yet it was enough to tickle his pride. Courtney's Fighting Scouts. The task now was to justify the second word of their title.

Saul hooked one leg over the saddle, balanced his notebook upon it – and while they rode he and Sean planned a thorough reorganization of the column.

When they halted at midday the planning was put into effect. A patrol of ten men in charge of the mules, for this duty Sean picked those who were fat, old or ungainly in the saddle. These men would also act as horseholders when the unit went into fight on foot.

From among his sailors, Sean selected the gunners to captain the four Maxim teams. The riflemen were divided into patrols of ten with the most likely men promoted Sergeant Patrol Leaders, and their warrants noted in Saul's little book.

It was well after nightfall when they offsaddled that night below the dark massif of the mountain. Mbejane was waiting with his men beside a small, well-screened fire.

'I see you, Mbejane.'

'I see you, Nkosi.'

In the firelight Mbejane's legs were coated with dust to the knees and his face was grey with fatigue.

'What news?'

'Old sign. Perhaps a week ago, many men camped over there below the river. Twenty fires not in lines as the soldiers make them. They left no little tin pots as the soldiers do when they have emptied them of meat. No tents, but beds of cut grass – many beds.'

'How many?' It was an idle question for Mbejane could not count as a white man counts. He shrugged.

'As many beds as there are men with us?' Sean sought a comparison.

'More.' Mbejane thought carefully before answering.

'As many again?' Sean persisted.

'Perhaps as many again – but no more than that.'

Probably five hundred men, Sean guessed. 'Which way were they moving?'

Mbejane pointed south-west.

Back towards Vryheid and the protection of the Drakensberg mountain. Yes, it was part of the Wynberg commando without doubt.

'What news from the kraals?'

'There is fear among them. They tell little, and that of no importance.' Mbejane made no attempt to hide his disgust, the contempt that the Zulu feels for every other tribe in Africa.

'You have done well, Mbejane. Rest now for we ride before the dawn.'

Four more days they moved south-west, Sean's trackers sweeping the ground ten miles on each side of their path and finding it empty.

The Drakensberg reared up like a serrated back of a prehistoric monster along the south horizon. There was snow on the peaks.

Sean exercised his men in the counters to a surprise attack. Riflemen wheeling out and dismounting in line to cover the Maxims as they galloped wildly for the nearest high ground. Holders gathering the loose horses and pelting away to the cover of the nearest donga or kopje. Again and again they repeated this manoeuvre.

Sean worked them until they leaned forward in their saddles to nurse aching backsides and cursed him as they rode. He worked them to the edge of exhaustion and then on to a new physical fitness. They sprouted beards, their faces reddened and peeled, then darkened with the sun, their uniforms darkened also, but with dirt. Now they no longer cursed him. There was a new feeling among them, they laughed more and sat solid in the saddle, slept soundly at night despite the cold and woke with eagerness.

Sean was moderately satisfied.

On the morning of the tenth day Sean was scouting ahead of the column with two of his troopers. They had just dismounted to rest among an outcrop of boulders when Sean picked up movement out on the plain ahead. With a savage lift of anticipation he scrambled down from the boulder on which he was sitting and ran to his horse for his binoculars.

'Damn it!' he mouthed his disappointment as he saw the lance blades glitter in the round strangely fore-shortened field of the glasses. 'Cavalry.'

Half an hour later they met the small patrol of lancers from one of the big columns that were driving south from the line of blockhouses. The young subaltern in command gave Sean a cigar, and the latest news of the war.

De la Rey and Smuts were rampaging north of Johannesburg in the Magaliesberg with forty thousand men chasing their three thousand. South in the Free State another of the great De Wet hunts was in full swing. But this time they would catch him, the subaltern assured Sean. Fifty thousand foot and horse had driven his commando into the angle between the blockhouse line and the flooded Riet River. In the east it was quieter. The commandos there lacked leadership and were lying up in the mountains around Komatipoort.

'So far it's quiet here also, sir. But I don't like the looks of it. This man Leroux is a nasty piece of work, clever man too. So far he's limited his activities to a few raids. Ten days ago about five hundred of his men hit one of our supply columns near Charlestown. Wiped out the guard and collected enough ammunition to fight a full-scale battle, then made off towards the mountains.'

'Yes,' Sean nodded grimly. 'We found one of his camps.'

'No sign of him since then, sir. We've been scouring the ground for him, but so far without luck.'

'What's his force?' Sean asked.

'He can muster three thousand, so they say. My guess is that he's getting himself poised for something really big.'

That night Mbejane came into camp well after midnight. He came to where Sean slept under the scotchcart and with him were two other men.

'Nkosi.'

Sean rolled on his side, instantly awake at the touch. 'Mbejane?' He crawled out from under the cart and stood up.

The moon was up, silver and round and bright. By its light he recognized the men with Mbejane and exclaimed with pleasure:

'By God! Hlubi! Nonga!' Then remembering his manners, 'I see you.'

He stepped forward grinning broadly to clasp their shoulders in turn. And each replied gravely as they returned his embrace. 'I see you, Nkosi.'

'Are you well?'

'I am well. Are you well?'

The catechism of Zulu greeting can be carried on for as long as there is time available. More than a year had passed since Sean had discharged them from his service outside Pretoria, and so Sean must ask each of them for news of his father, his brothers, his herds, and the journey they had made, before he could put his own question.

'You came through Ladyburg?'

'We came that way,' agreed Hlubi.

'You saw the Nkosana Dirk?'

Now for the first time they both smiled, white teeth in the moonlight.

'We sat in council with the Nkosizana,' Hlubi chuckled. 'He grows like a bull calf. Already he wears scars of battle, honourable blackening of one of his eyes.'

'He grows in wisdom also,' Nonga boasted. 'Saying aloud to us those things which are written in the book.'

Hlubi went on: 'He sends greetings to the Nkosi, his father, and asks that he be allowed now to leave his school and join with him once more. For now he is skilled in the matter of books and numbers.'

Sean laughed. 'And what of the Nkosikazi, my mother?' he asked.

'She is well. She sends you this book.' Hlubi produced a travel-stained envelope from his loin-cloth. Sean tucked it away inside his coat to be read at leisure.

'Now.' The formula of greeting completed, Sean could come to the present. 'What news of Mabunu? Have you found sign?'

Mbejane squatted on his haunches and laid his spear and shield beside him. The other followed his example. The meeting came to order.

'Speak,' Mbejane ordered Hlubi.

'We came through the mountains, this being the shorter way,' Hlubi explained. 'In the hills below the mountains we found the road made by many horses, and following it we came upon a level place surrounded by rock. The Mabunu are there with cattle and wagons.'

'How far is this place?' Sean asked eagerly.

'A day's long journey.' Thirty miles.

'How many Mabunu?' Sean asked and Mbejane explained, 'As many as camped at the place I told you of.'

It made sense, Sean decided. Jan Paulus would have split his force into smaller units, for reasons of supply and concealment, until such time as he needed them.

'We will go then,' he said and stood up.

Eccles woke quickly.

'Sergeant-Major. The guides have found a small Boer commando in laager below the mountains. Get the men mounted up.'

'Sir!' Eccles's moustache, rumpled with sleep, quivered like the whiskers of a hunting dog.

While around him the commotion of upsaddling began, Sean kicked life into the fire and in its yellow flickering light he tore a page from his notebook and licked the point of a pencil.

> *To all British troops in the field:*
>
> I am in contact with a Boer commando of 500. Will attempt to contain them pending your arrival. The bearer will act as a guide.
>
> S. Courtney (Major).
>
> 5th August, 1900. Time 00.46 hours.

'Hlubi,' he called.

'Nkosi!'

'Take this book,' he handed him the note. 'There are soldiers out there.' He swept his arm towards the north. 'Give it to them.'

45

Bunched into a compact column with the gallant little scotch-cart bouncing and jolting in the rear, Courtney's Fighting Scouts cantered southwards with the brown winter grass brushing their stirrups.

With Saul beside him and the two Zulus ranging ahead like hunting dogs, Sean rode in the van. He slouched easily in the saddle and tried with both hands to steady Ada's letter as it fluttered in the wind of his passage. It was strange to read the gentle reassuring words as he hurried into battle.

All was well at Lion Kop. The wattle grew apace – free from fire, drought or pestilence. She had hired an assistant manager who worked afternoons only; his mornings required attendance at Ladybury School. Dirk was earning his princely salary of two shillings and sixpence a week and seemed to be enjoying the work. The arrival of his school report for the period ended at Easter was the occasion for some concern. His average high marks for each subject were followed by the notation, 'Could do much better' or 'Lacks concentration'. The whole was summarized by the Headmaster, 'Dirk is a high-spirited and popular boy. But he must learn to control his temper and to apply himself with more diligence to those subjects he finds distasteful.'

Dirk had recently fought an epic bout of fisticuffs with the Petersen boy, who was two years his senior, and had emerged blooded and bruised, but victorious. Here Sean detected a note of pride in Ada's prim censure. There followed half a page of messages dictated by Dirk in which protestations of filial love and duty were liberally punctuated with requests for a pony, a rifle, and permission to terminate his scholastic career.

Ada went on tersely to say that Garry had recently returned to Ladyburg, but had not yet called upon her.

Finally, she instructed him to take pains with his health,

invoked the Almighty to his protection, anticipated his swift return to Lion Kop – and ended with love.

Sean folded the letter carefully and tucked it away. Then he let his mind drift, lolling in the saddle while the brown miles dropped steadily behind his horse. There were so many loose or ravel threads to follow – Dirk and Ada, Ruth and Saul, Garrick and Michael – and all of them made him sad.

Then suddenly he glanced sideways at Saul and straightened in the saddle. This was not the time to brood. They had entered the mouth of one of the valleys that sloped upwards towards the massive snow-plastered ramparts of the Drakensberg, and were following a stream whose banks dropped ten feet to the water that gurgled and tinkled over the polished round boulders in its bed.

'How much farther, Nonga?' he called.

'Close now, Nkosi.'

In another valley that ran parallel to the one Sean was following, separated from it by two ridges of broken rock, a young Boer asked the same question.

'How much farther, Oom Paul?'

But before answering, Vecht-Generaal Jan Paulus Leroux eased himself around in the saddle and looked back along the commando of one thousand burghers he was leading to a rendezvous at his laager in the mountains. They rode in a solid mass that clogged the floor of the valley, bearded men in a motley of dark homespun clothing, on ponies shaggy in their winter coats – yet Jan Paulus felt pride swell in his chest as he looked at them. These were the bitter-enders, veterans of half a hundred fights, men forged and tempered in the furnace of battle, razor-sharp and resilient as the finest steel. Then he looked at the boy beside him – a boy in years only for his eyes were old and wise.

'Close now, Hennie.'

'Eccles, we'll halt here. Water the horses. Loosen the girths but don't offsaddle. No fires but the men can rest and eat.'

'Very well, sir.'

'I am going forward to have a look at the laager. While I am away I want you to issue an extra hundred rounds of ammunition to each man. Check the Maxims. I should be back in two hours.'

'When will it be, sir?'

'We'll move forward at dusk, I want to be in position to attack as soon as the moon rises. You can tell the men now.'

As Sean and Nonga left the column and moved on foot up the valley, two men watched them from the ridge. They lay on their bellies among the rocks. Both of them were bearded. One of them wore a British officer's Sam Browne belt over his patched leather jacket, but the rifle that rested on the rock in front of him was a Mauser.

'They send spies to the laager,' he whispered, and his companion answered in the Taal.

'*Ja*, they have found it.'

'Go! Ride quickly to Oom Paul and say for him that we have three hundred khaki ripe and ready for the plucking.'

The other Boer grinned and wriggled backwards, working his way off the skyline. Once below it he ran to his pony and led it down into the grass which would muffle its hoof-beats, before he mounted.

An hour later Sean returned from his reconnaissance.

'We've got them, Eccles,' he grinned savagely at Saul and Eccles.

'They're about two miles ahead in a hidden basin of hills.' He squatted down and smoothed a patch of earth with the palm of his hand. 'Now here is the way we'll do it.' With a twig he drew quickly in the dirt. 'This is our valley. Here we are. This is the laager, hills here and here and here. This is the entrance to the basin. Now, we'll place two Maxims here, with a hundred men below and in front of them like this. I want you –'

Abruptly his earthen map exploded, throwing dirt into his eyes and open mouth. 'What the bloody –' he mouthed as he clawed at his face but the rest of it was lost in the blast of the Mausers.

Through streaming eyes Sean looked up at the ridge. 'Oh my God!' A fire haze of gunsmoke drifted across it like sea spray on a windy day, and he sprang to his feet.

'Into the river. Get the horses into the river,' he roared above the murderous crackle, the shrill fluting whine of ricochets and the continuous slapping of bullets into earth and flesh.

'Into the river. Get into the river!' He ran down the column shouting at the men who were struggling to clear their rifles from the scabbards of plunging, rearing horses. The Boer fire flogged into them, dropping men and horses screaming in the grass. Loose horses scattered along the valley, reins trailing and empty stirrups bouncing against their flanks.

'Leave them! Let them go! Get into the river!' Two of the mules were down, kicking, wounded in the traces of the scotch-cart. Sean tore the tarpaulin loose and lifted out one of the Maxims. A bullet splintered the woodwork under his hands.

'You!' he shouted at one of his sailors. 'Grab this!' He passed the gun to him and the man ran with it cradled in his arms and jumped over the river bank. With a case of ammunition under each arm Sean followed him. It seemed as though he ran waist-deep in water, each pace dragging with painful deliberation and his fear came strongly upon him. A bullet flipped his hat forward over his eyes, the ammunition cases weighted him down, and he blundered panic-stricken towards the river. The earth was gone abruptly from under his feet and he fell, dropping free until, with a shock that jarred his spine, he struck and toppled forward face-down into the icy water.

Immediately he scrambled up and, still clutching the Maxim ammunition, floundered to the steep bank. Above him the Boer fire whipped and sang, but the bed of the river was crowded with his men, and others still fell and jumped from the bank to add to the congestion.

Panting and streaming water from his clothing Sean leaned against the bank while he gathered himself. The stream of survivors into the river-bed dwindled and stopped. The Boer fire also stuttered out and a comparative quiet fell over the field, spoiled only by the groaning and cursing of the wounded.

Sean's first coherent thought was for Saul. He found him holding two pack-mules under the bank with Nonga and Mbejane beside him holding another pair. He sent Saul to take command at the far end of the line.

'Sergeant-Major!' Sean shouted, and with relief heard Eccles's reply from close at hand.

'Here, sir.'

'Spread them out along the bank. Get them to cut firing platforms.'

'Very good, sir,' and immediately he began. 'Here you lot, you heard the Major! Up off your backsides!'

Within ten minutes there were two hundred rifles lining the bank and the Maxim was sited and manned behind a scharnz of stone and earth. Those men who had lost their weapons were tending the wounded. This pitiful little group were gathered in the middle of the line, they were propped against the bank, sitting waist-deep in slush and their blood stained the water pinky-brown.

Sean climbed up on to one of the firing platforms beside Eccles and lifted his head to peer cautiously over the bank. The area in front of him was a sickening sight. Dead mules and horses with their packs burst open littering the grass with blankets and provisions. Wounded animals flopping helpless or standing quietly with their heads hanging.

'Is there anyone out there still alive?' Sean called, but the dead men gave him no answer. A sniper on the ridge ploughed a bullet into the ground in front of Sean's face and he ducked down quickly.

'Most of them managed to crawl in, sir. Those that didn't are better out there than in the mud here.'

'How many did we lose, Eccles?'

'About a dozen dead, sir, and twice as many wounded. We got off very lightly.'

'Yes,' Sean nodded. 'Most of their initial fire went high. It's a mistake even the best shots make when shooting downhill.'

'They fair caught us with our pants down,' mused Eccles and Sean did not miss the censure in his tone.

'I know. I should have placed look-outs on the ridge,' he agreed. You're no Napoleon, he told himself, and you've got casualties to prove it.

'How many of them lost their weapons?' he asked.

'We've got two hundred and ten rifles and one Maxim, sir, and I issued an extra hundred rounds to each man just before the attack.'

'Should be enough,' Sean decided. 'Now all that remains is to sweat it out until my native guide brings up reinforcements.'

For half an hour nothing happened beyond a little desultory

sniping from the ridge. Sean moved along the line talking to the men.

'How's it going, sailor?'

'Me old ma would have a fit, sir. "George," she'd say, "sitting in the mud is not going to do your piles no good," she'd say, sir.' The man was shot through the stomach and Sean had to force his chuckle through his throat.

'I could use a smoke, though. That I could.'

Sean found a damp cigar in his pocket for him and moved on. A youngster, one of the Colonials, was crying silently as he held against his chest the blood-soaked bundle of bandages that was his hand.

'Giving you pain?' Sean asked gently. The boy looked up at him, the tears smearing his cheeks. 'Go away,' he whispered. 'Please go away.'

Sean walked on. I should have put look-outs on the ridge, he thought again. I should have –

'Flag of truce on the ridge, sir,' a man shouted excitedly and Sean clambered up beside him.

Immediately a hum of comment ran along the line.

'They're hanging out their washing.'

'The bastards want to surrender. They know we've got them licked.'

Sean climbed out of the river-bed and waved his hat at the speck of white that fluttered on the ridge, and a horseman trotted down towards him.

'*Middag, Menheer*,' Sean greeted him. He received only a nod in reply and took the note the man proffered:

Menheer,

I expect the arrival of my Hotchkiss gun at any moment. Your position is not safe. I suggest you lay down your guns to prevent further killing.

J.P. Leroux, Vecht-Generaal,
Wynberg commando.

It was written on an irregular scrap of brown wrapping paper in High Dutch.

'My greetings to the General, *Menheer*, but we will hold out here a little longer.'

'As you wish,' the Boer acquiesced, 'but first you must see if any of these' – he pointed at the khaki figures that were scattered among the dead mules and horses – 'you must see if any of them are still alive. And you must destroy the wounded animals.'

'It is kind of you, *Menheer*.'

'You will, of course, make no attempt to pick up weapons or ammunition.'

'Of course.'

The Boer stayed with them while Eccles and half a dozen men searched the field, destroying the maimed animals and examining the fallen troopers. They found one man still alive. The air hissed softly from his severed windpipe and a froth of blood bubbles writhed about the hole. On a blanket they carried him down to the river-bed.

'Eleven dead, sir,' Eccles reported to Sean.

'Eccles, as soon as the truce ends we are going to recover another Maxim and the two cases of ammunition.'

They stood beside the scotchcart and Sean inclined his head to indicate the bulky, blue-metalled weapon that showed from beneath the tarpaulin.

'Very good, sir.'

'I want four men ready below the lip of the bank. Make sure each man has a knife to cut the pack ropes.'

'Yes, sir.' Eccles grinned like a playful walrus and drifted back towards the river, and Sean strolled across to the mounted Boer.

'We have finished, *Menheer*.'

'Good. As soon as I cross the skyline up there – then we'll start again.'

'I agree.' Sean walked back to the river, picking his way through the dead. Already the flies were there, swarming green and metallic, rising like a migrating hive of bees as he passed, then settling again.

Sean reached the bank and below him Saul crouched at the head of a bunch of unarmed men. Behind them stood a very disgruntled Eccles, his moustache drooping in disappointment. Instantly Sean saw what had happened – Saul had used his superior rank to take over command of the volunteers. 'What the hell do you think you're doing?' Sean demanded, and Saul answered him with an obstinate stare.

'You'll stay where you are. That's an order!' He turned to Eccles. 'Take over, Sergeant-Major,' and Eccles grinned.

This was no time to argue. Already the Boer horseman was

half way up the ridge. Sean raised his voice and shouted at the long line of men below the bank.

'Listen, all of you. No one is to fire until the enemy do. That way we may be able to spin it out a little longer.' Then less loudly as he spoke to Eccles. 'Don't run, just walk out casually.' Sean jumped down the bank and stood between Eccles and Saul. All three of them peered up at the ridge and saw the Boer reach the crest, wave his hat and disappear.

'Go!' Sean said, and all of them went. Eccles, the four volunteers – and Saul. Flabbergasted, Sean stared at the six of them as they strolled out towards the scotchcart. Then his anger flared. *The stupid little bastard*, and he went also.

He caught up with them as they reached the scotchcart, and in the strained silence of the suspended storm he growled at Saul:

'I'll fix you for this!' and Saul grinned triumphantly.

Still there was a puzzled silence from the ridge – but it could not last much longer.

Together Saul and Eccles slashed at the ropes that held the tarpaulin, and Sean pulled it back and reached for the gun.

'Take it.' He passed it to the man behind him. At that moment a warning shot cracked over their heads.

'Grab one each and run!'

From the ridge and the river came gunfire like a long roll of drums, and they ran doubled beneath their loads and dodging, back towards the river.

The man carrying the Maxim fell headlong. Sean threw the ammunition case he carried, it dropped short of the bank, but skidded forward and toppled over the edge. Hardly pausing in his run, he stopped and gathered the fallen Maxim and went on. Ahead of him first Eccles, then Saul jumped into safety and Sean followed them with the three surviving troopers.

It was over, Sean sat waist-deep in the icy water with the machine-gun clutched to his chest, and all he could think of was his anger at Saul. He glared at him, but Saul and Eccles knelt facing each other grinning and laughing.

Sean handed the gun to the nearest trooper and crossed to Saul. His hand fell heavily on his shoulder and he pulled him to his feet.

'You –' He could not find words cutting enough. If Saul had been killed out there, Ruth would never have believed Sean had not ordered it so. 'You fool,' he said and might have hit him, but he was distracted by the cries from the firing platform beside him.

'The poor bastard!'

'He's up.'

'Lie down, for God's sake, lie down.'

Sean released Saul, jumped up on to the platform and stared through the loophole in the scharnz.

Out in the open the trooper who had carried the Maxim was on his feet. He was moving parallel to the ban, shambling with a curious idiot gait, his hands hanging loosely by his sides. They were shooting at him from the ridge.

Held in the paralysis of horror, none of them went to him. He was hit and he lurched but tottered on with the Boer rifles hunting him, staggering in a circle away from the river. Then, suddenly they killed him and he dropped on to his face.

The gunfire stopped and in the silence the men in the river-bed began to move around, and talk of trivial things, avoiding each other's eyes, ashamed to have watched such a naked intimate thing as that man's dying.

Sean's anger was gone, replaced by guilty thankfulness that it had not been Saul out there in the open.

46

In the long period of stagnation that followed, Sean and Saul sat together against the bank. Though they talked little, the old sense of companionship was restored.

With a rush and rattle the first shell ripped the air above their heads, and with everyone else Sean ducked instinctively. The shell burst in a tall brownish-yellow spurt on the far slope. Consternation bushfired along the river.

'Lummy, they've got a gun!'

'Book me on the next train, mate!'

'Nothing to worry about, boys,' Sean shouted reassuringly. 'They can't reach us with that piece.'

And the next shell burst on the lip of the bank, showering them with earth and pebbles. One startled second they stood dazed and coughing in the fumes, and the next they fell on the bank like a band of competitive grave-diggers. Dust from their exertions rose in a pale brown mist over the river to puzzle the Boers on the ridge. Almost before the arrival of the next shell, each man had hacked out a small earthen cupboard into which he could squeeze himself.

The Boer gunners were alarmingly inconsistent. Two or three rounds would fly wildly overhead and burst in the open veld. The next would land squarely in the river spraying mud and water high in the air. When this happened the sound of sustained cheering drifted faintly down from the ridge, followed by a long pause – presumably while the gunners received the congratulations of their fellows. Then the bombardment would recommence with enthusiastic rapidity, which slowly wound down into another long pause while everybody rested.

During one of these intervals Sean peered through his loophole. From a dozen points along the ridge rose pale columns of smoke.

'Coffee break up there, Eccles.'

'The way they do things we can expect another white flag and a couple of their lads coming down with coffee for us as well.'

'I doubt it,' Sean grinned. 'But I think we can expect them to come down though.' Sean pulled out his watch. 'Half-past four now. Two hours to sundown. Leroux must try for a decision before dark.'

'If they come, they'll come from behind,' Saul announced cheerfully and pointed to the slope of ground that menaced their rear. 'To meet a charge from there, we would have to line the far bank and expose our backs to sniping from the ridge.'

Sean considered the problem for a minute. 'Smoke! That's it!'

'I beg yours, sir?'

'Eccles, get the men to build fireplaces of stone along the bed and set grass and branches ready to light,' Sean ordered. 'If they do come from behind we'll screen ourselves with smoke.'

Fifteen minutes of furious activity completed the work. At intervals of ten paces along the river-bed they built flat-topped cairns of stone that rose above the level of the water. On each was piled a large heap of grass and wild hemlock branches gathered from where they overhung the bank of the river.

A little before sunset, in that time of shadows and deceptive light, with a haze rising in the still, cold air to mask them, Leroux charged his horsemen at the river.

Sean heard a low drumming of hooves as though a train passed in the distance and started to his feet.

'Here they come!' somebody shouted.'The bastards are coming from behind.'

With the low sun at their backs throwing big, distorted shadows ahead of them, they swept down in a long line from the west.

'Light the fires!' bellowed Sean. They were lying flat on their horses, five hundred of them coming in at full gallop and shooting as they came.

'Maxims!' Sean shouted. 'Get the Maxims across!' The teams dragged the heavy unwieldy weapons from their emplacements and floundered with them across the stream. From each of the fires blue smoke spread and lifted. Men coughed and swore and splashed to their new positions. From the ridge a furious covering fire raked the river and then the field-piece crashed shell after shell amongst them.

'Fire at will!' Sean shouted. 'Hit the bastards. Hit them. Hit them hard.'

The din was appalling – gunfire and bursting shells, the hammering beat of the Maxims, shouts of defiance and pain, the thunder of charging hooves, crackling of the flames. Over it all a dense fog of smoke and dust.

With elbows on the rough shale of the bank, Sean aimed and fired and a horse went down, throwing rider and rifle high and clear. Without taking the butt from his shoulder he worked the bolt and fired again. Got him! swaying and twisting in the saddle. Drop, you bastard! That's it – slide forward and fall. Shoot again, and again. Empty the magazine. Hitting with every shot.

Beside him the matelot traversed the Maxim in a deliberate hammering arc. Fumbling, as he reloaded, Sean watched the Maxim scythe its slow circle of destruction, leaving a shambles of downed horses and struggling men, before its beat stopped abruptly and the matelot crouched over it to fit a fresh belt from the wooden case. A bullet from the ridge, fired blindly into the smoke, hit him in the back of the neck and he fell forward, jamming the gun, blood gushing from his open mouth over the jacketed barrel. His limbs twitched and jerked in the epilepsy of death.

Sean dropped his rifle and dragged the matelot off the gun, levered the first round of the belt into the breech and thrust his thumbs down on the buttons.

They were close now. Sean bore down on the firing handles to raise his fire, aiming at the chests of the horses. The sailor's blood fried and sizzled on the hot barrel, and the grass in front of the muzzle flattened and quivered in the continuous blast.

Above him a solid frieze of milling horses was outlined against the darkening sky, the men upon them pouring their bullets into the crowded river-bed. Wounded horses plunged down the bank, rolling and kicking into the mud.

'Dismount! Dismount! Go in after them!' an old burgher with a neat blond beard yelled.

Sean dragged the gun around to get him. The man saw him in the smoke but his right leg was out of the stirrup, his rifle held in the left hand, helpless in the act of dismounting. Sean saw his eyes were grey and without fear as he looked down into the muzzle of the Maxim. The burst hit him across the chest, his arm windmilled, his left foot caught in the stirrup as he went backwards and his pony dragged him away.

The attack broke. The Boer fire slackened, ponies wheeled away, and raced back for the shelter of the hills. The old burgher Sean had killed went with them, dragged upon his back with his head bouncing loosely over the broken ground, leaving a long slide mark of flattened grass.

Around him Sean's men cheered and laughed and chattered with jubilation. But in the mud there were many who did not cheer and with a guilty shock Sean realized he had been standing on the corpse of the sailor who had died over the gun.

'Our round, that one!' Eccles beamed. Callous among the dead as only an old soldier can be.

'Yes,' Sean agreed.

Out in the open a horse heaved itself up and stood shivering, one leg hanging broken under it. A wounded burgher started to cough in the grass, choking and gasping as he drowned in his own blood.

'Yes, our round, Eccles. Put up the flag. They must come down and collect the wounded.'

They used lanterns in the darkness to find the wounded and kill the horses.

'Nkosi, at a place where the river turns and the banks are low, they have placed men,' Mbejane reported, back from the reconnaissance on which Sean had sent him. 'We cannot escape that way.'

'I thought as much,' Sean nodded, and held out the open can of bully beef to Mbejane. 'Eat,' he said.

'What's he say, sir?' Eccles asked.

'The river is held in force downstream.' Sean lit one of the cheroots that he had recovered in the darkness from the saddle-bag of his dead horse.

'Ruddy cold sitting here in the mud,' Eccles hinted.

'Patience, Sergeant-Major,' Sean smiled. 'We'll give them until midnight. By them most of them will be down the other side of the ridge drinking coffee around the fires.'

'You are going to rush the ridge, sir?' Eccles obviously approved.

'Yes. Tell the men. Three hours' rest and then we'll take the ridge.'

'Very good, sir.'

Sean lay back and closed his eyes. He was very weary, his eyes felt gritty from the dust and smoke, his lower body was wet and cold, his boots heavy with mud. Lyddite fumes had given him a blinding headache.

I should have put a look-out on the ridge, he thought again. My God! What a mess I've made of this. My first command and already I've lost all the horses and damn-nigh half of my men. I should have put a look-out on the ridge.

47

They took the ridge a few minutes after midnight with hardly any opposition. The few Boer sentries made good time down the far slope and Sean looked down upon the Boer laagers. The camp fires glimmered in an irregular line along the valley. Men stood around them staring up at the ridge. Sean scattered them with a dozen lusty volleys, and then yelled, 'Cease firing. Eccles, get the men settled in. We are going to have visitors fairly soon.'

The Boers had built scharnzes along the crest which saved Sean's men much inconvenience and within ten minutes the Maxims were emplaced and Sean's two hundred unwounded men waited behind walls of rough rock for the situation necessitated a hurried War Council in the valley below. But at last they heard the first stealthy approach of the attackers.

'Here they come, Sergeant-Major. Hold your fire, please.'

The burghers worked their way up cautiously and when Sean could hear their voices whispering among the rocks he decided they were close enough and discouraged further intimacy with volleyed rifle-fire and the use of all his Maxims. The Boers replied with heat and at the height of the exchange the Hotchkiss gun joined in from the valley. Its first shell passed but a few feet over Sean's head, then burst in the valley behind him. The second and third shots dropped neatly among the attacking Boer riflemen and raised such a howl of protest that the gunners, their efforts not appreciated, maintained an aloof and offended silence for the rest of the night.

Sean had expected a determined night attack but it soon became clear that Leroux was fully aware of the danger of closely engaging an inferior force in the dark. He contented himself with keeping Sean awake all night, his burghers taking it in turn to come up and keep the short-range rifle duel going – and Sean began to have qualms about the wisdom of his offensive. Dawn would find him on a rocky ridge, facing a numerically superior force, with his line anchored at neither end, and short enough to be easily flanked and enfiladed. He remembered Spion Kop – and there was little comfort in the memory. But the alternative was to fall back on the river, and his hackles rose at the thought. Unless relief came soon, defeat was certain – better here on the high ground than in the mud. We'll stay, he decided.

In the dawn there was a lull but although the gunfire dwindled to an occasional crack and flash on the lower slope yet Sean could sense an increase of activity among the Boers. Ominous rustlings and the muted sounds of movement on his flanks confirmed his misgivings. But now it was too late to retreat on the river, for already the mountains were showing stark silhouettes against the dawn sky. They seemed very close, as close and unfriendly as the unseen multitude of the enemy waiting out there for the light to come.

Sean stood up. 'Take the gun,' he whispered to the man beside him as he relinquished the Maxim.

All night he had fought with that wicked clumsy weapon and now his hands were claws shaped to the firing grips, and his shoulders ached intolerably. He flexed them as he moved down the line, stopping to chat with the men who lay belly-down behind the scharnz, trying to make his words of encouragement sound convincing.

In their replies he sensed the respect they were forming for him as a fighting man. It was more than respect – closer to a tolerant affection. The same feeling old General Buller had evoked amongst his men. He made mistakes, a lot of men died when he led, but they liked him and followed cheerfully. Sean reached the end of the line.

'How's it going?' he asked Saul softly.

'Fair enough.'

'Any sign of the old Boer?'

'They're pretty close – we heard them talking a few minutes ago. My guess is they're as ready as we are.'

'We've got enough to finish this business.'

To finish the business! That would be his decision. When the massacre began, how much must he make then endure before he called for quarter, and they stood up with arms raised in the most shameful of all attitudes?

'You'd better get under cover, Sean. Light's coming fast.'

'Who the hell is looking after whom,' Sean grinned at him. 'I want no more heroics from you,' he said, and walked quickly to his station on the other flank.

The night lifted quickly from the land, and morning came as abruptly as it does only in Africa. The Boer laagers were gone. The Hotchkiss gun was gone. Sean knew that the gun and the Boer horses had been moved back behind the new ridge which now faced their position. He knew also that the rocky ground below him was crawling with the enemy, that they were on his flanks and probably in his rear as well.

Slowly, the way a man looks at a place before he begins a long journey, Sean looked around him at the mountains and the sky and the valley. In the soft light is was very beautiful.

He looked down the gut of the valley towards the grass plains of the highveld. His head jerked with surprise. He felt excitement lift the hair on his forearms. The mouth of the valley was blocked by a dark mass. In the uncertain light it could have been a plantation of wattle trees – oblong and regular and black against the pale grass. But this plantation was moving, changing shape, elongating. Birnam Wood to Dunsinane.

The first rays of the sun slanted in across the crest of the ridge and lit the lance-heads into a thousand minute dazzles.

'Cavalry!' roared Sean. 'By Jesus, look at them.'

The cry was taken up and thrown along the line, yelling, cheering wildly they fired down upon the tiny brown figures that were scurrying away to meet the Boer pickets who galloped in across the floor of the valley, each of them dragging a bunch of a dozen horses after him.

Then above the cheering and the gunfire, high above the sounds of hooves and the cries of panic, a bugle began to sing: 'Bonnie Dundee' – sharp and clear and urgently it commanded the charge.

Sean's rifles fell silent. The cheering faltered and stopped. One by one his men stood up to watch as the lines of lancers moved forward. Walk. Trot. Canter. Gallop. The lance heads dropped. Belly-high they flitted like fireflies in front of the solid dark ranks, and that terrible thing swept down upon the tangle of men and frenzied, struggling horses.

Some of the Boers were up now, wheeling away, breaking like game before the beaters.

'My God!' breathed Sean, tensing himself for the burst of sound as the charge struck home. But there was only the drum of hooves – no check, no distortion as the dark squadrons drove through the Boers. Precisely they wheeled, and came back. Broken lances thrown aside, sabres unsheathed, bright and long.

Sean watched a burgher dodging desperately as a lancer followed him. Saw him turning at the last moment and crouching with his arms covering his head. The lancer stood in his stirrups and swung his sabre backhanded. The burgher dropped. Like a polo player the trooper pivoted his horse and rode back of the Boer, leaning low out of the saddle to sabre him again as he knelt in the grass.

'Quarter!' growled Sean, the his voice rising shrilly in horror and disgust, 'Give them quarter. For the love of God, give them quarter!'

But cavalry gives no quarter. They butchered with dispassionate parade-ground precision. Hack and cut, turn and trample until the blades blurred redly – until the valley was strewn with the bodies of men wounded a dozen times.

Sean tore his eyes away and saw the remains of Leroux's commando scattered into the broken ground where the big cavalry mounts could not follow.

Sean sat down on a rock and bit the end off a cheroot. The rank smoke helped cleanse his mouth of the taste of victory.

Two days later Sean led his column into Charlestown. The garrison cheered them and Sean grinned as he watched his men react. Half an hour before they had bumped along, hunched unhappily on their borrowed mounts. Now they sat erect and jaunty, eating the applause and liking the taste.

Then the grin faded from Sean's face as he saw how his band was depleted, and he looked back and the fifteen crowded wagons that carried the wounded.

If only I'd put look-outs on the ridge.

48

There was an urgent summons from Acheson waiting for Sean. He caught the northbound express twenty minutes after arriving in Charlestown, hating Saul for the hot bath in which he left him, and for the uniform which Mbejane had persuaded a plump Zulu maid to wash and iron, hating him still more venomously for the invitation to be guest of honour at the officers' mess that night – and knowing that Saul would drink deep on Veuve Clicquot and Courvoisier which had once belonged to Sean.

When Sean arrived in Johannesburg the following morning, with soot from the locomotive adding a subtle touch to the fragrance he had gathered from two unwashed weeks in the veld, there was an orderly to meet him and conduct him to Acheson's suite in the Grand National Hotel.

Major Peterson was patently taken aback by Sean's turn-out, he eyed the stains and tears and dried mud with genteel horror at the contrast they afforded to the breakfast table's crisp white linen and splendid silver. The ripeness of Sean's odour impaired Peterson's appetite and he dabbed at his nose with a silk handkerchief. But Acheson seemed not to notice, he was in festive mood.

'Damned fine show, Courtney. Oh, damned fine. Proved your point entirely. We'll not have much trouble from Leroux for some time, I warrant you. Have another egg? Peterson, pass him the bacon.'

Sean finished eating and filled his coffee cup before he made his request. 'I want to be relieved of this command, I made a bloody mess of it.'

Both Acheson and Peterson stared in horror. 'Good God, Courtney. You've achieved a notable success – the most spectacular in months.'

'Luck,' brusquely Sean interrupted. 'Another two hours and we would have been wiped out.'

'Lucky officers are more valuable to me than clever ones. Your request is refused, Colonel Courtney.' So it's Colonel now, a bribe to get me into the dentist's chair. Sean was mildly amused.

A knock at the door prevented Sean continuing his protestation, and an orderly came into the room and handed Acheson a message.

'Urgent dispatch from Charlestown,' he whispered. Acheson took the paper from him and used it like a conductor's baton as he went on talking.

'I have got three junior officers for you, men to replace your losses. You catch them for us and hold them for my cavalry. That's all I want from you. While you're doing your bit the columns are going to start a series of new drives. This time we are going to sweep every inch of the ground between the blockhouse lines. We are going to destroy the crops and the livestock; burn the farms; take every woman, man and child off the land and put them in detainment camps. By the time we're finished there will be nothing but bare veld out there. We will force them to operate in a vacuum, while we wear them down with a relentless series of drives and raids.' Acheson slapped the table so that the crockery jingled. 'Attrition, Courtney. From now on it's a war of attrition!'

Those words had an uncomfortable familiarity for Sean. And suddenly a picture of desolation formed in his mind. He saw the land – his land – blackened with fire, and the roofless homesteads standing in the wastes. The sound of the empty winds across the land was the wailing of orphans, and the protest of a lost people.

'General Acheson –' he began, but Acheson was reading the dispatch.

'Damn!' he snapped. 'Damn and blast! Leroux again. He doubled back and caught the transport column of those same lancers who cut him up. Wiped it out and disappeared into the mountains.' Acheson laid the message on the table in front of him and stared at it. 'Courtney,' he said, 'go back and, this time, catch him!'

49

'Breakfast is ready, Nkosi.' Michael Courtney looked up from his book at the servant. 'Thank you, Joseph, I'm coming now.'

These two hours of study each morning passed so quickly. He checked the clock on the shelf above his bed – half-past six already – closed the book and stood up.

While he brushed his hair he watched his reflection in the mirror without attention. His mind was fully occupied with events that would fill this new day. There was work to do.

His reflection looked back at him with serious grey eyes from a face whose lean contours were marred by the big Courtney nose. His hair was black and springy beneath the brush.

He dropped the brush and while he shrugged into his leather jacket he flipped open the book to check a passage. He read it through carefully, then turned and went out into the corridor.

Anna and Garrick Courtney were seated at opposite ends of the long dining-table of Theuniskraal and they both looked up expectantly as he entered.

'Good morning, Mother.' She held up her face for his kiss.

'Good morning, Pa.'

'Hello, my boy.' Garry was wearing full dress, complete with crowns and decorations, and Michael felt a flare of irritation. It was so damned ostentatious. Also it reminded him that he was nineteen years old and there was a war going on while he sat at home on the farm.

'Are you going into town today, Pa?'

'No, I'm going to do some work on my memoirs.'

'Oh,' Michael glanced pointedly at the uniform and his father flushed slightly and applied himself to his meal.

'How are your studies, darling?' Anna broke the silence.

'Well enough, thank you, Mother.'

'I'm certain you'll have as little trouble with the final examinations as you had with the others.' Anna smiled at him possessively and stretched out to touch his hand. Michael withdrew it quickly and laid down his fork.

'Mother, I want to talk to you about enlisting.' Anna's smile froze. At the end of the table Garry straightened in his chair.

'No,' he snapped with unusual violence. 'We've been over this before. You're still a minor and you do as you're told.'

'The war is almost over, darling. Please think of your father and me.'

It began then. Another of those long wheedling, pleading arguments that sickened and frustrated Michael until he stood up abruptly and left the room. His horse was waiting saddled for him in the yard. He threw himself on to its back and swung its head at the gate, lifting it over, and scattering chickens as he landed. He galloped furiously away towards the main dip-tank.

From the dining-room they heard the hooves beat away until they had dwindled into silence. Garry stood up.

'Where are you going?' snapped Anna.

'To my study.'

'To the brandy bottle in your study,' she corrected him contemptuously.

'Don't, Anna.'

'*Don't, Anna*,' she mimicked him. '*Please don't, Anna*. Is that all you can say?' Her voice had lost the genteel inflexion she had cultivated so carefully. Now it contained all the accumulated bitterness of twenty years.

'Please, Anna. I'll stop him going. I promise you.'

'You'll stop him!' She laughed. 'How will you stop him? Will you rattle your medals at him? How will you stop him – you, who have never done one useful thing in all your life?' She laughed again, shrilly. 'Why don't you show him your leg and say, "Please don't leave your poor crippled Daddy".'

Garry drew himself up. His face had gone very pale. 'He'll listen to me. He's my son.'

'Your son!'

'Anna, please –'

'Your son! Oh, that's choice! He's not your son. He's Sean's son.'

'Anna.' He tried to stop her.

'How could you have a son?' She was laughing again, and he could not stand it. He started for the door but her voice followed him, cutting into the two most sensitive places in his soul; his deformity and his impotence.

He stumbled into his study, slammed the door and locked it. Then he crossed quickly to the solid cabinet that stood beside his desk.

He poured the tumbler half-full and drank it. Then he sank into his chair and closed his eyes and reached for the bottle behind him. He poured again carefully and screwed the cap back on to the bottle. This one he would sip slowly, making it last perhaps an hour. He had learned how to keep the glow.

He unbuttoned and removed his tunic, stood up and hung it over the back of the chair, seated himself once more, sipped at the tumbler, then drew towards him the pile of handwritten sheets, and read the one on top.

'Colenso: An account of the campaign in Natal under General Buller.' By Colonel Garrick Courtney, V.C., D.S.O.

He lifted it, laid it aside, and began to read what followed. Having read it so many times before, he had come to believe in it. It was good. He knew it was good. So too did Messrs William Heinemann in London, to whom he had sent a draft of the first two chapters. They were anxious to publish as soon as possible.

He worked on quietly and happily all morning. At midday old Joseph brought a meal to the study. Cold chicken and salads on Delft-ware china, with a bottle of white Cape wine wrapped in a snowy napkin. He worked as he ate.

That evening when he had altered the last paragraph on the final page and laid his pen on the inkstand, he was smiling.

'Now, I will go and see my darling.' He spoke aloud and put on his tunic.

The homestead of Theuniskraal sat on the crest of a rise below the escarpment. A big building of whitewashed walls, thatch and Dutch gables. In front of it the terraced lawns sprawled away, contoured by beds of azaleas and blue rhododendrons and bounded on the one side by the horse paddocks: two large paddocks for the brood mares and the yearlings, where Garry paused beside the low fence and watched the foals nuzzling upwards at the udders.

Then he limped on along the fence towards the smaller enclosure with its nine-foot fence of thick, canvas-padded gumpoles that contained his stud stallion.

Gypsy was waiting for him, nodding his almost snakelike head so that his mane flared golden in the late sunlight, flattening his ears, then pricking them forward, dancing a little with impatience.

'Hey, Boy. Hey there, Gypsy,' Garry called and the stallion thrust his head between the poles to nibble with soft lips at Garry's sleeve.

'Sugar, is that what you're after.' Garry chuckled and cupped his hands while the stallion fed delicately from them.

'Sugar, my darling,' Garry whispered in sensual delight at the touch of the soft muzzle on his skin and Gypsy cocked his ears to listen to his voice.

'That's all. All finished.' The stallion nuzzled his chest and Garry wiped his hands on its neck, caressing the warm and silky coat.

'That's all, my darling. Now run for me. Let me watch you run.' He stepped back and clapped his hands loudly. 'Run, my darling, run.'

The stallion pulled his head back between the poles and went up on his hind legs, whinnying as he reared, cutting at the air with his fore-hooves. The veins stood out along the belly and upon the tight double-swollen bag of its scrotum.

Swift and virile and powerful, it pivoted upon its quarters.

'Run for me!' shouted Garrick. The stallion came down into full gallop along the track worn by its hooves, sweeping around the paddock with loose dirt flying and the light dancing on his coat as the great muscles bulged beneath.

'Run.' Leaning against the poles of the fence, Garrick watched him with an expression of terrible yearning.

When he stopped again with the first dark patches of sweat dulling his shoulders, Garrick straightened up and shouted across the stable yard.

'Zama, bring her now!'

On a long rein two grooms led the brood mare down towards the paddock. Gypsy's nostrils flared into dark pink caverns and he rolled his eyes until the whites showed.

'Wait, my darling,' whispered Garrick in a voice tight with his own excitement.

50

Michael Courtney dismounted among the rocks on the highest point of the escarpment. For a week he had denied the impulse to return to this place. Somehow it seemed a treachery – a disloyalty to both his parents.

Far below and behind him in the forest was the tiny speck of Theuniskraal. Between them the railway angled down towards the sprawled irregular pattern of rooftops that was Ladyburg.

But Michael did not look that way. He stood behind his mare and gazed along the line of bare hills to the gigantic quilt of trees that covered them in the north.

The wattle was tall now, so that the roads between the blocks no longer showed. It was a dark smoky green that undulated like the swells of a frozen sea.

This was as close as he had ever been to Lion Kop. It was a forbidden land, like the enchanted forest of the fairy-tale. He took the binoculars from his saddle-bag and scanned it carefully, until he came to the roof of the homestead. The new thatch, golden and unweathered, stood out above the wattle.

Grandma is there. I could ride across to visit, there would be no harm in that. *He* is not there. *He* is away at the war.

Slowly he replaced the binoculars in the saddle-bag, and he knew he would not go to Lion Kop. He was shackled by the promise he had made to his mother. Like so many other promises he had made.

With dull resignation he remembered the argument at breakfast that morning, and knew that they had won again. He could not leave them, knowing that without him they would wither. He could not follow *him* to war.

He smiled ironically as he remembered the fantasies he had imagined. Charging into battle with *him*, talking with *him* beside the camp fire in the evenings, throwing himself in front of a bayonet meant for *him*.

From the look-out on the escarpment Michael had spent hours each day of the last Christmas holidays waiting for a glimpse of Sean Courtney. Now with guilt he remembered the pleasure he had experienced whenever he picked up that tall figure in the field of his binoculars and followed it as it moved between the newly planted rows of wattle.

But he's gone now. There would be no disloyalty if I rode across to see Grandma. He mounted the superb golden mare and sat deep in thought. At last he sighed, swung her head back towards Theuniskraal – and rode away from Lion Kop.

I must never come up here again, he thought determinedly, especially after *he* comes home.

51

They are tired, tired to the marrow of their bones. Jan Paulus
Leroux watched the lethargy of his burghers as they off-saddled
and hobbled their horses. They are tired with three years of
running and fighting, sick-tired in the certain knowledge of
defeat, exhausted with grief for the men they have buried, with
grief also for the children and the women with them in the
camps. They are wearied by the sight of burned homes scattered
about with the bones of their flocks.

Perhaps it is finished, he thought and lifted the battered old
Terai from his head. Perhaps we should admit that it is finished,
and go in to them. He wiped his face with his scarf and the cloth
came away discoloured with the grease of his sweat and the dust
of the dry land. He folded the scarf into the pocket of his coat
and looked at the fire-blackened ruins of the homestead on the
bluff above the river. The fire had spread into the gum trees and
the leaves were sere and yellow and dead.

'No,' he said aloud. 'It is not finished – not until we try for
this last time,' and he moved towards the nearest group of his
men.

'*Ja*, Hennie. How goes it?' he asked.

'Not too bad, Oom Paul.' The boy was very thin, but then all
of them were thin. He had spread his saddle-blanket in the grass
and lay upon it.

'Good.' Jan Paulus nodded and squatted beside him. He took
out his pipe and sucked on it. There was still the taste of tobacco
from the empty bowl.

'Will you take a fill, Oom Paul?' One of the others sat up and
proffered a pouch of springbok skin.

'*Nee, dankie.*' He looked away from the pouch, shutting out
the temptation. 'Keep it for a smoke when we cross the Vaal.'

'Or when we ride into Cape Town,' joked Hennie, and Jan

Paulus smiled at him. Cape Town was a thousand miles south of them, but that was where they were going.

'*Ja*, keep it for Cape Town,' he agreed and the smile on his face turned bitter. Bullets and disease had left him with six hundred ragged men on horses half-dead with exhaustion to conquer a province the size of France. But it was the last try. He started to speak then.

'Already Jannie Smuts is into the Cape with a big commando. Pretorius also has crossed the Orange, De la Rey and De Wet will follow – and Zietsmann is waiting for us to join him on the Vaal River. This time the Cape burghers must rise with us. This time . . . '

He spoke slowly, leaning forward with his elbows on his knees, a gaunt giant of a man with his unkempt, ginger beard wiry with dust and streaked about the mouth with yellowish grey. The cuffs of his sleeves were stained with the discharge from the veld sores on his wrists. Men came across from the other groups and squatted in a circle about him to listen and take comfort.

'Hennie, bring my Bible from the saddle-bag. We will read a little from the Book.'

The sun was setting when he closed the Book and looked around at them. An hour had gone in prayer that might more profitably have been spent in rest, but when he looked at their faces he knew the time had not been wasted.

'Sleep now, *Kerels*. We will upsaddle early tomorrow.' If they do not come in the night, he qualified himself silently.

But he could not sleep. He sat propped against his saddle and for the hundredth time re-read the letter from Henrietta. It was dated four months earlier, had taken six weeks to reach him along the chain of spies and commandos which carried their mail. Henrietta was sick with dysentery and both the younger children, Stephanus and baby Paulus, were dead from the *wit-seerkeel*. The concentration camp was ravaged by this disease and she feared for the safety of the older children.

The light had failed so he could not read further. He sat with the letter in his hands. With such a price as we have paid, surely we could have won something.

Perhaps there is still a chance. Perhaps.

'Upsaddle! Upsaddle! Khaki is coming.' The warning was shouted from the ridge across the river where he had placed his pickets. It carried clearly in the still of the evening.

'Upsaddle! Khaki is coming.' The cry was taken up around the camp. Jan Paulus leaned over and shook the boy beside him, who was too deep in exhaustion to have heard.

'Wake up, Hennie. We must run again.'

Five minutes later he led his commando over the ridge and southward into the night.

52

'Still holding southwards,' Sean observed. 'Three days' riding and they haven't altered course.'

'Looks like Leroux has got his teeth into something,' agreed Saul.

'We'll halt for half an hour to blow the horses.' Sean lifted his hand and behind him the column lost its shape as the men dismounted and led their horses aside. Although the entire unit had been remounted a week before, the horses were already losing condition from the long hours of riding to which they had been subjected. However, the men were in good shape, lean and hard-looking. Sean listened to their banter and watched the way they moved and laughed. He had built them into a tough fighting force that had proved itself a dozen times since that fiasco a year ago when Leroux had caught them in the mountains. Sean grinned. They had earned the name under which they rode. He handed his horse to Mbejane and moved stiffly towards the shade of a small mimosa tree.

'Have you got any ideas about what Leroux is up to?' he asked Saul as he offered him a cheroot.

'He could be making a try at the Cape railway.'

'He could be,' Sean agreed as he lowered himself gratefully on to a flat stone and stretched his legs out in front of him. 'My God, I'm sick of this business. Why the hell can't they admit it's finished – why must they go on and on?'

'Granite cannot bend.' Saul smiled dryly. 'But I think that now it is very near the point where it must break.'

'We thought that six months ago,' Sean answered him, then looked beyond him. 'Yes, Mbejane, what is it?'

Mbejane was going through the ritual which preceded serious speech. He had come and squatted half a dozen paces from where Sean sat, had laid his spears carefully beside him in the grass, and now he was taking snuff.

'Nkosi.'

'Yes?' Sean encouraged him and waited while Mbejane tapped a little of the dark powder on to his fingernail.

'Nkosi, this porridge has an unusual taste.' He sniffed and sneezed.

'Yes?'

'It seems to me that the spoor has changed.' Mbejane wiped the residual snuff from his nostrils with the pink palm of his hand.

'You speak in riddles.'

'These men we follow ride in a different manner from the way they did before.'

Sean thought about that for a few seconds before he saw it. Yes! He was right. Where previously Leroux's commando had spread and trampled the grass in a road fifty feet wide, since this morning they had ridden in two files as though they were regular cavalry.

'They ride as we do, Nkosi, so the hooves of the horses fall in the tracks of those that lead. In this way it is difficult to tell how many men we follow.'

'We know there are about six hundred. . . . Hold on! I think I see what you . . . '

'Nkosi, it comes to me that there are no longer six hundred men ahead of us.'

'My God! You could be right.' Sean jumped up and began to pace restlessly. 'He is splitting his commando again. We've crossed a dozen rocky places where he could have detached small groups of his men. By evening we'll be following less than fifty men – when that happens they'll break up into individuals, lose us in the dark and head separately for a pre-arranged rendezvous.' He punched his fist into the palm of his hand. 'That's it, by God!' He swung round to face Saul.

'You remember that stream we crossed a mile back – that would have been an ideal place.'

'You're taking a big risk,' Saul cautioned him. 'If we go back now and it turns out you're wrong – then you've lost him for good.'

'I'm right,' Sean snapped. 'I know I am. Get them mounted up – we're going back.'

736

Sean sat his horse on the bank of the stream and looked down into the clear water that sparkled over gravel and small round boulders.

'They will have gone downstream, otherwise the mud they stirred up would have washed down across the ford.' He turned to Saul. 'I'm going to take fifty men with me so as not to raise too much dust. Give me an hour's start and then follow with the rest of the column.'

'*Mazeltov*.' Saul grinned at him.

With a Zulu tracker on each bank Sean and Eccles and fifty men followed the stream towards the north-west. Behind them the mountains of the Drakensberg were an irregular pale blue suggestion against the sky and around them the brown winter-sere veld spread away in the folded complexity of ridges and the shallow valleys. In the rocky ground along the ridges grew the squat little aloe plants, holding up their multiple flowers like crimson candelabra while in the valleys the stunted thorn bushes huddled along the course of the stream. High, cold cloud obscured the sky. There was no warmth in the pale sunlight, and the wind had a knife-edge to it.

Two miles below the ford Sean was showing his anxiety by leaning forward in the saddle and checking the ground that Mbejane had already covered. Once he called, 'Mbejane, are you sure you haven't missed them?'

Mbejane straightened from his crouch and turned slowly to regard Sean with a look of frigid dignity. Then he shifted his war shield to the other shoulder and, not deigning to answer, he returned to his search.

Fifty yards farther on he straightened again and informed Sean. 'No, Nkosi. I have not missed them.' He pointed with his assegai at the deeply scarred bank up which horses had climbed, and the flattened grass which had wiped the mud from their legs.

'Got them!' Sean exulted in his relief; behind him he heard the stir of excitement run through his men.

'Well done, sir.' Eccles's moustache twitched ferociously as he grinned.

'How many, Mbejane?'

'Twenty, not more.'

'When?'

'The mud has dried.' Mbejane considered the question, stooping to touch the earth and determine its texture. 'They were here at half sun this morning.'

The middle of the morning; they had a lead of five hours.

'Is the spoor fat enough to run upon?'

'It is, Nkosi.'

'Then run, Mbejane.'

The spoor bellied towards the west then swung and steadied in the same persistently southward direction, and Sean's column closed up and cantered after Mbejane.

Southward, always southward. Sean pondered the problem – what could he hope to accomplish with a mere six hundred?

Unless! Sean's brain started to harry a vague idea. Unless he intended slipping through the columns of infantry and cavalry that lay before him and trying for a richer prize.

The railway, as Saul had suggested? No, he discounted that quickly. Jan Paulus would not risk his whole command for such low stakes.

What then? The Cape? By God, that was it – the Cape! That rich and lovely country of wheatlands and vineyards. That serene and secure land, lazing in the security of a hundred years of British rule – and yet peopled by men of the same blood as Leroux and De Wet and Jan Smuts.

Smuts had already taken his commando across the Orange River. If Leroux followed him, if De Wet followed him, if the Cape burghers broke their uneasy neutrality and flocked to join the commandos – Sean's mind baulked at the thought. He left the wider aspect of it and came back to the moment.

All right then, Jan Paulus was riding to the Cape with only six hundred men? No, he must have more. He must be riding to a rendezvous with one of the other commandos. Who? De la Rey? No, De la Rey was in the Magaliesberg. De Wet? No, De Wet was far south – twisting and turning away from the columns that harried him. Zietsmann? Ah, Zietsmann! Zietsmann with fifteen hundred men. That was it.

Where would they meet? On a river obviously, for they must have water for two thousand horses. The Orange was too dangerous – so it must be the Vaal, but whereabouts on the Vaal? It must be a place easily recognizable. One of the fords? No, cavalry used the fords. A confluence of one of the tributaries? Yes, that was it.

Eagerly Sean unbuckled his saddle-bag and pulled from it his

738

map-case. Holding the heavy cloth map folded against his thigh he twisted sideways in the saddle to study it.

'Here we are now,' he muttered and ran his finger south. 'The Padda River!'

'I beg your pardon, sir.'

'The Padda, Eccles, the Padda!'

'Very well, sir,' agreed Eccles with stolid features covering his bewilderment.

In the dark valley below them the single fire flared briefly, then died to a tiny glow.

'All ready, Eccles,' Sean whispered.

'Sir!' Without raising his voice Eccles placed affirmative emphasis on the monosyllable.

'I'll go down now.' Sean resisted the impulse to repeat his previous orders. He wanted to say again how important it was that no one escaped, but he had learned that once was enough with Eccles. Instead he whispered, 'Listen for my signal.'

The Boers had only one sentry. Secure in the knowledge that their stratagem had thrown off all pursuit, they slept around the poorly screened fire. Sean and Mbejane moved down quietly and squatted in the grass twenty paces from the high rock on which the sentry sat. The man was outlined darkly against the stars and Sean watched him intently for a full minute before he decided.

'He sleeps also.'

Mbejane grunted.

'Take him quietly,' Sean whispered. 'Make sure his rifle does not fall.' Mbejane moved and Sean laid a hand on his shoulder to restrain him. 'Do not kill – it is not necessary.' And Mbejane moved silently as a leopard towards the rock.

Sean waited straining his eyes into the darkness. The seconds dragged by – and suddenly the Boer was gone from the rock. A gasp, a soft sliding sound and stillness.

Sean waited, and then Mbejane was back as silently as he had left.

'It is done, Nkosi.'

Sean laid his rifle aside and cupped his hands over his lips, filled his cheeks and blew the long warbling whistle of a nightbird. At the fire one of the sleepers stirred and muttered. Farther off a horse stamped and blew softly through its nostrils. Then Sean heard a pebble click and the cautious swish of feet through grass, small sounds lost in the wind.

'Eccles?' Sean murmured.

'Sir.'

Sean stood up and they closed in on the camp.

'Wake up, gentlemen. Breakfast is ready.' Sean shouted in the Taal, and each burgher woke to find a man standing over him and the muzzle of a Lee-Metford pressing into his chest.

'Build up that fire,' Sean ordered. 'Take their rifles.' It had been too easy, he spoke roughly in the irritation of anti-climax.

'Mbejane, bring the one from the rock – I want to see how gently you dealt with him.'

'Mbejane dragged him into the firelight and Sean's lips tightened as he saw the way the man's head lolled and his legs hung.

'He's dead,' Sean accused.

'He sleeps, Nkosi,' Mbejane denied.

Sean knelt, beside him and twisted his face to catch the light. Not a man, a lad with a thin bitter face and the fluff of pale, immature beard on his cheeks. In the corner of his eye a stye had burst to matt the closed lashes with yellow pus. He was breathing.

Sean glanced up at the other prisoners. They were being herded away out of earshot.

'Water, Mbejane.' And the Zulu brought a canteen from the fire while Sean explored the hard swelling above the boy's temple.

'He'll do,' Sean grunted, and curled his lips in distaste at what he must do as soon as the lad recovered. He must do it while he was still groggy and bemused by the blow. From his cupped hand he splashed cold water into his face and the boy gasped and rolled his head.

'Wake up,' Sean urged quietly in the Taal. 'Wake up.'

'Oom Paul?' The Boer mumbled.

'Wake up.' The lad struggled to sit.

'Where . . . You're English!' As he saw the uniform.

'Yes,' Sean snapped. 'We're English. You've been caught.'

'Oom Paul?' The boy looked round wildly.

'Don't worry about him. He'll be with you on the boat to St Helena. Leroux and Zietsmann were both caught on the Vaal yesterday. We were waiting for them at the Padda and they walked right into the trap.'

'Oom Paul caught!' The boy's eyes were wide with shock, still dazed and out of focus. 'But how did you know? There must have been a traitor – someone must have told. How did you know about the meeting-place?' He stopped abruptly as his brain caught up with his tongue. 'But how . . . Oom Paul couldn't be on the Vaal yet, we left him only yesterday.' Then sickeningly he realized what he had done 'You tricked me,' he whispered. 'You tricked me.'

'I'm sorry,' Sean said simply. He stood up and walked across to where Eccles was securing his prisoners.

'When Captain Friedman arrives tell him to bring the column in to the garrison at Vereeniging and wait for me there. I am going ahead with my servant,' he said abruptly, then called across to Mbejane.

'Mbejane, bring my horse.' He would trust no one else to carry the news to Acheson.

The following afternoon Sean reached the railway line guarded by its blockhouses and flagged a northbound train. The next morning he de-trained with soot-inflamed eyes, tired and filthy, at Johannesburg station.

53

Jan Paulus Leroux checked his horse and behind him the tiny fragment of his commando bunched up and all of them peered eagerly ahead.

The Vaal is a wide, brown river, with sandbanks through which it cuts its own channel. The banks are steep and along them are scattered a few of the ugly, indigenous thorn trees which provide no cover for an army of three thousand men and horses. But Leroux had chosen the rendezvous with care. Here the tiny Padda River looped down through a complex of small kopjes to join the Vaal and among these kopjes an army might escape detection – but only if it exercised care. Which Zietsmann was not doing.

The smoke from a dozen fires hazed out in a long pale smear across the veld, horses were being watered on one of the sandbanks in the middle of the river, and a hundred men were bathing noisily from the bank, while laundry decked the thorn trees.

'The fool,' snarled Leroux and kicked his pony into a run. He stormed into the laager, flung himself off his horse and roared at Zietsmann.

'*Menheer*, I must protest.'

Zietsmann was nearly seventy years old. His beard was pure white and hung to the fifth button of his waistcoat. He was a clergyman, not a general, and his commando had survived this long because it was so ineffectual as to cause the British no serious inconvenience. Only great pressure from Delarey and Leroux had forced him to take part in this wild plan. For the last three days, as he waited for Leroux to join him, he had been harassed by doubts and misgivings. These doubts were shared by his wife – for he was the only Boer general who still had his woman with him in the field.

Now he stood up from his seat by the fire and glared at this red-bearded giant Leroux, whose face was mottled with fury.

'*Menheer*,' he growled. 'Please remember you are speaking not only to your Elder, but also to a Dominie of the Church.'

In this way was set the tone for the long discussions which were to fill the next four days. During this time Leroux saw his bold design bog down in a welter of trivialities. He did not resent the loss of the first day which was spent in prayer, indeed he realized that this was essential. Without God's blessing and active intervention the enterprise must fail, so the sermon he delivered that afternoon lasted a little over two hours and the text he selected was from Judges – 'Shall I yet again go out to battle against the children of Benjamin, my brother, or shall I cease?' and the Lord said, 'Go up; for tomorrow I will deliver them into thine hand.'

Zietsmann bettered his time by forty minutes. But then, as Leroux's men pointed out, Zietsmann was a professional while Oom Paul was only a lay-preacher.

The next and most critical question was the election of the Supreme Commander for the combined enterprise. Zietsmann was the older by thirty years, a factor heavily in his favour. Also, he had brought sixteen hundred men to the Vaal against Leroux's six hundred. Yet Leroux was the victor of Colenso and Spion Kop, and since then he had fought consistently and with not a little success, including the wrecking of eight trains and the annihilation of four British supply columns. Zietsmann had been second in command at Modder River, but since then he had done nothing but keep his commando intact.

For three days the debate continued with Zietsmann dourly refusing to bring the matter to the vote until he sensed that opinion had swung to his side. Leroux wanted command; not only for personal satisfaction, but also because he knew that under this cautious and stubborn old man they would be lucky to reach the Orange River, let alone force an effective entry into the Cape.

The card that won the hand belonged to Zietsmann, and it was ironic that he had it simply because of his inactivity over the last eighteen months.

When Lord Roberts had marched into Pretoria two years before, his entry had been offered only token resistance, for the Government of the South African Republic had withdrawn along the eastern railway line to Komatipoort. With them went the entire contents of the Pretoria Treasury, which totalled two million pounds in gold Kruger sovereigns. Later, when old President Kruger left for Europe, a part of this treasure went with him, but the balance had been shared out among the remainder of the commando leaders as their war chests to continue the fight.

Months before most of Leroux's share had been expended on the purchase of supplies from the native tribes, on ammunition from the Portuguese gun runners and on payment to his men. During a desperate night action with one of the raiding British columns he had lost the balance along with his Hotchkiss gun, twenty of his best men and a hundred irreplaceably precious horses.

Zietsmann, however, had come to the meeting with a pack-mule carrying thirty thousand sovereigns. The successful invasion of the Cape would depend largely upon this gold. On the evening of the fourth day he was duly elected Commander by a majority of two hundred, and within twelve hours he had demonstrated how well-equipped he was for the task.

'So we start in the morning, then,' one of the burghers beside Leroux grunted.

'About time,' another commented. They were breakfasting on biltong – sticks of hard dried meat – for Leroux had succeeded in convincing Zietsmann that cooking-fires were dangerous.

'No sign of Van der Bergh's men?' asked Leroux.

'Not yet, Oom Paul.'

'They are finished, or else they would have been here days ago.'

'Yes, they are finished,' agreed Leroux. 'They must have run into one of the columns.' Twenty good men, he sighed softly, and Hennie was with them. He was very fond of the boy, all of them were. He had become the mascot of the commando.

'At least they are out of it now – the lucky thunders.' The man had spoken without thinking, and Leroux turned on him.

'You can go too hands-up for the British, there is no one to stop you.' The softness of his voice did not cover the ferocity in his eyes.

'I didn't mean it that way, Oom Paul.'

'Well, don't say it then,' he growled, and would have continued, but a shout from the sentry on the kopje above them brought them all to their feet.

'One of the scouts coming!'

'Which way?' Leroux bellowed upwards.

'Along the river. He's riding to burst!'

And the sudden stilling of voices and movement was the only outward sign of the dread that settled upon all of them. In these days a galloping rider carried only evil tidings.

They watched him splash through the shallows and slide from the saddle to swim beside his horse across the deep channel. Then pony and rider, both streaming water, came lunging up the near bank and into the camp.

'Khaki,' shouted the man. 'Khaki coming!'

Leroux ran to catch the pony's head and demanded,

'How many?'

'A big column.'

'A thousand?'

'More than that. Many more – six, seven thousand.'

'Magtig!' swore Leroux. 'Cavalry?'

'Infantry and guns.'

'How close?'

'They will be here before midday.'

Leroux left him and ran down the slope to Zietsmann's wagon.

'You heard, *Menheer*?'

'*Ja*, I heard.' Zietsmann nodded slowly.

'We must mount up,' Leroux urged.

'Perhaps they will not find us. Perhaps they will pass us by.' Zietsmann spoke hesitantly, and Leroux stared at him.

'Are you mad?' he whispered, and Zietsmann shook his head – a confused old man.

'We must mount up and break away towards the south.' Leroux grabbed the lapels of Zietsmann's frock coat and shook them in his agitation.

'No, not the south – it is finished. We must go back,' the old man muttered, then suddenly his confusion cleared. 'We must pray. The Lord will deliver us from the Philistine.'

'*Menheer*, I demand . . . ' Leroux started, but another urgent warning shouted fromt he kopje interrupted him.

'Riders! To the south! Cavalry!'

Running to one of the horses Leroux vaulted on to its bare back, with a handful of its mane he turned it towards the kopje and flogged it with his heels, driving it up the steep rocky side, scrambling and sliding in the loose rock until he reached the top and jumped down beside the sentry.

'There!' The burgher pointed.

Like a column of safari ants, tiny and insignificant in the immensity of brown grass and open sky, still four or five miles distant, the squadrons were strung out in extended order across the southern hills.

'Not that way. We cannot go that way. We must go back.' He swung round to the north. 'We must go that way.'

Then he saw the dust in the north also and he felt his stomach slide sickly downwards. The dust drifted low, so thin it might have been only heat haze or the passing of a dust devil – but he knew it was not.

'They are there also,' he whispered. Acheson had thrown his column in from four directions. There was no escape.

'Van der Bergh!' whispered Leroux bitterly. 'He has gone hands-up to the English and betrayed us.' A moment longer he stared at the dust, then quickly he adjusted to the problem of defence.

'The river is our one line,' he muttered. 'With the flanks anchored on this kopje and that one there.' He let his eyes run back up the little valley of the Padda River, carefully memorizing the slope and lay of the land, storing in his mind each of its salient features, already siting the captured Maxims, picking the shelter of the hills and river bank for the horses, deciding where the reserves should be held.

'Five hundred men can hold the north kopje, but we will need a thousand on the river.' He vaulted up on to the pony and called down to the sentry, 'Stay here. I will send men up to you. They must build scharnzes along the ridge – there, and there.'

Then he drove the pony down the slope, sliding on its haunches until it reached the level ground.

'Where is Zietsmann?' he demanded.

'In his wagon.'

He galloped across to it and jerked open the canvas at the entrance.

'*Menheer,*' he began and then stopped. Zietsmann sat on the wagon bed with his wife beside him. A Bible was open on his lap.

'*Menheer*, there is little time. The enemy closes from all sides. They will be upon us in two hours.'

Zietsmann looked up at him, and from the soapy glaze of his eyes Leroux knew he had not heard.

'Thou shalt not fear the arrow that flieth by day, nor the terror that walketh by night,' he murmured.

'I am taking command, *Menheer*,' Leroux grunted. Zietsmann turned back to the book and his wife placed an arm round his shoulders.

We can hold them for this day, and perhaps tomorrow, Leroux decided from where he lay on the highest kopje. They cannot charge their cavalry against these hills, so they must come for us with the bayonet.

It is the guns first that we must fear, and then the bayonet.

'Martinus Van der Bergh,' he said aloud. 'When next we meet I will kill you for this.' And he watched the batteries unlimbering out of rifle-shot across the river, forming their precise geometrical patterns on the brown grass plain.

'*Nou skiet hulle*,' muttered a burgher beside him.

'*Ja*,' agreed Leroux. 'Now they will shoot,' and the smoke gushed from the muzzle of one of the guns out on the plain. The shell burst thunderously on the lower slopes and for an instant the lyddite smoke danced like a yellow ghost, swirling and turning upon itself, before the wind drifted it up to them. They coughed in the bitter-tasting fumes.

The next shell burst on the crest, throwing smoke and earth and rock high into the air, and immediately the rest of the batteries opened together.

They lay behind their hastily constructed earthworks while the shellfire battered the ridge. The shrapnel buzzed and hummed and struck sparks from the rocks, the solid jarring concussions made the earth jump beneath their bellies and dulled their ears so they could hardly hear the screaming of the wounded, and slowly a great cloud of dust and fumes climbed into the sky above them. A cloud so tall that Sean Courtney could see it from where he waited fifteen miles north of the Vaal.

'It looks as though Acheson has caught them,' murmured Saul.

'Yes, he's caught them,' Sean agreed, and then softly, 'The poor bastards.'

'The least they could have done was to let us be in at the kill,' growled Sergeant-Major Eccles. The distant rumble of the guns had awakened his blood lust and his great moustache wriggled with frustration. 'Don't seem right to me, seeing as how we been following the old Boer for going on a year and a half – the least they could have done was to let us be there at the end.'

'We are the cover guns, Eccles. General Acheson is trying to drive them south on to his cavalry, but if any of the birds break back through his line of beaters then they're ours,' Sean explained.

'Well, it just don't seem right to me,' Eccles repeated, then suddenly remembering his manners, he added, 'Begging your pardon, sir.'

54

Exultantly General Acheson traversed his binoculars across the group of hills. Vaguely through the dust and smoke he could pick out their crests.

'A fair cop, sir!' Peterson grinned.

'A fair cop indeed,' Acheson agreed. They had to shout above the thunder of the guns and beneath them their horses fidgeted and trembled. A dispatch-rider galloped up, saluted and handed Peterson a message.

'What is it?' Acheson asked without lowering his glasses.

'Both Nichols and Simpson are in position for the assault. They seem anxious to engage, sir.' Then Peterson looked up at the holocaust of dust and flame upon the hills. 'They'll be lucky if they find anyone left to fight up there.'

'They will,' Acheson assured him. He was not misled by the deceptive fury of the barrage. They had survived worse at Spion Kop.

'Are you going to let them go, sir?' Peterson insisted gently. For another minute Acheson watched the hills, then he lowered his glasses and pulled his watch from his breast pocket. Four o'clock – three hours more of daylight.

'Yes!' he said. 'Send them in.'

And Peterson scribbled the order and handed it to Acheson for his signature.

'*Hier Kom Hulle.*' Leroux heard the shout in the ceaseless roar of the shells, heard it take up and passed along the line.

'Here they come.'

'*Pasop!* They are coming.'

He stood up and his stomach heaved at the movement. Poisoned by the lyddite fumes, he fought his nausea and when he had controlled it he looked out along the river. For a second the veil of dust opened so he could see the tiny lines of khaki moving in towards the hills. Yes, they were coming.

He ran down his own line towards the river, shouting as he went.

'Wait until they are certain! Don't shoot until they reach the markers!'

From this corner of the kopje he could look out over every quarter of the field.

'Ja, I thought so!' he muttered. 'They come from two sides to split us.' Advancing on the frontage of the river were those same lines of tiny figures. The lines bulged and straightened and bulged again, but always they crept slowly nearer. Already the leading rank was moving up on his thousand-yard markers, in another five minutes they would be in range.

'They stand out well,' Leroux muttered as he ran his eyes along the rows of markers. While most of his men were building the earthworks along the kopjes and the river, others had paced out the ranges in front of these defences. Every two hundred and fifty yards they had erected those small cairns of stones, and over each they had smeared whitish grey mud from the river. It was a trick the British never seemed to understand, and as they advanced the Boer rifles had their range almost to the yard.

'The river is safe,' he decided. 'They cannot break through there,' and he allowed himself time to grin. 'They never learn. Every time they come against the worst side.' Then he switched his attention to the assault on his left flank. This one was dangerous, this was where he must command in person, and he ran back to his original position while around him and overhead the storm of shrapnel and lyddite roared on unabated.

He dropped on his belly between two of his burghers, wriggled forward unbuckling the bandolier from around his chest and draped it over the boulder beside him.

'Good luck, Oom Paul,' a burgher called.

'And to you, Hendrik,' he answered as he set the rear sight of his Mauser at a thousand yards, then laid the rifle on the rock in front of him.

'Close now,' the burgher beside him muttered.

'Very close. Good luck and shoot straight!'

Suddenly the storm lifted and there was silence. A vast aching silence, more shocking than the buzzing, howling roar of the guns. The dust and the smoke drifted away from the crests and after its gloom the sunshine burned down brightly on the hills and the golden brown plain, it sparkled with dazzling brilliance on the sweeping waters of the Vaal, and it lit each tiny khaki figure with stark intensity, so their shadows lay dark on the earth beneath them. They reached the line of markers.

Leroux picked up his rifle. There was one man he had been watching, a man who walked a little ahead of his line. Twice Leroux had seen him pause as if to shout an order to those who followed him.

'You first, my friend,' and he took the officer in his sights, holding him carefully in the notch with the bead obscuring his trunk. Gently he took up the slack in the trigger and the recoil slammed back into his shoulder. With the vicious and character-istic crack of the Mauser stinging his eardrums, Leroux watched the man go down into the grass.

'*Ja!*' he said and reloaded.

Not in simultaneous volley, not with the continuous wild crackle which they had used at Colenso – but in a careful, steady stutter which showed that each shot was aimed – the Boer rifles started the hunt.

'They have learned,' Leroux muttered as he worked the bolt of his rifle, and the empty case pinged away among the rocks. 'They have learned well,' and he killed another man. At two places on the ridge the Maxim guns began their frenzied hammer-ing bursts.

Before it reached the second row of markers, the first line of infantry no longer existed, it was scattered back in the grass, completely annihilated by the terrible accuracy of the Boer fire. The second line walked over them and came on steadily.

'Look at them come,' shouted a burgher farther down the line. Though they had seen it a dozen times before, all of these ragged farmers were awed by the passive, impersonal advance of British infantry.

'These men fight not to live but to die!' muttered the man who lay beside Leroux.

'Then let us help them to die,' Leroux shouted. And below him on the plain the slow inexorable ranks moved forward towards the third row of markers.

'Shoot, *Kerels*. Shoot straight,' Leroux roared, for now he could see the bayonets. He pressed a clip full of ammunition down into the magazine, and with the back of his hand brushed the clinging drops of sweat from his eyebrows, pushed the rifle forward and knocked down four men with his next six shots. Then he saw the change. At one place the line bulged as men began to hurry forward, while on the flanks it wavered and disintegrated as others hung back or crouched down behind pitifully inadequate cover.

'They are breaking!' Leroux howled excitedly. 'They won't reach the slopes.'

The forward movement faltered, no longer able to stand the mauling they were receiving, men turned back or went to ground while their officers hurried along the ranks goading them on. In so doing they proclaimed to the Boer riflemen that they were officers and at that range they did not survive long.

'They're finished!' shouted Leroux, and a thin burst of cheering ran along the ridge while the Boer fire increased in volume, flailing into the milling confusion of a broken infantry assault.

'Hit them, *Kerels*. Keep hitting them!' The following ranks overran the leaders, then in turn faltered and failed as the Maxim and Mauser fire churned into them.

Out on the plain a bugle began to lament, and as it mourned, the last spasmodic forward movement of the assault ceased, and back past the dead and the wounded streamed the retreat.

A single shell rushed overhead to burst in the valley beyond and immediately, as if in frustrated fury, the guns lashed the kopje once more. But in the jump and flash of the shells five hundred Boers cheered and laughed and waved their rifles at the retreating infantry.

'What happened on the river?' Leroux called in the tumult, and after a while the answer came back.

'They did not reach the river. They are broken there also.'

Leroux lifted his hat from his head and wiped the sweat and the dust from his face. Then he looked at the sunset.

'Almighty God, we give you thanks for this day. We ask your mercy and guidance in the days that are to come.'

The shellfire lashed the hills like the surf of a storm-driven sea until the night came. Then in the darkness they saw the fires of the British bivouacs spread like a garden of yellow flowers on the plains around them.

55

'We must break out tonight.' Leroux looked across the fire at Zietsmann.

'No.' The old man spoke softly, not looking at him.

'Why?' demanded Leroux.

'We can hold these hills. They cannot drive us from them.'

'*Ja!* We can hold them tomorrow – two days, a week – but then it is finished. We lost fifty men today from the guns.'

'They lost many hundreds. The Lord smote them and they perished.' Zietsmann looked up at him now and his voice gathered strength. 'We will stay here and place our trust in the Lord.' There was a murmur of agreement from those who listened.

'*Menheer.*' Leroux covered his eyes for a moment, pressing fingers into them to still the terrible aching. He was sick from the lyddite, and tired – tired to the depths of his soul. It would be easier to stay. There would be no dishonour in it for they had fought like no men before them. Two more days and then it would be over without dishonour. He removed his hands from his face. '*Menheer*, if we do not break out tonight we never will. By tomorrow we will not have the strength.' He stopped for the words came slowly, slurred a little from a brain dulled by the lyddite and the hammering of big guns. He looked at his hands and saw the suppurating sores on his wrists. There would be no dishonour. They would fight this last time and then it would be finished.

'But it is not a matter of honour,' he mumbled. Then he stood up and they watched him in silence for he was going to speak. He spread his hands out in appeal, and the firelight lit his face from below leaving his eyes in shadow, dark holes like the sockets of a skull. He stood like that for a while and his rags hung loosely on the gaunt wasted body.

'Burghers . . .' he started. But the words were not there. There was nothing except the need to fight on. He dropped his hands to his sides.

'I am going,' he said with simplicity. 'When the moon goes down I ride,' and he walked away from the fire. One by one other men rose and followed him, and all of them were men of his own commando.

Six men squatted in a circle and watched the moon as it touched the hills. Behind them the horses were saddled and the rifles stuck up from their scabbards. By each of the six hundred horses a burgher lay fully clothed, wrapped in his blanket and trying to sleep. Though the horses stamped and moved restlessly there was no jingling of bits for all of them were carefully muffled.

'We will say it again, so that each of us knows his part.' Leroux looked around the circle. 'I will go first with a hundred men and follow the river towards the east. What is your route, Hendrik?'

'South, through the cavalry until the dawn, then round towards the mountains.'

Leroux nodded and asked the next man:

'And yours?'

'West along the river.'

'*Ja*, and yours?'

He asked each in turn and when all had answered – 'The place of meeting is the old laager by the Hill of Inhlozana. Is this agreed?'

And they waited, watching the moon and listening to the jackals squabbling over the British corpses on the plain. Then the moon went down below the hills and Leroux stood up stiffly.

'*Totsiens, Kerels*. Good luck to all of us.' He took the reins of his pony and led it down towards the Vaal, while in silence a hundred men led their horses after him. As they passed the single wagon beside the Padda, old Zietsmann was waiting and he came forward leading a pack-mule.

'You are going?' he asked.

'*Ja, Menheer*. We must.'

'God go with you.' Zietsmann thrust out his hand and they gripped briefly.

'The mule is loaded. Take the money with you. We will not need it here.'

'Thank you, *Menheer*.' Leroux motioned to one of his men to take the mule. 'Good luck.'

'Good luck, General.' For the first time Zietsmann used his title, and Leroux went down to the perimeter of their defences and out into the veld where the British waited.

With the first pale promise of dawn in the sky, they were through and clear. Though twice during the night heavy outbursts of firing in the darkness far behind them showed that not all of the escaping bands had been so fortunate.

56

Sean and Saul stood beside the little scotchcart and Mbejane brought them coffee.

'My God, it's cold enough to freeze the hanger off a brass monkey.' Sean cupped his hands around the mug and sipped noisily.

'At least you've got a hood to keep your tip warm,' Saul retorted. 'We'd better get moving before we all freeze to the ground.'

'Dawn in an hour,' Sean agreed. 'Time to start walking our beat,' and he called across to Mbejane, 'Kill the fire and bring my horse.'

In double file with the scotchcart bumping along in the rear they started on the outward leg of their patrol. In the last four days they had covered the same ground as many times, tacking backwards and forwards across the beat that Acheson had assigned them. The grass was brittle with frost and crunched under the horses' hooves.

While ahead of them the Zulu trackers ranged like gundogs, and behind the troopers huddled miserably in their greatcoats, Sean and Saul picked up their endless discussion from the point at which they had left it the previous evening. Already they had reached so far into the future that they were talking of a federation under responsible government that would encompass all the territories south of the Zambesi.

'That's what Rhodes has proposed for the last ten years,' Saul pointed out.

'I don't want any part of that wily bastard.' Sean spoke emphatically. 'He'll keep us tied for ever to the apron strings of Whitehall – the sooner we get rid of him and Milner the better, say I.'

'You want to get rid of Imperial rule?' Saul asked.

'Of course, let's end this war and send all of them back across the sea. We can run our own affairs.'

'Colonel, it seems to me you are fighting on the wrong side,' Saul remarked, and Sean chuckled.

'But seriously, Saul . . . ' He never finished. Mbejane came out of the darkness, running with silent purpose so that Sean checked his horse and felt the skin along his arms prickle with nervous excitement.

'Mbejane?'

'Mabuna!'

'Where? How many?'

He listened to Mbejane's hurried explanation, then swung round to face Sergeant-Major Eccles, who was breathing heavily down his neck.

'Your birds, Eccles. A hundred or so of them, only a mile ahead and coming straight towards us.' Sean's voice was tight with the same excitement that made Eccles's moustache wriggle like an agitated caterpillar on the impassive oval of his face. 'Deploy in single line. They'll walk right on top of us in the dark.'

'Dismounted, sir?'

'No,' Sean answered. 'We'll gun charge them as soon as they show. But for God's sake keep it quiet.'

As Sean sat his horse with Saul beside him, the two files of troopers opened on each side of them. There was no talking; only the clicking of iron-shod hooves on rock, the rustling of men struggling out of their heavy greatcoats, and the soft rattle and snick of breech-bolts opening and closing.

'Once more into the breach, dear friends,' whispered Saul, but Sean did not answer because he was wrestling with his fear. Even in the cold of dawn his hands were damp. He wiped them on the thighs of his breeches and slid his rifle from the scabbard.

'What about the Maxims?' Saul asked.

'No time to set them up.' Sean knew his voice was hoarse and he cleared his throat before he went on. 'We won't need them – it's six to one.'

He looked along the silent line of his men. A dark line against the grass that was paling in the dawn. He could see that each of his troopers leaned forward in the saddle with his rifle held across his lap. The tension was a tangible thing in the half-darkness; even the horses were infected, they moved beneath their riders, shifting their bodies, nodding with impatience. Please God, let none of them whicker now.

And he peered ahead into the darkness. Waiting with his own fear and the fear of his men so strong that the Boers must surely smell it.

A patch of greater darkness in the dawn, ahead and slightly to the left of centre. Sean watched it for a few seconds and saw it move, slowly, like the moonlit shadow of a tree on the open veld.

'Are you sure they're Boers?' Saul whispered, and the doubt startled Sean. While he hesitated the shadow spread towards them and now he could hear the hooves.

Are they Boers? Desperately he searched for some sign that would allow him to loose his charge. Are they Boers? But there was no sign – only the dark advance and the small sounds of it, the click and creak in the dawn.

They were close now, less than a hundred yards, although it was impossible to tell with certainty for the dark, moving mass seemed to float towards them.

'Sean . . . ' Saul's whisper was cut off by the shrill nervous whinny of his horse. The sound was so unexpected that Sean heard the man beside him gasp. Almost immediately came the sign for which Sean waited.

'*Wie's daar!*' The challenge from ahead was in the guttural of the Taal.

'Charge!' yelled Sean and hit his horse with his heels. Instantly the whole of his line jumped forward to hurl itself upon the Boers.

Forward in the pounding hooves, forward in the shouting, in the continuous crackle of rifle-fire that sparkled along the line – with his fear left behind him, Sean spurred at them. Steadying the butt of his rifle under his right armpit, firing blind, blending his voice with the yelling of six hundred others, leading slightly in the centre of the line; he took his commando down upon the Boers.

They broke before the charge. They had to break for they could not hope to stand against it. They swung and drove their exhausted horses back towards the south.

'Bunch up!' roared Sean. 'Bunch on me!' And his line shortened so they charged knee to knee in a solid wall of men and horses and gunfire before which the Boers fled in wild despair.

Directly in Sean's path lay a stuggling, badly wounded horse with its rider pinned underneath it. Jammed into the charge he could not swerve.

'Up, Boy!' he shouted and lifted his horse with his knees and his hands, clearing the tangle and stumbling as they landed. Then forward again in the urgent, jostling clamour of the charge.

'We're gaining!' yelled Saul. 'This time we've got them.'

The horse beside him hit a hole and went down with its leg breaking like a pistol-shot. The trooper was thrown from it high and clear, turning in the air as he fell. The line closed to fill the gap, and pounded on over the grassland.

'There's a kopje ahead,' Sean shouted as he saw the ragged loom of it against the dawn sky. 'Don't let them reach it!' And he raked his spurs along his horse's ribs.

'We won't catch them,' warned Saul. 'They'll get into the rocks.'

'Damn it! God damn it!' groaned Sean. In the past few minutes the light had strengthened. Dawn in Africa comes quickly once it starts. Clearly he could see the leading Boers ride into the rocks, throw themselves from their ponies and duck into cover.

'Faster!' shouted Sean in agony. 'Faster!' as he saw the chance of quick success slip from his grasp. Already Mausers were talking back from the lower slopes of the kopje, and the last burghers were down and scurrying into the rocks. Loose ponies turned wildly into his line, empty stirrups flapping, eyes wide with terror – forcing his men to swerve into each other, dissipating the force of the charge. A loose pack-mule with a small leather pack upon its back climbed up through the rocks until a stray bullet killed it and it rolled into a deep crevice. But nobody saw it fall.

Sean felt the horse between his legs jerk and he was thrown with such violence that the stirrup leathers snapped like cotton and he went up and out, hung for a sickening moment and then swooped down to hit the ground with his chest and shoulder and the side of his face.

While he lay in the grass the charge spent itself like a wave on the kopje, then eddied and swirled into confusion. Dimly Sean was aware of the hooves that trampled about his head, of the sound of the Mausers and the shouts of the men who were swept by them.

'Dismount! Get down and follow them.' Saul's voice and the tone of it roused Sean. With his hands under his chest he pushed himself into a sitting position. The side of his face burned where the skin had been smeared away, his nose was bleeding and the blood turned the earth in his mouth to a gritty paste. His left arm was numb to the shoulder and he had lost his rifle.

Dully he tried to spit the filth from his mouth while he peered at the chaos about him, trying to make sense of it. He shook his head, to joggle the apathy from his brain, while all around him men were being cut down at point-blank range by the Mausers.

'Dismount! Dismount!' The urgency of Saul's voice brought Sean unsteadily to his feet.

'Get down, you bastards!' He took up the cry. 'Get down and chase them.' A horse brushed against him and he staggered but kept his balance. The trooper slid down from its back beside Sean.

'Are you all right, Colonel?' He reached out to steady Sean, but a bullet took him in the chest below his raised arm and killed him instantly. Sean stared down at the body and felt his brain click back into focus.

'The bastards,' he snarled and snatched up the man's rifle, then, 'Come on!' he roared. 'Follow me!' and he led them out of the shambles of struggling horses into the rocks.

In the next half-hour, grimly and irresistibly, they used their superior numbers to drive the Boers back up the kopje. Each outcrop of rocks was a strongpoint that had to be assaulted and carried, and paid for in blood. On a front of perhaps two hundred yards, the attack became a series of isolate skirmishes over which Sean could not maintain command. He gathered those men who were near him and boulder by boulder they fought their way towards the top, while the burghers in front of him held each position until the last moment and then fell back on the next.

The top of the kopje was flattened into a saucer with fifty feet of steep open ground falling away on all sides, and finally sixty burghers reached this natural fortress and held it with the determination of men who knew that they fought for the last time. Twice they threw the British from the lip of the saucer and sent them scrambling and sliding back into the shelter of the broken rock below. After the second repulse a heavy unnatural silence settled on the kopje.

Sean sat with his back to a rock and took the water-bottle

760

that a corporal offered him. He rinsed the slime of blood and congealing saliva from his mouth and spat it pink on to the ground beside him. Then he tilted the bottle and swallowed twice with his eyes tightly closed in the intense pleasure of drinking.

'Thanks.' He passed the bottle back.

'More?' the corporal asked.

'No.' Sean shook his head and looked back down the slope. The sun was well up now, throwing long shadows behind the horses that were grazing far out across the veld below. But at the foot of the slope lay the dead animals, most of them on their sides with legs thrust stiffly out. Blanket-rolls had burst open to litter the grass with the pathetic possessions of the dead men around them.

The men in their khaki and brown were as inconspicuous as piles of dead leaves in the grass, mostly British but with here and there a burgher lying amongst them in the fellowship of death.

'Mbejane.' Sean spoke softly to the big Zulu who squatted beside him. 'Find Nkosi Saul and bring him to see me here.'

He watched the Zulu crawl away. Mbejane had been left behind at the start of that wild gallop, but before Sean was half-way up the kopje he had glanced back to find him kneeling two paces behind, ready with a bandolier of ammunition for the moment when Sean needed it. Neither of them had spoken until this moment. Between them words were seldom necessary.

Sean fingered the raw graze on his face and listened to the murmured conversation of the men around him. Twice he heard clearly the voices of Boers from the saucer above them and once he heard a burgher laugh. They were very close, and Sean moved uneasily against the rock.

Within minutes Mbejane was back with Saul crawling behind him. When he saw Sean, Saul's expression changed quickly.

'Your face! Are you all right?'

'Cut myself shaving.' Sean grinned at him. 'Have a seat. Make yourself comfortable.'

Saul crawled the last few yards and settled himself against Sean's rock. 'Now what?' he asked.

'Ten minutes' rest, then we're going up again,' Sean told him. 'But this time with a little more purpose. I want you to work around the back of the kopje with half the men. Take Eccles with you. We'll rush their whole perimeter at the same moment. When you're in position fire three shots in quick succession then count slowly to twenty. I'll back you from this side.'

'Good.' Saul nodded. 'It'll take me a little while to get round – don't be impatient.' And he was smiling as he rose to his knees and leaned forward to touch Sean's shoulder.

Sean would always remember him like that: big mouth creased at the corners, smiling with white teeth through three days' growth of beard, slouch hat pushed to the back of his head, so his hair fell forward on to his forehead, and sunburned skin flaking from the tip of his nose.

The rock behind them was cracked through. If Saul had not leaned forward to make that gesture of affection he would not have exposed himself.

The sniper on the ridge had seen the brim of his hat above the rock and he held his aim into the crack. At the moment that Saul's fingers touched Sean's shoulder his head moved across the gap and the Boer fired.

The bullet hit Saul in the right temple, slanted diagonally back through his head and came out behind his left ear.

Their faces were but eighteen inches apart and Sean was smiling into Saul's eyes as the bullet hit. Saul's whole head was distorted by the impact, swelling and bursting like a balloon. His lips stretched so that for an instant his smile was a hideous rubbery thing and then he was snatched away and thrown sideways down the slope. He slid to a stop with his head and shoulders mercifully covered by a tuft of the coarse grey grass that grew among the rocks, but his trunk shivered and his legs danced and kicked convulsively.

For a slow count of ten Sean did not move nor did his expression alter. It took him that long to believe what he had seen. Then his face seemed to crumple.

'Saul!' His voice was a croak.

'Saul!' It rose higher, sharp with the realization of his loss.

He came slowly to his knees. Now Saul's body was still, very still and relaxed.

Again Sean opened his mouth but this time the sound he uttered was without form. The way an old bull buffalo bellows at the heart shot, that way Sean gave expression to his grief. A low shuddering cry that carried to the men in the rocks around him and to the Boers in the saucer above.

He made no attempt to touch Saul. He stared at him.

'Nkosi.' Mbejane was appalled at what he saw on Sean's face. His tunic was stiff with his own dried blood. The graze across his cheek was swollen and inflamed and it wept pale lymph. But it was the eyes that alarmed Mbejane.

'Nkosi.' Mbejane tried to restrain him, but Sean did not hear. His eyes were glazing over with the madness that had taken the place of his grief. His head hunched down on his shoulders and he growled like an animal.

'Take them! Take the bastards!' And he went up and over the rock in a twisting leap with the bayoneted rifle held against his chest.

'Come on!' he roared and went up the slope so fast that only one bullet hit him. But it did not stop him and he was over the lip, roaring and clubbing and hacking with the bayonet.

From the rocks four hundred of his men swarmed up after him and boiled over the lip of the saucer. But before they reached Sean he was face to face with Jan Paulus Leroux.

This time it was no match. Jan Paulus was wasted and sick. A gaunt skeleton of the man he had been. His rifle was empty and he fumbled with the reload. He looked up and recognized Sean. Saw him tall and splattered with blood. Saw the bayonet in his hands and the madness in his eyes.

'Sean!' he said and lifted the empty rifle to meet the bayonet. But he could not hold it. With Sean's weight behind it the bayonet glanced off the stock and went on. Jan Paulus felt the tingling slide of the steel through his reluctant flesh and he went over backwards with the bayonet in him.

'Sean,' he cried from his back. Sean stood over him and plucked the bayonet out. He lifted it high with both hands, his whole body poised to drive it down again.

They stared at each other. The British charge swept past them and they were alone. One man wounded in the grass and the other wounded above him with the bayoneted rifle and the madness still on him.

The vanquished in the grass, who had fought and suffered and sacrificed the lives of those he loved.

The victor above him, who had fought and suffered and sacrificed the lives of those he loved.

The game was war. The prize was a land. The penalty for defeat was death.

'*Maak dit klaar!* Make it finished!' Leroux told him quietly. The madness went out in Sean like the flame of a candle. He lowered the bayoneted rifle and let it drop. The weakness of his wound caught up with him and he staggered. With surprise he looked down at his belly and clasped his hands over the wound, and then he sank down to sit beside Jan Paulus.

In the saucer the fight was over.

57

'We're ready to move, sir.' Eccles stood beside the scotchcart and looked down at Sean. A massive scowl concealed his concern. 'Are you comfortable?'

Sean ignored the question. 'Who is in charge of the burial details, Eccles?'

'Smith, sir.'

'You have told him about Saul – about Captain Friedman?'

'Yes, sir. They will bury him separately.'

Sean lifted himself painfully on to an elbow and for a minute stared at the two gangs working bare to the waist on the communal graves. Beyond them lay the rows of blanket-wrapped bundles. A fine day's work, he thought bitterly.

'Shall we start, sir?' Eccles asked.

'You've given Smith my orders? Burghers to be buried with their comrades – our men with theirs?'

'It's all taken care of, sir.'

Sean lay back on the bedding that covered the floor of the scotchcart.

'Please send my servant to me, Eccles.'

While he waited for Mbejane, Sean tried to avoid contact with the man who lay beside him in the scotchcart. He knew Jan Paulus was watching him.

'Sean – *Menheer*, who will say the words for my men?'

'We have no Chaplain.' Sean did not look at him.

'I could say them.'

'General Leroux, it will be another two hours before the work is completed. You are wounded, and it is my duty to get this column with the other wounded back to Vereeniging as soon as I can. We are leaving the burial detail and when they're finished they'll catch us up.' Sean spoke lying on his back staring up at the sky.

'*Menheer*, I demand –' Jan Paulus began, but Sean turned angrily towards him.

'Listen, Leroux. I've told you what I'm going to do. The graves will be carefully marked, and later the War Graves Commission will send a Chaplain.'

There was very little room in the scotchcart and they were both big men. Now, as they glared at each other their faces were a foot apart. Sean would have said more, but as he opened his mouth the wound in his guts caught him and he gasped. The sweat broke out heavily across his forehead.

'Are you all right?' Jan Paulus's expression altered.

'I'll feel better once we get to Vereeniging.'

'*Ja*, you're right. We must go,' agreed Leroux.

Eccles came back with Mbejane.

'Nkosi, you sent for me?'

Mbejane, I want you to stay here and mark the place where they bury Nkosi Saul. Remember it well, for later you must be able to bring me back to it,' Sean mumbled.

'Nkosi.' Mbejane went away.

'Very well, Eccles. You can start.'

It was a long column. Behind the van rode the prisoners, many of them mounted two up. Then followed the wounded, each in a horse litter of poles and blankets, behind them the scotchcart, and finally Eccles and two hundred troopers of the rearguard. Their progress was slow and dismal.

In the scotchcart neither of them spoke again. They lay in pain, bracing themselves against the jolt and lurch, with the sun beating down mercilessly upon them.

In that dreamlike state induced by pain and loss of blood, Sean was thinking of Saul. At times he would convince himself that it had not happened and he would experience a rush of relief as though he had woken from a nightmare to find it was not reality. Saul was alive after all. Then his mind would focus with clarity and Saul was dead again. Saul was wrapped in a blanket with the earth above him, and they all had planned was down there with him. Then Sean would grapple once more with the unanswerable.

'Ruth!' he cried aloud, so that Jan Paulus beside him stirred uneasily.

'Are you all right, Sean?'

But Sean did not hear him. Now there was Ruth. Now there

was Ruth alone. He felt joy then in his loss, joy quickly swamped with guilt. For an instant he had been glad that Saul was dead, and his treachery sickened him and ached like the bullet in his guts. But still there was Ruth, and Saul was dead. I must not think of it like that. I must not think! and he struggled up into a sitting position and clung to the side of the scotchcart.

'Lie down, Sean,' Jan Paulus told him gently. 'You'll bleed again.'

'You!' Sean shouted at him. 'You killed him.'

'Ja.' Leroux nodded his red beard into his chest. 'I killed them, but you also – all of us. Ja, we killed them.' And he reached up and took Sean's arm and drew him down into the blankets. 'Now lie still or we'll bury you also.'

'But why, Paul. Why?' Sean asked softly.

'Does it matter why? They are dead.'

'And now what happens?' Sean covered his eyes from the sun.

'We go on living. That is all, we just go on.'

'But what was it about. Why did we fight?'

'I don't know. Once I knew clearly, but now I have lost the reason,' Leroux answered.

They were silent for a long time and then they began to talk again. Groping together for the things that must take the place of that which had filled these last three years.

Twice that afternoon the column halted briefly while they buried men who had died of their wounds. And each of these deaths – one a burgher and the other a trooper – gave poignancy and direction to the talk in the scotchcart.

In the evening they met a patrol that was scouting ahead of the big columns returning from the Padda River. A young lieutenant came to the scotchcart and saluted Sean.

'I have a message for you from General Acheson, sir.'

'Yes?'

'This fellow Leroux got away from us at the Padda. Zietsmann, the other Boer leader, was killed, but Leroux got away.'

'This is General Leroux,' Sean told him.

'Good God!' He stared at Leroux. 'You caught him. I say – well done, sir. Jolly well done.' In the past two years Jan Paulus had become a legend to the British, so that the lieutenant examined him now with frank curiosity.

'What is your message?' Sean snapped.

'Sorry, sir.' The youngster dragged his eyes away from Jan

Paulus. 'All the Boer leaders are meeting at Vereeniging. We are to give them safe conduct into the garrison. General Acheson wanted you to try to contact Leroux with the offer – but, that won't be difficult now. Jolly good show, sir.'

'Thank you, Lieutenant. Please tell General Acheson that we'll be in Vereeniging tomorrow.'

They watched the patrol ride away and disappear over a fold in the land.

'So!' growled Leroux. 'It's surrender then.'

'No,' Sean contradicted him. 'It's peace!'

58

The primary school at Vereeniging had been converted into an officer's hospital. Sean lay on his field cot and regarded the picture of President Kruger on the wall opposite him. In this way he was putting off the moment when he must continue with the letter he was writing. So far he had written the address, the date and the salutation: 'My dear Ruth'.

It was ten days since the column had returned from the veld. It was also ten days since the surgeons had cut him open and tied together those parts of his alimentary canal that the bullet had disrupted. He wrote:

> I am at this moment well on the way to recovering from a small wound received two weeks ago near the Vaal River — so please take no notice of my current address. [He started a new paragraph.]
>
> God knows I wish the circumstances in which I write were less painful to both of us. You will by now have received an official notification of Saul's death, so there is nothing I can add but to say that he died in circumstances of great personal gallantry. While about to lead a bayonet charge he was shot and killed *instantly*.
>
> I know you will want to be alone in your grief. It will be some weeks before the doctors allow me to travel. By the time I reach Pietermaritzburg I hope you will be sufficiently recovered to allow me to call on you in the hope that I may be able to give you some comfort.
>
> I trust that small Storm continues to increase in weight and beauty. I look forward to seeing her again.

A long while he pondered the ending, and finally decided on

'Your true friend'. He signed it, folded it into its envelope and laid it on the locker beside his bed for posting.

Then he lay back on his pillows and surrendered himself to the ache of loss and the dull pain in his belly.

After a while his physical pain dominated, and he glanced surreptitiously around the ward to ensure there were no nurses about.

Then he lifted the sheet, pulled up his nightshirt and began picking at the bandage until he had exposed the edge of the wound with the black horsehair stitches standing stiffly out of it like the knots in a strand of barbed wire. An expression of comical disgust curled his lips. Sean hated sickness – but especially he hated it in his own flesh. The disgust gave way slowly to a helpless anger and he glared at the wound.

'Leave it stand, old Sean. Looking won't make it better.' Sean had been so intent on the evil gash in his stomach that he had not heard the speaker approach. Despite the cane and the limp that dragged his right leg, Leroux moved silently for a big man. He stood now beside the bed and smiled shyly down at Sean.

'Paul!' Guiltily Sean covered himself.

'*Ja*, Sean. How goes it?'

'Not too bad. And you?'

Leroux shrugged. 'They tell me I will need this for a long time to come.' He tapped the ferrule of the cane on the floor. 'May I sit down?'

'Of course.' Sean moved to give him the edge of the bed and Leroux lowered himself with his bad leg stretched stiffly in front of him. His clothing was newly washed and the cuffs of his jacket darned; patches on the elbows, and a long tear in the knee of his breeches had been cobbled together with crude, masculine stitches.

His beard had been trimmed and squared. There were iodine-stained bandages covering the open sores on his wrists, but a red mane of hair hung to the collar of his jacket and the bones of his forehead and cheeks made harsh angles beneath the skin that was desiccated and browned by the sun.

'So!' said Sean.

'So!' Leroux answered him and looked down at his hands. Both he and Sean were silent then, awkward and inarticulate, for neither of them dealt easily in words.

'Will you smoke, Paul?' Sean reached for the cheroots on his locker.

'Thank you.' They made a show of selecting and lighting, then silence overwhelmed them again and Leroux scowled at the tip of his cheroot.

'This is good tobacco,' he growled.

'Yes,' agreed Sean and regarded his own cheroot with equal ferocity. Leroux coughed and rolled his cane between the fingers of his other hand.

'*Toe maar*, I just thought I'd come and see you,' he said.

'I'm glad of it.'

'So, you're all right then, hey?'

'Yes. I'm all right,' Sean agreed.

'Good.' Leroux nodded sagely. 'Well, then!' He stood up slowly. 'I had better be going. We are meeting again in an hour. Jannie Smuts has come up from the Cape.'

'I heard so.' Even the hospital was penetrated by rumours of what was happening in the big marquee tent pitched on the parade-ground near the station. Under the chairmanship of old President Steyn the Boer leaders were talking out their future. De Wet was there, and Niemand and Leroux. Botha was there and Hertzog and Strauss and others whose names had echoed across the world these last two years. And now the last of them, Jannie Smuts, had arrived. He had left his commando besieging the little town of O'Kiep in the Northern Cape and travelled up the British-held railway. Now they were all assembled. If they had gained nothing else in these last desperate years, they had at least won recognition as the leaders of the Boer people. This tiny band of tired and war-sick men was treating with the representatives of the greatest military power on earth.

'*Ja*, I have heard so,' Sean repeated, and impulsively he thrust out his hand. 'Good luck, Paul.'

Leroux seized his hand and held it hard, his mouth moved with the pressure of his emotion.

'Sean, we must talk. We have to talk!' he blurted.

'Sit down,' Sean told him and Leroux freed his hand and sank on to the bed once again.

'What must I do, Sean?' he asked. 'It's you who must advise me. Not these . . . not these others from over the sea.'

'You have seen Kitchener and Milner.' It was not a question, for Sean knew of the meeting. 'What do they ask of you?'

'They ask everything.' Leroux spoke bitterly. 'They ask for surrender without terms.'

'Will you agree to that?'

For a minute Leroux was silent, and then he lifted his head and looked full into Sean's face.

'So far we have fought to live,' he said and what Sean saw in those eyes he would never forget. 'But now we will fight to die.'

'And by this, what will you achieve?' Sean asked softly.

'Death is the lesser evil. We cannot live as slaves.' Leroux's voice rose sharply. 'This is my land,' he cried.

'No,' Sean told him harshly. 'It is also my land, and the land of my son,' and then his voice softened. 'And the blood of my son is your blood.'

'But these others – this Kitchener, this devil Milner.'

'They are a people apart,' Sean said.

'But you fought with them!' Leroux accused.

'I have done many foolish things,' agreed Sean. 'But, from them I have learned.'

'What are you saying?' demanded Leroux, and Sean could see the sparkle of hope in his eyes. I must say this carefully, thought Sean, I must be very careful. He drew a long breath before he spoke.

'As it stands this moment your people are scattered but alive. If you fight on, the British will stay until you have found the annihilation you seek. If you stop now, then soon they will leave.'

'Will you leave?' demanded Leroux savagely.

'No.'

'And you are British! The British will stay – you and those like you.'

Then Sean grinned at him. It was so sudden, so irresistible that grin, that it threw Leroux off balance.

'Do I look and talk like a *rooinek*, Paul?' he asked in the Taal. 'Which half of my son is burgher and which half British?'

Confused by this sneak attack Leroux stared at him for a long time before he dropped his eyes and fiddled with his cane.

'Come on, man,' Sean told him. 'Make an end to this foolishness. You and I have a lot of work to do.'

'You and I?' Leroux asked suspiciously.

'Yes.'

Leroux laughed, a sudden harsh bellow of laughter.

'You are a *slim Kerel*,' he roared.

'I'll have to think about what you have said.' He rose from the bed and seemed to stand taller now. The laughter filled out his gaunt features and wrinkled his nose.

'I'll have to think very carefully about it.' He reached out his hand again and Sean took it. 'I will come and talk with you again.' He turned away abruptly and limped down the ward with his cane tapping loudly.

Jan Paulus kept his word. He visited Sean daily, an hour or so at a time, and they talked. Two days after the Boer surrender he brought another man with him.

Jan Paulus stood a good four inches over him, but though he was slimly built the visitor gave the impression of size.

'Sean, this is Jan Christian Niemand.'

'Perhaps I am lucky we did not meet before, Colonel Courtney.' Niemand's voice, high in timbre, was crisp and authoritative. He spoke the perfect English he had learned at Oxford University. 'What do you think, *Oubas*?' He addressed Jan Paulus by the title which was obviously a private joke between them, and Jan Paulus chuckled.

'Very lucky. Otherwise you also might be using a stick.'

Sean examined Niemand with interest. Hard years of war had muscled his shoulders and he walked like a soldier, yet above the pointed blond beard was the face of a scholar. The skin had a youthful clarity which was almost maidenly, but the eyes were a penetrating blue, the merciless blue of a Toledo steel blade.

His mind had the same resilience, and before many minutes Sean was using all his wits to meet and answer questions that Niemand asked him. It was clear that he was being subjected to some sort of test. At the end of an hour he decided he had passed.

'And now, what are your plans?'

'I must go home,' Sean answered, 'I have a farm and a son – soon, perhaps, a wife.'

'I wish you happiness.'

'It is not yet settled,' Sean admitted. 'I still have to ask her.'

Jannie Niemand smiled. 'Well, then, I wish you luck with your suit. And strength to build a new life.' Suddenly he was serious. 'We also must rebuild what has been destroyed.' He stood up from the bed and Jan Paulus stood with him.

'There will be need of good men in the years ahead.' Niemand held out his hand and Sean took it. 'We will meet again. Count on that.'

59

As the train ran in past the great white mine dumps and Sean leaned from the window of the coach to look ahead at the familiar skyline of Johannesburg, he wondered how such an unlovely city still had the power to draw him back each time. It was as though he was connected to it by an elastic umbilical cord which allowed him a wide range. But when he reached its limit it pulled him back.

'Two days,' he promised himself. 'Two days I'll stay here. Just long enough to hand old Acheson my formal resignation and tell Candy Good-bye. Then I'll head south to Ladyburg – and leave this town to stew in its own evil juices.'

Near at hand a midday hooter howled from one of the mines, and immediately its cry was taken up and answered by the other mines. It sounded as though a pack of hungry wolves were hunting across the valley, the wolves of greed and gold. Those mines that had been forced to close during the hostilities were now back in production, and the black smoke from their stacks sullied the sky and drifted in a dirty mist across the crest of the ridge.

The train slowed, and the unexpected clatter and lurch of the points broke the rhythm of its run. Then it was sliding in along the concrete platform of Johannesburg Station. Sean lifted his luggage down from the rack above his head and passed it out of the open window to Mbejane. The exertion of lifting and carrying no longer caught in his guts; except for the irregular scar near his navel he was completely healed. When he strode down the platform towards the exit he held himself erect, no longer stooping to favour his stomach.

A horsedrawn cab deposited them on the pavement outside Acheson's headquarters, and Sean left Mbejane guarding the luggage while he pushed his way across the crowded lobby and climbed the staircase to the first floor.

'Good afternoon, Colonel.' The orderly sergeant recognized him immediately and jumped to attention with such alacrity that he overturned his stool.

'Afternoon, Thompson,' Sean told him. The honours of his rank still embarrassed him. Thompson relaxed and inquired with more than just the formal concern:

'How are you, sir? Sorry to 'ear about your belly, sir.'

'Thank you, Thompson, I am fine now. Is Major Peterson in?'

Peterson was delighted to see him. He made tender inquiries after the movement of Sean's bowels, for irregularity was often one of the unpleasant aftermaths of a stomach wound. Sean reassured him and Peterson went on:

'Have some tea. The old man is busy right now but he'll see you in ten minutes,' and he shouted for Thompson to bring tea before he returned to the subject of Sean's wound. 'Much of a scar, old chap?' he asked.

Sean loosened his Sam Browne belt, unbuttoned his tunic and pulled his shirt out from his trousers. Peterson came round the desk and inspected Sean's hairy stomach at close range.

'Very neat. Damn good job they did on you.' Peterson gave his expert opinion. 'I got one at Omdurman – one of those fuzzy wuzzies pegged me with his dirty great spear.' And he in turn partially disrobed and displayed his pale hairless chest. From common courtesy Sean was forced to cluck and shake his head at the small triangular cicatrice on Peterson's bosom, although secretly he was not impressed. The attention went to Peterson's head.

'Got another one – damn painful it was too!' and he unbuckled his belt and had his trousers half down when the interleading door opened.

'Hope I'm not interrupting anything, gentlemen?' General Acheson inquired politely. There were a few moments of confusion while they both attempted to dress and make the correct military salutations. Peterson had the nicest decision to make, one not covered by the Articles of War. It was one of the few occasions in history where a divisional commander was received by a senior field officer standing at rigid attention with his trousers round his ankles. Major Peterson affected a rather startling line in scarlet flannel underwear. Once Acheson had understood the reason for this irregularity of dress among his officers, he was strongly tempted to join in the exhibition, for he also had some fine scars, but he restrained himself admirably. He led Sean through to the inner office and gave him a cigar.

'Well, Courtney. I hope you haven't come looking for a job.'

'On the contrary – I want to get the hell out of this business, sir.'

'I think we can arrange that. The Paymaster will be relieved.' Acheson nodded. 'I'll get Peterson to draw up your papers.'

'I want to leave tomorrow,' Sean insisted, and Acheson smiled. 'You're in a big hurry. All right. Peterson can post them to you for your signature – your unit has already been disbanded so there is no point in kicking your heels around here.'

'Good!' Sean had anticipated resistance, and he laughed with relief.

'There are just three other items,' Acheson went on, and Sean frowned with quick suspicion.

'Oh?'

'Firstly, a parting gift from His Majesty. A Distinguished Service Order for catching Leroux – there will be an investiture next week. Lord K. would like you to attend personally.'

'Hell, no! If I've got to stay in Johannesburg – I don't want it.'

And Acheson chuckled. 'A surprising lack of gratitude! Peterson can post it to you also. Secondly, I've been able to bring a little influence to bear on the War Claims Adjustment Board. Although Parliament hasn't passed the Bill, they've gone ahead and sanctioned your claim.'

'Good God!' Sean was stunned. At Acheson's suggestion he had registered a claim for ten thousand pounds, his deposit in the Volkskaas Bank, which had been seized by the Boers at the outbreak of war. He had expected nothing from it, and had promptly forgotten about it. 'They haven't made a full award, have they?'

'Don't be naïve, Courtney.' Acheson chuckled. 'Only twenty per cent against a possible further adjustment once the Bill is through the House. Still, two thousand is better than a poke in the eye with a blunt stick. Here's their cheque. You'll have to sign for it.'

Sean examined the slip of paper with rising delight. It would go a little way towards paying off his loan from Natal Wattle. He looked up quickly.

'And the third item?' he asked.

Acheson slipped a small square of cardboard across the desk.

'My card – and a standing invitation to visit and stay as long as you like whenever you are in London.' He stood up and extended his hand. 'Good luck, Sean. And I'd like to think it isn't good-bye.'

In a rosy state of elation induced by freedom and the prospect of a loving farewell with Candy Rautenbach, Sean stopped the cab first at the railway station to reserve a seat on the following morning's southbound train, and to cable Ada of his home-coming. Then, on to Commissioner Street and the lobby of Candy's Hotel to ask for the proprietress.

'Mrs Rautenbach is resting, sir, and cannot be disturbed,' the clerk informed him.

'Good man!' Sean passed him half a guinea and ignored his squawks of protest as he climbed the marble staircase.

He let himself silently into Candy's suite and crossed to her bedroom. He wanted to surprise her; and there could be no doubt that he succeeded beyond his wildest expectations. Candy Rautenbach was not resting. In fact she was most strenuously employed in the entertainment of a gentleman whose tunic, hanging over the back of one of the gilt and red velvet chairs, showed him to be a subaltern in one of His Majesty's regiments.

Sean supported his subsequent actions on the hypothesis that Candy was his exclusive property. In the flood of righteous indignation that overwhelmed him, he took no account of the fact that his visit was a farewell gesture, that his relationship with Candy had been at best vague and intermittent, and that he was the following morning leaving to propose matrimony to someone else. All he saw was the cuckoo in the nest.

So that no discredit may reflect on the courage of the subaltern of the honour of his regiment, we must remember that his knowledge of Candy's domestic arrangements, if not those of her anatomy, was incomplete. She had been introduced to him as *Mrs Rautenbach* and now in this terrible moment as he returned to reality he assumed that the large and angry man who bore down on the bed, roaring like a wounded bull, was the one and only Mr Rautenbach come home from the wars. He made preparation for departure, which began with a rapid descent from the high four-poster bed on the opposite side to that of Sean's approach. In a condition of stark mental clarity induced by a super-abundance of adrenalin in the blood stream, the subaltern became aware of his own nudity which prevented flight into the public gaze, of the fact that Mr Rautenbach's threatening advance made such flight imperative, and finally that Mr Rautenbach wore the uniform and insignia of a full colonel. This last consideration weighed most heavily with him, for despite his age he came from an old and respected family with an impressive record of military service and he understood the decencies and orders of society of which one of the strictest was that you did not unite with the wife of an officer who outranked you.

'Sir,' he said, and drew himself up with dignity. 'I think I can explain.'

'You little bugger!' Sean answered him in a tone that suggested his explanation would have little consequence. Taking the shortest route, which was over the bed, Sean went for him. Candy, who had in these first few seconds been too preoccupied with pulling the coverlets over herself to take any active part in the proceedings, now shrieked and lifted the silk eiderdown in such a way that it wrapped around Sean's boots as he leaped over her, and became tangled in his spurs. Sean fell with a crash that reverberated through the whole building and startled the guests in the lobby below, and he lay for the moment stunned with his feet on the bed and his head and shoulders on the floor.

'Get out!' Candy shouted at the subaltern, as Sean began to stir ominously. Then she gathered up an armful of bedclothes and spread them over Sean, winding him and smothering him.

'Hurry up. For God's sake, hurry!' she entreated as her friend hopped with one leg in his breeches. 'He'll tear you to pieces.' And she pounced on top of the struggling, cursing mound of sheets and blankets.

'Don't worry about the boots,' and the subaltern tucked them under one arm, slung his tunic over his shoulders and placed his helmet on the back of his head.

'Thank you, ma'am,' he said, and then with gallantry, 'I sincerely regret any inconvenience I have caused you. Please give my apologies to your husband.'

'Get out, you fool,' she pleaded, clinging desperately to Sean as he heaved and swore. After he had left she stood up and waited for Sean to emerge.

'Where is he? I'll kill him. I'll murder the little bastard!' Sean threw off the bedclothes, scrambled to his feet and glared wildly around him. But the first thing he saw was Candy, and Candy was shaking with laughter. There was a lot of Candy to shake and most of it was white and round and smooth, and even if the laughter was a little hysterical it was still a very pleasing spectacle.

'Why did you stop me?' Sean demanded, but he was fast transferring his interest from the subaltern to Candy's bosom.

'He thought you were my husband,' she gasped.

'The little bastard,' growled Sean.

'He was sweet.' And abruptly she stopped laughing. 'And who the hell are you to come barging in here, anyway? Do you think you own the world and everything in it?'

'You belong to me.'

'Like hell, I do!' Candy exploded. 'Now get out of here, you big lumbering ox.'

'Put some clothes on.' Things were taking an unforeseen turn. Sean had expected her to be guilty and contrite.

'Get out of here,' she yelled, as her temper started to run. Sean had never seen her like this and he only just managed to field the large vase she hurled at his head. Frustrated in her desire to hear breaking china, Candy grabbed another missile, an ornamental mirror, which crashed with satisfying violence against the wall behind him. Her boudoir was furnished in splendid Victorian taste and provided an almost unlimited supply of ammunition. Despite Sean's nimble footwork, he could not remain unscathed for ever and finally he was hit by a gilt-framed picture of some nameless officer. Candy's taste leaned rather heavily towards martial men.

'You little bitch!' roared Sean in pain, and he launched a counter-attack. Candy fled, naked and squealing, but he caught her at the door, lifted her on to his shoulder and carried her kicking to the bed.

'Now, my girl,' he grunted as he arranged her, pink bottom up, across his lap. 'I'm going to teach you some manners.'

The first slap left a perfect red print of his hand upon her chubby cheeks, and stilled her struggles. The second slap had considerably less force behind it, and the third was an affectionate pat. But Candy was sobbing pitifully.

With his right hand raised, Sean realized with dismay that for the first time in his life *he was striking a woman!* 'Candy!' He spoke uncertainly, and was amazed that she twisted and sat up in his lap, clasped him about the neck and pressed a damp cheek against him.

Words welled up in his throat, words of apology, a plea for forgiveness – but his good sense prevented them from emerging and instead he demanded huskily, 'Are you sorry for your behaviour?'

Candy gulped and nodded shakily. 'Please forgive me, darling. I deserved that.' And her fingers fluttered at his throat and across his lips. 'Please forgive me, Sean. I'm so terribly sorry.'

They ate dinner in bed that evening. In the early morning, while Sean soaked lazily in the sunken bath and the hot water stung the scratches on his back, they talked.

'I'm catching the morning train home, Candy. I want to be home for Christmas.'

'Oh, Sean! Can't you stay – just a few days?'

'No.'

'When will you come back?'

'I don't know.'

There was a long silence before she spoke again.

'I take it then that I am not included in your plans for the future?'

'You are my friend, Candy,' he protested.

'Now, isn't that nice.' And she stood up. 'I'll order your breakfast.'

In the bedroom she paused and regarded herself slowly in the full-length mirror. The blue silk of her gown matched the blue of her eyes, but at this time of the day there were tiny creases in the skin of her throat.

I am rich, she thought, *I don't have to be lonely.* She walked on past the mirror.

60

Sean walked slowly up the gravel drive towards the Goldberg mansion. He walked between an avenue of 'Pride of India' trees and around him the green lawns climbed in a series of terraces towards the rococo façade of the house. It was a morning of drowsy warmth and the doves in the Pride of Indias cooed sleepily.

Faintly from among the ornamental shrubbery he heard the tinkle of laughter. He stopped and listened to the sound of it. Suddenly he was shy, loth to meet her again – unable to know how she would receive him for she had not replied to his letter.

At last he left the drive and crossed the carpet of lawn until he reached the lip of an amphitheatre. In the bowl below him stood a miniature replica of the Parthenon temple. Clean, white, marble columns in the sunshine, with a circular fish-pond like a moat around it. He could see the shapes of carp gliding slowly through the green water below the lily pads. The lily blossoms were white and gold and purple.

Ruth sat upon the raised marble edge of the pond. She was dressed all in black from her throat to her toes, but her arms were bared and she held them out and cried:

'Walk, Storm. Walk here to me.'

Ten paces away, her solid bottom solidly planted on the lawn, Storm Friedman regarded her mother seriously from under a bang of dark hair.

'Come on, baby,' Ruth urged her, and very deliberately the child leaned forward. Slowly she elevated her plump posterior until it was pointed towards the sky, displaying a laced and be-ribboned pair of pantaloons beneath the short skirt. She remained like that for a few seconds and then, with an effort, came up on to her feet and stood balanced precariously on her fat, pink legs. Ruth clapped her hands in spontaneous delight, and Storm smiled in triumph, displaying four large white teeth.

'Come here to Mummy,' laughed Ruth and Storm completed a dozen unsteady paces before abandoning this form of locomation as impractical. Dropping to her hands and knees she finished the course at a canter.

'You cheated!' Ruth accused, and jumped up to catch her under the arms and swing her high. Storm squealed ecstatically. 'More!' she commanded. 'More!'

Sean wanted to laugh with them. He wanted to run down to them and gather them both in his arms. For suddenly he knew that here was the whole meaning of life, his excuse for existing. A woman and a child. *His* woman, and *his* child.

Ruth looked up and saw him. She froze with the child held to her chest. Her face was without expression as she watched him come down the steps into the amphitheatre.

'Hello.' He stopped in front of her, twisting his hat awkwardly between his hands.

'Hello, Sean,' she whispered, then the corners of her mouth lifted in a shy, uncertain smile and she flushed. 'You took so long. I thought you weren't coming.'

A great grin split Sean's face and he stepped forward, but at that moment Storm, who had been staring at him with solemn curiosity, began a series of convulsive leaps accompanied by yells of:

'Man! Man!' Her feet were anchored against Ruth's stomach, which gave power to her thrusts. She leaned out towards Sean determined to reach him, and Ruth was taken by surprise. Sean had to drop his hat and catch Storm before she fell.

'More! More!' yelled Storm, continuing to bounce in Sean's arms. One of the few things Sean knew about babies was that they have a soft pulsing spot on the top of their heads which is very vulnerable, so he clung to his daughter in terror that he drop her and in equal terror that he crush her. Until Ruth stopped laughing, relieved him of his burden and said,

'Come up to the house. You're just in time for tea.'

They crossed the lawn slowly, each of them holding one of Storm's hands, so that the child need no longer concentrate on balancing and could devote her whole attention to the fascinating manner in which her feet kept alternately appearing and disappearing under her.

'Sean. There is one thing I have to know before anything else.' Ruth was looking down at her child, not at him. 'Did you . . .' She paused. 'Saul – Could you have prevented what happened to him. I mean, you didn't . . . ' Her voice trailed off.

'No, I didn't,' he said harshly.

'Swear it to me, Sean. As you hope for salvation, swear it to me,' she pleaded.

'I swear it to you. I swear on . . . ' He sought for an oath, not on his own life, for that was not strong enough. 'I swear on the life of our daughter.'

And she sighed with relief. 'That was why I did not write to you. I had to know first.'

He wanted to tell her then that he was taking her away with him, he wanted to tell her about Lion Kop and the huge empty house that waited for her to make it into a home. But he knew it was not the moment – not immediately after they had spoken of Saul. He would wait.

He waited while he was introduced to the Goldbergs and was left with them when Ruth took the child into the house to deliver her into the care of the nurse. She returned and he made small conversation during tea and tried not to let them see it in his eyes when he looked at Ruth.

He waited until they were alone together on the lawn and then he blurted it out:

'Ruth, you and Storm are coming home with me.'

She stopped over a rosebush and picked a butter-yellow blossom, then with a slight frown on her face she broke each of the tiny red thorns off the stem before she looked at him.

'Am I, Sean?' she asked innocently, but he should have been warned by the chips of diamond brightness in her eyes.

'Yes,' he said. 'We can be married within the next few days. It will take that long to arrange a special licence and for you to pack. Then I'll take you to Lion Kop – I haven't told you about . . . '

'Damn you,' she said softly. 'Damn your conceit. Damn your arrogance.' And he gawked at her.

'You stroll in with your whip in your hand, crack it once and expect me to bark and jump through the hoop.' She was working herself into a fury now. 'I don't know what dealings you've had with women before – but I for one am not a camp-follower, nor do I intend being treated like one. Did it ever occur to you for one single second that I might not be prepared to accept this favour you intend bestowing on me? How long did it take you to forget that I have been a widow for three short months? What supreme lack of perception made you believe I would run from one man's grave and throw myself into your condescending arms?'

'Buth, Ruth, I love you.' He tried to stop her outburst, but she shouted at him.

'Then prove it, damn you. Prove it by being gentle. Prove it by treating me like a woman and not a chattel – by *understanding*.'

Now his surprise gave way to an anger every bit as intense as hers, and in his turn he shouted at her.

'You weren't so bloody fussy on the night of the storm – or afterwards!'

As though he had struck her, she stepped back a pace and the mutilated rosebud dropped from her hand.

'You swine,' she whispered. 'Get out, and don't come back.'

'Your servant, ma'am.' He clapped his hat on to his head, swung round and strode away across the lawn. When he reached the gravel drive his steps slowed and he stopped and wrestled with his anger and his pride.

Then slowly he turned. The lawn was an empty sweep of smooth green. She was gone.

Ruth ran up the wide marble staircase, but by the time she reached her bedroom window he was half-way down the drive. From the height of the second floor his figure was foreshortened so he appeared massive, and his dark suit stood out clearly against the pale gravel of the drive. He reached the gates and stopped, she leaned forward eagerly across the sill of the window so he could see her more easily when he turned to look back. She saw him deliberately light a long black cheroot, flick away the match, adjust the hat on his head, square his shoulders – and walk away.

In disbelief she stared at the twin columns of the gate, and the dark green hawthorn hedge behind which he had disappeared. Then slowly she left the window and crossed to the bed and sat down.

'Why didn't he understand?' she asked softly.

She knew she would cry later, in the night when the real loneliness began.

61

Sean returned to Ladyburg in the middle of a misty Natal winter's day. As the train huffed over the rim of the escarpment, he stood on the balcony of his coach and looked out at the vast green stain upon the hills of Lion Kop. The sight of it moved him, but his elation was toned with dark colours.

This is the middle of the way. This year I will be forty-one years old. Out of all that striving and folly something must have emerged. Let me total my assets.

In cash I have a little over two thousand pounds (compliments of the War Claims Adjustment Board). In land I have fifteen thousand acres, with an option to purchase as many more. I have ten thousand acres of standing wattle which, in another year, will be ready for cutting. My loans against this are heavy but not oppressive, so I am a wealthy man.

In things of the flesh I have a number of grey hairs, a fine collection of scars and a broken nose. But I can still lift and carry a two-hundred-pound sack of mealies under each arm, I can eat half a young sheep at a sitting; without field-glasses I can count the number of head in a herd of springbok at a distance of two miles, and Candy who knows about these things made no complaint about my stamina. I am not yet old.

Apart from these things I have a son who belongs to me (and a son and a daughter who do not). Although I have lost the best of them, I have friends – perhaps more friends than enemies.

But as important as any of these is the purpose and direction I have at last achieved. I know what I want. My course is plotted and the wind stands fair.

These are my assets. These are mine to use and enjoy.

What are my liabilities? Borrowed money, the hatred of a brother and a son, and Ruth.

Ruth is gone! Ruth is gone! Clattered the crossties under the coach. Ruth is gone! Ruth is gone! They mocked him.

Sean scowled and forcibly changed the words in his mind. 'The wind is fair! The wind is fair!'

Over the months that followed Sean used his whole energy in the development of Lion Kop. He planned the cutting of his standing bark and decided to reap one-third of it a year before maturity, and another third in each of the subsequent two years. To replace it he used his two thousand pounds not to pay off his loans, but to plant the rest of his land to wattle. When this was done he had to keep busy. He bought himself a theodolite and a book of instruction in elementary survey, and mapped his lands, laid out his block of trees, pegged new roads for access to his plantations when the cutting began.

Once again he had nothing to do, so he went to see Dennis Petersen and spent a long day arguing the purchase of Mahobo's Kloof Ranch on which he had bought an option. He had no cash, and Jackson at Natal Wattle baulked at the suggestion of further loans. When Dennis refused to consider extended terms of payment, Sean called on Ronny Pye at the Ladyburg Banking & Trust. It was a forlorn chance and Sean was genuinely surprised when Ronny gave him a cup of coffee and a cigar, then listened politely to his proposition.

'You're putting it all on one horse, Sean,' Ronny warned him.

'There's only one horse in this race. It can't lose.'

'Very well.' Ronny nodded. 'Here's what I will do with you. I will advance you the full purchase price of Mahobo's Kloof, plus a further ten thousand pounds to develop it. In return you will give me a first bond on Mahobo's Kloof, and a second bond on Lion Kop after Natal Wattle Company's loan.'

Sean took it. A week later Ronny Pye called on Jackson in Pietermaritzburg. After the preliminary sparring Ronny asked him:

'Are you quite happy about those Notes you have out to Courtney?'

'The security is good.' Jackson hesitated. 'But he seems to be going a little wild.'

'I might be willing to take them over from you,' Ronny hinted delicately, and Jackson rubbed his nose thoughtfully to mask his relief.

Happily Sean flung his army of Zulus at the virgin grasslands of Mahobo's Kloof. He delighted in the long ranks of sweating, singing blackmen as they opened the rich, red earth and placed the fragile little saplings.

Dirk was Sean's constant companion in these days. His attendance in the schoolhouse became more sporadic. Convinced that Dirk would never become a scholar, Sean tacitly condoned the gastric disturbances that prevented Dirk leaving for school in the mornings, but cleared miraculously a few minutes later and allowed him to follow Sean out into the plantations. Dirk aped Sean's stance, his seat in the saddle, and his long reaching walk. He listened carefully to Sean's words and repeated them later without omitting the oaths. In the late afternoons they hunted quail and pheasant and guinea-fowl along the slopes of the escarpment. On Sunday when Sean rode across to his neighbours for a bush buck shoot, or a poker session, or merely to drink brandy and talk, then Dirk went with him.

Despite Sean's protest, Ada returned with her girls to the cottage on Protea Street. So the homestead of Lion Kop was a vast empty shell. Sean and Dirk used only three of the fifteen rooms, and even these were sparsely furnished. No carpets on the floor, nor pictures on the walls. A few leather-thonged chairs, iron bedstead, plain deal tables, and a cupboard or two. Piled in odd corners were the books and fishing-rods; a pair of shotguns and a rifle on the rack beside the fireplace. The yellow-wood floor was unpolished with dust and bits of fluff beneath the chairs and beds, dark stains left by the litter of pointer puppies; and in Dirk's bedroom, which Sean never visited, there was a welter of old socks and soiled shirts, school exercise books and trophies of the hunt.

Sean had no interest in the house. It was a place to eat and sleep, it had a roof to keep the rain out, a fireplace for warmth, and lamp-light so that he could indulge his new appetite for reading. With reading glasses purchased from a travelling salesman on his nose, Sean spent his evenings wading through books on politics and travel, economics and surveying, mathematics and medicine, while Dirk, ostensibly preparing his schoolwork, sat across the fireplace from him and watched him avidly. Some nights when Sean was engaged in correspondence, he would forget that Dirk was there and the boy would sit up until after midnight.

Sean was now corresponding with both Jannie Niemand and Jan Paulus Leroux. These two had become a political team in the Transvaal, and were already bringing gentle pressure to bear on Sean. They wanted him to organize the equivalent of their South Africa Party, and to lead it in Natal. Sean hedged. Not yet, perhaps later he told them.

Once a month he received and answered a long letter from John Acheson. Acheson had returned to England and the gratitude of the nation. He was now Lord Caisterbrook and from his seat in the House of Lords he kept Sean informed of the temper and mood of the English people and the affairs of State.

Sometimes, more often than was healthy, Sean thought about Ruth. Then he became angry and sad and desperately lonely. Slowly it would build up within him until he could not sleep, then he would go down at night to a friendly widow who lived alone in one of the gangers' cottages beside the new railways yards.

Yet he counted himself happy, until that day at the beginning of September 1903, when he received an embossed card. It said simply:

> Miss Storm Friedman requests the pleasure of the company of Colonel Sean Courtney, D.S.O., D.C.M., at a party to celebrate her third birthday.
> 4 p.m., September 26th.
> *R.S.V.P.*
> The Golds, Chase Valley,
> Pietermaritzburg.

In the bottom right-hand corner was an inky finger-print about the size of a threepenny-piece.

62

On the 24th, Sean left by train for Pietermaritzburg. Dirk came back from the station with Ada to his old room in the cottage on Protea Street.

That night Mary lay awake and listened to him cry for his father. Only a thin wooden partition spearated them. Ada's cottage had not been designed as a workshop and hostel for her girls. She had solved the problem by enclosing the wide, back veranda and dividing it into cubicles each large enough to hold a bed, a cupboard and a washstand. One of these was Mary's and tonight Dirk was in the cubicle next to hers.

For an hour she lay and listened to him weep, praying quietly that he would exhaust himself and fall asleep. Twice she thought he had done so, but each time after a silence of only a few minutes the tear-muffled sobs started again. Each of them drove needles of physical pain deep into her chest, so that she lay rigid in her bed with her fists clenched until they ached.

Dirk had become the central theme of her existence. He was the one bright tower in the desolation. She loved him with obsessive devotion, for he was so beautiful, so young and clean and straight. She loved the feel of his skin and the springy silk of his hair. When she looked at Dirk her own face did not matter. Her own scarred ruin of a face did not matter.

The months she had been separated from him had been an agony and a dark lonely time. But now he was back and once again he needed her comfort. She slipped from her bed and stood taut with her love, her whole attitude portraying her compassion. The moonlight that filtered in through the mosquito-screened window treated her with the same compassion. It toned down the mottled cicatrice that coarsened the planes of her face and it showed them as they might have been. Her twenty-year-old body beneath the thin nightgown was slender but full-breasted, innocent of the marks that marred her face. A young body, a soft body clad in moon-luminous white like that of an angel.

Dirk sobbed again and she went to him.

'Dirk,' she whispered as she knelt beside his bed. 'Dirk, please don't cry, please, my darling.'

Dirk gulped explosively and rolled away from her, folding his arms across his face.

'Shh! my darling. It's all right now.' She began to stroke his hair. Her touch evoked a fresh outburst of grief from him, liquid choking grief that spluttered and throbbed in the darkness.

'Oh Dirk, please . . . ' And she went into his bed. The sheets were warm and moist where he had lain. She gathered him, held his hot body to her bosom and began to rock him in her arms.

Her own loneliness at last overwhelmed her. Her voice took on a husky quality as she whispered to him. She strained to him – her need growing much greater than his.

One last covulsive sob and Dirk was silent. She felt the tension go out of his back and out of his hard round buttocks that were pressed into her stomach. Straining him even closer, her fingers moved down across his cheek to caress his throat.

Dirk turned towards her, turning within the circle of her arms. She felt his chest heave and subside as he sighed, and his voice stifled with misery.

'He doesn't love me. He went away and left me.'

'I love you, Dirk,' she whispered. 'I love you – we all love you, darling.' And she kissed his eyes and his cheeks and his mouth. The taste of his tears was hot salt.

Dirk sighed again and bowed his head until it was on her bosom. She felt his face nuzzling into the softness and her hands went to the back of his head and drew it closer.

'Dirkie . . . ' Her voice dried up in the strange new heat within her.

In the morning Dirk woke slowly, but with a feeling of wonder. He lay a while and thought about it, unable at first to place the formless shimmering sense of well-being that possessed him.

Then he heard Mary moving about behind the partition of her cubicle. The gurgle and splash of water poured from jug to basin, the rustle of cloth. finally, the sound of her door softly opened and closed, and her steps moving away towards the kitchen.

The events of the previous evening came back to him, crisp and stark in every detail. Not fully understood, but looming large to overshadow all else in his mind.

He threw the sheets aside and lifted himself on both elbows, drew up his nightshirt and contemplated his body as though he had never seen it before.

He heard footsteps approaching. Quickly he covered himself, pulled the bedclothes over and feigned sleep.

Mary came in quietly and placed a cup of coffee, with a rusk in the saucer, on the bedside table.

Dirk opened his eyes and looked at her.

'You're awake,' she said.

'Yes.'

'Dirk . . . ' she started, and then she blushed. It mottled the puckered skin of her cheeks. Her voice fell to a whisper, scratchy with her shame. 'You mustn't ever tell anybody. You must forget about . . . what happened.'

Dirk did not reply.

'Promise me, Dirkie. Please promise me.'

He nodded slowly. Not trusting himself to speak, his throat filled with a knowledge of domination over her.

'It was wrong, Dirkie. It was a terrible thing. We mustn't even think about it again.'

She walked to the door.

'Mary.'

'Yes.' She stopped without turning, her whole body poised like a bird on the point of flight.

'I won't tell anyone – if you come again tonight.'

'No,' she hissed violently.

'Then, I'll tell Granny.'

'No. Oh, Dirkie. You wouldn't.' She was beside the bed now, kneeling, reaching for his hand. 'You mustn't – you mustn't. You promised me.'

'Will you come?' he asked softly. She peered into his face, into the serene perfection of warm brown skin and green eyes with the black silk of his hair curling on to the forehead.

'I can't – it's a terrible, terrible thing that we did.'

793

'Then I'll tell,' he said.

She stood up and walked slowly out of the cubicle, her shoulders slumped forward in the attitude of surrender. He knew she would come.

63

In a hired carriage Sean arrived punctually at the Goldberg residence. He arrived like a column of wise men from the east. The seats of the carriage were piled with fancy-wrapped packages. However, Sean's limited knowledge of a three-year-old female's tastes were reflected in his choice of gifts. Every single package contained a doll. There were large china dolls that closed their eyes when reclining, small rag dolls with blonde plaits, a doll that passed water, a doll that squawked when its stomach was squeezed, dolls in a dozen national costumes and dolls in swaddling clothes.

Mbejane followed the carriage leading the gift which Sean considered a master stroke of originality. It was a piebald Shetland pony, complete with a hand-fashioned English saddle and a tiny martingale and reins.

The gravel drive was crowded with carriages. Sean was forced to walk the last hundred yards, his arms filled with presents. Under these circumstances navigation was a little difficult. He took a fix on the hideously ornamented roof of the mansion, which he could just see over the top of his load, and set off blind across the lawns. He was aware of the continuous and piercing shrieking which grew louder as he proceeded, and finally of an insistent tugging on his right trouser leg. He stopped.

'Are those *my* presents?' a voice from somewhere above the level of his knee asked. He craned his head out to one side and looked down into the upturned face of a miniature Madonna. Large shining eyes in an oval of innocent purity framed with shiny dark curls. Sean's heart flipped over.

'That depends what your name is,' he hedged.

'My name is *Miss* Storm Friedman of The Golds, Chase Valley, Pietermaritzburg. *Now* are they my presents?'

Sean bent his knees until he squatted with his face almost on a level with that of the Madonna.

'Many happy returns of the day, Miss Friedman,' he said.

'Oh, goody!' She fell on the packages, trembling with excitement while from the mass of fifty children who ringed them in the shrieking continued unabated.

Storm demolished the wrappings in very short order, using her teeth when her fingers were inadequate for the task. One of her small guests attempted to assist her, but she flew at him like a panther kitten with a cry of 'They're *my* presents!' He retired hastily.

At last she sat in a litter of wrappings and dolls and pointed at the single remaining package in Sean's hands.

'That one?' she asked.

Sean shook his head. 'No, that one is for your Mummy. But if you look behind you, you might find something else.'

Mbejane, grinning widely, was holding the Shetland. For seconds Storm was too overcome to speak and then with a sound like a steam-whistle she flew to her feet. Deserting her newly adopted children, she ran to the pony. Behind her a flock of small girls descended on the dolls, vultures when a lion leaves the kill.

'Lift me! Lift me!' Storm was hopping with delirious impatience. Sean took her up and the warm, wriggling little body in his hands made his heart flip again. Gently he set her on the saddle, handed her the reins and led the pony towards the house.

A queen riding in state, followed by an army of her attendants, Storm reach the upper terrace.

Ruth was standing beside the delicacy-laden trestle table with the parents of Storm's guests. Sean handed the lead rein to Mbejane. 'Look after her well,' and he crossed the terrace, very conscious of the many adult eyes upon him, thankful for the hour he had spent that morning at the barber's shop, and for the care he had taken with his attire – a brand-new suit of expensive English broadcloth, boots burnished to a gloss, solid gold watch chain across his belly and a white carnation in his buttonhole.

He stopped in front of Ruth and removed his hat. She held out her hand, palm downwards. Sean knew that he was *not* expected to shake that hand.

'Sean, how good of you to come.'

Sean took her hand. It was a measure of his feelings that he bowed to touch it with his lips – a gesture which he considered French, foppish and undignified.

'It was good of you to ask me, Ruth.'

He produced the box from under his arm and held it out to her. She opened it without a word and her cheeks flushed with pleasure when she saw the long-stemmed roses it contained.

'Oh, how sweet of you!' And Sean's heart did its trick again as she smiled full into his eyes, then slipped her hand into the crook of his arm.

'I'd like you to meet some friends of mine.'

That evening when the other guests had left and Storm, prostrated with nervous and physical exhaustion, had been put to bed, Sean stayed on to dinner with the Goldbergs. By now both Ma and Pa Goldberg were fully aware that Sean's interest in Ruth was not on account of his previous friendship with Saul. All afternoon Sean had followed Ruth around the lawns like a huge St Bernard behind a dainty poodle.

During dinner Sean, who was extremely pleased with himself, Ruth, the Goldbergs and life in general, was able to endear himself to Ma Goldberg and also dull Ben Goldberg's suspicions that he was a penniless adventurer. Over brandy and cigars Sean and Ben discussed the ventures on Lion Kop and Mahobo's Kloof. Sean was completely frank about the financial tightrope which he was walking, and Ben was impressed with the magnitude of the gamble and Sean's cold appraisal of the odds. It was just such a *coup* as this that had put Ben Goldberg where he was today. It made him feel nostalgic and vaguely sentimental of *the old days*, so that when they went through to join the ladies he patted Sean's arm and called him 'My boy'.

On the front steps, while he was preparing to leave, Sean asked, 'May I call on you again, Ruth?' and she answered,

'I'd like that very much.'

Now began what was for Sean a novel form of courtship. To his surprise he found he rather enjoyed it. Every Friday night he would entrain for Pietermaritzburg and install himself in the White Horse Hotel. From this base he conducted his campaign. There were dinner parties, either at The Golds or with Ruth's friends or at one of the local hostelries where Sean played host.

There were balls and dances, days at the races, picnics and rides over the surrounding hills with Storm on her Shetland bouncing along between them. During Sean's absences from Ladyburg, Dirk moved into the cottage on Protea Street and Sean was relieved that he seemed to accept it with better grace.

The time arrived when at last the first blocks of wattle were ready for the axe. Sean determined to use this as an excuse to inveigle Ruth away to Ladyburg. The Goldbergs froze up solid at the suggestion and only thawed when Sean produced a written invitation from Ada for Ruth to be her guest for the week. Sean went on to explain that it was to be a celebration of his first cutting of bark, which would begin at the end of the week, and that thereafter he could not leave Ladyburg for months.

Ma Goldberg, who was secretly delighted at having Storm all to herself for a whole week, exerted a subtle influence on Ben, and very grudgingly he gave his approval.

Sean decided that Ruth would be treated like visiting Royalty – the grand climax to his suit.

64

As one of the biggest landowners in the district and because of his war honours, Sean ranked high in the complicated social structure of Ladyburg. Therefore, preparations for Ruth's visit produced an epidemic of excitement and curiosity that affected the entire Ladyburg district. The flood of invitations he released sent women to their wardrobes and sewing-baskets, while the outlying farmers begged accommodation from relatives and friends nearer town. Other leading members of the community, jealous of their social status, rode out to Lion Kop with offers to provide entertainment on those three days of the week which Sean had left empty. Reluctantly Sean agreed – he had private plans for those three days.

Ada and her girls were inundated with orders for new clothing, but they still made one afternoon free and came up to the Lion Kop homestead armed with brooms and dusters and tins of polish. Sean and Dirk were driven from the house. They spent that afternoon riding over Sean's estate, looking for the best place to hold the big bush-buck shoot which would be the climax of the week.

With a gang of his Zulus, Mbejane hacked down the jungle of undergrowth around the homestead and dug the barbecue pits.

The Village Management Board met in secret conclave, infected by the general excitement and armed with strict instructions from their wives, they voted unanimously for a civic reception of Ruth Friedman at the station and a formal Ball that night. Dennis Petersen, who had Sean's consent to a barbecue on the night of Ruth's arrival, was placated with the promise that he would be allowed to make a short speech of welcome at the station.

Sean called upon Ronny Pye and was again surprised when Ronny agreed cheerfully to a further loan of one thousand pounds. Ronny signed the cheque with the satisfied air of a spider putting the final thread into his web, and Sean left immediately for Pietermaritzburg to visit a jeweller. He returned home five hundred pounds poorer, with a packet in his breast-pocket that contained a huge square-cut diamond set in a band of platinum. Dirk was at the station to meet him. Sean took one look at him and ordered him to the village barber.

The night before Ruth's arrival Sean and Mbejane fell upon Dirk in a surprise attack and dragged him protesting to the bathroom. Sean was astounded by the large quantities of foreign matter that he removed from Dirk's ears, and by the way in which Dirk's suntan dissolved so readily under an application of soap.

The following morning as her railway coach ground to a jerky halt in front of the station building, Ruth looked down on a mass of strangers surrounding the roped-off area in front of her. Only one family was not represented in the crowd, which included the young ladies and gentlemen of Ladyburg High School in their church clothes.

She stood uncertainly on the balcony of the coach and heard the hum of appreciative comment and speculation. Ruth had relieved the plain black mourning with a wide ribbon of pink around the crown of her hat, pink gloves and gauzy pink veil, which shrouded her face in a misty and mysterious fashion. It was very effective.

Convinced that there was some misunderstanding, Ruth was about to withdraw into the coach, when she noticed a deputation approaching along the roped-off passageway. It was headed by Sean and she recognized the thunderous scowl he wore as his expression of acute embarrassment. She felt an inexplicable urge to burst out laughing, but managed to keep it to a smile as Sean climbed up on to the balcony and took her hand.

'Ruth, I'm terribly sorry. I didn't plan all this – things got a little out of control,' he whispered hurriedly, then he muttered an introduction to Dennis Petersen, who had ponderously mounted the steps behind him. Now Dennis turned to face the crowd and spread his arms in the gesture that Moses might have employed on his return from the mountain.

'Ladies and gentlemen, citizens of Ladyburg, friends –' he

began, and from the way he said it Sean knew he was good for another half-hour. He glanced sideways at Ruth and saw that she was smiling. It came as a surprise to him when he realized she was enjoying herself. Sean relaxed a little.

'It gives me great pleasure to welcome to our fair town this lovely lady, friend of one of our foremost . . . ' Ruth's fingers found their way surreptitiously into Sean's hand, and Sean relaxed a little more. He saw the wide brim of Ada's hat standing out in the crowd and he smiled at her. She replied with a nod of approval towards Ruth.

By some curious twist of oratory, Dennis was now talking about the new water filtration plant and its benefit to the community.

'– But, my friends, this is only the first of a series of projects planned by your Board.' He paused significantly.

'Hear, hear,' Sean interjected loudly and clapped his hands. The applause was taken up by the crowd, and Sean stepped past Dennis to the rail of the balcony.

'On behalf of Mrs Friedman and myself, I thank you for your friendship and your hospitality.' Then, leaving Dennis on the balcony making helpless little movements with his hands and silently opening and closing his mouth, Sean spirited Ruth away, ran her through a rapid fire series of introductions and handshakes, gathered Ada and Dirk and got them all into the carriage.

While Sean and Mbejane fussed with the luggage, Ruth and Ada settled their skirts and adjusted their hats before meeting each other's eyes again.

'Although Sean warned me, I didn't expect you to be quite so lovely,' Ada said. Flushing with pleasure and relief, Ruth leaned impulsively across to touch her arm.

'I've been longing to meet you, Mrs Courtney.'

'If you promise to call me Ada, then I'll call you Ruth.'

Sean scrambled into the carriage, flustered and perspiring. 'Let's get the hell out of here.'

That week was to be remembered for many years. The usual Christmas festivities paled into insignificance beside it.

Matrons competed fiercely to provide food, mountains of it, prepared from their closely guarded recipe books. In between cooking they conducted old feuds, began new ones and worried about their daughters.

The young bucks competed on the gymkhana and polo field, then again on the dance floor. Dirk Courtney won the junior tent-pegging event. Then against a visiting team from Pietermaritzburg College he captained the school rugby team to an inglorious 30–0 defeat.

The young ladies competed with equal ferocity, covering it with giggles and blushes. The success of their efforts was measured in the outbreak of betrothals and scandals during the week.

The older men smiled indulgently, until, fortified with bottled spirit, they discarded their dignity and capered and panted around the dance floor. There were three bouts of fisticuffs – but these were between old enemies and none of them were really worth watching.

Only one family held aloof from the festivities. There were many of the young ladies who missed Michael Courtney.

During one of the infrequent lulls of the week, Sean managed to separate Ruth from Ada, and take her out to the homestead at Lion Kop. She moved silently through the empty rooms, appraising each with narrowed thoughtful eyes while Sean hovered anxiously behind her, certain that her silence was disapproval. In fact, Ruth was in ecstasy; a shell, a magnificent shell of a house, with no trace of another woman in it, waiting for her to bring it to life. She could imagine exactly the curtains she wanted, her Persian carpets sent down by Uncle Isaac from Pretoria and now in storage, would look just right once she had the yellow-wood floors polished to a gloss. The kitchen, of course, would have to be completely rebuilt – with a new double Agar stove. The bedroom . . .

Unable to contain himself, Sean blurted out:

'Well, do you like it?'

She turned slowly to him, the mists of thought clearing from her eyes.

'Oh, Sean! It's the most beautiful house in all the world.'

In this emotional moment, Sean put forward the proposition he had planned for that evening.

'Ruth, will you marry me?'

And Ruth, who had planned to hesitate and ask for a little time to consider, replied instantly:

802

'Oh, yes please!'
She was truly impressed with the ring.

65

The finale to the week was Sean Courtney's bush-buck shoot.

Sean and Dirk arrived at Protea Cottage with the dawn. They were dressed in rough hunting clothes and the leather gun-cases lay on the floor of the mule-wagon under Sean's feet. It took nearly fifteen minutes for Sean to transfer Ruth, Ada and her girls from the cottage to the carriage. In the same way a man might drive a flock of chickens towards the door of a henhouse. He would get them all moving slowly in front of him, down the path towards the carriage, clucking and fussing. Almost there when suddenly one of them would shriek softly and double back towards the cottage for a forgotten parasol or work-basket and the general movement would break down again.

The third time this happened Sean felt something snap inside his head. He bellowed. A vast hush fell over the ladies and two of them looked as though they might cry.

'Now don't get worked up, dear.' Ada tried to soothe him.

'I am not getting worked up.' Sean's voice quivered with the effort of restraint. 'But if everybody is not in the carriage by the count of ten – then I might easily get that way.'

They were all seated by the count of five and he drove out to the stockpens – a very ruffled rooster.

Carriages and mule-wagons carrying the entire population of the Ladyburg district were waiting in a disorderly tangle in the field beside the stockpen. Sean trotted past in a babble of greeting and comment. One at a time the waiting carriages wheeled into line behind him and the long convoy wound out towards Mahobo's Kloof Farm. The big shoot had begun.

In the middle of the line someone was playing a concertina and the singing started. It spread to each carriage in turn and blended with the sound of wheels and hooves and laughter.

Gradually Sean's irritation smoothed out. Ada's girls were singing *Boland Se Nooinentje* in the back seat. Dirk had jumped down from the carriage and with half a dozen of the youngsters from the village ran ahead of the horses. Ruth's hand touched Sean's leg uncertainly and as he turned and grinned at her he saw the relief in her answering smile.

'What a beautiful day, Sean.'

'Sorry I nearly spoiled it –' he answered.

'Oh, nonsense!' She moved closer to him and suddenly he was happy. All the preparation was worth it. Beside him Ruth laughed softly.

'What's the joke?' Sean reached out and took her hand.

'No joke. I just felt like laughing,' she answered. 'Look how green everything is.' She said it to distract him, to make him look away so that she could study his face. The subterfuge worked.

'The land seems so young now.' His eyes, as he looked at it, took on that gentleness she knew so well. By now she knew many of his moods and she was learning how to induce or redirect each of them. He was such a simple man, yet in that simplicity lay his strength. He is like a mountain, she thought. You know how it will be with the sun on it in the early morning. You know that when the wind is in the south there will be mist covering the crest, and in the evening the shadows will fall in certain patterns across the slopes and the gorges will look dark and blue. Yet also you know the shape of the mountain is unchanged, that it will never change.

'I love you, my mountain,' she whispered, and anticipated the startled expression before it flashed across his face.

'Hey?'

'I love you, my man,' she amended.

'Oh! I love you too.'

And now he is vaguely embarrassed. Oh, God, I could eat him! If I were to reach over and kiss him now in front of everybody . . . ! Secretly she savoured the idea.

'What devilment are you planning?' he demanded gruffly. He wasn't supposed to read her so accurately. Taken off balance she stared at him. Suddenly the mountain had shown that it understood exactly the way she felt when she looked at it.

'Nothing,' she denied in confusion. 'I wasn't . . . ' Before she realized fully what he was about, he had turned half-way in his seat towards her and lifted her bodily into his lap.

'Sean, no!' she gasped and then her protests were muffled. She heard the laughter of Ada's girls, the hoots of encouragement and applause from the other carriages, and she kicked and struggled, pushing with one hand against his chest and trying to keep her hat on with the other.

By the time he replaced her on the seat beside him, her hair had come down behind, her hat was off and her cheeks and ears were flaming red. She had been very thoroughly kissed.

'Nice shot, Sean!'

'Author! Author!'

'Arrest that man!' The cries and the laughter added to her confusion.

'You're terrible!' Ruth used her hat as a screen behind which she tried to control her blushes. 'In front of all those people, too!'

'That should keep you out of mischief for a while, me lass!'

And suddenly she wasn't so sure of the shape of her mountain.

The cavalcade turned off along the rough track from the main road, splashed through the drift, climbed the far bank and spread out among the trees. Servants, who had been waiting since the previous evening, ran to their masters' horses as they halted. Each vehicle disgorged a noisy blast of children and dogs, and then a more dignified trickle of adults. The women moved without hesitation towards the two huge marquees that had been erected among the trees, while the men unloaded the gun-cases and began assembling their weapons.

Still sitting on the front seat of the wagon, Sean opened the leather case at his feet and while his hands automatically fitted the barrels into the breech piece of his shotgun he allowed himself to review his preparations with a certain amount of satisfaction.

He had selected this site not only for the cool grove of syringa trees which provided shade above and a soft carpet of fallen leaves below, nor for the proximity of the tinkling stream where all the animals could be watered, but also because it was situated within fifteen minutes' walk of the first beat.

Days before a gang of Zulus working under Mbejane had cleared out all the undergrowth beneath the trees, had erected the marquee tents and the trestle tables, dug the cooking pits and even built two grass-walled pit latrines discreetly out of view of the main camp.

Huge log fires were burning in the cooking pits now, but by

noon they would have burned down to glowing coal beds. The trestle tables about which the women had already begun working were laden with food. There was a great deal of activity going on in that direction at the moment – most of it talking.

From the other wagons men were starting to drift towards him, buckling on their cartridge belts, hefting shotguns, chatting together nonchalantly in an attempt to disguise their excitement. Under instruction from Sean, Dirk had assembled a rabble of those males who were too young to handle shotguns but too old to stay with the women. These were making no effort to hide *their* excitement. Armed with *sikelas* (the Zulu fighting sticks) they were showing every indication of getting out of hand. Already one small boy was weeping loudly and massaging the welt he had received from a playful *sikela*.

'All right – shut up, all of you,' Sean shouted. 'Dirk will take you up to the beaters. But remember! Once the hunt starts, keep in the line and listen to what you're told. If I catch anybody running about or getting ahead of the line – I'll personally wallop the tar out of him. Do you understand?' It was a long speech to shout and Sean ended with his face flushed ferociously. This gave weight to his words and resulted in a respectful chorus of:

'Yes, Mr Courtney.'

'Off you go, then.'

Whooping, racing each other they poured away through the trees and a comparative peace descended on the camp.

'My God, let alone bush buck, that lot would drive elephant, buffalo and lion panic-stricken ahead of them,' observed Dennis Petersen dryly. 'How about our positions, Sean?'

Aware that he had their complete attention, Sean drew the moment out a little.

'We are going to drive the Elands' Kloof first,' he announced. 'Mbejane and two hundred Zulus are waiting at the head of the Kloof for the signal. The guns will take station at the tail of the Kloof.' Sean paused.

'How about our positions?'

'Patience. Patience.' Sean chided them. 'I know I shouldn't have to repeat the safety rules, but . . . ' and he immediately went on to do so. 'No rifles – shotguns only. You'll shoot only in an arc of 45 degrees directly ahead of you – no passing shots to either side. Especially you, Reverend!' That gentleman, who was notoriously trigger-happy, looked suitably abashed. 'My whistle will mean the beaters are too close – all guns up and unloaded immediately.'

'It's getting late, Sean.'

'Let's get on with it.'

'Right,' Sean agreed. 'I'll take centre gun.' There was a murmur of agreement. That was fair enough, the plum to the man who provided the hunt, no one could grudge that. 'On my left flank in this order, Reverend Smiley – since the Almighty will obviously send most of the game his way, I might as well profit by it.' A burst of laughter as Smiley wavered between horror at the blasphemy and delight at his own good fortune. 'Then Ronny Pye, Dennis Petersen, Ian Vermaak, Gerald and Tony Erasmus (you two fight it out in a brotherly fashion), Nick . . . ' Sean read from the list in his hand. This in strict order of seniority was the social register of Ladyburg, a proper and exact balancing of wealth and influence, of popularity and age. Apart from placing himself in the centre of the line, Sean had not taken much part in the preparation of the list – quite correctly Ada had not trusted his sense of social perception.

'That takes care of the left flank.' Sean looked up from the list. He had been so engrossed in reaching that he had not sensed the air of tension and expectancy which had fallen over his audience. A single horseman had crossed the drift and walked his magnificent thoroughbred into the camp. He had dismounted quietly and servants had led his horse away. Now, carrying a shotgun, he was walking towards Sean's wagon.

Sean looked up and saw him. He stared in surprise, while slowly elation mounted within him until it reached his face in a wide grin.

'Garry, glad you could make it!' he called out spontaneously, but Garry's face remained without expression. He nodded a curt greeting. At least he's come, exulted Sean. This is the first overture. Now it's up to me.

'You can take the first position on my right, Garry.'

'Thank you.' Now Garry smiled, but it was a curiously cold grimace and he turned away to talk with the nearest man. A small shiver of disappointment moved the crowd. They had expected something spectacular to happen. All of them knew of the feud between the Courtney brothers and the mystery that surrounded it. But now, with a feeling of anti-climax they turned their attention back to Sean's reading. Sean finished and jumped down from the wagon, and immediately the crowd moved away. Sean sought Garrick and saw him far ahead near the head of the long file of men that was strung out along the footpath that led to Elands' Kloof.

The file moved fast as the hunters stepped out eagerly. Unless he ran, Sean knew he would not be able to pass the men ahead of him and catch up with Garry. I'll wait until we reach the beat, he decided. My God, what a wonderful ending to this week. I have Ruth, now if only I can get back my brother and with him Michael!

From the shoulder of the gorge Sean looked down across Elands' Kloof. A deep slot of a valley, two miles long and five hundred yards wide at this end, but it tapered slowly upwards until it lost its identity in the high ground. The full length of it was clogged solid with dark green bush, a seemingly impenetrable mass above which a few tall trees reared up in a desperate attempt to reach the sunlight. Like the tentacles of a giant squid, creepers and vines lifted from the dark bush to overpower them and drag them down. Here on the shoulder the air was dry and wholesome – down there it would stink of damp earth and rotting vegetable matter.

Lingering as though suddenly reluctant to go down into the humid discomfort of the Kloof, the hunters gathered on the shoulder. Shading eyes against the glare, they peered up towards the head of the gorge where the beaters were a line of dark specks against the green spring grass.

'There go the kids,' someone pointed. Dirk was leading his band along the high ground above the Kloof.

Sean moved across to his twin brother.

'Well, Garry, how are things out at Theuniskraal?'

'Not bad.'

'I read your book – I think it's excellent. It certainly deserved the reception it got in London. Lord Caisterbrook wrote to me to say that your concluding chapter is giving the War Office much food for thought. Well done, Garry.'

'Thank you.' But there was an evasive lack of warmth in Garry's reply. He made no attempt to continue the conversation.

'Michael didn't come out with you today?'

'No.'

'Why not, Garry?' And Garry smiled for the first time, a cool, spiteful smile.

'He didn't want to.'

'Oh!' The hurt showed in Sean's face for an instant, then he turned to the men around him. 'Right, gentlemen, let's get down there.'

In position now, a line of men standing quietly in the gloom and stagnant heat. Each man's neighbour visible only as an indefinite shape among the leaves and vines and fallen trees. Few things sharp – the outline of a hat-brim, the glint of a random beam of sun on gun-metal, a human hand framed in a hole of dark green leaves. The silence heavy as the heat – spoiled by the nervous rustle of a branch, a hastily smothered cough, the click of a shotgun breech.

Sean hooked his thumb across both hammers of his gun and pulled them back to full cock, lifted the twin muzzles to the roof of leaves above his head and fired in rapid succession. He heard the deep booming note of the gun bouncing against the sides of the valley, echoing and fragmenting as it was thrown back upon itself. Then swiftly the silence closed in again.

He stood motionless, tuning his hearing as finely as was possible, but his reward was the thin drone of an insect and the harsh startled cry of a bush lourie. He shrugged, two miles of distance and the mass of vegetation would blanket completely the cries of the beaters and the clatter of their sticks as they thrashed the bush. But they were coming now, of this he was certain, they would have heard his signal shots. He could imagine them moving down the line, two hundred black men interspersed with the small white boys, chanting the rhetorical question which was as old as the drive hunt itself.

'E'yapi? Repeated over and over again, the accent on the first half of the word, shrilling it.

'E'yapi? Where are you going?'

And between him and the beaters, in that wedge of tangled bush, there would be the first uneasy stirring. Dainty bodies, dappled with grey, rising from the secret beds of fallen leaves. Hooves, pointed and sharp, splayed and driven deep into soft leaf-mould by the weight of tensed muscle. Ears pricked forward, eyes like wet black satin, shiny moist muzzles quivering and snuffling, corkscrew horns laid back. The whole poised on the edge of flight.

With the taint of gunsmoke in his nostrils, Sean opened the action of his shotgun and the empty shells ejected crisply, ping-ing out to leave the eyes of the breech empty. He selected two fresh cartridges from his belt and slid them home, snapped the gun closed and thumbed the hammers on to half-cock.

Now they would be moving. The does first, ginger-brown and dappled like roe-deer, slipping away down the valley with their fawns long-legged beside them. Then the bucks, the Inkonka, black and big and silent as shadows; crouching as they moved, horns flat against their shoulders. Moving away from the faint cries and the commotion, moving their mates and their young away from danger – down towards the waiting guns.

'I heard something then!' The Reverend Smiley's voice sounded as though he were being strangled, probably by the dog collar which showed as a pale spot in the gloom.

'Shut up, you fool!' Sean gambled his chance of salvation on the rebuke, but he need not have worried for the endearment was drowned by the double blast of Smiley's shotgun – so indecently loud and totally unexpected that Sean's feet left the ground.

'Did you get him?' Sean asked, his voice a little shaky from the fright. No reply.

'Reverend, did you get one?' Sean demanded. He had seen nothing, and heard nothing that might by the most generous stretch of imagination lead anyone to suspect the presence of a bush buck.

'My goodness, I could have sworn . . . ' Smiley's reply was in the kind of voice you would expect from beyond the grave. 'Oh dear, I think I must have been mistaken.'

Here we go again, thought Sean with resignation.

'If you run out of cartridges let me know,' he called softly and grinned at Smiley's injured silence. The shots would have turned the game back towards the beaters, they would be starting to mill now as they sought an avenue of escape. Perhaps moving out on the flanks. As if in confirmation of Sean's thoughts, a shotgun thudded out on the left, then another, then two more on the right.

The fun had started in earnest.

In the brief silence he heard the beaters now, their excited cries muffled but urgent.

A blur of movement ahead of him through the screen of branches, just a flick of dark grey and he swung the gun and fired, wallop of the butt on to his shoulder, and thud and scuffle and roll and kick in the undergrowth.

'Got him!' exulted Sean. Still kicking, the head and shoulders of a half-grown ram emerged from under a bramble bush. It was down, mouth open, bleeding, crabbing against the earth, leaving a drag mark through the dead leaves. Boom again, the mercy stroke, and it lay still. Head speckled with tiny buckshot wounds, eyelids quivering into death and the swift rush of blood from the nostrils.

The din of gunfire all about, cries of the beaters and the answering shouts of the gunners, the panic-stricken run and crackle in the bush ahead.

Inkonka, big one, black as a hellhound, three twists in the horn, eyes staring, lunging into the clearing to halt with head up and front legs braced wide, hunted, panting, wild with terror.

Lean forward against the gun, hold the pip on his heaving chest and fire. The bounce of the gun and the long blue gush of smoke. Knock him down with the solid charge of short range buckshot. Cleanly, quickly, without kicking.

'Got him!'

Another one, blundering straight into the gun line, blind with panic, bursting out of the undergrowth almost on top of Sean. Doe with fawn at her heels – let her go.

The doe saw him and wheeled left to take the gap between Sean and Garrick. As it dashed through, Sean looked beyond and saw his brother. Garrick had left his position and closed in on Sean. He was crouched slightly, the shotgun held in both hands, hammers fully cocked – and his eyes were fastened on Sean.

Garrick waited quietly during the initial stages of the beat. The tree-trunk on which he sat was soft and rotten, covered with moss and the orange and white tongues of fungus. From the inside pocket of his jacket he took the silver flask inlaid with carnelians. The first mouthful started his tears and numbed his tongue, but he swallowed it painfully and lowered the flask.

He has taken from me everything I ever had of value:

My leg: Garry looked down at the way it stuck out stiffly ahead of him with the heel buried in the damp leaf-mould. He drank again quickly, closing his eyes against the sting of brandy.

My wife: In the dark redness behind his eyelids he saw her again, as Sean had left her, lying in torn clothing with bruised and swollen lips.

My manhood: Because of what he did to her that night, Anna has never let me touch her body. Until then there was hope. But now I am forty-two years old and I am virgin. It is too late.

My position: That swine Acheson would never have thrown me out – but for Sean.

And now he will take Michael from me.

He remembered again the premonition of disaster that he had experienced when Anna reported to him how she had found Michael and Sean together on Theuniskraal. It had started then, each little incident building up. The day Michael had stared at the faded but bold entries in the leather-bound stock register. 'Is that Uncle Sean's handwriting?'

That battered saddle Michael had found in the loft above the stables; he had polished it lovingly and restitched the seams, fitted new stirrup leathers, and used it for a year. Until Garry had noticed the crude initials cut into the leather of the flap. 'S.C.' That night Garry had taken the saddle and thrown it into the furnace of the hot-water boiler.

Eight months ago, on Michael's twenty-first birthday, Garry had called him into the panelled study of Theuniskraal, and reluctantly told him of Sean's legacy to him. Michael had held the dog-eared sheet and read it through with his lips moving silently. Then at last he looked up and his voice was shaky. 'Uncle Sean gave me a half-share in Theuniskraal even before I was born. Why, Dad? Why did he do that?' And Garry had no answer for him.

This last week had been the climax. It had taken all Anna's and Garrick's combined influence and entreaties to prevent Michael responding to the invitations Sean had sent. Then the Zulu herdboy, whose duty was to follow Michael and come to Garrick immediately Michael crossed the boundary of Theuniskraal, reported that each evening Michael rode up to the high ground on the escarpment and sat there until after dark staring in the direction of Lion Kop ranch.

I am going to lose him. He is my son, even if Sean sired him. But he is my son, and unless I prevent it Sean is going to take that away from me also.

Unless I prevent it. He lifted the flask to his lips once more and found with surprise that it was empty. He screwed the stopper down and returned the flask to his pocket.

Around him the gunfire and the shouting began. From the log beside him he picked up the shotgun and loaded it. He stood up and cocked the hammers.

Sean saw him, coming slowly, limping a little, crouching, making no attempt to fend off the branches that dragged across his face.

'Don't bunch up, Garry. Stay in your position, you're leaving a gap in the line.'

Then he noticed Garry's expression. It seemed that the skin had been stretched tight across the cheek-bones and the nose, so the rims of his nostrils were white. His jaws were chewing nervously and there was a fine sheen of sweat across his forehead. He looked sick or deadly afraid.

'Garry, are you all right?' Alarmed, Sean started towards him – then stopped suddenly. Garry had lifted the shotgun.

'I'm sorry, Sean. But I can't let you have him,' he said. The blank double eyes of the muzzles were all Sean saw of the gun, and below them, Garry's knuckles white with pressure, as he gripped the stock. One finger was hooked forward around the triggers.

Sean was afraid then. He stood without moving for his legs were heavy and numb under him.

'I've got to.' Garry's voice was a croak. 'I have to do it – otherwise you'll take him. You'll destroy him also.'

With fear making his legs clumsy and slow, Sean turned deliberately away from him and walked back to his station. The muscles of his back were stiff with anticipation, knotted so tightly that they ached.

The beaters were close now, he could hear them shouting and thrashing the bush just ahead. He lifted the whistle to his lips and blew three shrill blasts. The shouting died away, and in the comparative silence Sean heard a sound behind him, a sound half-way between a sob and a cry of pain.

Slowly, inchingly, Sean turned his head to look back. Garry was gone.

Beneath him Sean's legs began to tremble, and a muscle in

his thigh twitched spasmodically. He sank down and sat on the carpet of soft damp leaves. When he lit a cheroot he used both hands to steady the fluttering flame of the match.

'Dad! Dad!' Dirk came pelting out into the tiny clearing. 'Dad, how many did you get?'

'Two,' said Sean.

'Only two?' And Dirk's voice went flat with disappointment and shame. 'Even Reverend Smiley beat you hollow. He got four!'

66

Ruth returned to Pietermaritzburg the afternoon following the hunt, Sean insisted on accompanying her home. Ada, Dirk and a dozen of the friends Ruth had made during the week were at the station to see them leave. Sean was trying to detach Ruth from the earnest discussion into which all women seem to fall on the eve of a major parting. His repeated, 'You'd better get aboard, my dear,' and 'The flag's up, Ruth', were studiously ignored by all of them until he found it necessary to take Ruth's arm and bundle her up into the coach. Her head reappeared instantly at the window to take up the discussion at the exact point where Sean had interrupted it. Sean was about to follow her when he saw Dirk. With a stab of guilt Sean realized how blatantly he had neglected Dirk during the week.

'Cheerio, Dirkie,' Sean called gruffly and the boy flew to him and wound his arms tightly around Sean's neck.

'Come on, Dirk. I'll be back tomorrow morning.'

'I want to go with you.'

'You have school tomorrow.' Sean tried to loosen Dirk's hold. The women were watching in silence now, and Sean felt himself flushing with embarrassment. *My God, he's not a baby any more – he's nearly fifteen*. He tried to keep his irritation from showing in his voice as he whispered:

'Stop that now. What will people think of you?'

'Take me with you, Dad. Please take me,' and Dirk quivered against him. The whistle blew and with voluble relief the women turned away and began talking at once.

'Do you think I'm proud of you when you act like this?' Sean hissed at him. 'Now, behave yourself and shake hands properly.'

Dirk clutched his hand, with the tears filling his eyes.

'Stop it this instant!' Sean turned abruptly and swung himself up into the coach as the train jerked forward and started sliding out of the platform.

Dirk took a few indeterminate paces after it and then stopped with his shoulders shaking uncontrollably, his eyes still fastened on Sean's face as it protruded from the window.

'Your father will be back tomorrow, Dirkie.' Ada laid her hand consolingly on Dirk's shoulder.

'He doesn't love me,' whispered Dirk. 'He never even . . .'

'Of course he does,' Ada interrupted quickly. 'It was just that he was so . . .' But Dirk did not wait her to finish. He shrugged her hand away, spun round and jumped blindly from the platform on to the tracks, ducked through the barbed-wire fence beyond and ran out across the fields to intercept the train as it made its first long turn on to the slope of the escarpment.

He ran with his face contorted, and the harsh grass brushing his legs, he ran with his arms pumping the rhythm of his racing feet – and ahead of him the train whistled mournfully and crawled out from behind the Van Essen plantation.

It was crossing his front, still fifty yards away, slowly gathering speed for its assault on the escarpment. He would not reach it – even though Sean's coach was the last before the guard's van – he would not reach it.

He stopped, panting, searching wildly for a glimpse of his father – but the window of Sean's compartment was blank.

'Pa!' He waved both arms wildly above his head. 'Pa! It's me. Me – Dirk.'

Sean's compartment moved slowly across his line of vision. For a few brief seconds he looked into the interior.

Sean stood sideways to the window, he was leaning forward with his shoulders hunched and Ruth was in his arms. Her head thrown back, the hat gone from her head and her dark hair in abundant disarray. She was laughing, white teeth and eyes asparkle. Sean leaned forward and covered her open mouth with his own. And then they were past.

Dirk stood like that with his arms raised. Then slowly they sank to his sides. The tension in his lips and around his eyes smoothed away. All expression faded from his eyes and he stood and watched the train puff and twist up the slope until with a last triumphant spurt of steam it disappeared over the skyline.

Dirk crossed the railway line and found the footpath that climbed the hills. Once he lifted his hands and with his thumbs wiped the tears from his cheeks. Then he stopped listlessly to watch a scarab beetle at his feet. The size of a man's thumb, glossy black and horned like a demon, it struggled with a ball of cow-dung three times its own size. Standing on its back legs, thrusting with its front, it rolled the perfect sphere of dung before it. Oblivious of everything but the need to spawn, to bury the ball in a secret place and deposit its eggs upon it, it laboured in silent dedication.

With the toe of his boot Dirk flicked the ball away into the grass. The beetle stood motionless, deprived of the whole purpose of its existence. Then it began to search. Back and forth, clicking and scraping its shiny body armour across the hard, bare earth of the path.

Watching its frenzied search dispassionately, Dirk's face was calm and lovely. He lifted his foot and brought his heel down gently on the beetle.

He could feel it wriggling under his boot until with a crunch its carapace collapsed and it spurted brown as tobacco juice. Dirk stepped over it and walked on up the hill.

In the night Dirk sat alone. His arms were clasped around his legs and his forehead rested on his knees. The shafts of moonlight through the canopy of wattle branches had a cold white quality, similar to the emotion that held Dirk's body rigid. He lifted his head. Moonlight lit his face from above, accentuating the perfection of his features. The smooth, broad depth of his forehead, the flaring dark lines of his brows set off the large but delicately formed plane of his nose. But now his mouth was a line of pain, of cold white pain.

'I hate him.' His mouth did not lose the shape of pain as he whispered the words, 'and I hate her. He doesn't care about me any more – all he cares about is that woman.'

'The vicious hiss of breath through his lips was the sound of despair.

'I always try to show him ... No one else but him, but he doesn't care. Why doesn't he understand – Why? Why? Why?'

And he shivered feverishly.

'He doesn't want me. He doesn't care.'

The shivering ceased, and the shape of his mouth changed from pain to hatred.

'I'll show him. If he doesn't want me – then I'll show him.'

And the next words he spat as though they were filth from his mouth, 'I hate him.' Around him the wattle branches rustled in the wind. He jumped to his feet and ran, following the moonlit road deeper into the plantations of Lion Kop.

A *meerkat* hunting alone along the road saw him and scampered into the trees like a small grey ferret. But Dirk ran on, faster now as his hatred drove him and his breathing sobbed in rhythm with his feet. He ran with the dry west wind into his face – he needed the wind. His revenge would ride on the wind.

'Now, we'll see,' he shouted suddenly as he ran. 'You don't want me – then have this instead!' And the wattle and wind answered him with a sound like many voices far away.

At the second access road he turned right and ran on into the heart of the plantations. He ran for twenty minutes and when he stopped he was panting wildly.

'Damn you – God damn you all.' His voice came catchy from his dried-out mouth.

'Damn you, then.' And he walked off the road and fought his way into the trees. They were two-year growth not yet thinned, and the branches interlaced to dispute his passage – hands trying to hold him, small desperate hands clutching at him, tugging at his clothing like the supplicating hands of a beggar. But he shrugged them away and beat them off until he was deep in amongst them.

'Here!' he said harshly and dropped to his knees in the soft crackling trash of small twigs and dry leaves that carpeted the earth. Hooking his fingers he raked a pyramid of the stuff, and he sobbed as he worked so that his muttering was broken and without coherence.

'Dry, it's dry. I'll show you then – you don't want – Everything I've done you've . . . I hate you . . . Oh, Pa! Why? Why don't you – what have I done?'

And the matchbox rattled. Twice he struck and twice the match broke in his fingers. The third flared blue, spitting tiny sparks of sulphur, burning acrid, settling down to a small yellow flame that danced in the cup of his hands.

'Have this instead!' And he thrust the flame into the pile of kindling. It fluttered, almost died and then grew again as a wisp of grass caught it.

Consumed instantly, the grass was gone and the flame died, gone – almost, but then a leaf and it jumped brightly, orange points of flame in the twigs. The first tiny popping and it spread sideways, a burning leaf swirled upwards.

Dirk backed away as the flame leapt jubilantly into his face. He was no longer sobbing.

'Pa,' he whispered and the flame fastened on to the living leaves of a branch that hung above it. A gust of wind hit it and sprayed sparks and golden orange flame against its neighbour.

'Pa.' Dirk's voice was uncertain, he stood up and wiped his hands nervously against his shirt.

'No.' He shook his head in bewilderment, and the sapling bloomed with fire and the fire whispered softly.

'No.' Dirk's voice rose. 'I didn't really mean . . . ' but it was lost in the pistol-shots of flame and the whisper that was now a drumming roar.

'Stop it,' he shouted. 'Oh God, I didn't mean it. No! No!' And he jumped forward into the heat of it, into the bright orange glare, kicking wildly at the flaming kindling, scattering it so that it fell and caught again in fifty new points of fire.

'No, stop it. Please stop it!' And he clawed at the burning tree until the heat drove him back. He ran to another sapling and tore a leafy branch from it. He rushed at the fire, beating at it, sobbing again in the smoke and the flame.

Riding joyously on the west wind, roaring red and orange and black, the flames spread out among the trees and left him standing along in the smoke and the swirling ash.

'Oh Pa! I'm sorry, I'm sorry – I didn't mean it.'

67

A shutter kept slamming softly in the wind, but this was not the only reason Michael Courtney could not sleep. He felt trapped, chained by loyalties he could not break; he was aware of the dark oppressive bulk of the Theuniskraal homestead around him. A prison, a place of bitterness and hatred.

He moved restlessly on his bed and the shutter banged and banged. He threw back the single sheet and the floorboards creaked as he stood up from the bed.

'Michael!' The voice from the next room was sharp, suspicious.

'Yes, Mother.'

'Where are you going, darling?'

'There's a loose shutter. I'm going to close it.'

'Put something on, darling. Don't catch cold.'

Stifling, beginning to sweat now in physical discomfort, Michael knew he must get out of this house into the cool freedom of the wind and the night. He dressed quickly but silently, then carrying his boots he crept down the long passage and out on to the wide front stoep.

He found the shutter and secured it, then he sat upon the front steps and pulled on his boots before standing again and moving out across the lawns. He stood on the bottom terrace of Theuniskraal's gardens and around him the west wind soughed and shook the trees.

The restlessness of the wind increased his own, so he must get out of the valley – get up on to the high ground of the escarpment. He started to walk, hurrying past the paddocks towards the stables. In the stable yard he stopped abruptly, his tall lean body caught in mid-stride. There was a glow, a soft orange glow on the far hills of Lion Kop.

Then Michael ran, shouting as he passed the grooms' quarters. He threw open the half-door of one of the stalls and snatched the bridle from its peg as he ran to his horse. Hands clumsy with haste, he forced the bit between the animal's teeth and buckled the cheek strap. When he led it out into the yard two of the grooms were standing there, bewildered with sleep.

'Fire!' Michael pointed along the hills. 'Call everybody and bring them to help.' He went up on to the bare back of his horse and looked down at them. 'Bring every man from the location, come in the mule-wagon. Come as fast as you can.' Then he hit his heels into the mare's flanks and drove her out of the yard, laying forward across her back.

Twenty minutes later Michael checked her on the crest of the escarpment. She was blowing heavily between his knees. Still five miles ahead, bright even in the bright moonlight, a circle of fire lay on the dark plantations of Lion Kop. Above it a black cloud, a cloud that climbed and spread on the wind to hide the stars.

'Oh God – Uncle Sean!' The exclamation wrung from Michael was a cry of physical pain, and he urged the mare forward again. Charging her recklessly through the ford of the Baboon Stroom so that the water flew like exploding glass, then lunging up the far bank and on along the hills.

The mare was staggering in her gallop as Michael kneed her through the gates into the yard of the Lion Kop homestead. There were wagons and many blackmen carrying axes. Michael hauled the mare back so violently that she nearly fell.

'Where is the Nkosi?' he shouted at a big Zulu he recognized as Sean's personal servant.

'He has gone to Pietermaritzburg.'

Michael slid down from his horse and turned her loose.

'Send a man to the village to ask for help.'

'It is done,' the Zulu replied.

'We must move all the livestock from the top paddocks, get the horses out of the stables – it may come this way,' Michael went on.

'I have sent all the wives to do these things.'

'You have done well, then. Now let us go.'

The Zulus were swarming up on to the wagons, clutching the long-handled axes. Michael and Mbejane ran to the lead wagon. Michael took the reins. At that moment two horsemen galloped into the yard. He could not see their faces in the night.

'Who's that?' Michael shouted.

'Broster and Van Wyk!' The nearest neighbours.

'Thank God! Will you take the other wagons?'

They dismounted and ran past Michael.

Michael stood with his legs braced apart, he threw his shoulders open as he wielded the whip and then sent it snaking forward to crack an inch above the ears of the lead mules. They lunged forward into the traces and the wagon bounced and clattered out of the yard.

As they galloped in frantic convoy along the main access road towards the plantations they met the Zulu women with their children from the location streaming down towards the homestead, their soft voices calling greeting and speed to their men as they passed.

But Michael hardly heard them, he stood with his eyes fastened on the pillar of red flame and smoke that rose from the heart of Sean's trees.

'It is in the trees we planted two years ago.' Mbejane spoke beside him. 'But already it will be close upon the next block of older trees. We cannot hope to stop it there.'

'Where then?'

'This side there are more young trees and a wide road. We can try there.'

'What is your name?' Michael asked.

'Mbejane.'

'I am Michael. The Nkosi's nephew.'

'I know.' Mbejane nodded, then went on, 'Turn off where next the roads meet.'

They came to the cross-roads. In the sector ahead were the young trees – ten feet high, thick as a man's arm, massed dark leaves and interlacing branches. Far out beyond them in the tall mature wattle was the line of flame. Above it a towering wall of sparks and dark smoke, coming down swiftly on the wind. It would be upon them in less than an hour at its present rate of advance.

A fire like this would jump a thirty-foot road without checking – they must cut back into the young wattle and increase the gap to sixty feet at the least.

Michael swung the wagon off the road and hauled the mules to a halt. He jumped down to meet the other wagons as they came up.

'Go on for two hundred yards – then start your boys in

chopping out the wattle towards the fire – we've got to widen the road. I'll start my gang here,' he shouted at Van Wyk.

'Right.'

'Mr Broster – go on to the end of the block and start working back this way – cut the timber out another thirty feet.'

Without waiting to hear more, Broster drove on. These two men, twice Michael's age, conceded him the right of command without argument.

Snatching an axe from the nearest Zulu, Michael issued his orders as he ran to the young wattle. The men crowded after him and Michael selected a tree, took his stance and swung the axe in a low arc from the side. The tree quivered and rained loose leaves upon him at the blow. Smoothly he reversed his grip on the shaft of the axe and swung again from the opposite side. The blade sliced through the soft wood, the tree sagged wearily away from him and groaned as it subsided. He stepped past it to the next. Around him the Zulus spread out along the road and the night rang with the beat of their axes.

Four times during the next half-hour fresh wagons galloped in, wagons loaded with men and driven by Sean's neighbours, until almost three hundred men were using the axe on Sean's lovingly planted and tenderly nursed wattle.

Shoulder to shoulder, chopping in wordless frenzy, trampling the fallen saplings as they moved forward.

Once a man yelled in pain and Michael looked up to see two Zulus dragging another back to the road with his leg half severed by the slip of a careless axe. Dark blood in the moonlight.

One of the neighbours hurried to tend the injured man and Michael turned back to the destruction of the wattle.

Swing, change hands and swing again, the solid *thunk!* and the tree swaying. Shove it over and struggle through the fallen tangle of branches to the next. Swing again, and smell the sweet bleeding sap – feel the ache in the shoulders and the sting of sweat in the burst blishers of the palms.

Then suddenly the other smell, acrid on the wind. Smoke. Michael paused and looked up. The men on each side of him stopped work also and the firelight danced on their naked, sweat-greased bodies as they leaned on their axes and watched it come.

On a front four hundred yards wide, ponderously it rolled down towards them. Not with the explosive white heat of a burning pine forest, but in the awful grandeur of orange and dark red, billowing smoke and torrential sparks.

Gradually the sound of axes died along the line as men stopped and watched this appalling thing come down towards them. It lit their faces clearly, revealing the awe that was on all of them. They could feel the heat now, great gusts of it that shrivelled the tender growth ahead of the flames – and suddenly a freak of the wind sent a bank of black smoke billowing down over the motionless line of men and blotted them out from each other. It cleared as swiftly as it came, and left them coughing and gasping.

'Back! Get back to the road!' yelled Michael and the cry was taken up and thrown along the line. They waded back through the morass of waist-high vegetation and assembled in small subdued groups along the road, standing together helplessly with the axes idle in their hands, fearful in the face of that line of flame and smoke.

'Cut branches to beat with!' Michael whipped their apathy. 'String out along the edge.' He hurried along the road, pushing them back into line, bullying them, cursing in his own fear. 'Come on, the flames will drop when they reach the fallen trees. Cover your faces – use your shirts. Hey, you – don't just stand there.'

With renewed determination each man armed himself with a green branch, and they re-formed along the road.

Quietly they stood in the daylight glare of the flames – black faces impassive, white ones flushed with heat and working anxiously.

'Do you think we'll be able to . . .' Michael started as he reached Ken Broster, and then he stopped. The question he had been about to ask had no answer. Instead he said, 'We've lost three thousand acres already – but if it gets away from us here!'

Involuntarily both of them glanced back at the tall mature wattle behind them.

'We'll hold it here,' Broster stated with a certainty he did not feel.

'I hope you're right,' whispered Michael, then suddenly Broster shouted:

'Oh Christ – look!'

For a moment Michael was blinded by the red glare and unsighted by the smoke. The fire burned unevenly. In places it had driven forward in great wedge-shaped salients of flame and left behind bays of standing wattle that were withering and browning in the heat.

From out of one of these bays, into the springy matt of fallen and trampled branches staggered a man.

'Who the hell . . . ' started Michael. The man was unrecognizable. His shirt ripped to shreds by branches that had also scourged his face into a bloody mask. He floundered forward towards the road, two slack exhausted paces before he fell and disappeared under the leaves.

'The Nkosana.' Mbejane's voice boomed above the thunder of the flames.

'Dirk! It's Dirk Courtney!' Michael started forward.

The heat was painful in Michael's face. How much more intense must it be out there where Dirk was lying. As if they knew their prey was helpless the flames raced forward eagerly, triumphantly to consume him. Whoever went in to rob them would meet the full fury of their advance.

Michael plunged into the brush and ploughed his way towards where Dirk thrashed feebly, almost encircled by the deadly embrace of the flames – and the heat reached out ahead of the flames to welcome him. Mbejane ran beside him.

'Go back,' shouted Mbejane. 'It needs only one of us.' But Michael did not answer him and they crashed side by side through the brush, racing the fire with Dirk as the prize.

Mbejane reached him first and lifting him, turned back for the road. He took one step before he fell and rose again unsteadily from the mass of branches. Even his vast strength was insufficient in this vacuum of heat. His mouth was open, a pink cave in the glistening black oval of his face, wide open and his chest heaved strenuously as he hunted air, but instead sucked the scalding heat into his throat.

Michael threw himself forward against the heat to reach him. It was almost a solid thing, a barrier of red shimmering glare. Michael could feel it swelling and tightening the skin of his face and drying the moisture from his eyeballs.

'I'll take his legs,' he grunted and reached for Dirk. A patch of brown appeared miraculously on the sleeve of his shirt – singed by the flames as though it had been carelessly ironed. Beneath it the heat sunk a barb of agony into his flesh.

Half a dozen paces together with Dirk between them before

Michael tripped and fell, dragging Mbejane down with him. They were a long time rising, all movement slowing down – but when they did they were surrounded.

Two prongs of flame had reached the area of fallen saplings on either side of them. This had slowed them and diminished their fury. But a chance gust of the wind and fuel had forced them to curl inwards on each other, spreading horns of fire ahead of Michael and Mbejane and leaving them enclosed by a dancing, leaping palisade of flame.

'Go through!' croaked Michael, his throat scalded and swollen. 'We must break through.'

And they churned their way towards the encircling wall. Through it, vague and unreal, he could see men beating at the flames – distorted phantoms trying desperately to open a path for them. Mbejane wore only a loin cloth, no breeches, coat nor boots to protect him, as Michael had. He was very near the limit of his strength.

Now looking at Michael across the body of the boy they carried, Mbejane saw a curious thing. Michael's hair crinkled slowly and then began to smoke – smouldering like an old sack.

Michael screamed at the agony of it, a hideous sound that shrilled above the roar and crackle of the flames. But agony was the key that unlocked the last storehouse of his strength. As though it were a rag doll he snatched Dirk's body from Mbejane's grasp and lifting it with both hands on to his shoulders he charged into the fire.

The flames reached to his waist, clawing greedily at him as he ran and the smoke eddied and swirled about him – but he was through.

'Help Mbejane!' he shouted at the Zulu beaters and then he was out on to the road. He dropped Dirk and beat at his clothing with his bare hands. His boots were charred and his clothing was alight in a dozen places. He fell and rolled wildly in the dusty road to smother it.

Two Zulus went in to help Mbejane. Two nameless blackmen, two labourers – men of no distinction. Neither of them wore boots. Both of them reached Mbejane as he tottered weakly towards them. One on each side they urged him back towards the road.

At this moment Michael rolled to his knees in the road and

despite his own agony watched them with a sickened fascination.

Leading Mbejane between them as though he were a blind man, they stumbled barefooted into the flames and stirred up a great cloud of sparks around them. Then the smoke rolled down over them and they were gone.

'Mbejane!' croaked Michael, and pushed himself to his feet to go to him – then:

'Oh God – Oh, thank God.' Mbejane and one of the Zulus stumbled out of the smoke into the arms of the men who waited for them.

No one went back for the other Zulu. No one went back for him until two hours later when the dawn had broken and the fire had been stopped at the road and the mature wattle had been saved. Then Ken Broster led a small party gingerly into the wilderness of still smouldering ash, into the black desert. They found him on his face. Those parts of him that had lain against the earth were still recognizable as belonging to a human being.

68

'Ladyburg in twenty minutes, Mr Courtney.' The conductor put his head round the door of the compartment.

'Thanks, Jack.' Sean looked up from his book.

'I see from this morning's paper that you're engaged to be married?'

'That's right.'

'Well, then, break clean, no hitting low – let's have a good clean fight and good luck to both of you.' Sean grinned and the man went down the passage. Sean packed his book into the briefcase, stood up and followed him.

On the balcony of the coach he stopped and lit a cheroot, then he leaned on the railings and looked out across the veld for his first glimpse of Lion Kop. This had become a ritual whenever he returned to Ladyburg.

This morning he was as happily content as he had ever been in his life. Last night, after conferring with Ma and Pa Goldberg, Ruth had set the wedding date for March next year. By then Sean would have completed his first cutting of bark, and they would take a month to honeymoon in the Cape.

Now, at last, I have everything a man could reasonably ask for, he thought, and smiled and in that moment he saw the smoke. He straightened up and flicked the cheroot away.

The train snaked up towards the rim of the escarpment, slowing as the gradient changed beneath it. It reached the crest and the whole vista of the Ladyburg valley opened below it. Sean saw the great irregular blot upon his trees, with the thin grey streams of smoke drifting wearily away across the hills.

He opened the balcony gate and jumped down from the train. He hit and slid and rolled down the gravel embankment. The skin was scraped from his knees and the palms of his hands. Then he was on his feet, running.

Along the road where the fire had been stopped men waited.

Sitting quietly or sprawled in exhausted sleep, all of them were coated with ash and soot. Their eyes were smoke-inflamed and their bodies ached with fatigue. But they waited while the black acres smouldered and smoked sullenly – for if the wind came up again it would fan the ashes to life.

Ken Broster lifted his head from his arm, then sat up quickly. 'Sean's here!' he said. The men around him stirred and then stood up slowly. They watched Sean approaching, he came with the sloppy, blundering legs of a man who has run five miles.

Sean stopped a little way off and his breathing wheezed and heaved in his throat.

'How? How did it happen?'

'We don't know, Sean.' In sympathy Ken Broster dropped his eyes from Sean's face. You do not stare at a man in anguish. Sean leaned against one of the wagons. He could not bring himself to look again at the vast expanse of smouldering desert with the skeletons of the tree-trunks standing out of it like the twisted and blackened fingers of an arthritic hand.

'One of your men was killed,' Ken told him softly. 'One of your Zulus.' He hesitated – then went on firmly. 'Others were hurt, badly burned.'

Sean made no reply, he did not seem to understand the words.

'Your nephew and your boy – Dirkie.' Still Sean stared at him dully.

'Mbejane also.' This time Sean seemed to cringe away from him.

'I sent them down to the homestead – the doctor's there.'

Still no reply from Sean, but now he wiped the palm of his hand across his mouth and eyes.

'Mike and Dirk aren't too bad, skin burns – but Mbejane's feet are in a hell of a mess.' Ken Broster spoke quickly now. 'Young Dirk got trapped in front of the flames. Mike and Mbejane went to get him . . . surrounded . . . down . . . picked him up . . . tried to help . . . useless . . . badly burned . . . meat off his feet . . .

To Sean the words were disjointed, meaningless. He leaned against the wagon. There was looseness in him, a lack of will. *It was too much. Let it go. Let it all go.*

'Sean, are you all right?' Broster's hands on his shoulders. He straightened up and looked around him again.

'I must go to them. Lend me a horse.'

'You go ahead, Sean. We'll stay on here and watch it for you.

Don't worry about it, we'll make bloody sure she doesn't start again.'

'Thank you, Ken.' Then he looked around the circle of anxious compassionate faces. 'Thank you,' he said again.

Sean rode slowly into the stable yard on Lion Kop. There were many carriages and servants, black women and children, but a hush came upon them when they recognized him. Surrounded by women, a crude litter lay near the far wall of the yard and Sean walked across to it.

'I see you, Mbejane.'

'Nkosi.' Mbejane's eyelashes were burned away giving his face a bland and slightly puzzled expression. His hands and his feet were bound loosely in bundles of crisp white bandages through which ointment had soaked in yellow patches. Sean squatted behind him. He could not speak. He reached out almost hesitantly and touched Mbejane's shoulder.

'Is it bad?' he asked then.

'No, Nkosi. It is not too bad. My wives have come for me. I will return when I am ready.'

They spoke together a little while, and Mbejane told him of Dirk and how Michael had come. Then he murmured, 'This woman is the wife of the one who died.'

Sean noticed her for the first time. She sat alone in the crowded yard, on a blanket against the wall. A child stood beside her; leaning forward, naked, holding one of her fat, black breasts with both hands as he fed from it. She sat impassively with her legs folded under her, a cloak of ochre-dyed leather draped loosely over her shoulders, but open at the front for the child. Sean moved across to her. The child watched him with large dark eyes, but without removing the nipple from his mouth and the corners of his mouth were wet with spilled milk.

'He was a man,' Sean greeted the woman.

She inclined her head gravely. 'He was a man!' she agreed.

'Where will you go?' Sean asked.

'To my father's kraal.' The high headdress of red clay enhanced the quiet dignity of her reply.

'Select twenty head of cattle from my herds to take with you.'

'*Ngi Yabonga* – I praise you, Nkosi.'

'Go in peace.'

'Stay in peace.' She stood, lifted the child on to her hip and walked slowly from the yard without looking back.

'I will go now, Nkosi.' Mbejane spoke from the litter. The colour of his skin was grey with pain. 'And when I return we will plant again. It was only a small fire.'

'It was only a small fire.' Sean nodded. 'Go in peace, my friend. Drink much beer and grow fat. I will visit you.'

Mbejane chuckled softly and signalled his wives to their places around the litter. They lifted him, young women strong from their work in the fields.

'Stay in peace, Nkosi.' Mbejane lay back painfully upon the soft mattress of fur, and they carried him out of the yard. They began to sing as they passed the gates, moving in double file on each side of the litter, stately and tall, their naked backs glistening with oil, rumps swaying together beneath the brief loin cloths, and their voices joined high and proud in the ancient song of welcome to the warrior returned from battle.

Gathered on the stoep of Lion Kop were many of his neighbours and their wives, come with sympathy and offers of assistance.

Ada was waiting for him as Sean climbed the steps.

'Dirk?' he asked.

'He is well, asleep now. Laudanum.'

'Michael?'

'He is waiting for you. He refused the drug. I've put him in your room.'

On his way down the passage Sean stopped at Dirk's room and looked in. Dirk lay on his back with bandaged hands folded across his chest. His face was swollen and laced with ugly red lines where the wattle branches had clawed him. On the chair beside his bed Mary sat in patient vigil. She looked at Sean and made to rise. Sean shook his head.

'No. I will come back when he is awake.' He went on down the passage to his own room.

Three of Ada's girls hovered and chirruped about Michael's bed like birds whose nests are endangered. They saw him and stopped their chatter. All Ada's girls held Sean in unexplained awe.

'Oh, Mr Courtney. His poor hands . . .' one little lass began, then blushed crimson, dropped a hurried curtsy and escaped from the room. The others followed quickly.

Sean moved across to the bed.

'Hello, Mike.' His voice was gruff, as he saw the blister that hung like a pale grape on Michael's cheek.

'Hello, Uncle Sean.' The raw places of his face and lips were smeared with yellow ointment. Sean sat down gingerly on the edge of the bed.

'Thank you, Michael,' he said.

69

Ronny Pye called early the following morning. With him came Dennis Petersen and both of them were wearing suits.

'Very fancy turn-out,' Sean greeted them. 'Business or social?'

'Well, you might say a little of each.' Ronny paused at the top of the veranda steps. 'May we come in?'

Sean led them to the end of the veranda, and they seated themselves before anyone spoke again.

'I heard about the fire, Sean. Terrible business. I heard there was a native killed and both Dirk and Michael were hurt. Terrible business.' Ronny shook his head in sympathy.

'Did you also hear that I lost four thousand acres of timber?' Sean inquired politely.

'Heard that also.' Ronny nodded solemnly. 'Terrible business.'

Ronny and Dennis glanced at each other furtively, and then looked down at their hands.

'Very nasty,' Ronny repeated and a silence fell upon them.

'Anything else worrying you?' Sean inquired politely.

'Well, now that you've brought it up –' Ronny reached inside his jacket and withdrew a long folded document tied with a red ribbon. 'Mind you, we don't have to discuss it today. Leave it until you feel better?'

'Talk!' Sean grunted.

'Clause eight.' Ronny spread the document between the coffee-cups on the table. 'In the event of the said security, namely, a certain block of wattle known as No. 2 block of Lion Kop Estates in extent approximately . . . ' Ronny hesitated. 'Guess there's no sense in me reading it all. You know what it says. That wattle was part of the collateral for the loan.'

'How long will you give me to raise the money?' Sean asked.

'Well, Sean, you understand there is no period of grace allowed in the contract. Seems to me you'll have to put it up right away.'

'I want a month,' Sean told him.

'A month!' Ronny was shocked and hurt by the request. 'See here now, Sean. I don't honestly – I mean, surely you've got the money. I mean why do you need a month. Just let us have your cheque.'

'You know damned well I haven't got it.'

'Seems to me –' Ronny offered delicately. 'Seems to me if you haven't got it now, there's not much chance you'll have it in a month. No offence, Sean, but we have to look at this thing from a business angle. If you follow me.'

'I follow you.' Sean nodded. 'And I want a month.'

'Give it to him,' blurted Dennis Petersen, his first contribution, and Ronny turned on him instantly with his face twisting into a snarl. The struggle he had within himself to smooth out his features and to restore his voice to its level and reasonable tone lasted fully five seconds.

'Well now, Dennis,' he murmured. 'That's an unusual way to look at it. Seems to me –'

'I spoke to Audrey before we came up here. I promised her . . . Anyway, we both agreed.' Dennis was staring out across the valley, unable to meet his partner's eyes.

Suddenly Ronny Pye chuckled. Yes, by God! It would be even better that way – watching this big arrogant bastard crawling round begging, with his hat in his hands. Sean would go to Jackson first and Ronny had telegraphed Jackson the previous afternoon. He had also telegraphed Nichols at the Standard Bank. By now the message would be spreading swiftly along the network of South African banking channels. Sean Courtney would find it difficult to borrow the price of a meal.

'All right then, Sean. As a special concession you can have a month.' Then all the laughter was gone and he leaned forward in his chair. 'You've got exactly thirty days. Then, by Christ, I am going to sell out under you.'

After they were gone Sean sat alone on the wide veranda. The sunlight on the hills was bright and hot, but in the shade it was cool. He heard Ada's girls chattering somewhere in the house, then one of them giggled shrilly. The sound irritated Sean, his frown deepened and he drew a rumpled envelope from his jacket pocket and smoothed it out on the arm of his chair. Awhile he sat in thought nibbling the stub of a pencil.

Then he wrote: 'Jackson. Natal Wattle'. And again, 'Standard Bank'. Then 'Ben Goldberg'. He paused and considered this last name on his list. Then he grunted aloud and scratched it out with two hard strokes of the pencil. Not from the Goldbergs. Leave them out of this.

He wrote again quickly, scrawling a single word – 'Candy' and below it 'Tim Curtis'.

That was all. John Acheson was in England. It would take two months to receive a reply from him.

That was all. He sighed softly and folded the envelope into his pocket. Then he lit a cheroot, sank down in the chair and placed his feet on the low veranda wall in front of him. I'll leave on tomorrow morning's train, he thought.

The windows behind him were open. Lying beyond them in the bedroom Michael Courtney had heard every word of their conversation. Now he stood up painfully from the bed and began to dress. He went out the back way and nobody saw him leave. His mare was in the stables, and on a borrowed saddle he rode back to Theuniskraal.

Anna saw him coming and ran out into the yard to meet him. 'Michael! Oh, Michael. Thank God you are safe. We heard . . . ' Then she saw his face and the raw, swollen burns on it and she froze. Michael dismounted slowly and one of the grooms led his horse away.

'Michael, darling. Your poor face.' And she embraced him quickly.

'It's nothing, Mother.'

'Nothing!' She pulled away from him, lips drawn into a tight, hard line. 'You run away in the middle of the night to that . . . that . . . Then you come home days later with your face and your hands in a terrible mess – is that nothing!'

'I'm sorry, Mother. Gran'ma looked after me.'

'You knew I'd be half-dead with worry, sitting here imagining all sorts of things. You didn't send word to me, you just let me . . . '

'You could have come to Lion Kop,' he said softly.

'To the home of that monster? Never!' And Michael looked away from her.

'Where's Father?'

'In his study, as usual. Oh, darling, you don't know how I've missed you. Tell me you love me, Michael.'

'I love you,' he repeated automatically and the sensation of suffocating was on him again. 'I must see Dad. It's very urgent.'

'You've just arrived. Let me fix something to eat – let me see to your poor face.'

'I have to see Dad now. I'm sorry.' And he went past her towards the house.

Garry was sitting at his desk when Michael walked into the study. Michael hated this room. He hated the high smoke-stained ceiling, the oppressive darkness of the panelled walls, the massive hunting trophies, he hated even the carpets and the smell of old paper and dust. From this room had issued the decrees and the pronouncements which had restricted and predetermined his life. This room was the symbol of everything from which he wished to escape. Now he glared around it definatly, as though it were a living thing – I've come back to extract from you what you owe me, he thought, you've had value from me, now pay me back!

'Michael!' Garrick's boot scraped on the wooden floor as he stood to greet him, and Michael winced at the sound.

'Hello, Dad.'

'Your mother and I, we have been so worried. Why didn't you send word to us?' The hurt was there in Garrick's voice. Michael opened his mouth to apologize in automatic guilt, but the words came out differently from the way he had intended.

'I was busy. I didn't have a chance.'

'Sit down, my boy.' Garrick gestured to one of the polished leather arm-chairs. He removed the metal-framed spectacles from his nose, but he did not look at Michael's injured face again. He would not think about Sean and Michael together.

'I'm glad you've come back. I was just working on the opening chapters of my new book. It's a history of our family from the time of your great-great-grandfather's arrival at the Cape. I'd very much like your opinion. I'd value it immensely. The considered opinion of a graduate from the South African College.'

The trap was closing. It was so obvious that Michael squirmed. He could almost feel the panelled walls moving in on him. He started to protest: 'Dad, I have to speak to you.' But already Garrick was adjusting his spectacles and shuffling through the papers on his desk, talking quickly.

'I think you'll like it. It should interest you.' Garrick glanced up and smiled at Michael with the eagerness of a child that brings a gift. 'Here we are. I'll start at the beginning. You must allow for it being the first rough draft. It's not polished yet.' And he began to read. At the end of each paragraph he searched for Michael's approval, smiling in anticipation of it. Until Michael could bear it no longer, until he shouted suddenly in the middle of a sentence.

'I want you to pay me out my share of Theuniskraal.'

There was a momentary break in Garrick's reading, just a flutter in his voice to acknowledge Michael's request and then he went on steadily, but his voice had lost its timbre and was now a lifeless monotone. He finished the paragraph, laid the sheet aside, removed his spectacles and placed them in their case. The lid of the case snapped shut against the tension of its spring and Garry lifted his head slowly.

'Why?'

'I need the money.'

'What for?'

'I need it.'

Garry stood up and moved across to the window. He stood before it with his hand clasped behind him. The green lawns flowed down to the fence that bounded the gardens, and upon them the poinsettia bushes were vivid patches of scarlet. Beyond, the land lifted into the first long roll, golden grass and scattered forest with the cattle feeding beneath and the massive silver and blue clouds piled above.

'It will rain tonight,' Garrick murmured, but Michael did not answer. 'We need it. Three weeks of dry, and the pasture is withering.' Still no reply and Garry returned to his desk.

'I hear there was a fire on Lion Kop last night.'

'There was.'

'They say that your uncle is finished. They say the fire finished him.'

'No!' Michael denied it quickly. 'That's not true.'

'Is that why you want the money, Michael?'

'Yes.'

'You want to give it to Sean?'

'I want to buy a share in Lion Kop Wattle. I don't want to give anything – it will be a business offer.'

838

'And what about Theuniskraal – it's your home. You were born here.'

'Please, Dad. I've made up my mind.'

'Did Sean suggest this?'

'He did not. He knows nothing about it.'

'It's your idea then. You thought it up all on your own. You're going to sell out your own parents for him. My God, what sort of hold has he over you that you would do that for him.'

Flushing a dusty brick colour, Michael kicked back his chair and jumped to his feet.

'You make it sound like treachery.'

'That's exactly what it is!' shouted Garrick. 'It's Judas's work. Your mother and I – we raised you with everything. We scraped to send you to University, we built our whole lives around you. We worked for the day you would return here to Theuniskraal and . . . ' He stopped, panting, and wiped from his chin the bubble of saliva that had burst through his lips. 'Instead you ran off to join that . . . that swine. How do you think we liked that? Don't you think it nearly broke our hearts? Of all people you had to go to him! And now, now you want half of Theuniskraal to take him as a gift – to buy his . . . '

'Stop that!' Michael warned him sharply. 'And before you go on remember where I got my half of Theuniskraal. Remember who made the original gift.' He picked up his hat and riding-crop and strode towards the door.

'Michael.' The terrible appeal in Garry's voice checked him.

'What is it?'

'Your share – it isn't very much. I hadn't told you before, but there was a time – when you were very young. The rinderpest. I had to –' He couldn't go on.

'What are you trying to tell me?'

'Sit down, Michael. Sit down and I'll show you.' Reluctantly, afraid of what he was about to hear, Michael returned and stood beside his chair.

Garry selected a key from the bunch on his watch-chain and opened the top drawer of his desk. He selected a rolled document, slipped it from its retaining ribbon and handed it without speaking to his son.

Michael spread it and read the words upon the cover.

'Deed of Mortgage'.

With a sliding sensation in his stomach, he turned the page.

He did not read it all. Words and groups of words stood out in bolder print, and they were sufficient:

'The Ladyburg Trust & Banking Co.' . . . 'A certain piece of land in extent approx. 25,000 morgen situate in the district of Ladyburg, Magisterial Division of Pietermaritzburg, known as the farm Theuniskraal' . . . 'All constructions, erections and improvements thereon . . . Plus interest at eight and one half per cent.'

'I see.' Michael handed the document back to his father and stood up.

'Where are you going?'

'Back to Lion Kop.'

'No!' Garry whispered. 'No, Michael. Please, my son. No – O God – No!' Michael left the room and closed the door softly behind him.

When Anna came into the room Garry was sitting behind the desk, sitting quietly with his shoulders slumped forward.

'You let him go!' she hissed. Garry did not move, he did not seem to hear.

'He's gone. Gone to your brother – and you let him.' Her voice was very low, but now it rose harshly and she shrieked at him. 'You useless drunken animal. Sitting here playing with your little books. You were not man enough to breed him – your brother had to do that for you! And you are not man enough to keep him – again your brother! You let him go. You've taken my son from me.'

Garry sat unmoving. He saw nothing. He heard nothing. In his head was a soft, misty greyness, and the mist blotted out all sight and sound. It was warm in the mist – warm and safe. No one could reach him here for it wrapped and protected him. He was safe.

'This is all you are good for.' Anna snatched a handful of the manuscript sheets from the desk in front of him. 'Your little pieces of paper. Your dreams and stories of other men – real men.'

She ripped the pages through and through again, then flung them at him. The pieces fluttered and swirled, then settled like dead leaves on his shoulders and in his hair. He did not move. Panting in her grief and anger, she took up what remained of the manuscript and shredded that also, scattering the tiny white scraps about the room.

70

The two of them stood together on the station platform. They did not speak. Most of the previous day and night had been spent talking and now there was nothing more to say. They stood together in quiet companionship – and a stranger looking at them would have known immediately they were father and son. Though Michael was not as tall, and he was lean beside Sean's bulk – yet the tone of the skin and the colour of the hair were the same. Both had the big Courtney nose and their mouths were wide and full-lipped.

'I'll telegraph as soon as I hit gold.' Sean had explained to Michael in detail the financial structure of Lion Kop. He had told him how he intended to find the money which would keep it from collapsing.

'I'll hold this end up.' Michael was to begin cutting the wattle which had survived the fire. They had ridden the previous afternoon through the plantations and marked the blocks which were ripe for the axe. 'Good luck, Uncle Sean.'

'Since we are working together now, Mike, I suggest you drop the "Uncle". It's too clumsy for everyday use.'

Michael grinned. 'Good luck, Sean.'

'Thanks, Mike.' They clasped hands, gripping hard, then Sean climbed up into the coach.

Jackson was friendly but firm and Nichols at the Standard Bank was very polite and full of sympathy. Sean caught the north-bound train for Johannesburg to fire his last two bullets.

'Colonel Courtney. How good to see you.' The reception clerk at Candy's Hotel came round from behind his desk to greet Sean. 'We were only talking about you last week. Welcome back to Johannesburg.'

'Hello, Frank. Putting on a little weight there, aren't you?' Sean prodded his waistcoat and the man chuckled. 'Tell me, Frank, is Candy . . . is Mrs Rautenbach in?'

'Ah! There've been some changes since you left, sir.' The clerk grinned with just a trace of malice. 'It's not Mrs Rautenbach any longer. No, sir. Mrs Heyns – Mrs Jock Heyns now!'

'Good God! She married Jock!'

'That she did. Two weeks ago – biggest wedding in Jo'burg since the war. Two thousand guests.'

'Where is she now?'

'On the water. Off to England and the Continent for six months' honeymoon.'

'I hope she'll be happy,' Sean murmured softly, remembering the loneliness he had seen in her eyes when he left.

'With all Mr Heyns's money? How can she be otherwise?' the clerk asked in genuine surprise.

'Will you be staying, Colonel?'

'If you have a room.'

'We always have a room for our friends. How long, sir?'

'Two days, Frank.'

Tim Curtis was Chief Engineer on the City Deep. When Sean spoke to him about a loan he laughed.

'Christ! Sean, I only work there – I don't own the bloody mine.'

Sean had dinner with him and his bride of two years' standing. At their urging Sean examined their newborn infant and secretly decided that it looked like an unweaned bulldog.

Extending his stay in Johannesburg, Sean visited the banks. He had dealt with most of them long ago, but the personnel had changed, so he was puzzled that the manager of each institution seemed to have heard of him.

'Colonel Courtney. Now would you be Colonel Sean Courtney of Lion Kop Wattle Estates down in Natal?' And when he nodded he saw the shutters come down in their eyes, like windows barred by a prudent householder against burglars.

On the eighth night he ordered liquor to be sent to his suite – two full bottles of brandy. He drank steadily and desperately. The brandy would not quieten the violent struggles of his brain, but seemed to goad it, distorting his problems and deepening his melancholia.

He lay alone until the dawn paled out the yellow gaslight of the lamps. The brandy hummed giddily in his head and he longed for peace – the peace he had found only in the immense silence and space of the veld. Suddenly a picture formed in his mind of a lonely grave below a little hill. He heard the wind moan over it and saw the brown grass sway. That was peace.

He sat up unsteadily.

'Saul,' he said, and the sadness was heavy on him for the pilgrimage he had promised himself and had not made.

'It is finished here. I'll go now,' and he stood up. The giddiness caught him and he clutched at the head-rail of the bed to steady himself.

He recognized the kopje from four miles off. Into his memory its shape was indelibly etched; the symmetrical slope of the sides cobbled with boulders that glinted dully in the sunshine like the scales of a reptile, the flattened summit ringed by a bolder stratum of rock, the high altar on which the sacrifice to greed and stupidity had been made.

Closer he could discern the aloe plants upon the slopes, fleshy leaves spiked like crowns and jewelled with scarlet blooms. On the plain below the kopje, in the short brown grass, stood a long line of white specks. Sean rode towards them and as he approached each speck evolved into a cairn of whitewashed stones and on each stood a metal cross.

Stiff from the long day in the saddle Sean dismounted slowly. He hobbled the horses, dropped saddle and pack from their backs and turned them loose to feed. He stood alone and lit a cheroot, suddenly reluctant to approach the line of graves.

The silence of the empty land settled gently upon him, a silence not broken but somehow heightened by the sound of the wind across the plain. The harsh tearing as his mount cropped at the dry brown grass seemed sacrilegious in this place, but it roused Sean from his thoughts. He walked towards the double line of graves and stood before one of them. Stamped crudely into the metal of the cross the words 'Here lies a brave burgher'.

He moved along the line of crosses and on each he read those same words. On some of them the printing was irregular, on one the 'r' in burgher had been replaced by a 'g'. Sean stopped and glared at it, hating the man who in his haste and unconcern had made the epitaph an insult.

'I'm sorry.' He spoke aloud, apologizing to the man who lay beneath it. Then he was embarrassed, angry at himself for the weakness. Only a madman speaks aloud to the dead. He strode away towards the second row of crosses.

'Leading Seaman W. Carter, R.N.' The fat one.

'Corporal Henderson C.F.S.' Twice in his chest and another in the belly.

He walked along the line and read their names. Some were just names, others he saw instantly and vividly. He saw them laughing, or frightened, saw the way they rode, remembered the sound of their voices. This one still owed him a guinea, he remembered the bet.

'Keep it.' He spoke and immediately checked himself again.

Slowly he went on to the end of the line, his momentum running down as he approached the grave that stood separate from the others – the way he had ordered it.

He read the inscription. Then he squatted down comfortably on his haunches beside it and stayed there until the sun settled and the wind turned cold and plaintive. Only then he went to his saddle and loosened the blanket-roll. There was no firewood and he slept fitfully in the cold of the night and the icier cold of his thoughts.

In the morning he went back to Saul's grave. For the first time he noticed that grass was growing up between the stones of the cairn and that the cross sagged a little to one side. He shrugged off his coat and went down on his knees, working like a gardener over the grave, weeding out the grass with his hunting knife, making certain the roots were removed. Then he went to the head and lifted the rocks away from around the cross. He tore the cross from the ground and re-dug the hole for it, setting it up again carefully, plugging the base with pebbles and earth and at last packing the whitewashed rocks firmly around it once more.

He stood back, brushed earth and flakes of whitewash from his hands and surveyed his handiwork. It still was not right, there was something missing. He thought about it, frowning heavily until he found the answer.

'Flowers,' he grunted and lifted his head towards the aloes on the kopje above him. He set off up the slope, picking his way through the litter of boulders towards the summit. His knife slipped easily through the soft thick stems and the juice oozed heavily from the wounds. With an armful he started back down the slope. Out to one side a patch of colour caught his eye, a sprinkling of pink and white among the boulders. He detoured towards it. Hottentot Daisies, each one a perfect trumpet with

845

a pink throat and a fragile yellow tongue. Delighted with his find, Sean laid aside his burden of aloe blooms and went in amongst them. Stooping like a reaper he worked through them towards the lip of a narrow ravine, gathering the flowers into posies and binding the stems together with grass. Finally, he reached the ravine and straightened up to rest his aching back.

The ravine was narrow, he could have jumped across it with little effort – but it was deep. He peered down into it without much interest. The cleft was floored with rainwashed sand, and his interest quickened as he made out the half-buried bones of a large animal. But what made him climb down into the ravine was not the bones, but the bulky leather object entangled with them.

Sliding on his backside the last few feet of the descent he reached the bottom, and examined his find. A leather mule-pack, double pouches, and the buckles of the harness almost rusted away. He tugged the whole lot loose from the sand and was surprised at the weight of it.

The leather was dry and brittle, faded almost white with exposure and the locks of the pouches were rusted solid. With his knife he slit the flap of one pouch and out of it cascaded a stream of sovereigns. They fell into the sand, clinking upon each other in a heap that glittered with merry golden smiles.

Sean stared at them in disbelief. He dropped the pack and squatted on his haunches over the pile. Timidly he picked up one of the discs and examined the portrait of the old President, before lifting the coin to his mouth and biting down upon it. His teeth sank into the soft metal and he removed it from his mouth.

'Well, damn me sideways,' he invited, and he laughed out loud. Rocking back on his haunches and lifting his face to the sky he roared out his jubilation and his relief. It went on and on until his laughter dried suddenly, and he sobered.

Cupping a double handful of the gold he asked it:

'Now, where the hell did you come from?' And his answer was in the grim face embossed upon each coin. Boer Gold.

'And who do you belong to?'

The answer was the same, and he let the coins trickle through his fingers. Boer Gold.

'The hell it is!' he growled angrily. 'Starting this minute it's Courtney Gold.' And he began to count it.

As his fingers worked so did his brain. He prepared his case against his own conscience, they owed him the balance outstanding on a train of wagons filled with ivory, they owed him his deposits in the Volkskaas Bank. They owed him for a shrapnel wound in the leg and a bullet in the belly, they owed him for three years of hardship and danger, and they owed him for a friend. As he stacked the sovereigns into piles of twenty he considered his case, found it good and proven, justified it and gave judgement in his own favour.

'I find for the appellant,' he announced, and concentrated his whole attention on the counting. An hour and a half later he reached the total.

There was a huge pile of coins upon the flat rock he had used as a desk. He lit a cheroot and the smoke he drew into his lungs made him lightheaded. His conscience had surrendered unconditionally and in its place was a sense of well-being. All the more intense for the period of depression through which he had come.

'Sean Courtney accepts from the Government of the one-time Republic of the Transvaal an amount of twenty-nine thousand, two hundred pounds, in full discharge of all debts and claims.' He chuckled again and began shovelling the gold back into the leather pouches.

With the heavy pack slung over his shoulders and with his arms full of wild flowers, Sean went down the kopje. He saddled his horse and loaded the pack on to his mule before he went to pile the flowers on Saul's grave. They made a brave show of colour against the brown grass.

He lingered another hour, fussing over his floral arrangements and resisting the temptation to thank Saul. For now he had decided the gold was not a gift from the Republican Government – but from Saul Friedman. This made it even easier to accept.

At last he mounted and rode away. As the man and his horses dwindled into insignificance on the great brown plain, a dust devil came dancing up from the south. A tall, spinning column of heated air and dust and fragments of dry grass, it weaved and swayed towards the graveyard below the kopje. For a time it seemed as though it would pass wide of it, but suddenly it changed direction and dashed down upon the double row of crosses. It snatched up the flowers on Saul's grave, lifted them, ripped their petals and scattered them widely across the plain.

847

72

With Michael beside him lugging the carpet-bag which was the heaviest item of luggage, Sean left the buggy and crossed the side-walk into the offices of the Ladyburg Banking & Trust Co.

'Oh! Colonel Courtney,' the young lady at the reception desk enthused. 'I'll tell Mr Pye you are here.'

'Please don't bother. I'll carry the glad news myself.'

Ronny Pye looked up in alarm as the door of his office flew open and the two of them walked in.

'Good morning, Ronny,' Sean greeted him cheerfully. 'Have you bled any good stones today, or is it still too early?'

Guardedly Ronny murmured a reply and stood up.

Sean selected a cigar from the leather box on the desk and sniffed it.

'Not a bad line in horse-dung you've got here,' he remarked and bit the end off. 'Match please, Ronny, I'm a customer, where are your manners?'

Reluctantly, suspiciously, Ronny lit the cigar for him. Sean sat down and placed his feet on the desk with ankles neatly crossed.

'How much do I owe you?' he asked. The question heightened Ronny's suspicion and his eyes settled on the carpet-bag in Michael's hands.

'You mean altogether? Capital *and* interest?'

'Capital *and* interest,' Sean affirmed.

'Well, I'd have to work that out.'

'Give it to me in round figures.'

'Well, very roughly, you understand, it would be around – oh, I don't know – say . . . ' He paused. That carpet-bag looked confoundedly heavy. Its sides bulged and he could see the tension in Michael's arm muscles as he held it. 'Say, twenty-two thousand, eight hundred and sixteen pounds, fifteen shillings.' As he named the exact figure Ronny dropped his voice in veneration the way a primitive tribesman might invoke the name of his god.

Sean lowered his feet. Then he leant forward and swept the papers that covered the desk to one side.

'Very well. Pay the man, Michael.'

Solemnly Michael placed the bag in the cleared space. But when Sean winked at him his solemnity cracked and he grinned.

Making no attempt to hide his agitation, Ronny plunged both hands into the mouth of the bag and withdrew two pouches of unbleached canvas. He loosened the draw string of one and spilled gold on to his desk.

'Where did you get this?' he demanded angrily.

'At the end of the rainbow.'

'There's a fortune here,' Ronny protested, as he dipped into the carpet-bag again.

'A goodly amount, I'll admit.'

'But, but . . . ' Ronny was scratching in the pile of coins, hunting for the secret of their origin like a hen for a worm. However, Sean had spent a week in Johannesburg and another two days in Pietermaritzburg visiting every bank and exchanging small parcels of Kruger coin for Victorian and Portuguese, and the coin of half a dozen other States. For a minute Sean watched his efforts with a smile of happy contempt. Then he excused himself.

'We'll be getting on home now.' Sean placed an arm around Michael's shoulder and led him to the door.

'Deposit the balance to my account, there's a good fellow.'

Further protest stillborn on his lips, and despair mingled with frustration, Ronny Pye watched through the window as Lion Kop Wattle Estates climbed up into the buggy, settled its hat firmly, waved a whip in a courteous farewell and trotted sedately out of his clutches.

All that summer the hills of Lion Kop echoed to the thud of axes and the singing of hundreds of Zulus. At each tree toppled and fell in a froth of heaving branches, men with cane-knives moved forward to strip the rich bark and tie it in bundles. Every train that left for Pietermaritzburg towed truckloads of it to the extract plant.

Each long day together strengthened the bonds between Sean and Michael. They evolved a language of their own, notable only for its economy of words. Without lengthy discussion each took charge of a separate sphere of Lion Kop activity. Michael made himself responsible for the maintenance of equipment, the loading and dispatch, all the paperwork and the ordering of material. At first Sean surreptitiously checked his work, but when he found no fault in it he no longer bothered. They parted only at the end of each week; Sean to Pietermaritzburg for obvious reasons, and Michael to Theuniskraal in duty. Michael hated those returns home, he hated Anna's endless accusations of disloyalty and her occasional fits of weeping. But even worse was the silent reproach in Garry's face. Early each Monday morning, with the joy of a released convict he set off for Lion Kop and Sean's welcome:

'What about those bloody axe handles, Mike?'

Only in the evenings they talked freely sitting together on the stoep of the homestead. They spoke of money and war and politics and women and wattle – and they talked as equals, without reserve, as men who work together with a common purpose.

Dirk sat quietly in the shadows and listened to them. Fifteen years old, but Dirk had a capacity for hatred out of all proportion to his age, and he used it all on Michael. Sean's handling of Dirk was in no way different; his school attendance was still spasmodic, he trailed Sean about the plantations and received his full share of rough affection and even rougher discipline – yet he sensed in the relationship between Sean and Michael a terrible threat to his security. Merely by reason of age and experience he was excluded from the evening discussions on the stoep. His few contributions were received with indulgent attention, then the talk would be resumed as though he had not spoken. Dirk sat quietly planning in lurid detail his assassination of Michael. On Lion Kop that summer there were small thefts and unexplained acts of vandalism, all of which affected only Michael. His best riding-boots vanished, his single dress shirt was ripped down the back when he came to don it for the monthly dance at the schoolhouse, his pointer bitch whelped a litter of four puppies, which survived only a week before Michael found them dead in the straw of the barn.

Ada and her young ladies began preparing for the Christmas of 1904 in the middle of December. As their guests, Ruth and Storm came down from Pietermaritzburg on the twentieth and Sean's frequent absences from Lion Kop left a heavy burden of work on Michael. There was an air of mystery in the Protea Street cottage. Sean was strictly excluded from the long sessions in Ada's private rooms, where she and Ruth retired to plan the wedding dress, but this was not the only secret. There was something else, which was keeping all the young ladies in fits of suppressed giggles and excitement. With a little eavesdropping Sean gathered it was something to do with his Christmas present from Ruth. However, Sean had other worries, chief of which was maintaining his position in the fierce competition for Miss Storm Friedman's favours. This included a heavy expenditure on sweetmeats, which were delivered to Storm without Ruth's knowledge. The Shetland pony had been left in Pietermaritzburg and Sean was required to substitute at the cost of his dignity and grass stains on the knees of his breeches. As reward he was invited to take tea each afternoon with Storm and her dolls.

Favourite among all Storm's dolls was a female child with human hair and an insipid expression on its large china face. Storm wept with a broken heart when she found that china head shattered into many pieces. With Sean's help she buried it in the back yard and they stripped Ada's garden of flowers for the grave. Sullenly Dirk watched the funeral. Storm was now completely reconciled to her loss and so thoroughly enjoyed the ceremony that she insisted Sean exhume the body and start again. In all the doll was buried four times and Ada's garden looked as though a swarm of locusts had descended upon it.

73

Christmas Day started early for Sean. He and Michael supervised the slaughter of ten large oxen for the Zulu labour force, then distributed pay and gifts. To each man a khaki shirt and short pants, and for each of their wives a double handful of coloured beads. There was much singing and laughter. Mbejane, risen from his sickbed for the occasion, made a speech of high dramatic content. Unable to prance on his freshly healed legs, yet he shook his spears, postured and roared his questions at them.

'Has he beaten you?'

'*Ai-bho!*' They hurled the negative back at him.

'Has he fed you?'

'*Yhe-bho!*' explosive accent.

'Is there gold in your pockets?'

'*Yhe-bho!*'

'Is he our father?'

'He is our father!'

All to be construed not too literally, Sean grinned. Then he stepped forward to accept the large earthenpot of millet beer that Mbejane's senior wife presented to him. It was a matter of honour that this be emptied without removing it from the lips, a feat which Sean and then Michael both accomplished. Then they climbed up into the waiting buggy, Mbejane took the reins and with Dirk on the seat beside him drove them down to Ladyburg.

After the first flurry of greeting and good wishes, Ruth led Sean into the back yard followed by everyone else. There stood a large object covered by a tarpaulin which was ceremoniously removed and Sean gaped at what Ruth had given him.

Its paintwork burnished to a high gloss, metal parts and polished leather upholstery sparkling in the sun – stood a motor vehicle.

Stamped in the huge metal wheel hubs, and below the mascot on the radiator were the words 'Rolls-Royce'.

Sean had seen these fiendishly beautiful machines in Johannesburg, and now he was overcome by the feeling of unease they had given him then.

'My dear Ruth, I haven't the words to thank you.' He kissed her heartily to delay the moment when he must approach the monster.

'Do you really like it?'

'Like it? It's the most magnificent thing I have ever seen.' Over her shoulder Sean noticed with relief that Michael had taken over. As the only engineer present, he was seated behind the wheel and speaking authoritatively to the crowd about him.

'Get in!' Ruth ordered.

'Let me look at it first.' With Ruth on his arm, Sean circled the Rolls, never approaching closer than half a dozen paces. The great headlights glared at him malevolently and Sean averted his eyes. His unease was slowly becoming genuine fear as he realized that he was expected not only to ride in the thing, but to direct its course and speed.

Unable to delay longer, he approached and patted the bonnet.

'Hey there!' he told it grimly. With an unbroken animal you must establish mastery from the first contact.

'Get in!' Michael was still in charge and Sean obeyed, placing Ruth in the middle of the front seat and himself nearest the door. On Ruth's lap Storm bounded and squealed with excitement. The delay while Michael consulted the handbook at length did nothing for Sean's confidence.

'Ruth, don't you think it wise to leave Storm behind – just this first time?'

'Oh, she isn't any trouble.' Ruth regarded him quizzically, then smiled. 'It's really quite safe, darling.' Despite her assurance, Sean stiffened in terror when the motor finally roared into life; and he held that pose, staring fixedly ahead, during the whole of their triumphal progress through the streets of Ladyburg. Citizens and servants boiled from the houses along their route and lined the road to cheer in wonder and delight.

At last they were back in Protea Street and when Michael stopped outside the cottage Sean escaped from the vehicle like a man waking from a nightmare. He firmly vetoed the suggestion that the family motor to church, on the grounds that it was irreverent and in bad taste. The Reverend Smiley was flattered that Sean remained awake throughout his sermon, and judged by Sean's worried expression that at last he was in fear for his soul.

After church Michael went out to Theuniskraal to eat Christmas dinner with his parents, but returned early in the afternoon to begin Sean's instruction. The entire population of Ladyburg turned out to watch Sean and Michael circling the block at a walking pace. By early evening Michael decided that Sean was ready for a solo circuit and accordingly he disembarked.

Alone at the wheel, sweating nervously, Sean looked at the sea of expectant faces around him and saw Mbejane grinning hugely in the background.

'Mbejane!' he bellowed.

'Nkosi!'

'Come with me,' and Mbejane's grin dissolved. He backed away a little. It was unnatural that a vehicle should move of its own accord – and Mbejane wanted no part of it.

'Nkosi, there is much pain still in my legs.'

Among the crowd were many of the Zulu labourers from Lion Kop, who had come down from the hills when news of the miracle reached them. Now one of these laughed in such a manner as to cast doubt on Mbejane's courage. Mbejane drew himself to his full height and withered the man with his eyes, then he stalked proudly to the Rolls, sat on the seat beside Sean and folded his arms across his chest.

Sean drew a deep breath and gripped the steering-wheel with both hands, his eyes narrowed and he scowled ahead down the road.

'Clutch in!' he muttered to himself. 'In gear! Brake off! Throttle down! Clutch out!'

The Rolls leapt forward so violently that both he and Mbejane were nearly thrown over the back of the seat. Fifty yards farther on the machine expired from lack of fuel, a stroke of good fortune because it was unlikely that Sean would have been able to remember the procedure for stopping it.

Grey of face and unsteady of limb, Mbejane alighted from the Rolls for the last time. He never rode in it again – and secretly Sean envied him his freedom. He was greatly relieved to hear that it would be weeks before more fuel could be sent up from Cape Town.

74

Three weeks before Sean's wedding Ada Courtney went into her orchard one morning early to pick fruit for breakfast. She found Mary there, dressed in her white nightgown, and hanging by her neck from the big avocado tree. Ada cut her down and sent one of the servants to call Doctor Fraser.

Between them they carried the dead girl to her cubicle and laid her on her bed. While Doc Fraser made a hasty examination Ada stood staring down at the face that death had made more pitiful.

'What depths of loneliness drove her to this,' she whispered, and Doc Fraser pulled the sheet over the corpse and looked across at Ada.

'That wasn't the reason – in fact, it might have been better if she were a little more lonely.' He pulled out his tobacco pouch and began to load his pipe. 'Who was her boy friend, Aunt Ada?'

'She had none.'

'She must have.'

'Why do you say that?'

'Aunt Ada, this girl was four months pregnant.'

It was a small funeral, just the Courtney family and Ada's girls. Mary was an orphan and she had no other friends.

Two weeks before the wedding, Sean and Michael finished the season's cut of bark and switched the Zulus to planting out the blocks destroyed by the fire. Together they drew up a draft Profit and Loss Account. Combining their rudimentary knowledge of accounting and arguing far into the night, they finally agreed that from fifteen hundred acres of wattle they had cut fourteen hundred and twenty tons of bark, to gross a little over twenty-eight thousand pounds sterling.

But here all agreement ended. Michael insisted that the stocks of material and expenditure on planting of new trees be carried forward, giving a net profit for the year of nine thousand pounds. Sean wanted to write all expenditure off against income and show a profit of one thousand, so they deadlocked and finally sent all the books to a qualified accountant in Pietermaritzburg. This gentleman sided with Michael.

They then considered the prospects for the coming season and were a little awed when they realized that there would be four thousand acres of wattle to reap and an expected gross of eighty thousand pounds sterling – always providing there were no more fires. That evening, without Sean's knowledge, Michael wrote two letters. One to a manufacturer of heavy machinery in Birmingham, whose name and address Michael had furtively copied from one of the huge boilers in the Natal Wattle Estate Company's plant. The other to the firm of Foyle's booksellers in Charing Cross Road, London, requesting the immediate dispatch of all and any literature on the processing of wattle bark. Michael Courtney had caught from Sean the habit of dreaming extravagantly. He had also acquired the trick of setting out to make those dreams become reality.

Three days before the wedding Ada and her young ladies set out for Pietermaritzburg by train and Sean, Michael and Dirk followed in the Rolls.

The three of them arrived dusty and bad-tempered outside the White Horse Hotel. It had been a nerve-racking journey. Sean had enlivened it by shouting incessant warnings, instruction and blasphemy at Michael, the driver.

'Slow down, for God's sake, slow down! Do you want to kill us all!'

'Look out! Watch that cow!'

'Don't drive so close to the verge!'

Dirk had done his share by demanding halts for urination, hanging over the sides, climbing tirelessly between the front and back seats and urging Michael to exceed the speed-limit set by Sean. Finally, in anger, Sean had Michael stop the car and administered corporal punishment with the birch of a melkbos tree cut from beside the road.

On arrival Dirk was met by Ada, and led away snivelling. Michael took the Rolls and disappeared in the direction of the Natal Wattle Company's plant, where he was to spend most of the following three days snooping and asking questions, and Sean went to find Jan Paulus Leroux, who had come down from Pretoria in response to Sean's wedding invitation. By the day of the wedding Michael Courtney had compiled a small volume of notes on wattle processing, and Jan Paulus had given Sean a minute account of the aims and objects of the South African Party. But in response to his urgings Sean had promised only to 'think about it'.

The wedding ceremony had given everybody much cause for thought. Although Sean had no qualms about marrying in a synagogue, yet he steadfastly refused to undergo the painful little operation which would enable him to do so. His half-hearted suggestion that Ruth should convert to Christianity was met with a curt rejection. Finally, a compromise was agreed, and Ben Goldberg persuaded the local Magistrate to perform a civil ceremony in the dining-room of The Golds.

Ben Goldberg gave the bride away and Ma Goldberg wept a little. Ruth was magnificent in Ada's creation of green satin and seed pearls. Storm wore an exact miniature of Ruth's dress and sparked off a minor brawl with the other flower girls during the ceremony. Michael as Best Man conducted himself with aplomb. He quelled the riot among the flower girls, produced the wedding ring on cue and prompted the groom when he muffed his lines.

The reception on the lawns was attended by a huge crowd of the Goldbergs' friends and business associates and by half the population of Ladyburg, including Ronny Pye, Dennis Petersen and their families. Garrick and Anna Courtney were not there, nor had they acknowledged the invitation.

Brilliant sunshine blessed the day and the lawns were smooth and green as expensive carpets. There were long trestle tables laden with the fruits of Ma Goldberg's kitchen and the products of Ben Goldberg's brewery.

Storm Friedman went from group to group of guests, boosting up her skirts to display the pink ribbons in her pantaloons, until Ruth caught her at it.

Having found his first taste of champagne very much to his liking, Dirk went on to drink six glasses of it behind the rose bushes. He was then copiously ill. Fortunately Michael found him before Sean did, and spirited him away to one of the guest bedrooms and left him there to languish.

With Ruth on his arm, Sean inspected the display of wedding gifts and was impressed. He then circulated among the crowds on the lawn until he reached Jan Paulus and fell into an earnest political discussion. Ruth left them to it and went to change into her going-away clothes.

The prettiest and most blonde of Ada's young ladies caught the bouquet. Immediately thereafter she caught Michael's eye and blushed to match the crimson carnations in her hand.

Amid a hum of appreciative comment and a snowstorm of confetti Ruth returned and, a queen ascending the throne, took her seat in the Rolls. Beside her Sean, in dustcoat and goggles, steeled himself, muttered his usual incantations and gave the Rolls its head. Like a wild horse the machine seemed to rear on its hind wheels and then tear down the driveway scattering gravel and guests. Ruth clutching desperately at a large hatful of ostrich feathers and Sean shouting at the Rolls to 'Whoa! There, girl,' – they headed out along the road that led through the Valley of a Thousand Hills to Durban and the sea, and disappeared in a tall column of dust.

75

Three months later, having picked up Storm from Ma Goldberg *en passant*, they reappeared at Lion Kop homestead. Sean had put on weight and both of them had that smugly complacent look found only in the faces of couples returning from a successful honeymoon.

On the front stoep and in the outbuildings of Lion Kop were the crates and packing-cases which contained wedding gifts, Ruth's furniture and carpets, and the additional furniture and curtains they had purchased in Durban. Ruth, ably assisted by Ada, threw herself joyously into the task of unpacking and moving in. Meanwhile Sean began a tour of inspection of the estate to determine how much of it had suffered in his absence, and he felt vaguely cheated when he found that Michael had managed very well without him. The plantations were trim and cleared of undergrowth, the vast black scar through their centre was nearly obliterated with freshly planted rows of saplings, the labour force was half as productive again under the new incentive payment scheme which Michael, in consultation with the Accountant, had introduced. Sean gave Michael a lecture on 'not getting too bloody clever' and 'learning to walk before you run' which he ended with a few words of praise.

Thus encouraged, Michael approached Sean one night when he was alone in his study. Sean was in a state of deep contentment induced by a meal from an enormous roast sirloin which he was digesting, by the fact that Ruth had finally agreed to his adoption of Storm and the change of her name from Friedman to Courtney, and by the prospect of joining Ruth in their gargantuan double bed just as soon as he finished his brandy and his hand-rolled Havana cigar.

'Come in, Michael. Sit down. Have a brandy.' Sean greeted him genially, and almost defiantly Michael crossed the Persian carpet and laid a thick sheaf of papers on the desk in front of him.

'What's this all about?' Sean smiled at him.

'Read it and you'll see.' Michael retreated to a chair across the room. Still smiling Sean glanced at the heading on the top sheet.

'Preliminary estimates and ground plan for proposed Tannin Extraction Plant. Lion Kop Estates.'

The smile faded. Sean turned the page and as he read he began to frown and then to scowl. When at last he finished he relit his dead cigar and sat in silence for five minutes while he recovered from the shock.

'Who put you up to this?'

'Nobody.'

'Where would you sell your extract?'

'Page 5. The outlets are listed there – and the ruling prices over the last ten years.'

'This plants needs 20,000 tons of bark a year – if we planted every foot of Lion Kop and Mahobo's Kloof to wattle we could only supply half of that.'

'We'd buy the rest from the new estates along the valley – we could offer a better price than Jackson, because we'd save railage to Pietermaritzburg.'

'Who would run the plant?'

'I'm an engineer.'

'On paper you are,' Sean grunted. 'What about water?'

'We'd damn, the Baboon Stroom above the falls.'

For an hour Sean poked and prodded at the scheme, seeking for a soft spot. His agitation mounted as Michael calmly met each of his queries.

'All right,' Sean growled. 'You've done your homework. Now answer me this one. How the hell do you propose finding seventy thousand pounds to finance this little lot?'

Michael closed his eyes as though he were praying, his jaw was a hard, thrusting line. And suddenly Sean wondered why he had never noticed the strength in that face, the stubborn almost fanatical determination. Michael opened his eyes again and spoke softly.

'A loan on Lion Kop and Mahobo's Kloof for twenty-five thousand, a notarial bond on the plant for as much again – and a public share issue on the balance.'

Sean jumped up from his desk and roared.

'No!'

'Why not?' still calmly and reasonably.

'Because I've spent half my life in debt up to here!' Sean grabbed his own throat. 'Because now at last I'm in the clear and I want to stay that way. Because I know what it feels like to have more money than I need, and I don't like the feeling. Because I'm happy just the way things are now – and I don't want to catch another lion by the tail and have him turn round and claw the hell out of me.' He stopped panting and then shouted: 'Because a certain amount of money belongs to you, but more than that you belong to it. Because I don't want to be that wealthy again!'

Lean and fast as an angry leopard, Michael came out of his chair and smashed a balled fist on to the top of the desk. He glared across at Sean, flushed angry red under his tan, quivering like an arrow.

'Well, I do! Your only objection to my plan is that it's sound,' he blazed. Sean blinked in surprise and then rallied.

'If you get it, you won't like it!' he bellowed, and Michael matched his volume.

'Let me be the judge of that!'

At that moment the door of the study opened and Ruth stood on the threshold and stared at them. They looked like a pair of game cocks with their hackles up.

'What on earth is going on?' she demanded. Both Michael and Sean looked up guiltily, then slowly they relaxed. Michael sat down and Sean coughed awkwardly.

'We are just having a discussion, my dear.'

'Well, you've woken Storm and just about torn the roof off.' Then she smiled and crossed to take Sean's arm. 'Why don't you leave it until tomorrow. Then you can continue your discussion at twenty paces with pistols.'

The pygmies of the Ituri Forests hunt elephant with tiny arrows. Once the barb is lodged they follow quietly and doggedly, camping night after night on the spoor until at last the poison works its way to the animal's heart and brings it down. Michael had placed his arrow-head deep in Sean's flesh.

76

At Lion Kop Ruth found a happiness she had never expected, had not believed existed.

Up to this time her existence had been ordered and determined by an adoring but strict father, and then in the same manner by Ben Goldberg. The few short years with Saul Friedman had been happy, but now they were as unreal as memories of childhood. Always she had been wrapped in a cocoon of wealth, hemmed in by social taboos and the dignity of the family. Even Saul had treated her as a delicate child for whom all decisions must be made. Life had been placid and orderly, but deadly dull. Only twice she had rebelled, once to run away from Pretoria and again when she had gone to Sean in the hospital. Boredom had been her constant companion.

But now suddenly she was mistress of a complex community. The sensation had been a little overpowering at first and from habit she had appealed to Sean for him to make the fifty decisions that each day brought forward.

'I'll make a bargain with you,' he answered. 'You don't tell me how to grow wattle and I'll not tell you how to run the house – put the damn sideboard where it looks best.'

Hesitantly at first, then with growing confidence and at last with sureness and pride she made Lion Kop into a home of beauty and comfort. The coarse grass and scrub around the home-stead fell back to make room for lawns and flower-beds, the outer walls of Lion Kop gleamed in a crisp new coat of white-wash. Inside, the yellow-wood floors shone like polished amber setting off the vivid Bokhara carpets and draped velvet curtains.

After a few disastrous experiments the kitchens began to yield a succession of meals that moved Michael to raptures, and even Sean pronounced them edible.

Yet, with a dozen servants, she had time for other things. To read, to play with Storm and to ride. Sean's wedding gift to her was a string of four golden palaminos. There was time also for long visits from and with Ada Courtney. The two of them established an accord stronger than that of mother and daughter.

There was time for dancing and barbecues, there was time for laughter and for long quiet evenings when she and Sean sat alone on the wide front stoep or in his study and talked of many things.

There was time for love.

Her body, hard from riding and walking, was also healthy and hot. It was a sculpture sheathed in velvet and fashioned for love.

There was only one dark place in her happiness – Dirk Courtney.

When her overtures were met with sullenness and her small specially cooked gifts were rejected, she realized the cause of his antagonism. She sensed the bitter jealousy which was eating like a canker behind those lovely eyes and the passsionately beautiful face. For days she prepared what she would say to him. The she found the opportunity when he came into the kitchens while she was alone. He saw her and turned quickly to leave, but she stopped him.

'Oh, Dirk, please don't go. I want to discuss something with you.' He came back slowly and leaned against the table. She saw how tall he had grown in the last year, his shoulders were thickening into the shape of manhood and his legs were strong and tapered from the narrow hips that he thrust forward in a calculated insolence.

'Dirk . . . ' she began and paused. Suddenly she was unsure of herself. This was not a child as she had imagined; there was a sensuality in that beautiful face she found disturbing – he carried his body with awareness, moving like a cat. Suddenly she was afraid, and she swallowed jerkily before she went on:

'I know how difficult it has been for you – since Storm and I came to live here. I know how much you love your father, how much he means to you. But . . . ' She spoke slowly, her carefully prepared speech forgotten so that she had to grope for the words to explain. She tried to show him that they were not in competition for Sean's love; that all of them – Ruth, Michael, Storm and Dirk – formed a whole; that their interests did not overlap, but that each of them gave to Sean and received from him a different kind of love. When at last she faltered into silence she knew he had not listened nor tried to understand. 'Dirk, I like you and I want you to like me.'

With a thrust of his buttocks against the table, Dirk straightened up. He smiled then and let his eyes move down over her body, slowly.

'Can I go now?' he asked, and Ruth stiffened. Then she knew there was no compromise, that she would have to fight him.

'Yes, Dirk. You may go,' she answered. She knew with sudden clarity that he was evil, and if she lost this contest he would destroy her and her child. In that moment she was no longer afraid.

Catlike, Dirk seemed to sense the change in her. For a moment she thought she saw a flicker of doubt, of uncertainty in his eyes – then he turned away and sauntered out of the kitchen.

She guessed that it would come soon, but not as soon as it did.

Every afternoon Ruth would ride out into the plantations with Storm's pony on a lead rein beside her. They made a game of finding Sean and Michael, following the labyrinth of roads that criss-crossed through the blocks of trees, guided by the vague directions of the gangs of Zulus until finally they ran them down and delivered the canteens of coffee and the hamper of sandwiches. Then, all four of them would picnic on the soft carpet of dead leaves beneath the trees.

This afternoon, dressed in riding habit and carrying the hamper, Ruth came out into the kitchen yard. The young Zulu nursemaid was sitting in the shade of the kitchen wall flirting with one of the groms. Storm was nowhere in sight, and Ruth asked sharply:

'Where is Miss Storm?'

'She went with Nkosana Dirk.' And Ruth felt the tingling premonition of danger.

'Where are they?' and the nursemaid pointed vaguely in the direction of the stables and outbuildings that sprawled away down the back slope of the hill.

'Come with me.' Ruth dropped the hamper and ran with her skirts gathered in one hand. She reached the first row of stables and hurried down them, glancing into each stall as she passed. Then into the feed rooms with the big concrete bins and the smell of oats and molasses and chopped lucerne mixing with the sharp tang of dung and dubbined leather, out again into the sunlight, running for the barns.

Storm screamed in terror, just once, but high and achingly clear, so the silence afterwards quivered with the memory of it.

The harness room. Ruth swirled in her run. *God, please No! Don't let it happen. Please! Please!*

She reached the open door of the harness room. It was gloomy and cool within the thick stone walls, anf for a moment the scene made no sense to Ruth.

Her back wedged into the far corner, Storm stood with hands lifted to shield her face – small fingers rigid, splayed open, spread like the tip feathers of a bird's wing. Her body shook silently with her sobs.

In front of Storm, squatting on his heels, Dirk leaned forward with one hand outstretched as though he offered a gift. He was laughing.

Then Ruth saw the thing in Dirk's hand move and she froze with horror. It uncoiled from around his wrist, and slowly reached out towards Storm, its head cocked back in a half-loop of its body, tiny black tongue vibrating between the grinning pink lips.

Ruth screamed, and Dirk jumped to his feet and spun to face her with his right hand hidden behind his back.

From the corner Storm darted across the room and buried her face in Ruth's skirts, weeping piteously. Ruth picked her up and held her tight against her shoulder, but she never took her eyes off Dirk's face.

'It's only a *rooi-slang.*' Dirk laughed again, but nervously. 'They're harmless – I was only having a joke.' He brought the snake out from behind his back, dropped it on to the stone-flagged floor and crushed its head under the heel of his riding-boot. He kicked it away against the wall, then with an impatient gesture he brushed the black curls from his forehead and made to leave the room. Ruth stepped across to block his path.

'Nannie, take Miss Storm back to the house.' Gently Ruth handed the child to the Zulu nursemaid and closed the door after them and slid the bolt across.

Now it was darker in the room, two square shafts of sunlight filled with moving dust motes fell from the high windows, and the quiet was spoiled only by the sound of Ruth's laboured breathing.

'I was only having a joke,' Dirk repeated, and grinned defiance at her. 'I suppose you'll run and tell my father?'

The walls of the room were studded with wooden pegs from which were suspended the harness and saddlery. Beside the door hung Sean's raw-hide stockwhips, eight foot of braided leather tapering from the butt handle into nothingness. Ruth lifted one down from the rack and flicked the lash out to lie upon the floor between them.

'No, Dirk, I'm not going to tell your father. This thing is between you and me alone.'

'What are you going to do?'

'I'm going to settle it.'

'How?' Still grinning, he placed his hands on his hips. Beneath rolled sleeves his upper arms bulged smooth and brown as though they had been freshly oiled.

'Like this.' Ruth flicked her skirt aside and stepped forward, using the whip underhand she sent the lash snaking out to coil around Dirk's ankle and immediately she jerked back on it. Taken completely off balance, Dirk went over backwards. His head hit the wall as he fell and he lay stunned.

To give herself space in which to wield the whip, Ruth moved into the centre of the room. Her anger was cold as dry ice, it gave strength to arms already finely muscled from riding, and it seared away all mercy. Now she was a female animal fighting for the survival of herself and her child.

She had learned to use a stockwhip in the process of becoming an expert horsewoman, and her first blow split Dirk's shirt from the shoulder to the waist. He shouted with anger and rolled on to his knees. The next blow cut down from the base of his neck along his spine, paralysing him in the act of rising. The next, across the back of both knees, knocked his legs out from under him.

On his belly Dirk reached for the pitchfork against the wall, but braided leather exploded around his wrist. He shouted again and rolled on his side to nurse the hand against his chest.

Ruth hit him and he writhed across the floor towards her like a wounded leopard with its hindquarters shattered by buckshot. Step by step Ruth retreated before him, and the long lash hissed and cracked.

Without mercy she beat him until his shirt hung in tatters

866

from his waist and shoulders, exposing the smooth white skin with the fat crimson welts superimposed upon it.

She beat him until his shouts turned to shrieks and finally to sobbing.

She beat him until he lay shivering, moaning, moving feebly with his blood sprinkled in dark blobs on the stone paving around him.

Then she folded the whip and turned to open the door. In the stable yard, standing in silent curiosity, were gathered all the grooms and the household servants.

Ruth selected four of them.

'Take the Nkosana to his room.'

Then to one of the grooms,

'Ride to the Nkosi. Tell him to come quickly.'

Sean came quickly; he came wild with anxiety and nearly tore the door off Dirk's bedroom in his haste. He stopped dead on the threshold and stared aghast at Dirk's back.

Stripped to the waist, Dirk lay face downwards on his bed and Ruth worked over him with a sponge. On the table beside her stood a steaming basin and the pungent reek of antiseptic filled the room.

'Good God! What happened to him?'

'I beat him with a stockwhip.' Ruth answered him calmly and Sean gaped at her, then dropped his gaze to Dirk.

'You did that?'

'Yes.'

The anger tightened Sean's mouth.

'Jesus God! You've cut him to pieces. You've half killed him.' And he glanced at Ruth. 'Why?'

'It was necessary.' The absolute assurance and lack of remorse in her reply, confused Sean. He was suddenly uncertain in his anger.

'What did he do?'

'I can't tell you that. It is something private between us. You must ask Dirk.'

Sean crossed quickly to the bed and knelt beside it.

'Dirk. Dirkie, my boy, what happened. What did you do?' And Dirk lifted his face from the pillow and looked at his father.

867

'It was a mistake. It doesn't matter.' Then he buried his face in the pillow once more, and his voice was muffled, so Sean had excuse for not believing that he had heard correctly.

'What did you say?' he demanded, and there was a short delay before Dirk replied quite distinctly,

'I said – it was my fault.'

'That's what I thought you said.' Sean stood up with a puzzled expression on his face. 'Well, I don't know why you sent for me, Ruth. You seem to have the situation fairly well in hand.' He moved to the door, looked back as though he were going to speak, then, changing his mind, he shook his head and went out.

That night in the quiet, exhausted minutes before sleep, Sean murmured against her cheek, 'I think you did today what I should have done years ago.' and then, with a sleepy chuckle, 'At least there's no doubt in anyone's mind as to who is the mistress of Lion Kop.'

77

There was a guileless simplicity in Sean's approach to life – in his mind any problem when met with direct action disintegrated.

If you became obsessed with a woman, you tumbled her. If that didn't produce the desired effect, then you married her.

If you wanted a piece of land or a horse or a house or a gold mine, then you paid your money and took it. If you didn't have the money, you went out and found it.

If you liked a man you drank with him, hunted with him, laughed together. If you disliked him, you either punched him in the head or subjected him to a ponderous sarcasm and mockery. Either way you left him in no doubt of your feelings.

When a son got out of hand you whaled the tripe out of him, then gave him an expensive present to demonstrate your affection. Now he admitted he had been tardy in the matter of Dirk; but Ruth had done a most effective job. It only remained for him to call Dirk into the study and shout at him a little. A week later he returned from a trip to Pietermaritzburg and with an embarrassed scowl presented to Dirk his peace offerings. The first was a brass-bound leather case, which contained a handmade shotgun by Greener of London; tooled silver inlay, glossy walnut stock and butt, and interchangeable Damascus barrels. The other was a two-year-old filly from the Huguenot stud at Worcester in the Cape. By Sun Lord out of Harvest Dance, Sun Dancer was an animal of the most distinguished blood in Africa and of surpassing beauty and speed. Sean paid a thousand guineas for her and considered he had got the best of the bargain.

As far as he was concerned there was no longer any problem with Dirk, and Sean could devote all his energy to furthering the three major ventures in which he was engaged.

Firstly, there was the matter of putting Ruth with child. Here he had her wholehearted co-operation. But their efforts, apart from providing a deal of healthy exercise and pleasure, were singularly unproductive. Sean remembered the deadly skill he had shown in their first encounter and was puzzled. Ruth suggested they keep in training until the rainy season began; she had developed a superstitious belief in the power of thunder. On one of his trips to Pietermaritzburg Sean saw a carved wooden statue of Thor in a junk dealer's window. He bought it for her, and from then on the god stood on their bedside table clutching his hammer and overlooking their strivings with such a knowing expression that at last Ruth turned him face to the wall.

Then there was Michael's Tannin Extract Plant. He had resorted to a piece of underhand villainy that shocked Sean and, he professed, killed his belief in the essential decency of mankind. Michael had visited each of the new growers along the valley, men who had followed Sean's lead in the planting of wattle, and after swearing them to secrecy had offered them shares in the Company. They were enthusiastic and with Michael at the head they visited Lion Kop in formal deputation. The meeting was conducted with so much verbal thunder and lightning thrown about that the Great God Thor might have been in the Chair. At the end Sean, who had teased the idea all the months since Michael had approached him and who was now as enthusiastic as any of them, allowed himself to be persuaded. He spoke for seventy per cent of the shares and the balance was allotted to the other growers. A Board of Directors, with Sean as Chairman, was elected and the Accountant was instructed to proceed with the registration of The Ladyburg Wattle Co-operative Ltd. For the first time Sean exercised his majority vote to crush the misgivings of the other shareholders and appoint Michael Courtney as Plant Engineer. Then, with an older director to act as a steadying influence, Michael was put aboard the next Union Castle mailship for England, a letter of authority in his pocket and Sean's warnings and words of wisdom in his head. Remembering himself at the age of twenty-three, Sean decided it necessary to point out to Michael that he was being sent to London to buy machinery and increase his knowledge of it, not to populate the British Isles nor to tour their hostelries and gaming establishments.

There was swift reaction from Jackson at Natal Wattle, who regretted that the contracts between the Tugela Valley growers and his company would not be renewed – and that owing to

870

heavy demands from elsewhere he could no longer supply seed or saplings. But Sean's seedbeds were now well enough established to meet the needs of the whole valley – and, with luck, their plant would be in production by the beginning of the next cutting season.

Before Michael and his chaperon returned flushed with the success of their mission, Sean had another visitor. Jan Paulus Leroux, weary of the three-year argument he and Sean had conducted with the aid of the postal authority, arrived at Ladyburg and expressed his intention of staying until Sean agreed to head the Natal branch of the South African Party and to contest the Ladyburg seat at the next Legislative Assembly elections. Two weeks later, after he and Sean had hunted and killed a number of guinea-fowl, pheasant and bush buck; had consumed huge quantities of coffee and more moderate quantities of brandy; had talked each other hoarse and had closed the last gap between them, Jan Paulus left on the Johannesburg train with the parting words:

'*Toe Maar!* It is settled then.'

The South African Party's platform was a Federation of the Cape, the Transvaal, the Orange Free State and Natal, under government responsible to Whitehall. It was opposed by extreme English and Dutch opinion – the jingoes who shouted 'God Save the King', and the Republicans who wanted the Almighty to treat the King differently.

After meeting with the men on the list Jan Paulus had given him, Sean began the campaign. His first convert was Ruth Courtney, won over by the prospect of the excitement associated with an election battle rather than by Sean's oratory. Now a week or more of every month was spent in travelling about Natal to attend political gatherings. Ruth rehearsed Sean in his speech – he had only one – until he was word perfect. She kissed the babies and played hostess to the wives, tasks in which Sean showed no special aptitude. She sat beside him on the platform and restrained him from going down into the audience to engage in hand-to-hand combat with hecklers. The way she smiled and the way she walked certainly lost no votes for the South African Party. From London Lord Caisterbrook promised his support, and it looked as though Sean could count on twenty-two seats out of the Assembly's thirty.

On the level ground below the escarpment, hard by the Baboon Stroom, the plant of the Ladyburg Wattle Co-operative took shape. It covered ten acres of ground and beyond it the cottages of the employees were laid out in neat blocks.

Despite Michael's vehement protests, Sean bowed to the will of his fellow directors and a consulting engineer was employed until such time as the plant was in production. Without him they would have lost a year's harvest of bark, for although Michael was eager and tireless, yet he was a young man with no practical experience. Even with the older man to help him, the plant was still a long way from ready before the season's cutting began. When at last the tall silver smoke stack began spewing smoke and the furnaces lit the night with a satanic glow, there were thousands of tons of bark piled up in the open-sided warehouses around the factory.

It was a wonderful season. Good rains had filled the bark with rich sap and when the year ended the Co-operative had shown a profit of ten thousand pounds on its first year's operation – Lion Kop Estates a profit four times greater. Sean had been in and out of debt as swiftly as a small boy visits the bathroom when sent to wash his face.

Despite the good rains, there were only three spectacular storms that summer. On each occasion Sean was away from Lion Kop on business. While the lightning leapt across the hills and the hammer strokes of thunder broke over the valley, Ruth stood at the window of their bedroom and lamented another wasted opportunity. Mbejane did much better – all his seed brought forth fruit and he reaped four fat sons that season.

78

It was a busy year for Dirk Courtney also. After his resounding defeat at the thin end of the stockwhip, Dirk and Ruth fell into a state of wary neutrality – but he conceded control of Lion Kop to her.

Storm Courtney he ignored, unless she was in Sean's lap or riding on his shoulder. Then he watched them covertly until he could find an excuse to interrupt their play or to get away from Lion Kop. His absences became more frequent; there were trips to Pietermaritzburg and the surrounding districts to play rugby and polo; there were mysterious night excursions to Ladyburg, and in the day he rode away at dawn each morning – Sean believed he rode to school until he received a note from the headmaster asking him to call.

After showing him the attendance register and a copy of Dirk's academic record, the headmaster leaned back in his chair and waited for Sean's comments.

'Not so good, hey?'

'I agree, Mr Courtney. Not so good.'

'Couldn't we send him to a boarding establishment some-where, Mr Besant?'

'Yes, you could do that,' Besant agreed dubiously, 'but would it serve any real purpose – apart from providing him with expert coaching in rugby football?'

'How else will he get his University entrance?' Sean was impressed with what higher education had done for Michael. He looked upon it as a sovereign alchemy for all the ills of youth.

'Mr Courtney . . .' The headmaster hesitated delicately. He had heard of Sean's temper and did not want a personal demonstration of it. 'Some young men are not really suited for University training.'

'I Want Dirk to go,' Sean interjected.

'I doubt that either Stellenbosch or Cape Town Universities

share your ambitions.' The schoolroom manner re-asserted itself for a moment, and Besant spoke with dry sarcasm.

'You mean he's stupid?' Sean demanded.

'No, no.' Hurriedly Besant soothed him. 'It's just that he's not, shall we say, academically inclined.'

Sean pondered on that awhile. It seemed a very nice distinction, but he let it go and asked:

'Well, what do you suggest?'

Besant's suggestion was that Dirk Courtney get the hell out of his school – but he phrased it gently.

'Although Dirk is only sixteen – he is very mature for his age. Say you were to start him at the Wattle Company . . . ?'

'You recommend I take him away from school, then?' Sean asked thoughtfully, and Besant suppressed a sigh of relief.

Dirk Courtney was apprenticed to the foreman boilermaker at the factory. His first action was to inform his journeyman that he'd be running this show one day and what was he going to do about it? That gentleman, forewarned by Dirk's reputation, regarded him dolefully, spat a long squirt of tobacco juice an inch from Dirk's gleaming toecap, and replied at some length. He then pointed to a kettle on the workshop forge and told Dirk to make him a cup of coffee, and while he was about it to remove his thumb from his posterior orifice. Within a week the two of them were cronies and the man, whose name was Archibald Frederick Longworthy, began to instruct Dirk in arts other than the fabrication of steelplate. Archy was thirty-six years old. He had come out to Africa after completing a five-year term in Leavenworth Prison for the intriguing offence of *Crimen Injuria* – and when he explained the meaning Dirk was delighted.

Archy introduced Dirk to one of his friends, Hazel, a plump and friendly girl who worked at the Ladyburg Hotel as a barmaid and dispensed her favours in the same cheerful manner that she did her liquor – but Dirk quickly became her favourite, and he learned some pretty little tricks from her.

Shrewdly, Archibald Longworthy examined the situation and decided that nothing but profit could come from friendship with Sean Courtney's heir. Besides which the boy was a lot of fun.

He could tumble a tart and swig gin with the best of them – also he had a seemingly inexhaustible supply of sovereigns.

In exchange Dirk hero-worshipped Archy, diverting much of his feelings from his father to his first real friend. Ignoring the grey wrists and neck which bespoke Archy's disaffection for soap and water, the pale wispy hair through which pink scalp showed, ignoring also the black tooth in the front of his mouth – Dirk invested him with the glamour and excitement of an old-time pirate.

When Dirk found himself to be suffering from a painless but evil-smelling condition, it was Archy who assured him it was only '*whites*' and went with him to a doctor in Pietermaritzburg. On the train coming home they planned their revenge with much laughter, comradely banter – and rising anticipation.

Hazel was surprised to see them in the middle of a Sunday afternoon, she sat up quickly as they came into her room overlooking the back yard of the hotel.

'Dirkie, you shouldn't come here in the daytime – your Pa will find out.' It was warm in the shabby little room, and the smell of cheap scent and a half-filled chamber-pot blended harshly with the odour of female perspiration. Hazel's thin chemise clung damply to her body and outlined the heavy hang of her breasts and the deep lateral fold around the level of her navel. There were dark smudges below her eyes and a curl was sweat-plastered down her cheek where the pillow had left little creases in the skin. The two of them stood in the doorway and grinned at her, from many experiences Hazel recognized the wolfish eagerness those grins masked.

'What do you want?' Suddenly she was afraid and instinctively she covered the deep cleft of her bosom with one hand.

'Dirkie here wants to have a little chat with you.' Carefully Archy closed the door and turned the key in the lock, then he ambled towards the bed. Manual labour had sheathed his arms in hard, knotty muscle and the hands that hung at his sides were disproportionately large and coated with coarse, blond hair.

'You keep away from me, Archy Longworthy.' Hazel swung her legs off the bed, the chemise pulled up to expose fat white thighs. 'I don't want no trouble, you just leave me alone.'

'You give Dirkie here a clap. Now Dirkie here is my friend and he don't like what you give him.'

'I didn't! It couldn't have been me. I'm clean – I tell you.' She

875

stood up, still holding the front of her chemise closed and backed away before him. 'You keep away from me.' Then as Archy jumped forward, 'No – don't! I'll . . . ' And she opened her mouth to scream, but Archy's hand closed over it like a great hairy spider. She struggled desperately, clawing at the hand over her face.

'Come on, Dirk.' Archy chuckled, as he held her easily with one arm around her waist. Uncertainly Dirk hesitated at the door, no longer grinning.

'Come on, man. I'll hold her.' With a sudden swing of his arm Archy hurled the girl face down on the bed, then jumped across to keep her mouth smothered in the pillow. 'Come on, Dirk, use this!' With his free hand Archy unbuckled the wide belt he wore. The leather was studded with blunt metal spikes. 'Double it over!'

'Hell's teeth, Arch – you reckon we should?' Dirk still hesitated, the belt hanging limply from his hands.

'You scared, or something?' And Dirk's mouth hardened at the gibe. He stepped forward and swung the belt in a full overarm stroke across the wriggling body. Hazel froze at the sting of it and she gasped explosively into the pillow.

'That's the stuff – hold on a second.' Archy hooked his thumb into the thin fabric of her chemise and ripped it down from the shoulder-blades to the hem. Her fat woman's buttocks bulged through, dimpled and white. 'Now, give it hell!'

Again Dirk lifted the heavy doubled leather, he stood poised like that while a sensation of giddy power buoyed him upwards to the level of the gods, then he swung his body down into the next stroke.

79

'He's unopposed,' Ronny Pye murmured, and beside him Garrick Courtney stirred uneasily.

'Have you heard him speak?' Ronny persisted.

'No.'

'He wants to throw in Natal with that bunch of Dutchmen up in the Free State and Transvaal.'

'Yes, I know.'

'Do you agree with him?'

Garry was silent, he seemed to be engrossed with the antics of the small herd of foals in the paddock in front of them as they chased each other on legs that seemed to have too many joints, clumsy in their fluffy baby coats.

'I'm sending twenty yearlings up to the show sales in Pietermaritzburg – should average about four, five hundred a head because they're all first-class animals. Be able to let you have a sizeable payment on the bond.'

'Don't worry about that now, Garry. I didn't come out here looking for money.' Ronny offered his cigar-case, and when Garry refused he selected one himself and began preparing it carefully. 'Do you agree with this idea of a Union?'

'No.'

'Why not?' Ronny did not look up from his cigar, he did not want to show his eagerness prematurely.

'I fought them – Leroux, Niemand, Botha, Smuts. I fought them – and we won. Now they're sitting up there in Pretoria calmly plotting to take over the whole country – not just the Free State and Transvaal, but Natal and the Cape as well. Any Englishman who helps them is a traitor to his King and his country. He should be put against the wall and shot.'

'Quite a few people round here think that way – quite a few. And yet no one is opposing Sean Courtney – he's just going to walk into the Assembly.'

Garry turned and began limping slowly along the paddock fence towards the stables, and Ronny fell in beside him.

'Seems to me and the others we need a good man to put against him – someone with a lot of prestige. Good war record, man who has written a book and knows what's going on – knows how to use words. If we could find someone like that, then we'd be happy to put up the expense money.' He struck a match and waited for the sulphur to clear before he lit his cigar and spoke through the smoke. 'Only three months to election time – we got to get organized right away. He's holding a meeting at the schoolhouse next week.'

Sean's political campaign, which had been ambling along mildly without causing much interest, suddenly took on new dramatic quality.

His first meeting in Ladyburg was attended by most of the local population – all of them so starved for entertainment that they were prepared to listen to Sean reel off the little speech that they had already read reported verbatim in most of the Natal newspapers. With hardy optimism they hoped that question time might be more rewarding – and some of them had prepared queries on such momentous matters as the price of hunting licences, the public library system, and the control of foot and mouth disease. At the very least it was an opportunity to meet friends from the outlying areas.

But, apart from Sean's employees, friends and neighbours, others arrived at the schoolhouse and filled the first two rows of desks. All of them were young men Sean had never seen before, and he eyed them with heavy disapproval while they laughed and joked loudly during the preliminaries.

'Where did this bunch come from?' he demanded of the Chairman.

'They came in on the afternoon train – all in one party.'

'Seems as though they're looking for trouble.' Grimly Sean sensed in them the slightly feverish excitement of men steeling themselves to violence. 'Most of them have been on the bottle.'

'Now, Sean.' Ruth leaned across and laid her hand on his knee. 'You must promise not to get worked up. Don't antagonize them.' Sean opened his mouth to reply, then left it like that as

Garry Courtney came in through the crowd around the doorway and moved across to sit with Ronny Pye in the back row.

'Close your mouth, darling,' Ruth murmured and Sean obeyed, then smiled and waved a greeting to his brother. Garry replied with a nod, and immediately fell into deep discussion with Ronny Pye.

Amid coughing and feet shuffling the Chairman rose to introduce Sean to men who had been his schoolmates, who had drunk his brandy and hunted with him. He went on to tell them how Sean had won the Anglo-Boer war virtually single-handed, how he had brought prosperity to the district with his factory and his wattle. Then he ended with a few remarks that had Sean squirming in his seat and trying to get two fingers into his collar.

'So, ladies and gentlemen of our fair district – I give you a man of vision and foresight, a man with a heart as big as his fists – your candidate and mine, Colonel Sean Courtney!'

Sean stood up smiling, to be rocked by a blast of jeers and catcalls from the front rows. The smile faded and his fists curled into great bony hammers on the table in front of him. He scowled down on them, beginning to sweat with anger. A light tug on the tail of his coat steadied him and his fists opened a little. He began to speak, bellowing above the shouts of 'Sit down!', 'Speak up!', 'Give him a chance!', 'Stand down!', and the thunder of booted feet stamping in unison on the wooden floor.

Three times in the uproar he lost the run of his speech and had to turn to Ruth for prompting, scarlet in the face with anger and mortification, while waves of derisive laughter broke over him. He ended up reading out the last half from his notebook – it made little difference that he stumbled and lost his place repeatedly for no one more than three feet away could hear a word. He sat down and a sudden silence descended on the hall, an air of expectancy that made Sean realize that this must have been carefully planned – and that the main entertainment was still to follow.

'*Mr* Courtney.' At the back of the hall Garry Courtney was on his feet, and every head was craned around towards him. 'May I ask you a few questions?'

Sean nodded slowly. So that is it! Garry planned this reception.

'My first question, then. Can you tell us what the name is for a man who sells his country to the enemies of his King?'

'Traitor!' howled the hecklers.

'Boer!' They stood up in a mass and roared at him. The pande-monium lasted perhaps five minutes.

'I'm taking you out of here,' Sean whispered to Ruth and reached for her arm, but she pulled away.

'No, I'm staying.'

'Come on, do as I tell you. This is going to get rough.'

'You'll have to carry me out first,' she flared at him, angry and beautiful.

Sean was about to accept the challenge, when suddenly the uproar ceased abruptly. Again, all heads turned towards Garrick Courtney, where he stood ready with his next question. In the silence he grinned maliciously.

'One other thing, do you mind telling us the nationality and faith of your wife?'

Sean's head jerked back. He felt the sickening physical jolt of it in his stomach, and he started to struggle to his feet. But Ruth was already standing, and she laid a hand on his shoulder to prevent him rising.

'I think I will answer that one, Garry.' She spoke clearly with just that trace of huskiness in her voice.

'I am a Jewess.'

The silence persisted. Still with her hand on Sean's shoulder, standing straight and proud beside him, she held Garry's stare across the room. Garry broke first. Flushing up along his neck, he dropped his eyes and shifted clumsily on his bad leg. Among the men in the front rows the same guilty reaction followed her words. They glanced at each other and then away, moving awkwardly in shame. A man stood up, and started down the aisle towards the door. Half-way there he stopped and turned.

'Sorry, Missus. I didn't know there'd be any of that,' and he went on towards the door. As he passed Ronny Pye he tossed a sovereign into his lap. Another man stood up, grinned uneasily at Ruth and hurried out. Then in twos and threes the others followed him. The last of them trooped out in a bunch, and Sean noted with relish that not all of them returned Ronny's sovereigns.

At the end of the schoolroom Garry dithered, uncertain whether to leave or to stay and attempt to brazen his way out of a situation he had so seriously misjudged.

Sean stood up slowly and encircled Ruth's waist with one

arm, he cleared his throat for it was choked with his pride of her.

'Not only that,' he called, 'but she's one of the best goddamned cooks in the district also.' In the laughter and cheers that followed Garry stumbled and pushed his way out of the room.

80

The following day Garrick Courtney announced his intention of contesting the Ladyburg seat as an Independent, but not even the Loyalist newspapers gave him an outside chance of winning – until six weeks before polling-day.

On that evening, long after dark, Dirk hitched Sun Dancer at the rail outside the hotel. After he had loosened the girth and slipped the bit from her mouth, he left her to drink at the trough and went up on to the sidewalk. As he sauntered past the bar he peered in through the large window with its gold-and-red-lettered slogan, 'Got a thirst, drink a Goldberg Beer!'

Quickly he checked the clientele at the bar for informers. There were none of his father's foremen – they were always dangerous, nor were Messrs Petersen or Pye or Erasmus present this evening. He recognized two of the factory mechanics, a couple of railway gangers, a bank clerk, a counter-hand from the Co-operative Society among the half-dozen strangers – and he decided that it was safe. None of these ranked high enough in Ladyburg society to carry news to Sean Courtney of his son's drinking habits.

Dirk walked to the end of the block, paused there for a few seconds, and then strolled casually back. But his eyes were restlessly checking the shadows for tale carriers. Tonight the main street was deserted, and as he came level with the swing doors of the bar he stepped sideways through them and into the warm yellow lamplight of the saloon. He loved this atmosphere – he loved the smell of sawdust, liquor, tobacco smoke and men. It was a place of men. A place of rough voices and laughter, of crude humour and companionship.

A few of the men along the bar glanced up as he entered.

'Hey, Dirk!'

'We've missed you – where have you been all week?'

Dirk returned Archy's greeting self-consciously and when he walked to take the stool beside him at the end of the bar counter he held himself erect and swaggered a little – for this was a place of men.

'Good evening, Dirk. What will it be?' The barman hurried across to him.

'Hello, Henry – is it all right tonight?' Dirk dropped his voice to a whisper.

'Should be – we aren't expecting any snoopers,' Henry reassured him. 'But the door behind you isn't locked.'

Dirk's seat in the corner had been selected with care. From it he could survey each newcomer to the room while being screened himself by the drinkers along the counter. Behind him a door led through the washup into the back yard – a necessary precaution when you're seventeen and both the law and your father forbid you liquor.

'Very well, then – give me the usual,' Dirk nodded.

'You're out late tonight,' Henry remarked as he poured gin into a tumbler and filled it with bottled gingerbeer. 'You been out hunting again?' Henry was a small man in his early fifties, with a pale unsunned face and little blue eyes, and now as he asked the question he winked one of them at Archy Longworthy.

'Did you get it tonight?' Archy took over the catechism.

Dirk laid a finger along the side of his nose. 'What do you think?' He grinned and they all laughed delightedly.

'Who was it? *Madame?*' Archy drew him out, playing for the other listeners, who were leaning forward still chuckling.

'Oh, her!' Dirk shrugged contemptuously. *Madame* was the code name of the wife of one of the railway drivers. Her husband ran the night train to Pietermaritzburg every alternate day. She was not considered much of a conquest.

'Who them?' Henry kidded softly.

'I'll let you know when I'm finished nesting there myself,' Dirk promised.

'A pretty one?' they insisted. 'Young, hey?'

'She's all right – not too bad.' Dirk tasted his gin.

'Man, you get so much you don't hardly 'preciate it any more,' Archy chided him, grinning at his audience, and Dirk bridled with pleasure. 'Come on, Dirk – tell us, man. Is she hot?'

For answer Dirk extended one finger cautiously and touched his glass, hissed sharply as though he had touched red hot steel and jerked his hand back with an exclamation of pain. They roared with appreciation and Dirk laughed with them, flushing, eager for their acceptance.

'Give us the story –' Henry insisted. 'You don't have to give us the name, just give us the details. Where did you take her?'

'Well –' Dirk hesitated.

'Come on, Dirk. Tell us about it.'

And of course he obliged. Telling it in detail so that the indulgent quality of their laughter changed and they leaned closer to him listening hungrily.

'Jesus! Did she say *that*?'

'Then what did you do?' they encouraged him.

And Dirk told them. He was a natural storyteller and he built up the suspense until there was a small island of attentive silence around him. But the rest of the bar-room was louder with laughter and voices than it had been when he entered. One group in particular were feeling their liquor.

'– So I took her hand,' Dirk went on, 'and I said, "Now I've got a little surprise for you." "What is it?" she asked, as though she didn't know. "Close your eyes and I'll show you." I told her . . .' And a voice rang loudly from across the room:

'– You take that big ugly bastard Courtney. What does he do except drive round in a big motor-car and make speeches.'

Dirk stopped in the middle of a sentence and looked up. Suddenly his face was pale. The man who had spoken was one of the group at the far end of the bar. He was dressed in a shabby overall of blue denim. A man no longer young, with the lines of hardship etched deep around his eyes and mouth.

'You know who gives him his money? I tell you – we give it to him. Without these he'd be finished – he wouldn't last a month.' The man held up his hands, they were calloused and the nails were split and ragged, encrusted with dark semi-circles of dirt. 'That's where he gets his money. Colonel Bloody Courtney.'

Dirk was staring across at the speaker; his hands lay clenched on the counter in front of him. Now suddenly the room was very quiet – so that the man's next words seemed even louder.

'You know what he pays – thirty-two pounds a month top journeyman's wages! Thirty-two pounds a month!'

'The minimum rate is twenty-five –' one of his companions observed dryly. 'I reckon you're free to move on to a better job – if you can find it. Me, I'll stay on here.'

'That's not the point. That big idle bastard's making a fortune out of us – I reckon he can afford to pay more. I reckon . . .'

'Do you reckon you're worth that much?' Dirk jumped up from his stool and shouted the question down the length of the counter. There was a stir of interest and every head turned towards him.

'Leave him, Dirk, he's drunk. Don't start anything,' Henry whispered in agitation, and then raising his voice and turning to the other, 'You've had enough, Norman. Time you were on your way. You old lady will be waiting dinner for you.'

'Good God!' Norman was peering in Dirk's direction, his eyes focusing blearily.

'Good God! It's Courtney's pup.'

And Dirk's face set into nervous rigidity. He began to walk slowly down the room towards the man.

'Leave him, Dirk.' To restrain him Archy caught his arm as he passed. But Dirk shrugged it off.

'You insulted my father. You called him a bastard!'

'That's right.' Norman nodded. 'Your daddy's a bastard all right. Your daddy's a big lucky bastard who's never done a full day's work in his life – a big, lucky, bloodsucking bastard. And he's whelped an equally useless pup, who spends his time . . .'

Dirk hit him in the mouth, and he went over backwards off the stool, flailing his arms as he fell. He hit the floor with his shoulders and rolled on to his knees spitting blood and a broken tooth from his mouth.

'You little bastard –' he mouthed through the blood. Dirk stepped forward with his left foot and swung his boot with the whole weight of his body behind it. The toe of his boot thudded into the man's chest and flung him on to his back.

'Christ, stop him,' shouted Henry from behind the bar. But they sat paralysed as Dirk stooped for the bar stool, lifted it above his head and then brought it down, swinging his body with it as though he were chopping a log. The heavy wooden seat hit the man in the centre of his forehead, it hit solidly for the back of his head was against the floor and could not give with the blow. It split his skull cleanly and twin spurts of blood shot from his nostrils into the sawdust on the floor.

'You've killed him.' A single voice broke the long silence that followed.

'Yes.' Dirk agreed. *I've killed him. I've killed a man.* It sang within him savagely. It came up and filled his chest so that he could hardly breathe. And he stood over the corpse not wanting to miss a moment of it. He felt his legs trembling under him, the muscles of his cheeks so tight with excitement they felt they must tear.

'Yes, I killed him.' His voice was choked with the violence of the pleasure that gripped him. His vision narrowed down so that the dead man's face filled the whole field of it. The forehead was deeply dented and the eyes bulged from their sockets.

Around him there was a sudden bustle of consternation.

'You'd better send for his father.'

'I'm getting out of here!'

'No, stay where you are. Nobody must leave.'

'My God, call Doc Fraser.'

'Doc's not wanted – get the police.'

'He was so quick – like a bloody leopard –'

'Christ, I'm getting out of here.'

Two of them stooped over the body.

'Leave him!' snapped Dirk. Don't touch him.' Jealous as a young lion of its kill. And instinctively they obeyed. They stood up and moved away. With them everyone else drew back, leaving Dirk standing alone.

'Get his father,' repeated Henry. 'Someone ride out and call Sean Courtney.'

An hour later Sean strode into the room. He wore an overcoat over his nightshirt and his boots had been pulled hurriedly over his bare feet. He stopped on the threshold and glared around the room, his hair in wild disorder from sleep – but when he entered, the atmosphere in the room changed. The tense silence relaxed and every face turned eagerly towards him.

'Mr Courtney – thank God you've come,' blurted the young police constable who was standing beside Dr Fraser.

'How bad is it, Doc?' Sean asked.

'He's dead, Sean.'

'Pa, he insulted . . . ' Dirk started.

'Shut up!' Sean ordered him grimly. 'Who is he?' he fired at the constable.

'Norman Van Eek – one of your fitters from the mill.'

886

'How many witnesses?'

'Fourteen of them, sir. They all saw it.'

'Right,' Sean ordered, 'get the body down to the police station. You'll be able to take statements from them tomorrow morning.'

'What about the accused . . . I mean what about your son, sir?' The constable corrected himself.

'I'll be responsible for him.'

'I'm not sure that I shouldn't . . . ' He saw the expression on Sean's face. 'Well, that will be all right, I suppose,' he agreed reluctantly.

'Pa . . . ' Dirk started again.

'I told you to keep your mouth shut – you've done enough damage for one night.' Sean spoke without looking at him, then to the barman,

'Fetch a blanket.' Then to the police constable, 'Get some of them to help you,' and he pointed towards the window which was lined four deep with curious faces.

'Very well, Mr Courtney.'

After they had shuffled out with the blanket-wrapped body, Sean glanced significantly at Dr Fraser.

'I'd better get down there – complete my examination.'

'You go ahead,' Sean agreed and the doctor packed his bag and went. Sean closed the door behind him and slammed the shutters across the window. Then he turned to the men who stood anxiously along the bar.

'What happened?' They stirred restlessly and looked everywhere but at him.

'You, George?' Sean selected one of his mechanics.

'Well, Mr Courtney, your Dirk went up to Norman and hit him off the stool. Then he kicked him as he was trying to get up, then he picked up the stool and hit him with it.' The mechanic stumbled hoarsely through his explanation.

'Did this man provoke him?' Sean demanded.

'Well, he called you a – begging your pardon, Mr Courtney – he called you a big, idle, bloodsucking bastard.'

Sean frowned quickly. 'Did he now! What else did he say?'

'He said you were a slave owner – that you starved your men. He said that he was going to get even with you sometime.' Archy Longworthy took over the telling of it with a note of interrogation in his voice as he glanced round at the others for support. After a few seconds there was a guilty nodding of heads

887

and a few murmurs of agreement. Archy took courage from it. 'He sort of hinted that he was going to wait for you one night and get even.'

'Did he say that in so many words?' Sean's presence dominated the room with such an obvious air of authority that when Archy looked again for support he found it in their faces.

'He said: "One night I'm going to wait for that big bastard – then I'll show him a few things."' Archy gave them the exact words. No one protested.

'Then what happened?'

'Well then he sort of picked on young Dirk. And "here's Courtney's brat," he said. "Yellow as his old man, I reckon!"'

'What did Dirk do?' Sean asked.

'Well, Mr Courtney, he just laughed – like a gentleman, sort of, nice and friendly. "Forget it," he said – "you've had too much to drink."'

A sudden thought occurred to Sean. 'What was Dirk doing in here, anyway?'

'Well, it's like this, Mr Courtney – a few weeks ago he lent me a couple of pounds. I asked him to call round here tonight so I could give it back to him – that's all it was.'

'He wasn't drinking then?' Sean asked suspiciously.

'Good Lord, no!' Archy was so obviously shocked at the suggestion that Sean nodded.

'All right, what happened then?' he pursued.

'Well, Norman went on ribbing him. Called him a coward and all that – I can't remember the exact words. But at last young Dirk lost his temper. He walked across and hit him off the stool. Well, I guess Norman deserved that – what do you think, boys?' Archy looked at them again.

'That's right – fair made my blood boil to hear him picking on Dirk like that.' The mechanic backed him up and the others murmured agreement.

'Well, then,' Archy took up the tale again, 'Norman's lying on the floor and pulls out his knife.' There was a rustle of astonishment from along the bar. One man opened his mouth and lifted his hand in protest, but suddenly embarrassed, he carried the gesture through and massaged his neck.

'Knife. What knife – where's it now?' Sean leaned forward eagerly. Standing beside him Dirk began to smile softly. When he smiled his face was beautiful.

'Here's the knife.' Henry, the barman, reached under the counter and brought out a large bone-handled clasp knife. Everybody in the room stared at it blankly.

'How did it get there?' Sean asked, and now for the first time he was aware of the sickly guilt-ugly faces in front of him. He knew then for certain it was a lie.

'I took it off Norman afterwards. We thought it best you should be the first one to know the truth – you being his father, and all.' Archy wriggled his shoulders ingratiatingly and smiled around at his witnesses.

Slowly Sean turned to the man nearest to him, the bank clerk. 'Is this the knife with which Norman Van Eek threatened my son?'

'Yes, Mr Courtney.' The man's voice squeaked unnaturally.

Sean looked at the man beyond him and repeated the question exactly.

'Yes, that's the one, sir.'

'That's it.'

'Yes.'

'No doubt about it – that's it.'

He asked each man in turn and each answered the same.

'Dirk.' Sean came last to him. He asked it slowly and heavily. Looking into the clear innocent eyes of his son. 'As God is your witness – did Norman Van Eek draw this knife on you?'

Please, my son, deny it now. Say it so they all can hear you. If you value my love – tell me the truth now. Please, Dirk, please. All this he tried to say, tried to convey it with the sheer force of his gaze.

'As God is my witness, Pa,' Dirk answered him and was silent again.

'You have not answered,' Sean insisted. *Please, my son.*

'He drew that knife from the hip pocket of his overalls – the blade was closed. He opened it with the thumbnail of his left hand, Pa,' Dirk explained softly. 'I tried to kick it out of his hand, but hit his chest instead. He fell on to his back and I saw him raise the knife as though he were going to throw it. I hit him with the stool. It was the only way I could stop him.'

All the passion went out of Sean's face. It was stony and hard.

'Very well,' he said. 'We'd better get home now.' Then he addressed the rest of the bar-room. 'Thank you, gentlemen.' And he walked out through the door to the Rolls. Dirk followed him meekly.

The next afternoon Dirk Courtney was released by the local magistrate into his father's custody on bail of fifty pounds, pending the visit of the Circuit Court two weeks later, when he was to stand trial on a charge of manslaughter.

His case was set down at the head of the Court list. The whole district attended the trial, packing the tiny Courthouse and clustering at each of its windows.

After a retirement of seven minutes the jury brought back its verdict and Dirk, walking out of the dock, was surrounded by the laughing, congratulating crowd and borne out into the sunlight.

In the almost deserted Courtroom Sean did not rise from his seat in the front row of chairs. Peter Aaronson, the defence lawyer Sean had imported from Pietermaritzburg, shuffled his papers into his briefcase, made a joke with the Registrar, then walked across to Sean.

'In and out again in seven minutes already – that's one for the record book.' When he smiled he looked like a koala bear. 'Have a cigar, Mr Courtney.' Sean shook his head and Peter thrust a disproportionately large cigar into his own mouth and lit it. 'I tell you truly, though, I was worried by the knife business. I expected trouble there. I didn't like that knife.'

'No more did I,' Sean agreed softly, and Peter held his head on one side examining Sean's face with bright, birdlike eyes.

'But I liked those witnesses – a troupe of performing seals. "Bark," you say to them – Woof! Woof! Just like magic. Someone trained them pretty well.'

'I don't think I understand you,' Sean said to him grimly, and Peter shrugged.

'I'll post my account – but I warn you I'm going to hit you with a big one. Say, five hundred guineas?'

Sean lay back in his seat and looked up at the little lawyer.

'Say, five hundred,' he agreed.

'Next time you need representation – I recommend a bright youngster name of Rolfe. Humphrey Rolfe,' Peter went on.

'You think I'll need a lawyer again?'

'With your boy – you'll need a lawyer,' Peter told him with certainty.

'And you don't want the job?' Sean leaned forward with sudden interest. 'At five hundred guineas a throw?'

'Money I can get anywhere.' Peter took the cigar from his mouth and inspected the fluffy grey ash at its tip. 'Remember the name, Mr Courtney – Humphrey Rolfe. He's a bright boy – and not too fussy.'

He walked away down the aisle lugging his heavy briefcase, and Sean stood up and followed him slowly. Pausing on the steps of the Courthouse he looked across the square. The centre of a small knot of men, Dirk stood laughing, with Archy Longworthy's arm around his shoulder. Archy's voice carried to where Sean stood.

'Don't let any of you get the idea you can tangle with Dirkie here – you'll end up with your teeth busted clean out the back of your head.' Archy grinned so that the blackened tooth showed. 'I say it so you can all hear me. Dirkie here is my friend – and I'm proud of him.'

You alone, thought Sean. He looked at his son and saw how tall he stood. Shaped like a man – broad in the shoulders with muscle in his arms, no fat on the belly and long legs dropping away clean from hips.

But he is only sixteen. He's a child – perhaps there is still time to prevent him setting hard. Then with truth he knew he was deceiving himself, and he remembered what a friend had said to him long ago:

'Some grapes grew in the wrong soil, some were diseased before they went to the press, and others were spoiled by a careless vintner – not all grapes make good wine.'

And I am the careless vintner, he thought.

Sean walked across the square. 'You're coming home,' he told Dirk harshly, knowing as he looked at the lovely face that he no longer loved his son. The knowledge nauseated him.

'Congratulations, Colonel. I knew we'd win,' Archy Longworthy beamed, and Sean glanced at him.

'I'll be in my office ten o'clock tomorrow morning. I want to talk to you.'

'Yes, sir!' grinned Archy happily, but he was not grinning when he left Ladyburg on the following evening's train with a month's pay in lieu of notice to compensate him.

81

With the storm of adverse editorial comment raised by Dirk's trial, Garry Courtney's chances in the coming election increased significantly. The jingo press spoke darkly of a 'surprise outcome, which thinking men will welcome as a true assessment of the worth of the two candidates for the Ladyburg constituency'. Only the Liberal papers reported the generous pension which the Ladyburg Wattle Co-operative Co. voted to Norman Van Eek's widow and orphan.

But everyone knew that Sean Courtney was still a long way ahead. He could be certain of the vote of the two hundred men employed at the factory and on his estates, the other wattle producers of the valley and their employees, as well as a good half of the townsfolk and ranchers – that was until the *Pietermaritzburg Farmer & Trader* devoted a full front page to the exclusive story of one Archibald Frederick Longworthy.

Mr Longworthy related how, by the threat of physical violence and loss of employment, he had been forced to perjure himself in court. How, after the case, he had been summarily dismissed from his work. The exact nature of his perjury was not revealed.

Sean cabled his lawyers in Pietermaritzburg to begin immediate proceedings against the *Farmer & Trader* for defamation of character, libel, contempt, treason, and anything else they could think of. Then, reckless of his own safety, he climbed into the Rolls and raced at thirty miles an hour in pursuit of his cable. He arrived in Pietermaritzburg to find that Mr Longworthy, after signing a sworn statement and graciously accepting a payment of fifty guineas, had departed without leaving a forwarding address. Legal advice was against Sean visiting the editor of the *Farmer & Trader* and laying himself open to a counter-suit of assault and battery. It would be two months before the defamation trial was heard in court, and the election was to be held in ten days' time.

All Sean could do was publish a full-page denial in each of the Liberal papers, then return to Ladyburg at a more sedate pace. There a telegram awaited him from Pretoria. Jan Paulus and Jan Niemand suggested that in the circumstances it might be better if Sean withdraw from nomination. Sean's reply went sizzling back over the wires.

Like a pair in harness, Garry and Sean Courtney swept up to the polling-day finishing line.

The actual voting took place in the Ladyburg Village Management offices under the beady eyes of two Government registration officers. Thereafter, the ballot boxes would be removed to Pietermaritzburg, where on the following day in the City Hall the votes would be counted and the official results announced.

On opposite sides of the square the opposing candidates set up the large marquee tents from which free refreshments would be served to the voters. Traditionally the candidate who fed the largest number would be the loser. Nobody wished to put *their* choice to additional expense, so they patronized the other man's stall. This day, however, both candidates served an almost equal amount of food.

It was a day that threatened the approach of the wet season, humid heat lay trapped beneath grey overcast clouds and the occasional bursts of sunlight stung like the blast of an open furnace door. Sean, suited and waistcoated, sweated with anxiety as he greeted each visitor to his stall with a booming, false *camaraderie*. Beside him Ruth looked like a rose petal, and smelled as sweet. Storm, demure for once, stood between them. Dirk was not there – Sean had found work for him on the far side of Lion Kop. Many sly eyes and snide sallies remarked his absence.

Ronny Pye had persuaded Garry not to wear his uniform. Anna was with him, pretty in mauve and artificial flowers. It was only at closer range that the ugly little lines around her mouth and eyes, and the grey hairs that were woven into the shiny black mass of her hair showed up. Neither she nor Garry let their eyes wander across the square.

Michael arrived and spoke first with his father, kissed his mother dutifully, then crossed to resume the argument Sean had broken off the night before. Michael wanted Sean to buy ten thousand acres of the coastal lowlands around Tongaat and plant it to sugar-cane. Within a few minutes he realized that this was not the best time to push his idea; Sean greeted each of his points with hearty laughter and offered him a cigar. Discouraged but not resigned, Michael went into the ballot office and, settling his problem of divided loyalty, deliberately spoiled his paper. Then he returned to his office at the wattle factory to whip his sugar estimates into shape for the next attack on Sean.

Ada Courtney never left the Protea Street cottage all that day. She had steadfastly denied appeals to join either camp, and refused to allow any of her girls to help in the preparations. She had prohibited any political discussion in her house – and ordered Sean to leave when he had disregarded this rule. Only after Ruth had interceded and Sean had made an abject apology, was he allowed to return. She disapproved of the whole business and considered it undignified and common that members of her family should not only be standing for public office but actually competing for it. Her deep distrust of and contempt for official-dom stemmed from the time the Village Board had wanted to place street lamps along Protea Street. She had attended their next meeting armed with an umbrella, and in vain they had tried to convince her that street lights did not attract mosquitoes.

However, Ada was the only person in the district who did not attend. From mid-morning until polling closed at five o'clock the square was jammed solid with humanity, and when the sealed ballot boxes were borne in state to the railway station, many of them climbed on the same train and went up to Pietermaritzburg for the official counting.

It had been a day of unremitting nervous tension, so a very short time after entering their suite in the White Horse Hotel, Ruth and Sean fell into exhausted sleep in each other's arms. When, in the early morning a brilliant electrical storm raged down upon the town, Ruth moved restlessly in her sleep, coming slowly back to consciousness – and to the realization that she and Sean were already engaged in the business that had been delayed so long. Sean woke at the same time and, for the few seconds that it took him to understand what was happening, was as bewildered as she – then both of them went to it with a will. By dawn Ruth knew that she would bear a son, though Sean felt it was a little soon to tell for certain.

After bathing, they ate breakfast in bed together with a renewed sense of intimacy. Ruth in a white silk gown, with her hair loosed into a shiny mass on her shoulders and her skin glowing as though she had been freshly scrubbed, was extreme provocation to Sean. Consequently they arrived late at the City Hall, much to the agitation of Sean's supporters.

The counting was well advanced. In a roped-off section of the hall ballot officers sat in silent industry at the tables piled with the small pink slips of paper. On a placard above each table was printed the name of the district and the candidates, and between the tables scrutineers paced watchfully.

The body of the hall was filled with a milling, humming swarm of men and women. Before it engulfed them Sean caught a glimpse of Garry and Anna moving through the press, then for the next ten minutes he was subjected to an orgy of hand-shaking, back-slapping and well wishes – interrupted by a bell and a complete silence.

'The result for the legislative assembly seat of Newcastle . . .' a high thin voice announced in the hush ' . . . Mr Robert Sampson 986 votes. Mr Edward Sutton 423 votes . . . ' And the rest was lost in a burst of cheers and groans. Sampson was the South African Party candidate, and Sean fought his way through the pack that surrounded him.

'Well done, you old son of a gun,' shouted Sean and beat him between the shoulder-blades.

'Thanks, Sean. It looks as though we are home and dry – I never expected a majority that size!' and they wrung each other's hands deliriously.

The morning went on with intervals of excited, buzzing tension exploding into applause as each result was announced. Sean's confidence rose as his party captured each seat they had expected, and one that they were resigned to lose – but then the bell rang again and in the same impersonal tone the Chief Registration Officer at last announced:

'The result for the legislative assembly seat of Ladyburg and the lower Tugela –' he felt the cold emptiness of apprehension in his stomach, and his breath burning up the back of his throat. Standing beside him he could sense the rigidity of Ruth's body and he groped for her hand.

'Colonel *Garrick* Courtney 638 votes. Colonel *Sean* Courtney 631 votes.'

Ruth's hand squeezed hard, but Sean did not reply to the pressure. The two of them stood very still, a tiny island of quiet in the surge and roar – in the triumphant cheers and despairing groans – until Sean said softly: 'I think we'll go back to the hotel, my dear.'

'Yes,' she answered as softly, and the sound of her voice was helpless pity. Together they started across the floor and a way opened for them. A passage lined by faces that bore expressions of regret, happiness, curiosity, indifference and triumphant malice.

Out into the sunlight and across the street to the rank of hire-cabs they walked together, while behind them the uproar was muted – sounding at this distance like the voices of wild animals.

Sean handed Ruth up into the coach and was about to join her before he remembered what there was still to be done. He spoke to the driver and gave him money before coming back to Ruth.

'Please wait for me at the hotel, my dear.'

'Where are you going?'

'I must offer Garry our congratulations.'

Through the screen of bodies that surrounded him Garry saw Sean approaching, and he felt his body tensing involuntarily – racked by that conflict of hatred and love he bore for this man.

Sean stopped in front of him and smiled. 'Well done, Garry!' he said and offered his right hand. 'You beat me in a hard straight fight – and I'd like to shake your hand.'

Garry took the words up with temerity, examined them with growing realization of their meaning and found that they were true. He had fought Sean and beaten him. This was something that could not be destroyed – something that Sean could never take away from him. *I've beaten him.* For the first time – the very first time in all my life!

It was an emotional orgasm so intense that for a long moment Garry could not move or make any reply.

'Sean . . . ' His voice choked up. He caught Sean's outstretched hand in both of his and held it with desperate strength.

'Sean, perhaps now . . . ' he whispered, 'I'd like to . . . I mean, when we get back to Ladyburg . . . ' Then he stopped and blushed scarlet with embarrassment. Quickly he released Sean's hand and stepped back. 'I thought you might like to come out to Theuniskraal,' he mumbled, 'some day when you're not busy. Look around the old place.' Then more eagerly, 'It's been a long time. I've still got Pa's old . . . '

'Never!' Anna Courtney hissed the word. Neither of them had noticed her cross the hall, but now she appeared suddenly at Garry's side. Her eyes were bright gems of hatred set in their patterns of wrinkles, and her face was white as she glared at Sean. 'Never.' She hissed again, and took Garry's arm. 'Come with me,' she commanded, and Garry followed her meekly. But he glanced back at where Sean still stood, and there was a desperate plea in his eyes. A plea for understanding, for forgiveness of this weakness.

82

Like one who lives in a hurricane belt, and recognizes the shape of clouds and the breathless hush that precedes high wind – Ruth knew she would have to deal with the brooding undirected rage which would be Sean's reaction to this failure of his plans. His moods came at widely spaced intervals and did not last long – but she feared those moods of his, and like the prudent householder forewarned of the hurricane's approach, she took precautions to minimize its wrath.

When she reached the hotel she sent an urgent summons to the Manager.

'In half an hour I want lunch served in the suite – not your ordinary bill of fare. Something really good.' The Manager thought a moment. 'Oyster! We have a barrel just arrived from Umhlanga Rocks.'

'Excellent.' Ruth liked the man's response to the emergency.

'Then I could do a smoked ham, cold venison, cold rock lobster, salads?'

'Excellent again. What about cheese?'

'Gruyère. Danish Blue. Camembert.'

'Wine?'

'Champagne?'

'Yes,' Ruth agreed instantly. She would shamelessly exploit Sean's weakness for it. 'A bottle of Veuve Clicquot – no, on second thoughts, three bottles.'

'I'll send the wine up first?'

'Immediately – with your best glass and a silver bucket,' Ruth told him.

Then she fled to her toilet. Thank the Lord for French perfume and this morning dress of grey silk she had been saving for just such an occasion. She worked quickly, but with skill, upon her face and hair, and when she was finished she sat quietly before the mirror and composed her features into an expression of peace. The effect was very satisfactory, she decided after critical contemplation. Since it was the way he had first seen it, Sean could never resist her hair in braids. It made her look like a little girl.

'Shall I open the wine, Madam?'

'Yes, please.' She called into the sitting-room, then went through to await the onslaught of the hurricane.

Ten minutes later it came wafting in like a gentle zephyr, with a cigar clamped between its teeth, its hands thrust deep into trousers pockets and a bemused expression on its face.

'Hey, now!' Sean stopped when he saw her, and removed the cigar. 'That's nice!'

The fact that he had noticed her appearance was proof that her weather forecast was hopelessly incorrect and she burst out laughing.

'What's so funny?' Sean asked mildly.

'Nothing and everything. You and me. Have a glass of champagne.'

'Mad woman,' Sean said and kissed her. 'I like your hair like this.'

'Aren't you disappointed?'

'About the result, you mean? Yes, I suppose I am.' He went to the central table and poured wine into the crystal glasses, handed one to her and took up the other.

'I give you a toast – the short, exciting political career of Sean Courtney.'

'You wanted to win so badly – but now . . . ?'

Sean nodded. 'Yes, I always want to win. But now that the game is lost . . . ' He shrugged. 'Shall I tell you something? I was getting a bit sick of all the speechifying and hand-shaking. I feel that even in my sleep I have a vacant grin on my face.' He crossed to one of the leather arm-chairs and sank down into it gratefully. 'There is something else also. Come here and let me tell you about it.'

She went to him, sat in his lap and slid her hand into the front of his shirt so that she could feel the soft springy hair of his chest, and the hard rubbery flesh beneath.

'Tell me,' she said, and he told her about Garry. He spoke slowly, telling her everything – about the leg, how it was when they were children, and finally, about Michael. She was quiet for a while, and he could see the hurt in her eyes that Sean had been another woman's lover. At last she asked:

'Does Garry know that Michael is your son?'

'Yes. Anna told him one night. She told him the night I left Ladyburg – he wanted to kill me.'

'Why did you leave?'

'I couldn't stay on. Garry hated me for siring his son – and Anna hated me because I would not go to her.'

'She still wanted you, then?'

'Yes. That night – the night I left, Anna came to me and asked me to . . . ' Sean paused. 'You know what I mean.'

'Yes.' Ruth nodded, hurt still and jealous, but making the effort to understand.

'I refused her – and she went to Garry and, in spite, she told him about the child. My God, what a poisonous bitch she is!'

'But if she wanted you, why did she marry Garry?'

'She was with child. She thought I had been killed in the Zulu war – she married him to provide a father for her child.'

'I see,' Ruth murmured. 'But why do you tell me this?'

'I wanted you to understand how I feel about Garry. After what he did to you at that meeting I can't expect you to have much sympathy for him – but he wasn't trying to hurt you, he was aiming at me. I owe him so much, I never seem able to pay him. That's why . . . '

'That's why you are glad he won today?' Ruth finished for him.

'Yes,' Sean answered eagerly. 'You see, don't you, how important this must have been to him. For the first time he was able to . . . able to . . . ' Sean fluttered his hands in frustration as he sought the words.

'He was able to compete with you on equal terms,' Ruth supplied them for him.

'Exactly!' Sean struck the arm of his chair with clenched fist. 'When I went to congratulate him, he was ready to meet me. He invited me out to Theuniskraal – just then that evil, bloody woman interfered and took him away. But somehow I know it's going to be all right now.'

A knock on the outer door interrupted him, and Ruth jumped up from his lap.

'That will be the waiter with the lunch,' but before she was half-way across the room, the knock was repeated with such insistence that it threatened to loosen the plaster.

'I'm coming.' Irritated, Ruth raised her voice and swung the door open.

Led by Bob Sampson a flood of men rushed into the room; jabbering and gesticulating they bore down on Sean.

'What the hell's going on?' he demanded.

'You've won!' shouted Bob. 'A recount, you won on a recount – by ten votes!'

'My God!' breathed Sean, and then so softly that only Ruth heard him, 'Garry. Poor Garry!'

'Open that champagne – send for another case. We're in solidly – all of us!' exulted Bob Sampson. 'So let's drink to the Union of South Africa!'

83

'Not even this once. Out of so many times, so many things – not even this once.' Already Garry Courtney was drunk. He lay deep in his chair with a tumbler held in both hands, stirring the brown liquid with a circular movement so a few drops slopped over the rims and stained the cloth of his trousers.

'No,' agreed Anna. 'Not even this once.' She stood with her back to him, staring out of the window of their suite into the gaslit street below, for she did not want him to see her face. But she could not control the harsh, gloating quality of her voice. 'Now you can go back to writing your little books. You've made your point – you've proved to yourself and the rest of the world how effective you are.'

Moving her hands slowly, she began to massage her own upper arms with sensual pleasure. A tiny shudder thrilled her so she moved restlessly and her skirts rustled like leaves in the wind. God, how close it had been – and she had been afraid.

'You're a loser, Garry Courtney. You *have* always been – and you *will* always be.'

Again she shuddered with the memory of her fear. He had so nearly escaped. She had seen it begin from the moment the first result was announced, every minute it had grown stronger. Even his voice had changed, deeper with the first hint of confidence in it. He had looked at her strangely, without submission, with the beginning of his contempt. Then the flare of rebellion when he had spoken to Sean Courtney. She had been truly afraid then.

'You are a loser,' she repeated, and heard the sound he made – half-gulp, half-sigh. She waited and when she heard the soft gurgle of brandy poured from bottle to glass she hugged herself tighter and now she smiled as she remembered the announcement of the recount. The way he had shrunk, the way he had crumpled and turned to he with all of it gone – the confidence and contempt wiped away. Gone! Gone for ever. Sean Courtney would never have him. She had made that oath – and now it would be kept.

As so many times before, she played over in her mind the details of that night. The night she had made the oath.

It was raining. She was standing on the wide stoep of Theuniskraal, and Sean was leading his horse up across the lawns of Theuniskraal. The damp linen of his shirt clung to his shoulders and chest, the rain had made his beard break out in tiny curls so he looked like a mischievous pirate.

'Where's Garry?' Her own voice, and his voice answering.

'Don't worry. He's gone into town to see Ada. He'll be back by supper-time.'

Then he was coming up the steps towards her, standing tall above her, and his hand on her arm was cold from the rain.

'You must take better care of yourself now. You can't stand in the cold any more.' And he led her through the french doors. The top of her head was on a level with his shoulders, and his eyes as he looked down at her were gentle with masculine awe of pregnancy.

'You're a damn fine woman, Anna. And I'm sure you're going to make a fine baby.'

'Sean!' She remembered how his name had come up her throat like an involuntary exclamation of pain. The fierce forward surge that had flattened her body against his, back arching to send her hips forward searching for his manhood. The coarse electric feeling of his hair in her hands as she pulled his face down and the taste of his mouth opened warm and moist.

'Are you mad!' As he tried to break away from her, her arms locked around his body and her face pressed to his chest.

'I love you. Please, Sean, please. Just let me hold you, that's all. I just want to hold you.'

'Get away from me!' And she felt herself thrown roughly on to the couch beside the fireplace.

'You're Garry's wife and you'll soon be the mother of his child. Keep your hot little body for him.' And his face thrust forward, close to hers. 'I don't want you. I could no more touch you than I could go with my own mother. You're Garry's wife. If ever again you look at another man I'll kill you. I'll kill you with my bare hands.'

Love congealing instantly, transformed to hatred by his words. Her fingernails raking across his cheek so the blood slid down into his beard, and he caught her wrists. Holding her while she struggled and screamed at him.

'You swine, you dirty, dirty swine. Garry's wife you say. Garry's baby you say! Now hear the truth. What I have within me you put there. It's yours – not Garry's!'

Then he was backing away from her. 'You're lying. It can't be.'

Following him now, speaking those cruel words softly. 'You remember how we said good-bye when you went to war? You remember that night in the wagon?'

'Leave me, leave me alone. I've got to think. I didn't know.' And he was gone. She heard the door of his study slam, and she stood in the centre of the floor while the storm surf of her anger abated and exposed the black reefs of hatred beneath.

Then she was alone in her bedroom, standing before the mirror – making her oath.

'I hate him. There's one thing I can take from him. Garry belongs to me now. Mine, not his. I will take that away from him.'

The pins pulled from her hair, so it tumbled to her shoulders. Her fingers tangling it into confusion. Teeth closing on her own lips so she could taste the blood.

'Oh God, I hate him,' she whispered through the pain. Tearing open the blouse of her dress, watching in the mirror the great pink bosses of her nipples already darkening with the promise of fruition.

'I hate him.' Pantaloons torn and discarded, bowls of face powder and cosmetics swept from the dressing-table to burst and fill the room with the pungent reek of perfume.

Then lying alone in the darkening room. Waiting for Garry to come.

Now she turned away from the window and looked down at Garry, triumphantly, knowing he could never escape again.

I have kept my oath, she thought, and crossed to the chair.

'Poor Garry.' She forced her voice to croon gently, and she stroked the hair back from his forehead. He looked up at her, surprised, but eager for affection. 'Poor Garry. Tomorrow we'll go home to Theuniskraal.'

She moved the bottle on the side table closer to his hand. Then she kissed his cheek lightly, and went on into the bedroom of the suite – smiling again, secure and safe in his weakness.

84

Four months passed quickly. Sean, distracted by the responsibilities of his office, the mountains of correspondence, the meetings and sessions, the petitioners and the schemers – offered only a token resistance to Michael's sugar plans. Michael went off to the coast, purchased the land, and became deeply involved with the seller's eldest daughter. This young lady had the dubious distinction of being one of the few divorcees in Natal. When the scandal reached his ears, Sean, secretly pleased that Michael's chastity was at last shed, boarded the Rolls and went off on a flying mission of rescue. He returned to Ladyburg with a penitent Michael in tow. Two weeks later the young lady married a travelling salesman and moved from Tongaat to Durban, whereupon Michael was allowed to return to Tongaat and begin the development of the sugar estate.

Ruth no longer accompanied Sean on all of his absences from Ladyburg. Her swiftly increasing girth and a mild malady which assailed her in the mornings kept her at Lion Kop, where she and Ada spent much time in the design and fabrication of babywear. In this Storm rendered assistance. The matinée jacket, which took three months to knit, was certain to fit the infant perfectly – provided it was a hunchback with its one arm twice as long as the other.

Kept busy from early morning to nightfall in the capacity of overseer on Mahobo's Kloof, Dirk found little time for distraction. Ladyburg was now well covered by Sean's espionage system, and Dirk's few visits were reported in detail.

But on the far side of Ladyburg, derelict and shabby from want of love, brooded the great homestead of Theuniskraal. In the night a single window showed a pale yellow square of light as Garry Courtney sat alone at his desk. In front of him lay a pathetically thin sheaf of papers. Hour after hour he stared at it – but no longer seeing it. He was dry inside, deprived of the juice of life and seeking its substitute in the bottle, which was always near him.

The days drifted into weeks, and they in turn became months – and he drifted with them.

Each afternoon he would go down to the paddocks, then, leaning against the heavy wooden paling, he would watch his bloodstock. Hour after hour he stood unmoving and it seemed that, in time, he left his own body and lived within those richly gleaming skins, as though his own hooves drove deep into the turf as he ran, as though his own voice squealed and his muscles bunched and moved in the savage mating of heaving bodies.

Ronny Pye found him there one afternoon; without Garry being aware of his presence, he came up silently and stood beside him, studying the pale intense face with the chisel-marks of pain and doubt and terrible yearning sculptured deep around the mouth and below the pale blue eyes.

'Hello, Garry.' He spoke softly, but recognizing the pity in his own voice he thrust it aside. There was no room for softness now, and ruthlessly he hardened his resolve.

'Ronny.' Vaguely, Garry turned to him, and when he smiled it was shyly. 'Business or social?'

'Business, Garry.'

'The bond?'

'Yes.'

'What do you want me to do?'

'How about coming into town – we can go over things in my office.'

'Now?'

'Yes, please.'

'Very well.' Garry straightened up slowly. 'I'll come with you.'

They rode together over the crest of ground and down towards the concrete bridge over the Baboon Stroom. Both of them silent – Garry because there was nothing in him, nothing to give voice to; Ronny Pye because of his sense of shame for the thing he was about to do. He was going to take a man's home from him and turn him loose upon a world in which he would have no chance of survival.

At the bridge they stopped automatically to rest their horses, and they sat without speaking, an incongruous pair. One man sitting quietly, slim and wasted, his clothing slightly rumpled, his face austere with suffering; the other plump, red-faced below

906

bright ginger hair, dressed in expensive cloth, fidgeting in the saddle.

There was little sign of life across the river. A long, tired smear of smoke from the wattle factory stack rising straight into the still hot air, a black boy moving cattle down to drink at the river, the huff and clatter and clang of a locomotive shunting in the goods-yards – but otherwise the town of Ladyburg lay slumbering in the heat of a summer afternoon.

Then on the open grassy plain below the escarpment, urgent movement caught Ronny's eye, and he focused his attention upon it with relief.

A horseman riding fast, and even at this distance Ronny recognized him.

'Young Dirk,' he grunted, and Garry roused himself and peered out across the river. Horse and rider blended into one unit, seeming to touch the earth so lightly they were bound to it only by a pale feather of dust that drifted low behind them.

'My God, that little bastard can ride.' In reluctant admiration Ronny shook his head solemnly and a drop of perspiration broke from his hairline and slid down his cheek. The horse reached the road and pivoted neatly, flattening into the increased speed of its run. Movement of such rhythmic grace and power that the watchers were stirred.

'Look at him go!' whistled Ronny. 'Don't reckon there's anything to catch that horse in the whole of Natal.'

'You think so?' Garry's voice was suddenly alive, and his lips were pursed in anger.

'I'm damned certain of it.'

'Mine. My colt – Grey Weather. Over a point-to-point course, I'd match him against any of Sean Courtney's stud.'

And those words gave Ronny Pye the idea. He turned it over in his mind while with slightly narrowed eyes he watched Dirk Courtney race Sun Dancer down towards the wattle factory. When horse and rider had disappeared through the tall gates, Ronny spoke softly:

'Would you back your colt with money?'

'I'd back him with my life.' There was savagery in Garry's voice.

Yes, thought Ronny, this way at least I will give him a chance. This way the fates will make the decision – there will be no blame to my account.

907

'Would you back him with Theuniskraal?' he asked, and the silence drew out.

'How do you mean?' whispered Garry.

'If you win, the bond on Theuniskraal is set aside.'

'And if I lose?'

'You lose the farm.'

'No,' snapped Garry. 'Christ, no! That's too much.'

Ronny shrugged indifferently. 'It was just an idea – you're probably wise. You wouldn't have much of a chance against Sean.'

Garry gasped sharply, that challenge had wounded deep as a lance. Made it a direct competition between Sean and himself; to ignore it would be to admit he could never win.

'I'll take the bet.'

'The whole bet? You'll cover my money with what you have left of Theuniskraal?'

'Yes, damn you. Yes. I'll show you how much chance I have against him.'

'We'd better get it down in writing,' Ronny suggested gently. 'Then I'll see if I can arrange it with Sean.' He touched his mount with his spurs and they moved forward across the bridge. 'By the way, I think it best we tell nobody about our little bet. We'll pretend it's just an honour match.'

Garry nodded his agreement. But that night when he wrote to Michael he told him about it, then went on to plead with Michael to ride Grey Weather in the race.

Two days before the competition Michael confided in his grandmother. Ada went out to Theuniskraal to try and dissuade Garry from this reckless gamble, without success. Garry was almost fanatical in his determination. The stake meant nothing to him – it was the prospect of winning.

And now he had Grey Weather and Michael to run for him. This time he would win. This time!

85

In the dark Sean walked with Dirk down the lane to the stables. The clouds banked along the escarpment were fired red by the hidden sun and the wind fretted through the plantations, so that the wattle moaned and shook.

'North wind,' grunted Sean. 'It'll rain before nightfall.'

'Sun Dancer loves the rain,' Dirk answered him tensely, and Sean glanced at him.

'Dirk – if you lose today . . . ' he started, but Dirk cut him short.

'I won't lose,' and again as though it were a vow, 'I won't lose!'

'If you'd only show as much determination in other things – the more important . . . '

'Important! Pa, this is important. This is the most important thing I've ever done.' Dirk stopped and turned to his father. He caught Sean's sleeve, clinging to him. 'Pa, I'm doing this for you – for you, Pa!'

Sean looked down and what he saw in his son's face, in that beautiful face, silenced the retort that he was about to make. Where did I go wrong with you, he asked himself with love stained by loathing. Where did you get this blood, why are you this way, demanded his pride and his contempt.

'Thanks,' he said dryly, freed his arm and walked on towards the stables.

Sightless in his deep preoccupation with Dirk, Sean was into the stable yard before he noticed Mbejane.

'Nkosi. I see you.' Mbejane rose solemnly from the hand-carved stool on which he sat.

'I see you also,' Sean cried with pleasure, and then controlled himself. A display of emotion in front of lesser persons would embarrass Mbejane. 'You are well?' he asked gravely, and restrained the desire to prod the swelling dignity of Mbejane's stomach, reminding himself that Mbejane's abundant flesh and fat had been carefully cultivated as a sign to the rest of the world of his prosperity.

'I am well,' Mbejane assured him.

'That you have come gives me pleasure.'

'Nkosi, on a day of importance it is right that we should be together – as it was before.' And Mbejane allowed himself to smile for the first time, a smile that within seconds became a mischievous grin that Sean gave back to him. He should have guessed that Mbejane would never miss a fight, or a hunt, or a contest.

Then Mbejane turned to Dirk.

'Do us honour today,' he commanded, as though he spoke to one of his own sons. 'Your father and I will be watching you.' He placed a huge black hand upon Dirk's shoulder as though in benediction, then he turned to gesture with his fly-whisk at the stable-boys waiting behind him.

'Bring the horse!'

Two of them led her out, her hooves ringing on the paving of the yard as she danced a little. Head up, moving greyhound-bellied, pricking her ears forward and back, she saw Dirk and wrinkled the soft velvet of her nostrils as she whickered.

'Hey, girl!' Dirk walked towards her. At his approach she rolled her eyes until the whites showed and her small dainty ears flattened wickedly against her neck.

'Stop that nonsense,' Dirk admonished, and she bared yellow teeth menacingly and reached with her slender snakelike neck. He put out his hand to her and she took his fingers between those terrible teeth and nibbled them tenderly. Then, finished with pretence, she snorted, pricked her ears and nuzzled his chest and neck.

'Where is her blanket? Has she eaten? Put the saddle and bridle in the car.' Dirk snapped a chain of questions and instructions at the stable-boys as he caressed Sun Dancer's face with the gentle hands of a lover.

So many contradictions in one person. Sean watched his son with sadness heavy upon him, oppressive as this red dawn. Where did I go wrong?

'Nkosi, I will walk down with the horse.' Mbejane sensed his mood and sought to end it.

'Better that a man of your station should ride with me in the motor-car,' Sean demurred, and took a fiendish pleasure in the shifty glance that Mbejane cast at the great gleaming Rolls parked at the far end of the yard. It has eyes like a monster, thought Mbejane and looked quickly away.

'I will walk with the horse and see that it comes to no harm,' he announced.

'As you wish,' Sean agreed. The small procession set off towards Ladyburg. The two grooms leading Sun Dancer in her red tartan blanket, and Mbejane following sedately with his small black sons carrying his carved stool and his spears behind him.

Two hours later Sean drove the Rolls into the field behind the stockyards. Staring straight ahead, both hands gripping the wheel so that the knuckles of his hands gleamed white – Sean did not hear the shouted greetings nor see the gala crowds and the bunting until the Rolls bumped to a halt in the grass and his hands unfroze slowly from the wheel. Then he exhaled gently and the rigid muscles of his face softened into a grin of uncertain triumph.

'Well, we made it!' He spoke as if he were not quite certain.

'You did very well, my dear.' Ruth's voice was also a little scratchy and she relaxed her protective hold on Storm.

'You should let me drive, Pa.' Dirk was lounging against the saddlery on the back seat. Sean turned furiously upon him, but Dirk was too quick. He flung open the door and was absorbed into the crowd that had gathered around the Rolls before Sean could assemble his words. Sean glowered after him.

'Hello, Sean. Nice to see you.' Dennis Petersen had opened the door at his elbow and Sean hastily rearranged his features into a smile.

'Hello, Dennis. Nice turn-out.'

'Everybody in the district,' Dennis assured him, as they shook hands, and then looked with satisfaction around the field. There were at least fifty carriages parked haphazard along the stockyard fence, an open wagon had been arranged as a refreshment stall with silver urns of coffee and piles of cakes laid out upon it. A dog fight was in progress near the gate, while small boys in already wilted church clothes shrieked and whooped and chased each other through the crowd.

'Who's responsible for the decorations?' Sean asked, surveying the flags and bunting that fluttered from the poles that marked the finishing line and from the wide roped-off lane that led up to them.

'The Board – we voted it last week.'

'Very nice.' Sean was looking now at the stockpen where the horses were. A solid barricade of humanity lined the railings, but he saw Dirk climb over and jump down beside Sun Dancer amid a splatter of applause from the onlookers.

'Good-looking lad.' Dennis was watching Dirk also, but there was something in his tone that added, *but I'm glad he's not mine.*

'Thanks.' The defiance in Sean's voice was not lost on Dennis and he smiled ironically.

'We'd better go across and talk to the other judges, Garrick is waiting.' Dennis jerked his head towards the carriage at the end of the line, and although he had been painfully aware of it, Sean looked at it for the first time.

Together with Pye, Erasmus and his father, Michael was standing beside it watching them. Tall and lean in tight black riding-boots, and an open shirt of white silk accentuating the breadth of his shoulders, he leaned against the wheel. Above him Ada and Anna sat together on the rear seat and suddenly Sean felt a twist of anger in his stomach that Ada should be there with *them.*

'Mother.' He greeted her without smiling.

'Hello, Sean.' And he could not fathom the tone of her voice nor her expression. Was it regret, or perhaps a reluctant rejection? For a long minute they held each other's eyes – until at last Sean had to break, because now, instead of anger, he felt guilty. But he did not understand the source of his guilt – it was only the sorrowful accusation in Ada's eyes that had given it to him.

'Anna.' He greeted her and received in exchange a stiff nod.

'Garry.' Sean tried to smile. He made a movement to lift his right hand, but as he did so he knew it would be rejected, for the same accusation that he had seen in Ada's eyes was also in Garry's. He turned with relief to Michael.

'Hello, Mike. You know you're going to get the pants thrashed off you?'

'I'm going to make you eat those words without salt!' And they laughed together easily, laughed with such obvious joy in each other that Anna moved restlessly in her seat and spoke sharply.

'Can't we get this over with, Ronny?'

'Yes,' Ronny Pye agreed hastily. 'Well, then. Where is young Dirk? We'd better go and find him.'

In a group they left the women and moved through the crowd towards the stockpen where Dirk stood laughing with two girls that Sean recognized as daughters of one of the factory foremen. They were both looking up at Dirk and reacting with such unashamed adoration that Sean felt a lift of indulgent pride. Casually Dirk dismissed the girls and came across to meet them.

'All set, Pa.'

'So I see,' Sean gruffed, and waited for Dirk to show courtesy to the men with him, but Dirk ignored them and spoke only to Ronny Pye.

'Let's hear it.'

'Well, then. A contest between Garry Courtney's colt Grey Weather and Sean Courtney's filly Sun Dancer. An honour match with no stake put up by the owners. Agreed?'

'Right,' said Sean.

Garry opened his mouth and then closed it firmly and nodded. He was sweating a little. He unfolded the handkerchief in his hand and wiped his forehead.

'The distance approximately five miles around four points. The points being firstly the posts that have been erected on this field, secondly the north-eastern boundary marker of the farm Theuniskraal.' Ronny pointed at the crest of the escarpment that stood above them, its slope golden with grass in the morning sun and smeared with streaks of dark green bush. 'Thirdly, the No. 3 dip-tank of Mahobo's Kloof farm, which you can't see from here as it is behind those trees.' Ronny's arm described a long arc along the crest of the escarpment and stopped pointing at the spires of a clump of saligna gums. 'But both of you know it?' 'Sure,' agreed Dirk, and Michael nodded. 'The fourth and finishing-point is the same as the starting-point – here.' He jerked his thumb at the two posts that fluttered gay with flags.

'Stewards have been posted at the Theuniskraal boundary and

the dip-tank – make sure you pass on the far side of them. The judges are Messrs Petersen, Erasmus and myself. All and any dispute regarding the running or interpretation of the rules will be decided by us. . . . ' Ronny went on talking and Sean felt his excitement mounting from his stomach and beginning to tingle along his forearms. It was taking a hold on all of them now, even Ronny's voice had an edge to it. Though Sean did not understand that the foxlike eagerness of his face came from the knowledge that this was a contest in which he stood to gain more than any of them. But Garrick understood fully, and his eyes watched Ronny's lips hypnotically.

'That's it, then,' Ronny finished and then to the riders, 'Get saddled up, and bring your horses to the start.'

The judges walked away and left the four Courtneys standing together.

'Sean . . . ' Garry spoke first, his eyes were stricken. 'I think you should know . . . ' but he did not finish.

'What?' Sean asked abruptly, and at the tone of his voice Garrick straightened up. The thing in his eyes changed shape, and became what Sean had never expected to see there – pride.

'It doesn't matter.' Garry turned away and walked purposefully towards his horse, and there was a spring in his stride and a set to his shoulders.

'Good luck, Mike.' Sean punched his arm.

'And the same to you.' Michael started after Garrick, then stopped and turned back to Sean. 'Whatever anyone else says, Sean, I know you didn't plan this.' Then he was striding away.

'What the hell did he mean by that?' puzzled Sean, but Dirk cut into his thoughts.

'Why did you have to do that, Pa?' he demanded.

'What?' Sean looked at him uncomprehendingly.

'Give him luck. Why did you have to give him luck? I'm riding for you – not him. I'm your son – not him!'

The two riders moved together towards the start, and buzzing with excitement the crowd went with them.

Sean walked beside Sun Dancer, with Dirk leaning attentively from the saddle to listen to him.

'Take it gently to the swamp, don't push her for she'll need all her steam in the mud. Michael will gain there, that colt is strong in the leg, but heavy. Follow him and let him break a path for you. Out of the swamp you can catch up and pass him on the slope, push hard there. You must lead him to the top and hold your lead along the crest to the dip-tank.'

'All right, Pa.'

'Now, when you start down again keep well out beyond the Van Essen plantation on to hard ground – that way you can cut the edge of the swamp. My guess is that Mike will come straight down and plough through the middle – but you must take the longer route – and use Sun Dancer's speed against Grey Weather's strength.'

They had reached the starting-posts and the crowd scattered and spread away to line the ropes. An open funnel of humanity faced the two horsemen, then the swamp with its deceptively lush papyrus grass concealing the glutinous mudholes. Beyond it the great soar of the escarpment. A long course. A hard course.

'Are both of you ready?' called Ronny Pye from the sidelines. 'Clear the field, please, Sean.'

Sean put his hand on Dirk's knee.

'Let's see what you can do, boy.' Then he ducked under the ropes into the crowd.

Sun Dancer was skittering nervously, coming up on her back legs and throwing her head so that the mane flew red-gold in the sunlight. She was sweating in dark patches on her shoulders. Michael was circling Grey Weather, keeping him moving gently, leaning forward and patting his neck, talking to him so that he switched his ears, cocking them half back to listen.

'Quiet, please, everybody!' Dennis was using a megaphone, and the buzz of voices descended into an expectant rustling.

'You're under starter's orders now,' he shouted at the riders, 'Turn wide, and walk up together.'

They swung away from the posts, and came together. Dirk touched Sun Dancer with the spur and she jumped back thrusting her quarters into Michael's leg.

'Keep your bloody animal under control,' he snarled at Michael. 'Don't crowd me!'

'Are you nervous, Dirkie?' Obediently Michael wheeled his mount aside.

'Damn you! – I'll show you who's nervous,' and Sun Dancer threw her head in protest, as Dirk sawed her with the curb.

'Come round, swing them round.' Dennis's voice through the megaphone boomed distortedly.

They turned in line and started walking up, twenty yards from the start, two horses with the sunlight glowing on their polished skins. Pale gold and dark red. The crowd sighed softly like wind in the grass.

Ten paces and Sun Dancer was pushing forward, lengthening her stride, crabbing a little.

'Hold your line! Keep together,' Dennis cautioned them, and Dirk yanked her back roughly. The rims of his nostrils were flared and white with tension.

Michael moved up beside him, holding his hands low. The big red colt stepping high in the exaggerated action of an animal under restraint.

Quickening together over the last five paces, their riders hunching lower in the saddles, they came to the posts.

'Go!' bellowed Dennis, and 'Go!' roared a hundred voices. Still in line, matching each other's stride, they changed from a walk into an easy, free, swinging canter. Both Dirk and Michael rising slightly in their stirrups to hold them from headlong flight. Half a mile ahead lay the swamp and beyond it five miles of mountain and rough, rocky ground, of donga and thornbush. They cantered down between the yelling lines and out of the funnel into the open.

The crowd broke and scattered to various points of vantage and Sean ran with them, unslinging his binocular-case, chuckling with excitement in the general confusion of shouts and laughter.

Ruth was waiting for him beside the Rolls and he caught her around the waist and lifted her on to the bonnet.

'Sean, you'll scratch the paintwork,' she protested, as she clutched at her hat and teetered dangerously on the high, round bonnet.

'The hell with the paintwork,' he laughed as he climbed up beside her and she clung to him for support. 'There they are!'

Far out across the field the two horses ran down towards the bright green of the swamp. Sean lifted and focused his binoculars, and suddenly they were so close he expected to hear the drumming of the hooves. Grey Weather was pulling ahead, forcing powerfully with his great shoulders lunging into each stride – and Sun Dancer trailed him with her neck arched against the pressure of the bit. On her back Dirk sat upright with his elbows pressed into his flanks as he held her.

'The little bugger is listening to advice,' Sean growled. 'I quite expected him to be using the whip already.'

Across the distance that separated them Sean could feel as a tangible thing Dirk's determination to win, he could see it in the way he held his shoulders, he could see it in the rigid lines of his arms. But what he did not see were the harsh lines of hatred in Dirk's face as he stared at Michael's back ahead of him.

The beat of hooves changed its tone, no longer ringing on hard ground, but dulling as they reached the swamp. Now lumps of damp clay flew from Grey Weather's hooves and a piece hit Dirk's chest and sprayed dirt on the white silk of his shirt. Sun Dancer's gait altered as she felt the soft ground.

'Easy, girl. Hey there, girl,' Dirk whispered and held her firmly with his knees to give her confidence. The grass brushed his stirrups and ahead of him Grey Weather splashed into the first mudhole, plunged through it and into the swamp proper. The tall papyrus engulfed him.

'The old man was right,' Dirk smiled for the first time. Michael was forcing a path through the reeds, flattening them for Dirk to follow with half the effort. Twice Grey Weather sunk to his belly in potholes of black glue, rearing and struggling to free himself while Dirk skirted them.

Both horses were shiny with mud, and their riders were soaked to the waist and splattered above. The swamp stank like an animal cage and marsh gas erupted sullenly as they disturbed it. Clouds of insects rose about them, a sakabula bird fled shrieking as they ploughed through the papyrus. One of the razor leaves lashed Michael's cheek and a thread of blood ran down his jaw washing the blobs of mud with it and dripped on to his shirt.

Then suddenly the ground firmed under them, the solid papyrus broke into clumps, thinned and was left behind and Grey Weather led them out on to the first slope of the escarpment. He was running heavily now, and grunting with each stride, while Sun Dancer moved up beside him.

'You're finished!' Dirk shouted at Michael as they drew level. 'I'll see you at the finish-line,' and he leaned forward in the saddle and gave Sun Dancer the spurs and the whip together.

Without pressing his horse Michael angled him off towards

the right, letting him move under slack rein to pick his own way and he began the first leg of the series of zigzags that would take him to the top.

On the steep ground below the crest Dirk used the whip incessantly, and Sun Dancer went up in a series of scrambling leaps with the loose rock rolling under her hooves. The sweat had washed away the mud from her shoulders and she landed with less control at each jump. 'Pull, you bitch. Pull!' Dirk shouted at her, and looked back in agony at Michael's sedate ascent. He was two hundred yards below and coming steadily. Dirk's movement caught Sun Dancer off balance and she landed awkwardly at the next jump, her hooves scrabbled and she started to fall. Dirk kicked his feet from the stirrups and jumped with the reins still in his hands. The instant he landed he leaned back on the reins to hold her, but she was down on her knees now, sliding back and she pulled Dirk down with her on to the level place below.

They struggled together and when at last he got her on her feet she was trembling with terror, dust and pieces of dry grass coated her muddy legs.

'Damn you! Damn you, you clumsy bitch,' whispered Dirk as he ran his hands over her hocks to check for damage. He glanced back at Michael and found him much closer now.

'Oh, God!' he blurted, snatched up Sun Dancer's reins and ran at the slope dragging her after him. Dirk came out on the crest with sweat pouring down his face and soaking through his shirt. Saliva had dried to a thick gummy froth in his mouth and he was panting harshly – but he had held on to his lead and Sun Dancer was over her trembling fit. She had recovered sufficiently to cavort a little as he mounted.

'This way, Dirkie!' The two stewards standing on the pile of stones that marked the Theuniskraal boundary were waving and shouting wild encouragement. Dirk clouted the spurs into her and was off again, galloping along the ridge, sweeping past them and on towards the clump of gums three miles ahead.

'Catch him, Mike. Ride, man, ride!' Faint shouts behind him – and Dirk knew without looking back that Mike had reached the top and was chasing him. He rode on, grimly mourning the time lost on the ascent and hating both Sun Dancer and Michael for it. At this point he should have led by four hundred yards – not fifty.

Directly ahead now was the gorge through which the Baboon Stroom dropped down the escarpment, its side choked with dark green river bush. Dirk found the path and turned away from the skyline aiming upstream at the ford. Without grass to muffle them Sun Dancer's hooves hammered in staccato rhythm on the hard-packed earth of the path, but also he could hear behind him like an echo the beat of other hooves – Michael was on to the path behind him. Dirk looked back under his own arm. Michael was so close that he could see the laughter lines creasing the corners of his mouth, and the mockery inflamed him.

'I'll show him –!' And Dirk started with the whip again, cracking it across Sun Dancer's flanks and shoulders so that she jumped forward with a new urgency. Down the steep bank of the river and out on to the white sandbank, he plunged with Grey Weather's nose drawing level with his boot. Into the dark green water they rode abreast, throwing up a veil of spray that sparkled in the sunlight, slipping from their saddles to swim beside the horses through the deep, while the current moved them down towards the falls. Up into the saddles again the instant the horses found the bottom and splashed towards the far bank. Out on to the sand, with water streaming from sodden clothing, shouting with excitement as they raced for the narrow path that climbed the far bank. First man on to it would hold the advantage.

'Give way! I'm leading – give me way,' screamed Dirk furiously.

'Make your own way!' Michael laughed back at him.

'You bastard!' Dirk used his knees and reins to thrust Sun Dancer's shoulder into Michael, trying to force him clear.

'None of that!' Michael warned him.

'You bastard – I'll show you.'

They rode knee to knee now. Dirk sat up quickly and twisted his foot, placing his booted toe under Michael's instep. With a sudden vicious lift of his leg he slipped Michael's foot from the stirrup and threw him sideways. As he felt himself going over Michael clutched desperately at the pommel, pulling the saddle with him so it slid on to Grey Weather's flank and the shift of weight forced the horse to disengage and slew away from the path. Michael went down on his shoulder into the sand and rolled with his knees drawn up against his stomach.

'That's for you!' Dirk yelled in defiance as he went up the

bank and out into the open veld again. Behind him in the river-bed Michael staggered to his feet, his wet clothing coated white with sand, and ran after Grey Weather who was trotting back towards the water with the saddle hanging under his chest.

'The dirty little swine. My God, if only Sean knew!' Michael caught the horse before it started to drink, wrestled the saddle on to his back again and clinched the girth.

'Now, I can't let him win!' He jumped up on to Grey Weather and booted him towards the bank. 'I can't let him win.'

Two hundred yards ahead Dirk's shirt was a white blob against the brown grass. As he rounded the dip-tank and pointed Sun Dancer's head at the ridge for the last leg, one of the stewards shouted:

'What happened to Michael?'

'He fell in the river,' Dirk called back. 'He's finished!' And his voice rang with triumph.

'He's leading – Dirk's leading!' Sean stood on the Rolls with his glasses trained on the clump of gum-trees, and now he was the first to spot the tiny figure of the horseman as it showed on the crest of the escarpment.

'Where's Michael?' Ruth asked.

'He can't be far behind,' Sean muttered and waited anxiously for him to appear. He had fretted while he watched Dirk's reckless ascent of the slope, and cursed him loudly for his brutal treatment of Sun Dancer. Then he had entreated him to *get a bloody move on* during the run along the ridge with Michael gaining steadily on him. When the two horsemen had veered away from the skyline to cross the Baboon Stroom they had disappeared from view and this was the first glimpse the spectators had received of either competitor since that moment.

'The little idiot's riding too wide. I told him to cut the edge of the swamp – not ride round it altogether.'

'Where's Michael?' Ruth repeated. Sean swung the glasses back and scanned the crest with the first twinges of concern.

'Not showing yet – he must have run into trouble.'

'Do you think he's all right? Has he been hurt?'

'How should I know?' Sean's anxiety made him irritable, but immediately he was penitent and encircled Ruth's waist with his arm. 'He can look after himself, that one. No sense fussing about him.'

Dirk was well down the slope now, leaving a thin trail of dust, for Sun Dancer skidded on her haunches most of the way.

'Still no sign of Michael?' Ruth moved restlessly against him.

'No. Not yet,' Sean grunted. 'Dirk can afford to miss the swamp – he's leading by a quarter of a mile.'

Suddenly a sigh of relief moved the crowd like a gust of wind through a field of wheat.

'There he is!'

'He's coming straight down the slope.'

'He can't make it unless he flies!'

Sean swung his glasses from Dirk to Michael and back, estimating their speeds and positions, allowing for Michael's delay in the swamp, but setting against that the additional distance that Dirk had to cover.

'It's going to be close –' he decided aloud. 'Dirk's got the edge, but it's going to be very close.'

Ada did not see it that way. Dirk was leaading and Dirk was going to win. She looked across at Garrick. He stood beside the finishing-post a hundred yards away, but even at that distance there was no mistaking the droop of his shoulders and the air of misery that surrounded him like an aura of defeat. Sun Dancer's hooves were slashing his life to threads.

Unable to bear it a moment longer, Ada jumped down from the carriage and ran through the crowd to where Sean stood like a triumphant colossus on the bonnet of the Rolls.

'Sean.' She reached up and touched his leg, but he was so engrossed he did not feel or hear her.

'Sean,' she shouted and tugged at his trouser-leg.

'Mother?' He turned vaguely to look down at her.

'I must talk to you,' Ada shouted above the sound of the crowd that was rising with excitement.

'Not now. They're coming in to the finish – climb up here where you can see it.'

'Now. I must speak to you now. Come down this instant!' Her tone shocked him, for a second he wavered and peered furtively back at the race. Then he shrugged with resignation and jumped down beside her.

'What is it? Please be quick – I don't want to miss –'

'I'll be quick.' Sean had never seen such a cold fury on her before. 'I wanted to say that I never thought I'd see that day when I had nothing left for you but contempt. Thoughtless you've been often – but never downright merciless.'

'Mother, I . . . ' He was bewildered.

'Listen to me. You set out to destroy your brother and you've done it. Well, I hope you have the pleasure of it. You've got Theuniskraal now. Enjoy it, Sean. Sleep well at night.'

'Theuniskraal! What do you mean?' He shouted at her now in his confusion. 'I didn't wager for the farm!'

'Ah, no,' Ada scoffed at him. 'Of course you didn't – you let Ronny Pye do that for you.'

'Pye? What's he got to do with it?'

'Everything! He helped you plan it. He helped you provoke Garry into this stupidity. He holds the mortgage on Theuniskraal.'

'But . . . ' Slowly the enormity of it all began to shape up in Sean's mind.

'You took his leg – now take Theuniskraal, but pay for it with my love.' She looked steadily into his eyes, but the pain was there clouding her own. 'Good-bye, Sean. We won't speak to each other again.' And she walked slowly away. She walked like an old woman at last, a tired and worn old woman.

Sean understood and began to run towards the finishing-line. He drove through the crowd like a shark through a shoal of sardines. Over their heads he saw the two horsemen galloping in across the field.

Dirk was leading, standing in the stirrups to thrash Sun Dancer with the whip. His black hair fluttered in the wind, and his shirt filthy with thrown mud. Under him the filly danced on flying hooves and the beat of them drummed above the rising roar of the crowd. Her body was black and shiny with sweat, and froth flew from her gaping pink mouth to form white lace on her chest and flanks.

Fifty hopeless yards behind her plunged the colt with Michael flogging his heels into him with despair. Michael's face was twisted in an agony of frustration. Grey Weather was finished, his legs loose with exhaustion and his breath sawing hoarsely with each stride.

Sean tore his way through the press of bodies that lined the guide ropes. He reached the front rank and shouldered two women from his path. Then he stooped and ducked under the rope into the open.

Sun Dancer was almost up to him, hammering down in a crescendo of hooves, her head nodding with each stride.

'Dirk! Stop her!' roared Sean.

'Pa! Pa! Get out of the way . . . ' Dirk screamed back at him, but Sean sprang to intercept him.

'Pa!'

Sean was in front of him, crouching with arms extended. Too close to swing Sun Dancer's head away from him, too late to stop her charge.

'Jump, girl, jump,' shouted Dirk and gathered the horse with his knees, feeling her respond with a bunching of her quarters; feeling her lift her forelegs against her chest and drive upwards in a high parabola. But sensing also the sluggishness of her exhausted body and knowing she had not gone high enough to clear Sean's head.

An aching moment as Sun Dancer lifted clear of the ground, the horrified groan of the crowd as her forelegs smashed into Sean and she twisted in the air, falling. Dirk thrown, his stirrup leathers parting like whip cracks. Then all of them down together in the grass. Shrill screams of women in the crowd.

Sun Dancer struggling up again with a foreleg swinging loosely from the knee, whinnying in the pain of broken bone.

Sean on his back, his head twisted to the side and blood from his torn cheek dribbling into his nose and mouth so that his breathing snored hoarsely.

Dirk with the skin smeared from elbows and one cheek, crawling towards Sean, kneeling beside him, raising both hands clenched, hammering down with them so that his fists splattered the blood, beating them into the chest and slack, unconscious face of his father.

'Why did you? Oh, God, I hate you.' Shock and fury and despair. 'For you! You stopped me, you stopped me.'

Michael dragging Grey Weather down on his haunches, flinging from the saddle, running to them, holding Dirk's arms, dragging him off, fighting him.

'Leave him, you little bastard.'

'He didn't want me to. He stopped me, I hate him. I'll kill him.'

The crowd surging forward, flattening the guide ropes, two

men helping Michael hold Dirk, the rest of them ringing Sean's body.

The cries and questions:

'Where's Doc Fraser?'

'Jesus, he's badly hurt!'

'Catch that horse. Get a gun.'

'What about the bets?'

'Don't touch him. Wait . . . '

'Got to straighten his arm.'

'Get a gun. For Christ sake, get a gun.'

Then a new silence on them, their ranks opening quietly and Ruth coming through to him running – Mbejane behind her.

'Sean.' She knelt beside him, clumsy in her pregnancy. 'Sean,' she began again, and the men about her could not look at her face.

'Mbejane, bring him to the car,' she whispered.

He slipped the monkey-skin cloak from his shoulder and let it drop, stooped over Sean and lifted him. The great black muscles of his chest and arms swelled, and he stood with his legs braced wide against the weight.

'His arm, Nkosikazi.'

She arranged the hanging arm comfortably across his chest.

'Bring him,' she repeated and together they walked through the crowd. Sean's head lolled against Mbejane's shoulder like that of a sleeping child. Mbejane laid Sean gently on the back seat with his head in Ruth's lap.

'My daddy,' she kept repeating, her face screwed up with horror at the blood and her tiny body trembling like that of a frightened rabbit.

'Will you drive us please, Michael?' Ruth looked up at him as he stood beside the Rolls. 'Take us to Protea Street.'

With Mbejane loping alongside, the big car bumped across the field through the throng of anxious watchers, then swung on to the main road and moved away towards Ladyburg.

86

While about him the crowds scattered slowly and drifted to their carriages, Dirk Courtney stood alone and watched the Rolls disappear in its own blown dust.

Waves of reaction shivered up his legs and turned to heavy nausea in his gut. The open gravel rash on his face burned like acid spilled upon the skin.

'You'd better go in and have Doc Fraser put something on your face.' Coming from his carriage with a heavy service revolver, Dennis Petersen paused beside him.

'Yes,' Dirk answered dully, and Dennis walked on to where two native grooms held Sun Dancer. Unsteadily on three legs, but quiet now, she stood between them with her head hanging dejectedly.

Dennis touched the muzzle of the revolver to her forehead, and at the shot she recoiled violently and dropped, shuddering. Her legs stiffened in one last convulsion, then she lay still.

Watching, Dirk shuddered in sympathy and then leaned forward to vent his nausea in the grass. It came up sour and scalding hot. He wiped it from his mouth with the palm of his hand, then he began to walk. Without direction, blindly, from the field towards the escarpment.

Over in his mind, keeping pace with his legs like the refrain of a marching song:

He doesn't want me. He doesn't want me.

And then savagely:

I hope he dies. Please let him die.

'Please let him die.' Anna Courtney said it softly, so that Garry standing below her seat in the buggy did not hear her. He stood with his shoulders hunched, and his head thrust forward in thought, hands hanging at his sides slowly folding and unfolding, then he raised one of them and squeezed the fingers into his closed eyelids.

'I'm going to him,' he said. 'God help me, but I'm going to him.'

'No! I forbid it. Leave him – let him suffer as I suffered.'

Slowly, bewildered, Garry shook his head.

'I must. It's too long, too much. I must. Pray God it's not too late.'

'Let him die.' Then suddenly it snapped in her head, broke under the weight of the hatred so long sustained.

She rose screaming in her seat. 'Die! Damn you. Die!' And Garry uncovered his eyes, and looked at her in alarm.

'Compose yourself, my dear.'

'Die! Die!' Her face was blotched with flaming spots of red, and her voice squawked as though she were being strangled. Garry scrambled up beside her and flung his arms around her protectively.

'Get away from me. Don't touch me.' She screamed at him; fighting from his embrace. 'Because of you I lost him. He was so big, so strong. He was mine – and because . . . '

'Anna, Anna. Please don't.' He tried to soothe her raving. 'Please stop it, my dear.'

'You, you crawling, crippled thing. Because of you.' And suddenly it had to come out, like pus from a canker. 'But I paid you back. I took him from you also – and now he's dead. You'll never have him.' She laughed, gloating, demented.

'Anna, Stop it.'

'That night – do you remember that night? Will you or he ever forget it? I wanted him, I wanted him big like a bull on top of me, I wanted him rutting deep like it was before – I begged him. I pleaded – but because of you. Because of his crippled little weakling brother. Christ, I hated him!' She laughed again, a shriek of pain and hatred. 'I tore my clothing and bit into my own lips, as I had wanted him to do. When you came – I wanted you to . . . but you, I had forgotten you were only half a man! I wanted you to kill him – *kill him!*'

Pale, so that the sweat on his face shone like water on white marble, Garry pulled away from her with loathing.

'All this time I thought he – I believed you.' And he half fell from the buggy, leaning against it for a moment to steady himself. ' . . . All this time wasted.' Then he launched himself and began to run, his bad leg jerking and catching under him.

'You want a lift, Garry?' Dennis Petersen drew level with him and called down from the carriage.

'Yes. Oh, yes.' Garry caught the handrail and dragged himself up beside Dennis. 'Take me to him, please, as fast as you can.'

87

Silent, deserted, the great house crouched over her. Dark with the shutters closed against the sun, brooding and immense, smelling musty as though old passions had died within its walls.

Anna stood alone in the huge central room and screamed its name.

'Theuniskraal!'

And the thick stone walls smothered the sound of her madness.

'He is dead! Do you hear me? I took him away from all of you.' And she shrieked in triumphant laughter, with the tears greasing her cheeks. 'I won! Do you hear me? I won!' And her grief distorted the laughter.

She picked up the heavy glass lamp and hurled it across the room; it burst and the paraffin sprayed wide, glistening on the walls and soaking into the carpet.

'Theuniskraal! Hear me! I hate you also. I hate him. I hate you all – all of you.'

She raged through the room, tearing down the gilt-framed pictures and smashing them so that the glass sparkled like tiny jewels in the gloom; she used a chair to smash in the front of the display cabinet and wreck the old china and glassware in it; she swept the books from the shelves into fluttering heaps, and threw their torn pages in the air.

'I hate!' she screamed. 'I hate!' And the great house waited silent. Exhausted with worn-out emotions – old and sad and wise.

'I hate you – all of you.' And she ran out into the passage, through the kitchens to the pantries. On the lowest shelf stood a four-gallon drum of methylated spirit and she panted as she struggled with the stopper. The stopper came out, the clear liquid welled and ran down the metal sides, and she picked the drum up across her chest and stumbled back into the kitchen.

It spilled down her skirts, soaking in, drenching the heavy cloth, forming a spreading pool on the stone flags.

'I hate!' She laughed and stumbled, staggering off balance, still clutching the drum she fell against the kitchen range. Hot metal scorched her clothing and burned through to the flesh of her hip, but she did not feel it. Her sodden skirts brushed over the fire-box, a tiny point of flame caught and grew. So when she ran on into the house a fiery train swept behind her.

Back in the central room, she poured from the drum over the books and the carpet, laughing as she splashed the long-draped velvet curtains.

Oblivious of the flames that followed, until her petticoats caught and burned against her legs. Then she screamed again at the agony of her tortured flesh and brain. She dropped the metal drum and it exploded, showering her with liquid blue flame, turning her hair and her face and her whole body into a living torch, a torch that fell and writhed and died before the flames reached the thatch of the roof of Theuniskraal.

88

They faced each other across the waist of the dhow, and the bright sunlight threw their shadows along the filthy planking of the deck. Two tall young men, both dark-haired and burned rich brown by the sun, both with the big Courtney nose – both angry. From the poop three of the Arab crew watched with mild curiosity.

'So, you won't come home, then?' Michael asked. 'You're going through with this childishness?'

'Why do you want me to?'

'Me? Good God, if I never see you again it would be too soon. Ladyburg will be a cleaner town without you.'

'Then why did you come?'

'Your father asked me.'

'Why didn't he come himself?' Dirk's bitterness echoed in his voice.

'He's still a sick man – his head. Hurt badly.'

'If he wanted me, he would have come.'

'He sent for you, didn't he?'

'But why did he want you to win – why did he stop me?'

'Listen to me, Dirk. You're young yet. There are many things you don't understand.'

'Don't I!' And Dirk threw back his head and laughed scornfully. 'Oh, I understand all right. You'd better get off this boat, we're just about to sail.'

'Listen, Dirk . . .'

'Get off. Run back to him – you can have my share.'

'Dirk, listen to me. He said if you refused to come – then I was to give you this.' From inside his coat Michael drew an envelope and offered it.

'What is it?'

'I don't know – but I expect that it's money.'

Dirk came slowly across the deck and took the envelope from him.

'Have you a message for him?' Michael asked, and when Dirk shook his head he turned and jumped down on to the wooden jetty. Immediately a bustle began behind him as the Arab crew cast off the lines.

Standing on the edge of the jetty, Michael watched the stubby little craft drift out on the waters of Durban Bay. He could smell the stench of her bilges, her sides were streaked with human filth, and the single sail that rose slowly as the crew hoisted the long teak boom was stained and patched like a quilt.

The wind took her and the pregnant belly of the sail bulged out, she heeled and thrust forward through the chop of dirty green water – headed towards the bar, where a low surf broke in languid lines of white.

The two half-brothers stared at each other across the widening gap. Neither of them lifted an arm or smiled. The dhow bore away. Dirk's face was a tiny brown fleck above the white of his tropical suit, then suddenly his voice.

'Tell him . . . ' Small in the distance. 'Tell him . . . ' and the rest of it was lost on the wind, in the soft lap and sigh of the wavelets beneath the jetty.

89

Below where they sat on the lip of the escarpment, the walls of Theuniskraal stood up like smoke-browned tombstones marking the burial ground of hatred.

'About time you started rebuilding,' Sean grunted, 'you can't stay on at Protea Street for ever.'

'No.' Garry paused before going on: 'I've picked out the new site for the homestead – there, beyond the number two dip.'

Both of them looked away from the roofless ruins, and they were silent again until shyly Garry asked, 'I'd like you to have a look at the plans. It won't be as big as the old house now that there is just Michael and I. Could you . . . ?'

'Good,' Sean cut in quickly. 'Why don't you bring them across to Lion Kop tomorrow evening? Ruth will want you to stay for dinner.'

'I'd like that.'

'Come early,' said Sean, and started to stand up from the rock on which he sat. He moved heavily, awkwardly – and Garry jumped up to help him. Hating the weakness of his slowly mending body, Sean would have brushed Garry's eager hands away. But he saw the expression on his brother's face and instead he submitted meekly.

'Give me an arm over the rough ground, please.' He spoke gruffly.

Side by side, with Sean's arm across Garry's shoulder, they moved to where the buggy waited.

Ponderously Sean climbed up and settled himself into the padded leather seat.

'Thanks.' He gathered up the reins and smiled down at Garry, and Garry flushed with pleasure and looked away to the infinite lines of young wattle trees that covered the hills of Theuniskraal.

'Looks good, doesn't it?' he asked.

'You and Michael have done wonders up here,' Sean agreed, still smiling.

'Courtney Brothers and Son.' Softly Garry spoke the name of the new company which had merged the lands of Theuniskraal and Lion Kop into one vast estate. 'Now at last it is the way it should have been long ago.'

'Until tomorrow, Garry.' Sean flipped the reins and the buggy rolled forward, rocking gently over the uneven surface of the new road.

'Until tomorrow, Sean.' Garry called after him, and watched until the buggy was lost to sight among the blocks of dark mature wattle. Then he walked to his horse and mounted. He sat a while watching the distant ranks of Zulu labourers singing as they worked. He saw Michael moving on horseback amongst them, stopping occasionally to lean from the saddle and urge them on.

And Garry began to smile. The smile smoothed away the lines from around his eyes. He touched the horse with his spurs and cantered down to join Michael.